Eternal Love

MAGGIE SHAYNE

BERKLEY SENSATION, NEW YORK

THE BERKLEY PUBLISHING GROUP
Published by the Penguin Group
Penguin Group (USA) Inc.
375 Hudson Street, New York, New York 10014, USA
Penguin Group (Canada), 90 Eglinton Avenue East, Suite 700, Toronto, Ontario M4P 2Y3, Canada
(a division of Pearson Penguin Canada Inc.)
Penguin Books Ltd., 80 Strand, London WC2R 0RL, England
Penguin Group Ireland, 25 St. Stephen's Green, Dublin 2, Ireland (a division of Penguin Books Ltd.)
Penguin Group (Australia), 250 Camberwell Road, Camberwell, Victoria 3124, Australia
(a division of Pearson Australia Group Pty. Ltd.)
Penguin Books India Pvt. Ltd., 11 Community Centre, Panchsheel Park, New Delhi—110 017, India
Penguin Group (NZ), 67 Apollo Drive, Rosedale, North Shore 0632, New Zealand
(a division of Pearson New Zealand Ltd.)
Penguin Books (South Africa) (Pty.) Ltd., 24 Sturdee Avenue, Rosebank, Johannesburg 2196,
South Africa

Penguin Books Ltd., Registered Offices: 80 Strand, London WC2R 0RL, England

ETERNAL LOVE

PRINTING HISTORY
Eternity: Jove mass market edition / December 1998
Infinity: Jove mass market edition / October 1999
Berkley Sensation trade paperback omnibus edition / November 2007

Berkley Sensation trade paperback ISBN: 978-0-425-21739-9

PRINTED IN THE UNITED STATES OF AMERICA

10 9 8 7 6 5 4 3 2 1

Contents

Eternity

This story is dedicated to
Sarah Osborne
Who died in jail on May 10, 1692.

Bridget Bishop
Who was hanged on June 10, 1692.

Sarah Good and her unnamed child
The baby died in jail just before its mother was hanged on
July 19, 1692.

Elizabeth How
Susannah Martin
Rebecca Nurse
Sarah Wildes
All of whom were hanged on July 19, 1692.

Reverend George Burroughs
Martha Carrier
George Jacobs
John Proctor
John Willard
All of whom were hanged on August 19, 1692.

Ann Foster
Who died in jail sometime after September 10, 1692.

Giles Corey
Who was pressed to death on September 19,1692.

Martha Corey
Mary Esty
Alice Parker
Mary Parker
Ann Pudeator
Wilmot Reed
Margaret Scott
Samuel Wardwell
All of whom were hanged on September 22, 1692.

And to
Sarah Destin
Who was pardoned when the madness of 1692 come to an end,
but who died in jail all the same, unable to pay her jail fees.

May we never forget.

The Witch Upon the Hill

Her eyes are black, the midnight sea,
Her hair, a sooty cloud
Her voice, the winds of fantasy,
Her heart like fire, and proud

I could not help but watch her
As beneath the moon she danced,
She whirled, she cast, she conjured
She sang a mystic chant

She soared into my soul that night
The starry sky her wings
She whispered secrets in my dreams
And spoke of sacred things

In my mind, she entranced me
Her kiss was magick-laced
Her touch, it left me trembling,
And craving her embrace

The skies obey her every wish,
The elements, her commands
She wields a power o'er me,
My heart lies in her hands

For her I'd cross the universe,
For her I'd swim the sea,
But what could an Enchantress want
with a simple man like me?

She came, and said, "I love you,
And likely, always will."
My heart, I pledge, forevermore
To the Witch upon the hill

— DUNCAN WALLACE

PART ONE

Chapter 1

I always knew I was a Witch.

The definition of the word has since broadened somewhat, and rightly so, I imagine. Today anyone with the determination to learn and practice the Craft of the Wise can call herself—and deservedly—a Witch. But in my time there were no books written to guide a seeker, save the books of the Witches themselves, but the grimoires were kept secret. Back then one was only a Witch if one was born to, or adopted by, another Witch. And even then the young one wasn't told all of the secrets. Some of them I didn't learn until much later.

My mother was a wise woman, a Witch, and from the time I was very young I was taught the ways of drawing on the power of the sun and the moon and the stars and of nature itself. Above all else, I was taught the importance of keeping all that I learned secret. For the penalty meted out to practitioners of the Craft in those days was harsh. Mother never told me just how harsh. I learned that when I was twenty and one, in a lesson so cruel its memory remains burned in my mind, though three full centuries have passed. And yet it was because of that cruelty that I first set eyes upon Duncan Wallace.

The key to my mother's ruin was her kindness. My father had died only a fortnight before, of a plague her simple folk magick could not fight. Many lives were lost in our small English village that brutal winter of 1689, and perhaps my mother simply could not bear to see one more death after so much grief.

At any rate, it was Matilda, the sister of my dead father, who came pounding on our door that dark wintry night. Looking startled at Aunt Matilda's state—wild hair and wilder eyes and not so much as a cloak about her shoulders—Mother drew her inside and bade her take the rocking chair beside the hearth to warm herself. I offered tea to calm her. But Aunt Matilda seemed crazed and refused to sit down. Instead, she paced in agitated strides, her skirts swishing about her legs, her thin slippers leaving damp footprints on our wood floor.

"No time to sit an' sip tea," she told us. "Not now. 'Tis my youngest, my little Johnny, named for my own dear brother who has gone to his reward. My Johnny has taken ill!" She whirled and grabbed my mother, gripping the front of her dress in white-knuckled fists. "I know you can help him. *I know*, I tell you! An' if you refuse me now, Lily St. James, I vow, I'll—"

"Matilda, calm yourself!" My mother's firm voice quieted the woman, though only for a moment, I feared. "I would never refuse to help Johnny in any way I can. You know that."

"I *don't* know it!" my aunt shrieked. "Not when you let your own husband die of the same ailment! Pray, Lily, why didn't you save him? Why didn't you save my brother?"

My mother's head lowered, and I saw the pain flare anew in her eyes—a pain that sometimes dulled but never died away.

"I tried everything I knew to help Jonathon. But I couldn't save him," she whispered.

"Perhaps because you brought the illness on him from the start."

"Aunt Matilda!" I stepped between the two, forgetting to respect my elders and tugging my aunt's arm until she faced me, rather than my mother. "You know better. My parents shared a love such as few people ever know, and I'll not stand by and hear you sully its memory."

"Raven, don't," Mother began.

But I rushed on. "No one can bring on such a plague as this, and well you know it!"

"No one but a Witch, you mean, don't you, Raven? *Raven*. She even named you for some dark carrion bird. Are you practicing the black arts as well, girl?" Aunt Matilda gripped my shoulders, shook me. "Are you? *Are you?*"

I could only blink in shock and stagger backward, pulling free of her chilled hands. My aunt *knew*. But how? How could she know the secret that had been only between my mother and me? Even my father had been unaware. . . .

"What makes you say such a thing?" my mother asked gently. "How can you accuse your own sister?"

"Sister-in-law and not by blood," Matilda reminded my mother. "And I know. I've always been suspicious of you and your Pagan ways, Lily. From the time you helped me birth my firstborn and somehow took away the pain. And later, when you nursed me through the influenza that should have killed me. You with your herbs and brews." She waved a hand at the drying herbs that hung upside down in bunches from our walls, and at the jars filled with philters and powders, lining the roughly hewn wooden shelves. "No physician could ease my suffering the way you did." She said it unkindly, made it an accusation.

Slowly my mother nodded, her serene expression never changing. "Herbs and plants are given by God, Matilda. Knowing how to use His gifts can surely be no sin."

"I saw you last full moon."

The words lay there, dropped like blows, as we stared at one another, my mother and I, both remembering our ritual beneath the full moon, when we chanted sacred words 'round a balefire at midnight.

"I know you have . . . powers. And I don't care if they're sinful or not. Not now. I need you to help Johnny. If you didn't conjure this plague, then prove it. Cure him, Lily. If you refuse . . ." Her eyes narrowed, but she didn't finish.

"If I refuse, you'll do what, dear sister? Bear witness against me to the magistrate? See me tried for Witchery?"

Matilda didn't answer. She didn't need to. I saw her answer in her eyes, and my mother saw it as well.

"You've no need of such threats," Mother told her. "All you had to do was ask for my help. I'll try my best for your son, just as I did for Jonathon. But Witchery or no, I may not be strong enough to help him."

"If he dies, I vow, I'll see you hang!" Aunt Matilda lurched toward the plank door, tugging it open on its rawhide hinges. "Gather what you need and come at once. I must make haste back to his bedside."

She left us in a swirl of snow, not bothering to close the door. I went and shut out the weather, then stood for a long moment, my hand on the door. I had a terrible premonition that the events of the past few moments would somehow change our lives forever. I didn't know how, or why, but I felt it to my bones. Drawing a deep breath, I turned to face my mother. I knelt before her, taking her hands in mine, staring up into eyes as black as my own. "Don't go to him," I begged her. "You cannot help him any more than you could help Father. And when he passes, she'll blame you."

"He is my own nephew," she whispered. She tugged her hands away, got to her feet, and began to make ready, taking sprigs of herbs from the dried bunches hanging on the wall, pouring a bit of this powder and a bit of that into her special cauldron. The one with the hand-painted red rose adorning its squat belly. She added steamy water from the larger cast-iron pot that hung in the fireplace to the brew.

"We should leave this village," I pleaded as I worked at her side, measuring, stirring, holding my hands above each concoction to push magickal energy and healing light into it. "We should leave tonight, Mother. Our secret is known, and you've told me how dangerous that can be."

"I can't break my vows," she said. "You know that. When someone needs help, asks me for help, I am bound by oath and by blood to try. And try I will." She looked into my eyes. "You should pack a bag and go to London. Take the horse. Leave tonight. I'll send for you when—"

"I won't leave you to face this alone," I whispered, and I flung myself into her arms, stroking her raven hair, so like my own, though hers was knotted up in back while mine hung loose to my waist. "Don't ask me to, Mother."

Her mouth curved in the first smile I'd seen cross her lips since my father's death. "So strong," she said softly. "And always, so very stubborn. All right, then. Come, let us hasten to Johnny."

We quickly packed our potions and some crystals and candles into a bag, pulled our worn homespun cloaks over our heads and shoulders, and stepped out into the brutal winter's night.

But my cousin was dead before we even arrived at my aunt's house. And we were greeted by a wild-eyed woman who'd once claimed us as kin, and the group of citizens she'd roused from slumber, all bearing torches and shouting, "Arrest them! Arrest the Witches!"

Cruel hands gripped my arms, even as I turned to flee. Accusations rang out in the night, and people stood round watching as my mother and I were surrounded, and then dragged over the frozen mud of the rutted streets. I cried out to my neighbors, begging for help, but none was forthcoming. And my heart turned cold with fear. As cold as the wind-driven snow that wet my face.

'Twas a long walk, the longest walk of my life. The poor shacks of the village fell away behind us as we were pulled and pushed along, and we emerged onto the cobbled streets that ran between the fine homes of the wealthy in the neighboring town. At last we stood before the house of the magistrate himself, trembling in the icy wind while our accusers pounded upon his door.

The man emerged in his nightclothes after a time, looking rumpled and irritated. "What's all this?" he demanded, white whiskers twitching.

"Two Witches!" shouted the man who gripped my mother's arms tightly. "The ones who brought this plague on us all, Honor."

The old man's eyes widened, then narrowed again as he perused us. Beyond him I could see the glow of a fire in a large hearth, and feel its heat on my face. I longed to go warm my hands by that fire. My fingers were already numb from the cold.

"What evidence have you against them?" the magistrate asked.

"The word of this one's own sister," said another, pointing at my mother.

"Matilda is not my sister," my mother said, her voice ever calm, despite the madness around her. I would never forget her face, beautiful and serene. Her eyes, so brave, no hint of fear in them. "She is the sister of my husband."

"Your husband who died of the plague!" the man cried out. "And now your nephew is taken as well."

"Many have been lost to the plague, sir. Surely you wouldn't accuse every bereaved family of Witchery?"

The man glared at my mother. "Matilda St. James bears witness, Honor. She's seen them practicing their dark rites with her own eyes."

" 'Tis a lie!" I shouted. "My aunt is maddened with grief! She knows not what she says!"

"Silence." The magistrate's command sent shivers down my spine. He stepped forward, glancing down at the woven sack my mother still clutched in her hands. "What have you there, woman?"

Mother lifted her chin, meeting his gaze. I could see the thoughts moving behind his eyes, the way he looked at us, judging us, though we were strangers to him.

" 'Tis only some herbs," she said softly, "brewed in a tea."

"She lies," the man said. "Matilda St. James said this woman was bringing a potion to cure her young son. But she feared the Witch would deliberately wait until it was too late to help the lad, and her fear proved true. A Witch's brew lies in that sack, Honor. Nothing less, I vow."

" 'Tis no potion nor brew," my mother told him. " 'Tis simply some medicinal tea, I tell you."

"Are you a physician, wench?" the magistrate demanded.

"You know that I am not."

"Give me the sack."

The hands holding my mother's arms eased their grip, and she gave her sack over. The magistrate opened it, pawing its contents, and I shuddered recalling the stones we'd put inside. Glittering amethyst and deep blue lapis, for healing. And the candles, made by our own hands and carved with magickal symbols to aid in Johnny's recovery. We would have set them around his bed, where they would have burned all night to protect him from the ravages of the plague.

The magistrate saw all of this, and when he looked up again, his eyes had gone cold. So cold I felt even more chilled despite the warmth from the fire at his back. "Put them in the stocks. We try them on the morrow. Perhaps a night in the square will convince them to confess and save us the time." He withdrew, leaving the door wide, and reappeared a moment later with a large key, which he handed over to one of the men. "See to it."

"No!" I cried. "You mustn't do this! We've done nothing wrong. Magistrate, please, I beg of you—"

His door closed on my pleas, and again I was pulled and dragged as I fought my captors. But my struggles were to no avail. And soon I found myself being forced to bend forward, my wrists and my neck pressed awkwardly into the stock's evil embrace. The heavy, wooden top piece was lowered as my own neighbors held me fast, and I heard the chain and the lock snapping tight.

I could not move. Could not see my mother, but I knew she was nearby, for I heard her voice, strained now, but steady. "Tell the magistrate he shall have my confession," she said. "But only if he will let my daughter go free. She knows nothing of this matter. Nothing at all. You must tell him."

The man to whom she spoke only grunted in reply. And then the villagers left us. In the town square, bent and held fast, we waited in silence for the dawn. The freezing wind cut like a razor, and the wet snow continued to slash at us. I shivered and began to cry, my face stinging with cold, my hands numb with it, my feet throbbing and swelling.

And then I heard my mother's gentle voice, chanting softly, "Sacred North wind, do us no harm. Ancient South wind, come, keep us warm." Over and over she repeated the words, and I forced my teeth to stop chattering and joined with her, closing my eyes and calling to the winds for aid. My mother's folk magick could not make iron chains melt away. But she could invoke the elements to do our bidding.

Within minutes the harsh wind gentled, and the snow stopped falling. A warmer breeze came to replace the bitter cold, and my shivering eased. I was still far from comfortable, bent this way, unable to relieve the ache in my back. But I knew my mother must be suffering far more than I, for her body was older than mine. Yet she did not complain. I took strength from that, and vowed to keep my discomfort to myself.

"Hard times await us, my daughter," she told me. "But whatever happens tomorrow, Raven, you must remember what I tell you now. Promise me you will."

"I promise," I whispered. "But, Mother, you mustn't confess anything to them. Not even to save me. I couldn't live if you were to die." The thought terrified me, and I pulled my hands against the rough wood that held them prisoner, though I could not hope to work them free. She was all I had in this world. All I had.

"Perhaps this is my destiny," she said softly. "But 'tis not yours."

"How can you know that?"

"I know," she whispered. "I've known from the day you were born, child. By the birthmark you bear upon your right hip. The crescent." Tears burned my eyes. But my mother went on. "You're a far more powerful Witch than I have ever been, Raven."

"No. 'Tis not true. I can barely cast a decent circle."

She laughed then, softly, and the sound of it touched my heart. That she could laugh at a time like this only made me love and respect her more than I already did, though I'd never have thought it possible.

"I speak not of the form of ritual, but the force, Raven. The power is strong in you. And you will need that strength. When this is over, child, you must leave here. Go to the New World. My sister, Eleanor, is there, in a township called Sanctuary, in the colony of Massachusetts. She is not a Witch, and knows nothing of our ways. She was born of my father's faithlessness and raised by her own mother and not in our household. But she is kind. She will not turn you away."

"Perhaps not," I said. "But *I* will not leave you behind."

"I fear 'tis I who will leave you behind, my darling. 'Tis the night of the dark moon, when our powers ebb low. But even were our lady of the moon shining her full light down upon us, I doubt I could save myself. Do not cry for me, Raven. Dying is part of living, a birth into a new life. You know this."

"Oh, Mother, stop saying such things!" I cried loudly, sobbing and choking on my tears.

When Mother spoke again, I could hear tears in her voice as well. "Raven, listen to me. You must listen."

I tried to quiet myself, to do as she wished, but I vowed she would not die tomorrow. Somehow I would save her.

"When 'tis over," she told me, "you must return to our cottage in the village. But do so by night, and be very careful. You mustn't be seen. Do not wait too long, child, lest they burn the house in their vengeance or award it to Matilda's family in return for her testimony against us. You must go back in secret. Gather only what you will need for your journey. Then go to the hearth. There is a loose stone there. Take what you find hidden beyond that stone."

"But, Mother—"

"And take the horse, if she is still there. You may sell her in some other village. But take care. Should you meet anyone, do not tell them your true name. And as soon as you can, book passage on a ship to the New World. Now promise me you will do these things."

"I'll not let them kill you, Mother."

"There is nothing you can do to prevent it, child. I'll have your promise, though, and I will die in peace because of it. Promise me, Raven."

Sniffling, I muttered, "I promise."

"Good." She sighed, so deeply it seemed as if some great burden had been lifted from her shoulders. "Good," she whispered once more, and then she rested. Slept, perhaps. I could not be sure. I cried in silence from then on, not wishing to trouble my Mother with my tears. But I think she knew.

When dawn came, it brought with it the magistrate, and beside him a woman, looking distraught with red-rimmed eyes. Behind them walked a man who wore the robes of a priest. He had an aged face, thin and harsh, with a hooked nose that made me think of a hawk, or some other hungering bird of prey. He was pale, as if he were ill, or weak. And then they came closer, and I could see only their feet, for I could not tip my head back enough to see more.

"Lily St. James," the Magistrate said, "you and your daughter are charged with the crime of Witchcraft. Will you confess to your crimes?"

My mother's voice was weaker now, and I could hear the pain in it. "I will confess only if you release my daughter. She is guilty of nothing."

"No," the woman said in a shrill voice. "You must execute them now, Hiram. Both of them!"

"But the law—" he began.

"The law! What care do you have for the law when our own child has become ill overnight? What more proof do you need?"

At her words my heart fell. She blamed us for her child's illness, just as my aunt had done. No one could save us now.

I heard footsteps then, and sensed the magistrate had gone closer to my mother. Leaning over her, he said, "Lift this curse, woman. Lift it now, I beg of you."

"I have brought no curse upon you, nor your family, sir," my mother told him. "Were it in my power to help your child, I would gladly do so. As I would have for my own husband and for my nephew. But I cannot."

"Execute them!" his wife shouted. "Michael was fine until you arrested these two! They brought this curse on him, made him ill out of pure vengeance, I tell you, and if they live long enough to kill him, they will! Execute them, husband. 'Tis the only way to save our son!"

The priest stepped forward then, his black robes hanging heavily about his feet and dragging through the wet snow. His steps were slow, as if they cost him a great effort. He went first to my mother, saying nothing, and I could not see what he did. But he came seconds later to me and closed his hand briefly around mine.

A surge of something, a crackling, shocking sensation jolted my hand and sizzled into my forearm, startling me so that I cried out.

"Do not harm my daughter!" my mother shouted.

The priest took his hand away, and the odd sensation vanished with his touch, leaving me shaken and confused. What had it been?

"I fear you are right," the priest said to the magistrate and his wife. "They must die, or your son surely will. And I fear there is no time for a trial. But God will forgive you that."

Pacing away, his back to us, the magistrate muttered, "Then I have little choice." And the three of them left us alone again. But only for a few brief moments.

"Mother," I whispered. "I'm so afraid."

"You've nothing to fear from them, Raven."

But I *did* fear. I'd never *felt* such fear grip me as I felt then, for within moments the priest had returned, and he brought several others with him. Large, strong men. People filled the streets as my mother and I were taken from the stocks. The people shouted and called us murderers and more. They threw things at us. Refuse and rotten food, even as the men bound our hands behind our backs and tossed us onto a rickety wagon, pulled by a single horse. I crawled close to my mother, where she sat straight and proud in that wagon, and I leaned against her, my head on her shoulder, my arms straining at their bonds, but unable to embrace her.

"Be strong," she told me. "Be brave, Raven. Don't let them see you tremble in fear before them."

"I'm trying," I whispered.

The wagon drew to a stop, and the ride had been all too short. I looked up to see a gallows, one used so often it looked to be a permanent fixture here. I was dragged from the wagon, and my mother behind me. But she didn't fight as I did. She got to her feet and held her head high, and no one needed to force her up the wood steps to the platform, while I kicked and bit and thrashed against the hands of my captors.

She paused on those steps and looked back at me, caught my eyes, and sent a silent message. *Dignity.* She mouthed the word. And I stopped fighting. I tried to emulate her courage, her dignity, as I was marched up the steps to stand beside her, beneath a dangling noose. Someone lowered the rough rope around my neck and pulled it tight, and I struggled to be brave and strong, as she'd so often told me I was. But I knew I was trembling visibly, despite the warmth of the morning sun on my back, and I could not stop my tears.

That priest whose touch had so jolted me stood on the platform as well, old and stern-faced, his eyes all but gleaming beneath their film of ill health as he stared at me . . . as if in anticipation. Beside him stood another man who also wore the robes of clergy. This one was very young, my age, or perhaps a few years my elder. In his eyes there was no eagerness, no joy. Only horror, pure and undisguised. They were brown, his eyes, and they met mine and held them. I stared back at him, and he didn't look away, but held my gaze, searching my eyes while his own registered surprise, confusion. I felt something indescribable pass between us. Something that had no place here, amid this violence and hatred. It was as if we touched, but did so without touching. A feeling of warmth flowed between him and me, one so real it was almost palpable. And I knew he felt it, too, by the slight widening of his eyes.

Then his gaze broke away as he turned to the older man and said, "Nathanial, surely 'tis no way to serve the Lord."

The kiss of Scotland whispered through his voice.

"You are young, Brother Duncan," the older man said. "And this no doubt seems harsh to you."

"What it seems like to me, Father Dearborne, is murder."

"'Thou shalt not suffer a Witch to live,'" the priest quoted.

"'Thou shalt not kill,'" the young Scot—Duncan—replied. And he looked at me again. "They've nay been tried."

"They were tried in the square by the magistrate himself."

"It canna be legal."

"His Honor's own child is ill with the plague. Would you have us wait for the wee one to die?"

The young man's gaze roamed my face, though he spoke to the old one. I felt the touch of those eyes as surely as if he caressed me with his gentle hands, instead of just his gaze.

"I would have us show mercy," he said softly. "We've no proof these women have brought the plague."

"And no proof they haven't. Why take the risk? They are only Witches."

The beautiful man looked at the older one sharply. "They are human creatures just as we are, Nathanial." And he shook his head sadly. "What are their names?"

"Their names are unfit for a man of the cloth to utter. If you so pity them, Duncan, ease your conscience by praying for their souls. For what good it might do."

"'Tis wrong," Duncan declared urgently. "I'm sorry, Father, but I canna be party to this."

"Then leave, Duncan Wallace!" The priest thrust out a gnarled finger, pointing to the steps.

Duncan hurried toward them, but he paused as he passed close to me. Then turned to face me, as if drawn by some unseen force. His hand rose, hesitated, then touched my hair, smoothing it away from my forehead. His thumb rubbed softly o'er my cheek, absorbing the moisture there. "Could I help you, mistress, believe me I would."

"Should you try they would only kill you, as well." My voice trembled as I spoke. "I beg you . . . Duncan . . ." His eyes shot to mine when I spoke his name, and I think he caught his breath. "Don't surrender your life in vain."

He looked at me so intently it was as if he searched my very soul, and I thought I glimpsed a shimmer of tears in his eyes.

"I willna forget you . . ." he whispered, then shook his head, blinked, and continued, ". . . in my prayers."

"If there be memory in death, Duncan Wallace," I said, speaking plainly, even boldly, for what had I to lose now? "I shall remember you always."

He drew his fingertips across my cheek, and suddenly leaned close and pressed his lips to my forehead. Then he moved on, his black robes rustling as he hurried down the steps.

"Do you wish to confess your sins and beg the Lord's forgiveness?" the old priest asked my mother.

I saw her lift her chin. "'Tis you who ought to be begging your God's forgiveness, sir. Not I."

The priest glared at her, then turned to me. "And you?"

"I have done nothing wrong," I said loudly. "My soul is far less stained than the soul of one who would hang an innocent and claim to do it in the name of God." Then I looked down at the crowd below us. "And far less stained than the souls of those who would turn out to watch murder being done!"

The crowd of spectators went silent, and I saw Duncan stop in his tracks there on the ground below us. He turned slowly, looking up and straight into my eyes. "Nay," he said, his voice firm. "'Tis wrong, an' I willna allow it!" Then suddenly he lunged forward, toward the steps again. But the guard at the bottom caught him in burly arms and flung him to the ground. A crowd closed around him as he tried to get up, and he was blocked from my view. I prayed they would not harm him.

"Be damned, then," the old priest said, and he turned away.

The hangman came to place a hood over my mother's head, but she flinched away from it. "Look upon my face as you kill me, if you have the courage."

Snarling, the man tossed the hood to the floor and never offered one to me. He took his spot by the lever that would end our lives. And I looked below again to see Duncan there, struggling while three large men held him fast. I had no idea what he thought he could do to prevent our deaths, but 'twas obvious he'd tried. Was still trying.

"'Tis wrong! Dinna do this thing, Nathanial!" he shouted over and over, but his words fell on deaf ears.

"Take heart," my mother whispered. "You will see him again. And know this, my darling. I love you."

I turned to meet her loving eyes. And then the floor fell away from beneath my feet, and I plunged through it. I heard Duncan's anguished cry. Then the rope reached its end, and there was a sudden painful snap in my neck that made my head explode and my vision turn red. And then no more. Only darkness.

Chapter 2

Duncan didn't even know her name.

He didn't even *know her name.*

And yet he felt as if he'd lost a treasured friend . . . more than that, even. 'Twas as if a part of his own soul had just been brutally murdered in the town square.

Her surname, St. James, he'd heard that much muttered in the streets. More than that he didn't know. Might never know.

"I tried," he whispered. "God knows I tried."

He'd been moved, beyond all reason, all logic, when he'd heard her strong, deep voice and the courage it held as it rang out over the spectators, shaming them as they should well be shamed. And he'd known then that he had to try. Though he had no idea now what he could have done, even had they let him pass. Even had he reached her again. Perhaps he'd been a bit mad.

Perhaps she truly was a Witch and had cast some spell, some enchantment, o'er his heart there on the gallows. He didn't know. He only knew that something had possessed him—some sudden, violent, *desperate* need to save her.

And that he'd failed.

She swung slowly from the end of a rope beside her mother, her life snuffed out far too soon. And he realized, by the cold dampness seeping through his robes and chilling his legs, that he knelt now, before the gallows. He seemed to have fallen right where he'd been standing when the trapdoor had jerked away from beneath the beautiful girl. And he remained there still, kneeling in the snow.

He got to his feet, but his legs felt weak and his chest hollow. Staggering forward, he snatched a blade from a local man's belt as he passed the fellow. Ignoring the man's outcry, he moved beneath the gallows, to gather the young woman's body into his arms. He held her tight to him as he sawed at the rope until it gave way. Her weight fell upon him, head resting on his shoulder like a lover's. Satin soft hair, snow damp and fragrant, brushed against his cheek. He closed his arms round her body and turned his face full into that hair to inhale it and to feel it and to commit it to memory—as well as to hide the inexplicable tears that welled up in his eyes. So warm, her face on his skin. So much as if she were only sleeping.

"What might you have been to me?" he asked her, his voice a strangled whisper. "What might we have been to each other?"

But he spoke to death, and death did not answer.

"Though it makes no sense, lass, my heart is broken. I didna know you at all, an' yet it feels so very much as if I did. As if I always have." He rocked her in his arms, and a sob choked him. "Can you hear me? Are you out there, somewhere, listenin', lass? I'll give you a proper burial, I vow it. An' your dear mother, too."

He held her close, enveloped in a sadness he could not explain and a new certainty about the path he'd walk in this life. And he owed her thanks for that, if nothing else, he realized.

A heavy hand fell upon his shoulder. "What sort of spectacle do you wish to make of yourself, boy?"

Duncan turned to see the murderer himself, Nathanial Dearborne, his own trusted mentor. "Do you ken what you've done this day?" he asked the man.

Nathanial's eyes narrowed, and he signaled to someone with a flick of his wrist. Immediately three men rushed forward to tear the beauty from Duncan's arms, even as he cried out in protest. They bore her away, dumping her body on the back of a rickety wagon where her mother already lay. The man in the driver's seat snapped the reins, and the wagon trundled away.

"Where are they takin' her?" Duncan demanded, addressing Dearborne but keeping his gaze riveted to that wagon—to *her*—until it rounded a curve and disappeared from sight.

"To the pit beyond the town. Best to get their kind as far from decent folk as possible, lad. You'll understand one day. This was . . . for the best."

" 'Twas murder," Duncan spat out, "an' sin of the most vile sort!" He glared at the man now that the wagon was gone from his sight. "I canna continue under the tutelage of a man who would condone it. My studies end here, today, Nathanial. I want no part of your priesthood, for you've shown it to be one of purest evil."

Nathanial's cloudy blue eyes narrowed, but not in anger, and he didn't shout "Blasphemy!" as Duncan had expected.

He simply said, "I'd hold my tongue, were I in your place, Duncan. You have no idea what sorts of forces you are dealing with."

"I willna hold my tongue. I *canna*."

Nathanial shook his head slowly. "You know the teachings of the Church. The elimination of Witches is our duty as Christians, Duncan. 'Tis imperative we wipe them from existence, rid the world of the scourge of Witchery."

Duncan searched the old man's face. He'd been close to him once, thought of him almost as fondly as he did his own father. No more. "An' what will you do next, Nathanial, when you've murdered them all? What will your next mission be? To rid the world of anyone else whose beliefs differ from your own?"

Nathanial smiled. "The Crusades attempted that and failed. I simply seek to do my duty, Duncan. And 'twill be a service to all Christians if I succeed."

"Nay," Duncan said. "Not all." And he turned from the man, feeling nothing now but loathing for him. A man he'd once thought to be closer to God than anyone he'd known. But Duncan realized now that Nathanial was nothing. Less than nothing. A killer who seemed to enjoy his work.

"Where are you going?" Nathanial demanded. "Don't turn your back on me, boy! Answer my question!"

With a glance over his shoulder and an awareness of the people looking on, listening in, Duncan replied. "I'm goin' to gather my things, Nathanial. An' then I'm goin' to see those two women get a proper burial. After that, I only know I'll be goin' as far away from you an' your kind as I can. You are no man of God, but a hypocrite an' a killer, an' I canna abide bein' in the same village with you."

Then he continued on his way without another word, hearing the gasps and whispers of the townspeople as he passed.

It surprised him when a hand fell upon his shoulder. Stopping in his tracks, he didn't turn around. For he knew that gnarled old hand well.

"Duncan, wait," Nathanial said. "Perhaps I was too harsh. 'Tis obvious this morning's work has distressed you. But there is truly no need to take such drastic measures. Surely you don't mean to leave here—"

"Aye, Nathanial, that I do."

"You cannot!"

Frowning, Duncan turned. Nathanial composed himself, tempered his voice. "Duncan, you've been like a son to me. Believe me, boy, were this action not necessary, I'd never have—"

"But you did. 'Tis done, Nathanial, an' there's no undoin' it now."

Lowering his head, Nathanial drew a breath. "I am ill, Duncan. Surely you know that."

"Aye, I know it. I've seen you growin' weaker by degrees, an' wished to God I could do somethin' about it, Nathanial. But I canna help you. An' being ill, even facin' death itself doesna give you the right to go about hanging innocents."

"I . . . I had no choice."

"An' I have no choice now," Duncan said. He turned away, having nothing more to say to the old man he'd once loved. But as he walked on, he heard Nathanial continue.

"'Tis because of the girl, isn't it? This is *her* doing."

Duncan kept walking.

"Damn her," Nathanial cried. "Damn her, she'll pay. I'll *make sure* she pays!"

"She's beyond your reach now, Nathanial."

"Oh, don't be so sure of that, my boy," Nathanial muttered.

Duncan turned then, only to see the old man walking away. He didn't know what Nathanial could have possibly meant by his words. But it didn't matter. The lass was gone now. Dead, and Nathanial was as responsible as if he'd pulled the lever himself. Duncan would never forgive the man.

He went to his stark room in the back of the church, to gather his meager possessions into a sack. He would never return here again; he'd meant what he'd said. This place had been his home for two years as he studied for the priesthood at Nathanial's feet. But that was over now.

What he had seen today—and what he'd *felt*—had changed him forever. He sensed it deep inside, though he had no idea how this change would manifest. He only knew he had to leave.

He only knew the strange beauty had touched him, touched his heart, and his soul, and his life, and that he would feel that touch for a long, long time to come.

Slinging his sack over his shoulder, he walked out again into the streets. People whispered and pointed as he passed. He didn't care. He would have liked a horse. It was a long walk to the place where they'd taken the girl and her mother. But he sensed it would be only the beginning of an even more distant journey. That the steps he took now were the first steps on the way to his destiny.

The darkness that descended on me when I reached the end of that rope was a temporary one.

I remember so clearly the sudden, desperate gasp I drew, the blinding flash of white light that stiffened my body and made me fling my head backward as I dragged in as much air as my lungs could contain. The rapidly fading pain in my neck and my head. And the shock I felt as I realized . . . I was still alive.

I was . . . alive!

I blinked my eyes open and looked around me, and then my stomach lurched. 'Twas daylight, morning. Still early, I guessed. I lay upon the ground with the bodies of the dead strewn around me. The bodies of hanged criminals, and those taken by the disease plaguing the area. This was the pit they'd dug for this purpose. Every so often men would come here with shovels to cover over the dead, and ready the place for another layer of victims of the plague and the gallows. But I was not dead.

I was not dead.

I sat up slow, gagging at the stench of rotting flesh, and looked around me, frantically searching for my mother. I'd had no idea her magick was strong enough to save us from the gallows, but it must have been, for I was alive, and she—

She . . . no. Oh, no.

I found her, and my heart shattered. She lay still, her neck broken, her eyes open but no longer beautiful or shining like onyx. They were already dulled by the filmy glaze of death.

"Mother! No, Mother, no!" I gathered her into my arms, sobbing, near hysteria as I held her close, and rocked her against me. "You can't be gone! You can't leave me this way. Why, Mother?" But she did not answer, and so I screamed my question again, to the earth and the sky and the corpses all around me. "Why am I still alive? Why do I live, and not my precious Mother? Why?" But I knew I would get no reply.

Not from the dead. Not from my mother. Her spirit no longer lived in this body. She was gone. Gone, and I was alone.

Eventually I sat back and looked down at her poor body, an empty shell, yes, but even so 'twould not remain here in this vile place. Not while my heart still beat on.

Gently I lifted her in my arms. I was taller, larger than she. But even then it shouldn't have been so easy to carry her. I thought perhaps 'twas my grief making me strong.

I made my way out of the pit and took my mother's body into the forest nearby. And there, I scooped away the snow, and scraped out a grave for her with no more than my two hands and a flat stone for a tool. My nails were split, my fingers bleeding and throbbing with cold when I finished, but I was beyond noticing the pain. I buried my beloved mother there, and then I lay upon her grave and cried.

When at last he reached the gruesome place of the dead, Duncan shuddered at the sight of the bodies strewn there. He pressed a handkerchief to his face, and even then the stench was sickening. And disease, too, hung on the very air here. One could smell it, almost feel it. Yet he searched for the dark beauty among the dead.

"Where are you?" he whispered as his gaze scanned the carrion. That she should be here in this filth even for a short time brought a fury more powerful than any he'd felt before surging through his veins. What was it about her that caused such reactions in him? Why did he care so deeply for a girl he didn't even know?

"Duncan!" a voice called, and he turned. "Come away from there afore you take ill!"

At the rim of the pit a young man Duncan had called friend since they were lads together in Scotland sat astride his horse. Samuel MacPhearson leaned on the pommel, looking down at him.

"I'll nay go until I find them," he said.

"Well, you willna find them, my friend, for they be elsewhere. I searched myself only an hour ago. Arrived here faster by horse, I suppose, than you could by foot."

"Are you certain?" Duncan asked.

"Aye. I wouldna lie to you about this, Duncan. I can see 'tis important to you. Or she is. Did you know the lass?"

"Nay," Duncan said, making his way to the edge. "But it felt as if I did." When he began to climb up, Samuel dismounted and bent to offer a hand. Duncan got his footing at the top and brushed at his soiled clothes. Homespun, and barely fitting. But all he had once he'd discarded the robes he no longer felt able to wear.

"Why were you looking for them, Samuel?" Duncan asked.

"Same reason as you, I'd guess. To bury them proper. I liked what was done no more than you did, Duncan." He looked out over the dead and grimaced. "I didna find them, though."

Duncan's heart twisted. "Where can they be?"

Samuel smiled, but 'twas bitter. "No doubt your friend Dearborne would claim they used black magick to rise up an' walk away. But I suspect there's a far more simple solution. Some relative came for their bodies in secret. It happens, Duncan."

Duncan nodded but met Samuel's eyes. "Nathanial Dearborne is no friend of mine."

"He was here, you know."

Duncan frowned. "Nathanial? Here?"

"Aye, lookin' for those two women himself, I do believe. An' if he got here afore me, Duncan, he must have run his horse ragged the whole way. I meant to ask him why that was, but he beat a hasty retreat when he saw my approach."

The thought of that bastard laying his hands upon the girl set Duncan's teeth on edge. "He didna find them? You're certain of that?"

"Certain as I can be," Samuel said. "He seemed to be still searchin' when I arrived, and he had no bodies o'er his saddle when he galloped away."

"What could he want with them?"

"Nothing good, I'll warrant."

"The bastard."

Samuel's brows rose in twin arches. "Ah, so your great teacher is a bastard, now, is he?"

Duncan sighed, looking at the ground. "You were right about him all along, Samuel, an' I should've listened to you. Aye, he's a bastard, an' a killer, an' I told him as much."

"Indeed," Samuel said, slapping Duncan's shoulder. "Half the town knows of it by now." He tilted his head to one side. "They're sayin' she bewitched you, Duncan. Stole your heart right there on the gallows."

Duncan lifted his head to meet his friend's eyes. "Perhaps she did," he whispered.

"Aye, I can see this has shaken you deeply."

"An' what's shakin' me more is that I willna know where she rests. Even that small comfort has been stolen from me. 'Twas wrong, what was done to her, Samuel."

Samuel nodded. "'Tis yet another reason I've decided to move on. I'm takin' Kathleen and leavin' this place. An' Duncan, my new bride an' I would be proud to have you come along with us."

Duncan searched Samuel's face. "Where will you go? Back to Scotland?"

"Across the sea, my friend. To the New World. They say 'tis far different there. Opportunity for every man. The rich an' the poor livin' as equals."

Taking a deep breath, Duncan thought hard about saying yes. He'd heard talk of this New World, this America, where religious persecution, 'twas said, did not exist. Wild and new and exciting. The idea appealed. But he had matters to attend to. Responsibilities to uphold.

"I'd like nothin' better than to do just that, Samuel. But not now. I must first return to Scotland to face my father with what I've done."

Samuel shook his head. "Angus will be furious, no doubt. He paid Dearborne an' the Church a goodly sum to take you in for trainin'."

"And I'll repay every bit," Duncan vowed.

"After you've repaid the debt to your father, Duncan . . . what then?"

Duncan shrugged, looking off into the distance, seeking something he couldn't name. "I dinna know. In truth, I just dinna know."

Samuel slapped his shoulder. "If you decide to join us in America, my friend, just come along. We'll welcome you gladly."

"Thank you," Duncan said. "I might just do that."

"I hope you will." Then Samuel frowned. "In the meantime, Duncan, I hope you'll put this day's doings behind you. You've a haunted look about your eyes that worries me."

"Haunted," Duncan muttered. "Aye, 'tis just the way I feel. I think that bonny lass will be hauntin' me for some time to come, Samuel. An' I doubt—rather seriously doubt—there's any way on God's earth I can put her memory behind me. I'm not even certain I want to."

Hours passed as I lay weeping atop my mother's grave. And then the day itself waned as well. 'Twas night again before I could even think of leaving her. Even wonder about what I was to do now. And 'twas then I recalled her words to me the night before. I had promised I would do as she asked. I had promised her. I must keep that promise. But first . . .

I dried my tears, tried to reach for the calmness necessary to do what must be done. I searched for that serene place inside me. My breathing deepened. My heartbeat slowed. In silence I pointed my forefinger at the ground and drew an invisible circle round my mother's resting place. And within that circle I sat, closed my eyes, and wished my dear mother goodbye.

For just a moment the wind whispered through the trees overhead in such a way that it seemed my mother's voice spoke to me. *Be strong, Raven. I am with you . . . always. . . .*

"Mother?" Rising, I looked all around me but saw nothing. Only the very thin sliver of the newborn moon appearing in the sky. Like a sign. To start anew. To find a way to go on.

'Twas what my mother would have wanted.

I brushed my fresh tears away and nodded. 'Twas time. But I did not close the circle I'd cast. I left it there, willing it to protect her unmarked grave from harm of any kind. That done, I forced myself to leave her there, so that I could begin doing what she'd asked of me.

I followed her instructions to the letter, sensing she might know, somehow, and be disappointed in me if I did not.

I went to our cabin under cover of darkness, and slipping inside I saw chaos. Our home had been stripped of anything we had of any value. Blankets and clothing, our copper and iron pots. Everything. Even my mother's precious cauldron, which I'd hoped to take with me that I might be reminded of her each time I brewed a magickal potion or used it in ritual. She'd painted a tiny red rose upon its face. It had been her most cherished possession.

But it was gone now.

Something glittered up at me from the floor, and I bent to scoop up a tiny bit of amethyst the looters had somehow missed. Caressing it as if 'twere a diamond, I placed the stone in my pocket.

Our dried herbs had been torn from the walls and trampled beneath booted feet. Not a stick of furniture nor even the braided rugs that had covered the floors remained, and I knew without checking the shed that the horse had been taken as well. They'd left nothing untouched.

I went to the hearth though, tugging at the smooth round stones until I found the very large one that came free at my touch. And then I set it aside and reached into the hole it left. There was a cloth bag there, stuffed full. Frowning, I pulled the bag out and sat down on the floor, untying its drawstring and looking inside. There was a smaller pouch within its folds, a pouch I found to be heavy with coin. And a dark, hooded cloak, lined with fur, all rolled up tight to make it fit in the bag. And there was a book. A beautiful leather-bound grimoire, filled with page upon page of my mother's delicate script.

I opened the cover and saw a necklace, a golden pentacle, with a cradle moon adorning one curve of its circle and the beautiful image of a goddess reclining in the moon's embrace. I lifted the pendant and beneath it, on the page, saw a note just for me.

My dearest Raven,

If you are reading this, you are on your own now. Do not mourn me, child. If my lifetime ended, 'twas only because it had served its purpose, and now I will go on to another. But for you, child, it is only the beginning.

Wear the pentacle, for it holds all the magick I ever possessed. My strength and my wisdom are within it, and they are yours to call upon so long as you wear it. But keep it near your heart, and not out for the world to see. 'Twas never mine to wear. I only held it in trust for you. It marks you as who and what you are.

In this book are all the secrets I've learned. But the one I will tell you now is the most important of all of them. My daughter, my beloved Raven, you are not like me. And the path before you will not be an easy one.

Raven St. James, you are an immortal Witch, a High Witch, though you've never known such beings existed.

When you suffer and die for the first time, you will know that what I say is true, for within a short while your body will revive itself. And from that moment on you will be stronger than before, and will never grow older.

I know this must shock you. But you are not the only one. There are others like you, though their numbers are few. And not all of them are good and pure of heart, as I know you to be.

The stories of them have been handed down through the generations of my family, and I will tell you all I know, and hope you put the knowl-

edge to good use, to keep you safe. But I fear there is much I do not know, Raven. Things you will have to learn on your own.

There are two kinds of immortal Witches. The dark, and the light. The evil, and the good.

In some previous lifetime, my daughter, you died while attempting to save the life of another Witch. Because of this, you were born into this lifetime with the gift of immortality. But this is only one of two ways that gift can be passed on.

The other way is far more sinister. By taking the life of an immortal Witch, one also takes that Witch's immortality, indeed, all of her power. I can imagine you crooking your delicate brow as you read this, wondering how one can kill someone who is immortal. There is but a single way, child. And that is to take the Witch's heart from her very breast, and to lock it up in a small box where it will go on beating forever. Whoever retains the box, retains the power. Witches created in this way are dangerous to you, Raven, for they are never content with the power they have acquired. They cannot be, for eventually, the captive heart will weaken, its life force drained by the dark one who took it. The Dark Witch begins to weaken, to grow pale and sickly just as any mortal suffering from the ravages of old age might do. And so the Witch must kill again and again, in order to survive.

Always beware of others like you, Raven. For you'll have no way of knowing whether they be dark or light. You will recognize them as Immortals, however. By the necklace many of them wear, one such as the one I give you now, and by the first touch of their hand. I do not know how or why that is, but I know 'tis true. Be careful, my love. Let no Dark Witch take your heart.

Hidden in the center of this book is a dagger that has been handed down through the generations of my family from time immemorial, just as this pendant was, to be held for the day when a special one was born to us. 'Tis as if they knew, somehow. It is yours, Raven, meant for you all along, I am certain. Keep it with you always and learn to wield it with skill. You will need to defend yourself from attack by those others. Above all, child, trust no one.

No one.

And know that wherever you are and for as long as forever, my love remains with you. Always with you.

Your loving mother,
Lily St. James

Blinking in shock at all I had read, I let the book fall open to its center and saw a jewel-encrusted dagger, tucked inside its sheath and hidden by the clever way my mother had cut away the centers of some of the pages. I took the weapon in my hands, turned it slowly, felt its weight, and tried to imagine myself using such a tool to do harm to another living being. The thought made me shiver. I did not believe I could ever do it.

But there was more to try to understand. More, so much that my mind could barely comprehend the enormity of it.

"Immortal," I whispered. And I knew, I already knew, 'twas the truth.

Chapter 3

The sack over my shoulder, my face concealed within the hood of the dark cloak my mother had left for me, I left the only home I'd ever known for the very last time. There was but a sliver of moonlight to guide me as the moon moved from its darkest void toward its first quarter. The thin slice of its gleaming white crescent was barely enough to light my way. I saw no one as I started down the worn dirt path on foot, more alone than I had ever been. But I should have sensed the presence. I was too wrapped up in sorrow and overwhelmed by grief to use my senses. Even as a mortal, I would have felt the danger, I thought later, for a Witch is more attuned to her senses than most. And since I'd quickened from a state of death, my senses were even sharper than before. They seemed to grow stronger and more acute with each passing hour. But for some reason that night, I tuned them out and focused only on my loss. My sadness. The fact that I'd lost the only person left with whom I'd had a special bond, a connection.

There was, I realized, one other, now. Another to whom I felt a powerful bond. An inexplicable link. A man whose touch made my heart flutter like the madly beating wings of a captive butterfly. A man . . . I must never, ever see again.

Those thoughts, those feelings, clouded my mind, dulled my senses, or at least made me ignore them. And then the cloaked figure stepped from a small copse of trees, into the path in front of me, and a harsh voice whispered, "I knew you'd come back here."

I came to a halt, narrowing my eyes to see his face, but it was hidden just as mine was, by the folds of a dark hood. My dagger was still secured inside the book, tucked deep in the bag that hung on my shoulder. I thought of it now, and wished I'd been wiser in heeding my mother's warnings. And yet part of me still believed this stranger to be no more than a simple mortal. He couldn't know who I was, much less *what* I was. Everyone here believed me to be dead.

"Who are you?" I asked him. "What do you want of me?"

And in a flash a dagger appeared in his pale, gnarled hand—a dagger so like my own that the sight of it took my breath away. "Not so much," he rasped. "Only your heart."

It couldn't be! But 'twas true, I realized as he lifted the blade and came closer and I backed away. Another immortal, one who wished to *kill* me. The horror of it was suddenly real, far more real to me than it had been as I'd read and scarcely believed the words of my mother's letter. I glanced around me desperately, but the snowy, twisting road and a few lightless, silent cottages were all I saw. No one would come to my aid. A breeze blew snow into my eyes and pushed at my hood, driving it down and away from my face, revealing me to him. Though I realized now he'd already known who I was. He had the advantage, then, for I had no clue as to his identity.

I walked backward, my eyes unalterably fixed to the blade, the way it gleamed when it caught a thin beam of moonlight. "I've no quarrel with you," I whispered, fear making my voice taut and low. "Leave me alone, I beg of you!"

His laughter came then, low and frightening. Harsh and raspy, that sound that made gooseflesh rise on my nape. "That's not the way this works, young one. A shame you won't live long enough to learn the rules of this particular game."

Suddenly he lunged forward, swinging the blade in a deadly arc. I jumped back, gasping as I felt its razor-sharp tip brush past my midsection. I slipped, damp slippers and numbly cold feet unwieldy on the snow-covered road. I nearly fell but caught myself. And he lunged again. I sidestepped this time, yanking the sack from my shoulder and swinging it at him with all my might. It caught him from behind and sent him stumbling forward. He went to his knees, and I turned to run for my very life. But within seconds I knew he was after me. I heard his steps keeping pace, gaining on me. Heard his breaths rasping in and out of his lungs as we ran. It seemed his lungs would burst if he pushed himself any harder. He seemed weak . . . it must have been desperation, then, that drove him on. My own heart pounded in my ears, and my breaths escaped in great puffs of silvery steam.

A tree's limb loomed before me, and I saw it only an instant before I would have run into it. I had to duck low, and as I did, I gripped the branch, pulling it forward with me, and letting it go when it would give no more. It snapped back, slicing the air with a high keen, and spewing snow, and I heard him grunt as it hit him. I thought he went to the ground again, but I could not be sure.

The woods along the roadside were my only hope. I could not fight him, whoever he was, no matter how old or weak he might be. I stood no chance of winning, for I knew nothing of battle. And he'd wielded his blade with the skill of long practice. Ahh, but the woods—they had been my haven all my life. I knew them as well as I knew the cottage where I'd lived. And I took to their protection now, running as fast as I could, never tripping or falling once. I'd bragged to my mother that I could traverse these woods blindfolded. Now I was forced to live up to the claim. I stepped into the deeper snow, shivering as its chill embraced my ankles, soaking through my stockings, and wetting the hem of my skirt. I knew my way, and chose a meandering deer path that bisected the woods at their deepest. And soon I was surrounded by the heady scent of pine and the whispers of those needled boughs brushing one and another with every breath of night wind.

I heard him enter the forest, crashing about like a lame bear. I heard his foul cursing as he hunted for me, and his labored breathing as he grew ever more frustrated. But *he* would not hear *me*. My soft slippers and light steps, though my feet were nearly frozen now, were all but silent. And yet I almost believed the monster could hear the thundering of my pulse and the roar of blood through my veins.

I kept moving, and soon I didn't hear him anymore. Breathless, I made my way to the far side of the small wood, emerging on the road that led to the harbor where the tall ships would be docked. I looked behind me often, but I saw nothing of my attacker. I had eluded him.

This time.

I realized now how very dangerous it was for me to remain in England. Word of my execution would spread quickly, and the tales of my body disappearing would make for wonderful gossip. If there truly were evil immortals out there who sought to take the hearts of their own kind—and I knew beyond doubt now that there were—they would find me all too easily here. I had to leave. Tonight.

So I continued on the road, eight miles to the harbor.

And there, tired from my long walk and shivering with cold, I paused, taken aback by the graceful beauty of those tall ships rocking gently upon the water. Naked masts rose high. The sliver of moonlight reflected back a hundred times from the surface of the briny deep and spilled generously upon the painted hulls. In fact, I thought, I'd never in my life seen anything quite so lovely as those majestic ships floating gracefully upon the water. Like powerful creatures at rest. And it might have been that I could see so much more than I ever had before. Yes, my night vision was getting sharper, but I could also see farther and pick out more details. Like the mermaid with the flowing golden hair, carved into the bow of one ship, and the words *Sea Witch* painted in elegant gold script along either side of her. Lovely.

I was jostled by several people as they passed, and I jumped, startled. There were people here. Many people, and Mother had warned me often that 'twas not safe for a young girl to come to the docks alone. Even more true now, I thought. If I were recognized . . .

Yet I had little choice. I had to leave England, and this was the place from which to do so. I simply pulled my hood closer, better to hide my face, and moved on. There were taverns where the seamen ate and drank, fought and swore. And women of the most disreputable sort, lounging with heavy lidded eyes and painted faces in doorways, calling out to every drunken man who staggered past. The stench of fish, and of liquor, hung heavy here. So much so that the salty fresh smell of sea air was nearly obliterated by it. I heard bawdy songs, off-key and slurred, coming from one establishment, and I dared not go inside. But 'twas not the drunken seamen I feared as much as recognition. Who knew which of these men had been in the crowd who'd watched as I was hanged only the day before?

Tugging at my hood again, I gathered my courage, and approached a woman in a ragged, revealing dress and smudged face paint. She stood near the entrance to a tavern, leaning tiredly against the building as if she'd been standing far too long. But she straightened at my approach.

"Can you direct me, mistress?" I asked her.

She perused me, top to bottom, and I kept my face lowered, one hand holding the hood in place. She smoothed her coppery curls with one hand. "You in hidin', are you?"

"Of course not." It startled me, how obvious I must be. Would she know? Would she guess? Would she alert someone in authority?

She only shrugged. "Yes, you are," she said, "but 'tis nothin' to me one way or the other. What are you doing here, missy? Lookin' to find yourself a seaman to warm yer bed?"

I felt my face heat, glad she couldn't see. "I only wish to know if there's a ship sailing for the New World tonight," I told her. "I need to book passage."

"Ahh, a runaway then? Is it yer man you be escaping?"

"Is there a ship or not?"

Her drawn-on brows arched high. But she concealed her surprise quickly, giving me a crooked smile. "Yer a spunky one, you are. You sure you want to leave? I could put you to work right here, if you like."

"I *have* to go to the New World," I whispered. "*Tonight.*" Several men passed and I fell silent, sensing their gazes on me. They didn't move on right away, and I was careful to keep my back to them. "Please," I said. "If you know of a ship . . ."

"Let's have a look at ye." She yanked my hood down suddenly, and I heard a soft gasp from the onlookers even before I jerked it up again. The woman was shaking her head. "Shame yer leavin'," she said. "Yer a pretty one, fetch a goodly price."

I lowered my head and turned to leave her. She wouldn't help me if I stood here begging her all the night through. I had no time to waste this way.

But then she surprised me. "Hold on, pretty one. There be a ship leavin' at dawn. The *Sea Witch.*"

I stopped, and slowly turned to face her again. "Not until dawn?" My disappointment must have been clear in my voice.

"Dawn is only a few hours off, girl."

"Is it?" I hadn't noticed. Nervously I glanced behind me, in search of the fiend who'd attacked me earlier. And then toward the group of young men who'd seemed so interested in watching us. They still huddled in the shadows not far away. And I still felt eyes on me. When I looked to the woman again, she was frowning, staring at me as if she'd seen something she hadn't before. Perhaps 'twas my fear that finally touched her.

"I can fetch the captain, bring him to you," she said. And there was a softness to her voice that hadn't been there at first. Speaking still lower, she added, "Come with me, girl. I can hide you just fine while you talk with Cap'n Murphy."

I jerked my head up suddenly. "And what makes you think I need to hide?"

She only smiled. "I been there, darlin'. I know the look. Come on, now." She took my arm and guided me around to the rear of the tavern, over the cobblestones that were blissfully free of snow, and through a door into a dark and musty room with several blankets strewn haphazardly upon a sleeping pallet, and little else. She lit a lamp and left me there, and 'twas only a short while later she returned with a finely dressed man who reminded me vaguely of my father, rest his soul.

He looked me over, sent an uneasy gaze to the woman, and then said to me in a gruff voice that seemed far too loud in the small chamber, "I understand you wish to book passage to the New World?"

"Yes," I said.

"'Tis not cheap."

I fished several coins from my bag. "I can pay."

Again he nodded. "I'll need . . . a name. To put in the books."

I knew the woman must have told him I was hiding, or running away. And I had no idea why he would help me on her say-so alone. But the looks they exchanged were familiar ones, and perhaps he trusted her judgment, as unlikely as that seemed. A man like him, a woman like her. Still, he made it clear he was asking for any name I cared to give him, and I gave him the first one that came to mind. "My name is Smith," I said in a soft voice, one quite unused to lying.

"Smith," he said.

I thought he battled a slight smile. He lowered his head, but crinkly lines appeared at the corners of his eyes. My father had lines like those when he smiled.

"It will not do. You'll need to be a bit more creative in the future, dear lady." He looked up again and winked. "'Tis more convincing that way. For now your name is Mistress Hunsinger. Rebecca Hunsinger, and you are traveling to visit your . . ." He rubbed his bearded chin.

"My aunt," I told him, relieved that at least that much was true.

"Of course." He took the coins I offered, examined them in his broad palm, then eyed the small bag from which I'd taken them. "Is this all the luggage you'll be bringing along?"

I lowered my head. "'Tis all I have."

He nodded thoughtfully. "Well now, look here. You've given me more coin than is needed. Perhaps you'll allow me to use the excess on your behalf."

I tilted my head to one side. "I don't under—"

"Certainly there's enough here for a simple dress or two, wouldn't you say, Mary?"

The woman nodded. "I know just where to find what she needs."

The captain pressed one of my coins into her hand. "Good. You'll send them along with one of the men, then. Meanwhile, Mistress Hunsinger, I have a feeling you'll feel better aboard the *Sea Witch*, behind the locked door of your cabin, will you not?"

I blinked in shock at these two strangers and their unexpected kindness. "Why are you helping me?"

The captain shrugged. "I'm known to be a good judge of character, mistress. But Mary here is even better. Perhaps one day, 'twill be me in need of help from a stranger."

"I'm grateful," I told them both. "You've no idea how much."

"Course we do, lass," Mary said. "Go along with Cap'n Murphy now. He'll see you safely to where yer goin'."

The man offered his arm, and I took it gladly. Eager to put England far, far behind me.

He'd seen her! The woman . . . the girl . . . the Witch . . .

But that was impossible. He'd watched her die, held her lifeless body in his arms, cried for her, even.

And yet, for just an instant he'd sworn . . .

Duncan had come with Samuel and Kathleen MacPhearson to the harbor, for they were two of the finest friends he'd ever known, and he'd be no kind of friend to either of them if he didn't see them off and wish them well. He'd long since exchanged his dark robes for plain breeches and a white shirt, and he'd joined them here.

With Kathleen settled in their cabin aboard the *Sea Witch*—Duncan had writhed in bitter irony at the name of the craft—he and Samuel had gone back to the docks for a pint of ale and a long goodbye. They'd been talking with some other men of their acquaintance outside one of the taverns, when he'd glimpsed the small form of the woman. And though she'd been concealed beneath a dark cloak and hood, something about her had caught his attention and refused to let it go.

As Duncan looked on, the whore to whom she spoke reached out and yanked the girl's hood down. And Duncan gasped aloud as he glimpsed her face. Her beautiful, haunting face. Huge dark eyes, and curling ebony tresses of hair. A face that had burned itself a place in his mind. He wouldn't mistake that face.

She'd tugged the hood up again, almost desperately. He'd only glimpsed her for a moment. And he knew what he thought he'd seen was impossible. And yet 'twas not possible he'd been mistaken.

He couldn't shake the feeling that overwhelmed him. The feeling that this was the same woman he'd seen die on the gallows. Though she couldn't be. She *couldn't be.*

He battled a burning need to see her more closely. To make sure. To know . . .

A spell. She must surely have been a Witch after all, and he was under her spell. Imagining her face on strange young women. Thinking of her eyes each time he closed his own. Catching the scent of her hair on every stray breeze. 'Twas unnatural!

And he was sounding like the fearful townsfolk who clamored to see Witches burned or hanged or pitched into the sea. What he felt may be magnified, exaggerated. But 'twas certainly natural. All too much so.

"Easy, my friend," Samuel said in a low voice, one hand on Duncan's shoulder. "She only looks like the dead girl. 'Tis not her."

"You saw?" Duncan asked.

"A brief glimpse of ebony locks is all I saw, an' all you saw, Duncan. Get hold of yourself."

"Nay, I saw more." He strained his ears to listen as the girl spoke to the whore, and he heard her saying she must go to the New World, heard the whore mention the *Sea Witch.*

"'Tis only the ale playin' tricks on your mind, Duncan," Samuel said softly.

Closing his eyes, Duncan whispered, "Aye. I suppose you're right."

But he didn't believe the words he spoke. And the woman . . . she'd be aboard that ship. That same ship, with Samuel and Kathleen. And if she were a Witch, they could be in danger. And if she wasn't, then she should be dead. Hell, either way, she should be dead. But he was compelled, obsessed perhaps. Whatever drove him . . . he had to be sure. He had to.

Lowering his head, rubbing his temples, willing his lips not to utter the words hovering on his tongue, he said them anyway. "Samuel, I've changed my mind. I'm comin' with you."

When he dared lift his head, 'twas to see his friend gaping. "Duncan?"

"I'm comin' with you," he said again.

"But . . . but the debt you owe your father . . ."

"I'll send him what I owe as soon as I find employment in the New World. As easy to pay the debt off from there as from Scotland."

Samuel stared and searched Duncan's face, concern etched on his own. And then he glanced over toward the cloaked woman and the whore, but the two were already hurrying away, around to the rear of the building.

"What made you change your mind, Duncan?" His sharp gaze probed Duncan's as he awaited an answer.

Duncan only shrugged. "A feeling," he said. "Just a feeling in my belly that 'tis the right decision. I can explain no more than that." He met Samuel's gaze. "Dinna ask me to."

Samuel nodded, but again stared off in the direction the women had gone. "I dinna *need* to ask, I fear. Duncan, think! You saw the girl die."

"Aye. I'm not likely to forget it, Samuel."

Still Samuel stared at him.

Duncan forced a smile. " 'Twas only a momentary lapse," he said. "An' my decision has naught to do with her. I only feel . . . a need to be away. To go to some shore so distant that I'll forget the blood I saw spilled here. Forget . . . forget *her*." But even as he said the words, he knew 'twas impossible. He'd never forget her.

Sighing deeply, Samuel nodded. "I'll take you at your word, for now. And be glad of it, too." He slapped Duncan on the shoulder. " 'Twill be the adventure of a lifetime, Duncan Wallace. I promise you that!"

"I have no doubt 'twill be all of that and more," Duncan said, but he wasn't smiling the way Samuel was. Instead he felt physically weak, and shaky, as if a fever were coming on, and atop that was an icy chill in his heart—indeed, in his very soul.

He was able to purchase space in a cabin for the passage to Boston Harbor in Massachusetts Bay Colony aboard the *Sea Witch*. He had his bag with him, the one containing all his worldly possessions, which amounted to a pathetically small bundle. He'd been planning to go on to Scotland as soon as he saw his friends off. But now his destiny seemed to be taking a sudden and unexpected turn. He was going to the New World, lured there, perhaps, by one of the very sirens he'd heard the seamen talk of. A Witch. A specter. A dead woman crooked her finger, and Duncan Wallace followed. He felt foolish, too foolish to tell Samuel the truth . . . that he still believed he'd seen her.

But not too foolish to make inquiries about her once he boarded the ship. He tried to be subtle. But though a few of the other passengers did indeed say they'd seen a woman such as the one he described aboard the *Sea Witch*, just as many denied it.

The ship weighed anchor at dawn, just as planned. And Duncan stood at the rail and watched England—and with it an entire phase of his life—disappear into the morning mist. Before his eyes it became a part of his past.

Except for her. She was present, in his mind, haunting him, always. In his dreams she came to him. He could not shake her image from his every thought. Duncan haunted the decks, searched every group of faces for her cream-skinned beauty, but never saw her. And finally he asked the captain himself. For if anyone would know, he would. He met the man at the helm, overseeing his navigator and manning the wheel. A stiff breeze mussed his silvery hair, but he faced it as if loving it, even as Duncan posed his question.

Captain Murphy shook his head slowly. "No. Sorry, but I can't say we've anyone aboard like that."

"Are you sure?" Duncan asked. And he knew he must sound desperate, but he'd *seen* her. He hadn't imagined it or hallucinated or dreamed it. He'd *seen* her.

The captain smiled. "I'm not so old I wouldn't notice a beauty such as the one you've described, son. No, I tell you, she's not aboard ship." Then the older man frowned, searching Duncan's face. "You don't look well, young man. You be feeling poorly?"

The man's face was more than speculative, and Duncan couldn't blame him. This ship had departed not far from a town ravaged by the plague of late. If Duncan showed signs of illness, the captain would have no choice but to put him off in a dinghy, for the protection of the passengers and the crew. And the truth was, Duncan wasn't feeling up to snuff, and hadn't been since boarding this vessel. And he was worried. But he was also taking great care not to touch anyone else physically, and he stayed well away from the others as he searched the decks for his mysterious beauty. He had no desire to spread illness, if indeed he were becoming ill.

Samuel, of course, had been far too busy, in the confines of his cabin with his new wife, to notice Duncan's behavior. All for the best.

"I'm fine," he told the captain. "Tired, though. An' a wee bit seasick, I fear."

The captain nodded, smiling. "It will pass, once your stomach gets used to the rocking," he said. "You haven't told me your name, lad."

"My manners are lacking. I am Duncan Wallace."

"I thought I detected a hint of the Scot in your voice."

"Aye, 'tis true."

"Captain Davis Murphy," he said, extending a hand.

Duncan couldn't shake, for fear of making the man ill. So he pretended to lose his footing, and gripped the rail. "If you dinna mind, Captain, I'll be goin' back to my cabin now."

"Of course."

As he left, Duncan felt the man's eyes on him. And he wondered if he'd fooled the captain even for a moment.

The journey was going to be exciting, I knew it from the moment we set sail. I spent much of my time sewing, mending my old clothes while wearing the ones the captain had sent to my cabin. I was grateful that I'd have presentable clothing to wear when I met my aunt Eleanor. But more of my time was spent on the decks of the magnificent vessel, staring out over the endless waters. I did so by night, of course, for I could not risk being recognized. But I loved the night, and always had. There was a magickal quality about wandering the decks alone, with no one else about save a few crewmen doing their jobs.

There was something about the sea that moved me. Such a magnitude of power surging beneath the tall ship. I was mesmerized by its endless rhythm, its mystery. And the wind that made those sails billow never let us down. I heard the captain remark more than once that he'd seldom seen the weather more cooperative. I only smiled to myself, and silently whispered thanks to my mother for all she'd taught me.

But as Captain Murphy approached me one night, I saw a certain grimness in his eyes. And I frowned at him. But he merely smiled in return, easing my mind somewhat.

"How are you enjoying the journey?" he asked me.

"Tremendously! I saw a great fish," I told him. "Big as a house, way off in that direction." And I pointed.

"Then your eyes are better than my lookout's, mistress. He's reported no such sighting."

I lifted my chin a bit. "No, neither did the crewmen I pointed it out to. I fear they didn't believe me."

"Of course they did. 'Twas a whale, dear girl. They've seen them before."

I nodded. A whale. My vision had reached a whole new level now, enabling me to see much farther than the mortals aboard. And my other senses were sharper, too. These things amazed me but troubled me, also, for they only served to remind me how very little I knew of my new nature.

"I have some news which might disturb you," the captain said. And as I tilted my head, he went on. "There's a man aboard ship who's been asking after you."

My heart froze. I swore it stopped beating as I recalled the hooded figure who'd attacked me. And the captain must have seen my reaction in my face, for he paled.

"What man?" I asked. "What did he look like?"

"Young, dark hair and brown eyes. Said his name was Duncan Wallace."

I caught my breath, but the captain was still speaking.

"There's no need for you to fear him. I told him no woman such as he described was aboard. But 'tis of no matter at any rate. I plan to put him off soon."

"Put him off?" I felt my eyes widen. He mustn't.

The captain nodded. "I'll wait until we reach a port, if I can, but if his symptoms continue, it will have to be sooner. I can't risk everyone aboard for the sake of one soul."

"I don't understand," I said, searching the captain's face. "I know you to be a kind man, Captain Murphy. Why would you do such a thing?"

The captain lowered his head. "I believe the man to be ill."

My eyes grew still wider. "No," I whispered. Not him, not the man I thought of nightly, the man who visited me in dreams I knew would never be more than that. "The plague?" I asked, breathlessly, thinking of my father, and little Johnny, and how helpless my mother and I had been to help either of them.

"I can't know that. But 'tis not a risk I can take."

I nodded slowly. Duncan Wallace. He was more than just a man who'd touched my soul. He was a priest, or would soon become one. A man who was associated in some way with the priest who'd murdered my mother. A man who'd tried to save us. Who'd seen us die. Was he following me? And if he was, then to what purpose? Did he know, or suspect that I lived still? Would he execute me again himself if he knew what I was? Was he working with that horrible old man? Or was there some other reason?

I could not trust him, despite his honorable and brave actions that cold dawn. Despite the feelings his touch had brought to life inside me. I could not trust him.

But I could not let him be put off this ship, for he would surely die. He'd tried to save my life, no matter what his intentions toward me now. I owed the man.

"I've had experience with the plague, Captain Murphy," I said quite softly. "I could easily tell by examining the man if it is that or some other illness."

The captain frowned at me. "You could be infected yourself, mistress. Even the ship's physician refuses to go near the man to examine him."

I shook my head firmly. "I won't become infected. I've cared for countless victims. I've never become ill." He still looked reluctant. "Surely you'd not wish to send a man to his death needlessly?" I asked him.

"Of course not. But, mistress, I thought you . . . you feared this Wallace."

I shook my head. "No, I do not fear him." I should, I thought, but somehow, I couldn't manage to convince myself to be afraid of the brown-eyed priest. I cleared my throat. "Nor do I trust him. Captain, if I could look on him without him seeing me . . ."

The captain lowered his head, rubbing his chin whiskers in thought. "There might be a way." Then he nodded. "Yes, I think it might work. Let me work on this now. Wait for me in your cabin. I'll come for you when all is ready."

I nodded my agreement. But I was not at ease as I returned to my cabin and waited there for word from the captain. I paced, nervous and frightened. I was taking a risk, I knew it. But as I thought of Duncan, of his eyes and the feeling, that sense of connection, that had passed between us there on the gallows, I knew I had no choice. Secretly, I'd longed to see him again. To thank him for what he'd tried to do. To feel that force moving between us once more. To touch his face, his hair, the way he'd touched mine. I'd longed . . . but secretly. It had been a fantasy. A dream I'd believed had no chance of coming true. Not ever.

And now it seemed . . . it would.

A tap came at my door, and I closed my eyes and stiffened my spine. "Who's there?"

"Captain Murphy."

I opened the door and faced the man. It had been more than an hour since I'd seen him last, and I wondered what he'd been up to, but I didn't have to wonder long.

"We put a sleeping powder into some food and left it for him. I peered in only moments ago. He's eaten every crumb and is resting quietly."

I nodded, battling a chill of foreboding. "Then I'll look in on him now. Take me to his cabin."

I started forward, but the captain caught my arm. "Are you sure, mistress?"

Solemnly, I nodded. And then I moved beside him into the passage, toward the cabin of Duncan Wallace, and with every step, my heart beat a bit faster.

Chapter 4

Just when Duncan had decided his illness was little more than a passing case of the sniffles, his fever climbed dangerously high, giving him renewed reason for doubt. He'd taken to his bunk, pulled the covers up to his chin, and drifted in and out of sleep, alternately freezing and sweltering, shivering and sweating. Each time he woke, he felt worse than the time before.

Damnation. He was thirsty. *Terribly* thirsty, and his throat felt so raw it hurt to swallow. Bleary-eyed, he reached for the pitcher beside his bunk, only to find it dry. And the flickering candle beside it was burning low. How long had he been on his back? Hours? A day? He thought he might be approaching delirium.

The knock at his door couldn't have come at a worse time. If anyone aboard saw him in this condition, they wouldn't hesitate to pitch him into the sea. And he couldn't say he would blame them. From his bed he called, "Who's there?" in a voice gone hoarse and thready.

"Steward, sir. The cap'n asked that I bring a meal down to you. Said you were feelin' a mite seasick, he did."

Closing his eyes, Duncan prayed there would be water. Or ale. *Any* liquid would sooth his parched, burning throat. "Leave it by the door," he called, softening his voice slightly because it hurt to speak any louder. "I'll come for it by and by."

"Very well."

He heard nothing more and waited a good while to be sure the man was gone. He still didn't believe he was sick with the plague. Miserable, feverish, aching, yes. But not dying. Not even close. Still, there was no use risking the health of others. When he felt it was safe, Duncan got to his feet, but his head began to spin the second he did so. He gripped the back of a chair, and it tipped over, toppling him to the floor along with it. Damnation. He was sicker than he'd realized. Could he not even walk on his own?

It seemed better not to try. The ship seemed to be rocking a bit more than usual tonight. Perhaps that was the blame. He crawled on all fours to the door, opened it, and glanced quickly up and down the passage. No one was in sight, so he hauled the tray inside. A fresh pitcher of ale stood upon it, and his thirst burned anew.

The food, the very sight of it, followed quickly by its aroma, made his stomach turn over. He dragged the tray to his bunk, managed to right the chair, and set the pitcher and cup upon it. Then he pulled himself to his feet and, leaning weakly against the wall, struggled to open the port-hole. He dumped the food into the sea, eager to have it out of sight. Perhaps his stomach would settle down some, then.

That done, he let the tin dishes fall to the floor and sank down onto his bed. It seemed he'd used every ounce of energy, all his strength, just to accomplish this one small task. He was disheartened to realize just how weak he truly was.

He managed to pour himself a bit of the ale, slopping too much of it onto the chair as he did. His hand trembled and his wrist felt barely able to lift the pitcher. Then he drank, *deeply*. Hellfire, he'd never been so thirsty in his life. He struggled to fill the cup again but gave up, deciding he was wasting too much of the precious liquid. This time he grasped the pitcher in both hands and tipped it to his mouth, gulping the cool, frothy brew, letting it numb and sooth his throat, and dull his pain. It warmed him some—eased the aches in his bones and joints.

As a student of the priesthood, Duncan had never imbibed in ale overly much. Even that night at the docks before leaving England, he'd only sipped at a single mug, making it last the entire time he'd spent in the tavern. He'd had wine, of course, in very small doses. It had never disturbed him. But suddenly he began to feel even more light-headed and dizzy than he had before. He glanced at the empty pitcher in his hands and realized he'd drained it. The flickering candlelight made him dizzier still, so he lay back on his bed, fully clothed, and closed his eyes. 'Twould pass. The spinning in his head would pass, if he just lay perfectly still.

How long he lay there, he had no notion. He drifted, dozed, woke again only to find his head still spinning. But when he blinked his eyes open this time, the candle's weak flame cast a dim glow upon a face.

Soft. Beautiful. Opalescent in the candle glow. The face of the woman he'd been dreaming about. The dead beauty. His Witch. His enchantress. Was he still dreaming, then?

She leaned over him, one hand sliding gently over his cheek, clasping his jaw and easing his mouth wider. She lifted the candle and seemed to be looking into his mouth. But he could only stare at her. The candlelight danced in her black eyes like the very flames of passion. Her lashes were as dark and thick as if she were a gypsy girl. And that hair. That magnificent hair, cascading and tumbling over her shoulders. Shamelessly free, and uncovered.

He moved his lips, tried to speak. "You . . . you're alive. . . ."

Her black eyes widened and snapped toward his, seemingly surprised to see him awake and staring back at her. Quickly, with a pinch of her fingers, she doused the candle and set it on the stand. And he heard her moving away, heard her soft, nearly silent steps crossing the floor.

"Please . . ." he whispered, and he reached out a weak hand toward her even though she couldn't possibly see it. He couldn't let her go, let her slip away again. He had to know. . . .

Hinges creaked as the door moved. Her voice, the voice of his fantasies, spoke softly. "'Tis not the plague, Captain, but merely a fever that will pass him by soon enough. If you keep everyone away, there will be no danger to the others aboard."

"Are you sure?" The captain sounded less than certain himself. "Because unless you are, mistress—"

"I am certain. I would not tell you so if I were not. I owe you a great deal, Captain Murphy. I'd never repay you by lying about a matter so grave."

The captain might have nodded, because he didn't utter a word. Duncan's head was swimming, and he was trembling with cold again, yet he strained to listen.

"I'll stay with him for a while," the enchantress said. "If you would bring some blankets, and the freshest water to be found, heated in a kettle. Just leave them outside the door."

"But if 'tis truly safe—"

"I only said 'twas not the plague. Though his illness is not deadly, Captain, 'tis most miserable. Best you spare yourself and anyone else from falling prey to it if you can."

"All right. I'll bring what you need. Shall I send the physician, as well?"

Duncan frowned when she spoke again, because her words made no sense to him.

"I can care for him far better than your physician can."

Then he heard the door close and tried in vain to see her in the dark room. Her footsteps brought her nearer, but he might as well have been blind, the room was so devoid of light of any kind.

Her weight sank onto the bed beside him. One of her cool hands stroked his fevered brow, while the other tucked his blanket more closely around him. Her touch was heaven, cooling, calming.

"You're going to be all right, Duncan Wallace. I promise you that."

He closed his eyes, sighing at the comfort her touch brought to him. "You . . . you're the Witch," he muttered. "I saw you die."

"No, Duncan. I'm but a stranger with a gift for healing. And you've never met me before. 'Tis the fever making you see another woman's face instead of mine."

She was lying. Even in this state, he knew she was. He lifted a hand, touched her hair, felt its silk just as before. He could even smell it, and he knew its scent was the same. "If you're not the woman I saw hanged in the town square," he whispered, "then light the candle and let me see your face."

"The candle has burned out."

He tried to sit up, to grip her shoulders, but she easily pushed him back down. He was too weak to fight her. Too sick. Sick. Damnation, he'd forgotten. "You should go, whoever you are," he told her. "You could take ill, as well."

"I've cared for many sick ones, Duncan, but I've never once become sick myself. You've no need to worry on that."

He frowned, and as she leaned over him, pressing her ear to his chest, he buried both hands in her hair, caressing its softness, committing each curl to memory.

She caught her breath and went very still. But she did not pull away. Was she closing her eyes as he was, then? Relishing the feel of his hands in her hair? The beat of his heart beneath her ear? He imagined she was, even thought he heard her sigh in pleasure, before she stiffened her resolve once again.

"Stop, now, Duncan," she said, but her voice was raspy and soft. "I'm only listening to your lungs, not embracing you."

He ran his fingers gently up and down her nape. "I canna stop thinking about you," he told her. "You've haunted me . . ."

"Don't say these things."

But he had to say them. Who knew when he'd get the chance again? "You mustn't leave me again. You must tell me the truth. How could you have survived the hangman's noose? How . . ."

She lifted her head away, and Duncan's hands fell limply to the bed. "You are burning up with fever and imagining things. I've never even seen a hangman, nor a noose, much less survived such horrors. I vow, your imagination is a fertile one, Duncan."

He sat up slightly, supporting himself on his elbow, so dizzy he could scarcely hold his head up. And when she moved close to him again, as if to ease him back down, he clasped her shoulders and drew her even closer. "Are you certain you willna catch this fever from me?"

"Of course," she whispered, and he heard the fear in her voice. The delicious fear. She wasn't pulling away, and she had to know what he intended.

"Good."

His lips found hers in the darkness as if by second sight. Soft, moist, so tender. He kissed her mouth the way he'd dreamed of doing since he'd watched her die. The way no man of his background should even consider doing. But 'twas as if he moved, and acted, without his mind's consent.

She tasted delicious. Sweet and cool and salty. Her lips were full and responsive, her tongue like satin when he touched it with his own. She shivered, or trembled. A soft sigh escaped her mouth, and he swallowed that sigh. His hands dived into her hair, and he deepened the kiss, parting her willing lips further, exploring her mouth, pulling her so close her breasts crushed to his chest. Her arms had gone around him, he realized, stunned. She was holding him, too, kissing him back. He lay back on his bunk, pulling her with him, until she lay stretched atop his body. He ran his hands down over her back and caressed her buttocks, and ached to be inside her, beyond the barriers of clothing.

She braced her hands against his chest and pulled her lips from his. "No," she whispered. "You . . . you're a priest."

"And how could you know that unless you are the woman I believe you to be?"

He felt her shake her head in denial. "The captain . . . he said . . ."

"He'd not have known it either, pretty one." Duncan closed his eyes, dizzy, and aroused to the point where it made him even more so. "I was only a student of the priesthood, lass. An' I gave it up the day I saw my teacher do murder."

She was silent for a moment. "You gave it up?" A slow breath, he felt it warming his face. "Because of . . . of what you saw?"

"Admit you're the one," he begged her. "I've feared for my sanity, lass. Tell me you're she who was hanged for Witchery in the town square. She who has haunted my mind ever since."

"I am not." But her voice trembled. "And you are quite drunk."

"Aye, I fear 'tis true. They brought me ale and I drank it as if 'twere water. I admit, I am unused to its sting."

"And you're half out of your head with fever."

"An' the other half with wantin' you." He pressed his palms to her back to bring her close, kissed her mouth again. His hands moved down her back, low on her thighs, and he bunched up her skirt to stroke the satin skin underneath. He arched his hips against her.

She pressed against him in return, and he heard her shuddering breaths. But she seemed to steel herself against him, and broke the kiss by turning her head to the side. Quickly she whispered, "When you gave up your studies, did you give up your beliefs as well, Duncan? Is it no longer a sin to fornicate?"

She said it in a clipped and harsh tone, and yet struggled to get enough breath for each sentence. As if she were as hungry for him as he was for her.

"I dinna ken *what* I believe. I've never . . . I've never wanted like this before. Perhaps you *are* a Witch, and I've fallen under your spell. . . ."

She jerked free of him so roughly he knew he'd said the wrong thing. He tried to open his eyes, but it was so dark and he was so disoriented, he couldn't be sure if they were open or closed.

"'Tis a typical male who would find a way to blame his lust on the object of it. I've put no spell on you, Duncan Wallace. And if I did, 'twould be a spell designed to sharpen your dull brain, not to make you desire me."

"Nay," he whispered, feeling cold and empty as he listened to the sounds of her getting to her feet, righting her dress. "You'd have no need of a spell to make me desire you, my beauty, because I already do."

"You're out of your head with the ale and the fever." He sensed she'd turned her back to him. "You know not what you say."

"Just tell me 'tis true. That you're alive. That 'tis not all of my imaginin'. 'Twill be enough to sustain me if only I know—"

"I am sorry, Duncan. But I cannot tell you what you wish to hear. If things were different, perhaps—"

"Dammit, woman, there is somethin' between us, an' well you know it. Somethin' alive an' real passed between you an' me on those gallows, an' you felt its power as much as I did, I know it. I saw it in your eyes. You stole my heart, lass . . . an' I dinna even know your name."

"You . . . are mistaken. . . ."

A knock at the door interrupted her, but Duncan thought he'd heard tears in her voice. He feared she was leaving when she answered that knock, but she didn't. She only took what was delivered and came back to him. He could sense the fever soaring high again. He was shivering cold, and damp with sweat, and his mind was wandering, drifting away before he forced it back with an effort. She brought him another blanket, and a cup of something hot and fragrant. She laid cool cloths, across his forehead. And then she told him to sleep. Gently she said the word. Again and again. Until he did.

But not soundly. Not so soundly he didn't know when she spoke again a long while later, after he'd drifted in and out of sleep, perhaps for hours. Her words fell in a songlike cadence, or a chant, perhaps. He opened his eyes and saw her standing above his bed. How long she'd been there, he didn't know. But moonlight spilled through the porthole now. A full moon, or nearly so. And she stood, bathed in that ethereal glow, and he could see her. He could see her with perfect clarity. Her eyes were closed, head tipped back, and she stood with her feet wide apart. Her left arm stretched upward toward the moon, her palm turned up as if to catch the pale moonlight that spilled into it. Her right arm was extended downward, toward him. She turned her palm down and pressed it gently to his forehead. And as she chanted, he felt energy flooding him. Filling him. Warm, potent, zinging energy.

Moon Goddess, Diana, send your healing hands,
Move through me, renew me, and heal this good man.

She repeated the chant three times as he lay there. And then she went rigid, eyes flying wide. And Duncan felt a surge of something white hot and tingling jolt right through his entire body. 'Twas sudden, and brief, and then 'twas gone.

He blinked his vision into focus and scanned the room, trying to understand what had just happened. Then he spotted her. She leaned on the back of the chair, head hanging down between her arms, her face curtained by her glorious hair. Breathlessly, she murmured, "Sweet lady, never has it been like that. . . ."

Duncan was breathless himself. But as he took stock, he realized . . . his head was clear. His pain gone. His throat, no longer sore. His head, no longer spinning. And he turned again to look at her, to see her and drink in the sight by the light of the moon—only to see her eyes widen in alarm.

"You're dreaming," she told him. "This has all been no more than a sweet dream."

"No, lass, 'tis no dream. An' what you just did—"

She held her palm toward him. "Sleep now, Duncan. Sleep."

A wave of drowsiness suddenly swept over him, and his eyelids felt so heavy he could barely hold them open. "Dinna go," he whispered. "I beg of you, dinna go. I dinna care what that was . . . what *you* are. I only need you to stay . . . please, angel . . . stay with me."

"Sleep," she whispered. "Sleep and regain your strength. You're exhausted. Rest, Duncan. Sleep."

His eyes fell closed, though he fought to keep them open. And he felt her lips, warm and soft upon his . . . all too briefly.

"If I could stay with you, Duncan, I would. Believe me I would. 'Tis better this way. I wish 'twere not true, but 'tis, Duncan."

He heard her leaving, heard the door creak open. Battling to stay awake, he forced words through his lips before losing himself to the veil of sleep that he could not resist. "I'll find you again. I swear I will. I'll find you. . . ."

I'd never felt the power surge through me as it did that night. No, nor had I ever before felt the other forces that came to life in my blood then. The ones that burned in me when Duncan pulled me into his arms, when his mouth mated with mine, when he whispered that he hadn't stopped thinking about me.

I'd never felt such things for a man. Not for any man. But I did now. For Duncan. From the moment our eyes had met I'd sensed there was something between us. Something new and powerful. I'd had no idea how powerful.

And yet, I could not trust him, could not tell him the truth. Secrecy was vital, especially from any man associated with the Church and her Witch-hunters. He'd told me he'd given it up. But wouldn't he tell me that even if he hadn't? Wouldn't that be the perfect way to fool me? To entrap me? Lure me into his trust, into his arms, into his bed, gain my confession and then haul me away? And what if I foolishly told him the only way I could be killed, what then?

No. I was weak where Duncan Wallace was concerned. My mother had trusted my own aunt Matilda, and now she was dead because of it. She'd written the words, emphasized them: *Trust no one. No one.*

I'd become hard that day they killed my precious mother. Harder than I had ever been before. But my hardness melted when Duncan's lips touched mine. My wisdom faded away like mist in the morning sunlight. He'd tried to protect me once, yes. But hadn't he just now accused me of bewitching him? Of making him want me by using some spell?

I'd heard it myself. Though he'd taken back the words, the sentiment that spawned them likely still lived in his heart. So 'twas best I not see him again. Not ever.

I remained in my cabin for the rest of that journey. The captain brought me my meals, spoke with me for a few minutes each day, and seemed concerned for my well being. He told me how Duncan had been quite crazed since his recovery, insisting a woman had come to him and made him well that night, demanding to know my name and where my cabin was. Most of the crewmen and passengers thought his bout of fever had warped his mind. Even his friends, the couple with whom he was traveling, seemed to fear for his sanity.

It disturbed me to let him go on unsure just what had happened that night in his cabin. To let him go on wondering how much of it had been real and how much a dream. But I had no choice. 'Twould do me no good to be with Duncan Wallace. Nor him, either. For what could come of it, after all? What could come of my falling in love with him? And I would—I knew I would. I'd have to watch him grow old, I'd suffer through losing him. He'd be forced to see me remain young and healthy, while he aged and withered. No. There was no point in following my feelings for him, none at all, for they would only lead to heartache for us both.

But often as I sat alone in my cabin . . . and more often when I sneaked up onto the decks in the wee hours before daylight, I wished it could be different. And when I thought of Duncan, of his kiss, a great heaviness seemed to settle atop my heart. It added its weight to the sadness already there, that which I'd carried with me from the night I'd lost my mother, and so I became quite melancholy. Silent and pale. I was told my eyes seemed haunted more often than not.

I'd mourned my mother for the whole of my journey, gone over the events that cost her life again and again, each time wondering if I could have done something to save her. But I knew this terrible grief, this near despair, was not what she would have wanted for me. She'd have wanted me to find my own life, to go on, somehow. She would hate knowing that I cried each time I thought of her. Her memory, she would say, should bring me warmth and joy, not sorrow. So eventually I vowed to try to make it so. I could not spend my life grieving. Not for her, and not for what might have been between Duncan and me, had our situations been different.

Often, in those long days of my solitary journey, I found myself thinking of the way Duncan had tried so valiantly to help us that day at the gallows. If he had succeeded, and died in the attempt, what would have been the result? I wondered if he would have returned to his next lifetime immortal, as I was. Such a thing seemed beyond belief to me. Surely not a priest, nor a man studying to become one! And yet the undeniable proof was in me. I had become immortal in just such a way.

I was changing daily—almost hourly—and these changes also occupied my thoughts. How far would they go? I wondered. Each day I grew stronger. My senses continued to sharpen themselves by gradual degrees. And I found that if I focused on my new nature, 'twas easier to escape my crippling grief. So many new and strange things were happening to my body.

I could hear conversations from a goodly distance, and hear them more clearly than before. I could see as sharply in the darkness now as I could by daylight, and had been able to do so since that night in Duncan's cabin, even after I'd extinguished the candle.

By the time we sailed into the harbor at Boston Town, I could hear the fish swimming beneath the waves. I could detect—even distinguish between—the scents of each person aboard. Duncan's above all others, and why that was, I did not know. I saw the purple line of the New World fully an hour before the lookout shouted "Land ho!"

Sanctuary was but forty miles from where the ship docked at Boston Harbor, and I was told 'twas a town on its own tiny peninsula that curved like a crooked finger into the sea. I was eager to see it. I waited, of course, until everyone had left the ship. Long, long after that I crept out of my cabin, half afraid Duncan would be waiting for me, even then. I even looked for him, searching the few faces I saw as I walked softly down the gangplank and along the dock and into the town. But he wasn't there. I saw him not at all.

And perhaps a very small part of me . . . was disappointed. I told myself how foolish that was, but the truth was a lot of the feelings I'd been having lately were foolish. It didn't stop me from having them, all the same. It didn't stop me from craving a man I could never have.

Chapter 5

꧁꧂

At Boston Town I purchased a horse with most of the coins still remaining in my purse. A fine black mare with fire in her eyes and spirit in her step. The livery man pleaded with me to take a more gentle animal instead, but I was insistent. From the moment my eyes met the animal's, and she gave a sassy shake of her dark, flowing mane, I knew she was the one for me. I called her Ebony, for that was her color.

I'd taken to carrying my dagger strapped round my thigh, held there by the red garter my mother had made for me long ago. All the Witches of her family had worn one, she'd said. 'Twas laughable that I still wore the garter, when my stockings were long since too tattered to wear.

Beyond the dagger, I had only the drawstring sack my mother had given me, all my worldly possessions tucked away inside. Armed with a crudely drawn map, and pitifully few coins, I set out at dawn on the day after the *Sea Witch* had docked, bound for Sanctuary. My new home.

I rode on narrow paths, amid forests of such grandeur I'd never seen their like. The trees towered to the heavens, their trunks incredibly large. I marveled at the natural beauty around me, the forces of nature I could feel thriving in this place. There was great power here. I sensed it the way an animal can sense the approach of a storm.

After riding for an entire day, I estimated my journey to be nearly half complete, and stroked Ebony's neck, praising her in soft words.

The dampness that coated my palm and her gentle nicker told me 'twas time to stop for the night. "All right, girl. Time you had some rest. And me, as well. Though one would not think I should be the one to feel so tired when you've been doing all the work."

The mare snorted as if in agreement, and I glanced at the area around me. Truly, there was little here. Woods that might be the homes of giants towered on either side of me. Ahead, there was only the dim outline of a well-worn dirt track, and even that vanished a short distance away as the sky turned dusky with twilight.

Sliding from the mare's back, I gathered the reins in my hands and went very still, closing my eyes, listening to my instincts to tell me which way to go. 'Twould be far from wise to camp beside the road, lest some ne'er-do-well come upon us in the night. Besides that, Ebony needed water. She'd last drunk at midday.

Softly I scented the breeze, waiting. And my senses did not let me down. I'd suspected as much. I could hear, very faintly, the trickle and splash of a stream off to the left. Moreover, I could smell the water.

I glanced at Ebony and realized I needn't have bothered. She smelled it, too, and looked eagerly off toward the woods in that direction. "Come on, then," I told her, and led her off the trail and into the darkness of the forest.

It took a long while to find that stream. It seemed we walked a mile, though it could not have been that far. But surrounded by the lowering darkness and towering trees, I felt the full extent of my solitude here more than I had since leaving the ship at Boston Harbor. I was alone, in a strange, new land.

And yet, not *quite* as alone as I might have been. Somewhere in this New World was Duncan Wallace. And I wondered if he might be staring in awe at the virgin forests, or gazing up at the same purple sky. I wondered if he thought of me.

Ebony tugged at her reins, and I glanced ahead to see the stream, wide and bubbling like an excited child. I released her, and she trotted to its banks and bent to drink from its crystalline waters.

Hands on my hips, I inspected the lush grasses here. "'Tis a good spot," I told the mare. "Tonight, we'll sleep right here." Using the length of worn and fraying rope the liveryman had given me, I picketed Ebony in a spot where she could reach both the sweet grasses and the water.

Then I tossed my bag on the ground to use as a pillow. My cloak would be my blanket, the grassy ground, my bed. 'Twould do quite nicely.

A twig snapped in the woods to my back, and I stiffened, turning to look around. I saw nothing, but for the first time I wondered what sorts of beasties might roam these woods. Large ones, if the size of the trees was anything to go by. I'd not expect an animal to harm me unless I provoked it. A Witch is in tune with nature, and its creatures, and I'd come to believe that even wild animals could sense that and know instinctively that I meant them no harm. But these might be new creatures, animals with which I'd had no experience.

A rustling sound came then, and I forced my brain to calm, my senses to open. Slowly I moved toward the center of the place I'd chosen as my camp for the night and stood there, still and silent for a long moment, letting my eyes fall closed and my breathing slow, and lengthen. Opening my mind, I sensed the intense energy of the earth thrumming beneath my feet, and instinctively I crouched down to place my palms flat to the ground, the better to feel it, to absorb it, and fall into harmony with the forces moving here. Then, after a moment, I rose again, gradually unfolding my body until I stood upright. Tipping my head skyward, opening my arms to the heavens, I let the energies of the sky above me flow into me.

When I felt the familiar sense of being in perfect harmony with all around me, I lowered my arms to my sides and opened my eyes, feeling confident again that nothing in nature would harm me here.

And then I saw him, peering at me from within the trees, so much a part of the forest he nearly blended into it. But once I'd spotted him, my eyes focused, and he became clearer and clearer to me. A red man, dressed in animal hide all adorned with beads. His long hair hung in streaks of dark and light, and his eyes were very dark.

I'd heard talk of these natives of the New World. Indians, they were called. Or savages. 'Twas said they murdered and raped at their pleasure, and took the scalps of their white victims. And a chill of unwelcome fear slithered up my spine as I held his gaze with mine.

He did not move. Nor did he look particularly savage nor bent on my murder. In fact, he seemed natural there, in the woods . . . as if he belonged there. As if he were even more in tune with his environment than I could ever hope to be.

And then I realized . . . this was his home. It had to be his home. The sense of that came to me too strongly to be a mistake. I'd simply walked in without knocking and decided to spend the night without an invitation.

Licking my lips, rather nervously, I said, "I'm sorry if I have intruded. I'd like to sleep here tonight. If 'tis all right."

He remained as he'd been before. Perfectly still, unblinking. Just watching me. And it occurred to me that he might not speak my language. So I spoke to him with my hands, as best I could manage. I pointed to myself, then folded my hands beneath my head, closing my eyes to indicate sleeping, and then pointed to the ground. Looking back at him, I waited.

He nodded, just once, and so slightly I might have mistaken it. I should thank him, I realized. But how did one make a sign for "thank you"?

Perhaps a gift. Kneeling, I opened my pack, searching my mind for something to give the man to show my gratitude and friendship, and finally found the small piece of glittering amethyst that I'd salvaged from my plundered home. But when I glanced up again, the man was gone.

I went to the spot where he'd been, but saw nothing, and the woods were so utterly undisturbed, I might have imagined him.

But I hadn't, had I?

I didn't think so.

Kneeling, I placed the stone on the ground, then returned to the grassy bank where my pack awaited.

I had a single biscuit in my pack, saved from my last dinner aboard the *Sea Witch*. I ate half of it, washed it down with water from the stream, and then lay down upon my pack, beneath my cloak, and slept. And dreamed that another man watched me from the shelter of the woods. A beautiful man whose face, it seemed, would haunt me until I died.

My nose woke before the rest of me. It twitched and sniffed and smelled something that made my stomach rumble. Then warm sunlight brushed my eyelids open, and the first thing I saw was food. Something golden colored and fragrant, resting on a slab of bark very close to my face.

Blinking and wondering vaguely if this were a dream, I sat up, grabbed the bark, and looked more closely. It was fish! Coated in something and cooked . . . still warm, in fact.

"Who in the . . ." I turned my head, scanning the woods around me, but saw no one. But it had to have been the red man I'd seen the night before.

I ate the fish eagerly, closing my eyes at the heavenly taste. And when I finished, and licked every crumb from my fingers, I leaned back, sighed in contentment, and muttered, "Savages, indeed. That man is kinder than many a white man I've known. Don't you agree, Ebony?"

The mare only looked at me. Getting to my feet, I gathered up all my belongings once more, making ready for the second leg of my journey. But before I left that place, I crept into the trees where I'd seen the man the night before and looked for the stone I'd left him.

The amethyst was gone.

Nodding in approval, I mounted the mare, and we meandered out of the woods, to the trail, and began our long trek again.

And again, we traveled all the day through. I hadn't expected it to take so long and, in fact, hoped to arrive at Sanctuary well before dark. I ate my remaining half biscuit, stale and crumbling now, at midday, and thought fondly of my delicious breakfast. But the trail seemed endless. Nightfall came, and still hours went by.

I was quite weary, and terribly hungry, when I finally rode into a small settlement with muddy paths running between a handful of small log structures more roughly built than any I'd ever seen before.

"Hello, mistress," a deep voice called.

I turned in the saddle to see a heavy man with whiskered jowls and curious eyes.

"Elias Stanton is my name," he said. "I be the town elder. What business have you in Sanctuary?"

"*This* is Sanctuary?" I asked, my heart sinking. I should have been glad, I suppose, that my journey was finally at its end. But this place was hardly what I'd expected.

The man's eyes narrowed on me, and I realized my tone might have offended him. "I hadn't realized I had come so far," I amended. "My name is Raven St. James." I saw no reason now to use a false name. My aunt would wonder why, if I did. "I am looking for my aunt, Eleanor Belisle. Do you know her?"

His bushy dark brows drew close. "I know her well," he said, and I sensed a grimness settling about him. "Have you traveled far, then?"

"All the way from England. My ship only arrived at Boston two days past, and I rode from there."

At that his frown changed to one of disapproval. "You traveled alone? Spent a night on the road? Unchaperoned?"

I'm afraid my chin lifted a little, when I likely should have assumed a humble and apologetic posture. "I had little choice, sir."

"Well now, such impropriety will not be tolerated here, mistress. You might learn it now as well as later. Unmarried young ladies do not go about—"

"I am not unmarried," I blurted. And my own words surprised me, for I had loathed liars for as long as I could remember. Yet the man's attitude reminded me so much of the arrogant priest who had murdered my mother that I could not help but wish to take precautions. "My husband died, during our crossing."

"You're a widow-woman, then," he said. His gaze roamed down my body, to my slippers, and up again. And I did not care for the shadow that darkened his eyes. Nor for the way his tongue darted out to moisten his lips. "'Tis still unwise to travel alone, mistress, but at least not quite as scandalous."

"I am weary, sir. My journey has been very long. Pray, direct me to the home of my aunt before I fall from the saddle."

"Ah, yes, your aunt. I'm sorry my news is not better," he said. "But your aunt has been taken ill. A physician came from Boston, as he does once a month when the roads are passable. He examined her and said there was nothing to be done."

"What ails her?" I asked, my heart in my throat.

"Old age," the man said. "Her heart has worn itself out. She's all of fifty years, you know." He shook his head sadly. "But 'tis good that you came. She needs caring for, being so far from Sanctuary proper. 'Twill be good for her to have you there."

"I'll go at once. If you'll just—"

"Yes, yes. Follow this road, mistress. It runs along the coast, all the way to the very tip of the peninsula. High on the cliffs above the sea is where she and that man of hers, God rest his soul, built their cabin. Though the good Lord only knows why. 'Tis no more than two mile."

"Thank you, sir." I snapped the reins lightly, and the mare, though likely as weary as I, lunged forward. Perhaps she sensed this journey's end was at hand. Or perhaps she simply found the little man as distasteful as I had.

I found the cabin just as the man had said, on the cliffs, with the mighty sea and its waves crashing below. But unlike Elias Stanton, I saw immediately why my aunt had chosen this site. I could envision no place more magnificent. Surely the gods themselves would gladly place their thrones along such majestic cliffs, while far below the rolling power of the sea paid homage.

The log cabin was humble but neat. And there was a crooked shed, which housed a cow and some hens, though the cow looked as if she'd been neglected of late, her ribs showing, her bag swollen. Though 'twas fully dark, no light shone from within the cabin. But of course, I could see quite sharply in darkness by now.

I took Ebony into the shed, relieving her of saddle and bridle, and rubbing her down as best I could with a rag that hung from a peg on the wall. Quickly I gathered hay from the small stack outside, and a pail of water from the well for her, and for the poor cow as well. And then I took up my sack and went to the cabin.

The door creaked as it opened, and I stepped inside to see a frail form hunched in a rocking chair beside a dwindling fire. I moved closer and softly whispered, "Aunt Eleanor?"

The graying head came up, turning slowly toward me in the dim room. The dying fire was the only light, so I stepped closer that she might see me better, and knelt beside her chair. "Aunt Eleanor, I am Raven, the daughter of your half sister."

Her parched lips parted, and her eyes widened slightly. "Lily's girl? You be Lily's little girl?"

"Yes, Aunt Eleanor. Lily's little girl."

"Saints be praised," she whispered, and tears brimmed in her clouded eyes. "Oh, mercy, child, I thought I would never live to see you." She opened her arms, and I embraced her. Her thinness made me wince, but though weak, she squeezed me tight. Sheer joy gave her that strength, joy at seeing me. A welcome I'd neither expected nor hoped for . . . from a woman who was all that remained of my family.

Family.

All at once so much emotion rose up inside me that I could scarcely speak and my eyes burned with tears. She would never know what such a welcome meant to me. Never. But I'd be grateful for it all my life. And I hugged her back just as firmly, though with great care.

"You're not to worry anymore," I told her. "I'm here now, and I'll care for you." I sat away slightly, and kissed her careworn cheek. "You'll be well again soon, Aunt Eleanor. I promise you that."

And, of course, she was.

I pampered my aunt in every way I knew. By day I took long walks in the woods, finding, growing wild in this lush land, many of the herbs and roots that would help her. I never told her of it, of course. My mother had warned me to trust no one, and though I was certain my dear aunt would never intentionally bring harm to me, I was equally certain it was best I never give her the means to do so. I seasoned the meals I prepared for her with the natural remedies for her weakening heart and made teas of the tonics I brewed. Hawthorn berries and devil's claw. Valerian root and chamomile, and wild garlic.

By night I performed quiet rituals over her bed as she slept, calling on all the powers of the Universe to aid in restoring her health. And of course, my magick was effective . . . though not as dramatic and shattering as it had been that night in Duncan's cabin aboard the *Sea Witch*. Never once did I feel the surge of power I'd felt when I'd called down the power to heal Duncan. Never once. And I wondered why.

I thought of him often. Mostly when I lay alone in my bed at night, wondering what would become of me. Would I live alone for all eternity? Would I ever stop seeing the longing in his deep brown eyes every time I closed my own?

In between struggling with these unanswerable questions, I milked and cared for the cow and the hens, so that we had fresh milk and eggs aplenty. More than we needed, in fact, so that each day I would ride into town and trade the excess for other goods. Vegetables and game and freshly caught fish. Good for my aunt's health, all of it.

Within a week Aunt Eleanor was strong enough to walk outside in the sunshine for a few minutes each day. Within two weeks she was gaining weight again, and the color had returned to her cheeks. After a month she was vigorous enough to supervise me as I planted a vegetable garden near the house. And at the end of my second month in Sanctuary, she was helping me gather eggs and nagging at me to take her to the Sunday meetings in the settlement.

I did not want to do this. The very idea of another clergyman, like the evil one back in England, glaring down at me with judgment in his eyes made me feel ill. And though this small church was no part of the Church of England, I was reluctant. But there was really no choice. I had to keep my secret, and attending services was necessary if I hoped to do so.

Since my arrival, no one had come to call on my aunt Eleanor, and I was quite happy to have it that way. People asked after her, of course, when I made my excursions into town. And each time I was asked, I would say that Aunt Eleanor was improving, and that we were fine and in no need of assistance. When they remarked that they hadn't seen me at the Sunday meetings since my arrival in Sanctuary, I replied that I dared not leave my aunt alone for that long.

I truly thought I was handling things well, and discreetly.

But when I walked beside my aunt into the meeting hall that first time, I knew that I hadn't. There were gasps and exclamations at the sight of my aunt's rosy cheeks and shining eyes and renewed vigor. And for the second time in my life, my neighbors began looking at me with suspicion in their eyes.

Duncan worked like a mule, pouring himself fully into physical labor. And not just to help his friends, though he told himself that was the reason. He was trying to make himself forget. Forget *her* and the brief flirtation with madness he'd suffered while he'd been ill aboard that ship.

But no matter how hard he worked, she haunted him still. Her eyes, gleaming black and full of mystery and promise. Her lips, full and tasting vaguely of honey as they moved in delicious, erotic response against his own.

It hadn't been real. He told himself that again and again as he worked by Samuel's side, sawing timber, building a cabin, hunting and fishing, and tilling the soil. Cutting firewood, harvesting vegetables.

And though he did the work of three men, Duncan still couldn't escape the memory of her. Neither the real memory, of her swinging from that noose, too beautiful and full of life to be dead, nor the false memory, the fantasy, of holding her body tight to his in a bed, of kissing her and begging her not to go.

He barely slept anymore. Each time he closed his eyes, he saw her there. She came to him in his sleep and loved him to the point of exhaustion. A gentle succubus. A seductive spirit. And though he knew 'twas only a trick of his mind that had created her, it felt just as real. Just as powerful.

He grieved her loss as if she'd been his lover. Ridiculous. But true, for she'd become his lover in his dreams. He was well and truly obsessed, and he knew that was no overstatement when he found himself searching the township of Boston for her. Everywhere he went, he sought her face, her hair. He was always, *always* searching.

And he feared he was cursed to do so for the rest of his life. For two full years had passed since that fateful voyage. And still, he found himself searching. 'Twas as if, though she'd died, part of her had remained alive inside him. Possessing him. He'd become depressed and moody, restless and irritable. And all the hard work in the colonies couldn't cure him.

Samuel and Kathleen had tried to convince him to return to the pulpit. How would they feel if they knew the thoughts that plagued him? The fire that burned in his loins for a dead woman? He couldn't do it. Not now, and perhaps not ever.

He'd earned enough by hiring himself out to help other settlers, and the debt he owed his father was finally paid in full. That goal reached, he felt adrift, directionless. The emptiness he felt threatened to consume him.

And then one day Kathleen returned from the marketplace with news that changed everything.

"I believe, dear Duncan, that I have found permanent and perfect employment for you." Her red hair danced in the breeze as she bent to set her basket of goods on the ground.

Duncan had been assisting Samuel in patching the roof, and looked down at his friend's pretty wife in surprise. "You've done what your husband and all his cronies couldna do, then."

"And it should not surprise you!" she teased, sending Samuel a wink and running a hand over her bulging belly. "There is a town two days' ride north. Sanctuary, 'tis called. Their minister was called away, Duncan, and they're sorely in need of a new one."

Duncan lowered his head then, disappointment washing over him. "I'm no priest, Kathleen. You know that. I canna be, not after seein' my own confessor, my mentor, commit murder."

He didn't tell her the other reasons, nor did he mention that it was that very same murder that kept him awake nights. The murder of the most beautiful creature he'd ever laid his eyes upon.

"You're the closest thing to one, Duncan. Your trainin' was all but complete when you left England. Besides, they don't want a priest, just a pastor."

"'Tis true," Samuel said. "I've heard of this place. Sanctuary is but a small settlement. They've no need of pomp and circumstance there. Only guidance and a stirrin' sermon of a Sunday morn. 'Tis not the Church of England we're discussin', after all."

"I've already spoken to the man makin' inquiries, Duncan," Kathleen continued. "He's at the Boar's Head, and he's hopin' you'll come by."

Duncan heaved a great sigh. "Samuel, you know my feelin's on this matter. We've discussed it before."

"Aye, I know them. But what better way to teach people tolerance and love for their neighbors than from the pulpit? You could change things, Duncan."

"Not all men of God are like Nathanial Dearborne," Kathleen said softly, sympathy for Duncan in her eyes. "I've known many fine, honorable men who preached to a flock. And so have you, Duncan Wallace. You cannot condemn the callin' because of the acts of one vile man."

Duncan knew she was right. "You're a wise woman, Kathleen."

"And well you know it," she said. "Come, Duncan. What harm will it do to speak with the man? You've certainly had no better offers. The pay is fair and includes a cabin for you to live in." She patted her round belly again. "And while I love havin' you here, I fear 'twill soon become crowded in this one."

"Nonsense!" Samuel cried. "I'd been plannin' to put Duncan to work as a governess, woman. Don't go chasin' him off now." He laughed and nudged Duncan with an elbow. "At least talk to the man."

Duncan shook his head in surrender and glanced down at Kathleen's gleaming eyes.

"His name is Elias Stanton," she said. "And he'll be leavin' town in the morn."

"I fear I'm outnumbered," Duncan said softly. And perhaps they were right, after all. Perhaps he could do some good in one small settlement . . . *if* he were to take the position. He probably would not. But 'twas high time he leave his friends to their new life, their new home, and growing family. Time he struck out on his own.

And perhaps he'd find a way in Sanctuary to exorcize the beautiful ghost from his soul. He'd failed to forget her in all this time and seemed to think of her even more since he'd come here. Again and again, he would close his eyes and see her body swinging from a rope. Feel her in his arms or catch the scent of her hair on a stray breeze.

"Duncan?" Samuel tapped his shoulder.

Duncan started from his morbid thoughts. "All right," he said. "I'll speak with this Stanton."

"Good," Kathleen said with a laugh. "I told him you'd be there directly. Off that roof with you. And wash your hands afore you go. If I had time I'd take a blade to that hair of yours, but I suppose there's naught to be done for it now."

"You'd best run, Duncan, before my wife domesticates you thoroughly."

"You make a good point, my friend." Duncan climbed down the ladder and washed his hands. Perhaps part of the void growing inside him was because he'd left what he'd once considered his life's work behind. In the various congregations scattered about here in the colonies, a preacher wasn't expected to be without sin, as it seemed he was in England. Here he was still considered a man, flaws and all. Which was as it should be. Ministers married and raised families. Desires of the flesh, then, should not necessarily mean he could not serve.

Perhaps he would give it a try. Perhaps he could fill the emptiness in his heart. And perhaps, by doing so, he'd rid himself of the woman who lived eternally inside his soul.

Elias Stanton looked like a man with many grave matters on his mind as he sat before a pint of ale at a slab table, across from Duncan.

He shook Duncan's hand but seemed distracted.

"I hope you didna wait long," Duncan said, apologetic.

"No. If I seem impatient, sir, 'tis only because I have many problems to tend to. However, finding a new man to minister to the township takes precedence over the rest."

"I hope your troubles are not too dire," Duncan said, curious. Elias rubbed his hairy chin, and Duncan thought he had jowls like a mastiff.

"Oh, quite dire indeed," he said. "Our town has a temptress nestled in its midst. A most improper young woman, truth to tell. An' I believe she's come to damn the souls of all the menfolk in Sanctuary."

Duncan tried not to smile, though the man's words amused him. "How shockin'," he said. "But surely the men of Sanctuary have enough moral fiber to resist such temptation?"

Elias shook his head slowly. "I'm in hopes you can help them in that regard," he said. "But 'twill not be easy. The girl is possessed of an unnatural beauty, and there is hellfire in her eyes. She's neither humble nor obedient. Nor devout, for she misses services as often as she attends them." He shook his head in disgust.

"Perhaps the girl is unaware of the effect she has on the men."

Elias took a long sip of ale, then set the glass down heavily. "She's aware. Even enticed *me* to impure thoughts. An' I tell you, not all our men have the moral fortitude and spiritual strength that I have. Some might be moved to do more than dream. They'll fall victim to her wiles, surely. And that will be their downfall. 'Tis why we cannot afford to go long without a minister."

"I see." Duncan wasn't certain he did. Was Elias saying that because he desired a woman, 'twas *her* fault?

"There's something evil about her," the man went on.

Duncan felt a cold chill dance up his spine. Damnation. Such ridiculous discussions were what led to more serious accusations. Accusations like the ones that had caused the death of his phantom lover. And suddenly he thought that perhaps this was why he'd been led to this man, to this position. Perhaps he'd get the opportunity to prevent such an atrocity from happening to another innocent young woman.

Aloud, he said, "We all have a darker side, Elias. We only learn to control it."

Elias frowned. "'Tis more than a dark side, I fear. Abundance seems to surround this girl. While others in Sanctuary simply get by from one year to the next, she and her aunt grow wealthier by unnatural measures, and in an unbelievably short time. Two years ago the girl rode into our town with little more than the clothes on her back, and one feisty mare. Now she is quite possibly more wealthy than I, the town's foremost elder! Imagine!"

"Aye. Imagine." So the man's pride was suffering, as well. Aye, Duncan thought, he had to take this position. He had to enlighten ignorant fools such as the one sitting across from him. Maybe he had a purpose in this life after all.

And there was something else, something Stanton had said, that had set off bells ringing in his mind. And then it hit him.

Two years ago.

Exactly when Duncan himself had come here. Exactly when the *Sea Witch* had docked at Boston Harbor. And if the ghost he'd seen aboard that ship *had* been real . . .

'Twas ridiculous. He was letting his thoughts run wild again.

But what if 'tis her?

"What is the name of this temptress?" he asked.

Elias sighed deeply and shook his head. "No matter," he said. "'Tis my responsibility to put a stop to her mischief, and I've taken steps already . . . precautions really. You need only concern yourself with the moral well being of the community. Keeping them strong and steadfast while I make sure she does no harm."

Duncan frowned. "What steps, exactly, are you referrin' to, sir?"

Elias shook his head. "We should be talking about you." And he began asking questions as to Duncan's background, his schooling and experience, and positions on various scriptural debates.

Duncan found it very easy to guess the answers the man most wanted to hear, and those were the ones he gave. He had decided he wanted this position—wanted it badly. Because despite how little sense it made, he had to see for himself that this woman of whom Elias Stanton spoke was not the same one who'd haunted him all this time. And because, even if she were not . . . he had a grim feeling things in Sanctuary were heading rapidly toward disaster. And this time, perhaps, he could do something to prevent it.

If that wouldn't exorcize his demons, he didn't know what would.

* * *

"You simply must come to meeting today, Raven. People will think it odd if you don't. The new minister is here!"

Aunt Eleanor fussed with the skirts of the new dress I'd made for her, then stopped herself. "Vanity," she said. "At my age one wouldn't think it a sin that would tempt me."

"Wishing to look one's best when greeting a newcomer is not vanity, Aunt Eleanor," I told her sternly. "'Tis simply good manners."

'Twas the beginning of my third summer with my aunt, and the cottage looked very different than it had when I had arrived. We'd truly prospered. And my knowledge of natural magick was only a small part of the reason why. At least part of our success was due to simple hard work and smart thinking.

We'd set aside fertile eggs and allowed the hens to hatch them, over and over, until we'd raised well over a hundred chickens. We sold most, and kept many more, enough to keep our business going, and supply half the town with eggs. We'd twice bartered for the services of a neighbor's bull, and our cow had produced twins both times. And, yes, I had used my knowledge of magick to help with that. All four calves had been female, and two would be producing milk and calves of their own very soon. Truly, we were doing exceptionally well.

We'd used our newfound wealth to hire the labor of some men, and now a small barn stood where the shed had been, and the chickens had a coop. We'd enlarged the hearth and built an oven among the cobblestones. And real glass, purchased in Boston, filled our windows.

"If you knew so much about good manners, child," my dear aunt said, "you would accompany me to church."

She made her eyes soft and pleading, like those of a child wheedling for a sweet. And again I marveled at how youthful and vigorous she had grown under my care.

"Please come with me, Raven."

I closed my eyes in defeat. "Oh, all right. But if he's as fond of shouting and pounding his Bible as the last one was, I shall get up and leave."

"You wouldn't!"

I smiled to let her know I was only teasing, and went to the bedroom we shared to fix my hair and put on one of my own new dresses, of shamelessly fine fabric and cut. I couldn't help but think 'twas a far cry from the rags, tattered stockings, and worn slippers in which I'd arrived.

Reluctantly I tied my hair into a knot at the back of my head, and covered it with the small white cap with its dangling ribbons, as was customary. 'Twas considered sinful for a woman to wear her hair loose, though I failed to see why those silly townsfolk said so. I wore my hair down and flowing all the time, unless I was in town. And I was often tempted to do so publicly as well, to show them what I thought of their conventions. However, I had not forgotten the lessons I'd learned. 'Twas best to keep my strange ways to myself.

I was not a fool.

Though, perhaps I had been behaving as if I were. That Aunt Eleanor's fortune had shifted so completely from the moment of my arrival had not escaped the notice of some. I could feel the eyes on me, hear the speculation in the whispers they shared as I walked among them. Perhaps 'twas time I convince Aunt Eleanor to sell the cabin and move away with me. I would not wait until it was too late a second time.

Sanctuary was becoming unsafe for me. I couldn't quite smell the danger on the air . . . yet, but I felt it drawing slowly, inexorably nearer.

We had acquired a modest wagon, and I hurriedly went outside to put Ebony into her harness. She hated towing the thing, and I couldn't say that I blamed her. However, the sight of my aunt and I riding double upon my horse's back would likely have caused some of the townsfolk to faint dead way. And Aunt Eleanor might well end up on the ground, at any rate.

My aunt came outside the moment I had the wagon ready, a large basket in her hands filled with food for the meal that would follow services. I helped her into the seat, then climbed in beside her and clicked my tongue at Ebony. She set off at a jaunty gait, and despite the fact that she detested it, she did look fine pulling the wagon, feet stepping high, her long mane dancing with every step.

'Twas a fine day in May, not yet summer, but feeling every bit as if it were. A warm breeze came in from the ocean, carrying that sea scent I so loved along with it, and caressing my face and hair. A few strands fell loose, but I was enjoying the ride far too much to fuss over them. We traveled the worn track they called the Coast Road, along the very edge of the peninsula, and 'twas well and good I trusted Ebony to stay on course, for 'twas more than I could do to stop gazing out at the frothy whitecaps winking at me from that broad blue expanse.

It could be said that I disliked and distrusted the people of Sanctuary. Elias Stanton in particular. But I was utterly enchanted with the place itself. The ground beneath me and the sky above. Sea to my left, and forest to my right. 'Twas like a magick circle unto itself. I felt the earth's power here as I never had before, and perhaps it wasn't all because of the forces moving in and around this wild, new land. Perhaps 'twas another bit of my new self making its presence felt. The ability to feel the places where Mother Earth's power pulsed strongest. I sorely wished I understood more about my own nature. I knew instinctively there was far more to it than what my mother had been able to tell me. And yet how could I learn? How could I know? It plagued me like an unsolved puzzle. Why this gift of immortality? Was there some purpose to it all?

We arrived in town, and Elias Stanton himself hurried to our wagon and reached for my hand to assist me from my seat. I took it, though his touch made gooseflesh rise on my arms. The man's gaze tended to linger on my form in ways that made me uneasy, and in his eyes I often glimpsed lechery, though on the surface, he acted every bit the gentleman. I knew 'twas a lie. I could see the worms in his soul.

"Ladies," he said. "So good to see you both." His hand lingered on mine, grasping briefly when I pulled. Then he cleared his throat, averted his eyes, and released me, turning to assist my aunt. "A fine day, is it not, Mistress Belisle?"

"Fine, indeed, Mister Stanton," she replied. "But 'tis not the weather I wish to discuss, as you might well guess."

"Ah, you're curious about our new pastor, no doubt," he said with a smile.

"Tell me about him," she urged. "Is he young or old? Plump or poor?"

"You will soon see for yourself," Elias responded. And turning, offered her his arm. She took it, and he offered the other to me.

I was loath to accept. But people were watching. And more than ever, I was wary. I sensed something . . . something that made the fine hairs on my nape bristle. But I could not name what that something might be. I took his beefy arm and tried to hide my distaste.

"I vow," Aunt Eleanor said, "nothing so exciting has happened in Sanctuary since . . . why, since my dear niece arrived and restored me to health."

"'Twas the Lord restored you to health, Aunt Eleanor," I said quickly, and I glanced at Elias from the corner of my eye. "I only took away your loneliness." To Elias, I said, "I do believe it may well have been the loneliness making her feel so poorly all along."

"Indeed," Elias asked, lifting his brows. "And are you a physician, Mistress St. James?"

My blood ran cold, and for a moment 'twas as though I was back in

England, shivering outside the magistrate's door while cruel hands held me fast and a demanding voice asked a similar question of my mother.

I blinked away the rush of fear that shot through me, and reminded myself I was no longer in England. That nightmare was behind me. And then I prayed it was true.

Fixing a smile to my lips, I said, "A woman physician? Oh, Mister Stanton, surely you jest. I wouldn't know where to begin!"

His eyes, when they met mine, were filled with dark suspicions and blatant lust. And as we approached the plank steps leading up into the church, he pretended to stumble and leaned toward me, brushing his forearm against my breast. That I knew beyond doubt it was deliberate might have been intuition. Or something more. But regardless, I knew.

Startled, I turned and backed away, only to collide with a solid chest. Two warm hands closed on my shoulders, and suddenly I felt light-headed and breathless. His scent touched me, embraced me, and I knew before I even looked upon him who he was.

"Pardon," a painfully familiar voice with a sweet Scottish lilt said from behind me. "Are you all right, lass?"

I stiffened, closed my eyes, opened them slowly. And then I turned, unable to do otherwise, and looked up into the face of the man . . . the man who, more than two years ago, had seen me die. The man who'd embraced me to the point of madness, made me want him as I'd wanted no other. The man who, by rights, should believe me to be dead. The man who'd told me he'd given up his ministerial studies. Duncan Wallace. Looking just as I'd seen him that first time, on the gallows. Once again dressed in the black robes of a clergyman.

Chapter 6

"So sorry, Mistress St. James," Elias blustered. He straightened away from me, but I barely felt his unwelcome presence anymore. "A damnable pebble caught in my . . . oh. I see you've met our pastor."

"St. James?" Duncan whispered, wide-eyed and suddenly pale.

If he revealed what he had seen on those English gallows . . . if he let on . . .

He suddenly gripped both my hands in his. His gaze never left my face but kept roaming it as if he couldn't believe what he was seeing. Panic caused my heart to pound. Panic . . . and his touch. His thumbs moved in gentle circles on the backs of my hands, and I thought he might not even be aware of it. I squeezed his fingers to remind him, and stared into his brown eyes, willing him to keep my secret. And then, reluctantly, I tugged my hands from his, though 'twas the last thing I wanted to do.

I remembered this man. Oh, he'd changed. He was no longer a handsome young priest, but a man grown now. And though it had been only two years, I knew that two years in this rugged new land were more than enough to bring about such changes. He was larger, broad across the shoulders and chest, and solid with strength. Even his neck seemed hard and corded with muscle. His hair was longer than before, but the same dark sable, pulled back with a thong. And his face . . .'twas harsher now. He looked weathered, as if he'd been through trying times.

All of this I took in, realizing that to his probing brown eyes, I was exactly the same. I had not changed. I never would. That he remembered me, too, was obvious.

"Do you know one another?" Elias asked, stepping closer, eyeing Duncan, and then me.

"No," I said softly. "We've never met." And I looked into Duncan's brown eyes, silently begging him to say the same.

He licked his lips once, then looked past me to Elias. "Aye, the lass speaks the truth. Had we met, I'd surely recall it," he said, his eyes laden with meaning. "Besides, I only arrived yestereve." And then, smiling, he turned to my aunt, who all but shouldered me aside to take his hand in welcome.

"I am so pleased to meet you, young man," she said. "I am Eleanor Belisle, Raven's aunt."

"Raven," he said softly, glancing my way once more. When his gaze touched my skin, 'twas as if he touched me himself. I could feel the warmth of his eyes. "So that's your name. You can't know how I've wondered . . ." Blinking, he shook his head and turned back to Aunt Eleanor. "I only hope I live up to your expectations, dear lady," he told her.

"Oh, I'm confident you will, Reverend." And taking my arm, my aunt urged me up the steps and into the church, leaving Duncan to greet other worshipers as they filed past. But I could still feel his eyes on me.

When the sermon was ended, I realized I hadn't heard a word. I'd been too caught up in the comforting sound of his voice to pay heed to the words he used. It didn't matter what he said, so long as he said it in those rich, deep tones, with the lilt of Scotland in every word. I couldn't stop staring at him, watching the graceful, powerful strides with which he would pace before the congregation as he spoke, and his magnificent hands gesturing to punctuate each line. His eyes met mine often. Those were the only times I would shake out of my state of blatant admiration of him enough to hear the words he spoke. Double entendres, shot like arrows at my heart as his dark eyes razed me in mingled anger and wonder and . . . something else. Scriptures about lies and deceit. And more, about desires of the flesh. The way they could burn a man, destroy him.

Was he bitter, then? Angry with me for leading him such a merry chase? It didn't matter. If anything, the harshness I saw in his eyes now only served to make him the more beautiful to me. I wanted the man. I knew it with a sudden, urgent pang that left me breathless. But I knew 'twas impossible. For he was a minister. And I was a Witch.

I must put him out of my mind.

I *must*.

I could not.

After the sermon and prayers concluded, the entire population of Sanctuary turned out for the mid-day meal to welcome the new minister. It was held outdoors since there was no building yet large enough to accommodate everyone for the meal.

I sat upon a blanket near a shade tree, putting out the food my aunt had brought along, when I felt his gaze on me again. And looking up, I saw him, Duncan Wallace, staring at me. He did not look away when I met his eyes. Instead, he inclined his head very slightly and then turned to go back inside the church.

He wanted me to come to him. He'd made it quite clear. My throat went dry as I rehearsed in my mind what I would say to him. I'd gone over it before, of course. Many times I'd tried to imagine what explanation I could concoct should I meet anyone who'd seen me hang. But always, I'd been imagining this man in my mind's eye. Secretly hoping, perhaps, that I would see him again one day.

"I left my shawl inside," I told my aunt.

She only looked at me and winked. "Best go and find it, then, Raven. Before someone else does."

I think she had some clue, even then, that I was truly going to speak privately with Duncan. But no hint of disapproval clouded her shining eyes.

I went inside and saw him sitting on a bench near the front of the church. My hands trembling, I went to him, stood before him, looking down, and thus having a view of the door beyond as well, lest someone come in and overhear the words he was going to say. Would he accuse me? Condemn me? I did not know.

Lifting his eyes to mine, he whispered, "'Tis true, then, after all. You *are* alive."

I swallowed hard. More than anything, I did not wish to lie to him. Not to him. But my mother's words seemed to ring in my ears. *Trust no one. No one!* I could not tell him what I was. Especially not while he wore minister's robes. Though it galled me to deny the truth to him.

"You say such odd things, Pastor. Of course I am alive."

Holding my gaze, he shook his head slowly, wonder in his eyes. "I saw you die, lass."

Feigning shock, I lifted a hand to my breast. "You have mistaken me for someone else, then. I've never died, else how could I be here?"

"Dinna lie to me, Raven. Not to me." He rose suddenly, tall and strong and so close his body was nearly touching mine. "I cut you down myself, held your lifeless corpse in my arms, and dampened your hair with my tears. I . . ." He broke off there, closed his eyes and lowered his head as if he were too overwhelmed to go on.

My throat seemed to swell closed. "You . . . cut me down? You *wept* for me?"

He looked into my eyes, and I felt an incredible yearning build within my soul.

"You've haunted my dreams since that vile day, Raven St. James. And now you stand here before me, as beautiful and alive as you were the first time I looked into your eyes when you stood so bravely upon the gallows."

I felt a stinging in my eyes, a burning in my throat. I could not deny who I was, for he would never believe me. No more than I would have believed him, had he told me he was not that young man I remembered so vividly. The lie, then. The one I'd concocted and honed in my mind over these past two years.

"I would know you anywhere," he told me, and his hands clasped my shoulders, warm and firm. I could feel him wanting me, just by his touch. And I wanted him, too. "I knew you on the ship," he said. "You came to me then, when I was ill."

He searched my face. I said nothing.

"Admit it to me, dammit! Have you any idea how many times I've doubted my own sanity since that night? Have you?"

"I'm sorry," I whispered. "Gods forgive me, I'm so sorry. Yes, Duncan, I came to you that night. I . . . they wanted to put you off, thought you carried the plague. I couldn't let them." With one trembling hand, I touched his cheek. "No matter the cost, I couldn't let harm come to you."

He nodded slowly, closing his eyes in relief. "I knew 'twas you. Even without the light. I'd know you even if I were blind, Raven."

"And I you, Duncan," I murmured, lowering my head. "I . . . I never forgot how you tried to help us."

"Then you will tell me the truth," he said softly.

I looked into his eyes . . . and I wanted to share this burden, this wonder, this miracle of what I was with him more than I'd ever wanted anything in my life.

And I lied to him.

"'Twas a trick, and nothing more." I had to avert my eyes in order to force the words out. I could not lie to him while looking into his eyes. "The dress I wore that day had a high neck. Do you remember?"

"Aye, I remember everything. The dress was brown, roughly woven, with small yellow buttons up the front, all the way to your chin. An' your hair smelled of lavender."

I was warm inside. His voice was like a caress upon my very soul. "Beneath the dress I wore a steel collar. No one could see it. It protected my neck from the noose."

His eyes narrowed, probed, and plumbed mine.

"An' where did you get this collar? They said you had spent the night in the stocks."

"A friend . . . he stole into the square and slipped it round my neck."

Frowning at me, Duncan shook his head. "Nay. Even with the collar, the fall could have broken your wee neck." And his forefinger danced across my neck as he said it, sending shivers down my spine.

"Could have," I said. "But did not."

His eyes were piercing, as if he sought to see inside my mind, to the truth hidden there.

"There was no life in you when I held you in my arms," he whispered. "You were not pretendin' that."

"No," I whispered, half afraid he'd see right through the lie. "I fainted. Perhaps from the fall . . . or the fear . . . I cannot say. But I woke in . . ." I shuddered at the memory. "In a horrible place."

His face softened then. Slowly he lowered his head. "Aye, I know about that," he said softly. Then meeting my gaze, he asked, "An' your mother? Did she wear this trick collar as well?"

I closed my eyes, my pain all too real. "Someone saw my friend and he had to run away, or be caught. There was no time for him to help her as he did me. When I woke among the dead, she was beside me . . . and . . ." Tears choked me and I could not go on.

His hand came to me, stroking my cheek. I wanted to clasp it in my own and press a kiss to his palm. But I only stood still, closing my eyes at the feelings his touch evoked. Weak with relief that I was feeling this man's touch again, as I'd so often dreamed of doing. Weak, too, with the remembered pain of finding my precious mother, dead.

"I went there," he said. "To the place where they took you. But you were not there. Nor was your mother."

I looked at him through my tears. "Why?"

"I couldna save you, lass. I thought . . . at least I might give you a proper burial."

I smiled gently at him, and he brushed a tear from my cheek.

"You're a kind man, Duncan Wallace," I said.

"Nay," he said softly, eyes going harder. "Not so kind, not when I'm lied to."

I swallowed hard. He could be a dangerous man, as well. Dangerous to me. To my life as well as my heart.

"Go on, lass. What happened when you woke?"

"I carried my mother into the forest and buried her there. She would have been pleased with the spot I chose, I think."

"She'd have been pleased," he said, "to know you survived."

"She knew," I whispered. And then I sniffed and impatiently dashed the tears from my face. "If you tell them what you know of me, Duncan—"

"I willna tell them."

I could only blink in surprise.

"I willna betray your secret, Raven. I swear it on all that I am. But you must tell me the truth. All of the truth."

I couldn't look him in the eye when he asked me that. "I can only tell you that I have never brought harm to another human being. Not in all my life, Duncan. On my mother's soul, I swear 'tis the truth."

His hand turned my face toward his again. He searched my face for a long moment, his velvet brown eyes as piercing as before. And then he nodded. "I believe you," he said. "But there is another question I have, and you must know what it is. I am a man of the cloth, Raven, a man of God, even though I abandoned my studies for the priesthood. And yet . . . and yet you've haunted my soul." He closed his eyes slowly. "I have to know the truth. Am I damning myself by lettin' you haunt my thoughts day and night? Am I, Raven? Are you, truly, a—"

The doors burst open then, and Elias Stanton, of all people, marched inside, saw us together, and stopped dead.

"Damning yourself?" I whispered, and anger swelled in my chest until I thought I'd burst with it. "How *dare* you?"

I took a single step toward the door and stopped when I saw the way Elias was staring from one of us to the other, his cheeks reddening with anger before he hid the emotion. Instead he painted his face with a false smile.

"Wondered where you'd gone, Reverend." Then he nodded at me. "Mistress St. James."

I acknowledged him with the briefest of glances, then turned to Duncan again. "Thank you for helping me find my shawl, Reverend Wallace," I said, my tone dripping ice. "Aunt Eleanor says I'd lose my head were it not for my neck keeping it attached."

"Then I'm glad your neck is intact," he said softly, and there was an apology in his eyes. One I refused to acknowledge. More softly, he whispered, "Very glad."

No. I would not feel this way for him. I would not.

Yet my knees were weak as I strode out of the church. And my heart, a quivering puddle.

'Twas midway through the afternoon when I drove our wagon over the worn path along the shore. My aunt prattled on about the sermon and the food and town gossip and such, but I paid little attention. I could think only of Duncan, the way he'd touched me. The look in his eyes. His promise that he would not betray me. I told myself I was angry with him for implying that my being a Witch could somehow damn his standing with his creator. And yet, I longed for the time when I might see him again. Certainly, my habit of skipping Sunday services was a thing of the past.

We were nearly home when I saw a woman in the road. Small and fair, with golden hair cut scandalously short, she was down on one knee, bending as if to tie the lace of her shoe. I drew the wagon to a halt before I spotted the pendant dangling from her neck, as she had no doubt intended me to see it. A pentacle, very like the one I wore.

As I caught my breath, I noticed the dagger that lay on the road beside her. And this was not only like my own, but identical to it.

The woman was a Witch. An immortal High Witch like me. I'd known 'twas only a matter of time before another one came for me. I'd known I should prepare myself for this day. But I wasn't prepared. Not at all.

When the woman's soft brown eyes met mine, I shivered. Perhaps I would not escape this time. Perhaps this day would be the last one I was to see. I was not willing to die. Not now, when I'd only just found Duncan again.

I was even less willing, however, to risk my aunt's safety. So, holding this strange woman's gaze, I handed the reins to Aunt Eleanor. "Go on to the cabin," I told her. "I'll be along soon."

"But, Raven . . . my goodness, girl, what's the matter? You've gone as pale as a wraith!"

"Nothing. I'm fine. I simply wish to speak with . . . an old acquaintance."

And the woman on the road straightened, gathering her dagger and slipping it into the sheath at her hip as she stepped off the track to allow the wagon to pass. She wore breeches, as a man would wear, and white stockings. Her shirt was white, with laces up the front, and she wore no cap upon her short, golden locks.

"You know this person?" Aunt Eleanor asked in surprise.

"I will tell you all about it . . . later," I promised. "Please, Aunt Eleanor, go on without me."

My aunt rolled her eyes and shook her head to make sure I knew of her displeasure, but after I stepped down, she did as I asked, snapping the reins. Ebony drew her away from me. Away from this strange woman, home to safety.

The Witch took a step forward, and I took an equal step back. And then she smiled, though only very slightly.

"You're right to be afraid, Raven St. James. But not of me."

"No?" I lifted my skirts to pull the dagger from its place at my thigh. "You'll understand if I choose caution over trust." I held the weapon in my hands, though they trembled.

The woman looked at it, then at me. For a very long time she stared at me, as if taking my measure. There was something else in her eyes. "You don't know me at all, do you, Raven?"

Narrowing my eyes on her, I said nothing, and it seemed for a moment a great sadness clouded her face. But she quickly dismissed whatever troubled her, chased it away to some dark corner, and lifted her chin once more. And then she drew her blade from its sheath, and I went rigid with fear.

But she simply tossed it. It landed at my feet, its blade embedded in the rich black earth. I looked down at it, blinking in surprise. Was this a trick?

"I am not one of the Dark Ones, Raven," she said.

"Then . . . then what do you want of me?"

She shrugged. "Would friendship be too much to ask?"

Still, I was hesitant.

Shaking her head, she untied the string that held her breeches, and as

I gasped, wide eyed, she tugged them low over her right hip, revealing the crescent mark blazed on the skin there. "Now will you believe I mean you no harm?" she asked, righting the breeches and looking not the least embarrassed.

"That proves nothing. We all have the crescent mark."

"My Lord and Lady, you really are as ignorant as a babe, aren't you?"

I said nothing, only waited for her to clarify.

"The Dark Ones bear the mark on their left flank, Raven. And the moon faces the opposite way. Did you not know even that much?"

Finally I lowered my dagger. "No," I said. "I'm afraid I did not."

"Then I was right to come to you."

I met her eyes, so strangely like the eyes of a doe. Innocent and liquid, while somehow dangerous at the same time. "I don't understand."

She sighed deeply. "I shall begin at the beginning, then. I am Arianna Sinclair, and I am nearly two hundred years old." I gasped in surprise, and maybe disbelief, but she only went on. "Several months ago I heard rumors of a lovely Witch hanged in a village in England, who'd been seen by some sailors alive and well only days later. And I thought to myself, she must truly be young if she took so few precautions to disguise her identity. So I set about the task of finding you, and here I am." She picked up her dagger, wiped its blade clean of dirt, and sheathed it at her side.

I shook my head slowly. "I still do not understand," I told her, no longer backing away in fear, relaxing my defenses. "Why would you want to find me?"

"The hanging . . . It was your first death, wasn't it, Raven?"

I nodded.

"Then you've much to learn. You see, young one, if I heard the rumors, if I could so easily track you down, then you must believe others will do the same. I'm here to help you, Raven. To teach you."

I stood before her now, my hands at my sides. She offered her hand, in friendship, I thought, and I took it.

And suddenly found myself twisted backward and held in small arms that had no business being so strong. My own dagger was wrenched from my hand and held to my heart, and I cried out, certain my life was about to end.

Her face close to my ear, she whispered, "First lesson, Raven. Trust no one."

I shuddered at the familiarity of those words, the way they echoed what my mother had told me. And then she released me and gently pressed my weapon back into my hand as my heart thundered against my ribs. I was breathing heavily from fear, pressing one hand to my breast as if to calm my racing heart.

"I would say, Raven, that it is a very good thing I was the first to find you."

"You weren't," I told her. And she crooked a golden brow. "Another one . . . a man, attacked me before I left England."

"And you defeated him?" Her tawny brown eyes were wide now with disbelief.

Ashamed, I lowered my head. "I escaped him. Barely."

"You survived," she told me. "There's no shame in living to fight another day, Raven. Come now, and take me to your home. I'll be needing a place to stay, and I suppose a silly dress so I can pass as one of *them*."

She expected my hospitality? After what she'd just done?

Smiling, she glanced at my dagger. "You can put that away. It will do you little good, anyway, until I've taught you to use it properly."

"I believe I'll hold on to it a bit longer," I responded.

And her smile grew wider as she nodded her approval. "Very good, Raven. You're a fast learner. You always were."

"And how would you know that?" I asked, studying her closely.

She laughed at herself, shrugging. "Oh, don't mind my cryptic comments. I'm a bit of a psychic, you know. I can read people. It's just something I picked up on. Besides, after what you've been through, having to flee for your life, start over, you'd almost have to be a fast learner, wouldn't you?"

She turned and began walking the road toward my home, glancing now and again at the tracks the wagon wheels had left in the dirt.

I had little choice but to follow her.

Chapter 7

Duncan paced the length of the spartan cabin he'd been given as shelter, turned, and paced back again. The fire snapped and popped loudly, drawing his gaze, and he found himself going still, staring into the flames, remembering.

The trapdoors dropping. The girl falling, the entire weight of her body hurtling toward the ground and then stopping short at the end of that rope. The way she'd jerked at the bottom. The way her head snapped. And then the way it had fallen upon his shoulder when he cut her down, as if her neck were boneless, or made of water.

Steel collar. There *had been no* steel collar.

The flames leaped and danced, and he thought of the fire he'd seen dancing in Raven's onyx eyes. Hellfire? he wondered. Or something else?

If he were truly a man of God, he'd tell what he knew. He closed his eyes and lowered his head. Nay. If he spoke out, she'd be arrested. Harmed. Killed, perhaps. He could not believe that to be God's will, no matter what she was.

Had she done something to him? Put some spell on him? Willed him to feel these things for her? Was such a thing even possible?

Heavy steps sounded outside, and he opened the door before old Elias Stanton could announce his presence. The man's face, whiskered jowls and all, seemed grim. And he said, "We have to talk. There's . . . something you need to be made aware of."

"Come in," Duncan said. And he wondered why he was irritated at the interruption. He ought to be glad to be distracted from thinking about her. To think of her was too confusing. Seeing her again—God, his preoccupation with the woman was bordering on obsession now that he'd seen her. 'Twas all he could do to keep himself from going to her. Right now, tonight.

"I had not intended to trouble you with this, Reverend Wallace, but upon seeing you in the church with Mistress St. James this morning, I felt it necessary."

"This concerns Mistress St. James, then?"

Elias nodded and, clasping his hands behind him, began pacing much as Duncan had been doing only moments ago. "Reverend . . . I fear the woman is trouble," he said. "You recall our conversation at the Boar's Head, do you not?"

Duncan nodded, and instantly knew what Stanton would say next.

"The temptress I spoke of is none other than Mistress St. James herself."

A cold hand seemed to clutch Duncan's heart when Elias's words confirmed what he had already guessed. He lowered his head, hoping to hide the flare of alarm that widened his eyes. *Nay. Not again.*

"I fear, my friend, she may be more than just a temptress. Much more."

"Say what you mean, Elias. I dislike guessing games."

Elias shrugged. "Surely 'tis obvious. The woman could easily be a practitioner of the black arts . . . a Witch."

The hairs on the back of Duncan's neck bristled, and he found himself instinctively defending her, not even giving his words thought before speaking them. "Dinna be ridiculous, Elias. Why would you think such a thing?"

Elias turned slowly, his eyes narrow. "She's unnaturally beautiful, is she not?"

Holding that gaze, Duncan nodded. "Incredibly beautiful," he said. "But why do you say 'tis unnatural?"

"Because of the way she flaunts it before the men of this congregation. I'll wager not a one has escaped her wiles. All of them lusting after her, I tell you, no matter how God-fearing they be. And that's her plan, Duncan. To lure us all into sin, and damn us before she moves on to the next God-loving congregation."

Duncan felt his lips pull into a grimace of distaste. The man was a fool. "Aye, no doubt the ruination of mankind is all the lass lives for."

He'd meant it as sarcastic and biting. Elias only nodded in enthusiastic agreement, which made Duncan sigh, and try another approach with the thick-skulled man. "You said before that even you have felt this Witchly allure she exudes," he said.

Lowering his head, Elias said, "Yes. Though it shames me to admit it."

"An' you dinna believe it could simply be the natural feelin' of attraction any man might feel when he sees a woman of such exceptional beauty?"

"Never," Elias denied flatly. "'Tis Witchery, I tell you. I be above desires of the flesh. Or was, 'til she worked her devilish wiles on me."

Nodding, Duncan said, "I'm glad you've come to me with this, Elias." And he was. Glad because in seeing how ridiculous the things Elias believed of Raven were, he could see more clearly how foolish he himself had been, only moments ago. Spells, indeed. He was drawn to the woman and had been since he'd first set eyes on her. And 'twas no more due to Witchery than was the sunrise or the changing phases of the moon. He desired her. And maybe more than that. Maybe . . . *much* more than that.

He searched Elias's face as he concocted his lies. And it occurred to him that he'd rarely lied in his lifetime, had always made an effort at utter honesty. But for her, for Raven, he lied without pause. Without the slightest hesitation.

He thought he'd likely be willing to do far more for her. Die for her, should the need arise.

"I've seen many Witches durin' my time in England," Duncan said. "An' I can tell you beyond any doubt, Raven St. James isna one."

Elias's face fell, eyes widening. "How can you be so sure?"

Duncan tilted his head. "Have you never *seen* a Witch?"

"No," Elias admitted. "But I was sure I had the day she arrived."

Searching for a plausible lie, then latching on to the first one he thought of, Duncan said, "The eyes of a Witch are two different colors. The left is green, and the right is blue."

"The hell you say!"

"Aye, Elias, 'tis true. And the forefinger of a Witch's hand is longer than the middle one."

Elias's eyes narrowed, and Duncan was certain he'd pushed it too far. Damn, he'd had the man believing him for a moment.

"But a skilled Witch," Elias speculated, "could likely disguise those

things. Don't you see, Duncan? Something is not right with the woman!
Her crops, her wealth. 'Tis not by natural means she succeeds at everything she sets her pretty hands to. All without a man to aid her!"

"Could it be that she is simply wise an' strong, an' perhaps a hard
worker?" Duncan put forth.

"I want you to go out there, Duncan. Mistress Foxgrove claims
they've taken in another strange young woman, and I tell you, she's likely
another of their coven."

"Their *coven*? Really, Elias, I believe your imagination—"

"Go out there tonight, Duncan. They liked you, the both of them.
Pretend to be making a social call. And see what sorts of things they keep
about that cabin. See how they behave when they're alone and not in the
public eye."

"You want me to spy on them?" Duncan asked, already formulating
the firmest refusal he could concoct.

"Yes. And if you won't, Duncan, I'll do it myself. However, I'm loath
to get that close to her. I fear she'd bewitch me even further. You're a
man of God, Duncan, surely you'd be far safer than I?"

Closing his eyes slowly, shaking his head, Duncan recalled the distaste
he'd seen in Raven's eyes when this man had touched her. She wouldn't
like him snooping around. And suppose Elias should find something?

He hadn't admitted it, even to himself, at least not consciously, but
Duncan knew there must be something to find. Some truth to Elias's suspicions. Raven *was* magick. Everything about her was mystical and potent. She'd cured him of whatever illness he'd been suffering aboard the
Sea Witch. He didn't doubt these things.

But she *wasn't* evil. No matter what else she was, she wasn't that.

And even if there were nothing for Elias to find in Raven's cabin, almost anything could be construed by his suspicious, fearful mind as evidence. At least if Duncan went himself, he could return with a favorable
report.

"All right, Elias," he said softly. "I shall go. But meanwhile, do one
thing for me?"

"Of course, Reverend."

"Tell no one else of your suspicions. Should you be wrong about
Mistress St. James, you could easily destroy her good name with such
gossip. And you wouldna wish to do that should she be innocent, would
you, now?"

He grunted and huffed, saying clearly that he *could not* believe her innocent, *would not* be proved wrong.

"Please," Duncan urged. "'Twould only send the town into panic."

Elias's face softened then. "All right, I shall keep my suspicions to myself . . . for now. Except for . . ." He narrowed his eyes on Duncan. "Never mind."

"Except for what?" Duncan asked, and he felt a cold foreboding in his heart. "Have you already spoken these suspicions, Elias?"

Elias averted his eyes. "'Tis of no concern to you," he said. "You'll report back to me upon your return?"

Shaking his fears away, Duncan faced the man. "Aye, I'll report to you, but on the morrow, Elias. 'Tis a long walk, an' I'll no doubt prefer sleep to conversation when I return."

"Tomorrow then," Elias said, and touching the brim of his hat, he backed out the door.

He wasn't going to her so he could spy on her, as Elias wished him to do. He was going to warn her. Duncan was certain she could have no clue what Elias suspected of her, or she'd have fled this place by now.

For just a moment, as he followed the road that led along the southern edge of the peninsula, overlooking the sea, he paused to wonder at the irony of what he was doing. Raven St. James had been convicted of Witchery and sentenced to death. He'd seen her die with his own eyes, only to find her alive and well, and again suspected of Witchcraft. And yet, he, a man of God, was about to warn her.

Worst of all, it wasn't that he disbelieved the accusations against her. Not that at all. 'Twas that he simply didn't care. *He didn't care.* He remembered all too well the way he'd seen her standing in the moonlight, felt the power surging from her hands into his body that night aboard the ship. It could have been a dream, but he didn't think so. And still, he didn't care.

He only wanted to see her again. To get to know all there was to know of her. To understand the workings of her mind and the mysteries of her soul. To know what she was thinking. And to see to it she remained safe from harm.

Nothing else mattered. And as little sense as that made, he didn't question it. It simply was.

Duncan knew what he would report to Elias, no matter what he found at Raven's cabin tonight. In the morn he intended to assure Elias all was as it should be, thus ending the elder's speculation.

But not, perhaps, ending his lust.

Duncan's flesh heated and he tugged at the too tight collar that suddenly chafed his throat. He wore an ordinary pair of breeches and a white shirt, this night. For some reason, he disliked the thought of going to Raven in the robes of clergy. He sensed the clothing threatened her, somehow, and that wasn't what he wished to do.

He didn't like thinking about the way Elias looked at Raven St. James. He didn't like Elias's insistence that all the men of Sanctuary must be looking at her the same way as he. And he didn't like that he himself was just as drawn to her as the rest. Because he wanted to believe that with him 'twas different.

At last her cabin came into view, and he saw the soft glow of candles in one of the windows. 'Twas a simple home, graying logs, set high on the cliffs overlooking the Atlantic. Pretty curtains of white, perhaps made by Raven's own delicate hands, hung in the few windows of imported glass. And the door was hand hewn, a single thick board sawed from what must have been a mighty oak tree once. The area around the house was lush with gardens. Herbs grew in tangled patches along with vegetables and flowering plants. All bathed tonight in the light of the moon, so that the place looked wild and untamed and mysterious. The waves crashing against the rocky shore far below were like a chorus, a magickal chorus. This place made him think of the enchanted palace where the sleeping princess of a fairy tale awaited rescue.

Duncan moved closer, lifted his hand to tap on the door, only to pause when the sound of singing reached his ears. Raven's voice, rich and beautiful, drifted over him like warmed honey. He'd heard that voice in his dreams often over the past three years. Heard it ringing out in condemnation of a crowd of bloodthirsty bigots. But he'd never heard it sweetly singing the words of a love song.

I've longed to taste your kiss, my love.
To hold you would be sweet bliss, my love.
My heart shall break, 'ere you wait too long.
Come to me, come love me, come answer my song.

"Raven," he whispered. His heartbeat quickened, and his stomach muscles clenched as if in response to her words. He steadied himself, or tried to, but he was shaken to the core. And even as he told himself not to, he leaned closer to peer through the window beside the door, where the pretty white curtains stood slightly parted.

Raven St. James reclined in a large metal tub, water and bubbles brimming around her. Her arms moved, long and graceful and shiny-slick with moisture. One hand squeezed a cloth she held high above her as she leaned back in the tub. Water trickled over her neck and shoulders. Bare skin glistened in the candlelight as she tipped her head back, eyes closed as if in some secret ecstasy. And he wondered if she were thinking of him as she continued to sing.

> *For two years, in secret, I've yearned, my love*
> *Forever it seems I have burned, my love,*
> *Your love is forbidden, you can't want me, too.*
> *Come to me, sweet Duncan, and tell me you do.*

She ran her fingertips slowly along the underside of her chin, tracing a path down over her neck, her chest, and lower, to where he could no longer see.

And then, quite suddenly, she stopped. Slowly she lowered her head and leveled her gaze on the very window he was peering through, and Duncan caught his breath. Her eyes met his—though he was certain she couldn't see him out here in the darkness. Still they met his, and held them. He couldn't look away. Not for the life of him. It seemed to Duncan as if every cell in his body came to vivid life in that moment, stirred by her gaze and aroused to action. He tingled with awareness. As if he were the one caught naked and she the one shamelessly looking on.

And as he remained there, riveted, he heard a voice call the woman's name from another room. Raven's head turned toward its summons. A brief glance toward the window again, and perhaps a very slight smile. So slight he could have easily imagined it. And then she rose from the water like a Pagan goddess of old, and Duncan felt himself burn. Rivulets streamed down her body. She gleamed in the golden light of the dancing candles. Gleamed and shone as she daintily stepped from the tub onto the folded rug beside it. She showed no shyness, no shame as she blotted herself dry with a small cloth. Nor should she, for she was truly magnificent to behold. Sensuality surrounded her like a nimbus, her every movement as graceful as a dance. And he was aroused, tempted as he'd never been before.

'Twas said by those who'd taught him that to bathe fully naked was sinful. To touch one's own body with the deliberate caress with which she'd run her hands over hers was to incite forbidden desires. Even to bathe too often was to embrace the sin of vanity. He'd never agreed with all of those teachings, and bathed often himself, feeling 'twas better to be vain than to stink. But for the first time, Duncan realized that perhaps there was wisdom in those particular teachings of the Church. For his loins were on fire as he watched her. She was, in that moment, the very temptress he'd been warned against.

But unwittingly. She was innocent. She couldn't know he was watching. And in fact, 'twas he who was to blame for the fire burning in his soul right now. For he had no business peering through the woman's windows. And yet, 'twas as if he'd been drawn there by some power beyond his will. And then held there by the force of her gaze.

She moved like a seductress, every inch of her body exposed to him as she turned and reached for a robe. And then she pulled it on, covering her feminine curves and delicate thighs and full, ripe breasts. And finally she moved out of the room, toward the sound of her aunt, calling her name once again.

"Is she as beautiful as you thought she would be?"

Duncan went rigid as the feminine voice came from behind him, and he whirled to face a small, fair woman he'd never seen before. "I . . . that is, I was only—"

"You're the preacher, aren't you?" she asked.

"Aye. Duncan Wallace, mistress." He fought to regain his composure.

"Well, Duncan Wallace, if I thought she'd mind your snooping, I'd gut you right here. Lucky for you I happen to know she wouldn't mind. Not at all."

He felt his face heating and lowered his head. "I wasna snoopin', as you put it, mistress. My attention was drawn by her singin', and—"

"Like a songbird," the woman interrupted. Then she turned toward the door and pulled it open. "Well, come on inside. You may as well let her know you're here."

Duncan, uncomfortable at being caught looking at Raven, and yet sensing somehow the small woman beside him held no judgment over him, stepped inside.

"Raven," the woman called. "You have a guest."

"Oh?" She stepped from the small bedroom, then went still as she met Duncan's eyes. "Oh," she whispered.

Was she embarrassed? Did she realize he might have heard the words of her song? His name floating from her lips with such longing? At that moment he battled the urge to sweep her into his arms, even knowing how inappropriate that would be. They barely knew each other. And yet it felt very much as if they did.

"I see you've met Arianna," Raven said, as if searching for something to say.

"She didna tell me her name."

"I got the distinct impression you couldn't care less about my name, Reverend," Arianna said. "Raven, take the man out for a moonlight walk. Show him the gardens, introduce him to Ebony, for heaven's sake."

"I . . . all right. If you want to, Duncan."

He nodded. "Aye, I'd like very much to walk with you, Raven. We have . . . much to talk about."

Nodding, she took a dark cloak lined with fur from a peg on the wall, and Duncan impulsively stepped forward, taking it from her hands. Moving behind her, he gently draped it over her shoulders. His fingers brushed the flesh of her neck before moving away. God, how he wanted to touch her.

"Th-thank you."

His hands settled there on her shoulders for a moment. He didn't want to take them away. But he had to, or she'd surely know the direction his thoughts were taking.

He opened the door and let her lead him outside. Her hair was still wet, and as he walked close beside her he could smell the scent of honeysuckle clinging to her skin.

She didn't show him the gardens, or introduce him to anyone named "Ebony." Instead, she led him out to the very edge of the cliffs. The wind gusted there, lifting her wet hair from her shoulders and snapping it like a whip. She faced the sea, staring out over the churning water, glancing down at the sheer drop to the rocks below.

"This is my favorite place," she said. "I love the sea."

It struck him that he'd been thinking the very same thing, as he'd been walking out here. That he loved the sea.

"There's a small island out there, not far at all from shore. It sits all alone. No one ever seems to go near. I've felt like that . . . alone. Isolated from the rest of the land and surrounded by an element very different from me."

"I've often felt that way myself," he told her. "As if I dinna quite fit in with the rest of mankind. Dinna . . . ken the way their minds work. Canna make sense of them."

She nodded, and was still for a moment. Then, "Why did you come?" She asked the question of him, but she didn't face him.

He stood beside her, staring out over the water just as she did. "I dinna know," he told her. "I was compelled to come, Raven."

She nodded.

"I couldna forget you, after that cold dawn in the square. But I've told you that."

"Yes." She turned to face him. "I believe a bond was formed between us on the gallows, Duncan. Easy enough to understand, really. You were the only man there who seemed to care."

"I did care," he said. And he clasped her shoulders now, stepping closer to her, staring down into those ebon pools. "One look into your eyes, and I cared more than I'd cared for anythin' in my life. Raven, I tried," he whispered. "I swear to you, I tried to stop them."

Her hand came up suddenly, palm flattening to his cheek, cupping it in a way that was somehow soothing. "I know you tried, Duncan. There is no reason for you to feel guilty for what they did. I knew you were no part of any of that. You risked your own life to prevent it, in fact. You don't need to convince me. I was there."

He nodded. And overwhelmed by feeling, by desire, he turned his face against her palm, let his lips touch it, kiss its tender center before rubbing his cheek against it once more. "Aye, you were there. So you know what I do. Raven . . . there is something here. Some powerful emotion between you and me. You must feel it."

She lowered her hand, and then her head. "I feel . . . desire for you, Duncan." Then she closed her eyes. "But 'tis a desire you believe will damn your soul."

He was stunned at the bluntness of it. He'd never met a woman who spoke so plainly. But he cleared his throat. "I dinna believe that at all. I spoke . . . without thinkin'. Raven, I burn for you, 'tis true. But I feel for you, too. And what I feel is the purest and most holy sort of carin' I can imagine. It canna be evil. It canna be damning. An' if 'twere . . .'twouldna matter, lass."

Slowly she lifted her head, met his eyes again. "And what do you propose we do about this feeling?"

Her black eyes fairly blazed. Duncan drew a breath, battled temptation. "We resist it, Raven. But only until we can be married."

"Married?"

The fire in her eyes seemed to cool, and she lowered her chin. He caught it in his hand and lifted it up again, until she faced him. "The Scriptures say 'tis better a man marry than to burn with lust," he said.

"What your Scriptures say means very little to me, Duncan." She sniffed and met his eyes. "My faith has only one rule."

"Only one?" He searched her face. "An' what *is* this rule you live by, Raven?"

"'An it harm none, do what thou will.'" She shrugged. "'Tis the only rule I've ever needed, the only one that makes sense to me."

"'Tis a good rule. But it doesna say, 'Thou shalt nay marry.'"

"Marriage between us . . . is something that can never be."

"But—"

"I will harm none, Duncan. To marry you . . . I'd harm *you*, you must see that. 'Twould ruin you. I stand convicted of Witchcraft and sentenced to death. And even here, the suspicions about me have begun to stir anew. No, I can be no preacher's wife."

"Were you my bride, Raven, they would no longer suspect you."

"Perhaps not," she said softly. "But would you?" She faced him, searching his eyes.

Duncan shook his head. "I will believe whatever you tell me, Raven. If you say you're innocent, I willna doubt it, I swear."

"And what if I can't claim innocence, Duncan? What if I am what they say I am?"

He gripped her shoulders, staring down into her eyes. "Are you?"

She lowered her eyes. "That's just it. I cannot tell you *what* I am. I've seen what trusting others can do, Duncan. Seen it in my mother's eyes just before they murdered her."

"You *can* trust me, lass," he said softly.

"But I can't. And you would want no wife who kept such dark secrets from you, Duncan."

"You're wrong," he said. "Raven, I dinna *care* what you are."

"How can you say that?"

"Because, lass, 'tis the truth."

She shook her head slowly. "Perhaps it is, at the moment. But you *will* care, Duncan. The time will come when you'll demand I tell all, and that is something I can never do." She cupped his face in her hands. "We cannot be together as husband and wife."

"An' I canna go on without you," he whispered.

"Then be with me, Duncan," she urged. "Come to me in the cloak of midnight, and in secret. For that's the only way a love like ours can be. A love for the moment, fleeting and precious. Forbidden, and consigned to darkness."

"'Twill be more," he whispered. "I vow, Raven, I will make it more." And then he pulled her into his arms and kissed her as he'd been dreaming of kissing her. And it didn't matter that she was keeping secrets, or that she hadn't denied the charges against her. All that mattered was this, holding her, alive and warm and real, in his arms, against his body.

And perhaps loving her this way was a sin. If it was, then he'd gladly be damned, because he couldn't resist . . . nor did he want to.

Chapter 8

﹏

He kissed me as I'd never been kissed by another. He kissed me as I'd been kissed only once—by him, on the *Sea Witch* as the fever and the ale mingled in his blood. I'd thought, in some secret part of me, that he wouldn't have touched me had he been sober and well.

But he was sober now. And healthy. And strong.

He swept me away there on the cliffs. His hands in my hair, touching it in some kind of wonder, as if he'd never felt anything so soft. His lips, brushing my neck and caressing my ear as he whispered sweet love words in his soft, Scot's lilt.

I'd told him I desired him. I dared not feel anything more. And yet I was not certain I could resist. He was like the sea, hurling its waves against the rocky shore below us, and slowly, steadily eroding the solid rock away. Bit by bit. As gentle, as softly as water, he wooed me. And the stone I thought was my heart began softening beneath his touch, even now.

"I've dreamed of this," I whispered. "Of you . . ."

"And I, lass . . . night after endless night."

His hands deftly untied my cloak, and it fell to the ground, shaping itself into a perfect nest. Then his hands touched the robe I wore, trembling, as if he knew there was nothing underneath. And perhaps he did know, for I'd sensed him watching at the window, glimpsed movement there as I'd bathed. One moment certain he had come to me, the next convinced I was only imagining what my mind told me.

Slowly, hesitantly, he parted my robe, and then the sea wind came in to complete his task, pushing it wide so it flew behind me like a cape. Duncan's gaze burned on my body, sliding up and down me as if he were glimpsing Divinity itself.

"You're almost too beautiful to touch," he whispered. Then he met my eyes. "An' far too beautiful not to."

His hands, tender and careful, came to me. Slid slowly from the column of my neck down the front of me, and I held my breath. At last he touched my breasts, palms skimming over them, pausing there as he closed his eyes.

"'Tis heaven I touch," he murmured.

"No, Duncan, 'tis earth itself." I pressed myself closer. "And I'll not break at your caresses."

At my word he squeezed, gently at first, with more pressure when I closed my eyes and released all my breath at once. And then he pulled me to him for more kisses, and his hands slipped around to the small of my back, and lower to stroke my naked buttocks, and my thighs. I shoved my hands between our bodies to tug at the laces of his shirt and breeches. He'd come to me tonight without the protection of his dark minister's robes. He'd come to me as a man. A man like no other.

And I knew it even more so when I'd undressed him fully and looked upon him. He hadn't been like this before. His chest had broadened, and his shoulders seemed capable of bearing any weight. His belly was tight and hard, hips lean. And he was aroused. Fully so, and the sight of him made my heart tremble. I touched him. Closed my hand around him, and understood, I think, the incredible magickal power of the mating of woman and man. I'd heard of it, of course. But never had it made sense to me. I saw it now, though. How he would fill me, complete me. How the scales of nature would hover for a time in perfect balance while I held him inside of me.

He breathed again only when I took my hand away. And then I lowered myself to the cushion of my cloak, reclining slightly, and opened myself to him. "Come, Duncan. I can wait no longer."

For an endless moment he stared at me lying there wantonly. The sea wind blew harsher, brushing over my nipples with its chilled breath, touching my secret places with icy hands. Goose bumps rose on my flesh, while inside I burned.

I lifted one hand to him, and he knelt. "I have never . . ." he began.

"Nor I," I whispered.

"We've been waiting then. For each other, I think." He looked into my eyes, expecting my agreement, but I said nothing. "Dinna tell me you dinna believe it, Raven, for I know you do. I know you as I know myself . . . somehow. We were meant to be, you and I."

"Perhaps," I whispered, but I could tell him no more. To let myself believe in his romantic notions . . . would only lead to heartbreak.

"I've been told it can be difficult for a woman . . . the first time." He knelt beside me. His fingertips danced over my neck and my shoulders.

"Not for me, Duncan. Not with you."

He kissed me again, so slowly, so deeply. "I'd nay harm you for the world, Raven."

"You won't." My words came in breathless sighs now.

He nodded, bent to nibble my ear, taste my neck. "My best friend . . . he says 'tis easier if the woman is . . . made ready."

I smiled, eager only to be on with it. I wanted him so much I could barely lie still. "How will you make me ready, Duncan? Rub me with sage like a turkey?"

Sitting back slightly, he looked at the nest between my legs, licked his lips. "Like this," he whispered, and then he touched me there. Gently he parted my folds and put his fingers on me, and I drew a gasp as a bolt of pleasure shot through my loins. Slowly he rubbed, exploring, watching my face so intently I thought he was trying to read my thoughts. When he pressed inside me, I cried out in delight, and arched my hips off the ground. How I wanted him.

"You've made me ready, then," I whispered.

"Oh, nay, lass. There is more my friend spoke of."

He bowed over me, and kissed me between my legs like a worshiper kissing the feet of a goddess. He opened me with his fingers, and kissed me again, and I moaned. And then his tongue snaked out, licking me, darting at the tiny nub that seemed to be the core of my desire, and then plunging inside as if he would devour me whole. Tears filled my eyes at the intensity of what he did to me, and I moved against him, pressing closer, losing myself to utter physical sensation as he probed and licked and tasted every part of me. My hands clenched in his hair as the tension in me tightened unbearably. Finally he moved up my body, nipping at my breasts, and then suckling them hard, no longer gentle, but seeming aroused beyond the ability to be so.

He settled atop me. I was so alive with sensation that when I felt him pressing inside me, 'twas as if lightning struck. I pressed my hands to his buttocks, gripping him tight, and I arched hard against him, to take him into me, all the way, all at once. There was a brief stab of pain, but I was so enraptured in pleasure that it felt good to me. Then he began to move, and I moved, too, sensing his needs, knowing his feelings as I knew my own. He fed at my mouth and my throat and my breasts by turns as he plunged himself into me again and again. He drove me nearer and nearer to something I'd never known. And finally the stars seemed to explode around me and I screamed his name, even as he stabbed deeper than before and cried mine.

He held me, slowly relaxing in my arms. Kissed my hair, my face, asked if I were all right, if he had hurt me.

"I am more than all right," I told him, running my hands over the wonderful expanse of his back, his shoulders. So firm and hard to my touch. "I never knew, Duncan. I never understood . . ."

"Understand this, bonny Raven." Framing my face with his hands, his directly above me, staring down with his heart in his eyes, he whispered, "I love you. I love you from the very depths of my soul. I would die for you, Raven St. James, an' never regret it for a moment."

I looked at him, guilt showing in my eyes, I think, when I bit my lip to keep from answering him in kind. The words bubbled up in my throat, but I refused to let them spill out.

"Nay, dinna look that way, my love. I know you dinna return my feelings . . . just yet. But you will, Raven. You will."

Lowering my lids to shield my true feelings from him, I shook my head. "I've given you all I have to give. My body. My virginity. And my promise, Duncan, that there will be no other man for me. Not ever."

"Truly?"

I nodded. "I do not lie."

"But canna quite trust me with the truth."

"I told you I—"

"Nay. 'Tis all right, Raven." He stroked my hair, staring down at me with love pouring from his eyes and spilling over me like the very elixir of the gods. "I am too in love to complain, to demand. I'll lie at your feet like a cur dog, awaitin' whatever crumbs drop from your fingers, and revelin' should you bestow even a pat on the head. Whatever you give me, I'll relish and cherish and return a thousandfold, lass. I vow it, until the day I die, I'll love only you." He lifted my hand, pressed his lips to my fingers. "And eventually, you'll see that I'd sooner die than betray you.

You'll ken that you can trust me as you can no other. You'll tell me all, my love, and you'll grow to love me, too."

I stared back at him, and wondered how he could miss what seemed to be bursting from my very soul, what must show in my eyes. I already did love him, too.

But if I told him the truth . . .

No, I couldn't. I'd be putting him at risk by trusting him. He'd be stripped of his position, driven from the town or worse, arrested and tried as my accomplice. And yes, there was more. There was that selfish fear, that gnawing certainty inside me that he would stop loving me if he knew the truth.

I'd never tell him. I'd never risk that. What we had—what we shared between us—would have to be enough.

Though I could never say it aloud, I would always, *always* love him.

Elias was waiting when Duncan made his way back to his cabin in town.

Duncan hadn't realized it, of course. He'd been humming to himself, happier than he could remember being, but at the same time battling a sense of dread. He'd sinned. He knew that. He didn't blame Raven for it, didn't even regret it, really. But he did wonder how he could put on his robes tomorrow morn and go about the town folk acting as if he were still their spiritual leader. Their Christian guide. How could he? None of them was likely to have committed the sins he had this night. He'd be pretending, playing a role that was utterly false.

But how *could* it be wrong to love this way? When he felt the emotion bubbling up from some bottomless well within him. It didn't *feel* sinful. It *felt* noble and pure and utterly . . . utterly *right*. It didn't even feel new, but ancient, as if it had been a part of him from the time before time was, if such a thing were possible.

He stopped humming when he reached his door, as doubts crept into his mind once again. But when he stepped inside, a deep voice chased those doubts away.

"Whatever could have taken you so long, Reverend Wallace? You've been gone for *hours*."

Duncan went stiff, searching the darkness and finally spotting Elias in the room's only chair, near the dying fire. "You told me to observe the women," he said. "So I did."

"Surely they're abed by now."

"Of course they are." Duncan walked to a table where a lamp sat and lit it, taking his time, setting the glass chimney in place with great care. Stalling as he sought an explanation in his mind.

"You remained out there, even after the women retired?" Elias asked, running short of patience, Duncan thought.

"Naturally," he replied.

"But why?"

It came to him slowly, and that's the way he spoke, slowly, carefully piecing the words together one by one. "You . . . obviously know naught of Witches, Elias." He paced to the hearth, tossed a pair of logs atop the coals, since Stanton had apparently been too lazy to do so himself. The flames licked up at the wood, searing the bark black and seeking the meatier wood beneath it. "Their . . . rites . . . are performed by night. Midnight bein' the, ah, the Witchin' Hour."

"Ahhh, the Witching Hour." Elias nodded, and his eyes took on an eager gleam in the lampglow and firelight. "And did they? Did they strip off their garments and dance naked beneath the moon at midnight? Did they kill a calf and drink its blood or mate with a goat possessed by their beastly master? Did they?"

Duncan's stomach clenched. He felt ill. And he knew with unrelenting certainty that Raven would never do such things as those of which Stanton spoke. If she were a Witch, then Stanton's ideas about Witches were pure fancy. There was something spiritual, something holy, about Raven St. James. He'd sensed it from the start.

"They did nothin' of the sort," he said very calmly. "They only slept."

Elias rubbed his chin. "Perhaps they knew you were still lingering about. They can sense such things, can they not?"

Duncan shrugged. "Nay, not in a man of the cloth," he replied. Anything, any lie, to relieve the man of his notions. Elias Stanton was dangerous to Raven. Duncan knew it to his bones.

Elias nodded thoughtfully. "Then perhaps 'twas simply not their night to practice their Pagan rites."

Closing his eyes, Duncan lowered his head. "There was naught in the cabin to indicate . . ."

"You seem so certain, Reverend. Are you sure they didn't bewitch *you*?"

He shook his head rapidly. "I'm utterly sure of that, sir."

"Hmm. Well, the situation bears watching. Just to be safe. Wouldn't you agree?"

Did he have a choice? Nay. He'd already made Elias wary of him. He had to keep the man's trust if he were to have any hope of protecting Raven from him. "I agree completely," he said. "Rest assured, Elias, I will be keepin' a very close eye on the goin's on at that cabin on the cliffs. A very close eye."

"Good." Elias got to his feet. "I'll let you get some rest, then. Good night."

And he hurried out the door.

Had Elias believed a word Duncan had said to him? There was no way to be sure. Raven should leave this place. She should leave at once. And he would warn her of that. Should have done so tonight as he'd intended, but . . . well, her touch, her kisses, had chased everything else from his mind. Tomorrow. Aye. He'd warn her of the danger that lived here in Sanctuary for her. He'd warn her on the morrow.

"You have the look of a woman well loved," Arianna said just as she lunged forward and swept her dagger in a deadly arc that could easily have gutted me on the spot. She looked all innocence this morning, with the early sunlight gleaming from her cropped golden hair, and her slight frame and small stature. But she could be a deadly opponent. I'd seen that right away.

And a good friend. I'd come to love her very much in the short while she'd been with us. So much so that I hoped she would never decide to leave. 'Twas as if I'd known her always, though that could not be possible.

"Perhaps there's no need to tell you so . . ." She slashed at me again, nearly nicking me this time, but I danced backward just out of reach of the gleaming blade. "But I think it a poor idea."

I thrust, she dodged. "Why?" I asked. "Is he not the most beautiful man you've ever seen, Arianna?"

"With perhaps one exception," she said with a careless shrug. "But he's also a man of the cloth."

"Which means he's in touch with the Almighty, just as we are."

"Which means he believes Witches should be put to death."

I went still, and so did she. Our blades raised, our bodies poised in ready crouches, we paused to catch our breath, and to lock gazes as she awaited my reaction to her words.

"Duncan tried to prevent the hanging that killed my mother," I said. "He's not like the rest."

"Can you be sure?"

I blinked, lowered my head. "I . . . yes, I'm sure."

Arianna shrugged. "I am not," she said. "And I'm equally doubtful of your judgment where he's concerned. I suppose 'tis lucky for you I'm here to watch out for you." She slashed at me again, neatly slicing the fabric that covered my middle this time.

I jumped back. "Be careful, would you? You could have cut me!"

"And what would it matter?" Arianna asked with a grin. "You're immortal. You would heal."

"'Twould hurt all the same," I replied, scowling, but lifting my own dagger to waist height before thrusting it forward in a quick darting motion, drawing back just as quickly.

"Better *I* hurt you than your preacher man, Raven. I've a feeling you'd recover from the nick of my blade far more quickly than from a broken heart," she said, and jumped sideways to avoid my blade. The act sent her off balance, and I leaped forward, shouldering her hard and sending her to the ground.

"Aha!" I shouted, and leaped on Arianna, straddling her middle, braced up on my knees. One hand gripped Arianna's wrist, immobilizing the dagger she still clutched, while the other held my own blade to my friend's throat. "I have you now!"

Arianna yanked one of her legs out from beneath me, planted a foot on my chest, and shoved hard, all in the space of a heartbeat. As I went sprawling onto my back, Arianna bounced to her feet without using her hands.

"Overconfidence is the quickest path to defeat. Never underestimate the enemy." Then she laughed. "That was good, though. You grow better every day."

"It does not feel as if I do."

"You do." Arianna's smile gentled. "You know I am only concerned for your safety, don't you? If I did not care for you, I'd keep my opinions to myself."

"I know, Arianna. I just happen to disagree."

"You could get yourself hurt. You know that."

She looked so sad, and I wondered if she spoke with the voice of experience. "I know," I said. "But 'tis worth the risk to have him, even for a little while."

She held out a hand. I took it, and Arianna pulled me to my feet, then spun me around and held me fast, her blade at my throat. "I cannot believe," she said close to my ear, laughter in her voice, "you fell for that one *again*!"

"Raven!"

'Twas Duncan's voice, startled and horrified. He came out of the nearby trees and into view, staring in utter terror at Arianna, her blade, my throat. "Let her go!"

Arianna glanced down into my eyes, her own sparkling with undisguised mirth. Then she looked at Duncan and shrugged. "Oh, all right. If you insist," she said. She released me, and then she threw her blond head back and laughed in a voice that rang with the clarity of bells.

I couldn't help it. I bent my head to hide it, but my shoulders shook as I, too, gave in to quiet laughter.

Poor Duncan only stood there, staring from one of us to the other in confusion. "I dinna ken . . . Raven, are you—"

"I'm fine, Duncan. Arianna and I were only . . . practicing."

He frowned, looking me over from head to toe and frowning even harder. "You're . . . you're wearin' *breeches*!"

"Being a man," Arianna said, "you've likely never tried to fight in skirts, but I can tell you, Duncan, 'tis no easy task."

I sent her a quelling glance and sought a plausible explanation. "We're learning to defend ourselves, Duncan. That is all. We're unmarried women living alone in a small settlement. We simply feel it the wise thing to do."

"The wise thing to do," he countered, "would be to marry."

The mirth fled me and regret replaced it in my heart. "Please stop asking. You know I cannot."

"You will, eventually." He came closer. "So, will you show me the finer points of combat with blades?"

"If I did, then how would I ever overpower you?" I asked.

"The same way you do now, my love, with a simple glance."

I smiled as he came to me, wrapped me in his arms, and hugged me so tenderly I nearly cried.

"How did you find us, Duncan?" Arianna asked him, even now sliding her blade into its sheath. "We thought coming here the height of discretion."

"Discretion is a fine idea," he replied. "For if 'twere someone besides me to see you both in breeches, fighting as if to the death, there would be scandal indeed in the streets of Sanctuary." He lowered his head. "More so than there already is." Then slowly he lifted it, met my eyes again. "Your aunt told me you'd gone walkin' in the woods. Once I got near enough, I simply followed the sounds of battle."

I smiled at that, but the smile he returned was a sad one.

"Something troubles you," I said.

"Indeed. Elias Stanton suspects . . ." He slanted a worried glance toward Arianna, as if about to say something she shouldn't overhear.

"Never fear," she quipped. "I know exactly what that fool suspects. More than likely, he suspects me of the same things."

"Aye, more than likely," Duncan agreed. Then he gripped my hands in his. "You should leave this town, Raven. At once. I dinna believe 'tis safe for you here."

I sighed deeply.

"You knew this day would come, Raven. We've spoken of it," Arianna said.

I nodded but met Duncan's eyes. "I'll not go. I'll not pack up and move away from . . ." I bit my lip.

"From what?" he pressed, squeezing my hands.

Closing my eyes, I whispered, "From you, Duncan. I don't want to leave you."

He smiled, then seemed to catch his lip between his teeth as if to stop its trembling. "You love me, lass. You either dinna ken it yet, or canna admit it to me, but you do. You love me."

"Stop it, please . . ."

"All right. All right." But he pulled me tight, kissed me softly, before he let me go and spoke once more. "I thought . . . I thought to go with you, Raven. If you'd have me."

My brows bent until they touched. "But all you have is here. Your home, your position, your friends in Boston."

"All I have, nay, all I *wish* to have, ever," he whispered, "is here, right here in my arms."

Pressing my lips tight, I averted my eyes. "My aunt Eleanor is not a young woman," I told him. "She'd never leave this place."

"She isna the one in danger here, Raven. You are."

Arianna spoke then, coming closer to the two of us. Though she disapproved of my relationship with Duncan, she seemed to understand it. And she would neither nag nor play the part of my judge. Witches didn't work that way. She'd voiced her opinion. Now she would leave it at that.

"I have to agree with the pastor on this point, Raven," she said, then she glanced at Duncan and lifted her brows. "Imagine that."

I saw Duncan smile at her, a tentative smile, and one Arianna returned, just as hesitantly. They would become friends, in time. I felt certain of that.

"It doesn't matter that you both agree," I said. "Eleanor's husband built that house for the two of them. She clings to her husband's memory by remaining there, and if she leaves . . .'twould be like cutting the roots from some great tree. She would wither and die."

"How can you know that, Raven?" Duncan asked.

"Oh, she can. Believe me, she can." Arianna lowered her head and shook it.

"She took me in when I had nowhere else to go, Duncan," I told him. "And in the time I've been with her, I've come to love her very much. She . . . she is all I have left of my own mother. Can't you see that?"

"Of course I can see it," he said harshly. "What I canna see is you dyin' *because* of it."

Meeting his gaze, I whispered, "She has only a year left in her, Duncan."

"She has . . . ?" He looked at me sharply, then at Arianna, who only lifted her brows and shoulders, and then turned to study a tree as if it held great interest. "How can you be sure of that?"

I lowered my eyes. The truth was, I'd studied the lines of Aunt Eleanor's palm, and I knew. I'd restored her health, she would enjoy what remained of her time on this plane, but when a person's purpose was done, they moved on, and all the magick in the Universe couldn't change that. "I simply know it."

He nodded. "Another of those things about which you canna tell me?"

"I owe her so much," I said, brushing past his question as if he hadn't spoken it. "I'll not ask her to give up the home she loves, leave the place where her dear husband lies buried, spend the last year of her life miserable. I cannot. 'Tis only a year, Duncan. Perhaps less. Surely Elias Stanton and his suspicions can be put off that long."

Duncan looked frustrated. He turned away from me, pushing a hand through his hair. But when he faced me once more, his jaw was set. "I'll see to it you're protected then. He willna harm you, Raven. I vow it on all that I hold sacred."

"You mustn't do that," I protested. "I won't have it, Duncan. Understand that."

"I love you more than my own soul, Raven, and because of it, I canna do otherwise. *You* understand *that*." He kissed me once more, hard, and walked swiftly away in the direction of town.

I watched him go, then sent Arianna a helpless glance. "What am I to do?"

"Teach me," Arianna said, "the spell that makes a man who looks like that one into your devoted servant."

I only shook my head at her. " 'Tis no spell, and well you know it."

"Perhaps not," she said. "A shame, though. I could have used it once."

I tilted my head. 'Twas the first hint she'd ever given me as to her past. "You . . . loved a man who didn't love you in return?"

"I loved a man," she said with a small, bitter smile, "who'd have been happy to see me dead."

"Then he was a fool."

She shook her head. "No, he was right. In the end I won his trust, if not his heart. And trusting me is what got him killed."

She turned and started back toward the house. I hurried after her. "Arianna?"

"I don't talk about that," she said, false gaiety in her voice. "It is history. I can't imagine what made me bring it up."

"But—"

"Please," she said, and there was a wealth of power in the word. "Let it be, Raven. And suffice to say that, having seen the way your Duncan looks at you, I am beginning to think I may have been wrong about him."

I went still and felt my heart swell. "Thank you for that," I whispered. "But as to this other . . ." She sent me a quelling look. "All right," I murmured. But I wondered. What kind of man could break a heart as strong as hers?

Duncan didn't come to me by day after that. Only by night. Nearly every night. We'd meet in the forests or on the cliffs above the angry sea. We'd love until we were spent and then lie naked in each other's arms, just resting. Just *being*.

I loved him more each time he smiled at me, each time he whispered my name. I wanted him with me always. And he came to me whenever the sun went down.

Except on my sacred nights, when I would make an excuse. I think he knew I was hiding something, one more secret added to the many I kept from him, but he never pressed. Only hoped endlessly that I would come to trust him enough to tell him my truths. If only he knew that I *did* by now. 'Twas for his own safety that he could not know the truth about me.

Once a month, when the moon was full, Arianna and I slipped away from the cabin very late at night, while Aunt Eleanor lay sleeping. Deep into the woods we'd venture, there to set a small balefire alight, and to cast a magick circle, invoke the elements to aid us in our work, and feel the power of our Goddess growing strong within us. We burned fragrant herbs and special candles we'd made ourselves with loving care and magickal energy. We left offerings of food and wine, or flowers we'd gathered for the occasion as a symbol of our love for the Divine.

I often pondered the nature of my religion and that of Duncan's. I knew, as I'd always known, that his God and mine were the same. Our beliefs about Him differed, as did our ways, but in the end, there was only One. I saw the Divine as every bit as much female as male, and addressed both aspects, by referring to them as my Goddess and my God, my Lord and my Lady. Followers of Duncan's faith no longer recognized the feminine Divine, but still prayed to Mary in times of need.

Prayer was another way in which we were at once the same and different. When in need, we both turned to Divinity for help. Duncan's way was to surrender his will to that of the Almighty, seeing it as a separate entity, and asking for assistance. My way was to connect to that same Source, only to do it believing it was *not* separate from me, just as the Earth and the Air and the very sunlight are not separate from me. I am but a small part of a very large being, and that being is the Universe Herself. When I make magick, I feel *Her* energy flowing through me and then direct that power to bring my will into being. For me, prayer is not a request, but a command, delivered with the very might and power and authority of the Almighty.

But the most important difference between Duncan's faith and mine was that I believed the religions of the world were simply many spokes on a single wheel, all springing from and leading back to the same, singular Source. And his decreed that there was only one way to salvation, and that anyone who chose another path was damned. Guilty of the most vile sin. Deserving of torture and death.

I wondered sometimes if he truly believed that. And if he did, how could he love me and still live with himself?

By the heavens . . . his feelings for me had to be tearing him apart inside. Or were they? I wanted to ask . . . but I couldn't very well begin a theological discussion with him and not reveal more than I wished to.

So I put my questions aside and lived in the moment. I was, for the first time in my life, truly happy. Knowing I'd see him each night made my days pass in a glow of pleasure. Holding him in my arms until the wee hours of dawn made my nights pass even more beautifully.

I suppose I should have known that it was too good to last.

Should have known. But didn't.

Chapter 9

To the Most Esteemed Nathanial Dearborne,

Your name is known even here in the Colonies, sir, where tales of
your skill and success in exposing the practice of Witchery are passed
from one man of God to another in tones of awe and admiration.
Such dark practices must be uncovered, wherever they hide, and
burned away by the light of righteousness. 'Tis for this reason I post
you now. The shadow of the Devil has fallen upon my own beloved
settlement of Sanctuary in the colony of Massachusetts Bay. A Witch
resides amongst us, of this I am certain. Her wiles and spells have
placed the souls of the entire population in dire peril. The Witch's
name is Raven St. James, and while I am convinced of her guilt,
there remains doubt in the mind of our settlement's pastor. I fear the
Rev. Duncan Wallace has lost the ability to see beyond her charms
and sorcery, and has perhaps himself fallen victim to her sinful en-
chantments.

I have heard, Reverend Dearborne, that you have, at times, traveled far in your quest to rid the God-fearing Christian world of the
scourge of Witchcraft, and 'tis my fondest hope that you will do so now.

*I beg of you, sir, come to Sanctuary. You may well be our town's only
hope.*

> *In God's most holy name, I remain,*
> *Elias Stanton,*
> *Sanctuary, Massachusetts Bay Colony*

Nathanial Dearborne received the letter three months after it was
written to him. Amazing, he thought, how his fame had spread even to
the New World. Amazing, and ironic. A High Witch, perhaps one of the
oldest dark ones in the world, known far and wide as a Witch-hunter of
the highest order.

But what better way to take the power of other Witches than to execute them and take their hearts before they revive?

He smiled to himself as he read the distraught words of this Elias
Stanton. He'd found her. At last he'd found the young Witch who'd so
thoroughly wronged him.

Raven St. James.

With Duncan, still with Duncan. How? Why? Did it matter? She was
a powerful Witch, Nathanial had sensed that from the start. More powerful than most so young. 'Twas the power of her ancestors, the power
of a long and unbroken line of natural Witches, all of it appearing col-
lectively in the first High Witch ever to be born to her family. Even she
hadn't been aware of the full extent of her powers.

But Nathanial had.

He'd been weakening when he'd come upon the girl in the stocks that
snowy morn. Barely functioning, and unsure how much longer he could
go on. He'd needed an immortal heart, *any* immortal heart, to revive
him, to restore his strength, his vigor. 'Twould give him the power to
seek out an older one before he began to decline once more. So he'd
touched the accused Witches as they stood imprisoned and bent over in
shameful display in the public square. He'd felt nothing when he'd
touched the mother.

But a jolt surged through him when his hand brushed over the girl's.
And he'd known, young and inexperienced though she was, he would
take her heart, just so that he might live to take others.

And then the rest of the knowledge had come to him, whispering
through his sharp mind like a breeze before he took his hand away. She
had a strong heart in her, Raven St. James did. A powerful heart. He
would not gain longevity by taking it, but instead, power. Magickal

power. And he wanted it for his own. He wanted her young, tender heart beating endlessly, imprisoned in a tiny wooden box. With the others.

Now, though, there was more driving him than just that. Events had taken an unexpected twist that day at the gallows. A twist that burned in his gut, and one he would not, could not forgive.

Raven had cost him a young man who'd been . . . almost . . . a son to him. She'd turned Duncan Wallace against him, and the hurt he felt was more than he'd allowed himself to feel in centuries. Damn her. *Damn her!*

Nathanial had had a son of his own, once, long, long ago. Before he'd known about immortality, before he'd taken his first heart, and thus stolen the gift for himself. So much time had passed that he remembered very little about that life—the life before. But he remembered the boy, and his love for him.

He hadn't thought it through, this endless life he'd managed to acquire for himself. He hadn't thought it through!

Nathanial's son had grown old. Died, eventually. As had his wife, and his friends and everyone and everything he'd ever known. So much pain swamped him then that he cursed his decision to kill his first Witch; to hold her heart entrapped in a small box, sucking the very life from it to extend his own lifetime.

He'd cursed his immortality. Briefly. He got over that in time.

But he'd never gotten over the loss of his son.

Duncan . . . Duncan had reminded him of the boy in some small way—had, perhaps, come close to filling the void that remained in Nathanial's heart after all these centuries.

Until Raven St. James had turned Duncan against him.

She'd pay. She'd pay with her very heart. If it took him a thousand lifetimes, Nathanial would make sure of that. He'd get her, take her heart, take her special brand of magick and make it his own. He'd repay her for thwarting him, not once, but twice, for he'd attempted to kill her when she'd returned to her former home after the hanging.

But he'd been weak. And she'd defeated him.

Only once before had he been defeated in battle by a woman. Only once. He hadn't been weakened, then, but at his strongest. But she had been a woman possessed of a fury beyond anything he'd ever seen. All because he'd murdered her lover. She'd nearly killed him, *would have*, had he not been clever enough to get away. He'd never face *that one* again if he had his way.

But Raven, he *would* face Raven.

And soon, for it seemed her day of reckoning was at hand. He knew where she was hiding. And as if the fates had decided to take his side for a change, he knew where Duncan was, as well. As if he were meant to go there, to dispose of the bitch once and for all, and to make Duncan come back to England with him. And he would. He would win Duncan back again, he would have Raven's heart. Not because he'd die without it. Not this time. No, this time it was sheer vengeance that drove him. He wanted Raven's heart . . . because she had taken his. She'd taken Duncan.

Duncan stood at the pulpit in the log structure that was his church, going over his notes for this morning's service. His sermons had taken a turn of late. He didn't preach about hellfire and the damnation of sinners anymore. He couldn't. To do so made him squirm inside, knowing that according to the beliefs he was supposed to be preaching, he was damned himself. But more and more he questioned those beliefs. More and more he felt with everything in him that loving Raven St. James could be no sin. No more so than breathing . . . because it came to him just as naturally.

He looked up when the groan of the heavy door announced a visitor, and quickly hid a frown of displeasure when he saw Elias Stanton coming in.

He looked ill, Elias did. Pale, weak somehow. The man came inside and sank onto a wooden bench as if his legs were too tired to carry him any farther.

Duncan set his notes aside and hurried forward. "Elias? Are you ill?"

Shoulders slumped, Elias only shook his head. " 'Tis no natural illness plaguing me, Duncan. 'Tis far darker than that, I fear." As Duncan frowned, Elias lifted his head, revealing the dark circles beneath his eyes. "But I've not come to you for that. You're no physician. 'Tis my soul needs cleansing, Reverend. I've come to confess. Will you hear me?"

Duncan blinked in surprise. "Aye, you know I will. But confession is nay part of our dogma here, Elias."

"Nonetheless . . ." He lowered his head once more.

Duncan nodded, clasping Elias's shoulder briefly. "Go on, then. Tell me what troubles you so. I'll help you if I can."

Tiredly Elias nodded. " 'Tis the woman."

And Duncan knew without asking what woman he spoke of, but he asked all the same.

"That St. James wench," Elias spat out. "Who else?"

A tingle of warning whispered through Duncan's limbs. He took the bench in front of Elias, turned sideways to look back at the bowed man, and warned himself to keep quiet. To give nothing away. To simply . . . listen.

"I thought myself strong enough in my faith to resist her, you know. Fool that I was. No man could withstand such an onslaught."

Swallowing the retort that leaped to his lips, Duncan only nodded. "What is it she's done to upset you so much?"

Elias brought his head up fast, and his eyes lost some of that tired look when they filled instead with anger. Rage.

"What has she done? Have you not seen it yourself, Reverend? The sidelong glances. The way she parades her beauty so proudly about this town. The devil is in her, I vow it!"

"I've nay seen anythin' of the sort," he said, too quickly, he knew.

"She's taken to haunting my dreams," Elias went on. "She comes to me by night, while I sleep. Tempts me to sin of the most vile sort while I'm helpless to resist. I tell you, only a Witch would be capable of such things!"

Duncan closed his eyes slowly. God, he'd been afraid of this. "Aye, only a Witch," he said slowly. "Or a man lustin' after an innocent. Take care, Elias, not to blame your own failin's on another."

"'Tis Witchery, I tell you! And I'm not alone in my opinion, Reverend!"

Duncan felt his eyes narrow on the man. "Aren't you, now?" And he waited, dreading what he was about to hear.

"I didn't speak of it to you at the time," Elias said slowly. "But I wrote to a man in England about her. A famous Witch-hunter. And now, at last, I have his reply." This as he tugged a folded sheet of vellum from within his coat. "He believes all the signs are there, Duncan. He says she's dangerous and that we ought to exercise extreme caution, that she could destroy us all! Read it for yourself!" He thrust the letter at Duncan.

Duncan recoiled from the sheet as if its very touch could burn him. "Nay, I've no need to read the words of a man like that. How can he judge and condemn a woman from across the sea, Elias? Think on this! He hasna even met her."

"A man with his experience has no need. Besides, he will. He's on his way here. Could arrive within a fortnight. Perhaps sooner. Then we'll see—"

Duncan surged to his feet. "You're bringin' a Witch-hunter here? To Sanctuary? Good God, Elias, do you know what you've done?"

Elias rose very slowly, staring hard at Duncan from head to toe. "I see. I guessed it long ago, but I doubted my own instincts. Now, though, I see it clear. All those nights you spend out there, on the pretense of spying on those women. She's got to you, too. Hasn't she, Reverend? Hasn't she?"

Duncan averted his eyes. "Dinna be a fool."

"Have you fallen even further than I? Has she lifted her skirts for you already? Have you been sampling her tender—"

Duncan lashed out, unable and utterly unwilling to restrain himself. His fist connected with Elias's face, and the man reeled backward, over the bench and onto the floor behind it.

"You dare!" Elias blustered, clutching his nose as blood ran from beneath his hand.

Duncan gripped the front of the man's shirt and lifted him to his feet. "Raven St. James is a fine and decent woman. I'll nay have you sullyin' her name, nor causin' her harm on account of your own rampant lust, Elias Stanton. You're a ruttin' pig of a man, with a mind so bent on the carnal there isna room for reason nor decency left in you anymore."

Elias stepped back and Duncan let him go.

"Leave her alone," he told the bastard. "I'm warnin' you, Elias, *leave her alone.*"

Elias sniffed, rubbed his nose again, and examined the blood on his fingertips. "I'll forgive you, Reverend. Only because I know the power of her spells on a man. She's obviously worked them on you as well. But she'll get what's coming to her. And I've half a mind to set the wheels in motion now, myself, rather than wait for the Witch-hunter's arrival as he advises in his letter. What more evidence do we need, after all?"

"Do you spread any more of this malicious gossip, Elias, I'll kill you myself."

The man's eyes widened, and he took a hasty step away. "You? A man of God, threatening murder?"

"Murder is what you have in mind for Raven. Dinna try to deny it."

Elias narrowed his eyes. "Raven, is it? I knew—"

"You know nothing. She's the innocent here. You're the sinner, Elias. As the leader of this church 'tis my duty to protect the flock from lechers like you."

Lowering his head, Elias shook it slowly. "You make me wonder, Reverend, whether she has enchanted you at all . . . or if perhaps you've been in league with her all along. Mayhap you be a Witch as well."

"Get out!" Duncan lifted a hand that shook with barely contained rage, and pointed toward the door. "Get out of my church. You soil it with your very presence."

Nodding twice, Elias turned and walked away.

Duncan released all his breath at once and sank onto the bench. Damn! Elias was dangerous, and this Witch-hunter, whoever he was, likely even more so. How many of the women in this town might be falsely accused, even executed, now that Elias had started this disaster? How many? Elias Stanton may well have lit a wildfire in Sanctuary that would spread until it consumed the entire settlement.

But it wouldn't consume Raven. Nay, not if it cost Duncan's life to prevent it.

He had to get to Raven, had to speak to her. She must leave this place, now. Right away.

But even now the parishioners were arriving for the service. God, there was no time. Afterward, then. He'd go to her tonight and he would make her understand the danger she faced here. He'd take the lass away from this place if he had to sling her over his shoulder and carry her all the way. Aye, he would!

He closed his eyes slowly and prayed to his God to watch over her in the meantime.

After the Sunday meeting, I lingered. Arianna didn't. She put on a good show, acting prim and pious in her humble, dark skirts, white cap always in place, hair discreetly tucked beneath it. But she hated the Sunday meetings, the townspeople with their false smiles and friendly words when all the while they were whispering their suspicions to one another in private. And as usual, she left as soon as possible. She always did, even if it meant walking all the way back to the cabin. But I was feeling generous today, so I told her to take the wagon. I'd walk home this time, if she couldn't wait to leave.

I was quite the opposite in my feelings about the Sunday meetings. Oh, the make-believe friendship of those backbiting locals riled me every bit as much as it did Arianna. But for me there was reason to stay. For I'd grown to cherish every moment I could spend near Duncan, even those moments when we had to pretend there was nothing between us. For he would shower love on me all the same—in a single glance sent my way and filled with fire, even as he spoke to one crowd of parishioners and I to another. In an accidental touch. In the very way his voice changed when he spoke to me. I knew I was always on his mind, in his thoughts, just as he lingered constantly in mine.

There were, of course, unpleasant experiences awaiting me each time I attended services. For Elias Stanton tended to pay nearly as much mind to me as Duncan did. Only his glances were dirty somehow, leaving me feeling stained when I chanced to meet his lecherous gaze, and even more so when he touched me "accidentally," which happened more and more often.

I was blessed today, though, because Elias did not attend services. Aunt Eleanor, too, had stayed at home, having awoken this morn with a crushing headache that kept her abed. And since Arianna had already gone with our wagon, I was to walk back to the cabin alone. Not that I minded. I was, in fact, looking forward to the walk, for the leaves were turning and beautiful, and Duncan was on my mind.

He'd tried several times to speak with me, and there was a new urgency in his eyes when they caught mine, but each time he'd been swept away by someone else begging a word or asking advice. No matter. He would come to me tonight. In the forest, beneath the stars, we'd make tender love. I'd spend my walk home dreaming of the evening to come.

It did not turn out that way at all.

I'd trekked only halfway, walking slowly along the worn track, singing to myself, bursting with the joy of the changing seasons, the scent of the autumn leaves and the sea at my side. But I was jolted out of my pleasure at the sound of a horse's clopping gait, and the rattling of the wagon it pulled. And when I turned, expecting to see Duncan coming to see me home, I caught my breath. For 'twas Elias Stanton manning the reins. He looked ragged, and there was a vacant look to his eyes that chilled me.

"Good morn, Mistress St. James," he called, drawing the rig to a halt right beside me.

"Good morn," I replied, my voice stiff. "We missed you at the meeting hall this morn." I hadn't missed him at all, but 'twas something to say.

"I had some thinking to do," he said. "Thinking . . . that was best done alone."

Something quivered inside me. Some sense of danger. I kept walking. But he snapped the reins to keep pace.

"I be on my way to call on your aunt," he announced, as if I might care where he were going.

"How thoughtful of you."

"Perhaps you'd care to ride the rest of the way in comfort, rather than taxing yourself by walking?"

I met his eyes, cold and menacing, revealing the lie of his voice, and I gave a quick shake of my head. "I thank you, sir, but I am enjoying my walk too much to end it so soon."

"Nonsense," he said. "A woman walking alone is unsafe. Come, ride with me."

"I walk this way often and never see another soul, Mister Stanton. I assure you, I'm perfectly safe."

Grunting deep in his throat, he stopped the wagon again, only this time he climbed down. Walking toward the horse, he took its halter in one hand. "I'll walk with you, then. Lord forbid some harm befall you while I ride safely away, unaware."

I lowered my head as my stomach clenched tight. "I prefer to walk alone." I blurted it, not softening the words or the tone in any way. There should be no mistake, I thought. I did not wish to walk with this man.

He understood all right, for his face darkened. He released the horse, and turned fully toward me. "The attentions of a man offend you, do they?"

I did not know what to say. "You are a married man, Mister Stanton. Surely you should not speak to me in such a way."

"Married, yes, and pious to a fault, but still subjected to the charms of a sorceress. Just as our preacher seems to be."

"I know nothing of sorcery! And the Reverend Wallace has never been anything but kind and perfectly polite toward me."

"That is not what I see in his eyes when they meet your own, lady. No. I see lust. The same lust that rears up in my own heart with each toss of your head."

"You're being ridiculous!" I backed away, but he caught my wrists in his cruel hands.

"I know of but one means to rid myself of your allure, Raven. And that is to sate this lust once and for all."

"Let go of me! Have you gone insane? Let me go!"

"No, mistress. I won't let you go."

He jerked me closer and mashed his face to mine. His mouth open and wet, his tongue lapping at my lips though I pressed them tight. I pulled backward, but he clung to me, held me fast to his body so that as I moved he moved as well, until my back was pressed to the trunk of a tree, and his flaccid body held me pinned there. I struggled frantically, but his perverted desire had caused him to have an overpowering strength, and I could not free myself, despite my own enhanced Witchly strength. He groped at the front of my dress, pawed at my breasts.

"Stop fighting, wench! You've brought this on yourself—visiting me in my dreams nightly as you do, tempting me to sin. I no longer rest at night. I cannot eat by day. You're draining the very life from me, woman, and now you'll pay!"

I had to stop him or be raped. The knowledge came clear to me just that quickly. I had no choice in the matter, and since I couldn't reach my dagger, I knew only one way. But it would take all of my focus.

Calm. I willed myself to go utterly calm. Forced my body to relax, and my mind to ignore what he was doing to me. I went inside myself, deep inside, to a place where his grunting and groping did not exist—as if they were happening to someone else and I was but a witness.

Closing my eyes, I whispered, chanted to Mother Earth, attuned to her, felt her strength beneath me and behind me and around me and, finally, surging from within me. I drew her energy up from the ground, centered that power until it thrummed in my veins, and then opened my eyes to find a focus for it.

The limb, above Elias Stanton's head.

With a shout of release, I sent the power shooting forth, and the limb cracked and split. It crashed down, smiting the man and knocking him to his knees, and then flat to the ground, with the limb heavy atop him. He did not move.

I had no wish to stay to see whether he was dead or alive. I ran, leaping into his wagon and snapping the reins hard. His horse reared up and raced forward, and in moments the brute was behind me, and my home, my haven, loomed ahead.

Arianna was waiting when I arrived. She stared at me as I wheeled the wagon to a stop. Then her face paled, and she ran forward even as I tried to climb down.

"Sweet Mother, what's happened!"

She gathered me gently into her arms, helping me down. And only as she stared aghast did I realize my dress was torn, my hair askew, my face hot and damp.

"This is Elias Stanton's rig," Arianna all but hissed. "He did this, didn't he? Raven?"

Trembling, beyond words, I merely nodded.

"I'll kill him." And even as she said it her dagger appeared in her hand. "Where is he? I'll cut out his liver!"

And finally coherent thought returned. Pushing my hair out of my face, head bowed, I said, "No, Arianna. Wait."

"For what?" Her face had reddened clear to her ears. "Did he rape you, Raven? Did he—"

"No. I'm . . . I'm all right. But Arianna, we mustn't speak of this. Not to anyone."

"And what should we do? Keep quiet and wait for that beast to try again?"

Drawing a deep steadying breath, I shook my head. "We should take the rig back into town. We should say the horse brought it in with no one inside, and that we're concerned about Elias. They'll send men out looking, and they'll find him in the woods, beneath a fallen limb. Alive . . . or, I think he was, when I left him there."

She scowled at me so intently I felt her anger washing over me. "So we cover for him, lie for him?"

"No, Arianna. For *us*. You know what they think of me in this town. No one would accept my word over his. Let them believe it an accident." Again, I glanced down at my dress. "Aunt Eleanor mustn't see me like this."

Lowering her head, Arianna blew a sigh. "Here, take my cloak." And she removed the cloak from her shoulders to cover mine, then gently smoothed my hair. "I'll do as you ask. But I still think he deserves to be drawn and quartered."

"He accused me of bewitching him," I muttered. "Of visiting him in dreams and driving him to . . . to this."

"His own lechery has driven him. Nothing more." She shook her head, eyeing the rig. "I'll bring Duncan."

"He must never know of this, Arianna. Please, don't tell him. He'd kill Elias, I know he would."

"The man *needs* killing."

"Please . . ."

She sighed, lowering her head. "You ask a lot of me, my friend."

"I know." I lifted my head. "Have I told you how grateful I am that you came to me, Arianna? I haven't, have I? But I should. You . . . you're the best friend I've ever had."

She blinked, looking away as if slightly irritated. "I would die for you, you know."

I frowned, confused by the power in that simple statement. "But why?"

She shrugged. "You did for me once."

"Whatever do you mean?"

Meeting my eyes, smiling gently, she said, "Perhaps it's time I told you the truth, Raven. You have this gift, this immortality, because in some previous life you died while trying to save the life of another Witch."

"I understand that, but—"

"That Witch . . . was me."

And before I could say another word, she leaped into Elias Stanton's wagon and snapped the reins.

There had been no love lost between Duncan and the mysterious, mischievous-eyed pixie who seemed to have become Raven's closest friend. They were polite to each other, but cool, and he sensed the smaller woman's disapproval. Understood it, even.

But when he saw Arianna driving Elias Stanton's rig into town that morn, her face expressionless and pale, he immediately felt his stomach tie in knots. He'd been steadily working to free himself of the people who seemed determined to have a word with him—and only now had he succeeded. He'd been about to start out to Raven's cottage on the cliffs.

The pace at which the wagon moved was enough to tell him something was wrong. Terribly wrong. When it stopped in a cloud of dust, Duncan joined the crowd gathering around Arianna, but her eyes were on him alone, and he sensed a silent message in them.

"Mister Stanton's horse arrived at our cabin with no driver," she said, calmly, as slowly as if she'd rehearsed her words. "We're concerned about his safety." She climbed down with grace, nimble as a sprite, ignoring all the shouted questions. "Perhaps some of you might wish to travel the Coast Road and search for him," she suggested.

Several men immediately shouted agreement and as they grouped off, and began making their plan, Duncan took Arianna aside. "What has truly happened?" he asked.

She averted her eyes. "Nothing good, Duncan. But I can say no more. I gave my promise to Raven, and I'll not break my word to her."

"Is she all right?" He nearly held his breath awaiting her answer.

"She's unharmed." Finally she met his eyes again, and he saw the concern there for her friend. "I'd have stayed with her myself and let that an-imal Elias rot. But it is you she needs, Duncan. Go to her."

He nodded quickly. Let the others search for Elias. He needed to see Raven, to assure himself she was well, and find out what this was all about. And then he had to take steps to get her away from here, to some-where safe.

What the hell had happened out there? God, he knew she'd been walking alone. But he hadn't seen her leave, and by the time he realized she'd gone it had been too late to prevent it. He should have gone after her, right then. Should have escorted her home, and to hell with what the town gossips would make of that. Damn Elias to hell if he'd touched her, frightened her in any way. He'd kill the bastard. He'd kill him with his bare hands.

"Come," he said to Arianna through clenched teeth. "We'll go to-gether." They were not friends, nay, yet he still wouldn't like the thought of her alone in this town should something rile the locals—should some-thing turn them against her.

"I think I should linger in town. See what the vermin has to say when they find him. If he's still alive, that is." Her frown was worried, more now than ever. And Duncan knew too well that Elias might speak his suspicions about her and Raven if he'd been provoked.

"I think it a bad notion, lass," he said.

She tilted her head, studied him. "Is that worry in your eyes, Duncan? For me?" Her smile was small and brief. "I'm grateful for the thought, but believe me when I tell you I can take care of myself."

He lowered his head. "Stay, then, if you're certain," he told her, speaking lower now. "But keep out of sight, Arianna. You might be judged guilty by association, does anythin' come of this."

She nodded, but when he turned to go, she clutched his arm. He faced her again, and she stared straight into his eyes. "So might you, Duncan. You should be well aware of that. Well aware of the risk in-volved."

"The only risk I'm concerned about is the risk to Raven," he told her. And meant it. "But I'm aware of it, aye. And willin' to face it. I'll have no regrets, no matter the outcome."

"You truly do love her, don't you?" Arianna whispered.

"Aye, with everythin' in me," he told her. Then he looked at her face, at the force of the emotions in her eyes, and added, "As much as you do, I'll wager."

"You must love her a great deal, then," she said softly.

Nodding, Duncan clasped Arianna's shoulder briefly, a gesture of friendship he thought long overdue. They'd reached an understanding between them, he thought. He and Arianna had one thing in common. They were both utterly devoted to Raven and determined to protect her at any cost. 'Twas a powerful bond they shared, and he thought they'd both finally realized that.

"Take care, lass," he told her. "You an' I have much to talk about when this is over. I'd like you alive an' well for the conversation."

She nodded, reaching out to briefly squeeze his hand in a gesture that told him she understood, and felt as he did. Their eyes met in silent communion, and then he turned and strode away.

Chapter 10

I felt soiled by Elias Stanton's very touch, could still taste his vile mouth on my lips, and feel his hands . . .

Aunt Eleanor lay asleep, perfectly peaceful and safe. She would not remain so . . . not if I stayed here with her any longer. Stanton, if he lived, would spread his accusations against me, and my aunt would be at risk. Christians did not treat Witches kindly, nor did they show mercy to anyone associated with them. I would have to leave her. And soon, I feared. Duncan had been right. If only I had heeded his warnings.

Without disturbing my aunt, I slipped back outside, a woven wash-cloth in my fist. I only wanted to cleanse myself of the stain of Elias's hands, rinse my mouth, scrub away the essence of his touch. But I was too frantic to carry water and fill the tub, much less wait for it to warm over the fire. No, I needed to wash *now*. At once. Every moment I waited made my stomach heave.

I hurried to the woods, to a stream there that emptied into the sea, and there I stripped off every stitch and plunged myself into the icy water. I drank in great mouthfuls of it, and spat it out again, over and over. I scrubbed at my arms, at my breasts, at my face. Everywhere he'd touched me. I scoured myself, but to no avail. Even then I didn't feel clean, so I scrubbed some more.

"Raven."

At the sound of my name whispered so hoarsely, I snatched my dagger from the rock at my side and whirled, raising it up, ready to gut the bastard if he came at me again.

But 'twas Duncan standing there on the bank, staring at me with eyes as wounded as dying stars. I parted my lips but could not speak. But I didn't need to speak. He knew me so well, knew at a glance my devastation, my shame, though he did not—could not—know their cause. He came to me, walked into the swirling, icy stream fully clothed, and gently gathered me into his arms.

"'Tis all right," he whispered, holding me close, turning and carrying me to the shore. "I'm here with you now, my bonny lass, and 'tis all right." His lips touched my hair as he held me like a frightened child in his arms. "What's happened to you, love? What's happened?"

"N-nothing . . ."

He lowered me to the soft, grassy bank, snatching up the cloth to begin rubbing me dry. So gentle, his touch. So careful as he pressed the water from my hair and wiped it away from my body. "You're freezin'," he whispered, and quickly picked up my dress. And then he stiffened, his hands tightened around my dress as he stared at it. I reached out, snatched it away, but 'twas too late. He'd seen the rips and tears down the front.

Slowly he looked at me again, his eyes more thorough this time.

"You're bruised," he whispered.

My hands flew to cover my breasts where I could feel the soreness Elias's cruel hands had left behind. But 'twas too late to hide the marks from Duncan's eyes.

"Stanton did this," he muttered.

I lifted my chin, swallowed hard. "It doesn't matter."

But Duncan's face reddened, his jaw clenched with anger. "Oh, it matters, lass. I'll kill him for this."

"No, please . . ."

He touched his fingers to my lips, silencing me. Then he quickly divested himself of his shirt, and then his coat, dressing me in both with such exquisite care I nearly wept.

"You mustn't take revenge on him, Duncan. 'Twould spell your ruin."

"Aye, an' what do I care about my ruin? Raven, darlin', I care only for you." Pushing my hair back away from my eyes, he stroked my cheek with the backs of his fingers. "Did he . . . ?"

"No." I saw the doubt in Duncan's eyes, held them with mine so he could see that I was being honest with him. "He would have, Duncan, though I fought. But a limb fell from the tree where he . . . where he . . ." I stopped, drew a shuddering breath, began again. "It might have killed him. I hope it did."

"If it didna kill the bastard, I'll do it myself."

"Please, Duncan, I've had all the violence I can bear."

"I'm sorry," he whispered. Then he gently pulled me close, cradling me in his arms, rocking me against his warm chest. I felt utterly surrounded by him, his strength, his love. "I'm so sorry, Raven. I should have been with you, should have protected you—"

"No, Duncan, do not for one moment believe any of this is your fault."

"I love you," he whispered, and he kissed me very softly, his lips on mine instantly erasing the memory of those other, cruel ones.

When he lifted his head away, I touched his face. "And I love you, Duncan Wallace. With all that I am, I love you."

He blinked, searching my face in wonder. "Do you know how long I've waited to hear you say those words?"

I bit my lip, realizing what I'd done. But 'twas too late to take the declaration back now. And it was true, more true, perhaps, than any words I'd ever spoken.

"We have to leave here," he said softly. "Tonight, Raven. There's nay time to wait. I want to take you away, to somewhere safe from fools like Elias and this other bastard who's on his way here even now."

I sat up a bit, frowning. "Who?"

"A Witch-hunter," he said, his voice grim. "I'd no idea until this morn, my love, but Elias wrote to some murderin' cur in England, and the man could arrive at any time. We must make haste."

I felt a shiver of utter dread creep up my spine.

"No, my lass, dinna be afraid," he told me, clasping my hand in his. "No one will ever harm you again, Raven. I vow it on my very life."

And those words made me shiver all the more.

Duncan stayed at my side as I packed a few belongings, and held my hand while I delivered my sad news to sweet Aunt Eleanor.

"You'll come back," she kept saying. And the hope in her eyes was so desperate that I couldn't divest her of it. "You *will* come back once you've taken care of this . . . this . . ."

"Business matter. 'Tis all to do with some property my father owned," I told her. "Very complicated and boring, but I must return to England to clear it up. And yes, of course I will come back."

She blinked back her tears. "I won't worry for your safety, at least. Not with Duncan going along to care for you." She hugged me gently, kissed my face.

"I promise to protect her as if she were my own," Duncan assured her.

I battled my tears, refusing to shed a single one in front of her.

"Don't be any longer than you have to, child. I'll be waiting for your return."

"I know you will, Aunt Eleanor." I squeezed her hands one last time. "I do love you, you know."

"Well, of course you do. Off with you, now. No sense waiting—my, but 'tis already near dark."

I knew it was. Duncan and I had deliberately waited for the night to fall. Like a dark blanket that would enfold and protect us. I finished with my goodbyes, and we stepped out into the night. It had always been our place, the place where we lived, where we loved. Night had been good to Duncan and me.

"I'm worried about Arianna," I whispered.

"Aye, I am, as well. The moment I get you safely away from Sanctuary, Raven, I'll return, an' I'll find her. I promise you that."

We were walking silently, hand in hand along the Coast Road. My belongings, what few of them I thought I would need, were in my pack, and Duncan carried it slung over his sturdy shoulder.

"Poor Aunt Eleanor," I said softly. "She was heartbroken when we told her that I must leave."

"Aye, no doubt, but she seemed to take the news in stride, all the same," Duncan said.

"Oh, she tried to put on a brave face . . . for my benefit," I told him. "But I saw through it. It broke her heart to say goodbye to me. I know it did, Duncan, for it broke mine, as well." I caught my lip in my teeth and swallowed back a sob. "I'll likely never see that dear woman again. 'Tis almost like losing my mother anew!" The hurt bubbled high in my chest, and tears spilled over.

Duncan pulled me close to his side, his arm strong and protective around my shoulders. "Nay, lass, you shall see her again. I'll see to it. We'll settle someplace safe, Raven, and the moment we do, I'll come back for her. Bring her to us."

I stared up at him in wonder. "You would do that for me?"

"Aye, lass. I'd do anythin' for you, and you ought to know it by now."

"I do know it," I whispered.

"Good." He drew my hand to his lips and kissed it.

'Twas fully dark now, but the light of a full moon made it nearly as bright outside as it might be at midday. We'd hoped to skirt the village unnoticed by waiting until the hour grew late enough. A frightening prospect, indeed. But I felt safe with Duncan at my side. Safe and loved, and yet sad beyond words. Someday I would lose him, just as I'd lost everyone dear to me. It would always be this way, I imagined. Goodbyes. So many goodbyes.

I didn't think I wanted to live to see the day I'd have to say goodbye to him. I didn't think I could bear it.

Running footsteps made my thoughts grind to a halt, and I reached for my dagger, spinning around and lifting it up. But then in the moonlight I saw Arianna's face, reddened and damp with perspiration. Wide-eyed and breathless, she came toward us. And I knew something was terribly wrong, but even then I couldn't restrain my joy at seeing her.

I flung my arms around her, felt the pounding of her heart and the rapid, deep breaths she drew. Her skin was hot and damp. "I've been worried out of my mind!" I cried. "Thank goodness you're all right."

"Not for long, I fear," she said, hugging me back before straightening away and eyeing first me, then Duncan as she fought to catch her breath.

"Something is wrong, then?" Duncan asked her. And she nodded.

Of course something was wrong, I thought. Ah, but what surprise was that? Nothing had been right today. Not today. Perhaps not ever again.

"Thank the fates I managed to catch up with you." Bending, hands braced on her knees, Arianna dragged in gulps of the bracing sea breeze that wafted up from the cliffs at our side. And slowly her breathing returned to normal.

"What is it, Arianna?" I asked.

"The townspeople. Stanton . . ."

"They found him, then? Alive?" Duncan's voice was grim, and I knew that in spite of his goodness, his generous soul, he truly wished the man dead.

"Yes, alive, and spewing venom. But delirious enough so no one paid much notice at first. But he finally recovered sufficiently to convince them he wasn't suffering delusions. He said you attacked him, Raven. Said you used Witchery to smash him with that limb and then left him to die."

I only stood still and silent, already knowing the answer to my next question. "And they believed him."

"They went out to the cabin in search of you. I raced ahead to warn you, Raven, but you'd already gone."

"Aunt Eleanor?"

She shook her head rapidly. "They've left her alone. I think they will continue to, Raven. You're the newcomer, the stranger here. She is one of their own."

"Thank goodness."

"I have no doubt they're on your heels even now," Arianna rushed on. "I cut through the forest to reach you first. Come, we must hurry."

Nodding, I grasped Duncan's hand all the harder and sent a longing glance down to the sea far below, where jagged rocks peered from beneath the surface only to vanish again with the waves. "What I wouldn't give for a boat. They have to know this road is the only way we can leave Sanctuary."

"Aye, they know it," Duncan said grimly. "But if they try to harm you, Raven, they'll have to go through me to do it."

"Duncan, no. You mustn't do anything to put yourself at risk. I—"

"Hold!"

I caught my breath, and whirled to see a mass of villagers streaming toward us and spreading like some oily pool to block our path. And when I spun the other way, I saw more of them. They carried torches. They shouted and accused. The very air around me snapped with the vibrations of their hatred, and their menace.

Trapped. Trapped here on these cliffs with no chance of escape.

"Stand aside," Duncan called, even as he gently moved me behind him. "I know what Elias has told you, but I'm here to bear witness that 'tis nothin' more than a pack of lies spun by a man sick with desire for a woman he can never possess."

"'Tis as Elias said," one man called to the others in a coarse voice. "She's bewitched even the preacher!"

They closed ranks around us. There was no way out.

"'Tis untrue!" Duncan shouted back. "I tell you, as a man of God, in the *name* of God, this woman is innocent."

"Blasphemer!" someone cried. "He's in league with her." And they surged forward like one living mass of evil, pressing ever closer on us from all sides. Duncan clung to me, shielded me with his own body, but I was torn from his sheltering arms by cruel hands. Hands that brought back memories I'd hoped never to have to relive.

'Twas as if the veil of time had melted away, and I was back in that poor English village. 'Twas as if I could feel the icy wind and the snow razing my cheeks, even though it was merely a crisp autumn night here.

"Get your hands off her!" Duncan roared.

But they held me all the same. And others held him, though they had a time of doing it.

Where was Arianna? I did not see her. She'd vanished.

The crowd stilled as Elias Stanton himself came forward, leaning heavily upon a staff and wearing a white cloth tied about his head. "This wench tried to murder me," he cried. "Moreover, she's guilty of fornication! With our own minister! A man of God, tempted to sin by a Witch!"

"End this curse! Free the preacher of her spells," someone called.

"Pitch her from the cliffs!"

"Nay!" Duncan tugged at the men who held him. Fought them, just as he'd fought them before, at the hanging. And 'twas just as useless. "I'll nay stand by and see you do murder! Nay, dammit!"

"Duncan Wallace," Elias intoned, "do you confess to the crime of fornication, and to the even darker sin of communing with a Witch?"

"I dinna confess anythin' to you, Elias! For 'twould be like confessin' to the devil himself!" Duncan shouted. But he stilled his struggling, standing straight and tall while lesser men clasped his arms. He faced Elias Stanton squarely. I'd never seen the like of him as he was that night. Standing with his back to the sea, the wind whipping his dark hair into chaos as the waves broke and crashed below, his eyes flashing.

"What of you, Elias?" he asked softly, and the men around us went silent at the power in his quiet voice. "Do *you* confess?"

"I've nothing to confess to, young man!"

"Nay? What of tryin' to force your attentions upon an innocent woman and then plottin' her murder to cover your own sins?"

Elias lowered his head and shook it slowly. "These men know me, Duncan. They've known me for years, and can vouch for my character. No, they'll not believe a come-lately preacher nor a Witch over one of their own." And lifting his head, he faced Duncan again. "Confess, Duncan. 'Tis the only way to save yourself."

"I'd confess gladly, if my doin' so would save her."

"Alas, her fate is already sealed, my friend. But for you, there remains some dim hope of salvation. Confess, son, beg forgiveness of God on your knees and—"

"Burn in hell, Stanton."

"Duncan, no . . ." I whispered the words, but it was too late. He'd damned himself already. Because of me.

Elias shook his head sadly and turned toward me. And his eyes were cold there in the darkness, beneath the light of a full moon. Cold and menacing. I had to save Duncan. Somehow, he must not be dragged into the depths of this mess I'd brought upon myself.

"Please, Elias," I whispered. "Duncan is innocent! He knows nothing of me or my ways! 'Twas all me. I bewitched him, just as you said. He doesn't even know what he's doing tonight. Spare him, for the love of God, spare him!"

Stanton looked upon me with utter hatred in his eyes. The men holding me were even now binding my hands behind me, and I saw they were about to do the same to Duncan. I searched the crowd for Arianna, praying to the Great Goddess that they hadn't put their hands on her as well, and sighed in blessed relief when I still didn't see her there. She must have slipped away. Please, I thought, please let her have slipped way.

"Disavow her, Duncan," Elias said softly. "Save yourself."

"Never!"

"Do as he asks, Duncan." I tried to move forward, to get closer to him, but there were too many of them holding me. Even with my strength I had no chance of overpowering them. "Please, trust me. Do as he asks."

Meeting my eyes, he only shook his head. "Not on pain of death, lass," he whispered. "Nay, not if it meant my own soul, would I speak against you."

"Don't listen to him," I pleaded. "He doesn't know what he's saying."

"Perhaps he'll come back to himself," Elias said, "when you lie dead and your spells are finally broken."

Elias looked at the men who held me, gave a nod, and I was lifted. I cried out to Duncan as they carried me to the edge, pleaded with him, prayed he'd understand. "They cannot kill me! Do you hear me, Duncan? They cannot take my life! Save yourself, Duncan, I beg you!"

But already he was tearing free of his captors, lunging forward, struggling to reach me. The men standing at my head and at my feet swung me like a feed sack, and then simply let me go. Out, out into the vast emptiness of space and wind and moonlight I sailed, and Duncan raced toward the edge. I hung in space for only an instant, long enough to see the horror in his eyes, and to know what he would do.

"*No!*" I screamed, and then I plummeted, and Duncan, my beloved Duncan, lunged out, reaching for me as if he could catch me somehow, and haul me back to safety. But he couldn't. He must have known he couldn't. And his reaching only resulted in him falling—he followed the course I took. The wind whistled past my ears, and my body tumbled and spun. I shouted my love for him but couldn't hear my own words for the crash of the sea below, drawing nearer—ever nearer. And then there was an impact, incredible pain. The snap and cracking of my bones as my body hurled itself upon the rocks and into the cold, salty water.

And then the pain blinked out, along with the light of life.

"Raven..."

I sucked in a sudden, sharp gasp, so deep it nearly burst my lungs when life returned to me once more. I opened my eyes, blinked the water away, and stared up at Arianna. She sat on the ground near the shore, my head cradled in her lap, the seawater streaming from my hair and soaking her clothes. She held me like a child, stroking my hair, caressing my face. Tears dampened her own lily-white cheeks.

"Raven," she whispered again. "Oh, sweet Raven, I'm sorry. I'm so very sorry."

And it all came back to me.

"Duncan!"

"Hush, now." She soothed, gentled me, but I struggled free of her comforting, struggled free and got to my feet.

"Where is he? Where is Duncan? Tell me!"

Arianna bit her lip as I scanned the shoreline in search of my love. And then I saw him.

His broken body lay upon a jagged cluster of rocks some distance out, waves reaching up at him, tugging him as if they wanted to carry him away in their crystalline arms. I ran into the water, shouting his name, crying uncontrollably. But when I reached him, I knew 'twas no use. Even as I clambered up onto the rocks where he lay and pulled him into my arms, begging him to wake up, to speak to me, I knew. He was as boneless as a rag doll, broken in so many places his poor body barely held its form. His face lay still and pale in the moonlight, blessedly unmarred. The blue of his lips, and his bloodless skin, the coolness of his cheek where I touched it, told a story too horrible to believe. I gathered his head to my breast, bowing over him, weeping as I'd never wept before.

"Oh, Duncan, no. Not now, not yet. You can't leave me so soon! For the love of the Goddess, why? Why couldn't I trust you with the truth?"

But I hadn't, and now he was dead. Because of me, he was dead. I'd never know his touch, his kiss again. Never look into his brown eyes. Never . . .

"Oh, why didn't I tell him! He'd not have died trying to save me if he'd known the truth of what I am!" I wailed my grief to the stars, ignoring the sloshing, splashing sounds Arianna made as she came out to where I was.

She stood waist-deep in the water, and gently she took my hand. "Come, love. Come away, now. You can do no more for Duncan here."

Shaking my head, I clung to him. "I can't," I whispered. "I can't leave him this way. Please . . ." The words were as broken as my heart, as my precious Duncan's body. *I* was broken. I felt I could never rise from that cluster of deadly rocks, never drag myself to the shore, never so much as lift my head again. The very life seemed to have fled me. And I thought then 'twould have been better if it truly had.

"The sea takes care of its own, Raven," Arianna said softly. "His body belongs to the sea now. But you know his soul does not. You know that. Let him go, Raven."

I shook my head and held him still closer, my face resting against his cool cheek. "I'll never see him again," I moaned. "Never again . . ."

"But you will." She kept stroking me, my hair, my back. "He'll live again, Raven, you know that, as well." She spoke louder now, perhaps hoping the strength and command of her tone would reach me.

But nothing could reach the dark place where I lived now. "What does it matter? He's lost to me."

Arianna drew my face toward her, staring intently into my eyes from where she stood with the ocean waves lapping at her waist. "He died trying to save your life, Raven. When he lives again . . . he'll be as we are. Immortal. His selfless act of love earned him the gift, don't you see?"

Opening my eyes, lifting my head, I released a breath. "'Tis true," I whispered. "And never was any man more deserving. But don't *you* see, Arianna? *I'll* never know him. Never find him again."

Arianna reached down to stroke Duncan's wet hair away from his face. "But you will. 'Tis the full moon, Raven, when our powers wax strongest. I . . . I couldn't save him. There was no time to cast a spell of enough magnitude to overwhelm so many bent on destruction. But I slipped away, to the woods. I did all I could, Raven. I did all I could."

And at last her pain made itself known to me. I'd been so immersed in my own . . . I covered her hand with mine, where it rested upon Duncan's face.

"I was actually growing to . . . to like the man," she whispered, tears welling in her eyes.

"I know you'd have saved him if you could, my friend."

She met my eyes, her own glistening. "More than your friend, Raven. Your sister. I am your sister."

Sniffling, I nodded. "Yes, you are as a sister to me, closer even than that—"

"No. No, you aren't hearing me. You truly are my sister, or were, a lifetime ago. And my sister you remain."

I frowned, shocked and surprised. And yet it was as if she were telling me something I already knew.

"I was the eldest," she said, "practicing the Craft behind our mother's back, in secret, with a group of Witches from our village. You never even knew, then—"

"But—"

She pressed a finger to my lips. "No, just listen. 'Twas many years ago, you know. I've waited a long while to tell you these things. So let me speak." In silence I nodded, and Arianna went on. "I didn't know what I was then. We were but girls, you and I, you a year younger, but always stronger."

"*I?* Stronger than you?"

She nodded. "The year was fifteen-ten. We lived in the village of Stonehaven, in the shadow of Castle Lachlan in the Highlands of Scotland."

"Scotland . . ." I closed my eyes, lowering my face to Duncan's once more. "'Tis where Duncan comes from, you know."

"Yes, I know."

"I didn't think I'd ever been there."

"You were born there. Once."

Sniffling, swiping away fresh tears, I nodded at her to go on.

"We were forbidden, of course, to play in the forests and lochs, but we did so all the same. I went too far into the water one day. My stomach cramped inexplicably, and I couldn't get back to shore." She touched my face, smiling gently. "You came for me, though, held me afloat and fought to get me to shore. And then there were others, the sons of Laird Lachlan himself. They swam out to help. But by then you'd been struggling with me for more than an hour. You were exhausted. Of course, they didn't realize it. They were concerned only with me, for I seemed to be the one in trouble. You never told them otherwise." She swallowed hard, loudly. "And when they eased me from your arms and drew me safely toward the shore, I looked back . . . and you were gone. Just slipped beneath the blue waters of the loch, leaving them so still 'twas as if you'd never been there."

Staring at her, I whispered, "I drowned."

"You drowned trying to save my life. The life of an immortal High Witch who didn't even know she was one at the time." She sighed slowly, and a tear slid down her cheek. "The lads went back after you, of course. And I stood there on the shore, knowing you'd left me, praying 'twas not too late to perform an incantation, so that I might know you again, one day. I called on all the powers of the Universe, Raven, and cast a potent spell. That when you lived again, 'twould be within my lifetime, and that you would look the same, and your name would again be Raven."

I tilted my head to the side, touched beyond measure at her words. "You did that for me?" I whispered.

"For me," she replied. "That I would have the joy of finding you again someday." She shook her head slowly. "Of course I had no idea then how long my lifetime would be. But the spell worked, Raven. I did find you, and you do look the same—older, yes, but just as you'd have looked before, if you'd had the chance to reach womanhood. And your name is Raven, just as it was then. And . . . and I love you, my sister."

A great sob welled up in my throat, choking the words. "I thought I had no family left . . . but I do. I have my sister."

She put her arms around me, held me tenderly for just a moment. Then stood back and stared hard into my eyes.

"I performed the same incantation tonight."

I frowned, searching her face.

"For Duncan. Even as he plummeted from the rocks, I hid myself in the forest and conjured with everything in me."

Now I looked at her, truly looked at her, though she blurred through my tears. And then I lowered my gaze to stare at Duncan's lifeless face. God, how I ached for him already.

"'Twas all I could think of to do," she whispered. "He will live again, Raven. He will look the same. And his name will again be Duncan. You'll find him again someday, I promise you."

Blinking in disbelief, I muttered, "When?"

"I've no way of knowing that. Nor is he likely to remember you, Raven, just as you had no memory of me when we met on the Coast Road that day. I did all I could do. I only hope 'twas enough to ease the grief I see in your eyes."

Closing my eyes, I clutched her chilled hand in one of mine, and clung to my lost love with the other. "'Twill be enough," I promised. "It shall have to be. 'Tis all I have." Then I opened my eyes and met hers. "You've given me hope where I had none before. How will I ever thank you for this?"

She shook her head. "I only wish I could have done more." Then she cleared her throat, lifted her chin. "Raven, we have to leave here. If you hope to live long enough to find this man of yours again, we have to go at once."

I stroked Duncan's face. "We should bury him."

"Listen to me," she said, and the urgency in her voice cut through the haze of mourning in my mind at last. "The Witch-hunter Elias Stanton sent for arrived only a short while ago. I overheard some of the men talking about it. Saying the man was furious that Elias had taken action, instead of waiting for his arrival as he'd instructed. Saying the man would be out here soon, that he insisted on seeing the spot from whence you were thrown."

My eyes widened, but I calmed myself quickly. "They can kill me as many times as they wish, Arianna. I've no fear of them."

"You don't understand. The Witch-hunter is an impostor, Raven. His name is Nathanial Dearborne and—"

"Nathanial Dearborne?" Now she had my attention. "The same arrogant priest who hanged my mother! I hope he does come. I'll—"

"He's no priest," Arianna whispered. "He's a High Witch. One of the Dark Ones, Raven. One of the oldest and most powerful I've encountered."

"You know him?"

Grimly she nodded. "'Twas he who murdered the only man I ever loved, and used me to do it. I nearly killed him then, but he escaped me. But it isn't me he'll be challenging this time, Raven. It's you he's come for. You can't best him in a fight and I can't protect you every minute of the day and night. If you want to keep your heart intact, we'd best not be here when he arrives."

Nathanial Dearborne, a dark High Witch. It made sense now. My mother's note had told me that I'd know another only when I touched them—and that tingling sensation, the one I'd become so used to since Arianna had come into my life—was the same one I'd felt when that beast touched my hand as I hung in the stocks. I simply hadn't made the connection before now.

"Duncan wouldn't want you risking your life to bury his empty shell, love," Arianna whispered. "Leave him to the sea, and come. He'd want you to stay alive, to await his return. You know he would."

I looked down at Duncan, lowering my head as tears rained from my face to his. "Yes. I suppose he would." Bending low, I kissed his cheek. "I love you, Duncan Wallace. In this lifetime and the next, I will always love you. I vow it on my heart."

And gently I eased his broken body from the rocks. Even as I did, an unusually large wave broke over us and swept him from my hands as it washed back out to sea. As if the sea were claiming him.

"Goodbye, my love," I whispered, but my words were only whispers, my pain so great I could speak no louder. And yet, I thought he might hear me.

Arianna touched my shoulders, and together we turned and made our way back to shore.

Nathanial Dearborne ran all the way to the base of the cliffs where she was supposed to have been thrown, but there was no sign of the dark-haired wench.

Nor of his beloved Duncan.

He clenched his hand into a fist and shook it at the heavens. Again! She'd eluded him *again*.

And this time she'd taken young Duncan Wallace into death with her! A death from which she could return . . . and he could not.

"Damn her," Nathanial whispered. And fury rose up to engulf him. Oh, Duncan would be back. Yes, he'd return. But when he did, he, too, would be a High Witch. One of the Light Ones, and as such, Nathanial's sworn enemy.

And if he knew Raven St. James, she'd manage to find the lad again, even then.

Then he paused, narrowing his eyes. What if she did? And what if, *when* she did, she found *him* as well?

Yes. Oh, he'd likely take the selfish bitch's heart long before then. He'd never stop trying to exact his vengeance. But if all else failed, he could use what he knew . . .

He could use Duncan . . .

If he could find the lad before she did.

But he would. He had to. He'd find a way. And he wouldn't rest until he'd exacted vengeance upon Raven St. James, until he'd cut out her heart and held it beating and bloody in the palm of his hand.

Chapter 11

Weak. Heavy. Languid. My body did not want to move, and I had no will to argue with it. Arianna gripped my forearm, tugging me along in her wake as we trekked into the woods. The village lay to the north, and the forest was but a thin strip of shelter between Sanctuary and the sea. And that might have been enough to protect us, if everyone in town truly believed me dead. They'd have no reason to suspect Arianna would have lingered in the vicinity for so long.

But there *was* someone who knew better. Nathanial Dearborne. And my gut told me he hadn't traveled all the way from England only to accept defeat so easily. No, he would be searching for us. I felt it in my bones.

And still, I felt no desire to move. I only managed to continue sloughing along, dropping one foot ahead of the other, for Arianna's sake. If I sank to the ground as I wished right to my soul to do, if I surrendered, she'd stay with me. I knew she would. And there would be yet another life lost because of me. More blood on my hands. Yet another one dead because of having loved me.

I would not let that happen. So I moved. But I felt numb, and dead inside. Truly, had it not been for Arianna, I'd have simply remained in the icy cold sea until Dearborne came for me. Not because of a desire to die, but because I had no desire not to. No reason to cling to my life. No will to fight for it.

I loved Duncan, and he'd been murdered, and my heart bled so profusely it seemed I could feel my life force draining away, bit by bit. Every breath drawn without him seemed to come a little harder. Every heartbeat cost more effort. Even lifting my head became too much work, so that I slogged through the forest without looking up. Head hanging, hair in my face, wet dress dragging through the brush. My only link to life, that small, strong hand gripping my arm. A lifeline. An undeniable force dragging me slowly forward, and maybe, inch by inch, out of the black swamp of deadly grief into which I had fallen. It sucked at me like quicksand, that grief. Pulled me under, choked me. But Arianna never let go. She refused to let it win.

And eventually, I surfaced enough to blink in the darkness and ask in a voice without life, "Where are we?"

She turned her head sharply, her steps ceasing all at once. But she did not remark on my finally having spoken. "Deep in the forest, heading south," she explained. "We got past the settlement, and we're well into the mainland by now."

It seemed it took my brain a long moment to process her words. They fell on my ears like meaningless noise and gradually worked through the machinery of my mind and made sense. "Already?" I asked her, not really caring, but vaguely aware of how disoriented I was.

"We've been walking for hours," she said, her eyes intense, probing mine. "It's nearly dawn, Raven."

Nearly dawn? How strange . . . how very . . . *wrong* that the sun would rise again now that Duncan was gone. It made no sense, somehow.

"Dearborne's following. We must keep moving." And she started forward again, tugging me into motion.

My legs hurt, and I glanced down to see that my dress was ripped to ribbons now. I could see bloodstains here and there. Obviously I'd walked like a blind person, through brush and brambles, never moving them aside, scratching my flesh and never feeling the sting. I felt it now. It began slowly, as my brain registered what my eyes were seeing, and told me that my legs should hurt. Then grew sharper, hotter. I lifted my hand to my cheek when that, too, began to pulse, and I discovered a long scratch there.

'Twould heal soon enough. That was part of the powers we both possessed, the rapid regeneration of any wounds we might suffer. Already, even the faintest bruise caused by my fall from the cliffs would have vanished. These new injuries would, as well. 'Twas one of the things we all had in common.

Our other powers were not so easily identified. For they were different from Witch to Witch, even in ordinary mortal ones. Some were gifted at divination, some at reading the stars. Some were psychic, some in touch with the spirit realm. Some could manipulate the weather, while others could communicate with animals. In immortal High Witches the area of power became magnified, and, Arianna had explained, other magickal gifts began to appear, and to grow. She'd told me that some of the very old ones had even mastered shape-shifting, though I doubted the validity of that tall tale.

My own powers were those of healing, always had been. But the longer I remained in this new form, this stronger, more sensitive, immortal form, the more I realized that my healing magick was only one very small part of my abilities.

There were more. Many more. Some, I'd discovered aboard the *Sea Witch* during my crossing. The acute hearing, the enhanced eyesight, and night vision. The ability to scent things, and people. And every spell I had cast since coming here had been incredibly potent, bringing immediate, incredible results. The fertility ritual I'd done for Aunt Eleanor's old cow had produce a successful mating the very next day, and twin calves, big and healthy. When I'd worked a charm to increase our flock of laying hens, the results had required a larger shed be built for them all! When I wanted a sunny day for Aunt Eleanor, or rain for our vegetable patch, it happened almost as soon as the thought appeared in my mind. And a prickling sense in the back of my neck usually warned me when danger was near.

'Twas there now.

"He's close," I said.

Arianna stopped walking, turned to scan the woods. "I know. I feel him, too. But I don't think he'll make a move when I'm with you, Raven. He knows I—"

An explosion ripped through the forest, and Arianna stopped speaking and jerked. Her jaw gaped, worked soundlessly, and I cried out as I saw the gaping wound in my beloved sister's chest. The blackened edges of the hole in the shirt she wore.

I reached for her, but Arianna's eyes rolled and she slumped to the ground. Whirling, I scanned the trees, and then I saw him. Nathanial Dearborne, there among the pines. In his hands he clutched a musket, which stank of sulphur and spewed black smoke from its dark, deadly eye.

"You bastard," I whispered. "I'll not let you take her heart. I will not!" In a heartbeat my dagger was in my fist, and the numbness was fleeing from my body. I may have had no reason to live a moment ago. Now, though, I had found one. Vengeance. "You killed my mother in the name of God, when you're nothing but purest evil. And I lost my love to the same vile lie. I'll not let you kill my sister as well!"

"Sister, is it?" He stepped forward, dropping the now useless weapon to the ground, knowing, perhaps, that should he try to load it again, I'd attack before he could finish the job. He pulled his own dagger from his hip, saluted me with it mockingly. "For now, Raven St. James, 'tis your heart I want, not hers."

"Then try to take it!" I shouted.

"Oh, I will. And long before your . . . *sister* revives to come to your rescue. It's almost too good. Not only do I get my vengeance on you . . . but on her, as well. Can you imagine her grief when she wakes to find your lifeless body lying at her feet?"

"The only corpse to litter this ground will be yours!" I cried, and crept closer, my blade before me, though my hand trembled.

He came a step closer to me as well, then another. "I've killed hundreds, over the centuries," he told me, his voice strong, sure. "How many have you taken, Raven?"

I blinked. He was trying to frighten me, to shake me. And he succeeded. I'd never killed. And despite all of Arianna's training, I doubted my skills now.

"I could kill you so very easily, so quickly," he said, coming still closer, then standing near enough so I could feel the heat rising from his body and see the fog of his breath appear and vanish again on the deadly blade he held. "So very quickly, you'd never know what happened." Then he smiled. "But I'm not going to."

I lunged forward, swinging my blade, and nicking his belly before he could jump back. He hooked a leg behind mine as I drew back from him in anticipation of his return thrust. Then he shoved me with his hand, so that I toppled backward to the ground.

He was upon me in an instant, straddling my chest and pressing me down into the earth so forcefully that I could scarcely draw a breath. Clutching both my wrists in one of his large hands, he pinned them to the ground above my head. He smiled down at me, a frightening grimace of a smile. "It's going to be slow, Raven," he said. "We have time."

"Why?" I whispered. "Why do you hate me so much?"

"You figure it out," he told me, and with his free hand, he sliced open the front of my dress, from my waist to my neck. Using the blade again, he parted it, baring my chest, my breasts. Then, the knife still in his hand, he touched me, the backs of his knuckles pressing to the center of my chest. "Right there," he said. "Beating so fast . . . so hard. It's strong, your heart. You'll stay conscious as I begin to cut it from you, you know. I know how to do it."

"Please," I whispered, a tremor working through me from head to toe. Suddenly I didn't want to die at all. Not at all, and most certainly not like this. "Please, I'm so young. What good can my heart possibly be to you?"

"You're so clueless, my dear," he whispered. "So very young, and naive." He traced a path on my breastbone with the cold tip of his dagger. "You have immense power in you. Wasted on one with no idea what to do with it."

"I . . . I . . ."

"And then there's vengeance," he went on. "Always a strong motivator." He traced the same path again, this time cutting me, but not deeply. Just breaking the skin and leaving a bloody outline of the pattern he drew.

I whimpered. He smiled wider.

"What have I ever done to you?" I cried.

"You took my s . . . you took Duncan. You turned him against me, and now you've cost him his life."

"B-but he'll return—"

"As my sworn enemy! All because of you! Damn you, Raven St. James!" Eyes blazing, he lifted the dagger high above me, blade pointing down.

I opened my mouth to scream, but the sound never emerged. There was, instead, a soft hissing sound, and then the thud of an arrow driving into Nathanial's chest. He looked surprised for just an instant, then fell over backward.

I scrambled to my feet, pulling my torn dress around me and searching the forest.

The silver-haired red man . . . the one who'd given me the fish for breakfast a full two years ago . . . he stood in the distance, his bow in one hand, his black eyes holding mine. My hands went to my face as relief swamped me and tears sprang to my eyes. And my dress fell open again. The man's eyes lowered, affixed upon my bared breasts, I thought at first. And then I realized that wasn't it at all. He looked at the place where Nathanial had cut me, and his eyes widened as the skin there drew itself together, and mended. I quickly covered myself, but too late. He'd seen.

And even if he hadn't, our secret would have been out. For when I turned, 'twas to see two other shirtless, dark-skinned men in buckskins, leaning over Arianna, then backing away as she sucked in her first new breath with a loud, desperate gasp. Her back arched off the ground, even as the hole in her chest closed in on itself and the younger men's eyes widened.

I lunged forward, uncertain what they would do to her. But the silver-haired man touched my arm, and when I turned, implored me with his eyes. Narrowing my gaze, I searched his face. And finally, seeing no ill intent there, I nodded once.

He in turn raised a hand to the other two, and they picked Arianna up even as she was blinking her eyes open and looking around her. Silver-Hair took my arm, his grip gentle, and the five of us marched away, through the forest. I tugged free once, turning back, realizing Dearborne would revive, that there was only one way I could ensure that he stay dead.

But the old red man met my eyes, shook his head once, and took my arm again.

"Another time, then," I whispered. "Another time."

His name, in English, was Trees Speaking. In his own tongue, 'twas impossible for me to pronounce, and my constant attempts only made the other members of his tribe laugh at me as we all sat around a central fire that night, in their village. Long, narrow buildings all covered in pale bark served as their homes, and it seemed many generations of a given family resided in each one. But the gathering place, which seemed to serve as many purposes as the meeting hall in Sanctuary, was the area around this central fire.

'Twas there we were taken, and urged to sit. The old one spoke in a tongue that was like something ancient and sacred to my ears, and people spilled from their homes and stopped whatever they were doing, to stare at us, with wide, shining dark eyes. In a moment they broke away, running in a dozen directions. A dark, beautiful woman brought cloaks of whisper-soft doe hide to drape gently over our shoulders, while another, a plump young woman with an infant strapped to her back in some ingenious contraption, brought bowls filled with something like stew. Another draped a dress across my lap, and another dropped beads atop it. And one by one every member of this clan gathered round the fire, all seeming to vie for the spots nearest Arianna and me. We kept exchanging glances and shrugging. Neither of us knowing what to expect, much less what to say as they spoke to us in words we could not understand.

Finally a young girl, perhaps twelve or even younger, began to speak to me in halting English.

"I know some . . . white man tongue," she said slowly. "My name Laughing River."

I was surprised at her knowledge of English. And yet should not have been. The settlers were all around these people. They'd be wise to learn their language, and obviously they were that.

"My name is Raven," I told the beautiful, sloe-eyed child.

"Raven?" And when I nodded, she turned to repeat the word to the rest in their tongue. Then turned to Arianna.

"I am Arianna."

Laughing River tilted her head. "Ahhhrrrr . . ."

"Arianna," my sister repeated.

"Ahhrranna." Laughing River nodded hard and said it again, with authority this time. Many in the circle tried to pronounce the name, but it only resulted in more laughter.

Laughing River pointed to the silver-haired elder. "Trees Speaking."

"Trees Speaking," I repeated. "'Tis beautiful."

"When Trees Speaking is born," she told me, and waved a hand toward the towering pines around us, "wind in trees tell all he is Shaman."

I tilted my head. "Shaman? What is a Shaman?"

Laughing River frowned hard. "Trees Speaking tell us you are Shaman, like he. He say you . . ." She moved her hands trying to express her words, and Trees Speaking spoke softly to her. She nodded hard, and translated. "He say you like him. You walk with spirits. You make powerful . . . medicine."

I blinked, and glanced at Arianna. She lifted her brows and looked at the girl. "Magick?"

"Yes! Magick!" Laughing River said, nodding hard.

"Is that what a Shaman does?"

"Yes."

She looked again at Trees Speaking, as I did. And then at those around him. They looked at him with respect, listened when he spoke, seemed to love the man.

"Then, I guess we are . . . Shamans . . . of a sort," Arianna finally said. I heard the relief in her voice, for it seemed obvious a person of magick would be treated far differently here than among the whites.

"White man fear Shaman," Laughing River said. And her eyes went sad. "Trees Speaking say white man try kill all who make magick."

I nodded. "Trees Speaking is telling you the truth, I fear. They don't understand us."

The girl translated, and the old man nodded. Then he spoke again, and the girl smiled. "Trees Speaking say no one hurt you here. Magick sacred, even white woman's magick. He say you stay."

I glanced at Arianna. She swallowed hard. "I don't know," she whispered. "I hate to drag them into this. Suppose Dearborne hurts them because of us?"

Laughing River quickly translated what was not meant to be shared, and to my surprise, the men around the fire burst into laughter. Our eyes must have registered our surprise, because the girl quickly explained. "They laugh because they know one white man no threat to them. They warriors, Crow-Woman."

Crow-Woman? I supposed it might be close to "Raven" from her point of view, but . . .

"No white man harm you here. Our warriors fierce. Strong." There was pride in her voice.

Trees Speaking rose from his cross-legged position on the ground and smiled down at us. "Show me," he said, very slowly, eyes narrow as he struggled to put the words together properly in his deep, raspy voice, a voice like the wind he was named for. "Show me . . . your ways . . . your . . . *magick*." Then he touched his chest, patted it three times. "I show you my ways . . . my magic."

I looked at Arianna and blinked. A sparkle appeared in her eyes. "There are many, many kinds of Witches, Raven," she whispered, "and not all of us use that particular word for what we are. Some call themselves Druids, some monks, some holy men." She glanced at Trees Speaking. "Some Shaman. He could teach us a great deal, I think."

Looking back at him, I recalled the way he'd watched me—perhaps, watched *over me?*—when I'd spent that lonely night in the woods so long ago. "Why not?" I replied. "We have nothing to lose."

A flash of sadness clouded her eyes, but she turned to Trees Speaking and nodded. "Yes. We'll stay."

Trees Speaking smiled broadly. And so we stayed.

We spent well over a fortnight at that Iroquois village, sharing knowledge and esoteric wisdom with Trees Speaking. And I realized that Arianna had been right. There were many kinds of Witches. He was practicing virtually the same belief system we did ourselves. We only called it by different names. Trees Speaking told us of the sacred importance of the circle, and how he worked within one when doing magick. And we told him we did the same. He spoke of calling upon the Divine spirit residing in things like the wind, and the water, and the earth itself, and we marveled at that, for we had, as well. He told us how the basis of his power was his belief that all life is truly linked together through a common source, and again, we were awestruck.

But there was more Trees Speaking taught us. Things we hadn't seen or practiced before. He taught us to hear what animals might be telling us by watching their movements and picking out signs and omens. He taught us the medicinal uses of many plants and herbs native to this land and growing wild within its forests. And perhaps, most amazingly of all, he taught us the secrets of invisibility.

I thought the man insane when he brought this up with us, but he only smiled, and, through Laughing River, explained. One doesn't truly vanish. One simply becomes so attuned to his surroundings that he blends into them, and onlookers don't see him there. He demonstrated this by hiding and asking us to search for him. When we did, we couldn't find him anywhere. But then he spoke, and we turned and saw him clearly, standing with his back pressed to a tree trunk. He insisted he'd been there all along. So we listened and practiced and learned, and tested our newfound knowledge by games of hide-and-seek with the villagers.

Each night Trees Speaking would whisper some of his beautiful words to me before I retired to a place of honor in his family's longhouse. He would move his hands over me and chant. And he told me he was working to mend my broken heart, for he could see it clearly in my eyes. Truly, my time there helped me far more than anything else could have done. By immersing myself in learning about these people and their ways and their magick, I was able to go on living. But the pain of losing

Duncan remained fresh and strong in me. I thought it likely always would.

Finally we had to move on. 'Twas not planned, nor even thought through. But we knew 'twas time to leave when one of the young men returned from a journey bearing meat and furs aplenty, and bringing news that shook me to the marrow. He spoke it to Laughing River, and her face paled, eyes widened. She turned to me, and I saw moisture spring into her shining eyes.

"Crow-Woman," she said. "Bear Killer say white women . . . die. Many, many killed."

I frowned. "I . . . don't understand. What white women? How were they killed, and why?"

She lowered her head. "White man say they . . . like you. Shaman. Witches."

My stomach convulsed, and my lips pressed tight as if to stop it.

Arianna's face went stony. "Where?" she asked.

"If you go they kill you, too!" Laughing River cried.

"Where, Laughing River?"

She closed her eyes. "Place called . . . Sa-lem Village."

"Salem Village." Arianna shook her head, closed her eyes. "I doubt there's a genuine Witch in the bunch."

"Does it make a difference?" I asked her.

"Of course not. They're executing innocents either way. Innocent Witches, or innocent women who know nothing of magick, wrongly accused."

I tipped my head back, searching the sky. "We have to go," I said softly. "We're stronger, more powerful, harder to kill—"

"*Much* harder to kill," she said.

"We have an obligation, then."

"We do," she agreed.

We stared at each other, both of us wondering what turn life would bring to us next. Both of us afraid, and yet a bit excited. My losing Duncan had done one thing for me besides cause me unspeakable pain. It had made me lose my fear of dying.

For the next six months Arianna and I were shadows in the night. We'd slip into Salem by darkness, freeing women from the stocks, and from the locked rooms where they were imprisoned. Often with their children, even babies, locked up with them. Filthy, malnourished, and thirsting, no blankets. Many had been tortured. And none of them seemed to have a working knowledge of the Craft of the Wise. Perhaps some genuine Witches had been hanged or burned when the madness had first run wild in Salem. Perhaps . . . but not now. Now anyone with a grudge could cry accusations against her enemy, and see that enemy tried, her very life in the balance.

'Twas the purest form of evil I'd seen since the day I set eyes on Nathanial Dearborne. And 'twas only much later that I learned that Dark Witch himself had been in Salem Village only a short while before the madness began. No doubt the bastard had been instrumental in starting this fire that swept through the place, destroying everything it touched.

We rescued dozens, Arianna and I. Women and children whose fates had been sealed. We took them deep into the forests and hid them there. Some had families still alive and not yet accused. So we located those loved ones and brought them out as well. Our band of outcasts and refugees numbered fifty and more by the time the fury in Salem ran its course. And at last we led them all southward, into Pennsylvania Colony and a Quaker settlement there.

The journey took nearly two months. Alone, they'd have perished. But Arianna and I were able to find food, to fish the streams, and gather roots and greens thanks to all Trees Speaking and his people had taught us, and they survived.

In their new village, they used false names, just in case. But they'd be safe in this place. I sensed it, and felt good about something for the first time since I'd lost Duncan.

And yet those we hadn't been able to save . . . how they haunted me. I knew their names, every one of them. Sarah Osborne. Bridget Bishop. Sarah Good and her tiny baby. Elizabeth How. Susannah Martin. Rebecca Nurse. Sarah Wildes. Martha Carrier. George Jacobs. John Proctor. John Willard. Ann Foster. Giles and Martha Corey. Mary Esty. Alice Parker. Mary Parker. Ann Pudeator. Wilmot Reed. Margaret Scott. Samuel Wardwell. Sarah Dastin. I knew not whether they had been of my own faith . . . nor did I care. They'd been living, breathing sisters of the human race. My sisters. And brothers. And children. My dear mother's face seemed to appear in my mind as I tried to imagine the faces of the women who'd died.

And Duncan's face hovered in my mind's eye when I thought of the Reverend George Burroughs, a minister who'd suffered the same fate as my beloved Duncan. Not being pitched from the cliffs, no. Reverend Burroughs was hanged. Choked to death by a rope, and I knew that feeling all too well. But just like Duncan, the man had died at the hands of his own flock. Had I been a Puritan in Salem then, I'd have renounced my faith out of sheer shame for what had been done in its name.

I wept for all of them nightly for a long, long time after that. Sometimes, when it's quiet and I'm alone, I still do. I cry for them . . . I cry for Duncan . . . I cry for myself, having lost him.

And my grief, it seems, is as immortal as my body, for it lives on still. Every bit as powerful, every bit as painful, as it was before . . . though three full centuries have come and gone.

PART TWO

Chapter 12

1998

Three hundred years later, on the anniversary of Duncan's death, I stood on the cliffs of Sanctuary, facing the sea. There was a lighthouse standing offshore now. It reached skyward from the tiny, lonely island where before there had been only seabirds and the occasional treasure hunter. Built a century ago, it had been used for a time, and then forgotten. Then it had been abandoned for the better part of five decades, its rounded glass looking like a lifeless, sightless eye. A sad reminder of the way time moved on all around me. The way the world grew and changed and evolved.

I did not.

There had been movement at the lighthouse a month or so ago. For a moment I'd felt an absurd hope spring up in my heart, a foolish joy the place seemed to be about to come back to life.

But I had not.

I was in limbo, living, but incomplete, waiting, always waiting for the return of my soulmate. My lover. I'd been many places in the endless years of my life. But wherever I roamed, I had but one purpose—to search for him. I scanned every sea of strange faces in search of the one I hoped to see.

In three hundred years that search had left me with nothing but disappointment.

I stood with my feet apart, arms spread wide, head tilted back. The sea wind whipped my hair behind me, and a soft glow painted my face as the full moon rose over the ocean. I knew, had always known, of the power in the moon. A physical tug, a pull. The waves felt it; the tides changed because of it. Animals felt it. Coyotes and wolves bayed in response. Lunatics felt it, stirring the sickness in their minds.

Witches felt it.

The surge of power within growing stronger and peaking with the moon. At the full moon I felt I could do anything. I was invulnerable, invincible, and as powerful as the Goddess herself. And I had only one focus for the immense power the full moon gave to me.

Duncan.

But something was different tonight. Perhaps it was only the endless longing in my heart—heaven knew it had been often enough before—but I felt more hopeful than usual. I felt as if . . . as if perhaps he were near.

And yet I couldn't trust my own feelings where Duncan was concerned, for "wishful thinking" was real and powerful and sometimes too potent to distinguish from true intuition.

Standing at the eastern edge of the circle I had cast, I spread my arms and felt the wind on my face. "Mighty Energies of the East, Sacred Ones of Air, I call on you to attend this circle and empower these rites." Immediately the wind in my face sharpened.

To my right, facing South, Arianna stood in the same position I had, arms spread outward and upward. She'd kept her blond hair short, and it ruffled in the breeze like the feathers of a golden bird preparing to take flight. Softly she intoned, "Ancient Energies of the South, Blessed Ones of Fire, I call on you to attend this circle and empower these rites."

As I watched her, Arianna's face glowed, just for a moment, as if someone held a candle before her, but no candle was there. Only the balefire we'd built, but that was behind her, in the circle's center. Her huge brown eyes flicked open, and she tilted her head as if she'd felt that warmth on her face.

Solemnly, I crossed to the opposite side, the west. "Healing Energies of the West, Ancient Ones of Water, I call on you to attend this circle and empower these rites."

Dampness . . . dotting my face, my forearms. I blinked at the mist that rose from the ground to leave its kiss of moisture on my skin. Truly some powerful magic would be worked here tonight.

Arianna had moved to the North now, and in a strong voice she called, "Powerful Energies of the North, Eternal Mother Earth, I call on you to attend this circle and empower these rites."

And then I started, because I felt the earth herself rumble beneath me. A deep-throated vibration welled up from the ground, trembling against my feet and shaking my body so slightly I might have imagined it. When my wide-eyed gaze shot to Arianna's, she met it, and nodded once. She'd felt it, too.

I moved to the center of the circle, then, to invoke the fifth element, that of spirit. And then together we said the words that would bring the presence of Divinity to our circle this night. When we finished it seemed that the circle pulsed more powerfully with unseen energies than it had ever done before.

Meeting Arianna's eyes, I saw that she knew what I did. Something had changed. Something was happening. I'd planned to recite an incantation, to cast and to conjure this night, just as I had on every Esbat night for the past three hundred years. I used every power I possessed to ensure that when Duncan returned, as I knew he would one day, he would come here. To Sanctuary. To me. Over and over I'd willed the elements and every force of the astral plane to bring Duncan back here, to the place where I'd lost him. I could not hasten his return; it would have been wrong of me to try. His soul would incarnate again only when it was ready, when the time was right. But my greatest fear was that when he did live again, I'd never find him. The world was a big place, after all.

And though I sought him everywhere I went, I always returned here, where I waited. Endlessly waited, for his return.

But tonight was not the same as all those other nights when I'd worked my magick. As I stood in the center of my circle this night, with the large flat stone before me and the tools of my craft spread out upon it—cauldron and blade, wand and pentacle, censers and candles—I felt something different.

The winds of the four directions seemed to spin and whirl about the two of us as Arianna and I knelt before the altar, and she looked up into my eyes.

"No conjuring tonight, Raven," she whispered. "Something's not right here. I *feel* it."

Blinking, I lowered my head. "Perhaps the Universe is angry with me. . . . Plotting to make Duncan come here even if it's against his wishes is not exactly ethical."

She shook her head. "I've never seen the elements react this way to a tiny bit of arguably manipulative magick before." She moved closer to me as the whirlwind swept around us, around the balefire and the altar stone at the circle's center. The swirling action of the wind on the flames was something to see, for they narrowed and lengthened as if the fire reached toward the heavens. A loud cry made me look up fast, gripping Arianna's hand as I did, only to see a large raven land upon the stone altar. It looked at me, tilted its shiny black head, and looked at me again. The balefire's flames leaped with a snap and a hiss, and I gasped as in the brighter light of the fire, I saw more clearly.

"Look! He's injured!"

Arianna squinted, leaning closer, and saw the tiny droplet of blood that clung, quivering, to the bird's gleaming breast. It trembled as if in time with the tiny rapid heartbeat. I reached out very slowly. "Come, namesake. Let me tend that for you."

But the bird only squawked once more and, lifting its great wings, pumped them mightily and flew away.

Still staring at the spot where the bird had been, I whispered, "What does it mean?"

Arianna squeezed my hand. "The Druids said Ravens brought warnings. I don't know, Raven, it was as if he were trying to tell you something."

"But what?" I saw the blankness in her eyes, and rubbed my hands over my chilled arms. She wouldn't speak it, but I knew what she was thinking. A raven—with a wound over his heart. It could well portend my death. Even now there might be a Dark One lurking, waiting to . . .

"You've survived their attempts before, Raven," Arianna whispered, as if reading my thoughts. "You're as good with your blade as I am now. You can defend yourself."

I nodded, but the chill of fear still danced barefoot over my spine. "Let's close the circle, Arianna. Something feels . . . wrong."

"All right." Quietly then, we performed the closing rites, and then gathered up our tools and turned our backs to the sea, facing the giant of a house.

It had begun as a simple home built on the site of my dear aunt Eleanor's cabin. But it had . . . grown. We had money enough. Two talented Witches with several centuries to accumulate wealth would always have money enough to do whatever they wanted. Adding on to the house had become a bit of a hobby. A tradition. Almost an inside joke. The rambling structure was so utterly outragous now it would no doubt have drawn curious sightseers from town in droves . . . under normal circumstances.

But we were *Witches*. We cast spells over the place, and wove astral shields to protect it. It wasn't invisible, of course. But it blended in with the woods if one viewed it from the east, with the sea if one viewed it from the west, the sky if one looked at it from below. There were ways to avoid notice. There was magick.

Of course, we came and went often . . . and sometimes were forced to let years pass between visits, just to make sure the locals never became suspicious.

It was easier now, though. Sanctuary boasted few actual residents. Oh, there were the lobster men on the north shore, and the shop owners on the south. Innkeepers scattered hither and yon, and a handful of restauranteurs. But most of the people who came here today were vacationers in search of a coastal getaway and some autumn foliage. That log village with its mud tracks that I'd ridden into so long ago was long forgotten now. A tourist-trap had emerged in its place. It was no longer even part of Massachusetts, but of Maine, which itself had been a part of Massachusetts Bay Colony three hundred years ago.

As we approached the sprawling home we'd created, I felt Arianna nudge my ribs. "Shall we add a new wing this visit? Georgian this time?"

She was attempting to cheer me, I knew. "We did that in thirty-seven, love," I said, pointing to the stately brick section that housed our overflowing library, our favorite sitting room, and a small alcove for . . . for whatever purpose we could think of. I'd thought as we'd built it how Duncan would love it. How we could sit there together, in that alcove, and reminisce, and . . .

Tears welled up in my eyes. I rarely spent a day when they didn't.

"Oh," Arianna said. "Well, Victorian, then? Or Gothic? Gothic would be so poetic for a pair of Witches, don't you think?"

"You're forgetting the west wing, Arianna. With the gargoyles we imported from France in eighteen-ninety-nine lining the roof."

"Right, that slipped my mind." She pouted. "Do we have a colonial wing?"

"Complete with a cobblestone hearth," I said, smiling, letting my friend draw me out of my contemplative state. "Face it, Arianna, we have everything except a log cabin sprouting from this house of ours."

"A log cabin . . ." Arianna said, clasping her chin and tilting her head as she studied the many roofs, some steep, some shallow, some flat, some slate, some steel, some shingled, all sporting chimneys—cobblestone, brick, block, and steel. "No," Arianna said thoughtfully. "Logs would simply clash."

The laughter burst from me just as she'd intended it to. And she smiled at my reaction as she reached for the back door. "It's good to see you laugh, Raven," she said softly, pulling our door open, smiling back at me. "It's so seldom that you do." Then her smile died as she stared past me, out toward the sea, and a curious frown creased her brow. "Oh, look."

"What is it?" I turned to follow her gaze and saw that the old light-house standing dark and lonely on its tiny island was coming alive again. A light came on in one of the lower windows. Why it should thrill me so, I had no idea. Seeing a light in formerly dead eyes . . . perhaps somewhere inside it reminded me of my long wait, and my hope that my dead lover would be restored to me one day soon. Another light came on, followed by another. And for just an instant I felt a shiver as an icy finger trailed a path up my spine.

"Just what we need," I muttered. "A new neighbor—and so close." A reaction that made far more sense than the one I truly felt.

"Raven," Arianna whispered. "Raven, look . . ."

She pointed to a dark shape moving in the sky, and as I squinted and it moved into the moonlight, I realized it wasn't one shape but several; a dozen or more ravens, flying toward the lighthouse. One by one they landed atop it, or around it. And then in chorus they began to shout.

Drawn by invisible hands, I walked toward them, until Arianna clasped my shoulders, drawing me to a halt.

"Come inside, Raven."

"I should go there," I whispered. "They're telling me something, don't you see?"

"Yes. And what if what they're telling you is 'Stay away from here, Raven St. James!' What then, hmm?"

I blinked, shaking my head. "I don't think—"

"The Celts used to say that when evil preachers died, they were transformed into ravens," she blurted.

And I blinked, my stomach clenching. The only evil preacher I knew—had ever known—was Nathanial Dearborne. The bastard who'd killed my mother and hunted me all my days. How many times had I barely escaped his blade? How many more would there be before one of us paid the ultimate price?

Perhaps it was he the birds warned me of. Perhaps he'd caught up to me again after all these years. He was long overdue for another attempt. And maybe he'd finally found our haven, the place we'd kept so secret we'd hoped no other immortal would ever know we came here.

"Why is that bastard so determined to have my heart?" I whispered.

"You know why, Raven."

I closed my eyes. "Because of Duncan."

"Yes. Because of Duncan. And because of your magickal power—you've always known how special it is, Raven. You have a healing gift like no other, and you're able to draw luck and good fortune to you like no Witch I've known."

I closed my eyes. "I've lived three hundred years without the man I love. You call that luck or good fortune?"

"You know what I mean. The wealth, Raven. The way you and your aunt prospered back then, and the way we do now."

"Any Witch could do that."

"I lived two hundred years before I found you again, Raven. And I never managed it."

"You got by."

"Getting by is irrelevant. Have you looked at our bank statements lately?"

I sighed. Making good financial decisions had always come as naturally to me as breathing. It wasn't something I was overly proud of, but I doubted I could help it if I tried. If I bought a stock, it skyrocketed. If I opened a bank account, the interest rate went up. If I bought so much as a lottery ticket . . .

"And now there's your age, as well," Arianna went on. "Nathanial would get a lot of life force from a heart three centuries strong. Besides all of that, the more times you thwart him, the more angry and determined he becomes. You know that, as well."

Lowering my head very slowly, I said, "I'm going to have to kill him, aren't I?"

Arianna nodded. "I'm afraid it's the only way you'll ever find peace." She searched my face. "You've killed before, Raven. He wouldn't be your first."

"Yes," I admitted, "but only in battle, when it was forced on me. Only when I had no choice. It takes something from me when I take a life, Arianna. I die a little each time."

"The bastard needs killing," Arianna told me.

"But not by me. Not unless he forces me to." I bit my lower lip. "We'll leave here for a while. Tomorrow. I'd rather avoid confrontation if I can."

Tipping her head skyward, Arianna rolled her eyes. "Raven! Why must you be such a pacifist? After three centuries of living as a being who must kill or be killed, how can you cling to that mortal idea of morality? I swear, if I get the chance, I'll cut out that black heart of his myself." I looked at her harshly. "I *will*!" she vowed. "I've owed that bastard for a long time. But he's as slippery as a snake where I'm concerned."

"He does avoid you," I said, contemplating. "It's as if he's always out there, watching us, waiting. Every time he's attacked me since Duncan, it has been when you and I were apart. In Virginia, when I stayed behind to care for that ailing woman, while you went off to find her husband. In California, when I sat on the beach thinking of Duncan while you slept soundly in the beach house. In New York when we got separated in that crowd at the theater . . ."

"Because he knows I can take him."

"I suspect you're right," I told her. "And that's why he never gives you the chance. It's me he comes after. Always me . . . and those I love."

"So you'll run from him again," Arianna went on. "And what if Duncan returns here while you're hiding from Dearborne? What if you miss your chance to find him again?"

I only shook my head. "That won't happen. We can keep watch from a safe distance."

"He won't come after you if I'm here, Raven."

"You can't watch over me twenty-four hours a day, Arianna."

"But we're not even sure Dearborne is here yet!" she wailed.

I turned to stare out at the night sky, at the full moon, and even as I did, a dark cloud eclipsed its golden face.

"He's here," I whispered. "I feel it. He's here."

Duncan stood near the curving glass windows of the lighthouse for a long time. Alone, as utterly alone as he'd always been.

She'd been out there again tonight.

The same woman, he was sure of that. The same one he'd glimpsed that first night he'd come here, a month ago. When this had been just another job, and not one he particularly wanted at that. Not that restoring a century-old lighthouse wasn't exactly the kind of thing he loved best . . . just that it meant spending months surrounded by water. And he hadn't been over the fear of water all that long. Heights barely gave him a second thought anymore, but the water . . .

Still, he'd agreed to come out here, take a look at the place. And he still wasn't exactly sure why he'd done that when he'd been certain this was one restoration job he'd be turning down. He only knew that a strange sort of pit-of-the-stomach feeling had started gnawing at him from the moment he'd set foot in this tourist mecca town. And when he and the owner left shore in a small motorboat the first time to head out to the lighthouse, the physical reactions, the cold sweat and rapid heartbeat he'd been expecting, hadn't come. They'd been overpowered by different reactions, unexpected ones as he stared back at the peninsula, and the cliffs at its tip. A clenching sensation in his stomach. An empty well opening in the vicinity of his heart. A tightening in his throat that made it hard to swallow.

All of that only got worse once he was inside the lighthouse, discussing the renovations with the owner, who wanted to fix it up and sell it. Already, he'd been reconsidering his earlier decision not to take on the job.

Then he'd glimpsed her. Through these very windows. She stood like some kind of sea goddess, on those cliffs, with the wind lifting her satin hair like a flag. Her face turned up to the rising moon as if she were drinking in every moonbeam. And he'd lost track of what the owner was saying, of what he was supposed to be doing here as he'd watched her, mesmerized. Someone said, "So how much do you want for this place?" and he realized later it had been him.

And now he owned it. *Him.* The guy who'd had a crippling, inexplicable fear of water ever since he'd been a toddler had bought himself an old abandoned lighthouse surrounded by the stuff. And he wasn't even sure why.

But he was pretty sure it had something to do with *her.*

She'd been out there again tonight, soft breeze fingering her long, dark hair, yellow moonlight bathing her face. There had been another one with her, a tiny blond, but he'd barely noticed. The two had gone inside now . . . back into that twisted-up mishmash of a house that towered up there.

Odd, that house. He'd commented on it to lighthouse's former owner, and the guy claimed he'd never even noticed the place.

How could anyone not notice *that?*

He shook his head and looked at the place atop the cliffs once more. The bonfire burned low, and by and by the blond one came back outside with a pail of water to pour over it. But of the dark one, he saw no more.

The cell phone bleated, and Duncan reached for it, still watching for a glimpse of the woman on the cliffs as if he were some sort of stalker.

God, what was wrong with him? He jerked his gaze away deliberately and answered the call. Just before he brought the phone to his ear, he thought of his father, and almost laughed at himself. He often got an inkling of who was on the other end when the phone rang.

Then his jaw dropped when he heard his father's voice on the other end. "Is that you, Duncan? There's so much static . . ."

"Father?"

"Ah, then it *is* you. Good."

Duncan licked his dry lips. His father wouldn't be calling unless . . . "Is something wrong?"

"No, no. I heard you'd bought a lighthouse . . . on an island of all things! Couldn't believe it."

Frowning, Duncan shook his head. "It's true. To be honest, Father, I can't imagine you'd be all that interested."

His father cleared his throat. "I know we haven't been . . . close . . . since you left home."

"Since I left home?" If he sounded sarcastic, he ought to. His father had ignored him most of his life . . . and Duncan often wondered why the man had bothered adopting him in the first place. As a newborn, no less. He couldn't imagine a less paternal man. There had been nannies, an entire staff to care for him, until he'd been old enough to ship off to boarding school, followed by summer camp, followed by an expensive, private college. He'd barely known his father.

But he'd always wanted to. A relationship with the cold, distant man was something he'd craved in secret all his life. Sometimes he thought that might be the answer to that emptiness, that ache in his heart that he'd never been able to explain.

"I'm in Sanctuary, son."

Duncan's thoughts ground to a halt. "You're . . . where?"

"In town. I arrived on Monday."

Blinking, Duncan gave his head a shake to clear it. "You've been in Sanctuary for three days? And you didn't even call me? No, no, that's not the surprise, the surprise is that you'd bother calling me now. What do you want, Father?"

There was a long pause. "I want . . . to *be* your father, Duncan."

The breath seemed to have been stolen from Duncan's lungs. He couldn't inhale, and couldn't speak until he did. How long had he imagined his father saying those words? How many nights had he dreamed them, wished for them, as a child? And why, why had his father waited so long? Why couldn't he have started this conversation years ago, when a little boy had needed it so badly? Why now?

Swallowing, Duncan said, "I'm a grown man with my own business and my own life. I don't *need* a father now."

"I know. Duncan, I know, believe me. My mistakes . . . well, they're too numerous to mention, but I'm well aware of every last one of them. I want to start over, to try to . . . to make up for the past. Please, give me that chance."

Duncan had to close his eyes, because they burned. When he spoke, his voice was gravelly, coarse. "Do you mean it?"

"I do, son. I swear to you, I do."

But Duncan was almost afraid to let himself believe it. He'd wanted this too badly for too long to trust that it could be real.

"You aren't convinced," his father said. "But you will be. I sold my house, Duncan. And today I bought a new place, the old courthouse right here in Sanctuary."

Frowning, Duncan took the phone away from his ear, stared at it for a moment, as if he could read his father's expression through it somehow. Then he brought it back.

"That's how serious I am about this. I want to be close to you, close enough so that we can work on . . . on building a relationship, Duncan. I want to start over with you. Will you let me try?"

Blinking the moisture from his eyes, Duncan nodded. "Sure, Dad. Sure, we can both try."

His father sighed in relief, and Duncan could almost imagine the stern face cracking in a rare smile. "Meet me for breakfast tomorrow?" his father asked. "Here in town, at the Coast Road Café?"

With a quick swipe at his eyes, Duncan said, "Okay. Around eight?"

"Perfect," his father said. And then he hung up without another word.

Duncan set the phone down after a long moment. He told himself not to hope for too much, not to invest any emotions in this apparent softening of his father's hard heart. It would only lead to disappointment. But he'd had plenty of that over the years. He should be used to it by now.

Kneeling, he resumed the unpacking he'd been in the midst of when he'd become distracted by the dark woman on the distant cliffs. It was the first box. He traveled a lot. Always searching, it seemed, though he could never quite figure out what for. But wherever he went, this was always the first box he unpacked. His collection, the one he'd been accumulating ever since the fourth grade, when he'd bought the first piece at a five and dime with his allowance money. He thought the fascination might have begun when he'd read that poem by Edgar Allan Poe . . . or maybe the love of the birds had already been there, and that was why the poem had affected him so deeply. Why, that haunting refrain "Nevermore" could still bring tears to his eyes.

Either way, he liked them. Had over a hundred now. And the tiny sills along the insides of all these curving windows would be the perfect shelves for them.

He opened the box, removing the protective paper that cushioned them, and began removing his collection of ravens, one by one, placing them carefully, just so. And as he did, he whispered the words of the poem he sometimes heard in his sleep.

"Take thy beak from out my heart, and take thy form from off my door!
Quoth the Raven, 'Nevermore.'"

Chapter 13

Duncan was early. His father wasn't at any of the round, lion-footed stone tables or their matching rock-hard benches outside the Coast Road Café. And the inside of the place was all but deserted. Too nice a day for anyone to want breakfast inside, he figured. The foliage-seekers filled almost every available spot outside—uncomfortable stone benches notwithstanding. The tourists wore cardigans and sunglasses. The locals wore flannel and baseball caps with the names of their favorite products on them. John Deere. Mack. GMC. His father fit into neither group, but Duncan would spot him easily enough. He'd show up in his traditional funereal suit with his thin ribbon of a tie dangling.

Duncan glanced at his watch. Twenty minutes. Daddy dearest wouldn't be a minute early, either. Well, he'd walk, then. He was too nervous to stand still, or grab a table and wait. Besides, it was high time he got to know this town a bit, if he was going to live here.

The sun blazed so brightly from the clear blue sky that the hillsides nearby seemed fluorescent. The air had a bite to it, but it was invigorating rather than chilling. Made a man want to taste it.

Something had lifted his spirits this morning. He had a good feeling, and he hoped he was intelligent enough that it wasn't because of his father's apparent change of heart. That would be a foolish mistake. It didn't seem as if it was, however. Something else lingered in the air. Expectation. A sense that something big was going to happen. A feeling that he ought to be holding his breath.

He often got . . . feelings . . . intuitions about things. But he'd never had one like this before.

Strange.

He walked a full block, then stopped dead in his tracks and stared. Across the street a woman stepped out of a small shop. She carried boxes, empty boxes, stacked inside one another. They towered so tall in her arms that they hid her face. But it didn't matter. He knew her.

He knew her.

Sure he knew her. She was the woman who stood on the cliffs in the middle of the night. The woman he was compelled to watch. That was all.

It doesn't feel *like that's all, though. It feels like something more.*

When she turned and that long ebony hair swung around her shoulders, his heart did a crazy leap in his chest. He couldn't make his legs work, could barely make his *mind* work. He could only stand there, staring at her, wondering why the hell she got to him this way. Cars passed back and forth between them, traffic increasing as the morning aged, but they didn't disturb his intense study of her. He couldn't have looked away even if he'd wanted to.

She shifted the boxes to one side, balancing them on her hip. She wore black. Leather, he thought. A snug leather dress with a zipper that traced a path up the front of her, cool metal, he imagined, pressing to her center and running right between her breasts. The hemline hugged her thighs. Below that her legs were encased in black stockings that ended at short, laced-up boots with pointy toes.

His gaze rose once more. Her head turned toward him, slowly. Very slowly. As if she sensed him there, looking at her. Her dark, dark eyes met his, locked on them, held them. Then widened, and the boxes fell from her hands. The smaller ones spilled out of the larger ones when the stack tumbled in the stiff autumn wind. Her hair danced with the breeze, moving in apparent slow motion. Her lips parted, seemed to form his name.

She stepped off the sidewalk and into the street. Into the traffic. Eyes glued to his, blinking rapidly now, but never glancing to one side or the other, she came closer.

He did manage to look away—but only when the shadow loomed and the horn blared. The traffic—she was stepping right into the traffic, and there was a truck, and—

He opened his mouth to shout a warning. Before he made a sound, the dark enchantress lifted a hand toward the rumbling vehicle—like a traffic cop signaling "stop"—and abruptly the truck skidded to the left as if something had shoved it. Something *big*. It came to rest neatly against the curb. She never even looked at it, never took her eyes from his, just kept coming. The wind blew harder, and her hair writhed and twisted like Medusa's.

And suddenly Duncan felt an icicle of fear slide up his spine. Why?

She stepped up onto the sidewalk. Came closer. Tears, he could see them now. Welling deep in her eyes, glimmering, spilling over. Wet black lashes shining, dampening her cheeks. Longing so intense he could *feel* it, flowing from her eyes with the pain and the tears. Closer. And she was so close now she was nearly touching him. God, was he dreaming this? Her body brushed his and he felt a snapping, crackling electricity spark between them as she tipped her head back, searched his face. A trembling hand rose to touch his cheek, brush at his hair, and he felt it again. Delicate brows drew together. She tilted her head slightly to one side, and she whispered, "Duncan?"

"Yes," he said, amazed he could speak at all with the force of these unnamed, and utterly illogical, emotions swamping him. He felt absurdly like pulling her into his arms, like kissing her endlessly. It was an effort to keep his arms at his sides, and the muscles flexed and his fists clenched as he reminded himself to do just that. "How did you know my—"

"Duncan?" she asked again, both hands running over his face now, as if she couldn't believe he were real. Her breaths came faster, and the tears flowed like rivers. "Oh, Duncan . . ." There was more, but the words were garbled and choked out on sobs so he only got bits and pieces. "Waiting" and "centuries" and "living without you." Not that it mattered what she said. Not to him, because it was what she *did* that had his full attention.

She pressed herself against him, twisted her arms around his neck, and she kissed him. Even with the sobs making her hiccup and gasp, she parted her lips over his, so that he tasted the salt of her tears. She clung to him as if she'd never let go. And something happened to him. He didn't know what. Something. It was as if he were someone else, someone who knew this woman and returned her wrenching emotions fully. He wrapped his arms around her slender waist and it felt . . . familiar. The shape, the size of her, the way her body rubbed against his. And he bent over her—just the right amount to compensate for the differences in their heights. He returned her kiss. But it was more than a kiss. It was like . . . coming home when he touched his mouth to hers.

His mind seemed to shut down. It no longer mattered who he was, or who she was, or how insane this entire encounter was. All that mattered was the taste of her mouth, and its warmth. The texture of those lips moving against his, that tongue as soft and rough as velvet when he stroked it with his own. The feel of her waist clasped in his hands, or of her hair when he touched it, plowed his fingers into it, rubbed it against his cheek. Sweet. God, she was sweet. And small and pliant in his arms. And he wanted her. He wanted her with a power and a passion that exploded inside his mind. His hips arched against her belly. She didn't even pull away.

He fed from her mouth, and his head spun. His heart pounded, and it felt as if something stabbed into it, but he ignored the sudden pain as his lips slid around to her jaw, and lower, to suckle the skin of her neck. No matter where he put his mouth he found sweetness, salt, softness, heat. And wanted more.

Panting, he lifted his head to stare down into her eyes. Still wet with tears, but wide and deep and incredible, they gazed back at him. He couldn't speak above a whisper, felt dizzy, weak, and entirely disoriented.

"Who are you?" he managed to ask her. And next he'd ask who *he* was, he thought vaguely. Because for a few minutes there it was as if he'd lost his own identity. This shock, this dizziness, must be the aftermath of that temporary lapse.

She blinked up at him, and Duncan saw the fire in her eyes flicker and, slowly, begin to fade.

"Not that it matters," he went on, very quickly. To hell with the fear of losing himself, losing his identity or even his soul to her . . .

Odd thought, isn't it?

His only fear now was that she wouldn't let him kiss her again. "I mean, it doesn't matter," he blurted. "Not at all. I just—"

"Oh, Duncan." The words were a sigh. Unspeakably sad, then riding away on a stray breeze. Closing her eyes, she untwisted her arms from his neck, took a step backward. "Oh, sweet Duncan, I didn't mean to do it this way." She shook her head slowly. "What must you be thinking right now? You don't even know me, do you?"

He swallowed hard, reaching up with one hand, stroking her cheek, and absorbing a tear into his fingertips. "Oh, yeah," he whispered. "I know you. I've seen you on the cliffs . . . I've watched you . . . from the lighthouse."

"*You* live in the lighthouse?"

He nodded, watching her face, wishing he could kiss her again. But even now the confused yearning of that moment was fading, and he was beginning to realize how weird all this was, and to feel self-conscious about losing his head with a total stranger. Practically making love to her in the street.

Still wanting to.

"How did you know my name?" he asked, maybe because it was all he could think of to say—to distract himself from thinking of her taste, and wanting more. To ground himself in something solid and logical and practical. To grab hold of the first rational thought to come into his mind in several minutes, and cling to it for dear life.

"I know a lot of things about you, Duncan." She closed her eyes, lowered her head again. "But I'm messing this up. Badly." And she looked up at him again. Like the sun emerging from behind the clouds. "I meant to take it slowly. To give you time to get to know me again and—"

"Again?"

She nodded. "Yes. But don't worry about that now. Don't worry about anything now. I'll explain it all, Duncan, and this time I'll tell you everything. I won't keep anything from you this time, I swear it."

Frowning, he studied her and wondered for the first time if this beautiful young woman were, perhaps, slightly insane.

Good, Duncan. Better that than wondering what happened to your own sanity just now, isn't it?

"This time?" he said, pretending not to hear his own mocking thoughts. God, how her black eyes gleamed. She reminded him of something . . . some . . . *one.*

"All that matters now, Duncan, is that you're here. You're here." Her beautiful lips curved into a smile so enticing he found he really didn't care if she were sane or not. "You're really here."

He found himself smiling back at her, a reflex beyond control. "Yes, I certainly am."

She shook her head from side to side. "You don't sound the same."

"The same as what?"

She shook her head again. "You've lost the lilt of the Highlands. But beyond that . . ." She stroked his hair once more, tugged a strand away from his head and ran it between her fingers. "Beyond that, you're the same. Lord, but I've missed you so much. And to think I thought it was *him.* And I left poor Arianna home packing, convinced we had to go away and—"

"Go away?" She sounded crazier all the time, but for some reason the idea of her leaving here shook him. His hands were on her shoulders now, and he battled a rising tide of panic that usually only crept up on him this way when he tried swimming or looked down from some substantial height. "But you can't. Not now, not when—"

"Oh, but we're not going away. No, Duncan, not now, I promise you that. I'm not about to leave you when I've only just found you."

He sighed his relief. "I'm glad."

"Are you?"

He nodded. "We . . . we know each other, don't we?" he said, a little uncertain.

A cloud covered the light in her eyes. "We did . . . once. I'd hoped you might remember, but Arianna told me you wouldn't. It's all right, Duncan."

He licked his lips, swallowed hard. "I can't imagine meeting you and not remembering," he said.

She shrugged, averting her eyes. "It was a long time ago."

He tilted his head, studying her face. "You do seem . . . familiar to me. Maybe that's why I've been . . ." He let his words die. Maybe that was why he'd been so drawn to her, so compelled to watch her from the lighthouse. Maybe he *had* known her once.

"Well, if I'm a bit familiar to you, then that's something, isn't it?"

"I'm half afraid you're mistaking me for someone else."

"There could never be someone else, Duncan. Not ever." Lowering her head slowly, she whispered, "There's so much we need to talk about. So much I have to tell you."

"Apparently so."

She drew a breath. "This must seem so strange to you."

"It's . . . yeah. It's strange." She bit her lip, and he rushed on. "Strange in a very nice way," he added, and he caught her chin, lifted it so he could look into those mesmerizing eyes of hers. "Tears," he said. "They've got no business filling eyes like these."

She sniffed, and the tears welled deeper and spilled out onto her cheeks. "Will you hold me, Duncan? I know it makes no sense to you now, but I need to feel your arms around me more than I need to draw another breath right now."

She didn't have to ask twice. He pulled her close, and she nestled in his arms. She fit herself against him as if she were custom-made for him to hold. Her arms around his waist, her cheek resting on his chest. Her hair just below his face so its scent wafted up to entice. Something stirred a memory when he smelled that scent. Lavender and honeysuckle. He'd smelled it before, he knew he had.

For a very long time he stood there and just held her. It felt . . . potent. Emotions more powerful than any he'd ever known roiled around inside him, and he couldn't even figure out why. But he didn't want to let her go. Hell, he'd hold her like this forever if he had time.

Time.

Damn, the *time*.

He glanced at his watch, realized he was late now for his meeting with his father. Almost decided to let the old man sit alone all morning. But his conscience gave a twist. No, he'd wanted this chance with his father for too long to blow it when it finally came. He had to at least try.

"I'm sorry," he told her as he stroked her hair and gently lifted her head from his chest. The regret he heard in his voice was genuine. He didn't want to leave her. It made his knees weak, made his head ache to entertain the idea! Clenching his jaw, he forced the words to come. "I have to meet someone. I swear, if it wasn't so important, I'd—"

"No, it's all right. I . . . I should go, talk to Arianna before she has the entire house packed up." She shook her head. "Besides, I need to . . . put my head on straight. Seeing you . . . it made me forget everything I'd planned, everything I wanted to say."

A lump came into his throat. "I . . . will I see you again?"

Her smile was soft, edged with sadness and joy all at once. "I'll come to you, Duncan. Tonight, I'll come to the lighthouse. We'll talk then. I promise you, all of this will make sense then."

He nodded slowly, doubting anything she had to say could make any of this make sense. But he didn't care. All that mattered was that she would come to him. She'd be with him. Tonight, and that was only hours away, and if she hadn't made that promise, he didn't think he'd be able to walk away from her right now. "I'll be waiting," he told her.

Leaning forward and up, she pressed a gentle kiss to his lips. Then, stepping away, she turned to go.

"Wait," he said, and she stopped, glanced back at him. "I don't even know your name."

She blinked, as if to cover something in her eyes. "No, you don't, do you? It's St. James. Raven St. James." Then she turned again and hurried away.

Duncan stood staring after her until she was out of sight. Raven.

Raven?

My God, what the hell was going on here?

"Duncan?"

Blinking out of his stupor, he half turned toward the voice that called his name. His father stood three feet away, on the sidewalk, hands thrust into the deep pockets of the long black coat that made him look like a mobster's grandfather.

"Hello, Father."

His father frowned, and the additional lines lost themselves with all the others on his face. It was a stern face, narrow and pale. Steel-gray hair, too long for a man his age, surrounded it. He looked like winter, Duncan thought. He'd always looked that way. Never seemed to change.

"I waited a good fifteen minutes at the café," he said, his voice a monotone.

"I was on my way there." He met the old man's eyes, wondered if there would be a confrontation, accusations and defenses now. No, he wouldn't defend himself to his father. He wouldn't apologize. He was an adult.

His father's gaze wavered first, and the man sighed. "No matter. I was just on my way back to the old courthouse building. Walk with me, Duncan?"

Duncan nodded, turning around and falling into step beside his father. Awkwardly trying to think of some light conversation, some casual words to break the ice. "So how have you been?"

"Same as always. And you?"

Duncan shrugged. His father spoke without making eye contact. It was a trait Duncan had never really become used to. "The business is going well," he told his father at length.

"Yes, well, it should. There will never be a shortage of old buildings in need of restoration."

"I hope not."

"You bought that lighthouse." He made a clicking sound with his tongue, gave his head a shake, but other than that didn't break his stride or raise his head. "I found that surprising."

"So did I."

The old man did look up then. Sharply, quickly, scanning Duncan's face in one sweep of his pale eyes and then facing the sidewalk again.

"I bought it on impulse," Duncan explained. "I'm not sure why. As soon as I saw it, I knew I had to stay there."

"Mmm." Their shoes tapped in sync over the sidewalk. Passing traffic. Dry leaves rustling against bare limbs in the breeze. Silence.

"You regret it yet?" his father asked.

Duncan sent the man a sideways glance. "No. No, I don't."

"So you'll be staying around here for a while."

He thought of the woman. Raven. Tonight. "Yeah, I think so."

"Then I have a proposition for you." The old man paused and waved a hand. Duncan followed it to the square flat-topped building, made of deep gray stone blocks. Broad stone steps, with pillars top and bottom, led the way to the entry, which was by itself impressive with big, dark double doors attached with brass bells. "This is it."

It took Duncan a minute to process the announcement. "The old courthouse? The one you bought?"

Nodding, his father mounted the steps. "Come, I want you to see inside. My apartments are above, on the second floor, but it's the ground story you'll be interested in, Duncan. I've already acquired some of the most—" He broke off there, turning his key in the lock and swinging the doors wide, and Duncan joined him. "Here, see for yourself."

Duncan stepped inside. His father reached for a light switch, and then stood back and waited while Duncan's gaze skimmed the crates, the boxes, the odd items stacked hither and yon, the large wooden items standing in one corner of the room. Were those . . . were those *stocks*?

Finally his gaze fell on a sign. The Gothic letters printed in red on a black background read: YE OLDE WITCH MUSEUM.

He blinked. "What *is* all this?"

"Just what it looks like," his father said. "A tourist trap, but a money-maker, Duncan, I guarantee it."

"A *Witch* Museum?"

Nodding, his father moved around, touching first one box and crate and then another. "Torture devices, antique stocks, handwritten confessions—"

"And you don't think it's slightly morbid?"

"Ah, Duncan, don't be foolish. It's all in fun."

Gee, do you suppose it was fun *to the women who saw this stuff firsthand?*

"Besides," his father went on, "what do people come to this part of the country for, if not this? Why is Salem doing such a booming business, eh? This will succeed, Duncan, I'm sure of it." He slapped Duncan's shoulder—the most physical contact he'd made with his son in a dozen years. And as always, a shock of something like static electricity sparked where they made contact. Duncan stiffened, and pulled away instinctively. Oddly, it reminded him of the static he'd felt when the strange beauty touched him . . . and yet it had been different with her. Pleasant and exciting, rather than slightly repulsive the way it always was with the old man. Duncan had never understood it, and assumed he simply tended to conduct static more than most people.

His father's lips thinned for a moment. Then he acted as if nothing had happened. And nothing had. Nothing new, anyway. "I hoped we could work on it together. Partners. You and I."

Duncan lifted his head slowly to meet his father's eyes. "You . . . you want me as your partner?"

His father nodded. "Yes, son, I do. It will give us a chance to . . . well, to make up for the past. Time to get to know each other, the way we should have done long ago."

Duncan couldn't believe it. A lump came into his throat, but he swallowed it down. "I . . . I don't know what to say."

"I'm an old man, Duncan. When a man gets to be my age, he starts to think . . . starts to wish he'd done certain things in his life a little differently . . . starts to understand what's really important."

Nodding, Duncan had to look away. "I've waited a long time for a chance like this."

"Then take it, Duncan." His father's hand returned to his shoulder. Jolted him, then tightened there. "What do you say? Partners?"

Duncan faced his father and said nothing. How many times had his father made false starts like this? How many times had he seemed to want to get closer, only to pull away again, without explanation? And, God, even if he were sincere this time . . . something about the idea of putting these relics on display seemed crude. Repugnant, even.

"Duncan?"

"I . . . I don't know." *Say no*, some inner voice told him. And yet he wanted so much to be close to this cold man. Had wanted it for so long. "I . . . I'll think about it."

"That's good enough."

Good enough. When nothing Duncan had ever done had *ever* been good enough.

God Almighty, Duncan thought. Could this day *get* any stranger?

Chapter 14

"Raven."

I turned around, holding my hair to the back of my head in a temporary bundle and craning my neck to glimpse the effect in the mirror behind me. Then I frowned. "Maybe I should just leave it down."

"Raven—"

"What do you think, Arianna?" Letting my hair fall, finger combing it slightly, I arranged it over my shoulders. "Yes, I'll leave it down." With a firm nod I faced the four-poster bed and the clothing draped over every inch of the mattress and hanging from the foot. "I just wish I knew what to wear."

"Raven, will you stop for one minute and *listen* to me?"

Smiling—I hadn't been able to stop smiling since that morning—I faced Arianna. "This is all because of you, you know. If it hadn't been for your spell . . ." I closed my eyes, tipped my head back, and mentally saw my beloved Duncan again. "He looks just the same. It's as if . . . as if he never left me."

"No, Raven. It is *not* like that at all." Arianna stood close, gripped my shoulders, and the warm, familiar tingle passed from her body into mine as she stared hard into my eyes. "He *did* leave you. For you, everything seems the same, but it's not, love. Not for him."

I sighed softly. Poor Arianna, trying so hard to protect me from my own hopes and dreams. She just didn't understand. "I know he may not remember me now, but he will. And he'll love me again, and—"

"And how do you know it will happen that way?" she asked me.

I blinked. A finger of doubt crept into my brain, but I banished it. Ignored it. Pretended it didn't exist just as I'd been pretending all day.

Just as I'd been pretending for three hundred years.

I'd spent all this time waiting for his return—none of it pondering how things might have changed between us.

"It has to happen that way," I told her.

"Yes, that's just the way I was thinking, Raven, when I set out to find my little sister more than three centuries ago. But your reaction was quite different. Do you remember?"

I did remember. And the doubt in my heart grew larger. "But—"

"You thought I'd come to kill you. You drew your blade, Raven. You'd have fought me—perhaps to the death. To you I was a stranger. Nothing more."

My heart contracted at her words. Slowly I lowered my head. "You're right." Drawing a deep breath, I met her eyes. "But we're sisters again now, Arianna. Closer, even, than that."

"But our past together is just as gone. The life you led before is lost to you. You remember none of it. Not our father, a lowly saddle maker, nor our mother, nor our poor cottage in Stonehaven. Not the loch where we played . . ." She closed her eyes. "Our closeness now is based on this lifetime . . . we've built it together over centuries, Raven. It's strong, and it's real, but it's not the same. It can *never* be the same."

Turning slowly, eyes downcast, I felt tears well up and burn my eyes. "I . . . I hadn't thought . . ."

"I know. That's why I'm trying to *make* you think. Raven, Duncan may look the same, bear the same name, but he is *not* the same. To him, you're a beautiful stranger who kissed him on the street one day."

My head came up sharply. "*He* kissed *me*, too!"

"Of course he did. But, Raven, you could fling yourself into the arms of any red-blooded, heterosexual male and he would do the same. You're a beautiful woman. Duncan is a man."

"No," I said. Biting my lip, I paced to the bed, snatching up a dress, eyeing it through my tears. "There was something there, something between us, Arianna. I *felt* it."

"Yes. *You* felt it. But did *he*?"

The fabric of the dress crumpled in my fists, I slowly lifted my head, faced her, bit back a sob. "He . . . he doesn't love me?"

"He doesn't *know* you." Arianna came closer, took the dress gently from my hands, and laid it on the bed. Then she cupped my face and wiped my tears away with her thumbs. "I only want you to be aware . . . to be careful, darling. He'll fall in love with you again, I don't doubt it for a moment. But, Raven, he's going to need time. And so are you. Time to get to know him again. He might be very different from the man you remember. You might decide you don't even want—"

"I will never decide *that*!" I sniffed, brushing at my wet eyes. "I love him, Arianna. I will always love him."

"I know," she said softly. Turning, she fingered the clothes on the bed, pausing on a sheer, soft dress of ivory silk. "This one, I think." She gathered the dress up, draped it gently over my arm. "It won't be easy for him, you know. He's going to have a lot to deal with, when you tell him. He's immortal now, Raven. A High Witch like us, with maybe no clue that he has some fledgling powers coming to life inside him. You must remember what a shock learning of your own nature was to you, how difficult it was to accept, to understand."

"I remember." I let the robe I wore fall from my shoulders to the floor, then pulled the dress over my head. But the bubbling excitement I'd felt all day ebbed now. I was suddenly unsure, afraid. What if Duncan . . . what if he never loved me again?

"Be gentle when you tell him. Go slowly, love. Slowly." She guided me to the mirror, lifted a brush to my hair, and smoothed it with long, soothing strokes. "And don't expect too much all at once."

I nodded, staring at Arianna's reflection beside mine in the mirror. We stood in sharp contrast to each other, she so fair with her sunshine hair, cropped short around her face. With her pixielike features and huge brown eyes. Me, so dark, long ebony curls, jet-black eyes and lashes and brows.

"It must have hurt you, all those years ago," I said. "To find me and realize I had no memory of you."

She nodded. "I don't know what I was expecting. An emotional reunion, I suppose. If I'd given it any thought I'd have realized that wasn't going to happen."

I turned toward her. "But it *did*. You *are* my sister, Arianna. You're the sister of my soul. And while my mind may not remember our past together . . . my heart has never forgotten. The feelings live on there."

She dipped her head, shielding her eyes from me. "Truly?"

"Oh, yes. Truly."

Lifting her head, smiling and misty-eyed, she hugged me tight. "I do love you, little sister."

"And I you," I told her.

Finally she stepped away, looking me up and down. "Well, put your shoes on and go, then. This man of yours has kept you waiting quite long enough, don't you think?"

I nodded emphatically. "More than long enough," I told her.

Duncan paced. He wore jeans. Jeans should be okay, right? They were the all-purpose, fit-for-any-occasion uniform of the twentieth century, after all. He hoped jeans were all right.

He hoped she'd come. She said she would, but any woman crazy enough to kiss a man she didn't even know in broad daylight on a busy street might not be too good at keeping her word. Or even remembering she'd given it.

No. She'd come. And who was he kidding, anyway? There was more going on here—with him, with her, with *them*—than just an impulsive kiss on a busy street.

It *had* been a busy street. Too busy.

And that was part of it, the way she held up her hand and that truck skidded to the side like it had been pushed there. That was . . . that was . . .

That was nothing. The driver must have locked up his brakes and jerked the wheel. That was all. It was nothing.

But she knew his name. She knew his name, and then there was *her* name. Raven. And he'd been collecting ravens all his life, been fascinated by them. Had books on them, paintings of them, and miniatures everywhere. Wooden ravens, stone ravens, cheap plastic dime-store models, and some made of glass. The large one, carved of pure black onyx, that was his favorite. Three hundred bucks he'd paid for that bird, even while asking himself why the hell any sane man would plunk down that kind of cash for a hunk of rock. He looked at it now, perched on a pedestal table all its own like a queen holding court. His fingers stroked its cool hard feathers.

But that was beside the point. Her *name* was *Raven*. And *that* was . . . weird. Not to mention that since he'd come here there had been real ravens stalking him. Okay, not stalking him, but he'd sure as hell seen more of the big black birds perched around this lighthouse than he'd ever seen in one place in his whole life.

Oh, but there was more. There was *her*. The obsession he'd had with her since that first time he'd laid eyes on her, over there on the cliffs, doing whatever it was she did on full-moon nights.

And she knew his name.

He felt nervous and jittery, and not like himself at all. He kept fighting smiles and warm, fuzzy emotions and even a tear or two, and he didn't know why. He felt as if he'd stepped out of reality and into the Twilight Zone.

The soft hum of a motor jerked him back to himself, and he braced his hands on the sill to stare out the window. Then he tensed. The small johnboat came closer, and he peered, squinted. She sat in the stern, one hand on the outboard motor's rudder. She wore white, or off-white. Something soft and flowing. It rippled with the breeze as the boat came closer. And then she steered toward shore and cut the motor. Tipped it up, so its prop rose from the water, dripping beads of the sea back into itself. The boat moved forward of its own momentum for another second or two, stopping only when its nose scraped along the shore. And then she was stepping out.

So graceful, he thought. She didn't even get her feet wet.

She bent at the bow and gave the boat a tug to pull it more securely onto dry land. Then, turning, she faced the lighthouse. He should have gone out to help her. Some gentleman he was, standing here gawking at her while she manhandled the boat on her own. Not that it had seemed to give her any problem. She must be stronger than she looked.

His throat was dry. His stomach, queasy. She started forward, and he turned, went to the door, opened it, and stood there wondering what was happening to his stable, boring life. His solitary, predictable, lonely life.

And then she was standing there, facing him, looking uncertain, a little afraid, utterly beautiful, and he knew that old life was gone forever. Nothing would ever be the same again. Why he knew it, or how, didn't matter. It was real, gut deep, and true. Telling himself it made no sense didn't negate that certainty in the least.

"Hello again," she said.

Was that a slight waver he detected in her voice?

"I'm . . . glad you came." Or was he? Yeah. He was. "Come in." He stepped aside to let her pass, holding the door for her. She moved past him. The front door led directly to the main room, which he'd made into a living room for himself. A curved sofa fit perfectly to one concave wall.

Above it the windows looked out on the sea, on the cliffs and her home beyond them. No curtains. He hadn't wanted anything blocking his view.

But she wasn't looking at the view, or even at the paint cans and tarps, or the stepladder in the corner. She was looking at the birds. Staring at them, one by one, blinking, and then turning to him with a question in her eyes.

"Yes," he said, wondering just how much of himself he wanted to reveal to her. Wondering if he even had a choice about that. "They're ravens. I've been collecting them since I was a kid."

Her lower lip trembled. She caught it in her teeth.

"Quite a coincidence, isn't it?"

Meeting his eyes, holding them with some kind of magnetic force he couldn't resist and didn't want to, she shook her head, first to one side, then the other. "I don't believe in coincidence."

He shivered. "What, then?"

Licking her lips, she lowered her head, freeing him at last to look away. But he found he didn't want to. "I don't want to frighten you, Duncan," she said very slowly, and it seemed she chose each word with great care. "But there *are* things you need to know. Things I have to tell you."

He nodded. "Like . . . how you knew my name, for example."

"Yes."

"It all sounds very mystical."

"Some might call it that."

"I think you should know I'm pretty much a skeptic where anything . . . you know . . . *flaky* is concerned."

A tiny frown knit her brow as she tilted her head. A look so startlingly familiar it hit him like a blow to the solar plexus and took his breath away.

"Flaky?"

"Paranormal." He waggled his fingers in front of him. "Supernatural."

"Oh. Well, that's all right. It's all quite . . . *natural*, Duncan. It's just that most people don't know . . . or understand it."

"But you do?"

She nodded.

They were still standing in the middle of the room, facing each other. He didn't know what to do with his hands, so he stuck them in his pockets. "Why don't you sit down. You want some coffee or a beer or—"

"No, thank you." She sat. On the sofa. And now he had to go and sit beside her. There was a tension between them, something that made his skin tingle and his nerves jump. Something that made him want to touch her, pull her closer. If he sat down next to her, it would be hard not to.

"Well, *I* want a beer," he said. And he fled into the kitchenette. Not much of a kitchenette so far, actually. Just a mini-fridge, a card table with a hot plate on top, two folding chairs, and a couple of boxes full of supplies. And tools. There were tools everywhere. He took a beer out of the fridge, popped the top, and went back in to join her.

She'd turned sideways on the couch, one leg folded beneath her, arm resting on the back as she stared out the window. She didn't turn to face him when he came in. "What made you buy this place?" she asked.

"The view." He blurted it before he thought better of it.

Turning, she smiled gently, a tremulous little smile that he suspected contained a wealth of emotions, though he couldn't guess what they might be. "You're fond of the sea, then?"

"Actually, I've always pretty much detested it." Safe subject. His personal neuroses never failed to cool things down with women, whether he intended them to or not. He usually kept them to himself. This time, though, he needed things to cool down a little. Maybe if she thought he was nuts . . . hell, they'd be pretty much even then, wouldn't they?

He sat down, took a long pull from his can. "I've had a fear of water since I was a kid. Even baths were a major trauma when I was real young."

She didn't look as if she thought he was nuts. Instead she nodded. "Yes, I can see why."

"Funny. I never could." He lifted the can to his lips.

"Heights, too, I'll bet?"

His hand froze with the can in midair. He blinked slowly, said nothing, and then took a larger gulp of the cool brew than he'd intended.

Licking her lips, she went on. "But you moved into a lighthouse, on an island, despite your dislike of water. And all because of the view?"

He lowered his head. "Sounds pretty crazy, doesn't it?"

"No. There's a reason for it. For all of it."

He took another sip of beer before facing her again. "And you know what it is?"

She nodded.

"Well? Don't keep me in suspense, Raven. I'm dying to hear your theory."

Drawing a deep breath, she lifted her chin. "You've lived before."

Ahhh, so that was it. She was some kind of a psychic, or considered herself one. Well, it was interesting, if not exactly earth-shattering.

"You were born over three hundred years ago, in Scotland. Later you lived in England, where you were studying for the priesthood. And then—"

He choked on his beer, set the can down, and swiped his mouth. "The priesthood," he repeated. "Me."

"Yes. But you gave it up and came here. You lived right here in Sanctuary. And when you died . . ." She closed her eyes. "You died right there," she whispered, pointing. "On the rocks below those cliffs you can see so clearly from this window. And that's probably why you came into this lifetime with a fear of the water, and of heights, and part of the reason why the view from these windows affects you so deeply."

Her words made his stomach cramp and turn, and his spine tingle, and his jaw clench. But they were utterly ridiculous, and there was no reason in the world he should feel any reaction at all.

"Next you'll tell me that we knew each other in this . . . past life."

She got to her feet. The ivory dress slid down her legs, brushing her calves. The light was behind her, and he could see her silhouette through the soft fabric. And that feeling, that craving he had no business feeling, stirred to life in him all over again. Then he realized she was crying. Not noisily. She wasn't a noisy crier, he suspected. It was just one silent tear, glimmering on her cheek.

He rose, too, and touched that tear, absorbed it into his fingertip. "I wasn't making fun," he told her.

"But you don't believe me."

"I told you I was a skeptic." When she would have turned away, he touched her shoulders, gently keeping her there, facing him. "Why does any of it have to matter, Raven? I like you. I'd . . . like to get to know you. Can't we forget about all this hocus-pocus stuff and just be two people who just met? Two people who . . . maybe . . . could feel something for each other, given time? Hmm?"

She seemed to search his face. "It would be easier, maybe, if we could. But there's more, Duncan. So much more. And it does matter . . . especially to you."

He shook his head. "It really doesn't matter in the least to me. But it does to you, doesn't it?"

"It does. To both of us." She cleared her throat. "We . . . were . . . you and I were . . ."

Frowning, he probed those black eyes of hers. "Lovers?" he asked her.

"Oh, Duncan, it was so much more than that. So very much more. When you held me, touched me, it was a kind of magick beyond anything I'd ever felt. And it was the same for you, I know it was. . . ." She bit her lip as if to stop the words.

Too late, though. That irrational desire for her was sizzling through him now, and no amount of reasoning would vanquish it. "I suppose that would explain," he whispered, and he let his hands slide from her shoulders, down her arms, and to her waist, "why I want you so badly right now."

He leaned down, and he kissed her. Tentatively, lightly, so that she could object if she wanted to. The power of his attraction to her . . . was that what made such a jolting awareness between them? Was it something chemical? Something physical?

She didn't object. Her lips formed his name against his, and then she melted into his arms. Her mouth parted, her arms twisted around his neck, and she kissed him back.

Warm, she was so warm, and soft, and her taste was like a drug that he couldn't quite get enough of. He bent over her, deepening the kiss, hands at the small of her back holding her close, then burying themselves in her hair, and then slipping lower again while his tongue dove into her mouth. He gathered the dress up until he could touch her bare thighs, run his palms over them. Heat met his hands. Her skin seemed to be burning him. Fevered . . . for him. And when he explored the soft mound of her buttocks and found it bare, he knew this was what she'd come here for. He cupped her there, squeezed her and pulled her hips tight to his. The soft sound she made was like a plea.

So he turned her, and scooped her into his arms. He kept marauding her succulent mouth as he carried her up the curving stairs to the bedroom above. Glass all around . . . the old light in the center, and the mattress on the floor. It was all he had here . . . all he'd needed. Until now. Now he needed something more, and it was a need more powerful than any he'd felt in his life.

He laid her on the mattress, knelt beside her, and peeled the dress away. And then he looked at her.

There was no shyness in her, none of the first-time nervousness other women had displayed. She lay still, proud and naked and utterly beautiful. He stripped off his shirt and tossed it aside.

Her soft small breasts rose and fell with every breath, quivered with every heartbeat. Their centers like sweetmeats, dark, dusky rose, their peaks hard, elongated, expectant. He bent over her slowly, saw her close her eyes, arch her back. And when his mouth hovered a hairsbreadth from her, she clasped his head and pulled him down, until he took her nipple in his mouth and suckled, and nipped, and tugged at it. Then he moved away, stretching his body out alongside hers, twisting his arms around her slender waist, pulling her against him. Her breasts against his naked chest, her body tight to his, her longing as intense as his was as he kissed her again.

Rocking his hips against her, he muttered, "God, lass, it's been so long," and was barely aware of his own words as he reached for the button of his jeans.

A buzz made him pause. He closed his eyes, sighed in agony as the sound grew louder. Another boat. Dammit, who the hell could be coming out here now?

He met her eyes as the sound grew louder and then died. Someone was here. No question. And his own little launch sat outside, so they'd know he must be home. Suddenly protective of her, he reached for a blanket, drew it to cover her even as he got to his feet.

"I'm sorry," he whispered. "God, you have no idea *how* sorry. But I'll get rid of them. I'll be back."

I knew it would be a mistake to let him make love to me. But how could I resist him? How could I resist my own burning need to hold him inside me again, after all this time? I craved him just as I had before . . . no, even more so. I loved him. I loved him, and none of the things Arianna said made a difference in that.

He trotted down the stairs, pulling on his shirt. I heard his steps cross the floor, and the creak of those hinges as the door swung open. And then I heard him say, "What in the world are you doing out here?"

Curious, and suddenly sure he wouldn't be returning as quickly as he'd promised, I pulled my dress on, and found my shoes, which I'd kicked off at some point. One lay in one direction, one in another. I slipped them on, then crept to the stairs. Then down them. I was quiet, not wanting to interrupt Duncan and his guest, just eager to glimpse the visitor.

At the bottom of the stairs I paused. I could see through the main room to the door at the far end from here, and so far, I remained unnoticed.

But as Duncan spoke, the other man's head came up. He met my eyes, finding me there unerringly, as if he'd known exactly where I was. And my blood rushed to my feet. Dizziness swamped me, and I nearly lost my balance. Because the man I hated above all others, the man who had tried to kill me more times than I could count over the centuries, *Nathanial Dearborne*, was staring back at me, and the message in his eyes was clear. He meant to have my heart this time.

And just when I thought my shock and surprise had reached the precipice of a dozen lifetimes, I heard the words that chilled me to the bone.

Duncan said, "Come in, Father."

Chapter 15

I stepped off the bottom step and darted to the side, out of their sight. Pushing open the first window I came to, I rapidly clambered outside. What was wrong with me? Was I a fool? I hadn't even brought my dagger tonight! It was at home, tucked away in a drawer in my bedroom, and I was helpless. A sheep awaiting the slaughter. How many times had Arianna told me I must carry it with me always? *Always!*

I ran to my small boat, shoved it away, and then leaped inside. Taking the oars from the floor, I dipped them, and stroked with all my strength. The craft shot away.

And then I paused, looking back. What about Duncan? What if it were him Nathanial was after?

But no. Duncan had called the man Father.

Father.

I shuddered again, sick to my soul. But how, why? And was Duncan safe?

I closed my eyes, searched my mind, sought the wisdom of the ancient Witches whose blood flowed in my veins. If Nathanial meant to have Duncan's heart, he'd have had it by now. Duncan never would have lived to reach adulthood. It was obviously something else the bastard was after.

Me. It was me. He must have known that if he remained close to Duncan, he'd find me, eventually. And suddenly I knew with great clarity exactly what Dearborne intended. I knew it as surely as I'd known Duncan when I'd seen him again standing on the sidewalk in town. He would use Duncan . . . to get to me. But once he took my heart, his need of his *son* would be as dead as my lifeless corpse would be. He might very well intend to kill Duncan, too. But only after he'd cut the living heart from *my* chest.

There was only one thing for me to do. Kill him. Kill him before he could hurt Duncan.

I would not again be the cause of my lover's death. Not again.

"It's really not a good time, Father."

"No? And why not?" His father stepped inside, pulling the door closed behind him and idly stroking the antique dagger he insisted on carrying. He'd had that thing belted to his hip for as long as Duncan could remember. But then, his father had always been fascinated with antiques. His collection of obscure books on the occult was probably the largest around. Nathanial loved things salvaged from the past. Duncan figured the dagger must be his favorite piece. That he likely treasured it the way Duncan treasured his own onyx raven.

Raven.

He glanced uneasily toward the stairs. But the sound of a motor drew his head back around. He ran to the window, to look out, only to see Raven's small boat churning steadily away from the island, heading toward the rocky shore. "Damn."

His father looked over his shoulder. "Who . . . ?"

"A girl. A strange, beautiful girl. I can't believe she left like that."

"I should apologize. I didn't know you had . . . company."

Duncan eyed his father then, immediately doubting the man. Her boat had been right outside, after all, and . . . No. He'd never build a relationship with his father if he kept doubting every word the man said.

"It's all right. I'm sure I'll see her again." With a longing glance through the windows, he sighed and told himself to focus on the *other* stranger in his life. His father. "You want a beer?"

"Only if you have no wine."

"I detest wine." He headed into the kitchen, bit his lip, then turned to look back into the living room and forced a smile. "I'll make a point to buy some, though." It felt fake, this jovial attitude. This farce of friendship. And it hurt to realize just how strained things between him and the old man had become. God, could this ever work? Or was it too late?

Maybe, Duncan thought, it was too late a long time ago.

His throat tightened on that thought. He grated his teeth and re-solved to give it a chance. Again. One last time.

When he joined his father with a beer—in a glass, in deference to Nathanial's sensibilities—he found the old man holding one of the miniature ravens in his hands. The tip of his thumb kept running across the bird's wooden breast. It gave Duncan a chill, though he couldn't say why. He had to resist the urge to snatch his treasure away and replace it lovingly in its spot. But his hands itched to do just that.

Instead he held out the beer.

Clutching the bird too tightly in one hand, his father took the glass with the other. "So tell me about this mysterious beauty. Are you . . . in-volved with her?"

"I just met her."

"Really? You'll have to introduce me sometime."

No way in hell.

And just where did *that* thought come from?

"Maybe. Sometime," he said. "But right now, I'd rather talk about why you're here."

Nathanial shrugged. "Can't a father visit his son without a reason?" He set the bird down carelessly, and it tipped onto its side with a clunk that set Duncan's teeth on edge.

Instinctively he reached for it, set it upright in the spot where it be-longed. As he did, he stroked its back, almost as if he were soothing it. As if it were real. Man, he *was* losing it.

"I'd like you to come to the courthouse—er, that is, the museum to-morrow."

"Oh?"

Nathanial nodded, his pale blue eyes skimming the furniture, the floor, lighting, everywhere but on Duncan. "I've already taken care of most of the paperwork involved. Acquired the proper permits, and so on. There's still the advertising to be done, but that won't be a problem. Still, Duncan, there are physical aspects to this project that a man of . . . of my age—"

"Oh." Was this his father? The cold, brutally independent, utterly se-cretive man he knew, asking for his help? "Look, I'm not real comfort-able with this Witch Museum idea," Duncan began.

"I know, you made that clear this morning. Still, there are all those crates to unpack, you know. The sign to hang. Shelves to be assembled and placed. All of that."

And maybe *that* was why he'd asked Duncan to be his partner. He could handle the business end himself, and money was no problem. So all he wanted was a strong body for the grunt work.

Duncan frowned, looking away. He was jumping to conclusions. Judging Nathanial according to the pattern he'd set in the past. If this "one more try" routine were going to have any chance of working, he'd have to try to curb that tendency. But hell, old habits died hard.

"Besides," Nathanial went on, "if you do decide to be my partner, I'll want your input on things." He looked at Duncan's face, very briefly. Not his eyes, just his face. "I do hope it doesn't upset you that I've done so much of the early work already."

"No, of course not." So maybe it *wasn't* just a set of strong arms the old man wanted. A spark of hope flared in Duncan's chest. A tiny kernel of belief in the man he'd always *wanted* to believe in.

"We need a gimmick," his father said. "A hook to draw in the tourists for the grand opening."

Duncan lowered his head. Part of him was ready to agree, while the other part grimaced in distaste. And still another part warned him not to hope for too much where his father was concerned.

Slowly he said, "I suppose if I *were* going to get involved in this—and I'm not saying I am—but if I were, I might suggest Halloween for the grand opening."

Nathanial slapped his knee, sloshing beer from his glass onto the couch cushion. "There, you see! That's the kind of brilliant idea I'd hoped you'd generate. It's perfect. The holiday most sacred to Witches, as the grand opening of the Witch Museum."

Duncan felt the blood leave his face. "I didn't realize . . ."

"It's perfect," Nathanial said again.

"No, Dad, it's not. Look, it was a bad idea. I spoke without thinking it through. Given the origins of the holiday . . . hell, it would be offensive."

"Nonsense. It's the perfect date, I tell you."

"You don't think it's like opening a Nazi war crimes museum during Passover?"

"Not at all!" Nathanial rubbed his chin. "I hope we can be ready, though. It's only a couple of weeks away."

His father's face seemed more animated to Duncan than it ever had as he talked about his plans—talked about *their* plans. It didn't *feel* right, this idea of a museum devoted to relics of the Witch trials. Not that he knew much about the subject. But it sent an odd feeling up his spine to think about it.

Yet, his father was speaking to him as if he gave a damn—for the first time in Duncan's memory. Besides, he hadn't even seen the items to be put on display yet. Maybe it wouldn't be as bad as he thought.

He . . . hoped not.

Who was he kidding? He'd seen enough. Those stocks.

"I can't be your partner, Father. It doesn't mean we can't try to work on things, but—"

"Does it mean you can't help an old man unpack a few crates?"

Sighing, Duncan shook his head. "No, it doesn't mean that, either. I'll help with the heavy work, all right?"

"Wonderful. Wonderful. As I said, there are the shelves and the sign, and . . ."

Duncan turned, barely hearing the animated buzz of his father's voice now, as he gazed across the water to the mainland. It was too dark to see the cove far to the west of the cliffs, where Raven kept the small boat. There must be a path from there up to the house atop the cliffs. Perhaps he'd walk it one day soon.

He had to see her again. He knew that much. Crazy or not, he couldn't seem to shake the woman's image from his mind. And even if it turned out she was a raving lunatic, he had a feeling it would always be this way.

When I slammed the front door, Arianna leaped off the sofa, as startled as if a gunshot had gone off beside her ear. One hand pressed to her chest, she drew a deep breath and stared wide-eyed at me. "What in the name of the Gods are you trying to do, *scare* the heart out of me?"

I met her brown eyes, and she stared into mine. And then her face changed. She came forward, one hand going to my shoulder. "What is it? What's wrong?"

Lifting my chin, I swallowed hard. "Nathanial Dearborne," I told her.

The roses drained from her cheeks. "You've *seen* him?"

I closed my eyes. "Oh, Arianna, what am I going to do? I didn't expect this! Even *he* couldn't be this clever, this low, as to set himself up as . . . as . . . Sweet Goddess, I can't even say it."

Gripping my shoulders, she steered me backward to the velvet settee in the Edwardian parlor. I went easily, my bones like water.

"Go on," she whispered. "Tell me what he's done."

I met her eyes, but they swam in my tear-hazy vision. "I don't even know. I only know I was with Duncan, at the lighthouse, when Dearborne came to the door. And when he opened it . . ." I bit my lip, shook my head in reborn disbelief. "Duncan called him *father*, Arianna."

"*What?*"

I nodded, reaffirming what I'd said. "I don't know how, but that beast has managed to set himself up as Duncan's father. And Arianna, I think . . . I think he was planning all along to use Duncan to get to me."

"That's impossible. Raven, listen to what you're saying. No Witch, neither Light nor Dark, could manage a spell so powerful. To choose the soul who would incarnate as his own child . . . It can't be done."

I met her gaze, my own narrow. "So you believe it's coincidence?"

Arianna lowered her head, shook it. "Of course not. It can't be that, but there's simply no way Nathanial could have . . ." And then her head came up again, slowly. "Unless . . ."

"Unless?"

"Do you suppose Duncan is Dearborne's *adopted* son?"

I blinked. "That's it. It has to be."

"And if that's true, then you're right. It has all been a part of Dearborne's plan to get to you. Otherwise he'd have killed Duncan by now. He has to know the man is immortal."

"Oh, he knows." I got to my feet, too upset to sit still when every nerve in my body seemed to be squirming. "He knew Duncan would find his way to me again, one day. Somehow, he knew."

Pushing both hands through her hair, Arianna paced away from me. "This is not good."

"And *that's* an understatement."

"What are you going to do, Raven?"

I faced her. "What choice do I have, Arianna? I'm going to kill Nathanial Dearborne."

She gripped my shoulders. "Oh, no. Not so fast, my friend. In the first place, if you murder the man Duncan thinks of as his father, he is going to hate you."

"That's just a chance I'll have to take. Dearborne is out for my heart, Arianna, and you must realize that once he has it, Duncan's could easily be next."

"I know, I know, but—"

"Then what would you suggest I do? Wait for him to attack? Let *him* decide when and where and how it will be? No. My best advantage will be to surprise him. He won't be expecting me to make the first move."

"That's because he thinks you have half a brain, Raven." I scowled at her. "You can't beat him." She stated it flatly, dropped it as if it were a proven fact, with no room for doubt. "You know it, *I* certainly know it, having faced the man in battle myself . . . and Nathanial Dearborne knows it. You won't stand a chance."

"You told me I was as good as you now."

"I lied."

I blew a sigh and turned away.

"Let me do it, Raven," she said.

I stiffened and stopped in my tracks. "You didn't lie," I said very slowly. "I am as good as you. You're trying to protect me."

"Duncan can't blame you if I'm the one who does it."

I went to her, took her hands in mine firmly, and made my gaze as penetrating as I could. "I won't let you fight him for me, Arianna. You beat him once, yes, but that was centuries ago. There's no way to be certain you could do it again. He's had time to improve."

"So have I," she said.

"And so have I. The difference is, this is my battle, not yours, Arianna."

She averted her eyes, but they slid back to mine. She understood, I knew she did. Didn't want to accept it, but she would. I knew her well enough to know that.

"If you insist on fighting him yourself, Raven, then please, please wait. Put it off, just for a little while."

"Why?" My suspicion had to come through in my voice.

"Not to give me a chance to do it for you, love. But . . . because there might still be a way out of it. If there is, you should take it, because if you fight him, you'll die."

"He's going to force me to face him sooner or later, Arianna."

"If you die . . . Duncan might be next. You said it yourself."

I couldn't reply to that. She was right, and there was nothing else for me to say. "So I put it off, if I can. But what if there *is* no way out of this? How is delaying it going to help matters then?"

"The delay will give us time, Raven. Time to find out exactly what his plans are, maybe what his strengths and weaknesses are, as well. And knowledge is power."

I nodded, hesitantly, but even so I couldn't deny the relief I felt in knowing I wouldn't have to face Nathanial right away. Unless he attacked me.

"You'll have to avoid him. And in the meantime, you can work on making Duncan see him for what he really is. So if you do manage to survive the battle, he won't hold it against you."

"Do you really think that's possible?"

"Anything's possible. Including your winning this thing. If we work very hard between now and then. Are you willing?"

"Work is something I'm entirely willing to do—if it will help me rid the world of that bastard."

"No time like the present," Arianna said. There was a familiar hiss as she drew her blade and faced me, dropping into a ready crouch. "Let's get to it."

Sighing softly, I felt my lips pull into a reluctant smile. "Damn," I whispered. "You can make me smile no matter how bad things get, you know that?"

"Don't smile," she said, though she was disobeying her own order even as she said it. "Fight."

So we fought.

Arianna and I walked side by side along the route that led through the center of Sanctuary the next day. All but invisible, or we tried to be. We'd honed our talent for blending in with our surroundings, drawing so little notice we might as well have been invisible—one of the skills we'd learned from Trees Speaking long ago. Invisibility, he'd taught us, was not a physical state, but a mental one. It came in handy when one needed anonymity. And an immortal Witch living in a mortal world always needed that.

"Did you learn anything at the café?" I asked softly, leaning close to her.

"My waitress—Shelly, the redhead—said she didn't recognize the name, but that *someone* had recently moved into the old courthouse building on Main."

I nodded. "Jeremy at the herb store heard that someone was converting the courthouse building into some kind of museum."

Arianna frowned. "That makes no sense. Why would Dearborne want a museum?"

I shrugged. "One way to find out."

She nodded in agreement and we turned at the corner, walked to the old courthouse building, a truly lovely structure. I remembered when it had been built just over a century ago, all the hoopla of the brass band playing as the mayor cut a ribbon and the townsfolk applauded. Women in layered skirts and bonnets. Whiskered men in bowler hats. Children in knickers, pushing hoops with sticks.

Arianna's arm came across my middle to stop me, so I bumped into it with my next step, then paused to look at her. "Look," she said, pointing.

I did. And saw the two of them, Nathanial smiling in that frozen way he had, so that it didn't look like a smile at all, but an icy grimace suitable for a Halloween mask. And Duncan, looking slightly confused, a bit uncertain, but so hopeful.

Of what, I wondered?

My heart felt as if it were in the grip of a large, contracting fist, just for a moment. It did every time I looked at Duncan. I could still barely believe I'd finally found him again. After all this time.

My narrow gaze returned to Dearborne. The man who would try to tear us apart all over again.

"We'll wait," Arianna said, drawing me with her toward the park, just across the little circle that made up the center of Sanctuary. There was a fountain in the center of the circle, pavement all around it. This was the point of the teardrop-shaped Coast Road. From here, the road ran out along the northern edge of the peninsula, broadening, circling around near our home on the very tip, and then running along the southern coast all the way back to this very spot. From here one could also head northwest, back into the mainland.

We sat down on a bench near the fountain—a piece I'd always found vaguely distasteful. A scene of a group of Puritans gathered round their preacher, a mean-looking fellow, book in one hand, the other one pointing skyward. It was sculpted in bronze. The water flowed up through its base and cascaded down several levels to pool at the bottom.

"What, exactly, are we waiting for?" I asked, staring back toward the courthouse.

"For them to leave," she said. "We'll take a look inside when they do."

"They'll lock it up."

"Not if we make them forget to." Arianna turned halfway to study the fountain. "Does this guy remind you of anyone?" She tipped her head toward the bronze preacher.

"Arianna, that's manipulative magick and you know it."

"Ah, but with harm to none," she told me. "And you didn't answer my question."

I glanced at the sculpture. "Certainly not Duncan," I told her. "He never looked like that. So haughty and threatening. When he wore the robes of clergy, they seemed more like blankets than bronze. Inviting, warm. Safe."

She sighed, lowering her head. "You really do still love him, don't you?"

"You know I do."

I met her eyes, and Arianna pitched a penny into the well, making a wish in silence. "I wasn't talking about Duncan, anyway," she said softly. "Look at the eyes, the belly. No doubt the artist underplayed its true girth. Look at the jowls, Raven."

I did, and then my own eyes widened. "My goodness, you're right. He resembles Elias Stanton!"

Laughing, Arianna got to her feet, turning to face the sculpture. "Hello, Elias, you filthy old pig. Did some Witch get angry enough to turn you to bronze, I wonder?"

"Oh, what a thought," I said. But on looking, even I wondered if it could be true, though I'd certainly never heard of a Witch, even an immortal High Witch, with that kind of power. Still, the resemblance was uncanny. And in a moment I was laughing, too.

And then the courthouse doors swung open, and Duncan emerged, his father behind him.

We sat down at once, as if on cue, and I focused my attention on the color and texture of the bench. Sun-bleached granite, hard and cool, slightly rough. Focus, focus, until my body seemed to soften, and to blend in with the bench on which I sat.

Arianna's gaze remained on the two men while I did this, and I knew she was willing them to leave the door unlocked. Sending her thoughts, though gently. If she were too obvious, too aggressive, Nathanial might well sense her thoughts. If she were too gentle, on the other hand, he would be unaffected. If she were perfect, "thinking" at him with just the right amount of force, he'd simply forget to lock the door.

Seconds later Nathanial and Duncan came down the steps and toward us. Arianna put her back to the fountain, and she, too, went still and quiet and granitelike. Sinking into the granite, my body melding, it seemed, with the stuff, I watched as Duncan and his father approached us and kept on walking, passing within five yards of where we sat and never even noticing we were there.

When they were out of sight, I pulled myself from the heavy, slumberous pose of stone as if waking from a short nap. I drew a breath, wondered if I'd breathed during that time. Granite benches didn't, so I might have forgotten to myself.

"All right," Arianna said. "Let's go."

"I don't like this."

"Oh, for heaven's sake, do we want to know what's going on in there or not?"

"Well, yes, but—"

"Then come on!" She took my hand, and together we crossed the curved portion of street and headed up the courthouse steps. Arianna gripped the ornate doorknob, gave it a twist. "Unlocked. Lord and Lady, I *am* good." She pushed the door open, and the next thing I knew, we were standing inside.

It was a large room, the entry hall. Towering vaulted ceiling and gleamingly finished cherry woodwork everywhere. On the floor were boxes and crates in various shapes and sizes. Standing hither and yon were small stands and shelves, some assembled, some still in pieces.

And in one corner a large, old object that made me gasp and look again. Old, rough wood, rusted hinges. Stocks.

My stomach convulsed a little, and I gripped Arianna's hand, squeezed it, and inclined my head so she'd see them as well.

"That vile bastard," she whispered. "Look, Raven." And as I met her gaze, *she* nodded toward something. So I turned.

The huge sign, elaborately painted in elegant Gothic letters of black on a shining red background, stood upright, propped against a pair of crates. It read: Ye Olde Witch Museum.

But it got worse. Underneath in smaller block letters it went on: Genuine relics from witch trials around the world.

Bile rose in my throat. For a moment I neither moved nor breathed.

Arianna had no such reaction. She bent over the nearest box, tearing the cover off and pushing aside the protective paper. "Candleholders," she said. "A pentacle, a staff . . . my Goddess, they have some Witch's *staff*. And there's more. Shackles, fire irons . . . Raven, these are instruments of *torture*."

Shaking my head from side to side, I, too, opened a box. "Diaries," I said, gently opening the cover of one such book, so old and fragile its pages were like butterfly wings. "Oh, no, it's a *grimoire*. And there's an athame, and . . . and a cauldron." I closed my hands around the small, stout iron pot, with its three squatty legs, lifted it, and saw the rose painstakingly painted by hand on the front. "No," I whispered. "No, not this." Tears burned in my eyes, and anger rose to overwhelm the sickness all of this brought upon me, as I stared for the first time in well over three centuries at my mother's own sacred cauldron. It had been taken with every other possession when the villagers—or *someone*—had ransacked our home in England.

My fury, my outrage, became a deep buzz in my ears, and a red haze formed before my eyes, so that I didn't even hear the sounds of Duncan and his father opening the front door.

Not until Nathanial Dearborne said, "Oh, good. Trespassers."

Chapter 16

Duncan stood in the huge arching doorway, not sure what to think, much less what to say. Raven St. James stood facing him, one of his father's antiques in her hands. A pot of some kind. Stout black iron, encircled by slender, pale fingers that moved restlessly over its surface. Red nails, glossy red, and smooth, and he thought of fire. Wondered if it showed when his blood heated, and quickly lifted his gaze.

She wasn't looking at him, though, and that surprised him. Instead, she stared at his father, and the hatred in her eyes was second only to the horror he saw there. Potent emotions that shook him. Then they worried him.

Beside her was her blond pixie of a friend, who didn't look any more amused than Raven did. Unlike Raven, though, *she* hadn't lost the power of speech.

"I didn't see any signs," she said softly. "Last I knew, the courthouse was public property. Besides, the door was unlocked."

"It's not public property anymore," Nathanial said, and he spoke softly, his voice odd. Challenging. A dangerous edge to it and a frisson of something he couldn't hide. Something that sounded a lot like fear.

Duncan felt the tension in the room, thick enough to slice through, but he didn't know why.

"It's privately owned now," Nathanial went on. "And you know that."

"Ease up, Father," Duncan said sharply. He didn't know what the hell Raven and her friend were doing in here, but he didn't like the edge to Nathanial's voice. "They said they didn't know."

"They knew," Nathanial said.

"Oh? And are you a mind reader?" the blonde asked, glancing down at the wooden sign on the floor. "What's the meaning of this?"

"I think it's fairly self-explanatory. It's a museum. We're going to open it on Halloween—or, um, should I say, *Samhain*?"

The blonde gasped. Raven's eyes went wider and her lips parted. Her words were spoken so softly it was as if they emerged without a single breath pushing them. "Even *you* couldn't be this vile, Nathanial Dearborne."

"Wait a minute," Duncan said in confusion. "You two *know* each other?"

Nathanial didn't look at him. Neither did Raven. The blonde only glanced his way briefly, then focused on the other two again, her gaze nervous, darting. Her stance poised, knees very slightly bent, as if she were ready to spring into action. What was she expecting here? An actual *fight*?

Raven lifted the cauldron. "This . . . it was my mother's. But you already knew that, didn't you?"

Duncan stepped forward, touched Raven's shoulder, putting himself between her and his father in the process. His hand on her was gentle, and he squeezed slightly, instinctively wanting to calm and comfort her, even though it looked very much as if she'd come here to pick a fight with his old man.

Maybe because that was an emotion he could understand.

"Raven, look again. Come on, that pot must be a hundred years old."

"Three hundred," his father said from behind him, but Raven blurted the same words at the same moment. And Duncan only blinked and told himself this was all some kind of twisted dream.

"Regardless of who it belonged to, it's mine now," Nathanial said. "And it will be put on display with the other items confiscated from executed Witches."

"No, Father. It won't." Duncan's tone was hard, firm. He didn't know why, but the idea obviously made Raven sick inside. And the paleness of her skin, the wideness of her eyes, was all it took to tell him which side he had to take here. Right or wrong.

"You're a murdering thief, Nathanial Dearborne," Raven stated passionately.

And it surprised him. His father might be an insensitive, argumentative, unfeeling bastard, but he'd done nothing to deserve that.

"Raven . . ." Her friend's voice held a warning. But Duncan didn't let her finish.

"My father's political correctness might be in question here, Raven," he said, still standing between them, both hands on her shoulders now when she moved to step around him. "But I don't think he's a murderer or a thief."

Finally she looked at him. He'd been waiting, expecting, hoping she would. But when she did, he wished she hadn't, because there was such intense pain in her eyes. Round, wounded eyes, searching his for something he didn't think she'd find. The woman was traumatized, that was clear now. By him, by his father, or by the things she saw here, he didn't know. Nor did he know why it stabbed at his heart to see her hurting like this—but it did.

"You're involved in this obscenity as well," she whispered.

Unsure how to answer, he hesitated. And then it was too late. She tried to speak, swallowed hard as if she couldn't, as if something were blocking her throat, and then tried again. "So this is what he's made of you, is it, Duncan? How could you be involved in something like this? How *could* you?"

"Like father, like son," Nathanial almost sang.

Whirling, not even aware he was about to move, he snatched his father's lapels in fisted hands and glared at the man. "Not another word, dammit."

But Raven's hand was gentle on his shoulder, easing him aside. He didn't have to move, but he did. He looked down at his hands, trembling as he clutched the front of his father's jacket, and he wondered what the hell he was doing. She touched him, and he let go—shocked, angry, but unsure where to direct that anger.

Shaking his head slowly, he stepped aside. "Someone tell me what the *hell* is going on here."

He shouldn't have moved. It left Raven facing his father, and whatever was between them, it was potent and it was ugly.

"It ends here," she whispered.

His father tensed, Duncan frowned, and Raven's hand shot to her waist, disappearing beneath her draping, dark blouse. Duncan got the sickening sensation that she'd pull a gun in a moment. Instinct took over.

He swept his father behind him with one arm and gripped her wrist with the other, stopping it where it was.

She met his eyes, and hers were hurting. And there was a message in her eyes, or he thought there was. *Him or me, Duncan. Him or me.*

Her friend lunged forward, clasping Raven's hand in hers and dragging her away from Duncan, both from his touch and his sight, blocking her with a small, slender body. But he could still see Raven's hand, and just beneath the hem of her blouse a small jeweled hilt clutched in her fingers. *My God, a knife?*

"No, Raven," the blonde whispered. "Not here. Not now."

For one tense moment Raven's white-knuckled grip remained tight, half hidden in the folds of the blouse. But then it relaxed and the blood flowed back into her small hands as she lowered them to her sides.

"I think you'd both better leave," Duncan said. His hands were shaking, his vision blotchy with the shock of knowing she'd just come very close to attacking his father with a knife. And here he was wondering just what the bastard had done to her to make her want to gut him.

Some chance he had of building a relationship with the man, he thought grimly, when he trusted him so little. Or maybe it was just that he knew him so well.

No, it was neither of those things. It was Raven. He'd defend her against the Devil himself or God Almighty without giving it a second thought.

The women hadn't moved.

"Go on. We'll talk later, Raven."

"You don't understand what he's doing," Raven said, very softly. "I know that. But even so, you ought to know how wrong this is." Her friend released her and stepped aside. Raven lifted her head, dark eyes wet, probing. "These were the most cherished possessions of real women. Wives, mothers, daughters, sisters. Grandmothers, Duncan. Some were Witches, but most didn't even know what a Witch truly was. And regardless of that, they were people. Human beings, Duncan. And here you have the plunder, the booty taken from them after they were brutally tortured and murdered." Her voice grew louder with every sentence. "You have the weapons that hurt and killed them. The hot irons that seared their flesh until they broke or until they died. The stocks that held them like cattle in the streets. You have objects they considered sacred. And you plan to put them on display on Samhain, of all times!"

He lowered his head. "No," he said. "I don't."

"And just why does this bother you so much, anyway?" Nathanial boomed, reaching for the cauldron Raven held, only to have her pull it away, holding it protectively at her side. "Anyone would think you considered *yourself* a Witch the way you're taking on."

Duncan blinked. Instantly the image of Raven standing on the cliffs in the light of a full moon, head back, arms extended skyward, wind blowing the dark gown she wore . . .

"You do," Duncan said softly, without judgment. "You do consider yourself a Witch, don't you Raven?"

She swallowed, faced him, a new fear lighting her eyes.

"Oh, do tell him," Nathanial urged with a smirk. "He won't hang you for it, after all."

"Shut up, Father." He searched Raven's face. "You don't have to answer that if you don't want to."

At those words her eyes welled with tears. "I won't lie to you again, Duncan. I don't *consider* myself a Witch, I *am* a Witch. I live by the Witches Creed, which tells us to do harm to no one. But there are those who don't. There are those who harm who they will without a hint of remorse. Some who even *enjoy* the harm they bring." And she shot a poisonous glance at his father.

Duncan felt his eyes widen. "I'm not even certain I believe there are such things as Witches."

"How can you doubt it when there are four of them in the room right now, Duncan?"

He looked at the blonde, then at his father. But that was only three. "Oh, *come on* now—"

"You've no idea what you were born into this time around, Duncan. You're a High Witch, like Arianna and me, a Witch of the Light. But your father isn't. He's one of the Dark Ones, and he means to kill me—"

Duncan threw up his hands. "That's enough."

"You know you have powers, Duncan," she rushed on. "Think about it. Haven't you ever known things before they happened, sensed things, heard someone's thoughts, wished for something and had it come about almost instantly? Haven't you ever—"

"*That's enough.*"

She fell silent.

"I'm trying to understand you, Raven, but you're way over my head with this. I think the best thing would be for you and your friend—"

"Arianna," the blonde said.

"Arianna." Duncan glanced at her, saw recognition in her eyes, as if she knew him. But she couldn't. Then he returned his gaze to Raven. "It would be best if you went home. You're angry. My father's angry. Go home, Raven."

"Is that what you truly want?"

Those eyes of hers—God, they had something so powerful pouring out of them he could almost believe her nonsense. Right. She was a Witch and his father was a murderer. "You just tried to pull a knife on my father," he told her . . . or was he reminding himself? "If it were anyone else, Raven, I'd be calling a cop."

"If you were any kind of a son, you'd have done just that!" his father yelled.

"I didn't let her kill you," he said softly. "Leave, Raven. I need to have a talk with my father."

"Dammit, Duncan, this man you call your *father* is nothing to you! He can't be! He conspired and plotted to get control of you from the moment you were born, but I tell you he's not your father. He's evil."

"Have it your way, Raven." Duncan reached for the phone. He had no intention of calling any cop on her, but she'd have no way of knowing that, and right now he just wanted her to leave so he could sort this out—and make his father tell him what the hell was going on between the two of them.

"He hanged my mother and me in a snowy square in England in the winter of sixteen eighty-nine, and you were there, trying to stop him!"

Duncan paused with the phone in midair. Because when she said those words an image passed through his mind—one so vivid it startled him. He saw two women, one unmistakably Raven, the other looking like an older version of her. They stood on a gallows with nooses draped round their necks. He saw his father wearing pastoral robes, eyes gleaming and cruel, and himself on the ground below, struggling against men who held him back. Raven and her mother faced the crowd, chins high, proud, unafraid, and then the floor fell away from beneath them and—

He closed his eyes fast and tight, lowered his head and pinched the bridge of his nose hard, as if to pinch away the disturbing image and the physical reaction it had evoked in him. Dizziness spun his brain wildly. He thought he might vomit.

"Duncan?"

He blinked, shook himself, met her eyes.

She stared back at him, and he kept doubting himself. Doubting she was the disturbed, confused beauty she appeared to be. Doubting everything he'd ever known or believed in. "I'm sorry," he said softly. "But you really do have to leave."

Tears brimmed, but she lifted her chin. Looking a lot like she did on that gallows in the vision or whatever the hell it had been. "All right," she whispered. "All right, if that's what you want."

She turned away from him, heading for the door.

"Leave the cauldron," Nathanial commanded.

"Father—"

"No. It's . . . it's all right." She looked at the pot she clutched, eyes tormented. But she set the cauldron down, stroked it lovingly, then pressed a kiss to her fingertips, and her fingertips to the rose painted on the front. That was when the tears spilled over. That was when Duncan's insides churned, and his throat tightened up.

Facing the door unblinkingly, she strode through it like a martyr to the flames.

Arianna shook her head hard. "You're going to pay, Dearborne," she stated. "This is one time you won't wreak your havoc and walk away unscathed. I'll see to that, I vow it."

"You're no part of this, Arianna," he said in a low voice.

"Oh, I'm a part of it. Make no mistake about that." Then she swung her gaze to Duncan's. "And you—I'm beginning to wonder if you're even worthy of her this time around."

Then she, too, sailed out the door.

Duncan shook himself, pressed his hands to his temples, closed his eyes, and tried to clear his head. "What the hell just happened here?"

When he looked up, he saw his father quickly wiping an expression of fear away from his face as he stared after the blonde woman who'd just left—watching so intently it was as if he were afraid she'd burst back in at any moment. But . . . Raven was the one who'd all but threatened him with a blade.

Nathanial covered the look quickly, and shrugged. "We were accosted by two admittedly attractive, but seriously disturbed women who think they're some kind of Witches, and who take offense at our establishment." He waved a hand. "That's all."

"No, Father, that's *not* all. Those two 'attractive but seriously disturbed women' acted as if they *knew* you."

"Yes," Nathanial said, rubbing his chin and moving to a window to watch as the two moved away down the street. "That *was* rather strange, wasn't it?"

"Well, is it true? Do you know them?"

Nathanial faced Duncan, put one hand on his son's shoulder, as fatherly a gesture as he'd ever made. But he took that hand away again very quickly. Just as well. There was that static again. Duncan was always getting shocks from Nathanial on those rare occasions when the man deigned to touch him.

"I swear to you, son, I've never seen either of them before in my life. And you can believe that. I'd sooner cut the heart from your chest than lie to you."

Lowering his head, Duncan released all his breath at once. "I just wish I knew what the hell their problem is," he muttered. Then he glanced at the pot, and recalled the pain in Raven's eyes when she'd had to set it down and leave it behind.

Forget about her, he told himself. Unbalanced, crazy women who broke into houses and accused innocent men of murder while wielding blades did *not* make the best love interests.

If he could just convince himself of that, he'd be far better off.

He couldn't sleep. The events of the day kept replaying in his mind.

Nathanial had spent the rest of the afternoon showing Duncan around Sanctuary. The old man hadn't even been angry when Duncan told him he couldn't in good conscience have any part of his Witch Museum. He'd said he understood, and that he hoped the incident with the two women wouldn't derail things between Duncan and him. He said he respected Duncan for defending the woman, that he'd been far too angry to think rationally himself, and that he regretted having been so harsh with her. He said he hadn't been himself lately, and apologized for it.

And the part of Duncan that was still a desperate, lonely son aching for a father . . . wanted to believe him.

Wary, burned too often not to know how foolish the still small gleam of hope was, he nonetheless gave the old man the benefit of the doubt. One more time. One more chance.

Jesus, when would it be enough?

There had been a strained banter between them that day. At lunchtime his father insisted on buying.

It was almost as if they were . . . real. A real father and son for the first time. It had never been this way before. Not because he was adopted, Duncan knew that had nothing to do with it. But because his father had never seemed to care.

Now he did . . . or . . . he was pretending to.

So why, just when things were going so well, did a mysterious beauty have to come along and throw a wrench into the works? Why did Raven have to show up now and make him doubt his father even more than he had before?

Why was this tiny voice whispering in his mind that he ought to be with her tonight? He ought to be with Raven.

Duncan closed his eyes, rolled over in his bed, told himself to forget about her. Sleep eluded him like some rare butterfly flitting away from a clumsily swung net. And as for forgetting about Raven . . . hell, he knew better, didn't he? Not why, not how . . . but he knew he couldn't forget her. It was as if she were already a part of him, even before he'd met her. As if she'd somehow wheedled her way into his soul and waited there like a spider in the center of a web. Waited for him to stumble into Sanctuary, into her sticky clutches. And now the more he struggled, the more entangled he became.

A Witch. He sighed, rolled again, punched his pillow. A *Witch* of all things. Hell, the way he was feeling, maybe she *was*.

I sat alone in a darkened room. Arianna was out. Making herself scarce, knowing I needed some time alone. Privacy to lick my wounds. She wouldn't have gone far, though. Not with that predator so close. She'd be watching over me like a tigress guarding a cub. My big sister. Three hundred—over four, since she'd lost me the first time—and she still played the part.

It made me feel warm inside. And it was a warmth I needed, because everything else suddenly seemed cold and dark and barren.

I'd been sitting there a long time, bathed in candleglow, smothered in a cloud of incense. A round table that had a pentagram painted on its surface sat in front of me, with a few tools laid out and ready. A slip of paper with Duncan's name on it stood in the center, to represent him, since I had no photo. Surrounding it was a ring of stones. Fluorite to bring past life memories. Bloodstone to remove the blocks in his mind that prevented those memories from coming. Around the stones were purple candles, for purple is the color of hidden knowledge. And in each candle I had engraved Duncan's name in sacred runes, along with the spiral of rebirth and the eye, representing the conscious mind. My herbs stood ready.

It was manipulative magick I was about to perform. The memories were his, but if his conscious mind were ready for them, he'd have regained them himself by now. And yet I knew he might be in danger from the very man he called his father. Unless he could remember, unless he could know the truth, he'd be defenseless.

This was the Temple-room. Sacred space, because Arianna and I had made it so. This place was used only for magick, on nights when we preferred to work indoors, whether it be due to the weather or for some other reason.

The reason tonight was privacy. I didn't want Duncan spying on me, because I would know he was there, in that lighthouse, staring out across the waves. I'd know his gaze was on me, burning over my skin. And knowing that tonight would only distract me from the work to be done.

I'd been still for a very long time, chanting, breathing, keeping my mind utterly blank until I had descended into an altered state. My body was limp, and I could barely feel it now. I was sinking into my soul, connecting to the utter essence of my spirit, because that is the where the power pulses strongest. That is where my connection to the Universe lives. Only when I felt that connection open, felt the power flow freely through me, did I move. Slowly, very slowly, I opened my eyes, focused on the candle flames, and then on the censer, where charcoal burned, heating the powdered incense I'd sprinkled atop it. Now I added other herbs.

I sprinkled rosemary and watched it turn cherry red, sizzling and popping and sending its scent to the heavens, as I whispered, "Sleep."

A pinch of dried marigold petals went next, crackling, blazing up briefly only to settle into a gentle smolder again as I whispered, "Dream."

Then the holly, dropping from my fingertips in tiny green bits, and burning with the rest as I whispered, "Remember."

Settling again into a comfortable position, legs crossed, eyes falling half closed, I watched the smoke rise steadily as the herbs burned, releasing their magick. And I continued to chant those three words over and over. I only hoped it would work. For without the memory, Duncan might never believe me. And unless he did, he'd be putting his life in grave danger. I wouldn't lose him again—especially not to the likes of Nathanial Dearborn.

Funny, he thought he smelled something. A smoky, pleasant scent that . . . Nah, he must have been imagining it. There was nothing now.

Scent or no scent, his eyes were finally getting heavy. Lids drooping as his body relaxed bit by bit. Better. Sleep wasn't eluding him now, but coming closer. Timidly, but steadily, and finally curling up beside him like a favorite pet. He drifted away, relieved that he was finally able to.

And then he forgot all that, because his bed seemed to be tilting back and forth . . . as if his island had become a boat, rocking on the waves. His throat was dry and sore, his skin burning hot. He was sick. Damn, when did he get sick, anyway? He'd been fine just . . .

Wait, someone was there. Hands, cool and soft on his forehead. For just a moment he saw Raven's face in the glow of a candle, saw her hair, tumbling freely over her shoulders. "'Tis you, lass," he whispered in a brogue not his own. And then he realized that it couldn't be her, because Raven was dead.

Dead. No, that wasn't right, but even as he thought that, the images faded from his mind. He wasn't on a boat anymore, and her hands were not on his skin, nor was she soothing away his fever. No. The hands on him now were hard, strong, callused ones. And he struggled against them.

In front of him was a gallows, and upon it he saw Raven, with her mother beside her, and his own father standing with his gnarled hand on the lever. "Do you confess?" his father demanded.

"My soul is less stained than yours, Nathanial Dearborne. You're a murdering thief. You enjoy the harm you cause. You stole my mother's cauldron." Raven said those things, and Duncan sensed he was mixing her words together with more recent ones. But it didn't matter. His father's hand closed around the lever.

"Nay!" Duncan screamed. "I willna watch her die!" But he heard the horrible groan of the hinges, and the sudden slam of the trapdoor flinging open, slamming downward. He even heard the snap of delicate bones when the two women plummeted to their deaths.

And then he was standing there in the snow, gathering Raven's broken body into his arms, cutting the filthy rope away from her bonny neck, kissing her hair, her face. He couldn't believe the force of the pain that engulfed him. He felt empty inside, crippled, devastated. He'd lost her. *Lost her!*

"Dinna die," he whispered hoarsely. "You canna die, Raven, I love you."

Her body stirred, then, and he brushed the hot tears from his eyes to look down at hers, and saw them open. "Don't cry, my love," she whispered. "See? I'm not dead."

He felt his heart leap in fear. Sitting up in bed his eyes flew open wide, and he drew in fast, open-mouthed gasps in an effort to catch his breath. His skin beaded with cold sweat, and real tears burned paths on his face.

"Damn!" He flung back the covers, put his feet on the floor—not far away, since his bed was but a mattress—and then leaned over, elbows braced on his bent knees. "Damnation, lass, what're you doin' to me?" Then he clapped a hand over his mouth, for he'd shouted the words in some other man's voice. The accent . . . Scottish and archaic and . . .

"What's the matter with me?" he whispered in his own voice.

Her. That was what. It was all her. Raven St. James. What he could do about that, he didn't know. Was she really some kind of Witch? Could she possibly have powers he never would have believed in? Making him utterly obsessed with her? Making him think of her ahead of his own father, for God's sake? Subconsciously, at least.

Right, right. And making him dream crazy dreams and wake up speaking with an accent. It wasn't even possible.

But some small part of his mind didn't believe that.

All right, all right, enough. There was a library in town. First thing tomorrow he'd go there and read up on this nonsense. He'd find out once and for all if there *was* such a thing as magic, or Witchcraft, or whatever she called it. And then he'd confront her, armed with at least a small amount of knowledge, and he'd tell her to stay the hell out of his life. And out of his father's life.

And most of all, out of his *mind*.

Chapter 17

"I need to see him. Alone. Without worrying about that bastard Nathanial bursting in on us at any moment." I paced, as I'd done most of the night, wringing my hands and wondering if anything I could say or do would ever make a difference, when I could see so clearly the feeling in Duncan's eyes for that bastard. He cared for Nathanial. Dearborne had *made* him care. Learning the truth was going to break Duncan's heart. And for that I hated Nathanial even more.

But Duncan had to know. He had to.

"I have to make him believe me," I told Arianna.

"He doesn't *want* to believe you."

She sat at the table in our small breakfast room. The octagon-shaped area was completely surrounded by windows, and the sun streamed in like a warm yellow waterfall, drenching us both. Arianna bit into her bagel and sipped orange juice. I was too ill with tension to eat a bite.

Chewing, she mumbled, "As for you seeing him alone, that won't be hard to arrange. I doubt it will help anything, though." She swallowed, sipped, set the glass down. "I don't remember Duncan being so dense last time."

"He didn't love the man last time, Arianna." My stomach churned at the words, and in my mind I heard those I hadn't spoken. *Back then, it was me he loved.*

I closed my eyes, ignoring the self-pitying voice in my head, talking above it to drown it out. "In those days everyone believed in Witches and magick, though they barely knew the meaning of the words. Today no one does."

"Today no one believes in *anything*," Arianna said. "It's pathetic." I sighed my agreement, while she tilted her head in thought. "But there's nothing we can do about that. What I *can* do, though, is keep Nathanial out of your hair long enough for you to see Duncan alone. He probably isn't going to listen, but I suppose you have to try."

"Of course I have to try."

She nodded. Rising, she moved closer to the glass windows that surrounded us, shielding her eyes and facing the sea. "Duncan is still at the lighthouse. And I don't see any other boats there. Go on, pay him a visit before he decides to go into town to babysit the so-called father."

I blinked, stopped my pacing, and studied her stance, the tilt of her head, the shape of her brow. Everything. In three centuries you begin to know a person too well to miss anything. Even the slightest change in Arianna's breathing would have told me a tale.

"You won't confront him," I said, looking hard at her. "You won't even let him know you're there."

"Not unless it looks as if he's heading out to interrupt you. And then, I swear, I'll make it casual. Public, even."

"You won't challenge him?" I asked, suspicious.

"He wouldn't take me up on it even if I did, Raven. The man has an agenda, and I'm not on it. Not yet, anyway."

I believed her, and nodded at last. "All right. Now is as good a time as any, I suppose." I glanced down at my clothes. Unremarkable. Jeans, a snug black T-shirt with a flannel shirt pulled over it in deference to the autumnal chill in the air.

"Don't even think about changing. He might leave while you primp. He already left the island once this morning. Thank goodness he came back in short order. You might not be so lucky next time."

I sighed, shaking my head.

"Go, will you?"

I knew she was right. I was only putting it off . . . out of fear, really. His reactions . . . well, so far they'd fallen short of what I'd hoped for. I didn't expect they were going to improve now that I'd accused his father of murder and not only claimed to be a Witch, but informed Duncan he was one, too. He probably thought I was a lunatic. And goodness only knew what kinds of lies his father had told him after I'd left that horrible place yesterday.

Arianna looked at me, making her eyes big and impatient.

"All right." I sighed. "I'm going."

My big sister smiled, touched a hand to her blade, and then got to her feet.

We parted at the door, Arianna heading into the small garage where we kept our car—an old Volkswagen Bug we'd both grown too fond of to replace—while I walked toward the cliffs. We rarely used the Bug while we were in residence out here. Walking to and from the village was so much more pleasant, and less damaging to the earth and the air. But I supposed in this case Arianna felt she might need the advantage of speed on her side. She could beat Nathanial back here and signal me if anything went wrong.

I hoped nothing would.

The path began at the top of the cliffs, wandered at angles down them, zigging this way and that way and finding the shallowest route. As I started my descent I heard the VW's deep, froggy-voiced motor come to life, growl a few times, then fade as it moved away toward town.

The path was old. It had been here longer than I, and, Aunt Eleanor had confided, longer than she, as well. I often wondered whose feet had first trodden here, and if they'd been feet at all, or perhaps paws or hooves.

Sand-covered stone lay beneath my feet, slippery and gritty all at once. A chill breeze blew salty moisture onto my face, dampening the flannel shirt I wore with its misty droplets. I could smell the sea, taste the salt when I licked my lips, and feel it leaving wet sloppy kisses on my hair.

At the bottom my johnboat sat on the narrow strip of sand, dry and safe. I pushed it into the water and hopped aboard, then, crouching in the stern, tugged the rip cord and started the motor. All that remained then was to steer the little craft as the propeller whirled and pushed me forward. I sat down, felt the dampness of the sea creeping through the denim of my jeans, wished I'd brought something dry to sit on.

And then the shore was fading behind me and Duncan's island grew larger, closer. I bit my lower lip as I stared ahead, wind blowing my hair back and chilling my face until my nose went numb and my cheeks burned with cold.

He heard my approach. I knew it a moment later when he stepped out onto the front step and stood there, hands deep in his pockets as he watched me all the way in. His face, so beautiful, just as it always had been to me. Those deep brown eyes, and dark, thick brows. His full lips and strong jawline.

But that beloved face was expressionless this morning. It told me nothing of how he felt at seeing my approach. And I wondered if perhaps he might not *know* how he was feeling about that.

When I killed the motor and stepped out, he came down to the beach. Bending beside me, gripping the squared-off nose of my vessel, he tugged it up, out of the water. Then he stood facing me, and I straightened and turned to face him in return.

"I decided last night to tell you to leave me alone," he said. No greeting. No welcome. Just that.

"Did you?"

He nodded, his eyes roaming my face like a touch. "I can't do it, though. I've been rehearsing the words from the moment I saw you start down that path, to the boat, and the whole time you were crossing. But it didn't help."

"I'm glad of that."

He sighed, lowered his head, no longer looking at me. "Raven, I got some books on this . . . this Witchcraft thing. This morning. Now I haven't had time to read a lot, but—" He broke off, perhaps because I was smiling at him, slightly, but smiling all the same. "What?"

"Why?" I asked him. "Why did you go to get the books, Duncan?"

He took his time about answering, licking his lips, looking skyward as if for help. "Because I thought you were crazy, and I didn't want to think that, so I thought if I understood what you were talking about, I might see that . . . that it made some kind of sense."

I nodded. "And not because you were curious about your own . . . abilities," I said softly.

"I don't *have* any abilities."

"Oh."

He looked down at his feet, quiet for a long moment, while I stood, waiting, knowing.

"Sometimes . . . I know who's calling when the phone rings." He shrugged, looking up again. "Sometimes I reach for it before it rings without even realizing it. And then it does." He shook his head as if to negate everything he said. "But that's nothing."

"Of course."

"I mean, everyone does that. It's like when you hum a song and then flick on the radio and it's playing. Or when you wish the guy ahead of you on the highway would change lanes just before he does. . . ."

"Or when you mentally tell the red light to turn green and it happens," I added with a nod.

"Exactly."

"Exactly," I repeated.

"That stuff happens to everyone."

I didn't speak. He looked at me, as if awaiting my confirmation, my agreement. I met his eyes and shook my head. "No, Duncan. It doesn't."

He looked away, hands plunging into his pockets. "Yeah, it does," he said. "It has to."

I was trying to go carefully, gently. He didn't seem ready for any of this, and I was pushing it on him. But I didn't have a choice. "It's my fault you're having trouble accepting all of this, Duncan. I didn't explain things as well as I could have."

He shook his head. "Maybe not, but it's all right now. I think I understand. There's nothing supernatural going on here. And as for Witchcraft, according to the books, it's pretty much just a belief system based on—"

"No."

He looked at me, brows knit in frustration.

"For some, that's all it is—those things you've found in the books. A religion, a belief system one can study and learn and adopt. But those things are not what it is to us, Duncan. We're different. We were born different. Witches, yes, but not like all those others practicing the Craft. Most of them don't even know we exist, for it's a secret we guard of necessity. We're born with something extra, senses beyond the five. Weak, unpracticed, raw, but real."

I was losing him. I could see the skepticism in his eyes even now, but like a fool I rushed on, because it had to be said. "We . . . we're *immortal*, Duncan."

"Immortal." He closed his eyes and bent his head. "Dammit, dammit, *dammit*," he whispered. His voice was harsh, raspy, emotional. Then he looked up again, his hands gripping my shoulders gently as he probed my eyes, and his were worried, filled with some kind of concerned sympathy that was all wrong. "It doesn't matter," he said. "I told myself it did, that I should stay the hell away from you, but I can't do that, Raven, no matter how . . ." He stopped himself, closed his eyes briefly, then went on. "Listen to me. I have a wonderful therapist in Boston. He helped me beat my fear of heights, and the water thing, helped me deal with all the baggage my father has dumped on me over the years and—

hell, he even helped me get rid of the dreams . . ." He stopped there, his voice trailing off as he frowned hard.

"Dreams?" I swallowed the hurt I'd felt at his insinuation that I was mentally unstable, and focused instead on Duncan. On *his* pain, *his* confusion.

"Damn, I'd forgot all about the dreams."

I sighed at the way his face paled, just slightly, and closed my hand around his, turning him, beginning to walk beside him along the shore. "Tell me about the dreams."

He shook his head quickly, jerkily. "It was a long time ago. I was only a little boy. They . . . they don't mean anything."

I squeezed his hand. "Please," I said softly. "I'd like to know about them."

He lowered his head, and his head clutched mine tighter, reflexively, I thought. I could feel the tremor of pain move through him. He was quiet for so long I didn't think he was going to tell me. And then he began to speak in a soft, halting voice.

"I used to dream of a woman." He shivered. "Holding me, crying . . ." His voice grew even softer. "She kept whispering my name and . . . saying she didn't want to let me go."

He looked at my face. I hoped my tears didn't show. "The doc said it was a memory of my birth mother, embedded in my subconscious."

I caught my lower lip in my teeth to remind myself to think before speaking. To go gently. Lifting my gaze, I looked out across the water, toward the shore a short distance from my home. To the place high on the cliffs, beside the Coast Road, where I'd lost him three hundred years ago. I felt that crushing pain again, that crippling grief. My heart contracted at the memory of his beloved broken body lying lifeless on those rocks, and suddenly, going gently seemed like the least important thing in the world.

"Do you see those jagged rocks thrusting up out of the water, just offshore?" I asked, pointing. I didn't wait for a response. "That's where I found your body, Duncan. That's where I found you, and I thought it would kill me. I went to you, slogged through the waves out to where you were, and gathered you close, and held you against me and cried. I cried your name, and told you I couldn't let you go, and that I refused to go on alone, without you."

The old tears welled up in my eyes again. I didn't look at Duncan, but out there at those rocks, reliving the nightmare as I spoke. I half expected him to interrupt, but he didn't. So I went on.

"Arianna had cast and conjured even as your body plummeted from the cliffs, Duncan. She willed that when you lived again you'd look the same, and that your name would be the same so that I'd be able to find you and know you, and love you again."

I faced him, so that the sight of him alive, and whole, and here beside me could chase my most heartbreaking memory from my mind. Hands trembling, I reached up to stroke his face. "And that's exactly what happened."

I could see his skepticism. But I could also see the man I loved, alive and well behind his eyes, yearning to escape—to love me again.

"If I'm immortal, then how did I die?" he asked slowly.

"You weren't immortal then, Duncan. I was, though. They pitched me from those cliffs for Witchery. You tried to save me. You're immortal now because in that other lifetime, you died trying to save the life of a Witch. That's how the gift is earned."

Shaking his head, sighing heavily, confused and frustrated and torn between his instinctive knowledge that I spoke the truth and his absolute certainty that all I said was impossible. He turned away. I drew my dagger. "Look at this," I told him.

Slowly he turned. I did something then I was taught never, ever to do. I handed my blade over to another being. I gave Duncan my only means of defense. And he frowned as he turned it over and examined it.

"The man you call your father has one just like it, doesn't he? One he carries with him everywhere he goes."

Slowly Duncan's dark gaze rose from the blade, to my eyes. "Yes. He does. But that doesn't mean—"

"I know it isn't enough, alone. But there is more, Duncan. More that I can show you . . ." I stepped closer to him, my hands, trembling, going to the button of the jeans I wore. Duncan went utterly still, his gaze riveted to my fingers as he dropped my blade to the sand.

"You have a birthmark, Duncan. When we were together in the lighthouse, you only took off your shirt. So I couldn't have seen it. But I know about that mark all the same. It's in the shape of the crescent moon, and it's on your right hip."

Blinking, he said nothing. But I saw the amazement in his eyes. And then they darkened as I tugged my zipper down, and pushed the jeans down over my hips. They tripped my feet, making me clumsy, so I stepped out of them, right there on the shore in the biting October wind. I lifted the T-shirt slightly, moved the panties I wore so my right hip was revealed to him, and whispered, "Look."

He did. And then the color drained from his face.

"We're all born with the crescent, Duncan. That's how I knew you had it."

"That . . . that can't be real. You . . . you put it there." I could hear the desperation in his voice.

"Do you really think so?"

His knees bent. I never knew whether he knelt deliberately or simply lost the ability to stand, but the result was the same. Duncan on his knees in the sand, his face very close to my hip. I felt his warm breath on me there, and closed my eyes. This was no time to let carnal desires overwhelm me. But then his fingers came to me, running over the crescent, tracing its shape, making me shiver more even than the cold wind was doing.

"Madness," he whispered, so close I could almost feel the movements of his lips. "This is utter madness. . . ." And then his mouth touched my hip. His lips moved over it, pressed to it, parted as if to taste my skin, leaving it damp and vulnerable to the wind. I drew in a jerky, noisy gasp when his tongue ran along the mark, hot and wet. Hungry.

Shuddering, I sank into the sand in much the same way he had done, until I knelt before him, facing him, seeing the desire burning in his eyes just the way it used to do. "Duncan," I whispered.

He kissed me—pushing me backward into the sand, pressing me down with his body, he kissed me. And it was as if he felt the frustration of the three hundred years of waiting as desperately as I did. Or maybe it was a different frustration. That of wanting so badly to remember and not being able to. I didn't know. I only knew he wanted me as much as I wanted him, for I could see it in his eyes and feel it in his touch. He wasn't gentle. I didn't want him to be.

Already atop me, he ate at my mouth with unrestrained greed, then lapped a path over my throat. One hand gripped and squeezed my breast while the other battled my flannel shirt, and the T-shirt underneath, relentlessly striving to bare my body. As if he couldn't wait, his mouth closed on that breast, despite the T-shirt barrier. The shirt grew wet from his nursing, my nipple felt sore, deliciously hurting when he bit and tugged at it. And at last he shoved the clothes away, tearing them over my head, shoving my panties down now as his hands closed on my buttocks, fingers parting, exploring the dark, damp places of me. His mouth found my breast without defenses now, exposed, and returned to applying exquisite torture.

One hand moved around to the front of me, cupped me, and then two fingers pushed my folds apart, wide apart, while another stabbed up into me. I arched against him, whispered in his ear, "Don't make me wait, my love. I've waited so long already."

His breath shuddered out of him, but he complied, loosening his own jeans, pushing them down, and then pressing his erection against me. A second later he filled me, and the sigh that initial thrust drove from my lungs seemed to contain all the longing of the past three centuries—for it all melted away with that first joining. It was as if I'd come home.

I held him, kissed him, moved with him there in the sand, told him I loved him over and over. My hands on his back, his shoulders, feeling him, knowing him so well. And then I forgot everything as Duncan drove me higher—to points beyond those where conscious thought existed. To a place where only feeling lived. My body writhed with pleasure as I cried his name aloud and clutched him tight with every part of me, and he cried mine, when he emptied his passion into me.

Then he was still, braced up on his elbows, staring down into my face with something—wonder? Awe—sparkling in his eyes. His fingers tangled in my hair, and he bent to kiss me.

"You're going to be all right, Raven. I promise you that. I'm going to make you all right."

Blinking away the haze of pleasure, slowly understanding that he still didn't believe me, I felt all my joy fall to the ground like the dying spark of a falling star.

"You still don't believe me."

He stroked my forehead, pushing my hair away. "There's something to what you're saying, I realize that. The birthmarks . . . that's too much to be coincidence, I know. And whatever it is, it's feeding this . . . this . . ."

"Fantasy? Delusion?"

He smoothed my hair again, kissed it. "Don't worry about that now, Raven. All that matters is that you get past it. I want you well, because I . . . I feel something for you. Something I can't explain."

"I've *already* explained it."

He kissed me again, my forehead this time. "I'm going to call my doctor and force my father to go along with us on this. Arianna, too, if she's involved. Then I'll take you there myself, and we'll get to the bottom of this, one way or—"

"Your so-called father has the mark as well, Duncan."

He stopped talking, went silent, looked down at me with such sweet sympathy and genuine worry in his eyes that I almost laughed at him.

"I know you think I'm insane, but before you drag me off in a strait-jacket, at least do me the honor of checking. Nathanial Dearborne bears the same mark we do, but his is on the left flank, just as it is with all the Dark Ones."

"Raven, you have to let this go—"

"He adopted you, didn't he?"

Rolling off me, slowly righting his clothes, Duncan nodded. "But that has nothing to do with any of this."

"No? Then why do you both have the mark? Not heredity, Duncan. Look at the man. Find a way and you'll see I'm right. He wants me dead, Duncan, and that's why he adopted you."

"No," he said.

"He used you, Duncan. He knew you'd find me again one day, and when you did, he would as well. Because he wants me dead."

"Stop it, Raven. He wouldn't—"

"My Goddess, I wouldn't be surprised if he were even instrumental in getting your natural parents to give you up. Perhaps he even harmed them once he realized who you were! All just to—"

"That's enough!" Duncan sprang to his feet, glaring down at me. "God, I must be as crazy as you are to have let this happen."

I gasped, cut to the quick. But slowly I sat up, gathering my clothes, retrieving my dagger from where it lay in the sand. "I'm sorry it hurts you, Duncan, but it's true. All of it, and you have to know."

"It's impossible, that's what it is. You're spinning yarns too farfetched to even be called a fairy tale, and expecting me to turn against my own father based on them. God, Raven, do you know what a vile thing that is to say? That he had something to do with my birth parents dying in that accident?"

I lifted my head, met his eyes. "Then they *are* dead." I lowered my eyes. "That bastard."

He fell silent and lowered his head.

"Duncan . . ."

"He's my *father*," he whispered.

I'd gone too far. I knew it then. "I'm sorry, Duncan. . . ."

"Get back in your boat and go home, Raven. I . . . I thought I couldn't say it, but it turns out I can after all. Stay the hell out of my life. Stop playing with my head. Leave me alone, and more important, leave *my father* alone. If you go anywhere near him, I'll have you tossed in jail. Understand?"

Blinking, I nodded. "I understand. But you should understand something, too, Duncan. That man murdered my mother, and probably yours as well. He's tried to kill me more times than I care to remember, and brought nothing but grief to me all my life. But none of that matters to me. *You* are what matters to me, Duncan. And if it takes my very life, I'm not going to let him hurt you. You won't die because of me. Not this time."

He closed his eyes. I got to my feet, pulled on my jeans.

"I love you Duncan. You loved me, too, once, so much you gave your life trying to protect me. So don't feel badly if I return the favor this time around, okay? It'll only be karma evening things up."

He whirled on me. "What the hell are you saying? Are we making some kind of suicide pact now?"

"No. If I die it will be at Nathanial's hand. And if it happens, Duncan, no matter what you believe now, I want you to leave here. Get away from him as fast as you can, because you'll be next."

I turned to leave, striding toward my boat.

"Dammit, Raven, wait!"

I stopped. Duncan ran up behind me, catching my shoulders and spinning me to face him. Then he kissed me, hard and long and deep. And when he stopped, I saw moisture in his eyes.

"Do you have any idea what I feel for you? No matter what kinds of ridiculous tales you spew, I . . . Raven, it's powerful, this feeling. It could be so much, if you'd just let it be. I think about you all the time, dream of you at night, *ache* for you, for Christ's sake. It's going to kill me to lose you, and I know that sounds like bull, because this is so new, between us. But that's what it feels like."

He searched my eyes, shaking his head, and the wind lifted his hair as it was lifting my own.

"Please, just let all this nonsense go. Stop harassing my father, stop spinning these fantasies. And just . . . just be with me. Just be with me, Raven."

Tears blurred my vision, but I blinked them back. "I tried it that way last time." I sniffed. "Then you used to beg me to trust you with the truth, the entire truth, the parts you sensed I was keeping from you. I didn't . . . and you died because of it. So this time I'm telling you all my secrets, Duncan. But you don't believe them, don't even want to hear them. You want me to pretend they don't exist, like I did before. And just be with you. The way I did then. But I can't. No matter how wonderful the memory is of all those nights in your arms, I can't do it to you again,

Duncan. Because the memory of the way it ended is pure agony." I touched his cheek. "It would kill me this time, I swear it would."

He frowned so hard his brows touched.

"Know this much," I whispered. "I love you. With every breath I take, I love you Duncan Wallace, just as I have for three hundred years while I wandered this earth in search of you, mourning you, aching for you. Utterly alone, I waited all this time to find you again. And now that I have, you won't have me." I lowered my head. "Your father and I have to settle things, Duncan, and when it's over, one of us will be dead. If it's me, don't mourn. Just get away from him."

He shook his head. "You won't be hurting my father, Raven, and he won't be hurting you. I'm going to protect you from each other. And you . . . from yourself."

I nodded. "And if it comes to a choice between him and me?"

"Jesus, Raven, he's my *father*."

It was as if he drove a blade straight into my heart. But I said nothing. Just walked to my boat.

Duncan watched her go, a tear rolling down his cheek. Why did it have to be this way? What kind of madness was inside her that she had it in for his father the way she did? God, would she really try something? And why? Why did he fall in love for the first time in his life with a woman who had so many problems?

And why was this insistent feeling in his gut telling him she was perfectly sane, and that everything she'd said made some kind of sense?

He wanted to make it all go away. To love her so much she'd forget about all of this. To hold her and cherish her and exorcize whatever demons must be tormenting her.

But he also wanted to continue building a relationship with his father. A real one, a genuine one. The one he'd been hoping for and dreaming about since he was old enough to dream.

Hell. He couldn't risk that Raven might actually try to harm Nathanial. She wouldn't, though. She wouldn't *really*.

As for the rest of it—his dreams, his memories, the fact that she'd called him Duncan Wallace—a name he'd never heard before, but that sounded perfectly familiar when she said it—the dagger, the birthmarks—all of those things, he refused to think about. For now.

Or thought he did.

But they were there, niggling at his mind, eating away at his disbelief. Making him wonder.

Two hours later he arrived at the courthouse in town, determined to be his father's shadow until he knew for sure just how much of a threat Raven was to him. Until he knew for certain she was imagining things when she said his father wanted her dead.

When he got there, Nathanial did something so out of character that Duncan *knew* he was sincerely changing.

He handed Duncan the small black iron pot that Raven had tried to steal the other day.

"What's this about?" Duncan asked, confused.

"I want you to give it to that girl. Raven . . . what's-her-name. You know who I mean."

Duncan could only stare at his father in surprise.

Nathanial shrugged. "Hell, son, it seems to mean something to her. I suppose in her poor twisted-up mind she must think all that she was saying was true. I have no reason to fight with her. So I thought, as a gesture of friendship, I'd let her have the damned pot." He shrugged. "Call it a peace offering."

Taking the pot from his father's hands, Duncan shook his head slowly. "That's really kind of you," he said. "It must be worth—"

"It's only money." Nathanial waved a hand in dismissal. But his eyes seemed to be watching Duncan's face very closely. As if he were doing this for a specific reason, and that reason had to do with Duncan's reaction. As if it were a part of this whole act he'd been perpetuating. This whole "I-want-to-be-your-father" game the old man had been playing for reasons Duncan didn't understand.

And now I'm just letting Raven's madness poison my mind against my own father. Just what I don't want to do.

But he'd been suspicious of his father's motives long before Raven had come onto the scene. Hell, he'd been suspicious of his father for most of his life, particularly whenever the coldest man he'd ever known started making fatherly overtures toward him.

He just wasn't sure anymore how much of that feeling was his own gut instinct, and how much was the power of suggestion Raven St. James wielded.

"Frankly, son," Nathanial went on, "part of me wanted to call the police, swear out a complaint, something like that. But I realize she . . . well, she means something to you."

"You do?"

"She does, doesn't she?"

Blinking, wondering just when his father had become sensitive enough to pick up on something like that, he nodded. "Yeah. She does."

"That's why I decided it would be better to make peace than to wage war. For your sake."

"For my sake."

"I don't want her coming between us," he said, very softly.

And a tear shimmered in Nathanial's pale, cold eye. A real tear? Duncan didn't know. He'd never seen his father shed one before.

Jesus, between the two of them, they were ripping his heart to shreds.

Swallowing hard, feeling a softness he hated toward the hard man who was his father, he reminded himself not to believe too strongly, not to hope for too much. And he made a decision. One way or another, he was going to get a look at Nathanial's left hip. Tonight.

Chapter 18

⁂

"Why don't I pay the girl a visit tonight?"

Duncan paused in his constant, sickening perusal of the place—his father had been busy today—and felt a new chill lift the hairs on the back of his neck. "What girl?" But he didn't really need to ask.

"You know," Nathanial said. He stood in the center of the room, hands on his hips, looking around just as Duncan had been doing since he'd arrived here. Duncan had refused to take part in things, until his father had hurt his back trying to set up shelves, and Duncan had somehow ended up jumping in to help. He'd been here ever since. Shelves stood everywhere, all of them filled with "artifacts." It made Duncan sick to look at them.

"The self-proclaimed Witch," Nathanial went on. "I can deliver the cauldron along with an invitation to our grand opening. Maybe smooth those pretty ruffled feathers of hers, hmm?"

Straightening, Duncan sent his father a look of disbelief. He didn't like being here. Didn't like *himself* right now, for giving the old man the benefit of the doubt. Wasn't he surrounded by proof of the man's true nature? Wasn't all of this just a little too cruel to be the result of ignorance or even narrow-minded bigotry?

"I don't think visiting Raven St. James is a very good idea, Father."

"And why not? It's the least I can do! After all, you were making inroads with her before I stepped on her delicate toes with this museum. I'm well aware I messed things up for you."

"No, you didn't." He lowered his head, shook it, couldn't quite bring himself to tell his father that he thought Raven might be a bit . . . confused. Maybe because when he said it aloud he realized that he didn't believe it. Not really.

"Still, I fear I got off on the wrong foot with the woman. And she *is* a local. I'd rather not have the locals turning against me before I even begin. Maybe I can make her see reason."

"She doesn't seem to know what reason is," Duncan muttered. Then again, neither did he just now. "Besides, she'd never agree to see you."

"I've thought of that. Still, I want to gift her with the pot, personally, an overture of friendship. You'll just have to arrange it *for* her."

Duncan turned from surveying yet another shelf and faced his father slowly. "What do you mean?"

"Set us up. She'll never agree to meet with me, but she *would* if she thought she were meeting you. So ask her to meet you somewhere. Someplace . . . private. I . . . wouldn't want to embarrass her, after all. And then I'll meet her instead, gift her with the cauldron, and become her friend."

His father's eyes were as still as glass. His lips smiled, but the rest of his face seemed frozen, expectant.

"I don't think I can do that," Duncan said.

"Nonsense! Of course you can. It's the only way it will work. I can see you care for the girl, son. This way she and I will mend our fences and she'll see I'm not the monster she thought. That ought to smooth things over substantially between the two of you. Don't you think?"

Swallowing the dryness in his throat, Duncan nodded. "It might." No way. No way in hell. And what was he reacting to? His own gut instinct? The cold look in his father's calculating eyes? Or maybe Raven's crazy stories were making him feel this icy foreboding in the pit of his stomach.

"Well then?"

Duncan shook his head firmly. "It would be too cruel, Father. She thinks you're some kind of murderer. Can you imagine how frightened she'd be to show up somewhere and find you there, waiting?"

"Yes," Nathanial said. "I can."

Duncan blinked. He'd never seen his father's eyes look so dead. What the hell was happening here? Wasn't it obvious? Nathanial was trying to manipulate him into setting Raven up. The question was why?

He wants me dead, Duncan.

No. Not that, it wasn't that. Nathanial might be a cold, mean SOB, but he was no killer.

"What do you say we grab a late dinner, hmm?" Anything to change the subject. He didn't like discussing Raven with his father. It seemed like some kind of blasphemy.

He wanted her. Maybe even needed her. Probably loved her. My God, he probably loved her.

But he needed her sane, dammit, with all these delusions blown out of her mind.

Unless of course, they *weren't* delusions.

And now who's crazy?

"Dinner?" Nathanial said. He glanced at his watch. "Damn, boy, dinner was hours ago! You should have said something. I got so caught up in this project I lost track of the time."

"I've been doing that lately myself."

"It's late to go out." His father frowned in thought.

"We could order in," Duncan suggested. "If you'll tolerate pizza, I'll tolerate wine."

"Ahh, we'll dine in that quaint style . . . early redneck. Perhaps even put one of those . . . videos into the machine and stare mindlessly at it."

Was he being hatefully sarcastic, or joking around? Tough to tell. He'd never *heard* his father joke around before. "You don't have a VCR," he reminded the old man. "But I'm sure we can find something on TV. It's Monday night. Should be a football game on."

"Ahh, yes, the sport of champions. Well, I'm willing if you are."

"Great. What do you like on your pizza?" Duncan picked up the phone, punched buttons.

His father shrugged, not even looking at Duncan. "I can't imagine it much matters." Then he sighed. "Perhaps we could invite your friend here. Not that blonde she had with her. I . . . I didn't like that one. Still, your Raven could join us in this modern-day ritual. It would give me a chance to get to know her."

Duncan's hand tightened on the phone and he knew without a doubt he didn't want his father anywhere near Raven. "You're like a dog with a bone about this, aren't you? She wouldn't accept. Just give her some time and space, and maybe she'll come around."

"And if she doesn't?"

"Then she doesn't." Duncan shrugged. "It doesn't matter."

"Oh, but I'm afraid it does, Duncan, my boy."

Before he could ask what his father meant by that, the pizza guy answered the phone to take Duncan's order. And by the time he hung up, his father was off on another subject. As if he'd forgotten all about Raven.

But Duncan had a feeling that might be an illusion.

So far, neither Raven nor Nathanial was proving to be what either seemed.

I paced outside the courthouse, a safe distance away, but close enough to watch the door. Duncan was inside, and he hadn't left yet. There had been a delivery boy, a pizza box, and the mouth-watering aromas had reached me. Spices, tomato sauce, cheeses, and fresh crust. My stomach rumbled. I'd been too tense and worried and . . . yes, heartbroken, to eat today, and now I regretted it. But I didn't regret being out here. I glimpsed Duncan in the doorway, just briefly. Dark, and beautiful, forbidden to me just as he'd always been. By choice this time, rather than by vows. But just as forbidden. Just as unreachable. His dark hair played with a stray breeze as he handed the delivery boy some bills. And when the boy left, Duncan stood there a moment longer, head cocked to one side, eyes scanning the benches and the fountain and the park beyond. Scenting the air like a wolf, I thought. He knew I was there. Sensed my nearness somehow. He probably didn't even realize it, but he did.

And yet it seemed he'd deny the connection between us with his dying breath. Why must he be so stubborn?

Sighing as he moved inside and the door closed again, I sank onto the stone bench beside the fountain, elbows on my knees, head in my hands.

"Raven . . ." The harsh, familiar whisper brought my head up fast. Arianna came skulking from the shadows like a Halloween spirit. "What are you *doing* out here?"

"You must have radar," I told her. "It's barely been an hour since I slipped away."

"I don't need radar and you know it." She came closer but didn't sit. Instead she stood over me, feeling taller than me for a change, I thought. Her short hair riffled like dove feathers as she looked down at me from those huge brown eyes. Her Peter Pan stance, I called it, when she stood like this. Legs shoulder-width apart, hands planted on her hips, elbows pointing to either side of her. Give her a hat and a feather, and she'd probably fly. The leggings she wore, and the green velvet tunic that reached to midthigh enhanced the image considerably. I almost smiled.

"Are you going to tell me what you're up to, or sit there inspecting my wardrobe?"

I shrugged. "Peter wore less jewelry, of course," I muttered. She frowned harder. "Then again, so do most of the royals."

"Are you mocking me? After I came all the way out here worried half to death about you and—"

"Hush, Arianna. I love you, you know that."

"Then talk to me." Her hands lowered to her sides, and she paced. "It's to be tonight, isn't it? You'll go after him tonight."

"Yes." I drew my dagger, ran my thumb across its edge to test its readiness. A nervous habit I'd repeated a dozen times today. "It's time."

"You're not ready."

"And I'll not become any *more* ready by putting it off."

"He'll kill you."

"Duncan is in danger!"

She rolled her eyes. "Duncan should have listened to you in the first place." Then she paused, glaring at the courthouse as if trying to send it up in flames with the sheer force of her gaze. "I'm beginning to hate them both."

"Not Duncan," I protested. "You're my sister. You can't hate the man I love, Arianna."

"I can if his foolishness gets you killed."

I closed my eyes. I didn't want that to happen. And I knew it was possible. I just wished she wouldn't remind me quite so often.

"So what are you waiting for? Having second thoughts?"

I shook my head. "Duncan's inside. I'm afraid he's going to spend the night. He thinks he needs to protect his . . . *father* from me."

Arianna lifted one brow. "His *father* could probably roll a bus onto its side without breaking a sweat, as old as he is."

I wasn't being fair, I knew that. Duncan had said he meant to protect both of us, from each other. But it still felt like betrayal to me.

Arianna eyed me. "What if he's weakening?" she asked suddenly. "Maybe that's why Nathanial is so determined to have you this time, Raven. Maybe he needs a heart soon. You . . . um, you didn't tell Duncan about that part of it, did you?"

"There are a lot of things I didn't get around to telling him," I whispered, averting my eyes.

"So what *did* you do all that time you were with him this morning? Or need I ask?"

My chin dipped lower. "It doesn't matter."

"I beg to differ! It certainly *does* matter. If he made love to you, Raven, then he must care. And if he cares, he'll believe you over Nathanial." I looked at her, my doubt in my eyes. "He *will*!" she insisted.

"He thinks I need mental help." I heaved a deep sigh, leaned over, and trailed my hand in the icy-cold water that rippled in the fountain. Soft blue lights lit it from below, so my hand seemed to glow in the choppy water. Pink lights illuminated the flow that spilled from above, tumbling down the stairlike layers of the statue's base, and losing itself in the pool.

"He'll believe you if you just give him time."

"There *is* no time. I can't let him go on being so close and so damned vulnerable to a man who could kill him at any moment. And I can't just wait for Nathanial to come for me. The waiting is going to drive me insane. I can't eat or sleep, and that will all work to the old man's advantage. You know that."

"What I *know* is that your lack of appetite and restful nights has nothing to do with Nathanial, and everything to do with Duncan."

I shook my head. "It doesn't matter." My gaze returned to the courthouse. My vigil began anew. The lights still blazed from the windows.

"You can't go through with this," Arianna said, apparently reading my eyes as easily as I could read hers. "Not tonight, not with Duncan right there."

"I didn't think I could kill Nathanial in front of Duncan," I told her. "But it doesn't look as if I have a choice. Besides, when he sees his father wield that blade with every intention of doing me in, when he sees the old man's skill—his *well-practiced* skill—then perhaps he'll know I told the truth all along." A light flicked off on the lower level. But seconds later one came on upstairs. "Still," I said, sheathing my blade, getting to my feet, "I'll spare Duncan seeing it if I can."

"How?"

I shrugged. "He has to sleep sometime." I started forward, crossing the cobbled street so reminiscent of old England. But Arianna's hand on my shoulder stopped me, and I turned. "This will be a fair fight," I told her before she could speak. "I won't have murder on my conscience. I won't attack Nathanial with the odds stacked in my favor. You'll stay out of it, no matter what. I want your promise on that."

Lifting her chin, my sister swallowed hard. "I don't want to lose you again, Raven."

It was not often I'd seen tears in Arianna's eyes, but I did now. All her harshness and brass melted into twin pools that shimmered in her eyes.

"I know." I hugged her gently. Stroked her short hair, kissed her face. "If I'm meant to triumph over him, I will."

She nodded, sniffled, and straightened away from me.

"If I fall . . ." I began.

"If you fall, I'll kill the bastard myself," she told me.

I met her eyes and knew there would be no talking her out of it.

His father had seemed averse to the idea of Duncan staying over. That reaction offended Duncan slightly, hurt him a little, and prodded his suspicious mind a lot. Still, he'd talked the old man into it. No way was he leaving Nathanial alone tonight. He was half afraid the old man would head out after Raven the minute he was alone—and half afraid she'd come after him instead.

There was a guest room overlooking the circle, the park, and the fountain. His father's room was on the opposite end of the hall, overlooking the road that led back to the mainland. There appeared to be several bedrooms in between, but the doors were all closed, and Duncan didn't want to let his father know how little he trusted him by peering inside those other rooms as they passed. Still, he thought there was likely no reason he couldn't have used any of the in-between rooms. And then he wondered why his father would want to keep him at a distance.

It didn't matter though. This one was fine. He'd sensed something, got that little shiver up the back of his neck earlier when he'd looked out on the town circle. That same prickly awareness he got when *she* was near. Not Witchcraft. Just intuition. Normal intuition. He hadn't seen anyone outside, but it was dark. And he doubted a nightbird like Raven would be seen if she meant not to be.

Going to the window, he stared down at the circle again. And again, saw no one. So he paced, and he waited, and he battled the growing feeling that something was going to happen tonight. To distract himself from it, he tried to figure out how he could check his father for the birthmark, and wondered if his intention to do just that made him as crazy as Raven was. Probably. He couldn't understand why he *wanted* to believe the woman so much when he *knew* that everything she said was just part of some grand delusion. And it wasn't that he wanted her to be right about his father. Just that he wanted her to be sane. No, it wasn't that, either. It was something else. Something deep inside him, so deep he couldn't reach it. Couldn't examine or explore it. But it was there. Knowledge. Truth. Buried, but present, and whispering every once in a while. Words that he couldn't quite hear. Reality that he couldn't quite grasp.

Closing his eyes, lowering his head, he wondered what his shrink would think about this latest crisis. That he'd fallen head over heels in love with this particular woman from the second he'd set eyes on her. And why, for heaven's sake? What was it about her?

Her eyes. Dark, as black as midnight, and full of mystery and onyx fire.

Her hair. Tangled silk. As twisting and writhing as Medusa's, but gleaming and glossy and soft. Tempting his fingers and his lips to touch it. Threatening to bind him up and never let him go.

Her skin, like moonlight. Warm, when he touched it. Responsive against his lips. Sweet and salty and as addictive as a drug.

Her laugh, though she laughed very little. And her voice, deep and rich, slightly coarse. Whiskey and roses, that was what her voice was like. If whiskey and roses could sing in harmony, they'd sound like Raven St. James. It seemed he'd known her voice before he'd ever heard her speak. It seemed he'd known exactly the way she would sound.

But there's more. Her courage. The way she faced that crowd from the gallows, shamed them all, she did, an' never once cried out as she plummeted to her death! Aye, an' the way she refused to confess to anythin' when she'd done nothin' wrong. An' her strength. When the bastard Elias Stanton attacked her, tried to rape her, she laid him out cold. Damn near killed him. The way I wanted to do when I saw her later—her dress torn, her satin skin bruised, scrubbin' herself raw in the crystalline cold o' the stream. I didna think I'd ever seen anythin' so pain-filled as her eyes that day. An' . . .

Duncan went very still. Utterly still. "What the *hell* was all that? Where . . ." He looked around the room, as if he expected to see someone else there. But the someone else wasn't in the room—the other man was inside him, inside his head, spewing memories that did *not* belong there!

None of those things had happened!

And yet they kept flashing. Bits and pieces. He was kissing her bruised skin as she cried, and trembled. He was whispering, "No one will every hurt you again, lass. I swear it on my life." He was facing his father, only they both wore robes, and he was demanding to know where Raven's body was being taken. And then he was there, searching a horrible place filled with the stench of death and decay, livid because he couldn't find her there.

"Stop!" he moaned, pressing his hands to the sides of his head and turning in a slow circle. "Stop, dammit!"

Nay, Duncan, I willna stop. I canna. You must remember.

The lights had gone out at last, and I had slipped inside by means of a small window in the back. Silently I crept up the stairs, my dagger in my hand, at the ready, lest Nathanial be aware of my intent, and be lying in wait around some dark corner.

The stairs creaked as I mounted them, and I went still. But only for a moment. Testing the next step with care, I moved to the top, and there I paused, looking up the hall and down. Unsure which way to go. And finally turning left, and tiptoeing down the hall.

Just outside the door at the end, I heard Duncan's anguished, "Stop, dammit!"

My heart leaped into my throat, and I kicked the door open, springing inside and landing in a ready crouch, dagger high, eyes darting.

He stood by the window. His back to the pane, staring at me. His face seemed tormented, unsurprised, too caught up in whatever was eating at him to feel startled at my rather dramatic entrance. But I saw that he was alone in the room, and slowly sheathed my blade. "I . . . I heard your voice. I thought . . ."

"Thought what? That my father was in here trying to murder me?"

I didn't nod. It seemed the wrong time to speak ill of his father. "Where is he?" I asked.

"You think I'm going to direct you to his room so you can attack him in his sleep?"

I lowered my head. Turning, I glanced back down the hall to calm the rising goose bumps on the back of my neck. I saw no one, and then I closed the door. Moving forward slowly, I reached up, touched Duncan's face.

"What's wrong?"

His eyes moved over my face as if he couldn't look at me enough to suit him. And then he closed them. "What *isn't* wrong would be a better question."

"Okay, what isn't wrong?"

He met my eyes, smiling a sad, sarcastic smile. "Nothing."

"That's very good."

"The woman I think I'm falling in love with has just broken into my father's house, kicked in my bedroom door, and jumped in wielding a knife. And I ought to be calling the cops and having her hauled off to a rubber room somewhere. And instead I'm standing here wishing I could . . ." He let his voice trail off.

"You love me?" I whispered.

One hand rose to delicately cup my chin, and then he lowered his head, holding my eyes with his until mine fell closed, and his lips pressed to mine.

So tenderly he kissed me. As if he thought I might break. And when he straightened away, I stared at him in wonder. "Does this mean . . . does this mean you . . . believe me?"

He shook his head sadly, walked to the bed, sat on its edge. "I don't believe anything. Not even my own feelings right now."

"Oh."

"Will you tell me something?"

I put my back to the window, half sitting on its sill, so I was facing Duncan, and the door beyond him. "I'll tell you *anything*," I promised.

He drew a deep breath, blew it out. "Was there ever a time when you were . . . attacked?"

I nodded. "Many have tried to kill me."

"Now, that's something I don't understand," he said quickly. "You keep saying how my father has tried to kill you, but then you claim to be immortal."

"There is only one way to kill an immortal, Duncan. And that's to cut the still-beating heart from his breast."

"God," he said, turning his head away in disgust. Then he closed his eyes, cleared his throat. "But I got off the subject. The attack I asked you about . . . this man wasn't trying to kill you, he was trying . . ." He looked away, and it seemed he couldn't finish.

Finally I understood. "To rape me?"

Duncan nodded. "Did it ever happen?"

"Once. It was Elias Stanton, the pig. Claimed I'd bewitched him into feeling desire for me, and so it was his right to act on it—teach me a lesson."

Duncan closed his eyes. "When did it happen?"

"Sixteen ninety-two. I remember it well, Duncan. It was later that night I lost you."

Lifting his head slowly, meeting my eyes, he said, "Tell me more."

I searched his face. "Are you sure you want to hear this?"

"I think . . . I have to hear it."

I nodded, licked my lips. "I was walking home from town, when he approached me. I resisted, he pursued. I wound up with my back to a tree, while he groped at me. In the end, he was on the ground with a heavy limb atop him, and I was racing back to my aunt's home in his wagon." I closed my eyes. "I told Arianna, but not Aunt Eleanor. It would have killed her had she known. I couldn't even face her. I felt . . . contaminated. So I went to the stream, stripped off my torn clothes, and plunged myself into that icy water, and I scrubbed and scrubbed. But it did no good. I could no more rid myself of the memory of his vile touch than I could wash away the bruises." I shuddered at the memory. But then I opened my eyes and faced Duncan again. "Then you came. And it was all right."

Duncan bit his lip. His jaw was taut, as if he were bearing a great weight and straining to support it. "Why would my father want to kill you?"

I blinked. He jumped from one subject to another so fast it made my head spin. "I told you that you died trying to save my life, and that was how you earned the gift of immortality."

"Something I still think is impossible."

"Yes, I know." I sighed. "So pretend it's fiction, a story I'm telling to entertain you."

"That's exactly what it is." But he said it as if trying to convince himself. His gaze held mine for a long moment. But it was Duncan who finally looked away.

"There is another way one can gain immortality, and that's the way the Dark Ones, the evil ones, go about it. They gain it, Duncan, by stealing it. When they take the heart of another immortal, and keep that still-beating heart captive in a small box far away from the ever-young body of their victim, they hold that victim's power as well. The first kill gives them immortality. But they need more. The ones that come later increase their strength and powers, and replenish their life force when it weakens and dims. They use the hearts like . . . like a child's toy uses batteries. Drain them all but dry, then toss them aside for another."

"And you think my father is one of these . . . these *Dark Ones*?"

I nodded. "I'm a powerful Witch, Duncan. He wants that power for his own, and each time I've thwarted him he's become more determined to have it." I lowered my head. "But it's not just the power. He hates me because he blames me for coming between you and him three hundred years ago. And here I am, doing it all over again."

He shook his head. "It's so far-fetched."

"But you're starting to wonder, aren't you?"

He looked at me, saying nothing. "I called a lawyer this morning, after we talked. Asked him to find out any details he could about the car accident that killed my birth parents."

I nodded, trying not to show him how deeply those words touched me, moved me. He was trying to believe me . . . or maybe trying to prove me wrong, but at least giving me the benefit of the doubt. "Thank you for that."

He nodded, drew a breath, lifted his eyes to mine. "Don't go after my father, Raven. Please, for my sake. Not yet. Give me some time to find out what . . . what the hell this is about. Time to understand."

I lowered my head. Was he giving me the benefit of the doubt after all? Or just trying to distract me, to protect his father?

"Please. I don't believe he's this evil being you think he is. Raven, if you knew what he told me tonight, how he wants to make peace with you, you'd—"

The bedroom door flung open, and the old man stood there, dagger clenched in his fist, black satin robe held around his rail-thin, beanpole of a body with a sash. In a half crouch, just as I had been, he lunged into the room.

I flew forward to meet him, quickly putting myself between Nathanial and Duncan. And though we faced each other, blades at the ready light and nimble in our hands, the old man still tried to feign innocence.

"What is *she* doing here?" he asked. "Did she try to hurt you, Duncan?"

"You know I'd sooner die than hurt him," I answered before Duncan could.

"If you insist," he rasped, and he lunged at me, swinging the blade in a deadly arc.

"Stop!"

Duncan's cry pierced my mind, but I didn't straighten or take my eyes from his father. I knew better than to glance away, even for an instant, from a cold-blooded snake poised to strike.

"Dad, come on, this is insane. Raven, Christ, if you ever cared for me . . ."

Nathanial lunged again, but I dodged his blade with easy grace.

"Father, tell her about the pot. Give her the damn pot. You said you wanted to mend fences with her. Go on, go get the pot and—"

"That cauldron is worth nine hundred dollars," he muttered.

"But you said—"

"He lied, Duncan," I whispered. "He's been lying to you all along."

"Shut up and fight me, wench," Nathanial snarled.

"No, Raven," Duncan said softly. "If you love me, please, Raven, don't. He's an old man, please. . . ."

"He's an old man, all right. Centuries old, how many, even I don't know." I lunged, feinted, dodged. "You killed my mother, you son of a bitch, and now you've stolen Duncan from me. You *will* pay. But not to-night."

Again, my blade flashed out, easily slicing the sash that held his robe together. I leaped past the man, dodging his returning slash, hooking the robe with my blade and tugging it back. Far enough. "There, Duncan!" I cried, knowing full well that crescent was in full view, if only for a moment. And then I landed in the hall. One hand on the rail, I vaulted over, landing on the floor of the foyer below, and then I spun around even as Nathanial's footsteps pounded into the hall after me.

There. My mother's cauldron sat on a shelf. Looking up, I saw Nathanial leaning over the rail, hatred blazing from his eyes. I gathered the cauldron in one arm. "Thanks for the token of friendship, Dearborne!" I cried. "Unfortunately, it was never yours to give."

And as he raced for the stairs, I left the building by the front door and vanished into the shadows where I knew Arianna would be waiting.

Chapter 19

It was there. The mark Raven had told him about was there, just as she'd said it would be. Dark, bloodred, on his father's left hip.

But that didn't mean . . .

Jesus, how long was he going to keep denying it? Everything she'd shown him, everything she'd said—the flashes and dreams that kept haunting him. This feeling that he knew her, that he loved her . . . there had to be some reason for all of it.

God, just not the reason she said.

He raced into the hall, down the stairs, catching his father at the door, and gripping the man's arms from behind. "Stop! I'm not going to let you go after her!"

The ease with which Nathanial broke Duncan's grip was shocking. He was old. He had no business being so strong. But he didn't run off in pursuit of Raven. Instead he turned, eyes as cold as ice.

"I suppose you'd rather I wait for her to sneak back in here. To kill me in my sleep. Is that what you want?"

"Of course not!" Duncan pushed both hands through his hair, sighing. "Look, she didn't hurt you, didn't even try. Because I asked her not to." And he knew that much, at least, was true. "She's not going to come back here tonight."

Nathanial's eyes narrowed. "She stole my blasted pot. I should call the police—"

"You were going to give it to her anyway."

"Mmmph." It was a growl, not an affirmation. "I changed my mind when I saw her in your room with her blade."

"Yes." Duncan moved past his father, closed the door, then turned to face the old man again. "It's just like yours, her blade."

Nathanial's head came up slowly. "It's similar."

"And so is the mark on your hip."

"Seen that much of her, have you?"

Duncan looked away. He wasn't going to answer that. "She knows you, knew you before you came here. You lied to me when you denied that."

Nathanial thrust his small blade into the sheath at his hip, turned away, muttering under his breath.

"God, you even wear that thing to bed?"

"I wear it everywhere," his father replied without facing him.

"It's time for you to tell me what this is all about. I want to know. And I mean *everything*."

His back still to Duncan, his father kept walking. "No, you don't." Then he paused. "And even if you do, it's not your business, Duncan. This is between her and me, and will remain that way."

"For how long? Until one of you is dead?"

A long sigh emerged from his father's lips. A raspy one. But he said nothing. And a moment later he kept walking, up the stairs, to his room. He closed the door firmly.

Duncan sank to the floor, holding his head in his hands. He didn't know what to think, what to do, who to believe. It was obvious there was a fierce enmity between Nathanial and Raven. They had a past, those two. A violent one. Raven was all too willing to tell him all about it . . . but the things she told him surpassed belief and even the most distant realms of possibility. His father, on the other hand, would tell him nothing. And Raven's version of things was looking more and more like the truth.

He knew one thing. There would be no killing, no dagger wielding, no bloodletting tonight. Not tonight. He'd make sure of it.

He couldn't sleep anyway, so he played the part of sentry. And long after dawn, while his father still slept, he called the lawyer he'd contacted the day before. He called the man at home—woke him up, judging by the thickness of Jack Cohen's voice.

"What did you find out?" Duncan asked without preamble.

It took a moment for Jack to identify him, another for him to figure out what it was Duncan wanted. They were acquaintances, not friends. Jack had done some work for Duncan's restoration business, helped out with contracts periodically over the last several years, and Duncan had his home number. For emergencies only, Jack had told him when he'd scrawled it on the back of a business card.

Hell, if this wasn't an emergency, Duncan didn't know what was.

"I have office hours, you know," Jack finally said.

"This is too important to wait. What did you find out about the accident that killed my birth parents?"

Jack sighed, hesitated. "It . . . was easier than I expected to check into it. You had their names and everything, so—"

"What did you find out?" Duncan asked again.

Jack cleared his throat. "This isn't the kind of thing I like to tell someone over the phone," he said. "But, uh . . . there *was* no car accident. Your parents were murdered, Duncan."

His throat closed off. He closed his eyes, drew a breath. "How?"

"A mugging. Wallet stolen. The cops figured they must have resisted, tried to fight back."

Opening his eyes, Duncan whispered, "Shot?" *Please, please, please say yes.*

"No. No, it was, uh . . . it was a knife."

A knife. Or maybe an antique dagger with a jeweled handle.

"Did they get the guy?"

Another sigh. "The case is still unsolved. I'm sorry, Duncan, I wish the news had been better."

"So do I," Duncan said. "So do I." He put the phone down and turned to see his father coming down the stairs.

Nathanial paused, frowning. "You're up early!"

"Couldn't sleep." Duncan reached for his coat, hanging on an antique tree near the door.

"You're leaving? But what about breakfast? We really do need to talk, Duncan."

"We can talk later." Duncan pulled the coat on, then eyed the old man. "When you're ready to tell me the truth. Right now there's . . . something I have to do."

Lowering his brows, Nathanial said, "You're going to see *her*, aren't you?"

"Yes. So don't bother charging out there to confront her, because I'll be there to prevent it."

He disliked the harsh, condemning tone of his own voice, and the way his father flinched and paled slightly at every word. Even though things looked bad, he had to remember his father might not be guilty of a damn thing. All of this could be . . .

His chin fell. Could be what? Coincidence? Some elaborate con? Bullshit. It was none of those things and he knew it.

Still, his tone gentled, almost as if there was still some part of him, some fatherless child inside, who *wanted* to believe the old man innocent. "I'll be back later on."

"She's crazy, you know. She'll try to turn you against me, Duncan. Don't let her."

"Look, all I want to do is fix this, make it all right, get at the truth. And I *will*."

His father shook his head slowly. "I only wish you could. Make it all right, I mean. But you can't, Duncan. You're dealing with things you don't understand. The way things are . . . is the way they've always been. It can't be changed."

"Anything can be changed."

His father lowered his head tiredly. "I wish that were true. I'm . . . I'm *tired*. You've no idea how tired."

Narrowing his eyes, searching his father's face, Duncan took a step closer. "Tired of what?"

When Nathanial looked up again, his skin seemed pale, and dark circles seemed to have appeared beneath his eyes overnight. "Death. Life. All of it. I'm an old man, Duncan, and I ought to know it. I ought to just let go, but I can't. I can't. Maybe she'll be the one to end it. Maybe it's time someone did."

"Father, what the hell are you talking about?"

Nathanial shook his head. "Nothing. I sound as crazy as she does, now, don't I?" He smiled softly. "Go on, go to her. Do what you have to do, Duncan. We never know how much time we have left. We ought to spend it doing what we want."

"You'll be all right?"

"Fine. I promise. Go on, go."

Sighing, suddenly uncertain his father should be left alone just now—but even more certain than before that he had to see Raven, he finally nodded, and left. He walked the two miles to Raven's house. A pleasant walk, or it would have been if there hadn't been so many unanswered questions swamping his brain. He walked along the Coast Road with the sea crashing to the shore below, giving him slight goose bumps and making him walk as far to the left of the road as possible. Raven's story about him having been tossed from these very cliffs kept creeping into his mind, but he pushed it away. Still, it was sunny. The air held a brisk chill that invigorated, but no real wind. And the sound of the waves was pleasing, even if looking down on them did make him dizzy.

He paused once, near those very cliffs she'd pointed out to him—the place where she claimed he had died. Swallowing a lump of foreboding, he stepped closer to the edge, stared down at the froth and rocks below, expecting the slight dizziness that still hit him from time to time when he looked down from on high.

It didn't come. Instead, there was a flash. Darkness, moonlight. Dancing red-orange torches and men all around him. Holding him. Holding . . . *her*.

"Disavow her, Duncan. Save yourself."

"Never!"

"Do as he asks, Duncan. Please, trust me! Do as he asks."

Tears glittering on her cheeks in the moonlight.

A soft rending of his heart as he looked into those dark eyes. "Not on pain of death, lass. Nay, not if it meant my own soul would I speak against you."

They carried her to the edge. Duncan broke free of those who held him, ran forward, reached for her.

"They cannot take my life!" she cried. "Save yourself, Duncan, I beg you!"

They pitched her over the side, and he lunged for her, and then fell with her into the abyss.

Duncan pressed a hand to his head and staggered backward, away from the edge. God, what *was* that? A memory? A hallucination? Real or imaginary?

The image, the dream, was gone. But the feelings . . . the emotions . . . remained. Pressing out from somewhere inside his chest. Expanding, making it hard to breathe.

"God, what is happening to me?"

When he arrived at Raven's driveway, he heard voices, and the rhythmic chink of metal clashing against metal. Was his father here before him, then? Were Nathanial and Raven fighting to the death, even now? A beat of panic pulsed in his throat, and he rushed forward, following the noise around to the rear of the house, and stopped in his tracks when he saw Raven and her blond friend wielding their deadly little daggers as if they meant to kill each other.

He lunged forward, then stopped. They were . . . laughing. Swinging those double-edged blades and ducking, rolling and springing to their feet again, and *laughing*.

My God, they *were* insane.

But graceful. So skilled in their movements that it started to resemble a dance the way they circled and lunged and dodged. Then Arianna let loose with a spinning kick that looked like some kind of martial arts move, and Raven's dagger sailed from her hand to land point down, in the dirt, its jeweled hilt quivering.

Arianna leaped forward, her blade to Raven's throat. "I have you now!" she shouted, a beautiful smile on her face.

"No, don't!"

The shout was wrenched out of him, a knee-jerk reaction he hadn't planned. The two women stilled, turning toward him. Raven looked surprised, but not the least bit afraid. Arianna, on the other hand, straightened, sheathed her blade, and rolled her eyes.

"Isn't *this* familiar?" she said, her tone sarcastic.

And it was. He had a dizzying sense of déjà vu all of a sudden. It was as if he'd done this all before. He had to close his eyes to regain his balance.

But then Raven was coming to him, stroking his hair with those loving fingers. "Are you all right?"

"More to the point," Arianna said, "are you *alone*?"

He drew a steadying breath. "Nathanial is back at the courthouse. I wouldna . . . *wouldn't* . . . bring him here." Then he gazed at Raven to see if she'd noticed his slip—God, for an instant it felt as if that stranger inside had leaped to the surface and taken over.

Raven's hair was tousled, and his fingers ached to smooth it. Her cheeks gleamed pink with exertion and her eyes sparkled.

"It's all right," she said. "We were only practicing. We do it all the time." She didn't mention his slip, but she'd noticed. He knew she had.

"I don't even want to ask why," he said.

"To stay sharp . . . you'll pardon the pun." Arianna smiled at her own joke. "So when people like Nathanial come for us—and they do, Duncan—we're ready."

"So you believe this nonsense, too? About immortal High Witches and beating hearts in little boxes . . . ?" He shook his head, not wanting to think about it anymore.

"I see Raven *did* get around to telling you a few things," Arianna said. "Well, Duncan, old friend, you might as well come inside. If you won't believe your lover, then perhaps you'll believe me. I'm far older than she is anyway. Just over five hundred, actually."

"You'll have to give me the name of your plastic surgeon."

She lifted her golden brows. "You can still joke about it. I think that's a good sign. Do you drink coffee, Duncan, or is it still strong English tea you prefer?"

Strong English tea was exactly what he preferred. But how did *she* know that? "To be honest, I think I could use a beer about now," he told her.

"Used to go straight to your head," she replied with a smile. "I think you need all your wits right now. So tea it is." She turned and led the way inside.

Raven gripped his hand and followed. "I was so afraid to leave you with Nathanial last night. Was there any trouble after I left?"

"He's my father, Raven."

"As if *that* means anything."

They walked into a pretty room, with a fireplace flickering from one wall, and claw-footed furniture of deep cherry wood all around.

"You two sit. Talk. I'll get that tea." Arianna left them there.

Raven took a spot on the love seat, and Duncan sat beside her. He took her hands in his, stared into her eyes. "I want you to end this feud with my father," he said. "It doesn't matter whether all of this other stuff is true or not. Nothing matters right now except that it has to end."

She closed her eyes. "Do you think I *want* to fight him? Duncan, believe me, I don't. I'd end this if I could."

"You can. I can help. I don't think he wants this any more than you do, Raven."

"He has no choice, Duncan."

Duncan closed his eyes. What now? Would she tell him more far-fetched tales?

"Didn't you understand what I told you last night, Duncan? The Dark Ones take hearts, and keep them, and eventually, they use up the power. The hearts weaken, perhaps even die if they're tapped long enough in this vile way. I don't know. But I do know they weaken, and as they do, so does the Dark Witch who holds them. They need to take more, to kill again and again, in order to continue living."

He swallowed hard. "You can't truly believe this," he said, but in a hoarse whisper, because somewhere inside him, he knew it was true. It *couldn't be*. But it had to be.

"It's why he wants me," she went on. "He could have taken your heart, Duncan, but you're young, and you've never even wielded the power of nature. Your heart might sustain him for a few decades at most. Mine would give him centuries."

He only stared at her, wrestling with what she'd said. Arianna came in with the tea. She set the tray down and stood there looking from one of them to the other. "He's never going to believe you until you show him, Raven."

"I know."

"So?"

Sighing heavily, Raven got to her feet. She bent to a drawer in an end table and pulled it open. And then she pulled out a small-caliber weapon. It looked like a derringer. Duncan's blood rushed to his feet.

"What the hell are you—"

Raven handed the weapon to Arianna, then stood facing her friend. "Go on, do it. Let's get this out of the way."

Arianna pointed the gun squarely at Raven's chest, from a distance of no more than two feet.

"My God, no!" Duncan lunged between them just as Arianna pulled the trigger.

Fire tore through his chest even as the explosion rang in his ears. Warmth oozed and he drew a hand upward, pressed his palm hard against his sternum, and felt the blood pulsing from beneath it. "Jesus Christ," he said, but the words were slurred, and he sank to the floor. "Jesus Christ, you shot me. You freaking *shot* me."

Raven snatched a towel from somewhere and pressed it to the wound. But she seemed more interested in keeping his blood from staining her carpet than in halting its flow. "I'm sorry, Duncan," she whispered. Sitting down, she cradled his head in her lap. "You'll be all right. In a moment."

Her words were fading. Why wasn't someone calling 911? My God, were they just going to sit there and watch him . . . ? "I'm *dying*. . . ." he rasped.

"Only for a moment," Arianna said. "You'll be a believer very soon, Duncan. I swear, I don't know why Raven didn't just shoot you in the first place. Would have saved so much time." Then she grimaced at his chest. "It is *messy*, though."

"The phone . . . Someone call . . . an amb—"

"Oh, you're well beyond that, Duncan. No ambulance would do you any good now." Arianna tipped her head back and laughed, and Duncan tried to call her a bitch, but he wasn't sure the word was audible.

Raven bent closer, pressed her lips to his. And everything went black.

It felt as if he'd grabbed a bare wire with about 220 volts going through it. The jolt split him, surging up his breastbone, and for an instant he figured he must be in some operating room somewhere, with a surgeon opening his chest.

He arched up, tipped his head back, and dragged in a ragged gasp, starved, it seemed, for oxygen. And then his body relaxed and the power surge faded. He opened his eyes.

He was still in Raven's house. On the sofa now, stretched out, shirtless. His head felt achy, light, still buzzing with the remnants of whatever current had zapped through him.

"For the love of Christ," he muttered. "You still haven't called an ambulance?"

"No need, Duncan." Raven sat beside him, brushed his hair off his face. "Come on, sit up."

"Yeah, right."

"Sit up, Duncan." Her hands slid under his shoulders, and she eased him into an upright position. Arianna sat nearby. A basin of blood-tinted water at her side, with a pink-stained washcloth floating in it looking like a donor organ. His heartbeat quickened at the sight, and he instinctively pressed a hand to his wounded chest to keep himself from bleeding to death.

And then he frowned, because there was no pulsing warmth oozing now. No sticky residue on his skin. His fingers probed, and then he bowed his head, staring at his bared chest. His *clean* bared chest.

No blood. No wound. He blinked, pressing both hands to his chest now, moving them, pressing again, searching for the bullet hole. It had seemed gaping before. Maybe it was just smaller than it seemed, and . . .

"There's nothing there, Duncan," Arianna said. "You died. Right there on the floor. We cleaned you up, and put you on the couch. In less than an hour the wound healed and you revivified. You're alive now, and there's no hole in your chest because you're immortal."

He gaped at her, then stared up at Raven.

"I know it's shocking the first time," she whispered. "I know how difficult this is for you to believe. But, Duncan, we didn't mean to. Arianna was aiming at me—"

"Oh, but this is so much better. Really drives the point home."

"Arianna, *please!*"

Arianna shrugged, making a lip-zipping motion with one hand. Raven turned to him again. "From now on, you won't age. You're going to start noticing other changes, as well. You'll get stronger. Your other senses will sharpen. And your ability to manipulate nature, to do what we call magick, will be far stronger than it was before. Although, since you've never *been* a practicing Witch, I don't suppose you'll notice that."

Again, he looked at his chest. "I can't believe this."

"Get him a mirror, for heaven's sake," Arianna said in exasperation.

"You have to believe it, Duncan. It's true."

"It's true," he whispered. "It can't be . . . but it's true."

"Yes." He searched her eyes, and she repeated the word. "Yes, Duncan."

His head was whirling. Unreal. It was all so unreal.

"I want you to read this," Raven said. And she pressed a very old book into his hands. So old its pages were curled and yellow, and the leather cover cracked in places. "This is three hundred years old. It was what my mother left for me."

"Your mother?"

She nodded. "You see, I didn't know, either. Not until Nathanial Dearborne hanged my mother and me in a snowy square as you looked on, fighting to prevent it, but unable to. That was the first time we met, Duncan, on the gallows just before I was to die. And something happened between us there, some connection was made. But it was over before it even began, or so I thought. We were hanged. Our bodies were pitched into a heap of the dead, where criminals and victims of the plague were dumped. That's where I awoke. But my mother didn't. Nathanial came for me there, intent on taking my heart before I could revive. And he must have been desperate then, because as young as I was, it wouldn't have sustained him long. I *was* a powerful Witch, though, even then. And perhaps it was my magickal skill he sought. Or perhaps it was because you'd turned against him that day. You'd taken my side over his, and when he killed me, you hated him for it. You went to the place of the dead, too, looking for my body. You intended to give me a decent burial. But I awakened before either of you arrived, and I carried my mother into the woods and buried her there. And then I went home to find this book. Our cottage was ruined, had been plundered. My mother's sacred cauldron, with the rose painted on the front, was gone. But the book she'd left for me, hidden behind a loose stone in the hearth, remained."

Duncan opened the book reverently, scanned the first page—and knew, though it seemed impossible, that these really were her mother's words . . . and really had been written some three centuries ago. So sad, his eyes grew damp as he read them, and then he met Raven's again. "But I found you again after that, didn't I, Raven?"

She nodded. "I booked passage on a ship to the New World. You boarded the same ship. And later came to this very town, as its new minister, and met me again. But even then I didn't tell you the truth. I didn't trust you enough, Duncan. So when they pitched me from the cliffs for the crime of Witchery, you lunged after me, trying to save me."

Yes. Because it had seemed better to die trying to save her than to go on living without her.

How did he know that?

"If you'd known that I couldn't die . . . you wouldn't have fallen from those cliffs. You died because I didn't trust you with the truth. And that's why I've been so determined to tell you everything this time."

He stilled as the one memory that had remained intact came rushing back to him. The dream he'd had as a child, the one he'd thought had to be of his birth mother, came back to him now. Clearer than before.

"You found my body on the rocks," he said. "You were crying. God, it hurt me to see you crying. I wanted to touch you, to tell you it was all right, but I couldn't. I was . . . hovering above, somehow. You held me. You wouldn't let me go."

"Yes," she breathed, tears springing into her eyes. "Yes, Duncan, that's exactly the way it happened."

"And . . . *you* were there," he said, turning to Arianna. "You protected her, told her they were coming for her, made her let me go, and took her away from the danger."

Arianna nodded.

"The last thing I remember is watching the waves sweep my body away, swallow it up." He closed his eyes as a chill rushed through him. It was a terrifying memory. But real. And there. He recalled the clothes she wore, and those he'd been wearing. He remembered the differences in her speech as she held him and spoke to him. Old, arcane.

"My God, it's true, isn't it?"

Raven nodded. "Yes, Duncan. It's true."

"And my father . . . ?"

"Is one of the Dark Ones. He wants my heart, and likely yours, too."

Duncan shook his head slowly. He knew it was all true, all of it. And still . . .

He blinked his burning eyes dry. "People can change," he whispered, and he knew he was grabbing at straws. "If it's been as many years as you say it has, Raven, then how do you know he hasn't changed?"

She closed her eyes. "Oh, Duncan, I know you want that to be true, but he can't change. If he stops taking hearts, he'll weaken and die."

"But save his own soul."

"He sold his soul long ago."

"But there's a chance, Raven. There's a chance you're wrong about him. I've *seen* the changes in him since he came here. He's been kinder, more *real* than before."

Arianna got to her feet. "Why would the old man change after all this time? What motive could he possibly have to suddenly value his soul at all?"

Duncan looked at her squarely. "He has a son now."

The sorrowful looks the two women exchanged let him know they didn't believe him for a minute. He wasn't sure he believed it himself. But he wanted to. God, how he wanted to.

"I have to give him a chance," he said, turning to Raven. "I *have to*. He's the only father I've ever known, Raven. I . . . I care for him."

"Even though he might have killed your birth parents to get his hands on you, Duncan?"

"I don't know that," he insisted. "I . . . don't *want* to believe that."

Raven's eyes went round and soft, and she nodded. "All right. I . . . I understand."

"You're giving him a second chance," Arianna snapped. "A second chance that's liable to cost Raven her life, do you realize that?"

"Let him be, Arianna."

But something cracked in Duncan's heart. Was Arianna right? Was he making a huge mistake? He stared into Raven's eyes and hoped to God he wasn't. "I won't let him hurt you," he promised. "I swear it, Raven."

"I know you'll try," she whispered. Then she lowered her head. "Go on, go to your father, Duncan. Do what you feel you must."

Chapter 20

Duncan supposed he must have walked back into town. The evidence was there. He stood on the cobbled circle, the fountain on his right splashing as if the entire world hadn't just tilted off its axis. The courthouse loomed in front of him like some big, shadowy giant. No curtains yet on the lower floors. Nathanial had never been fond of frills or fluff. So the windows stood empty . . . just like the old man's eyes.

So he was here, and he hadn't brought the car in the first place, so he must have walked. He didn't remember the trip. Only the haze that had been descending over his brain—or was it a haze burning away, revealing a light too bright to look upon?—ever since he'd finally understood that Raven St. James was *not* delusional. But immortal. And so was he.

Immortal.

My God. It was so immense a concept his brain couldn't seem to grasp it. He kept thinking it must have been a dream, that it couldn't really have happened. No one had shot him. He hadn't bled. He hadn't died only to come back to life again on Raven St. James's sofa. But he knew that was bull. It *had* happened. And he needed to swallow it before it choked him. Swallow it, get over it, and figure out what the hell to do next.

Stop this ridiculous urge that kept surfacing . . . to test it. Jump off a

roof or step in front of a bus just to see what would happen. Stupid. If a
bullet in the chest wouldn't kill him, what the hell would?

He closed his eyes and swallowed. Damn, it was as if he had to think
about every step. Go to the door, open it up, step inside, speak to his father. His mind was so busy turning this over and over, examining it from
every angle, he kept forgetting to pay attention to what he was doing.
Forgetting to *breathe*, for God's sake.

"Duncan?"

He looked up, drew himself out of his mind, and met his father's
darting gaze. An old man. A weathered, careworn face, a little paler than
it was a couple of weeks ago. He was no killer. And he certainly had
aged, hadn't he? Didn't Raven say immortals stop aging? So why hadn't
Nathanial?

*Who are you kidding, Duncan? Can you remember him ever looking any
different? He's* always *looked like a man in his sixties.* Always.

He shook his head as if to clear it. "Father," was his greeting.

"Did you see her?"

Duncan nodded.

"Well? What did she say? Did she fill your head with lies and fantasies
again? Did she—"

"She said she'd like peace as much as you would, Father," Duncan interrupted. Tired—he sounded tired. *Felt* it, too. "She said if you'd be
willing to drop this ridiculous feud, so would she." It wasn't *precisely*
what she'd said, but he was confident he spoke nothing but the truth.
And she *did* say she wasn't pursuing this battle because she *wanted* to.

His father's brows bent, eyes narrowed, but instantly all of that
stopped. His face went as still as stone, and slowly he averted his eyes.
"Good," he said, and then he let his shoulders slump a little. "You can't
imagine my relief."

Duncan studied the old man with a practiced eye, but he couldn't
judge a thing, couldn't be objective, was all too aware that he wasn't in
control of the situation. He never had been.

"Relief?" he asked Nathanial. "Is that what you're feeling?"

Slowly his father's head came up. "You think *I'm* the one who started
this with her? She's the one who came in here screaming accusations and
trying to come between us!"

"Come between us? You could park a semi between us, Father, and
that's been true all my life. Long before she came into our lives."

"She's *always* been in our lives." Nathanial's head lowered. "I've been
trying to change that, son."

"Why?"

The brows crooked, the face puckered. "Why do you keep asking that?"

"Because I want to know. Was this a change of heart, *Dad*? Or is that just where it's leading?"

He held his father's pale eyes for once, willing the man to look at him, face him. And slowly he saw the knowledge dawn there. The realization that Duncan knew the truth.

"I was shot tonight, Father. Right in the chest." He touched the spot with one hand. "Point-blank."

His father seemed to go even whiter. "That's . . . that's ridiculous. Look at you, you're . . . you're fine."

"Yes, I know. Because I'm immortal." Nathanial's eyes fell closed. "And so are you," Duncan added.

There was a long taut strand of silence hanging in the air between them. Until it was broken by his father's ragged sigh, and this time when the old man's shoulders slumped, Duncan believed it was for real.

Duncan bent his head, knowing by his father's reaction that it was true. His father was immortal. And if he'd kept that truth to himself all this time, how could Duncan expect him to be honest now?

Sighing deeply, Nathanial said, "I can't talk to you about this now."

"No, not now," Duncan agreed tightly. "Not for the past thirty-five years, and not now."

"Duncan, you don't understand—"

"Or maybe I just don't want to."

Nathanial faced him. "I'm no immortal, Duncan," he said, and suddenly Duncan saw the shadows underneath his eyes. "Far from it, in fact. I'm sick, Duncan. I'm . . . I'm dying."

Duncan actually reeled backward at those words. "But—"

"That's why I came here, bought this place. To be close to you. To make up for all that time . . . to be your father just once . . . before it was too late." Shoulders shaking, the old man sank into a chair. And the sounds he made were as close to heartbreak as anything Duncan had ever heard.

Slowly, questions swirling still, he stepped closer. A hand went to his father's shoulder, and then he knelt and stared up into the old face. "That can't be."

"It is. I . . . I don't know what fantasies that pretty young thing has been weaving, Duncan. She's . . . she's disturbed. And tricky. I've dealt with her before, it's true. I don't know how she made you think you'd been shot, and convinced you of all this nonsense. Starter pistol, blanks, blood capsules . . . perhaps even some kind of hallucinogen. She does claim to be a Witch, you know. Maybe it was a spell of some sort. I don't know. I don't care. It doesn't really matter in the scheme of things."

Duncan swallowed hard. He tried to fit what his father said with what had happened this morning at Raven's, knew intellectually that it didn't fit, didn't make sense, but set it aside for now. He'd hear what his father had to say. He'd listen to the lies. One last time. And it *would be* the last time.

"Every day I get weaker, son. I don't have much time left. I don't want to spend it arguing over some girl."

Just as Raven said . . . They weaken in time, and have to kill again. . . .

Nathanial lifted his head, eyes imploring, looking suddenly very much like the eyes of a dying old man.

"I should have told you sooner. I'm sorry for that."

Duncan knew better, he *knew* better. Hadn't he just been wondering about his father's unusual strength? Hadn't he just been noticing how the man had never changed?

"This confrontation has taken a lot out of me, I'm afraid."

"Rest, then," Duncan said. Because he needed time, time to think, to figure out what Nathanial could have to gain with this latest ruse. "I'll, uh . . . I'll make us some dinner."

"I've no appetite," his father said, and he got slowly to his feet. "I'd like to go to bed."

"But there's so much more to talk about." He faced his father, made his voice firm. "I want the truth, and I'll have it before this night is over."

"And what does it matter now? I told you, Duncan, I'm *dying*."

"So you'll take the truth to your grave with you?" He felt mean. Cruel. Hell, he was being heartless, but he'd had it with the lies. "I know damn well it was no parlor trick Raven pulled on me this morning. I *felt* the heat of that bullet that plowed through my chest, Father, and I had a hole the size of a golf ball to show for it. It was my blood all over me, not some trick capsule."

His father closed his eyes, shook his head, and turned toward the stairs. "You won't let up on me, will you? Even now?"

"I'm sorry. I need to hear the truth, and I'd like to hear it from you."

"All right, then." Nathanial mounted the bottom step, moved up one, then another. "You'll hear it. But not now. Come back in an hour, Duncan. Come back in an hour and I'll tell you everything. *Everything*. I promise."

Duncan breathed deeply, trying to clear his head. His father was dying. It would have been easier to believe than anything else he'd heard today. But he didn't believe it. Oh, he might be weak, maybe feeling poorly. Raven said the hearts wore out in time.

He swallowed the bile that rose in his throat, marveled that he was referring back to conversations he'd considered nothing more than symptoms of mental illness only a few hours ago. He was exhausted, drained.

"All right. Rest. But I'm not going anywhere. I'll be here waiting. And we *will* talk."

Without looking back, his father climbed the stairs, seeming old. Weak. Sick.

Duncan sank to the floor, glanced at the empty crates all around him. Crates that had held the most cherished possessions of murdered women. It was wrong, what his father was doing. Just wrong. He'd known it from the beginning.

And he knew other things, too. Raven wasn't lying to him.

She wouldn't. The things she said about Nathanial were absolutely true. If she said he'd killed, then he had. If she said he wanted her heart, then he did. He'd hoped his father could be capable of change, but he doubted that now.

As for his father . . . he would lie to Duncan without batting an eye. Duncan sighed. He'd give the old man some time, let him rest or get his story straight or whatever he was doing up there. And then he'd get the answers he needed. He'd insist on that. An hour. Two at the most, and then he'd make Nathanial tell the truth, for the first time.

I picked up the phone when it jangled.

Nathanial Dearborne's voice rasped at me. "I need a heart. I wanted yours, but I'm out of time, Raven. Duncan's will have to do."

My throat went dry. I swallowed, tried to speak. "No," was all I managed.

"You or him, darling. You or him. I won't wait long."

Lowering my eyes to shield them from Arianna's probing ones, I said, "Where are you?"

I tried to keep my face expressionless as the man who'd been hunting me for most of my life told me where to meet him.

Slowly I replaced the receiver, keeping my eyes carefully turned away from Arianna's curious, probing brown ones.

"Who was that?" she asked.

The lie stuck in my throat. I loved her—lying to her made me physically ill. But I forced the words anyway. "Duncan. He . . . wants to see me. To . . . talk."

"Does he?"

"Yes. I, um, said I'd meet him."

"Where?"

I looked up quickly, knowing I'd stumbled, and forced a smile that felt as weak as it probably looked. "Someplace private. Perhaps he's beginning to remember after all."

"Why are you lying to me, Raven?"

I looked away fast. "I'm not. Is it so hard to believe he might want some time alone with me?"

"It is when I combine it with the look on your face. You look shaken." She gripped my chin, tilted my head to the side and stared down at me as if she were a sergeant inspecting some soldier's rifle. "No, Raven, this isn't the face of a girl rushing off to meet her lover."

"I'm no girl." I pulled myself free of her grasp, tried to act huffy when all I felt was guilt for lying to the best friend I'd ever known. My sister. "I'm over three hundred, for heaven's sake. And you know how important this is to me. Can you blame me for being nervous?"

She only kept looking at me.

"I'd better get ready."

"Yes. Don't keep him waiting."

I swallowed hard and headed from the room into one of our countless corridors and up one of the many sets of stairs. Arianna didn't follow. My room was my refuge, and I needed it right now. I think she sensed that.

The small, oval portrait I'd labored over for months stood on the night table beside my bed, bearing little physical resemblance to Duncan, but holding his essence all the same. The face I'd blurred, but his dark gleaming eyes shone from their deep wells, and his tumbling satin hair tempted my fingers just as it always had. His shadowed jawline spoke of feelings, immense feelings, all bubbling inside him in search of escape. It captured him, my experiment in painting.

I paused a moment, to run my fingertip over the image of Duncan's face. "For you," I whispered. "I do this for you."

A tear burned at the back of my eye. Sadness welling up, not because I might be about to die, or worse. I hated to think of what that sort of death was truly like. For it wasn't death, really, but a kind of limbo. The body alive, but inanimate. The heart beating, but captive, providing life force to a foreign body. And yet that wasn't why I cried.

I cried for the love Duncan and I had once shared. The love I'd spent so many lifetimes searching for, only to realize, at long last, that it wasn't coming back to me. A once-in-a-lifetime kind of love like ours had been was just that. Once in a lifetime. I'd never find it again. All these years I'd naively believed that Duncan would feel just the way he had before when I finally found him again. But he didn't. Perhaps he couldn't. Oh, he was attracted to me, drawn to me—even claimed to love me. But it was only a faint echo of what we'd had before. And that was all it would ever be. I supposed it was time I accept that.

Yes. Difficult though it was, it was time.

And this was not the moment to let the knowledge weaken me. I needed to acknowledge, accept, and move beyond it. Tonight I would fight for my life, as I'd done so many times before. My opponent was the most powerful foe I'd ever be likely to face. He could kill me very easily. I'd need to be sharp, to be quick. I'd need to be smart and I'd need to be ruthless.

Or I'd die.

Sniffling, I drew my hands away from the portrait on the stand and opened the table's drawer. From inside I took a velvet pouch and, pulling it open, removed the agate pendant. No stone was more protective than agate, and this one had been charged with a spell to make it even more so. I fastened the chain around my neck, then turned to the door.

Nathanial had given me thirty minutes. No more time for dawdling. I left my haven, my bedroom, grabbing a cloak on the way. The dark blue velvet one that hung by the door, because it reminded me of that one I'd worn long ago. The one left to me by my mother. I pulled it snug around me as I tapped down the stairs. Swathed in those soft, warm folds, I felt protected. Safe.

But I wasn't. I was far from safe. And there wasn't much I could do about it.

I left on foot, by the Coast Road, and I knew Arianna must be watching me. She knew me too well to have believed my lie. But it didn't matter. All that mattered was that she not follow me. Or that I lose her if she did. I wouldn't have her jumping between Nathanial's blade and mine, and dying in my place.

I walked quickly and with purpose, but not so quickly that I didn't take time to *feel*. The sea wind in my face, tugging at my hair. The tiring sun, already relaxing on the western horizon, warm on my skin, bright in my eyes.

When I'd gone around a bend in the road, I turned sharply left, cutting down the steep cliff's face. There was one instant when Arianna could have seen me change direction, but only an instant. And I hoped the road's curve hid me from her sharp eyes for long enough.

Pebbles clattered away beneath my feet, and I slipped, gripped a sharp rock, scraped the skin of my palm, but held on. Digging in with fingers and the toes of my shoes, I managed to keep from falling, and slowly inched my way to where this steep face melded with the path I'd taken so many times. Here, the going eased. When I reached my boat, I took it, hoping Arianna would never think to check. And then, keeping close to shore, I paddled back the way I'd come. Avoiding rocks, bounding on waves as they tumbled toward shore, but unable to go out further, for fear Arianna would spot me from above. I moved past the point where our house stood high above, and in the other direction, until the cliff's sheer face eased again, shallowed, melted. There I rowed toward shore.

My feet got wet when I stepped out, and a wave rolled in at the same time, but I barely noticed. Too busy looking for a place to hide my craft. I dragged it into some brush, laid some loose branches and weeds over it, and brushed off my hands, satisfied that at least it didn't leap out and shout my presence to anyone who happened to pass this way. A trained eye would still spot it, but not unless they happened to be looking. And if I'd done everything right, Arianna would have no reason to be looking for me here.

That done, I stood still, ocean at my right, and the woods to my left. The woods where I would meet Nathanial. My hand touched the hilt of my blade, closed around it, and remained there. I glanced out at the whispering trees. They glowed with soft green-yellow auras as the sun sank behind them. Like magick, a brief, luminous magick, that faded away, and the light with it.

And I felt its loss. No light now. Nothing. Just me, and the woods, and the darkness, and out there somewhere, Nathanial Dearborne, and his bloodstained blade.

He didn't intend to fall asleep. And when he woke, head thick and eyes foggy, he had the oddest sensation that it hadn't been sleep. Not really. It had been something else. Something foreign, and malignant. Its remnants made him shudder as if something slimy had slipped over his spine. He felt soiled.

He got up, didn't even remember sitting down, but he apparently had. And then he remembered his conversation with his father, and the reason he hadn't left when Nathanial had gone upstairs to nap.

He didn't trust him.

But now, there was more.

There was an old man on a gallows, the rising sun painting his bony face, a light of malicious glee in his pale eyes as his hand caressed the lever. There was a girl more afraid than any he'd ever seen before, and yet so brave she shamed everyone else there. There was a warmth, an intense, magnetic *warmth* that seemed to melt from her eyes into his when she looked up at him.

"Believe me, mistress, I'd help you if I could."

"They'd only kill you as well, did you try."

He felt it. Felt *her*. All of her. Her innocence, her power, her allure. Her beauty, not just the way she looked but the beauty inside her. He felt it flowing through him like warm honey, cleansing everything ugly from his soul. Filling every empty spot there was in him.

"I willna forget you."

"If there is memory in death, Duncan, I shall remember you always."

He remembered that moment. He'd been wearing loose black robes, and Nathanial had, too. He'd fallen in love with her, with Raven, right then. With that look, that intense moment of feeling, all of it magnified a thousand times by the imminent presence of the Reaper.

And then he heard it again. That sound. The creaking, the slam, the horrible snap of a slender neck when it reached the end of a rope. It sickened Duncan, and his face contorted in remembered anguish as the memory played out in his mind. And then he was there, beneath the gallows. Holding her, his tears wetting her hair. Her body so soft, so small in his arms. Innocence. Utter innocence snuffed out without a thought. And Nathanial . . .

In his mind he looked up at the man. Nathanial looked back. Smiling.

"God, no . . ." The words were a rasp, a whisper, as Duncan shook the memories away, blinked the past from his eyes and turned to face the stairs the way Raven had faced those of the gallows. Fists clenched at his sides, he strode up them.

"It's time, Nathanial," he muttered as he moved upward. Somehow he couldn't bring himself to call the man "Father." Not now. "And you'll tell me the truth. For once in your life, you'll tell me the truth."

At the top he turned toward Nathanial's room, stepped up to its closed door, and gripped the knob, not bothering to knock.

But when he twisted, he felt resistance. "Unlock this door and let me in. We need to talk. *Now.*"

There was not so much as a breath in answer. Duncan's stomach clenched. "Nathanial?"

Nothing.

His heart tripped, and he thought of Raven, and for once, he wasn't worrying about her hurting his black-hearted *father*. He was worried about Nathanial hurting her. Stepping backward, he slammed his shoulder into the door, then stumbled through when it split and fell beneath the force of the blow.

"You'll grow stronger than you were before." Raven's voice whispered through his mind. He managed to keep his footing, barely, but the splintered wood on the floor shocked him. He *was* stronger.

He turned, then, toward the bed. It was perfectly made, not a rumple, not a wrinkle. Beyond it the window stood open, its curtains billowing inward like ghosts.

"My God, he's gone after Raven. . . ."

Duncan raced to the window. Hands braced on its sill, he looked out, but his father was nowhere in sight. Not only that, but the sheer drop, and the distance to the ground loomed huge. No way out but to jump. "Quite a feat for a weak, dying old man, isn't it?" he asked himself, and then his shoulders sagged. He'd done it, hadn't he? Given Nathanial the benefit of the doubt in spite of what Raven had said. And now Arianna's warning rang over and over again in his mind. *It could cost Raven her life.*

God, he'd been a fool.

He remembered the gallows. Then the cliffs. He couldn't lose her again. He *wouldn't.*

"Duncan! Duncan, are you here?"

He spun around at the sound of Arianna's voice and called back to her. "Here. I'm coming." Then he ran down the stairs to greet her.

"Where is he?" She didn't bother with preamble, and he could see she was breathless, wide-eyed, pale with worry.

"I don't know. He did something to me, made me sleep, and slipped away. I'm afraid he's gone after Raven."

"She had a call a half hour ago," Arianna said, turning in a slow circle, pushing one hand through her blond locks. "She told me it was you, that you wanted her to meet you somewhere."

He shook his head. "I didna call her."

She glanced at him sharply, even as he bit his tongue, but didn't remark on his speech.

"Nathanial, then," Arianna said after a moment. "I thought as much. She's gone to meet him." Closing her eyes, she tipped her head back. "But I don't know where. I tried to follow, but she gave me the slip. Damn her for being so protective of those she loves."

"Why would she go to fight him?" Duncan asked desperately. "I believed her, not him. And she promised she wouldn't."

"Oh, don't kid yourself, Duncan. Nathanial knows exactly how to get Raven to dance to whatever tune he plays. All he had to do was threaten one of us." She tilted her head. "Probably you, since I was safe at her side when the bastard called."

Duncan felt a crushing sensation in his chest. "She'd face him down to protect me?"

"She'd die for you, Duncan. Just as you would have for her . . . *did* for her . . . once."

He brushed past her, yanked the door wide. "We have to find her."

Her hand on his shoulder brought him up short, but he didn't turn. She spoke to his back. "I don't think she can beat him. Prepare yourself, Duncan. By the time we get to her . . . it may be too—"

"Don't even think it."

Chapter 21

I waited, paced, and grew restless. When the sun had descended fully beyond the western horizon to sleep in some distant place far beyond the trees, I shivered. The air cooled all at once, and gooseflesh rose on my arms and the back of my neck.

An owl hooted three times, and I turned my head quickly toward the sound. The people of Old Sanctuary would have said it was an omen, a warning of death. Accurate. There *would* be a death tonight. The only question was, would it be mine? Or Nathanial's?

A chill worked up my spine, settling right between my shoulder blades, as if someone's eyes were on me. I looked behind me, but there was only the sea. Waves rolling gently over the stony beach, pausing there like a breath held in anticipation, and then receding in a slow-motion sigh.

Swallowing my fear, I turned to face the forest again. I stiffened my resolve, drew my blade, and walked forward. One step, then another, and another. I reached the edge of the woods and paused there, sensing the presence of my enemy. I couldn't see him, but I knew he was near, and likely had been ever since I'd arrived.

My fingers tightened on the hilt of my blade, and I stepped through the first line of trees and into the darker area beyond. "Where are you?" I called out.

"Waiting," he answered, and his hoarse voice had little substance. Like the voice of a ghost. He must be weakening. No, it wouldn't do to underestimate him. Perhaps that was only what he wanted me to think.

I moved forward a few more steps, which took me beyond the clusters of trees on this side and into a small clearing. Pines towered all around me, a circle made by nature. Standing in a half crouch on a carpet of grass, I moved my fingers on the hilt and scanned the shadows that loomed amid the trees.

I didn't see him. Didn't hear him. Instead, I *felt* him; the crushing impact of his aged body when he hurled himself at me from behind. The red-hot trail his blade left as it arched across my back.

I hit the ground hard, face first, but rolled fast and sprang to my feet again. He'd knocked the wind out of me, taken me by surprise, and sliced my flesh. I pulsed with pain, felt the blood dampening my blouse, soaking through it, to stain the cloak.

Facing him, I reached to the ties at my neck and pulled, then tossed the cloak aside. "You had the advantage, Nathanial," I told him, careful to keep the pain from my voice. "And wasted it."

"Too eager to see my enemy bleed, I suppose."

"No more than I am." I lunged and swept my dagger's tip across his soft belly, drawing away just as quickly and avoiding his return thrust. We battled, fought, nicked and cut each other, but neither scored a killing blow.

We circled each other, both of us breathless, then lunged again, slashing and stabbing in a tangle of blades and limbs and then drawing back again.

I was tiring, panting.

He danced forward, I danced back, into the thickest cluster of trees. Then I focused on the pines. Their scent, the stringy, sticky bark, the needles that whispered their secrets all around me with every breath of a breeze that passed through them. In effect, I vanished. Melded with the pine trees and, in silence, thought of Trees Speaking and all he'd taught me.

When Nathanial pursued me, he slowed, stilled. His eyes darting this way and that as he searched for me. Then narrowing as he understood.

"You're very good," he whispered. Then thrust his dagger into the trunk of the tree nearest him. "*Very* good. But you can't keep your focus long. I'll find you, Raven."

Not long, he was right. But long enough.

My feet are roots, sinking deep into the rich, black earth.

I curled my toes. I wouldn't move. Not yet. To move would break the enchantment. I'd wait until he turned his back to me. It would give me the advantage I needed if I hoped to survive.

My body is still and strong, and my skin is like bark. The blood in my veins is pine sap, sticky and smelling of the very spirit of Earth herself.

Nathanial came closer, jabbed another tree.

My arms are limbs. Each nerve ending a fine needle, quivering, sighing on the breeze.

I could feel my heart pounding, hear it in my ears as Nathanial came still nearer, stabbing his blade into first one trunk and then another, until he reached the one right beside me. So loud, that beat in my chest. So strong with fear as I stood motionless, praying he wouldn't hear it. *It's the pulse of life through my trunk. It's the thrum of the spirit in me.* I told myself anything to keep the image alive, the image I projected, the only thing between Nathanial's blade and my heart right now.

He came closer, lifted his blade, tilted its tip up and spasmodically clenched his fist on the hilt.

Just as he thrust it at me, I let the image dissolve and dodged to the side. He missed me cleanly, but stood grinning at me all the same. "You can't outwit me, Raven," he said. "Never that. I'm too old, too clever to be fooled by your tricks."

I couldn't even argue it. "So I see. Then I suppose my only hope is to outfight you."

"We both know you cannot."

"We'll see." I lurched, swinging my blade, and when he dodged the blow, I leaped and kicked him hard in the belly. A loud grunt gusted from him as he doubled over. By the time he got his breath and straightened again, I was racing through the trees, taking an uphill course. If I could tire the old man, I might stand a chance of beating him. Maybe. If he were as desperate for a heart as he'd claimed, he should be weak. He should lack stamina.

He'd shown no signs of it so far, though. And if he'd lied . . .

I wouldn't think of that now.

He gave chase. I knew when I paused for a breath and heard him crashing through the pines, branches snapping, needles raining to the ground in his wake like minuscule raindrops, whispering down.

Higher, then. And I ran on.

And then the trees parted before me, opening all at once onto a sheer drop to the sea. Planting my feet, I nearly overbalanced. My arms whirled backward twice, then I went still, blinking at the vista spread out below my feet. Endless space, and below it, jagged rocks winking and blinking up at me as the waves covered and uncovered them. White froth.

"Oh, now, this *is* amusing."

I turned slowly, faced Nathanial. He stood in a powerful crouch, and if his face was flushed, it was with excitement, not exhaustion. His eyes gleamed. He wasn't tired. If anything he was thriving on this battle. "You made a grave mistake, didn't you, Raven?"

Grimly I knew Arianna had been right. I didn't have the skills to beat him. I'd never beaten him. And if I fought him now, he would kill me. And then perhaps he'd kill Duncan.

But if I didn't . . .

He'd promised he would go after Duncan anyway.

I couldn't die here. I had to survive, even if it meant running from this fight. At least that way I would be alive to warn Duncan, to protect him, or try to. Goddess, I should have listened to Arianna in the first place. She'd *told* me I couldn't beat him.

I looked to the left, to the right. In the distance I saw two forms coming toward me. Far below, they moved along a path leading up to these cliffs. And as I stared down at them, focused my vision, I saw the woman's soft blond hair riffling in the breeze, and then the dark locks of the man beside her. Arianna . . . and Duncan. As if sensing my eyes on them, they both looked up. Duncan pointed, and I saw his lips move. It was likely he called my name, though he was too far away for me to hear him. Then the two ran. They'd be here soon.

I met Nathanial's eyes again. Cold.

"Yes," he said, having seen my thoughts in my eyes. "But by the time they arrive, you'll be dead. And I'll be gone. And know this as you die, Raven. I will take Duncan's heart, too, once you're out of the way. Your friend can't protect him forever."

I narrowed my eyes on him. He was lying. I saw it there clearly. He wouldn't take Duncan's heart unless he had to. And he wouldn't even attempt it while Arianna was nearby. He feared her.

But there was no time to work this out in my mind any further, because he leaped at me. His blade drove directly at my midsection, and though I moved to block the thrust, I moved too late. Hot steel sank deep into my belly. Burning pain, terrible pain. I cried out, but all that emerged was a gurgling sound and a mouthful of blood.

He jerked the blade out again. Then he reached for me. And I knew he would hold me and carve into my chest, rip out my heart, end it all now. I took a single step backward as he reached for me. And there was nothing there. Air. I fell into its breath. In silence I plummeted. No sound at all. Not until the impact.

Duncan ran. His lungs worked in a way he'd never felt them work before. Efficiently. Powerfully. The beat of his heart seemed like an engine. Unstoppable, strong. His legs pushed his body to speeds greater than he could have reached before. But he didn't marvel at these changes. Only noted them and felt grateful, because it meant he could reach Raven faster.

He could still see her, facing his father—or the man he'd called his father—on the cliffs. Nathanial moved closer, until Raven seemed trapped.

"We're not going to make it in time," Duncan rasped.

"We have to." Arianna's voice was a monotone of utter determination.

Then Nathanial drove forward, and Raven went stiff. Duncan could see her eyes widen, see her lips move, and the scarlet that bubbled from them. She looked down, then toward him. And Nathanial jerked his blade from her belly.

"No!" Duncan screamed with a voice that rolled like thunder, like the words of the gods themselves; his command broke the silent pause on that cliff. "Dammit, Nathanial, leave her alone!"

But it was as if no one heard. Nathanial reached out. Raven stepped back and into oblivion. She didn't even cry out. Just fell. *Just fell.* He could hear her clothes snapping like flags in the wind, see her hair fluttering. He screamed her name in anguish. His head felt as if it were exploding, splitting, when her body hit the rocks below. A shock went through him. Pain, horror, devastation . . .

And memory. The clear, vivid memory of all of this happening before.

His heart filled with long-repressed emotions, unbearable emotions he realized had been there all along. Condensed, perhaps, and bottled up somewhere. But the bottle had shattered and the feelings swelled until he didn't think he could contain them. And then he was running, clambering, half climbing, half falling, sending a shower of rocks down the cliffs before him, hearing their plunking sounds as they hit the water. Sliding, skinning his hands and chin and every other part of him, tearing his clothes, he made his way to the bottom.

And then he paused on the shore and searched the unforgiving waves for her.

There.

She lay faceup, half submerged. Her head and one shoulder and arm were sprawled on a sloped rock. The rest of her body submerged, broken, as the waves tugged at it, so steadily and greedily that she'd be swept out to sea soon.

He moved as if entranced. Sloshing into the water, walking out deeper, deeper, then swimming. He'd kicked free of his shoes at some point. He wasn't certain when. But he reached that rock and pulled himself up onto its slick surface. And then he gathered her broken body into his arms.

Limp. So limp, so shattered. A porcelain doll smashed and tossed aside.

"No," he whispered. "No, not now. God, Raven, not now."

Her hair, long, dripping with seawater that streamed over her face and shoulders. He gently smoothed it, stroked her face with his hand as his tears came. Burning hot, like acid on his cheeks, they flowed. They fell, and mingled with the water on her lips.

He clung tighter, pulling her full against him, rocking her slowly and weeping without control, without shame. So tightly, he held her body pressed to his, her lifeless head heavy on his shoulder. The enormity of it crushed down on him all at once. To have loved her this much, this damn much, so much it was every part of him, every cell, every breath, his soul, his life . . . all his lives . . . How could he not have known? How could he not have *felt* this? And now, now when he finally *did* feel it, and know it and recognize it for what it was, and remember it . . . she was gone. She was gone. Oh, God, she was gone!

He kissed her face, her hair, as sobs rose up and tore at his chest, threatening to split him in two. Now he understood how she'd felt all those years ago, when she'd held his lifeless, broken body on these rocks. Now he understood what she'd faced . . . all those years alone. God, they stretched out before him like a desert, where every grain of sand was a shard of glass, and which he had to cross barefoot without a sip of water.

"I willna," he whispered. "I canna do it, Raven. I dinna know how you did, but I canna. I canna go on without you, lass."

She had, though. Her strength must be an awesome thing, to enable her to survive with this kind of pain. Three hundred years. Three centuries, she'd dealt with it.

"An' when you found me again, what did I do? God, Raven, what did I do to you? I trusted *him*, believed *him*." He let her head fall backward, staring down at her face, so pale and still and lovely. "How that must have hurt you. How could I hurt you like that? You . . . you, Raven, my soul, my heart. How many times will I lose you this way? How many times?"

Still. So still. So dead. He closed his eyes and held her, loving her with everything in him, and another memory came to him. He was standing there, holding her in his arms for the first time. Beneath a gallows as he sawed at the filthy rope with a pilfered blade. And held her, and cried for the woman he didn't even know.

But he had. He'd known her then, somehow. Some way. His soul had recognized hers. His heart had known hers, and he'd loved her. He'd loved her from the first moment he'd set eyes on her.

"I told you I wasna the man you remembered, Raven. But I am. I'm Duncan Wallace, an' I was born in 1675 in the land of the Scots, the land of my father an' his before him. I'm the man who loved you all those lifetimes ago, an' I love you still, Raven St. James. I love you still."

He drew a breath, somehow got to his feet, and holding her cradled as carefully as if she were made of ice crystal, he drew her with him as he made his way to shore. He wouldn't leave her to the sea. He couldn't. Something was niggling at him through his anguish. A faint, desperate hope that wouldn't leave him alone. He didn't want to let the hope form fully, for fear 'twould only destroy him if it turned out to be a false one. But as he stepped out of the waves and carried her onto the shore, he couldn't suppress it any longer.

He laid her down, in the lush green grass, in a spot dotted with tiny blue forget-me-nots. And then he sat beside her, leaned over her, and gently spread her hair to dry in the grasses. "That first time I held you, lass, that first time I wept for you . . . you were nay dead then. You survived that noose. You told me you were immortal. You told me you couldna die unless the bastard took your heart." He closed his eyes, recalling the thrust of Nathanial's blade, but he'd been so far away. He couldn't tell. . . .

"Tell me that bastard didna do that."

Gently he touched the front of her torn, bloodstained blouse. Even the cool kiss of the ocean hadn't washed those stains away. Nothing would, and he hoped nothing would wash them from Nathanial's hands, either.

His heart in his throat, he prayed in silence. *Please . . . please, dinna let it be. . . .*

Opening her blouse, he stared down at her chest. Pale, beaded with droplets of seawater, but unmaimed. There was no gaping hole, no wound near her heart.

He spread the blouse further and saw the wound she *had* suffered, the deep cut of Nathanial's blade, high in her belly. But even as he looked, that wound began to heal. Its edges puckered and pulled in on themselves as if magnetized. One side met the other, pressed like a kiss, and seemed to meld before his eyes.

Stunned, he drew his gaze upward, focused on her face, afraid to believe, afraid to hope . . .

"Raven?"

And then she went rigid, back arching off the ground, hands clenching fistfuls of grass at her sides, heels pressing the earth. Her neck arched as well, chin pointing skyward, and she sucked in a harsh, greedy breath. It made him think of electrocution, that brief seizure. Her eyes went wide, too wide, for just an instant. And then her body relaxed again, and she lay limp on the ground, blinking slowly, staring at him from unfocused eyes.

"Raven," he whispered. "Raven, Raven, Raven." He slipped his arms around her, beneath her, lifting her gently against him, holding her close, but not close enough. It would never be close enough. She hugged his neck, so pliable in his arms, melting there. His hands burying themselves in her hair, he drew her head back slightly, and then he pressed his lips to hers, kissing her more deeply, more urgently than he had in this lifetime. Kissing her the way he had before, in that other time, when he'd known what she was to him. Because he knew it now. He finally knew it now.

She blinked in confusion when he lifted his head away. Her slender, perfect fingers touched his cheeks, touched the tears there as she frowned. He couldn't speak, couldn't put the overwhelming things he was feeling into words. Not yet, not yet. He felt as if he'd been lost . . . wandering and lost, and searching . . . and now he'd found her. He'd found himself. He'd come home.

He bent and kissed her again, and this time he didn't stop. His hands pushed her blouse away, caressed her breasts, felt them warming, felt her entire body warming to his touch. He kissed her neck, her shoulders, her belly, where that wound had been. He kissed the place where her heart beat in her chest and willed that it would always remain there, strong and alive and full of love for him. He kissed her hips as he undressed her. Her thighs. Her center, where he lingered. How he loved her. *How he'd always loved her.*

She whispered his name with her heart in her breath and her hands in his hair, and he tasted more of her, wanted to devour her, make her truly a part of him, take her inside him somehow and keep her there, cherished and safe. Always safe.

When she cried out, he moved up over her body once more. He ran his hands over her flesh. Living and warm. Over limbs, alive and responsive now, no longer limp and broken. Did she know what she was to him? Could she know? My God, was it even possible that he was that much to her, as well?

Yes. It shone from her eyes and danced on the tiny, tremulous smile on her lips as she opened to him, held him, drew him down, took him inside her. She held his gaze as he moved, and she moved with him. Rocked him, loved him. He stared right into her eyes, into her soul, it seemed, as he made love to her. And the pounding of her heart and the pounding of his own blended with the pounding of the waves against the shore until it was all one. All one . . . and he felt as if he and she were one. A single soul that had been split for a time, united again at long last. She never blinked, nor did he. And when her lips parted and her breaths came in short little gasps, and he rode her faster and harder and deeper, their gazes remained locked. He felt their souls connect and touch, through their eyes.

She cried out his name, those black eyes widening. He felt the pressure build inside him, and then the explosion as he spilled into her, his entire body quivering with the force of his release. And in that moment, he saw himself in her eyes. As if he truly *had* merged with her, as if his soul really did live inside her.

And only then did those eyes fall closed.

He relaxed atop her, sliding slightly to the side, to ease the burden of his weight. "I have so much to tell you," he whispered.

She nodded. Kissed his head. "And I you. I'd been thinking, Duncan, that our chance had passed. That we could never be as we were before." Her hand stroked his hair. "But I know now that I can't go on without you, Duncan. So whatever you can give me, it will be enough. I'll *make* it be enough."

He lifted his head, stared down into her eyes. "You dinna ken what this was, do you, lass?"

She smiled slightly. "You sound like the Highland lad you were so long ago. Are you lapsing into a brogue you don't even recall, Duncan?"

"Am I? I dinna care if I am. It doesna matter. Nothing does right now, except . . ." He licked his lips, swallowed hard. "When I saw you on the cliffs . . . when I saw you fall—"

She sat up straight, eyes flying wide. "Nathanial! The bastard nearly had me! Duncan, we have to . . ." She paused, looking past him. "Oh, no," she whispered, and her face went pale.

"What is it?"

She snatched her clothes, wet and tattered, throwing them on haphazardly. "Arianna! She was with you. Where did she go, Duncan, where—"

He gave his head a shake. He'd completely forgotten about Raven's friend. "We . . . we were together when you went over the edge. I dinna ken where she went then, Raven. I was only thinkin' of you, trying to get to you. When I did . . . she wasna with me."

Her face crumpled, and her fingers went to her lips. Openmouthed, she sucked in a breath and got to her feet, righting her clothes as best she could. "She's gone after Nathanial." Closing her eyes, she shook her head. "He's better than either of us knew, Duncan. He'll kill her."

"We'll stop him." He helped her to her feet, and when she stumbled, held her tight to his side. "Are you sure you're all right?"

Raven nodded. Always so strong, so determined. "I love her, Duncan."

"I know. I can see it."

"He probably ran back to his lair—that obscenity he calls a museum. He doesn't want to face Arianna. He fears her. . . . She fought him once . . . nearly beat him, I think."

"That's where we'll go. It'll be all right, Raven, I promise. He's never goin' to hurt you, nor anyone you care about, ever again. I swear it."

She stared up at him, and he saw the questions in her eyes. Maybe because he'd spoken with such passion just now, maybe because she sensed he meant every word.

"Later," he promised, bending to plant a quick, tender kiss on her mouth. "I'll tell you everythin' later."

He took her hand, closed his eyes briefly in ecstasy as he realized how good it was to hold that hand in his again . . . and together, they ran.

Chapter 22

Damn!

She'd done it, Nathanial thought viciously. Raven St. James had come between him and Duncan all over again. And she'd gotten away with it!

He'd had the woman! Had her right in his hands, impaled on his dagger, and *still* she managed to escape him! He should have held on to her, should have . . . but what use were *should haves* now? She'd escaped him. Fallen from those cliffs, to send his soft-hearted son scurrying after her. Once again Duncan had chosen Raven over Nathanial, even now, when they were supposed to be father and son. Even now.

But not her fair-haired companion. No, Arianna hadn't been distracted for a moment. She'd headed *up* the cliffs, not down. And Nathanial had known then that she was coming for him.

He should have left this town, this state, perhaps this country, right then. Should have fled Arianna's wrath without hesitation. He could seek out some weaker immortal once he was safely away, take the first heart he found and get stronger. But to leave without the hearts he'd already taken—those he kept captive in small wooden boxes—would be to leave whatever vitality remained. So he'd returned to the old courthouse, to the small room at the top where he kept them, locked away from prying eyes inside their tiny wooden prisons. Some beat so weakly now they could barely be heard. He suspected they'd stop one day. But they hadn't. Most were no longer strong enough to support life, yet they kept beating on. One beat an hour, one beat a day. Were they truly immortal? Would they beat eternally? Somewhere, perhaps, in the dusty tomes he'd collected over the centuries, he might find an answer to that puzzle. An explanation. But he hadn't yet.

If *she* arrived in time, he never would. And there would be no time to take his books or his journals with him.

Quickly he opened a large case and set it in the middle of the floor. And then he snatched the most recent kills, the strongest hearts, from the shelf, carefully setting those boxes inside.

Speed was of the essence here. He couldn't face *her*, not now. She'd nearly beaten him once long ago, when he'd mistaken her for easy prey in Scotland. She'd been younger then. Weaker. He'd been at his best.

And she'd nearly killed him.

He would never forget the power of emotion again. Even as he'd battled, losing ground with every thrust, he'd wondered at her strength, her power. And reading his mind, it seemed, she'd uttered her curse. "You took the man I loved," she'd all but growled. "And I'll kill you for it."

She nearly had. He'd run. Fled for his life, from a mere infant of a High Witch. And a woman, at that.

Thrusting the memory away, he closed his case, hefted it, and turned toward the doorway. Never again would he underestimate the power of hatred.

"It wasn't the power of hatred, Nathanial."

Her voice brought him up short. She stepped into view, into the doorway, blocking his escape. Arianna, a tiny mite of a woman standing with her legs wide, hands planted on her hips.

"So you truly *do* read my thoughts?"

"I hear thoughts sometimes. Yours are like poison. I'll be glad to end them forever. But in the meantime, Nathanial, know this. Hatred *has* no power. The power that nearly killed you then was the power of love. My love for one of the many you murdered. And it's that same power that will destroy you now."

He took a step backward, setting the case on the floor to free his hands. "Which one was he, this victim of mine? It's been so long . . . I can scarcely remember them all. Was he the barbaric Celtic warlord? The Mayan Shaman?" He shrugged. "Not that it matters. They all died on their knees, begging for mercy."

"I can hardly wait to see how you do," she said, and drew her dagger, held it lightly, tossed it from one hand to the other. "But to remind you, his name was Nicodimus, and he died with the blade of a coward in his back."

She'd kill him. Nathanial knew it beyond a doubt. *If* he played by the rules.

He swallowed hard. "Will you kill me unarmed, Arianna, or give me a chance to draw my blade?" His hand inched toward the leather pocket at his side. He'd known she might get here before he could escape. He wasn't a fool. He'd prepared for this.

She narrowed her eyes. "I'll kill you in a fair fight or not at all," she told him. "Go on." And she nodded.

He drew the weapon from its sheath. Not his dagger. But a crude and inelegant handgun, the killing machine of the modern age. She sucked in a breath, but he simply leveled the barrel and pulled the trigger.

The impact sent her backward into the hall. She hit the stairs and tumbled, head over feet. Her body crashed down upon the first landing, bounced off the wall, and continued its brutal descent to the ground floor. Finally she came to rest at the bottom in a twisted, broken tangle.

Nathanial descended slowly, smiling to himself, and making certain she could hear his footsteps. He replaced the handgun, and drew out the blade as he approached her prone, battered form. She couldn't move. Dying, she was dying. He'd make sure it was permanent.

"It's a shame you prefer a fair fight," he said, and he crouched over her, gripped her blouse in one fist, and tore it open. Sliced the center of her silken bra so that her breasts spilled free. "I prefer a sure win, myself."

"Raven . . . will kill you for this. . . ."

"Oh, I'm sure she will try." He positioned the tip of his blade just to the left of the center of her chest. "Do you ever wonder about the bodies, Arianna?" he asked, pressing a little, drawing a droplet of blood, and hearing her suck air through her teeth. "They die, but don't really. They remain ever new, ever young. Do you suppose their minds are still alive, as well? Do you suppose they *know* that they've been buried alive?"

He smiled slowly at the terror in her brown eyes, and then he drove the blade in to the hilt.

Raven went still, eyes bulging, and screamed out loud. Her hands pressed to her chest, and she dropped to her knees.

Duncan was beside her in a heartbeat. They'd just stopped his car, got out, and had been running toward the courthouse when she'd suddenly . . . suddenly *what*?

"What's wrong? Raven, what—"

She didn't answer, just lifted her wounded, watering eyes toward the courthouse, and screamed, "Arianna! *Arianna!* Noooooo!"

He didn't know what to do. Didn't want to leave her, but he had to go inside, and sensed what he would find once he got there. He scooped her into his arms, and headed for the car, intending to lock her in where she'd be safe while he went to see to Nathanial.

Halfway there she squirmed free and hit the ground running. He saw her pull that dagger from her hip as she went. Could barely keep up with her speed. Damn, he didn't want her going in there if what he thought was true.

She burst through the front door, cried out, and raced ahead. Duncan entered on her heels, only to find her on the floor, holding Arianna's blood-soaked body in her arms, sobbing hysterically. Arianna was a slick, scarlet shimmer. Raven was rapidly becoming one, too. He saw the gaping, jagged hole in Arianna's chest, and then he looked away, unable to bear the sight.

It only took a footstep from above, and a glimpse of Raven's eyes to set him into motion. Nathanial would pay. He'd pay for this.

"Kill him," Raven whispered through gritted teeth, her voice raw.

Duncan nodded once and took the blade Arianna had given him from its place at his side. Carefully he stepped over the body at the foot of the stairs and headed up. And then he paused, because he swore he heard a whisper.

"Take mine, too."

He turned quickly. But Raven only knelt, crying, and Arianna couldn't have spoken a word. Still, he knelt and took Arianna's blade from where it lay on the floor beside her, blessedly away from the spreading crimson pool. He tucked it into the back of his jeans, and continued up the stairs.

The sound came from the room at the top. It lay up a second flight, and through a door.

Duncan stepped into the room to see his self-proclaimed father opening the window, a suitcase at his side. His hands were coated in Arianna's blood, his sleeves stained with it. Atop the suitcase sat a small wooden box, fresh blood dripping down its sides, a soft beat coming steadily from within. Arianna's heart.

"Damn you to hell for this," Duncan said softly.

Nathanial turned. He met Duncan's eyes, closed his own. "Not you, Duncan," he whispered. "I'll face any of them, but not you."

Duncan stepped forward. "Maybe I havena been immortal long enough yet to understand. You're willin' to fight with women, but not with a man?"

"Not with my son."

"I'm not your son," he said very softly. "The only father I knew was Angus Wallace, and he's been dead over three hundred years. I suppose I had another, this time around. But 'twasna you, Nathanial Dearborne. 'Twas never you."

Nathanial lowered his eyes. "So you remember."

"Aye. I remember the man you were. A killer in the guise of a priest. Makin' a mockery of the faith you pretended to serve."

"It's all true. But you don't understand, Duncan."

"I understand that you had my birth parents murdered just to get your hands on me. Raised me without a hint of love, all so I'd lead you to Raven one day."

Again, Nathanial nodded, confirming what Duncan had still hoped, in some tiny corner of his mind, he would deny. "It began that way, Duncan. But the truth is . . . I've come to care for you, boy. Just as I did before."

"I can see how you care for me. 'Twas clear in the way you tried to murder the woman I love."

"I might have died without another heart."

"You think that makes it all right? You kill others just to prolong your own life, an' you think that makes it all right?"

Nathanial shook his head slowly. "It's the way things are for us, Duncan. The way it's always been. . . ."

"Not for you," Duncan uttered quietly. "Not anymore."

Nathanial closed his eyes. "I don't want to kill you, Duncan, but I will if you make me."

"I rather thought you would. An' that says it all. Dinna you think . . . *Father*?"

Duncan lunged forward, still seeing Arianna's blood, Raven's pain, in his mind's eye. Nathanial dodged, and then drew his own blade, attacking, stabbing, fighting as fiercely as an animal, a rabid animal.

"You've no chance against me, Duncan. I've seven hundred years of practice!"

Duncan tried again, but this time Nathanial kicked and the blade went sailing out of Duncan's hand.

He heard Raven, her footsteps rushing up the stairs, through the door. "Don't, Duncan! Don't fight him! I didn't mean—I wasn't thinking!" Nathanial lifted his blade and came at him. Raven ran into the room behind him and cried out. And Duncan stood where he was. One hand flashed behind him, to close around Arianna's blade. He brought it forward just as Nathanial lunged at him. And the blade sank into the old man's chest, deeply and brutally, though Duncan hadn't even thrust it. 'Twas Nathanial's own forward motion, his attack, his own hatred, that killed him.

Blood welled, warm and thick, spilling over Duncan's hands, and he took them away, disgusted. Sickened.

For a moment he stood, looking down at the man he'd called father, the man who lay dying. "I wanted your love," he said. "I wanted it more than you know."

Blinking slowly, his eyes already glazing over, Nathanial whispered, "You had it, son. I *did* love you . . . in my way. . . ." His eyes fell closed, briefly. But then they opened again. His hand snatched the front of Duncan's shirt with surprising strength, and he pulled him close. "I'll prove it to you now," he managed, and then he whispered something in Duncan's ear. A second later his breaths stopped, his hand went slack, and Duncan straightened away from him.

Duncan's throat closed off and he turned away, eyes burning. Raven enfolded him in her arms. Held him tight to her, where he belonged. Nathanial hadn't loved him. That wasn't love. Even with that one final gesture, it wasn't love. Guilt, maybe. *This* was love, this thing he felt right here, this woman he held, who was healing him even now. This was love, and 'twas all he needed. All he had ever needed, or ever would.

"Don't mourn him, Duncan. The world's better off without him. He was evil."

"I know." He looked down at her, kissed her lips, finding some soothing elixir in her taste that eased his heartache. "But he's still evil. He'll . . . he'll revive . . . ?"

"I'll do what has to be done."

He stepped away from her, searched her face. "Nay, lass. I canna ask you to do that—"

"I'll do it, Duncan. . . . I'll do it because I love you." She touched his shoulders, kissed his face. "If you knew, my darling, if you knew what you were to me . . . What you still are to me, you'd understand. Let me do this for you."

"What I . . . still am?" he asked her. Lowering his head, he shook it slowly. "I doubted you. I called you crazy and gave my father more chances than a saint deserves, while refusing you so much as the benefit of the doubt. I nearly got you killed, Raven—"

"No." She shook her head hard. "No, Duncan, it was your father who nearly killed me. You had no part in that."

"An' Arianna? Will you tell me now that *her* blood doesna stain my hands?"

Raven took his hands in hers, holding them tightly. "This is the way we live, Duncan. The Dark Ones pursue us, and when we meet them, we fight. Sometimes . . ." Her eyes filled, though she blinked against the tears. "Sometimes we die. Arianna knew that as I do, and she'd never have blamed you. She cared for you, Duncan. And I love you now, as I always have."

"Do you, lass?"

She nodded. "I always will," she told him.

Sighing, he nodded. He'd tell her the truth—that he *did* remember, that he *was* the man she'd been searching for all this time . . . that he loved her. By the Gods, *he loved her!* But first he wanted to give her something. A gift. A gift he knew how to give . . . because of an evil man's dying words. And they might have been lies for all he knew. But he had to try.

"I'll take care of Arianna," he whispered, saw her close her eyes in stark pain. Then he picked up the small box, felt the chilling thrum of its beat from within, and carried it down with him.

I took Nathanial Dearborne's heart. Not because I could grow strong by draining its power, but because it was the only way he would remain dead. The only way I could be sure. I would burn it, and his body, when this gruesome task ended. I would free his soul, and perhaps on some other plane, he'd learn what this long lifetime had been about. Perhaps he'd live again one day, a decent, loving man. A father, perhaps, who would learn the meaning of the word.

Gently, I placed Nathanial's heart in an empty box on the shelf, but as I did so, I couldn't help but notice all the other boxes, and the weak, slow beats emanating from them. His victims. All his victims. I'd burn this place. I'd destroy the hearts that lived on here, beating endlessly while the bodies that had once owned them lay in some nightmarish state between life and death. I'd burn them all and, in so doing, set their captive souls free.

Sighing, I felt my heart breaking for all of them, but mostly for my sister, my Arianna, my beloved best friend and kindred spirit. I felt empty, lost without her. As lost as I had been all those years without Duncan.

Had I ever told her, I wondered, how very much she meant to me?

Crying, I washed my hands in a basin of water, and then I went down the stairs.

Arianna's body was no longer there, tangled and bloody. Duncan had moved her to an antique chaise fit for a goddess. He'd draped a sheet over her as she reclined there. And for that, I was grateful.

Duncan awaited me at the foot of the stairs. His dark hair tousled, his eyes swirling cauldrons of emotion. I saw so much there as his intense gaze locked with mine; pain, grief, shock. And something more. He took me into his arms when I reached him. I thought he needed to hold me as much as I did him, just then. To feed from my strength, to bolster me with his. Together we were so much more than either of us was alone. But that couldn't be what he was feeling. Maybe three centuries ago, but not now.

"I have to tell you some things, Raven. An' I hope you'll do me the honor of listenin' before you interrupt."

Smiling just a little, tears still spilling from my eyes, I stepped back and looked up at him. "Your Highland lilt is back, Duncan. I . . . it was upstairs, but I was too . . ." I frowned hard, searching his face. "What does this mean?"

"I thought you liked my lilt."

"I do. I just don't understand why it keeps slipping into your speech."

"'Tis more than the accent that's come back to me, Raven."

I blinked . . . then blinked again and searched his eyes. "Duncan?"

"I love you, lass," he said very softly. "I've been fallin' in love with you all over again, ever since I found you, Raven, but 'tis more than that now. It has come back to me. All of it, all you were to me, an' all I was to you. All we still are to each other." He closed his eyes, searching for words as his strong hands kneaded my shoulders in time with the beat of my heart.

I tried to speak and couldn't.

He opened his eyes, and they were wet. "When I saw you fall . . .'twas like a doorway into the past opened up wide. An' God, my sweet bonny lass, when I held your poor broken body in my arms on those rocks, I knew. . . ." He cradled my face in his hands, his eyes poring over me. "You're everythin' to me, Raven. *Everythin'*. You always were.

My mind might have forgotten for a little while, but my heart remembered you, lass, from the moment I set eyes on you again. I love you, Raven."

I touched his face, searched his eyes, and saw him there. Duncan Wallace, the man I'd loved so long ago, alive again, fully alive at last. "Duncan . . ." I collapsed in his arms, wanting to weep for joy. "Oh, Duncan, hold me. Hold me forever."

"We'll never be apart again, love. Never again, I vow it to you." He kissed me with such passion and love, and held me cradled against his chest, wrapped warmly in his arms.

"You truly remember everything?"

"Aye," he said softly. "The night I watched you through the cabin windows, bathin', singin' like a siren, an' drawin' me near. The first time we made love on the cliffs with the sea crashing below us . . . all of it."

I could barely breathe, so tight was my chest. I closed my eyes. "And how you died . . . just because I didn't trust in you enough to tell you the truth?" I asked him.

He stepped back slightly so he could see my face. "I'd die a thousand times for you, Raven St. James. An' even that wouldna show you the limits of my love. I canna . . . I canna find the words . . . there *are* no words. 'Tis beyond somethin' as mundane as language. 'Tis beyond anythin' physical . . . 'Tis pure, Raven. Spiritual. Holy. You . . . are a part of me. Even death couldna change that."

"No. Not even death," I told him.

"I need you the way I need air," he whispered, and my heart soared. He held me tight and kissed me, so tenderly, so deeply, that I knew he truly meant every word. "An' I believe all that happened to us was just as 'twas meant to happen. Had it been different, I'd be long dead by now, an' you with no hope of seein' me again."

I closed my eyes. "I can't even imagine living with that kind of pain."

"I want to take your pain away, my love," Duncan whispered. "All your pain. An' I think I can. I think so long as I'm with you, you'll never hurt again. Not if I can prevent it."

I lifted my head and glanced toward the sheet-draped body of the other person I'd come to love beyond reason. And my joy dimmed beneath a fresh onslaught of sorrow. The sister of my soul lay dead and beyond my reach.

"No one can ease this pain," I said very softly. "Not even you, Duncan, though I love you with everything in me. I'm so glad you've come back to me. Truly come back, at last. So long, I've waited. And maybe . . . maybe someday Arianna will find her way back to me as well."

Duncan looked toward where Arianna lay, and his eyes widened for just an instant. Then he smiled, a tentative, wary smile. "Maybe sooner than you think," he said. He took my hands in his, staring down into my eyes. "Nathanial . . . he said somethin' to me as he lay dyin'."

I tilted my head, frowned up at him. "I don't under—"

"He said, 'The heart beats on. The body only rests. Put it back.' An' then he repeated, it. 'Put it back,' he kept sayin'. *'Put it back.'*"

I shook my head, and my breath caught in my throat. "P-put it back?"

Duncan nodded. "Aye. So . . . I did."

"But . . ." I looked toward the chaise. Blinked my eyes as the sheet seemed to move. And then it moved again. "It can't be. . . . Arianna?"

The body beneath the sheet went stiff, the arms rigid, the sheet flinging aside as a desperate gasping sound filled the room. The sheet fluttered to the floor, revealing Arianna's body, arching and taut . . . then relaxing back to the chaise. Still, unmoving, eyes closed.

I took a step forward. "Arianna?" I whispered, almost afraid to hope. . . .

Her eyes opened. Arianna blinked, looked around, and then sat up fast, wide-eyed with fear. "What—Where—" Her hands clawed at her chest in search of the remembered wound.

I ran to her. "Arianna . . . Arianna, it's all right. It's okay, I'm right here."

She stared at me, shocked and disoriented. Slowly she tugged at the remnants of her torn blouse and stared down at her chest. Even now, I could see the lines of the jagged cut, barely visible in her flesh, fading fast.

"How . . . how did you . . . what . . ."

I stroked her hair. "It's over, Arianna. You're all right." My smile was watery and my chest nearly bursting with emotion. I hugged her close. "You're really all right."

"B-but . . ." She hugged me back, but she was trembling. "He took my heart," she whispered.

"I know, I know, darling. But now I've taken his. And yours . . . yours beats still, back inside you, where it belongs."

"But—"

"'Twas Nathanial," Duncan said from behind me. His hands clasped my shoulders. Then he reached down and stroked Arianna's hair as she lifted her head to stare up at him. "He seemed to want to clear his conscience," Duncan explained. "So he told me how to bring you back."

Sitting back away from me, Arianna gazed up at him. "But how could he know that? *I* didn't even know that . . . and . . . and . . ." Her eyes widened and her voice became a soft croak, barely audible. "He has other hearts here. . . ."

"Well, yes, weak ones. Nearly lifeless, some of them. But—"

"Don't you see?" She grasped my shoulders, shook me gently. "My Goddess, Raven, *don't* you *see?*"

I met her eyes, and slowly shook my head.

She swallowed hard and seemed to gather herself. "Never mind. Never mind, I . . . this isn't the time. We have to get out of here. Cover this up. My God, if they find this place, the blood, his body up there like that . . ."

"You're right," I said.

She got to her feet, holding the sheet around her and moving slowly forward, until she stood toe to toe with Duncan. "You . . . you did all right for a newborn."

He lifted a brow. "Aye, I suppose so. Better than you, at least." And I saw a teasing gleam in Duncan's eyes.

"He'd never have taken me without cheating," Arianna said, looking a bit more like herself, I thought. Slightly mischievous, cocky, arrogant.

"I have no doubt," Duncan returned.

She smiled, tilted her head. "You saved my life . . . returned my life, more precisely."

He nodded. "You did the same for me, that night when I died, with your castin' and conjurin'." He stared at me then, but continued speaking to Arianna. "You gave me back my life."

"Ah, so you finally got your head straight, did you?"

"I got my heart back, just like you," he said. "An' I'll never let her get away from me again."

"And I'll never let mine slip away, either," I promised him.

Arianna put one hand on Duncan's, one on mine, and drew the two together. "A love like yours is so precious," she said, and her voice got a little gruff, drawing my gaze to the tear that shimmered in her eye. "And a second chance is a gift beyond measure. Not everyone gets that. Cherish it."

The tear spilled, glistening on her cheek, rolling slowly downward.

"Arianna?" I whispered, instantly concerned.

"No. No, we have work to do tonight. And when it's done, we celebrate. This is no time for tears. Tears make their own time. Tears . . . be-long in private. Come." And she drew us out, out of that house of death, and into the night.

Hand in hand, Duncan and I walked away from sadness and loneli-ness and grief. And for the first time I could remember, the future looked bright . . . and it would be. As long as we were together.

Epilogue

※

Hours later we stood far away from the courthouse as its red-orange flame licked up into the night sky. Duncan and I stood arm in arm, watching the fire. And I felt like a Phoenix. I'd survived the flames, I'd risen from the ashes, and now, at last, I would live again.

Duncan's arm was around me, strong and firm, just as I remembered it. *He* was just as I remembered him. Just as I loved him, and I loved him still.

Apart from us a little, Arianna knelt. She'd gathered all the small boxes with their weakening, barely beating hearts, and they sat around her in a circle. In her hands she held the other box, the one that held the heart of Nathanial Dearborne. She'd taken all of these, along with all of Nathanial's books, from the house before we'd set it alight. I suspected she wanted to work a special ritual over them before putting them to the torch and freeing their captive souls once and for all.

Staring at the flames that even now devoured Nathanial Dearborne's body, Arianna lifted the box that held his heart high above her. In silence Duncan and I closed our eyes and aided in empowering her spell by joining our will with hers as Arianna spoke in a low but powerful voice.

"Thy spirit is free, and separate from thee. Thy body's no more, thy spirit can soar! I release thee, Nathanial Dearborne, and commend thy spirit to the light."

Then she lifted the box higher, for the heart beat on.

"The life in this heart, this heart does not own. Return to thine own hearts, return to thy home!"

I caught my breath as at last I realized her intent. "Arianna, no. You mustn't—"

"As I will it," she cried, her voice ringing with sheer force, "so mote it be!"

The sound of the beating from within that box grew suddenly louder, suddenly deafening, and then all at once, the box burst into flames. I caught my breath as the blazing thing tumbled from Arianna's hands to the ground, snapping and crackling as if soaked in some propellant. In seconds it flickered and died, leaving only ashes. Arianna sighed and relaxed. Nathanial's heartbeat was silenced now. Utterly, completely silenced.

She sank to the ground, lowered her head. And one by one the soft, weak thrum of the dying hearts in the boxes around her grew stronger, louder, until they all pumped with the steady rhythm of life.

I lowered my head into my hands. "Oh, Arianna," I whispered. "What have you done?"

"The hearts live on, the bodies only rest," she told me. "That's what Nathanial said, isn't it?"

"Yes. But these were nearly gone. You should have helped them pass, Arianna, helped them find release, and peace. Now who knows how long they'll go on beating from those prisons?"

Slowly she shook her head. "No. We don't know that they'd ever have stopped beating entirely, do we?"

"Well, no, but we could have cremated them—"

"It would have been too much like murder," she declared.

"Those hearts were not strong enough to sustain life, Arianna."

"And now they are," she shot back. "Now they're as strong and as healthy as they were when he stole them."

"But I don't understand."

Duncan's hand closed around mine. "I do," he said. He met Arianna's eyes. "You're goin' to put them back."

She smiled gently, and nodded. "If I can find the bodies they belong to. Nathanial kept journals and diaries among all those books of his. There might be clues there. If it worked for me . . . Well, there's a chance."

I stiffened, and stepped forward. "You . . . you're *leaving* me?"

"Yes, my darling." She cupped my cheek with her palm, leaned forward, and kissed me very gently, very briefly. "It's time. This is your time, yours and Duncan's."

"No!" I cried. "No, you don't have to leave. We *want* you with us. Tell her, Duncan!"

"She knows," he said softly. "But I think this is her time, too. *Her* second chance . . . maybe."

Arianna's lips pulled tight, and her eyes welled with tears. "One of these hearts . . . means more to me than my own," she said, then she bit her lip, but her tears fell anyway. "If there's a chance in a million that I can find him . . . that I can restore him . . . I have to try."

I blinked, searching her face. "You . . . you loved him."

She said nothing, but I could see the truth in her eyes. So I hugged her close, held her a long time. "I will never be more than a wish away," I promised her. "And you'll come back to me. Promise me you will."

"You know I will, little sister."

Sniffling, I released her. Arianna gathered the small boxes, the six hearts of Nathanial's victims, and gently packed them in a satchel. Then she zipped it tight and gathered it up. "I love you, you know," she told me. Then she glanced at Duncan. "*Both* of you."

"If you need us—" Duncan began.

"Ha! Me? Need help? You do make me laugh, Duncan." But she said it with a wink and a smile. Then her smile died. "Take care of each other," she whispered, just before she turned and walked away, disappearing into the night.

But not from my life. She'd return to tell me all about her adventures, and this mysterious man she sought. I knew she would. We were sisters, and always would be. Nothing could change that.

Just as nothing could change the love Duncan and I shared. A love beyond mortality. Beyond life, or death, or the forces of evil.

"Well, we should get started, too," he said.

"Get started?" I turned toward him, and he gently brushed the tears from my eyes.

"I guess you didna believe me, did you lass? When I said I'd see to it you never hurt again."

"Of course I did, but—"

"Then we'd best get started. I've lots of time to make up for, you know. Three hundred years of lovin' to give to you. Three hundred years of sweet nothin's to whisper into your ears, an' of gifts, an' of kisses an' pamperin'."

I nodded. "And I suppose I have three hundred years of magick and of fighting to teach you."

"Aye. But first, we travel."

I tilted my head.

Duncan smiled and kissed my nose. "We dinna want that stubborn sister of yours to get too far ahead of us, do we?"

"We're . . . going with her?"

"Aye, we're goin' with her."

"But why?"

He stared down at me, his dark eyes growing darker, even as the light of that distant fire danced its reflection in their depths. "If you could see the joy in your eyes right now, love, I'd point to it, an' I'd tell you, 'That's why.' I love you, Raven St. James. What makes you happy, makes me happy. I love you. *I love you, lass.*"

I closed my eyes when he kissed me again, and I knew it was true. The darkest night of my soul had ended, though it had been three centuries long. Dawn had finally broken, and my heart was whole again.

Infinity

Arianna

Darkness
unfurled its shroud upon my soul,
long before Death could take *his* toll

I walked in place,
breathed air without taste
A blind man with eyes
A dead man alive
A corpse animated
A hunger unsated
A soul made of stone
A heart with no home

Sunlight
spilled Her gold and warmed my skin,
though I fought not to let Her in.

I emerged from the grave,
by the magick She gave
The dirt in my eyes,
swept away by Her sighs
A dead man, reborn
Night gave way to morn
My hunger She sates
My fear She abates
My soul, She does own
My heart has come home

Infinity
unfolds through space and time,
as soft I hold Her hand in mine

I've found Her again
and a love without end
As Her kiss I taste,
my tears are erased
My grief-crippled soul,
at Her touch is made whole
And the gift from above,
is the joy of Her love

—NICODIMUS LACHLAN

Prologue

I am lying in a shallow grave, immersed as if in the bowels of some great, black sea. I know not how long I have been captive in this void, nor do I care. But something has disturbed me, has stirred me to consciousness . . . of a sort. A sound. A steady beat, pulsing ever more strongly, forcing me back to the realm of coherent thought.

And thought alone.

The silk that once wrapped my body has rotted away. I have no coffin. Black, rocky soil is my tomb. But I am not dead. As dead as I can be, perhaps, and that is my greatest fear. I am . . . *immortal*.

I do not want this . . . to think. To know. To remember. But that drumbeat in my mind will not release me. And bit by bit, my mind clears, my past resurfaces.

My name . . . do I even know my own name?

I grasp in the darkness of my mind, fighting a momentary panic, and find it there . . . Nicodimus. That is my name . . . Nicodimus.

The beat that stirred me grows louder, as faint memories taunt me through the mists of my mind. There is no light, no return of feeling or sense. Only of awareness. Horrible, wrenching awareness. A living nightmare. The knowledge that I have been buried alive.

And the beat grows still louder.

Gods, it is my heart! It is near. I sense it drawing closer to me the way a lodestone can sense the north. I feel its beat growing stronger when logic tells me it should be weakening . . . slowing, fading, as its power is steadily drained by its greedy captor.

And yet, the proximity of the organ matters not. My heart is no longer my own, and without it, here is where I shall remain. I wonder, can the heart of an immortal ever cease its endless beating? And if it should, will the soul of its rightful owner find blessed release at last?

If not, then what remains for me? A living mind trapped in this undying body. A living soul held captive in a dead man's grave. How long can this go on? How long?

Forever.

The answer comes to me as if riding a whisper-soft breath. *Her* breath.

At the first thought of her, those teasing, distant memories break free at last, and rush through my mind all at once in a chaos of emotion too agonizingly shrill and sharp to bear. Images and fragments, painfully vivid, blindingly bright . . . that all begin with . . .

Arianna.

Arianna.

Arianna . . .

PART ONE

Chapter 1

1511,
Stonehaven Village,
in the Scottish Highlands

I rode my faithful Black, and he stepped high, as though he knew the man he bore to be of an utterly different breed than those others who surrounded us. Beside me rode an old friend . . . a mortal, chieftain of his clan, and laird as well. Joseph Lachlan welcomed my visit. He called me his cousin because I claimed to be. But though I supposed I might be some distant relative of his, the link was too old to trace now. I used the name and claimed the clan Lachlan only when it suited me.

Joseph didn't doubt me, nor did he ask why I might need to retreat here for a time. And that was just as well, for I couldn't have told him the answers had he questioned me. The truth was that resting from the constant battle was only one of the reasons I'd come.

Another was the skulking, dark robed pair who'd been following me on and off over the previous seven centuries. Always silent, always faceless within the caves of their hoods. But I didn't need to look upon their faces to know. I'd avoided them sometimes. On other occasions, they had vanished without explanation. But more often than not, I'd fought them. Sometimes one at a time, frequently both together. Once I had nearly bested Kohl, but he fled before I could finish the job. And once—this last time—the two immortal brothers had done the same to me, and *I* had fled. To Stonehaven—my sanctuary.

I feared very little, almost nothing. But there was a cold dread in the pit of my stomach where my oldest and most bitter enemies were concerned. And it came, I believe, of knowing exactly why they had stalked me so doggedly, and for so long.

They blamed me for the deaths of their sister and their nephews . . . my wife and my sons. And they would never stop until they had taken my heart.

Or I theirs.

So I had come here to rest from the endless fighting. I put it from my thoughts in order to focus on the other reason I had returned to Stonehaven—the more important one. Her. The girl who had drawn me back here time and time again over the past seventeen years.

"You never age, Nicodimus," Joseph remarked. "You look to be the same fair lad I last saw five years past."

I sent a cocky grin his way. "And you've grown wrinkles about your eyes, Joseph. Soon I'll mistake you for my father." Joseph was perfectly bald, his pale head as shiny as his cheeks and his bulbous nose. He did have brows and lashes, but of a hue so pale it seemed as if he were entirely hairless. When he smiled, as he often did, it seemed even his bald head smiled along.

"No hope of that, lad. Your father was twice the man I'll ever be." Joseph lowered his chin. "I do miss him. But havin' you here on occasion is almost like havin' my dear cousin back with me again."

I had to avert my eyes. Joseph had never known my father. He had known only me. But when he'd seen me die at his side on a field of battle, I'd had no choice but to stay away for many years. And when I returned—as I had been compelled to do—I had simply claimed to be my own son. He had believed me.

"My father often spoke similarly of you, Joseph," I said after a pause. I nudged Black's sides with my heels. The stallion trotted forward along the narrow, twisting paths of the village, chickens scattering in his wake. A fat man rolled a barrel of ale from a rickety wagon into the daub-and-waddle hovel that passed as the village tavern, while across the way a woman hurled wash water from a window hole where no glass had ever stood.

I'd seen London and Rome, Paris and Constantinople, great cities all around the world. Yet I marveled at how this tiny hamlet had grown. For when I had lived there it had borne no name. My home had been a thatched straw hut, cured hides stretched over the walls had served to keep out the cold. The meat I killed, my wife had cooked over a fire on the dirt floor.

Anya. Beautiful Anya. Meek, gentle, fragile. I could see her still, in my mind. Soft brown hair and eyes like the palest winter sky, her belly swelling with our third child as she watched over the other two. And I could see our boys. Jaymes, growing taller by the day and too skinny to stand up to a windstorm, though he ate more than his brother and I together. He had his mother's coloring, Jaymes did. And Will, a head shorter, but strong, already looking more man than boy. Hunting at my side, and outdoing me now and again. Begging to fight beside me as well.

The old pain trembled and howled and threatened to break free. I caught it with a will of forged steel, and forced it still and silent.

"The village hasna' changed since last you were here," Joseph said, pulling me out of my thoughts.

Ahead of me, the crofters' cottages leaned crookedly, their thatched roofs showing wear. I caught myself studying the villagers we passed, with their well-worn kilts and haggard faces, and realized I was seeking the golden child as I did on each visit. But I did not see her there. And it occurred to me then that I might not even recognize her at first glance, after so long.

I nearly smiled at the unlikelihood of that.

She stood out from the rest of the villagers the way a diamond stands out among bits of coal; her dark brown eyes gleaming against ivory skin. Her corn-yellow hair. Her upturned bit of a nose, and the gleam of life in her little girl eyes. And more. A spirit, a fire, undefinable, yet all but gleaming in its brilliance.

She had been a child, barely twelve years of age, when last I had seen her. She would be . . . seven and ten now. Quite possibly wed—though people here now married later than they used to. I'd made Anya my wife when I'd been but four and ten. But things changed a great deal in seven long centuries. And wedded or not, this girl, Arianna, was likely still unaware of what she truly was.

"Is that saddle maker still in the village, Joseph?" I asked abruptly. "Sinclair, wasn't it?"

"Aye. Is your saddle in need of repair?" Joseph eyed it, likely seeing that it was perfectly fine. Likely thinking that I never paid him a visit but that I needed repairs done to my saddle.

"Only a bit of loose stitching at the girth," I told him. "But I ought have it checked before I leave again."

Joseph nodded. "'Twas a cursed bad year for poor Sinclair. Cursed bad."

My head swung toward him. "Was it?"

"Aye." Joseph's lips thinned, and his bald head joined his brow in a frown. "Lost a daughter, he did."

At those words, my heart seemed to ice over. I had been watching the girl all her life, awaiting the time when I would explain her own nature to her. When she was old enough, and mature enough to understand and deal with the truth. Perhaps I had waited too long. I tried to speak, but couldn't.

Joseph never seemed to notice the force of my reactions. He was involved now in the telling of his tale. "Nearly lost the both of his girls, that sad day. Over a year ago, 'twas. They'd been up to no good, playin' in the loch when their father had forbidden it. My lads were about, heard the shoutin'. Kenyon pulled the one to safety, an' Lud went back for her sister. But 'twas no use . . . she drowned in the muddy waters of Loch Haven."

"Drowned?" I asked, nearly holding my breath.

"Aye. And young Arianna has ne'er been right since the day the loch claimed her sister."

I lowered my head and released my breath all at once. So Arianna was alive . . . Not that she could have died by drowning. She'd have revived . . . but to what?

Joseph nodded toward some distant point. "See for yourself, Nicodimus. She's there now, at the grave. 'Tis no place for a lass of ten and seven to be spendin' all her time. An' alone, no less! She's forever walkin' about alone." He ran a hand over his head, and slowly shook it.

I frowned, knowing exactly what Joseph implied. It was said that only a Witch walked about all alone. Only a Witch. And Arianna *was* one. But she couldn't know that. Not yet.

"Perhaps if I were to have a word with her," I suggested.

Joseph drew his mount to a halt, frowning at me. "Do you think it wise?"

"Why not? I've lost loved ones myself. I know a bit of what she's feeling." I knew, I realized, far too much of what she was feeling. It was a feeling she would have to get used to, for in time she would lose everyone and everything she knew. I sighed as I looked at her. Slight, so slight. Barely larger than she'd been at twelve. A golden wisp of a girl, the picture of innocence. She would have to learn to be hard. To close herself off. She would have to learn to stop caring, as I had done.

Looking worried, Joseph nodded all the same. "Take care, my friend. Dinna spend too long with her. She's promised to the cobbler's son, but even he's beginning to shy away. There's been some talk. . . ."

"What sort of talk?"

Joseph shrugged. "Ah, I pay it no mind, nor will I tolerate anyone persecutin' the poor lassie. We must make allowances, after all. Grief can twist a mind in all manner of—"

"*What sort of talk*, Joseph?"

Joseph cleared his throat. "Some claim she slips out alone in the dead of night. An' she's been seen speakin' to The Crones more than once. What people will make of it . . . well, you can guess as well as I."

The Crones . . . the outcasts. The word "Witch" was never spoken aloud here. The people were too superstitious to dare it. Everyone in the village knew what the three old women were, yet The Crones were tolerated. Their shack outside the village at the edge of the forest was left alone. That happy state would likely continue, so long as only good fortune smiled down upon the flocks and the crops and the crofters here. As for the blue-blooded Christians of Stonehaven, most would no more exchange a public greeting with The Crones than eat from the trough of a pig. But they visited the old women every now and then, for a potion to cure the croup or a charm for good luck. In secrecy. In hypocrisy.

I turned again to stare at the girl. She knelt beside the grave of her sister off in the distance. Perhaps she knew more than I'd thought she possibly could. It would explain her visits to the village Witches. But who was there to tell her? I'd never met another High Witch, Dark nor Light, in this part of Scotland. Never. And our secrets were seldom shared with anyone else. I'd ascertained years ago that The Crones were mere mortals, and knew nothing of our existence.

"I'll speak with her," I said. "Before she lets the gossips ruin her."

Joseph nodded. "Perhaps 'twill do some good at that. Shall I wait at the tavern, then?"

"If the owner still brews that secret recipe of his."

"Heather Ale?" Joseph asked with a crook of his invisible brow that resulted in new wrinkles appearing in his forehead. "That he does, Nic. That he does." Joseph gave a wink, and wheeled his horse about, heading away.

I turned my attention toward the cemetery once more, and nudged Black's sides until he leapt into a spirited trot. Stopping him a short distance away from the girl, I tied him to a scraggly tree, then walked to where Arianna Sinclair knelt. For a moment, I only stood still and silent, looking at her.

Arianna had changed. In five short years she'd grown from a waif into a woman. And that aura of vitality that had always surrounded her seemed stronger than ever before. Her golden hair draped about her shoulders like a shawl of spun sunlight, moving in the breeze every now and again. And I'd been wrong when I'd concluded she had not grown, for she had. Her breasts swelled now, a woman's breasts, straining the fabric of her homespun dress. Her hips had also taken on a sweet roundness, while her waist remained small.

Kneeling, spine straight, chin high, she lifted a fist, and let some herb or other spill from it atop her sister's grave, as she muttered soft words under her breath.

A spell. For the love of the Gods, had the girl no sense? In full daylight?

"What is it you're doing?" I called. I expected her to stiffen with surprise and perhaps fear at being caught. The lesson would do her good.

She didn't start, didn't turn to face me. "Should anyone *else* ask, I'm plantin' wild heather upon my sister's burial site."

"And if *I* ask."

"I think, Nicodimus, you know better than to ask."

I blinked in surprise. Just how much *did* she know? And the familiarity of her tone with me . . . as if she knew me far better than she did. We'd spoken only a handful of words to one another in the past. Polite greetings at most, though my interest in her had always been more than that of a stranger. She was my kind. A rarity in itself. She was without a teacher, and . . . and something about her spoke to me on a level I had never understood.

The herbs gone, she pounded her fist thrice on the ground; a time-honored method for releasing the energy raised in spellwork. Then she lowered her head for but an instant. Finally, she rose, brushing her hands on her skirts and facing me. Her velvet brown eyes hadn't been so large before . . . nor so haunted. "It has been a long while since your last visit here," she said.

"Long enough so I must wonder how you could have recognized my voice."

"'Twas nay your voice, Nicodimus. Although 'tis true, you speak distinctly enough."

"Do I?"

"Aye," she said. "Almost like a Sassenach, rather than a true Scot. Careful, an' slow, without a hint of an accent, so a body could never guess where you truly come from."

"I come from right here," I told her.

She shrugged, and I wasn't sure whether she believed me or not. "Regardless of *how* you speak," she went on, "I knew you were there long afore you did."

Her words gave me pause. If that were true, her natural powers were incredibly advanced—particularly for one so young. "How?" I asked her.

She shrugged again. "I always know when you're near. Have since . . . why since I was a wee bairn toddlin' along and clingin' to my mam's skirts . . . an' you came ridin' into the village alongside Laird Lachlan. Do you recall?"

I did. It had been then I had first set eyes on her, and I'd known— even before I'd seen the crescent shaped birthmark on her chubby right flank—that she was one of us. "I remember it well."

Arms crossed over her middle, she sent me a steady look, and I studied her in return. Her small, upturned nose was the same as before. But her face had thinned. No babe's plumpness to her cheeks. Not now. It was a woman's face, touched by sorrow.

"I always wanted to ask you about it—that feelin' I get when you're near. But it seemed I should remember my place, and be neither impertinent nor disrespectful."

"But you've changed your mind about those things now?"

She glanced toward her sister's grave and her eyes grew darker, her voice softer. "They seem less important to me now than the dust in the highland wind, Nicodimus." Her eyes were round and filled with pain— and something else: rebellion. A dangerous wildness flashed from somewhere deep within her, and seemed to fit with the way her hair snapped whiplike with the wind, while her skirts flew about her ankles and bare, dirty feet.

"Propriety has its place, Arianna."

"Propriety," she whispered, looking directly at me again. "Society. Lairds and chieftains and crofters and slaves. What good is it, I ask you? What does any of it truly mean? Who cares whether a woman wears her hair unbound until she bears her first child, and bound up tight thereafter? Or if she walks about alone, or if she addresses a laird by his given name? What arrogant fool made up all these ridiculous rules that have us all hoppin' and scurryin' to obey?"

"You're angry," I said softly. "I understand that, Arianna . . ."

"Aye," she replied. "I am angry. 'Tis meaningless, all of it!"

Her voice had grown louder with every word, until I gripped her hands gently in my own and felt the jolt of awareness that occurs when one of our kind touches another. She looked at me quickly, shocked by that heat, wondering at it, I knew, but I said only, "Keep your voice low." And I inclined my head toward the village nearby, where already several sets of speculative eyes were turned our way. Hands shielding careworn faces from the morning sun. Squinting, searching gazes trying to see who dared raise her voice in the cemetery, of all places.

Arianna followed my gaze and saw her curious neighbors. She sent them a defiant glare with a toss of her head that reminded me of Black when he is agitated and smelling a battle; the way he shakes his mane almost in challenge. I moved to take my hands from hers, but she closed hers tight and clung with a strength that surprised me.

I looked down at our joined hands, and for the first time a ripple of alarm zigzagged up my spine to tap at my brain. For this was no child clinging to my hands. This was a woman, young and beautiful and full of fire. And her hands were slender and strong and warm.

"You *want* to make them gossip about you. Is that it?" I asked her.

"Let them gossip. I dinna care."

I took my hands away. "Do you care what pain you cause others, Arianna?" I asked, in a second attempt to put her firmly in her place, to let her know that what she might have been thinking just now when our hands were locked together, could never, never be. She was hurting, full of anger, confused and lonely for her sister. That was all it was. "You're promised to the cobbler's son," I reminded her.

She tilted her head to one side and shrugged. But it seemed her rant had ended, for her face no longer seemed like that of a warrioress about to do battle. "*I* never made any such promise to Angus MacClennan. Nor do I intend to abide by it. An' believe me, that clod has no tender feelin's where I'm concerned."

"No? Why, then, do you suppose he's asked for your hand, Arianna?"

She smiled slowly, eyes sparkling now with mischief. "You can guess as well as I. He wants a servant. Someone to cook an' clean an' mend for him. But mostly, he wants someone to lift her skirts when he demands it. Someone to relieve his manly needs with so he'll nay have to hide in his da's woodshed an' do it himself—"

"*Arianna!*"

"What?"

She was all wide-eyed innocence, but I saw the gleam beyond it. I only scowled at her.

"A tender young girl isna supposed to ken such things, I suppose!" Again that expressive toss of her golden locks. "Nay, we're to blindly agree to be some man's slave an' his whore in exchange for our room and board. Well, it willna be me, Nicodimus. Not ever."

I had to bite back a smile. So bold and outspoken, and so damned determined. "A wife should be none of those things, Arianna."

"Name one who isna *all* of those things," she challenged me, leaning slightly forward, hands on her hips, legs shoulder width apart in a cocky stance.

"Your mother," I said.

She lost a bit of her cockiness. "'Tis different with my mam."

"Why?"

"Because my da loves her, I suppose."

"And are you so certain your cobbler's son doesn't love you?"

She peered up at me from beneath her dark lashes. "Not so much as he loves his hand on certain nights in his da's woodshed."

I had to look away. To laugh aloud would only encourage her. And she needed no encouragement.

For a moment I thought about how seldom it was that I found myself inclined toward laughter. Genuine laughter. "I like you, Arianna," I said. "Just take care to bite your tongue from time to time. Not everyone appreciates a sharp wit and bold talk from a young woman the way I do."

She smiled up at me, all but glowing. And I thought I would enjoy spending a bit of time with Arianna while at Stonehaven this time, getting to know the astounding young woman she had become. And then I was shaken out of my thoughts, for she suddenly grabbed my hands and held them, and her thumbs caressed the hollows of my palms in slow circles. She stared up at me, her inquisitive eyes probing mine.

"You're different from other men, Nicodimus. I've sensed it always. You pay no more mind to the world and its silly conventions than I do. You . . . you're like me, somehow."

I averted my eyes. "I don't know what you mean."

"Dinna you? You're supposed to be Laird Lachlan's kin, yet you dinna live in his keep. You bathe just as often as you like, without a care that the church calls it vanity."

"And just how would you know how often I bathe?"

Her smile was slow, and it stirred something to life deep within me. "You smell good, Nicodimus. Clean. I like the way you smell." I looked away from the heat in her eyes. Her palm came to my cheek, turning my head until I faced her again, and then it remained there. "An' what's more, you dare to talk openly and all alone to the girl half the clan thinks is crazy—"

"And the other half thinks is dabbling in Witchcraft," I interjected, hoping to shock her into silence. She saw too much, this girl. And she was looking far too closely, tampering with parts of me that no one had dared come near in a very long time. Her touch . . . rattled me. Relief sighed through my chest when her hand fell away from my cheek at last.

"An' what if I am a Witch?" she shot back, undaunted.

I stared at her in surprise. She was all fire and life and utter defiance, boldly blurting words that could easily get her killed. "'Tis no business of mine what you are, Arianna," I told her. "And no business of theirs, either. Do as you will."

She rolled her eyes. "I intend to do just that!"

I gripped her shoulders to make her listen. "But keep it to yourself, for the love of heaven! If you can't conform, then *pretend* to conform. And never, ever again must you say something so foolish aloud! For your own sake, girl, take the advice of one older and wiser. One who would like to see you live to grow into womanhood."

"I'm a woman already," she told me, chin high, hair sailing in the breeze. "A woman like no other woman you've ever known." She swayed slightly closer to me, gaze locked on my lips.

I dropped my hands from her shoulders and staggered backward as her bold, enticing eyes flashed fire at me. I'd come to her to try to help her. Instead, I felt as if I were under attack. Her forces battered my innermost tower, and I had a feeling they could bring it to rubble with minimal effort.

"An' since you've mentioned it," she went on, "just *how much* older and wiser are you, Nicodimus?" She smoothed the front of her dress as she spoke, her fingers brushing very near to her breasts, but her eyes never left my face.

I saw her meaning in those eyes. Saw it clear, for she didn't seem the least bit inclined to hide it from me. It unsettled me, shook me to my bones. I'd never thought of her in that way . . . not until this very moment—or perhaps a few moments ago, when I'd seen her again, a woman grown.

"Too old for what you have in mind," I said, hoping I sounded mildly amused and sardonic. "Go find your cobbler's son now, and torment him in my stead."

But even as I turned to leave her, my mind spun its arguments. She would be eighteen in a fortnight. Oh, yes, I knew the date of her birth. I knew more about her than she knew about herself. I was over seven centuries old . . . and yet at the time of my first death, I'd been twenty and eight. Physically . . . I still was. And never more aware of it.

"You're meant for me, Nicodimus," she called as I walked away. "You must ken that as well as I."

I froze where I stood. She came toward me, but didn't stop when she reached my side. Instead she kept walking, brushing past me, and dropping a kiss upon my cheek as she did. The touch of her lips sent heat through me all the way to my toes. "You'll be mine one day," she whispered. "An' then, Nicodimus, I will know all the secrets you hide behind your sapphire eyes."

A shiver raced up my spine as I watched Arianna walk away, golden hair dancing in the wind. She walked proudly right up to where a crowd of crofters stood pretending not to watch her antics. Her chin jutting high, she nodded hello to each of them, her entire stance oozing defiance—as if she were silently daring anyone to chide her for going about alone. Or for kissing a guest of their laird so boldly.

Or for muttering incantations over her dead sister—and in the daylight at that.

Daring them.

No one took the challenge.

She was right when she said she was a woman like no other. For there had never been another who touched my soul the way she did.

Chapter 2

"Just what do you think you're about, Arianna?" her mother whispered harshly.

Arianna turned back toward the darkened cottage from which she'd just emerged, and hugged her dark cloak tighter 'round her shoulders. Her mother opened the splintery wooden door wider, and peered out at her. "I thought you were sleepin', Mam."

"How is a mother to sleep when her child roams about in the night like a wraith?"

Lowering her head, Arianna whispered, "I was only goin' for a walk. I couldna sleep."

Mara Sinclair shook her head, glanced up and down the path as if to be sure none of the neighbors were watching, and then stepped outside. She wore a nightshift that reached to her ankles and covered her arms to the wrists, over which she had thrown an old shawl for both warmth and propriety's sake. Out of long habit, Mara began twisting her long, gold and gray hair into a knot even as she sent her daughter a disapproving stare.

The sight of it made Arianna's temper rise. "Why do you do that?" she asked. When her mother tilted her head in confusion, she continued,

"Your hair. Leave it, Mam. Just this once, dare to ignore the rules of this foolish society and leave it."

With firm motions, her mother finished the job of binding up her hair and met Arianna's stare. "You so disapprove of me. Of all I am, all I stand for. I vow, Arianna, I dinna ken what's happened to you."

"You ken exactly what's happened to me, Mam. I've lost my sister," Arianna said.

Mara pressed one hand flat to her chest, and held the other up as if to ward off her daughter's words. "Dinna speak of Raven to me!" It was a shout. But then she bit her lip, tempered her voice. "I canna bear it, child."

Arianna shook her head. "Dinna call me 'child,' Mam, for I am a woman grown. An' I willna obey without question the way a child would do. The way . . . you do."

Her mother lifted her head slowly, staring at Arianna with hurt in her eyes. "Nay. You never did, lass."

"You scold me for my silence. You say I'm broodin' an' that I willna talk to you. Yet when I try to express my grief for my dead sister, you silence me. What am I to do?"

"Talk to me of something else," her mother whispered, gaze lowering, lids shuttering her eyes at once. "*Anything* else."

"I *think* of nothing else," Arianna said.

"Oh, but you do, lass," her mother said, speaking slowly and meeting her daughter's eyes once more. "You think of wherever it is you go on these midnight walks o' yours. An' of late, you think of Laird Lachlan's comely cousin. I've seen you spyin' on him now and again."

Arianna searched her mother's face. Barely a line in her skin and yet she looked old all the same. It was more than the gray in her once pure golden hair. It was something deeper than any wrinkle could ever be.

"Aye," Mara went on. "I've seen the way you look at Nicodimus, lass." Reaching out as if to stroke Arianna's hair, she paused and lowered her hand. Arianna told herself she'd have ducked away from her touch all the same. And yet she felt the pain of longing for her mother's caress, having been denied it. Not since Raven's death had her mother touched her in love. Instead they only hurt each other, over and over.

"Dinna wish for what you canna have, child," Mara warned. "He's far too old, an' above you as well. The kin of a chieftain, while you're but a saddle maker's daughter."

"You know nothing about Nicodimus Lachlan," Arianna said, feeling as if her mother were attacking her. "He cares no more for the silly ways of society than I, an' I *can* have any man I wish! You'll see!"

Mara frowned. "Child, you'll find only disappointment should you go dreamin' of such things. 'Tis young Angus you'll wed, an' none other."

"I've told you before," Arianna replied slowly. "I willna marry that whelp!"

"Hush!" Again her mother glanced around, seeking watchers in the night. More concerned, Arianna thought, with what her fellow clansmen and kin might think than with her daughter's feelings.

"You think I'm nay good enough for the likes of Nicodimus Lachlan, dinna you? You think I'm nay pretty nor smart enough. But I *am* equal to him. Equal to any man, be he peasant or king!"

When there was no immediate reply, Arianna met her mother's gaze again, saw her eyes soften, dampen. "I certainly believe you equal to any man, daughter. 'Tis the man you might have a wee bit o' trouble convincin' of it."

Arianna sighed hard, and shook her head in disgust.

"Child, we used to be so close, you an' I. Do you recall? I'd sit an' comb your hair, an' sing to you 'ere I tucked you in to sleep. . . ."

Arianna closed her eyes in response to a rush of pain. She missed those times. "An' Raven would sing along," she said, caught up in the memory for just a moment, in spite of herself. "She had such a beautiful voice. And when she—"

"Nay, you mustn't!"

Arianna lowered her head slowly. "You blame me," she whispered.

"Whatever are you—"

"Speak the words, Mam. 'Tis high time we spoke the truth, you an' I. You blame me for my sister's death. I was the elder. I should have protected her. She drowned because of me. I—"

"Nay, child!" Her mother reached for her, and perhaps wouldn't have stopped halfway this time. But Arianna ducked away before she could find out. "'Tis untrue, Arianna," her mother rushed on. "Your da an' I have ne'er once blamed you for what happened."

Holding back her tears, Arianna lifted her head. "Of course you do," she whispered. "An' I canna dispute it, for I blame myself as well." Sniffling, Arianna turned to walk away.

"Come back here! Arianna, where do you think you're goin', lass?" her mother demanded in a voice gone harsh.

"I'm goin' where I want," she cried. "An' doin' what I want, an' I'll marry who I want, as well. I'll nay be good nor obedient ever again, Mam, for I've seen the truth of where goodness and obedience find their reward! At the bottom o' some murky loch is where!"

"Arianna . . ."

"Raven was the good one," Arianna whispered, shaking her head and backing slowly away into the night. "She was the good one. It should've been me who drowned, Mam. It should have been me!" Arianna turned and raced away into the night.

She refused to cry. Instead she worked her rage out by running as fast as she could over the rutted paths of the village and beyond them, toward the woods. When her lungs burned and her muscles screamed, she slowed to a trot and then to a walk. Her heart thrummed and her breath rushed in and out of her heated body like the wind in the trees around her. And then she rested, waited . . . and listened. The nighttime woodland sounds would soothe her. They never failed to help her regain control when her tight grip on it faltered.

Soft, pine-scented air caressed her face, stroked her hair, filled her lungs. Padded feet stepped over the ground off to the left. Three steps, then a pause. Then an airy sound . . . sniffing. A wolf. Yes, a wolf. Nodding in affirmation, she moved a little farther, stopping again at a familiar scent that tickled her nose. Standing still, she inhaled softly, closing her eyes. She smelled the heather growing thick on the moors, and rich earth and night air. She didn't smell the wolf, though the old women had told her such a thing was possible. The wolf could smell her, they'd said. So why shouldn't she be able to detect his scent in the night air?

She put all else from her mind as she made her way to The Crones' cottage just inside the edge of the woods. She chased away her sorrow, her guilt, her rage, and replaced them by focusing on her senses, on honing them as The Crones had taught her, on feeling as if she were one with everything around her. On trying to detect the scent of a wolf in the night.

"You're late," a rich, female voice announced, and Arianna looked up to see Celia, her skin smooth and unlined, her silver hair loose and flowing over her shoulders as if she were a young girl. Her smile was warm, and despite her scolding tone she enfolded Arianna's hands in her own. It was the sort of touch Arianna had been craving from her mother. What would she have done this past year without the companionship of these three women?

A small fire danced in the clearing beside the crooked little shack The Crones shared. The light of the fire was bathing their faces, gleaming in their eyes, throwing shadows upon their worn woolen shawls. Their home was a humble one, built of rough-hewn plank boards and filled with knotholes. It had weathered to near black over the years, and had moss growing on one side and vines creeping up the other as if embracing the wood. Its thatched roof sagged in the middle, as if it were tired to the point of exhaustion. The wild tangle of growth in the back looked to be a weed patch, but was in fact a garden of herbs and plants with healing properties. But no matter how untended this place looked, there was magick here. Arianna had known it from the first time she'd come to these three women and pled with them to teach her their ways.

"My mam tried to stop me," she explained.

"An' you came anyway?" Celia asked with an arched brow.

"I'm a woman grown. I'm a Witch. I do as I will."

Celia tilted her head. She exchanged an indulgent glance with her two companions. They each smiled and shook their heads helplessly. "Do what thou wilt is but a part of the Rede, child. Tell me the rest," Celia said.

"I dinna—"

"Tell me the rest."

Sighing, Arianna muttered, "'An' it harm none, do what thou wilt.'"

"Exactly," Celia said. "Do you think you harmed your mother tonight, child?"

"Nay! I dinna so much as touch her."

Celia's eyes narrowed. Arianna knew full well what she meant. She also knew that she likely *had* hurt her mother tonight—and that she would have to make it right.

Celia nodded, seeming to read Arianna's face. "Come," she said, and led Arianna closer to the fire. Arianna nodded her greetings to Leandra, the eldest of the three, a woman whose face was so lined it resembled the surface of the trembling sea. Her snow-white hair was piled atop her head, and when she spoke it was with the voice of gravel. Then Arianna turned to Mary, plump and always smiling, with steel-gray streaks in her thick ebony mane.

"Merry meet," Arianna said.

"An' to you, lass," Mary returned. "You ought be lookin' forward to this night's ritual."

Arianna smiled broadly. For a year and a day The Crones had been teaching her, letting her observe, answering her questions. But tonight, for the first time, she would be welcomed into the sacred circle as a

Witch. And after her initiation, she would be allowed to participate in a magickal rite. She could barely contain her excitement.

So far, The Crones' "magick" had consisted mostly of concocting herbal remedies for various ailments, and they *had* managed to raise a cooling wind one hot summer's night. Arianna had been mildly disappointed. She'd been expecting explosions of smoke and light, thunderbolts, and evildoers changing into toads.

She'd been hoping. . . .

Well, what she *really* wanted to learn from the old women would take far more magick than what they'd shown her so far. But Arianna had learned one thing. Even in their minor workings, there was real power. Magick was real. Knowing that made Arianna certain she would one day learn what she needed to know.

Perhaps even from The Crones. For it may be that they were simply saving the stronger sorts of magick for later on.

"Tonight, you become one with us, Arianna. Our own sister in the Craft of the Wise." Leandra smiled, and more wrinkles appeared in her face before the smile died. "And then, we conjure rain," she said with a nervous glance at the sky. "For unless we get some soon, the crops could well begin to wilt."

"Aye," Arianna said, "and those fool villagers would no doubt blame you for it."

The three Crones exchanged glances, but didn't speak their fears aloud. Still, Arianna sensed their worry.

"Come, let us cast the circle," Leandra said.

I followed Arianna that night. I had been watching her often at night, hoping I could keep her out of harm's way, certain from what Joseph had said that she was too reckless to heed my warnings. I was right.

She went to The Crones on the night of the full moon just as I had suspected she would. Dammit, didn't she realize what a risk she was taking by sneaking out to that croft alone? What could happen to her if she were found out?

I followed, of course, and hid myself in the trees just beyond reach of the dancing firelight's glow.

Then I forgot why I had come. My mind became too involved in the beauty of what I witnessed.

The beauty of Arianna.

By the time I reached the edge of the clearing, the four of them had cast their circle, and were well into their ritual. Arianna had removed her dark cloak, and beneath it wore a garment of flowing white, which reminded me sharply of the ritual robes of my first teachers—an order of Druid priests. In Arianna's golden hair was a ringlet of flowers, and as I looked on in silence, I realized this was some sort of initiation rite. Arianna knelt in the center of the circle, near the fire, and one by one each of the old women presented her with a gift.

Apparently, Arianna had studied long enough to be recognized as one of them now. It was almost laughable. Gods, if those Crones only knew.

In silence, one of the old women gave her a book. I recognized it as a *grimoire*, in which spells and rituals and ancient knowledge would have been painstakingly copied. The second old woman presented her with a pendant that I couldn't see in detail. The third gifted her with a dagger.

This made me peer more closely, for it seemed to be a very special dagger. One much like the one I carried—like the one *we all* carried at our sides.

But The Crones didn't know of our existence, or of their student's true nature. Did they?

There was no time to ponder this mystery, for the initiation rite concluded, and the four of them moved on to whatever magickal working they had planned for this night. I crept nearer, so I might hear them.

"Dinna be disappointed if the spell doesna work right away, child," the one who looked to be the eldest said softly. "It oft' takes several tries before the rains come. We simply repeat our rite until they do."

Arianna nodded and took the small pouch the old woman handed her, looping its drawstring 'round her wrist.

"In honor of your initiation, Arianna, we've decided to let you perform tonight's incantation."

I saw Arianna's huge eyes widen in surprise. "Oh, but I—"

"You know what to do, lass," the plump one said with a smile, patting Arianna's arm. "We've taught you well."

"Aye," said the third, the one who seemed to personify grace, and whose face defied her years. "An' besides, 'tis in the grimoire."

Drawing a deep breath, Arianna opened the book. She clutched the dagger in her right hand. The pendant hung 'round her neck. The three Crones moved to the center of the circle, surrounded the balefire, and slowly began to move in a deosil direction. Arianna stood close to the fireside, so they were circling her, as well. Laying the dagger upon the open book, she opened the small pouch the old one had given her, and withdrew herbs, which she pitched into the dancing flames. Her face was a study in concentration as she worked.

Something about her touched me just then. I couldn't have said exactly what. But it had to do with the golden fire glow on her cheeks, and the light in her eyes. Or perhaps with the curve of her lips, or the slender grace of her neck.

Lowering her gaze to the book, she began to read the words written there in a voice that came soft and uncertain.

Ancient Forces of the Sky . . .
Winds and Clouds and Rain on high . . .
Rainbow Goddess, hear my cry . . .

I saw Arianna's shoulder's grow straighter, saw her chest expand as she inhaled, and I knew she was feeling it; the surge of power. In our kind, it was magnified, and in a rite like this, she would *have to* feel it. She may not know it for what it was, but its essence would fill her; the very essence of the Divinity she'd called upon.

She lifted her head, chin pointing skyward, and her voice came louder now, and firm.

Mother Earth is parched and dry,
Without thy dewy kiss, we die,
I call forth rainclouds. Draw thee nigh!

I glanced skyward, saw the barest hint of shadow crossing the face of the full moon. Quickly I fixed my gaze on Arianna again. Partly concerned for her, and for the reactions of her teachers, but mostly . . . I felt pride.

Her body seemed to elongate and tense as she let the book fall to the ground, and lifted her arms over her head, dagger pointing at the sky. Her voice came as strong as thunder then, deeper than before, echoing unnaturally in the night.

I call forth the rain!
I call forth the rain!
I call forth the rain!
And as I will it, so mote it be!

A clap of thunder punctuated her command. The wind came then. A harsh downward sweep of it sent her white robe snapping behind her and her golden hair sailing. The Crones stopped circling, went still, and looked at one another with wide eyes. Then they were staring at Arianna as if they had never seen her before, and looking skyward as if in fear.

Arianna noticed none of it. She remained as she was, arms stretched to the sky, eyes closed, body buffeted by the wind as she silently commanded the rain to fall. She seemed completely lost in the power she wielded.

Dark clouds surged as if from all directions, collecting in one grim mass overhead, blotting out the face of the moon. Thunder rumbled. Lightning cut a jagged swath across the sky. Then the sky opened, and the rains poured down.

Arianna's eyes blinked open. Her face still tipped back, she parted her lips as if to taste the raindrops that pummeled her. Slowly she lowered her arms and her head smiling as she sought approval in the faces of her teachers. But instead she found only shock in their eyes.

"I . . . I did it," she said. I could barely hear her words over the pounding rain.

Shaking her head slowly, the plump one backed away, and quickly walked the perimeter, chanting a closing rite as she did.

"Celia? Leandra? Did I . . . did I do something wrong?"

It was the elder who spoke. "Go home, child. This rite is ended. We'll speak of this on the morrow." She turned and walked back toward the cottage as Arianna stared helplessly after her.

The third gripped Arianna's shoulders. "I hope to heaven you know how to stop it, Arianna. Suppose it goes on until we're all swallowed up by floodwaters?"

Arianna looked wounded, then angry. "If I've the power in me to call forth the rain, then I can certainly halt it. An' I dinna ken why you all act as if you've suddenly discovered a demon in your midst! I only—"

"Celia!" the old one called from the cottage.

With a sigh, Celia turned and walked away, leaving Arianna alone in the deluge she'd summoned forth.

Arianna turned and strode back toward the village, filled with too many emotions to count. Gods! The power that had surged through her! Such a feeling had only come to her once before; as she'd knelt on the shore of that dark-water loch, moved beyond reason to shout her commands to the sky.

She'd made it rain. *She had made it rain!*

And yet The Crones had seemed stunned, and almost fearful of her afterward. She'd expected them to beam with pride. It was all very odd, and she had no idea what to think. She only knew she felt powerful. She could wield magick and command the elements to do her bidding. Her hair and her dress were even now soaked through with proof of it!

When Arianna turned to walk along the muddy path to her home, Nicodimus stepped out of the shadows in front of her, arms crossed over his broad chest, rust-and-gold hair plastered to his head. "This has to stop, Arianna."

She didn't jump, didn't cry out in surprise at his sudden appearance. She'd sensed him there in the instant before she'd seen him. So she simply stopped walking and stood facing him as the rain continued to beat down upon them both.

"Whatever do you mean?" she asked, feigning innocence.

"You know what I mean. The penalties for Witchcraft are not to be taken lightly. And if you continue on this reckless course, you'll surely be found out."

She tilted her head to one side, studying him. "An' how is it you know about me and my so-called reckless course?"

His eyes, when they probed hers, were piercing and sharp. "I've been watching you."

"Aye, so you have. I wondered if you'd admit it."

He lifted one brow slightly higher than the other. "You knew, then?"

"I have felt your eyes on me more than once since last we spoke." She shrugged. "'Tis all right, Nicodimus. I've watched you, as well."

That seemed to take him by surprise, for he looked up sharply. "Have you?" She nodded. "But why?"

"Why? What a silly question. For the same reason you've watched me, of course. We're connected, you and I. Linked together in some way . . . some way I've yet to understand. But you obviously feel it, too. Just as I do." She stared up at him, and when he said nothing, planted her hands on her hips and narrowed her eyes. "You're not goin' to deny it, now, are you?"

"I . . ." He seemed to think deeply before he spoke, his eyes studying her, as if seeing more than anyone else ever had. Or ever could. Pushing his wet hair away from his forehead, he pursed his lips, set his jaw. "I did not come here to speak of such things, Arianna, but to warn you."

"Warn me?" She shrugged. "I fear nothing, Nicodimus, so there's no reason to warn me of anything at all."

"I think there is."

Sighing, she rolled her eyes. "Speak your warning, if you must. I canna promise I'll heed it."

"You'll heed it," he said, and she thought she detected a hint of a threat in his voice. As if he intended to make certain she did. But he didn't say so. "You mustn't visit The Crones anymore," he told her. "There's no more they can teach you. And already they begin to wonder about you, Arianna. To fear you."

"Fear me? What rubbish, Nicodimus! Why would they—?"

"Because, foolish girl, you're a far more powerful Witch than any of them. More powerful than any Witch they've ever known. They have realized that even if you haven't yet."

His hands closed on her shoulders as he went on. The delicious tingling of his touch rocked her, and she closed her eyes in response, but he barely seemed to notice.

"They brew herbal potions to cure the croup while you cast spells to bring the dead back from their graves! Can you not see the difference?"

She blinked in shock as the import of his words sank in, but she did not pull free of his grip. Somehow he already knew her ultimate goal— something she hadn't dared confess to anyone.

He took his hands away, looking at his palms and shaking his head. He'd felt it, too. That sizzling jolt. That heat that had no place amid this cold, pounding rain.

She swallowed hard and voiced the suspicion she'd always harbored about him. "What do you know of spells, Nicodimus? Dinna tell me you're a Witch yourself."

"What I am or am not is between me and my Creator, Arianna. You'd do well to take a lesson from that."

She shrugged as if she didn't care, but took his refusal to answer as an admission. "Why should I heed your advice if you dinna even trust me enough to tell me your secrets?" she asked.

"I trust no one with my secrets. I have lived too long and seen too much to make that mistake." He studied her eyes for a moment, and his expression seemed to soften. "But I'll tell you a little of what I know, if you will promise to stay away from The Crones from now on."

She lowered her head. "I will promise this much. I shall be more careful, and will think about your warnings."

He dipped his head to search her eyes, seemed to resign himself to the fact that she would promise no more, and nodded. "All right. Then

I'll tell you this much. Your sister will come back one day, Arianna. We *all* come back," he said softly. "The Crones must have taught you that much, at least."

She nodded. "Some would call those words blasphemy, Nicodimus."

"And some would call them truth," he countered. "But you cast a spell when your sister died, didn't you, Arianna? A spell to make her coming back . . . different."

"How do you know?"

He lifted a golden brow, tilted his head.

She sighed. "Kenyon an' Lud Lachlan told you how I shouted it to the heavens, did they? I made them swear ne'er to say a word."

He kept his gaze riveted to her eyes, only the raindrops, a misty curtain, between them. "What sort of spell was it, Arianna?"

Closing her eyes, she told him what she'd told no one, not even The Crones. "My sister sank into the cold embrace of that dark water," she said, lowering her head slowly as the pain of that day renewed itself in her soul. "I lay upon the shore, fighting to breathe, choking water from my lungs, searching for her. And Laird Lachlan's sons, Kenyon and Lud, they both went back for her. Frantic, shouting. But I knew she was already gone. I felt it somehow. Like a large, heavy stone where my heart should have been."

Nicodimus sighed, and when she looked up at him, he squeezed her shoulders. "I know the feeling well, child. Go on."

"I felt anger, rage, an' . . . something else. Like some other voice tellin' me what to do, only . . . nay aloud. I heard with my heart, with my soul, nay my ears. I knelt up, an' lifted my fists to the heavens, an' I demanded that my sister be returned to me. Aye, Raven will live again, but when she returns, she'll look the same, and bear the same name, and I'll know her again, for she will come back afore my lifetime is ended. Those are the words I shouted, the commands I sent forth, an' I tell you, Nicodimus, when I did so I felt as powerful as the Goddess Herself."

Nicodimus expelled his breath. "That is because it was Her power you wielded, Arianna." He turned slightly away from her. "Within your lifetime," he muttered. "Sweet child, if only you knew how long that might be."

"Nicodimus?"

He faced her again, and she searched his eyes, not understanding what he'd meant. But he shook his head at her as if to tell her to forget about it. "Do you have any doubt your spell will be effective?" he asked.

Her chin came up. "None whatsoever."

"And who taught you such a conjure, Arianna?"

Slowly, she shook her head. "No one. As I said, it came from . . . within me. 'Twas as if the very Queen of Heaven put the words to my lips . . . or something."

"Or something indeed." His brows drew together. "You've no need of those village Witches any longer. There is no more they can teach you."

"But there is so much more I need to learn." She sighed heavily, pacing away from him, wringing her wet hands. "I want Raven back *now*, Nicodimus. I canna bear the loneliness without her."

When he didn't answer, she turned to face him again, only to glimpse a bleak expression in his eyes before he managed to shutter them. But deep in his eyes, she could still see a shadow of pain. Rivulets of rainwater ran down his corded neck, dripped from his chin. She wanted to wipe the drops away with her hands. With her lips.

Finally, he whispered, "I know how much it hurts. But there's nothing you can do to make her come back to you any sooner. Believe me, I've searched the world over for such a spell. It doesn't exist."

"Nay, it must," she whispered, clasping the plaid at his chest in her fists, staring up at him, pleading with her eyes.

"It doesn't. I would not lie to you about this, nor would I speak the words unless I knew them to be true. There is no way to raise the dead from their graves, Arianna. It *cannot happen*."

"Nay . . ." Her knees buckled. She collapsed at his feet, kneeling weakly in the mud. It was as if she'd been hit in the belly by a giant fist, the very breath forced out of her. She couldn't draw any air for a moment. For she knew, instinctively, that he spoke the truth. He wouldn't lie to her, not about this. So there was no way to hasten Raven's return. It was almost as if she'd lost her sister all over again at that moment. For she'd existed on a hope that had suddenly disappeared.

Gently, Nicodimus bent over her. He closed his big hands 'round her waist, lifted her to her feet again. "I regret taking your dream away. But 'tis best you know . . ."

She leaned against his chest and would have fallen once again had his arms not come 'round her to hold her upright. Sobs burst from her all at once, her tears mingled with the rain that soaked his clothes. He lowered his head and she felt his lips grazing the top of hers, heard his comforting whispers. "You cast your spell, Arianna, and I believe you cast it true. It will work. She'll come back to you one day, you have to believe it. Cling to it, child. At least it is something."

Sniffling, Arianna lifted her head, searching his face with her damp eyes. "Aye. 'Tis more than you had, is that what you're sayin'?"

He nodded. "Yes. It is more than I had."

"Who did you lose, Nicodimus?"

Licking his lips, he set her gently away from him, cleared his throat, schooled his features. Hardened them. "If you must practice your rites, Arianna, do it alone and in some secret place where you won't be found out. It is safer that way. That is what I came here to tell you, nothing more." He turned to go.

Arianna caught his arm and he stopped, his back to her. "*You ken all of it, dinna you?*" she whispered. "You ken the ways of magick, and far more than those village Witches understand. You have the secrets I've been seekin' all my life."

"I know nothing beyond what I've told you."

Slowly she moved around until she was in front of him again. She smeared the tears from her cheeks with one hand, and gripping his forearm with the other she probed his eyes. "I've been driven to learn the ways of the mystics, Nicodimus. Driven by some force deep inside me that I dinna even ken. An' drawn to you like a moth to the candle's flame from the first time I set eyes on you. And now I ken why. You can teach me, Nicodimus. You can tell me the things I need to learn."

"You're mistaken."

"Am I?"

He nodded.

"An' what of this, then?" Abruptly, she released his arm, and stepping back, bunched her skirts in both hands and lifted them high, baring her right leg and her thigh, and finally her hip, where the mark of a crescent moon stood in dark contrast to her pale skin. Clouds parted as if on command, and moonlight spilled down onto the birthmark as if in a caress. Nicodimus's gaze fixed to it in much the same way.

She saw him tremble, saw the sweat bead upon his upper lip. His hands reached out, and she closed her eyes in anticipation of his touch there on her bare hip. She held her breath, and felt the heat of his hands as they hovered a hairbreadth from her skin . . .

But he only took her skirts from her hands to lower them. If his fingers brushed her thigh as they passed, it was purely unintentional, though that touch left a burning trail of forbidden pleasure in its wake.

"Do not," was all he said.

Breathless, shivering, she stared into his eyes as if daring him to deny the truth. "You bear the mark, same as I do, Nicodimus."

He caught his breath. "How can you know that?"

She lowered her eyes. "I told you. I've watched you just as you've watched me. I've peered from my da's croft as you rode through the village upon that magnificent black stallion, an' I've spied on you from the tall reeds near the loch, long before the sun has risen in the sky. You go there to bathe in the coolness of the wee hours."

"You have no right—"

"Aye," she whispered. "I do. That mark you bear upon your hip gives me the right. An' if that were not enough, Nicodimus, there is the stirring I feel deep in the pit of my belly when you step, naked and wet, out of that water into the glow of the early sun, lookin' as wild an' magnificent as Cernunnos Himself. We're bound to one another somehow. When you touch me, I feel a force pass between us that is more than ordinary desire. An' you know 'tis true, Nicodimus. For you feel it, too."

"Arianna—"

"What does the crescent birthmark mean?"

He closed his eyes only briefly. So strong and steadfast, while she trembled at his very touch. "You're a young girl. The time when you'll need to burden yourself with all of this is far away yet. Far away. When it comes, when you need to know . . . I'll tell you. I promise you that." He stroked her hair with his big hand. "For now, that will have to be enough for you." He lowered his head, shaking it slowly. "An' as for this other—"

"Us wantin' each other, you mean?"

His jaw clenched. "You're too young, and I am too old for either of us to entertain such a ludicrous notion, Arianna."

But he didn't deny it was true. It wasn't an admission, nor even much of a concession. But it was something. He wanted her, too. She knew that as he turned and she watched him stride away. But it wasn't enough. She wanted a good deal more than a promise and a pat on the head from Nicodimus Lachlan.

A good deal more.

"You'll be mine, one day, Nicodimus. Heart an' soul you'll be mine. You canna see it, but deep down in your soul, you already are."

Nicodimus stiffened, but kept on walking.

Chapter 3

✥

Arianna was a girl in need of rescue. Yet at the same time, she was a woman . . . a woman in need of a man. And I knew that made her dangerous to me. I had a weakness in me for a woman in trouble. And with her that weakness seemed trebled. I had long ago vowed never to care again, and I feared that rescuing Arianna would mean breaking that vow. Already I felt the slow burn of desire for her in my blood. And more. A softness. A weakness. A vulnerability.

Just as there had been before . . . for Anya.

It had been a furious battle, between my own clansmen and those who dwelled in the lowlands. I no longer remember precisely when nor why it began, but in the year 764, I rode into battle beside my father, bow at my side and a quiver of arrows on my back. I fought bravely that day. I killed as many men as any of the other warriors, though I had but four and ten years, and this was my first battle. They congratulated me, my clansmen. Slapped my shoulders and sang my praises as we rode through the defeated village. Wounded men raced out of our path while women cowered.

As I looked around me, I saw her for the first time. A bit of a girl with wild hair as red as the sun before a storm. She tugged a wounded man by the arm, dragging his body from the path, though it was obviously more than she could manage alone. Her eyes met mine, and she stopped what she was doing, staring at me in silence.

Another man, younger than the wounded one, strode up to her and slapped her sharply across the face. "I told you to get him inside, Anya. Do it. *Now*."

"Yes, Marten." She lowered her head in submission and began tugging at the man again. I drew my horse to a halt before her.

"Leave him," I said.

She looked up at me, wide-eyed. Her eyes were the palest blue I had ever seen. The blue of water, or ice. A thin, weak blue. And they showed me her soul.

"Leave him," I told her again, my voice more gentle this time, for she was small and timid and afraid.

She slanted a glance at the one who'd slapped her, as if seeking his permission.

"Anya," I said, calling her by name. "He's too heavy for you. Let this brute who slaps small women carry him instead."

She let go of the unconscious one's arm, and he thumped downward to the dirt.

"You," I said, addressing the young man now. "Are you her husband?"

"Her brother," he said, all but spitting the words at me. "An' she'll do as I tell her or suffer the consequences."

The men around me muttered, but didn't interfere. "No," I said softly. "You'll both do as *I* tell you. Marten, is it? If you want that wounded man carried inside, do it yourself." He didn't move. I pulled an arrow from my quiver. I'd fired them all in the midst of the battle, and I'd had to run about plucking arrows from dead men in order to rearm myself. The tip was bloodied. I strung the arrow, but before I lifted my bow, Marten had slung the old man—his father, I guessed—over his shoulder and was lugging him away. Anya turned to follow.

"Wait," I said, and she stopped, her back to me. "Does he strike you often?"

Her body seemed to stiffen. "Only when I do not work fast enough, or do my work well enough to suit him."

"And how often is that?" I asked softly.

I saw her shoulders slump. "Every day."

My stomach churned with the urge to kill the bastard. "Is he the only one who treats you this way," I asked. "Or does your father join in as well?"

She turned to face me. "My father is far harsher than Marten, and my other brother, Kohl, is just as bad." Her eyes flashed with the first life I'd seen in them. "And now that you and your clan have defeated ours in battle, it is bound to be even worse. Our women will bear the brunt of their anger. While you ride away with the spoils."

"Spoils?" I lifted my palms and looked at the men around me. "Have we taken any spoils?"

They all answered in the negative. It had never been our custom to loot a defeated enemy's village. I looked back at Anya once more. "But perhaps we should. I am the victor this day, after all. I ought to take a token of this battle back with me."

Her eyes widened slightly. She took a step backward as I held out my hand to her.

"Come with me, Anya," I said. "Come with me and no man will ever raise a hand to you again."

She simply stood there, her brows crooked together as if she couldn't understand. She took a hesitant step forward, then went still as a man yelled her name.

I turned to see what had to be the second brother rushing toward us, and I quickly leapt to the ground, snatched up a sword, and grabbed Anya's hand.

"Let go of her!" Kohl shrieked, and then he cried, "Marten! Marten, they're taking Anya!"

By the time Marten came running, likely after having dropped his father headfirst, I was lifting the girl onto my horse. I swung up behind her. She neither helped me nor resisted. And I remember wishing she'd give some indication whether she wished to come with me or not. I'd likely have taken her either way. It was my right to do so. But mostly I hated the thought of those men treating her so cruelly.

Marten and Kohl rushed me, and I could have easily killed one or the other of them with a single swipe of my sword, but I chose not to. Not in front of their sister. Instead, I simply kicked my stallion's sides, and we lunged forward. Tipping my head back, I bellowed a victory cry, and carried my prize away. And Anya whispered, "Goodbye, my brothers." Her voice was neither jubilant nor sad.

I'd made a pair of lifelong enemies that day. Their vengeance had cost me dearly, and would again, I knew. And yet here I was, once again, tempted by a woman in need of rescue.

Yet, I could not quite envision Arianna ever taking the abuse Anya had. I imagined the man who would lift a hand to her would suffer a thousand deaths before she'd satisfied her need for vengeance. She needed rescuing only from herself. And that, she needed badly. For if she continued on the course she'd set, only disaster awaited her.

I went into the village often. Daily, in fact. And each time, I made it a point to see her, to watch her movements. But from a distance, for my own peace of mind. Being close to her was far too disturbing to me.

Most often I found her at the grave of her sister—not mourning, but focusing very intently with a look of stubborn determination on her pretty, elfin face.

One morning I found her near the loch, sitting on the grassy bank alone—always alone. She stared out at the blue-green waters that had taken her sister, a haunted expression in her eyes. I'd vowed to watch over her, to keep her from ruining herself, if I could, but to do so without interacting with her any more than necessary. If she knew how often I observed her, she would read more into my actions than was truly there. And that would feed her romantic notions about the two of us. Besides, sparring with her was exhausting . . . and yet exciting to me.

So I'd decided to stay away. But the picture she made there that morning was one so heartbreaking that I started forward. No one deserved to be as lonely as Arianna looked at that moment.

As soon as I took a step forward, I saw a young man approaching her, and decided to wait . . . and to watch.

He had to be the cobbler's son of whom Joseph had spoken; the lad to whom she was betrothed. His proprietary hand on her arm gave me to know as much. The way she shook it off only made me smile as I crept closer amid the rushes to watch this little scene play out amid a backdrop of sparkling water and rocky hillsides. The keep loomed tall and gray beyond them, looking almost like an extension of the cliffs beyond it. Its backdrop was the sky, the fluffy clouds drifting lazily past the sun.

"You've mourned your sister long enough," the lad was saying. Angus MacClennan was his name, I recalled. "It looks bad for you, Arianna, sitting out here all alone. 'Tis long enough, I tell you."

Arianna tilted her head to one side, studying him curiously. "How can one know how long is long enough? If I still miss her, if I still weep for her when I'm alone at night . . . then I still mourn her, Angus. And I *do* miss her. And I *do* weep for her. And I sometimes think that I loved her so much . . . a lifetime of mourning her wouldna be 'long enough.'"

Lowering his head, properly shamed, he whispered, "I didna mean you should stop missing her, Arianna. Only that 'tis high time you be happy again."

"An' how would you suggest I do that?"

He shifted his stance. Arianna remained where she was, sitting carelessly on the bank, knees wrapped within the folds of her arms, glancing at the boy occasionally only to return to her contemplation of the waves. It looked as if he was a bit of a nuisance to her, like a fly, and would get no more attention than one.

"You've long been promised to me," he said, seeming to choose his words with great care and forethought. "I want us to go forth with our lives, Arianna."

"Speak plainly, for heaven's sake."

He cleared his throat, thrust out his chin. "I want us to marry."

"Why?"

Very frank, very blunt, and spoken so quickly poor Angus nearly fell over backward. He blinked his surprise. "What sort of question is that?"

"A good one, I think. Why do you want to marry me?"

"Arianna, you're nigh on ten and eight! And I nearly twenty!"

"So we should marry because we are of a certain age, then." She frowned, shaking her head, still staring at the water. "Hardly seems reason enough to me."

Pushing both hands through his carrot-colored hair, Angus spun in a circle. Then he stopped and stared down at her. "Ahh, I see. So 'tis declarations of love you be wantin', is that it?"

She said nothing, but I saw her close her eyes as if in dread of what was to come.

Sure enough, young Angus rounded on her, dropping to one knee. "I love you, fair Arianna. I want you to be my wife. To bear my children. To—"

"So, you love me, do you?" she interrupted.

He licked his lips. "Aye. Do you nay believe it?"

She shrugged. "Why should I believe it? 'Tis the first time you've spoken of love, Angus, and only now because you think 'tis what I wish to hear. So tell me, what is it you love about me?"

"I-I dinna ken—"

"Well, do you love the way I go about alone when 'tis deemed improper?"

"Nay, not that, but—"

"Then 'tis the way I speak my mind, be my thoughts impertinent or not?"

"Nay, of course not, lass. But I—"

"Nay? Then it must be the way I mourn my beloved sister. . . . Oh, nay, for you've already told me you dislike that about me."

"You talk in circles!" he shouted. "I-I love your hair, lass, and your eyes, and the figure you fetch in your dresses." He gave a nod, looking quite satisfied with himself.

"My hair will turn gray and fall out in time. My eyes will dull and lose their glow amid the wrinkles that will pucker my face, and as for the figure I fetch, 'twill go to this childbearing you've spoken of soon enough. What will remain of your so-called love, then, Angus?"

He looked as if he'd been hit between the eyes for a moment. Then he frowned at her. "It willna matter," he said, his voice growing sharper now. "'Tis time, Arianna, canna you see that?"

"Why?" she insisted. "Tell me why. Tell me now or go away. Why, Angus?"

"My mother is ailing, woman!" he blurted all at once. "How much longer do you expect her to run that household and care for me and my da and my younger brothers? 'Tis *your* place, an' the time has come for you to take it."

She rose, and the look in her eyes as she glared at him made me shiver, even from the distance between us. I actually feared for the lad for just a moment. I rose from my hiding place in the rushes without a thought.

"'Tis *nay* my place." She poked him in the chest with a forefinger. "'Tis neither *my* mother, nor *my* household, nor *my* brothers need carin' for," she said, poking him three more times. "I willna marry you, Angus. Not now and not ever, so you might as well stop with your askin'."

"You . . . you . . ." His face reddened. "You canna do that! You're my betrothed! You canna—"

"Katie McDaniel would swoon on the spot should you ask for her hand. Go find you a woman who wants you, Angus. 'Twill never be me. I'd sooner go to prison, for that's what life as a wife here would be like. Prison. Servitude. But there is more than that out there awaitin' me, an' I'll find it someday. I vow I will, or die in the search."

He stared at her, dumbfounded. "Who's been puttin' such wild notions into yer head, woman?" Then he looked at the ground when she didn't answer. "Can it be true, what they're sayin'? Can it be true, after all?"

"Can what be true?" She looked exasperated with the entire discussion.

Angus lifted his head, and with a sigh of apparent surrender, reached out to her. "No matter. No matter at all, not now. Will you give me your hand, then? A gesture of friendship in parting?"

I went stiff, a little chill of warning creeping into my nape. Even as I started forward, she offered her delicate hand. Angus took it and gripped her hand hard. Too hard. I saw the alarm in her eyes, saw her try to pull free, and I raced toward them. But Angus had a blade in his free hand now, and with a ruthless swipe of it, he cut her. Blood sprayed from her wrist and she screamed. The sound cut right to my heart. Angus jumped backward, wide-eyed, terrified, first at the way she bled, and then as he caught sight of me bearing down on him.

"I dinna mean . . . They say a Witch doesna bleed when ye cut 'em! They say a Witch doesna bleed—"

My fist crushed the better part of his face, and when he landed hard on his back, he was blessedly silent. I turned and gathered Arianna close as her knees began to give. I closed my hand firmly around her wrist, slowing the blood flow with pressure. I didn't want her to die, only to revive into a new life; an endless life of fighting just to stay alive. Not yet. Not when she was so young, so innocent. She'd never survive.

"There, lie back, lass. I have you."

"I'll kill him," she whispered through grated teeth. "That simpering, superstitious lout!" She lifted her head to eye the wound. "I'll bleed to death."

"You know I won't allow that to happen. Lie back, Arianna."

She did, reclining half across my lap, her side pressed to my chest. I tore a strip of cloth from her skirt and wrapped her wrist up tight. She winced in reaction and bit her lip. "I'm sorry it hurts you, lass."

"Fear not, Nicodimus. I'm committin' every bit of this pain to memory, so that I can visit it back upon him."

"Hush." I tied a knot in the makeshift bandage. "You'll need stitching. Can you stand?"

She nodded, and then clung to my neck as I got to my feet. She tried to stand without aid and wobbled a bit. I eased her into the crook of my arm. "Come down to the water's edge, and I'll wash some of the blood away."

"My head is spinning," she whispered, but she walked beside me, lowering her head as she sank down into the grass beside the water. This time, she remained sitting up on her own, as I tore at my clothing and used the scraps to bathe her with loch water. Gently, I wiped the blood from her slender forearm. She sat still and silent, contemplating the loch as before. I rinsed the scrap of cloth, squeezed it out, and moved to her face, wiping as carefully as I could. Then I paused, my heart tripping, as I saw a teardrop slip down her cheek.

"Don't cry, Arianna," I said, and I washed it gently away.

She whispered, "'Tis ironic, dinna you think? Now both the Sinclair sisters' blood nourishes this water."

"Then this water must be very special indeed," I said softly.

She met and held my gaze. Her eyes were so brown and deep . . . and filled with far more pain and wisdom than a girl of nearly eighteen should know. She touched a palm to my cheek. "You likely saved my life just now, Nicodimus."

I shook my head, and concentrated on cleaning her face, trying to keep my touch cool and impersonal. "'Twould take more than a cut such as that one to do you in."

She opened her mouth as if she would argue the point, but as she did, she spotted her beau on the ground. Her eyes widened, and I followed her gaze to where he lay. His nose broken, lip bleeding. I supposed I hit him a mite harder than I should.

"Mercy," Arianna said with a gasp. "Have you done him to death?"

"I think not. He moaned a moment ago. And don't pity him, Arianna. He didn't get half the beating he deserves." I scooped her up into my arms, cleaner now. At least not covered in enough blood to send her mother into a dead faint should she catch sight of her. "I never could abide a man who'd harm a lady."

Looking back at the lad, she told him softly, "Think how surprised you'll be, foolish Angus MacClennan, when you learn once and for all that Witches *do* bleed."

I knew exactly what she was thinking, though it didn't take any magick to do so. Her thoughts were writ clear across her face. "If you think you can go about wielding magick for such petty causes as vengeance, lass, then you've had poor teachers."

She blinked up at me. "Are you admittin' you know of such things personally, Nicodimus?"

I scowled at her. "I'm only saying young Angus has done you a favor. He'll consider this proof of your innocence." I nodded toward her bandaged wrist. "Though I'd like to throttle him for it, all the same."

Her smile was sweet and slow. "You care for me far more than you know," she whispered.

I ignored that remark, finding it far too close to the truth. "When word gets out that Angus cut you and you nearly bled to death, then the speculation about you might well die." I glanced down at her. "At least until you do something to revive it all over again."

"Superstitious fools, all of them. They'll never let it die. They'll say the blood was an illusion, a trick, that I conjured the blood to appear and flow just to fool him." She tilted her head. "At last Da canna expect me to marry the whelp now."

"Ahhh, you owe him for two favors, then."

She glared at me, and then sighed. "Where are you takin' me, Nicodimus?"

"To the keep."

"The keep," she whispered, and her eyes turned to stare off at the fortresslike structure. Her slender arms clung more tightly to my neck, and her head rested upon my shoulder as I strode with her along the craggy path up the hill to the massive stone structure at its top.

"Surely you've been in the keep before, Arianna," I said teasingly. "You've nothing to fear there."

"Aye, I've been inside before. An' I dinna fear it, Nicodimus. You've misread me entirely. I was born to live in a castle keep, and one far finer than this. . . ." She smiled up at me. "Just as I was born to be with you, Nicodimus."

Chapter 4

Arianna rocked against Nicodimus's broad chest when he scooped her up into his arms and strode toward the keep. His arms were clamped securely around her, like some sort of protective armor. His scent surrounded her, warm and musky and male. And this close to him, she could see the tiny bits of stubble that made his cheeks appear shadowed. Beautiful, he was. She'd never known a man so beautiful. And she knew she'd never felt so safe. She didn't like the idea that she needed a man to make her feel this way. She'd never *needed* a man for anything, and she'd vowed she never would. But wanting a man, well, she supposed that was a far different matter. *Not* wanting this one, with his angular face and his wizard's eyes, *that* would be impossible.

Behind them, she heard Angus groaning. Raising her head to look back over Nicodimus's shoulder, Arianna saw that Angus's face was a mottled mess as he stirred himself to sit up. Nicodimus didn't so much as glance backward at the boy. And she knew, even more surely now than she'd known before, that he felt something very powerful for her. It was there in the hard set of his jaw, in the furrow between his brows. In the way he cradled her against his hard chest so carefully even while his broad strides ate up the distance to the keep. And in the way he paused ever so briefly, and closed his eyes tight when the wind blew her hair into his face.

Arianna felt a rush of uncertainty when he carried her through the outer gates and into the courtyard. Sounds of clanging metal rang in her ears. Men practiced with their swords, fighting one another in mock battle. Off to the left, there were men who shot arrows at straw stuffed targets fashioned in the shapes of men. Everywhere she looked, curious eyes in sweaty, wary faces seemed to greet her. To a man, they stopped what they were doing when they saw Nicodimus carrying her past. She could almost hear their thoughts as they stared at her. *What sort of trouble has the fool girl got into this time?*

Laird Lachlan would not be pleased with her. True enough, Angus's attack had not been her fault, but the laird would not likely see it that way. She was the one whose behavior had stirred suspicious minds to wild speculation. She was the one who'd caused the tongues to wag.

She couldn't help but stiffen in nervous anticipation as Nicodimus carried her nearer to the huge, banded doors.

Nicodimus looked down at her as he strode closer. "What is it, Arianna?"

She shrugged, averting her eyes. "I'm hardly dressed proper to be visitin' the keep. Look at me. Barefoot."

"You've been barefoot every time I've seen you." His gaze was indulgent and slightly amused.

"My dress is but poor tartan, an' stained with blood an' loch water at that, Nicodimus. Perhaps I ought simply return to my mam an' let her tend the wound."

When he didn't immediately respond, she peered up at him, only to see his deliciously full lips curving at the corners. "Was it not you I just heard telling your beau that there was more awaiting you in this world than a dirt-floor croft and a life of servitude? Or was that some other barefoot hellion?" He shook his head.

"So you were spyin' on us the whole time, were you?"

"I'd say 'tis a good thing I was." She pressed her lips shut tight, but he ignored her lack of response. "Joseph will have to know what happened sooner or later, Arianna. I cannot believe a girl of your spirit is afraid of her own chieftain."

"I'm nay afraid of any man!"

Nicodimus lifted one brow. "Good. You've no need to be. And don't worry yourself about your state of dress, Arianna. You shame the sun, and I think you know it. What you might be wearing has little to do with it. And I doubt it would have any bearing on Joseph's mood at any rate."

A thrill of warm liquid pleasure spilled into her belly. "Are you sayin' you think I'm beautiful, then, Nicodimus Lachlan?"

Nicodimus's eyes darkened from a gleaming topaz-blue to the shade of sapphires at midnight. "You're beautiful. But there is more than mere beauty shining from those brown eyes."

"What more?" Her words came out on a breathless whisper.

He seemed to force his lingering gaze away from her face, and with a ragged sigh and a sharp shake of his head, resumed walking. "It is dangerous ground I'm treading. Best we speak of something else."

"Tell me," she whispered. "Tell me what *you* see when you look into my eyes, Nicodimus."

He looked down at her once more, and it almost seemed as if he could see right to her soul. He held her gaze with his, exerting some unseen force, even when she would have looked away. His eyes probed for a long moment, and what she saw in them . . . It was so intense, so powerful that it nearly frightened her.

An instant later the large, arching door opened, and he never answered her question. Laird Joseph Lachlan appeared in the doorway, a strikingly beautiful woman at his side. Arianna had seen the dark, exotic woman in Stonehaven before. She seemed to come and go as irregularly as Nicodimus himself did. But she seldom set foot in the village, and seemed to hold herself aloof from the clan in the keep. No one seemed to know from whence she came. That she was a foreigner was obvious. That she was well liked and welcomed by the clan chieftain, equally so. And if Laird Lachlan trusted her, then that was enough for his clan. Few asked questions.

But from the first moment Arianna had seen her, she'd burned with curiosity over the woman's background. The mysterious woman exchanged a lingering, searching glance with Nicodimus that made Arianna want to leap from his arms and claw out her eyes. 'Twas obvious they knew one another. And well.

Her eyes were ebon, slanted, and lined in black. Jewels dangled from her ears and a single ruby pierced her nose. So many bracelets adorned her wrists that they made music when she moved, and around her neck she wore at least as many pendants on chains. She was willow slender, and very tall—taller than most men, in fact. Her hair hung to her waist, blue-black and shining, and perfectly straight. And her skin was a flawless shade of bronze.

She met Arianna's gaze, and her expression did not change. She was stone-faced, no smile of welcome, no frown of concern. Nothing. Just a gaze that made Arianna feel measured and weighed and judged all at once.

"Come, bring her inside," Laird Lachlan said, stepping aside, holding the door. "I saw you comin' and summoned Nidaba. What's happened to her?"

Arianna stiffened in his arms as Nicodimus swept through the doors and into the great hall. Endless distance loomed above her, to the concave ceiling. She shivered at a chill so deep it seemed to reach out and touch her bones.

"Her devoted husband-to-be cut her," Nicodimus said. "To see whether she would bleed, he claimed."

The sound of conversation abruptly ceased as people in the great hall all turned toward Arianna. A lad with his arms loaded down with wood for the fire, the men who stood 'round the plank table deep in some discussion, the women performing various chores—everyone stared at Arianna so intently she thought their looks were burned into her skin. Nidaba muttered a word Arianna didn't recognize, but from the sound of it, it might have been a curse. She had no inkling whether it was directed at her or at Angus. The woman looked briefly into Arianna's eyes and then away.

"I will tend the girl," she said, her voice as deep and rich as a vat of spring honey, with an accent too exotic to identify. "Bring her to my chamber."

There was no trace of the highlands in Nidaba. Her dark skin was sun-kissed, her nails long and curving, with tiny stones somehow affixed to them. And her dress was as scandalous as any other Arianna had seen her wearing. Black and tight and anchored only at one shoulder, leaving the other, and both arms, completely bare.

She was frightening, and Arianna did not fear much. She bristled, and told herself she could hold her own against the strange woman, should the need arise.

The chieftain turned and waved a hand to those in the chamber. "Go about your business. The lass is nay in need of your gawkin' at her." His voice lower, as they scurried away, he said, "Angus MacClennan is a foolish lad, if ever there was one." He ran one hand over his bald head and sighed, walking beside Nicodimus as Nidaba led the way through an arching doorway and into one of the many dark stone corridors. Nicodimus carried Arianna past what seemed like endless doors, and his steps echoed like ghosts all around them. While Arianna had often been in the great hall and the kitchens, she had never before been in the private wing or invited into the chambers of those who lived here. And yet, she couldn't stop looking ahead, at Nidaba. The woman's black dress seemed to be made of some magickal fabric that shimmered when she moved and clung to her like skin.

"He could have killed her!" the laird muttered angrily. "How many daughters does he think her poor family can stand to lose?"

"You can see the damage gossip can do, Joseph. The tongue-waggers who started this ought to be horsewhipped," Nicodimus said quickly.

"Aye, indeed. Gossip can be a deadly thing, Nic. A deadly thing."

Arianna cringed a bit, knowing Nicodimus likely believed her own behavior had brought this upon her as much as the gossip of the villagers had done. He had warned her, hadn't he?

Nidaba opened a door, and they stepped into a large chamber. It was far different from the dark, rather barren parts of the keep Arianna was familiar with. The room seemed to be of some other world, filled with the most incredible collection of exotic items Arianna had ever seen. Glittering stones of purple and blue and pink, some colorless, some multihued, lined shelves on the walls. And there were daggers—countless different shapes and sizes, all from different lands, Arianna thought, perhaps even . . . different times. They hung on the stone walls, some crossing one another, some forming triangles, some fanning out like the tail feathers of some beautiful, deadly bird.

Nidaba waved a beringed hand toward her fur-covered bed, and Nicodimus lowered Arianna onto it. Then he stepped aside to let Nidaba move closer to her. The woman's black eyes met hers, and the ruby in her nose seemed to glow. Arianna shivered. And then the woman touched Arianna's forearm, clasping it to begin removing the makeshift bandage.

A jolt surged from her hand into Arianna's arm the instant the strange woman touched her. Just the way it had at Nicodimus's touch. Arianna's eyes widened. Nidaba paused, met her gaze, and seemed to will her to keep silent. Aloud, she said, "I have no need of you two men. You may go, take refreshment. I will bring her along to you when we've finished."

Arianna sought Nicodimus's eyes, her own pleading. She didn't know this woman. Nidaba frightened her, when she'd long prided herself on fearing nothing; not man, nor beast nor death itself.

"I'll stay," Nicodimus said, very softly. "She's been through a shock, and you're a stranger to her, Nidaba."

Nidaba's dark, probing gaze never left Arianna. "I am a stranger to most of the clan Lachlan. But few look at me with such wide eyes as these." Her hand clasped Arianna's chin as she studied her face, and Arianna fought to hide her inexplicable fear of the woman. "You are right to be afraid, young one, of those you do not know. However, I mean you no harm . . . just now." As she unwrapped the wound, she whispered, "I am not one of the Dark Ones."

Arianna only frowned, puzzled.

And when Nidaba saw that she hadn't understood, the woman sent Nicodimus a questioning look, to which he responded with a quick subtle shake of his head. There was another long gaze between them, but it broke off when Nicodimus came to the other side of the bed to watch over her as the dark woman worked. The laird himself, not some servant, fetched water and a cloth, and brought fine whiskey for her to sip, while Nidaba cleansed and then stitched the wound, and Arianna clutched Nicodimus's forearm in pain.

Twice, Arianna saw Nidaba move one hand over the cut in a circular motion; saw her lips moving as she whispered some words too soft to hear. Almost as if . . . as if she were casting a spell.

But nay. She couldn't be. Could she?

When the laird left the three of them alone in the room, Arianna cleared her throat, gathered her courage, and blurted the question on her mind. "Are you a Witch, Nidaba?"

Nidaba's hands stilled. Then she lifted one forefinger, and taking the needle, pricked it. A ruby-red droplet welled from the tiny puncture, and Nidaba met Arianna's eyes. "I bleed. Therefore, I cannot be, can I?"

Silent for a moment, looking from Nidaba to Nicodimus and back again, Arianna realized it was meant to be a joke. Though the strange woman never smiled.

"I am serious," Arianna insisted. "Is it only when I touch the hand of another Witch that I feel that . . . that surge of . . . of whatever it is that I felt when I touched you just now, Nidaba? Or when I touch Nicodimus?"

Nidaba met Nicodimus's eyes, her eyebrows raised.

"But it canna be that," Arianna continued, shaking her head. "I feel nothing when I touch Celia's hand, nor Leandra's nor Mary's."

Nidaba tilted her head. "And who are they?"

"The Crones," Nicodimus explained.

"Ahhh," she said. "The mortal village Witches."

Arianna frowned at them both while Nidaba bent to her work once again. "'Mortal'? What do you mean, Nidaba?" But Nidaba didn't answer. "Nicodimus, what did she mean?"

Nicodimus cleared his throat. "Nidaba is not quite fluent in our language, Arianna. It is not her native tongue."

"Do you think I dinna ken as much?" Arianna said with a toss of her head. "The entire clan kens she's a foreigner." Arianna looked at her. "Where do you come from, Nidaba?"

"I believe you know it as Sumeria," Nidaba answered without looking up. Her hair hung over her face like a black satin curtain.

Arianna blinked. She was uncertain, but she thought Sumeria to be the name of some long ago desert land; a place that no longer existed. She must be mistaken. She certainly didn't want to show the two of them her ignorance by asking.

"And, how do you two know each other?" she went on, burningly curious about the nature of their relationship.

"Why do you ask?" Nicodimus asked her.

She shrugged. "You seem . . . well acquainted."

"We are."

Nidaba's head was still bent over Arianna's wrist, but not so much that Arianna missed the slight smile at Nicodimus's answer. "Nicodimus and I have been . . . acquainted . . . for a very long time. Longer than you could even begin to guess."

"Then . . . you are close. Close . . . as friends are close?" Arianna pressed.

The needle jabbed her, and while up to now she hadn't felt a hint of unnecessary pain under the woman's ministrations, this time it hurt. "The curious rabbit who pries into the scorpion's lair," Nidaba said softly, "gets stung."

"You did that apurpose!" Arianna all but shouted.

Nidaba said nothing more as she wrapped Arianna's arm in a clean, soft cloth. When that was done, she straightened, and began putting her things away. "Finish the whiskey," she told Arianna. "The pain will ease soon."

The door opened and the laird peered inside. "How is she?"

"She will be fine," Nidaba replied. "But it could have been far more serious, had Nicodimus not been nearby."

"Aye, I thought as much. Rest awhile there, lass," the laird bade Arianna. "You'll take dinner here in the keep. An' I'll have no argument about that. Fear not, I'll send word to your mother with the same two men I'm sendin' to bring young Angus back here. A night in the dungeon might give the lad somethin' to think about 'ere next he harms a lassie. We dinna tolerate such behavior in the clan."

"No," Nicodimus said, almost under his breath. "No, we never have." And he exchanged yet another secretive glance with Nidaba.

Arianna forced herself to exercise the manners her mam had taught her. "I'm very grateful to you, Laird, and to you, Nidaba." It galled her to thank a woman she sensed might be closer to Nicodimus than she was. But she had no choice. The strange woman *had* helped her.

"Then you'll repay us by saying nothing of Nidaba's healing skills to those vicious gossips in the village," the laird responded. And as Arianna frowned at him, he explained, "If they persecute you for your strange ways, child, think what they'd make of her, did they learn she was a gifted practitioner of the healing arts. Nidaba is an old and valued friend, an' I'll nay subject her to such gossip."

Those words, and the truth behind them, made Arianna's chin raise. Women who practiced healing with any degree of success would soon raise the same suspicions in the superstitious members of the clan that Arianna herself had raised among them. "Aye," she said softly. "If 'tis my silence you want, you have my word on it, Laird. But were I you, Mistress Nidaba, I would march among the crofters proudly, and challenge anyone to say an unkind word and survive my wrath. Those ignorant fools need a lesson. 'Tis high time they had one, in fact, an' I—"

"And you're just the one to deliver it," Nicodimus finished for her. "Have you not learned a thing from all of this, Arianna?"

Nidaba looked from Nicodimus to Arianna, a worried glint in her strange eyes. "I approve of your spirit, child. And, if it is your own destruction you seek, you are going about it very well."

"My own . . . ?" Arianna shook her head. "That's not it at all."

"If that is true, then perhaps you will listen to someone a great deal older than you, Arianna. Sometimes it is better to wait in silence—to choose one's battles with wisdom rather than to rush headlong into each and every fight because of foolish pride."

Arianna blinked at the soft, poetic cadence of Nidaba's voice. She spoke slowly, deliberately, her tones deep and musical and hypnotic.

"I come here," she went on, "to rest from strife and conflict, Arianna. Lachlan Keep is a haven to me, as it is to Nicodimus. I have no wish to stir up trouble here, among Joseph's clan. There will be enough awaiting me when I leave these walls."

Arianna frowned, tilting her head to one side. "If your life is so filled with trouble, perhaps you ought to stay here for good."

"My troubles would find me soon enough," she said, and there was a sadness in her eyes that made Arianna think perhaps she'd jumped to the wrong conclusions when she'd judged the woman to be her rival and her enemy.

"What sorts of troubles do you—"

"No, child. You know nothing of these things. Not yet."

"Rest until dinner, lass," the laird said again. "Come, Nidaba. I could use some of that wisdom of yours myself as I ponder what to do with the lass. I've spoken to some of the clansmen, and the talk Angus has already spread will no doubt make matters far worse. Decisions will need be made regarding the lassie's safety."

Nidaba nodded as Arianna frowned, and the two left the room, the laird's head gleaming as much as Nidaba's nose ring did in the flickering lamplight. Turning her puzzled gaze on Nicodimus, Arianna asked, "What did the laird mean by that?"

Nicodimus sighed deeply, and sat down upon the edge of the bed. "Arianna . . ." He drew a breath and let it out slowly. "It is fairly obvious now that you cannot simply return to the village. Not when the talk about you has reached such a crucial point that people are out to cut your pretty flesh just to see whether you bleed. It is too dangerous."

"But I *did* bleed. Surely that should prove something to them."

"You said yourself that it meant nothing, and I fear you were right. If Angus is spreading more wild tales already . . . You're in danger here, Arianna."

She narrowed her eyes. *"Danger,"* she spat. "If my own clan is ignorant enough to come for me, let them. Next time I'll be ready."

"No, child, you're not nearly ready for such as that."

"Why will everyone nay stop callin' me 'child'? I am nay a child!"

His lips crooked as if he battled a grin.

Sitting up in the bed, Arianna frowned at him. "Nor am I ready to allow the laird to decide my fate! Nicodimus, I'll nay stand for it!" She swung her legs to the floor, went to stand, but Nicodimus gripped her arms in his, his touch tender, but firm enough to still her.

"All the laird has done up to now is show you his kindness, care for your wounds and invite you to dine here, Arianna. I'd suggest you try gratitude instead of rebellion, just this once. Wait to see what your chieftain has to say before you decide to flay him alive for it."

She blinked, released all her breath at once, and lowered her head. "You're right. I . . . I'm sorry. I'll try to behave better. Some things . . . just dinna sit well with me, Nicodimus."

"I know. And persecution of those whose ways are different is one of those things. Being told what to do is another. I'm aware of it. You wear your principles wrapped about you the way a knight wears his master's colors. What you don't understand is that Joseph shares those same concerns with you. It is why I come here when I need a rest from the . . . from the battles I fight. Why Nidaba has taken refuge here as well. Because he's not like the others out there."

She hung her head, a bit ashamed. "I suppose you think I'm actin' like a child."

"No. Like a warrior in search of a war. But you've no battle to fight here, not with me, nor with Nidaba, nor with Joseph. I promise you that."

She nodded slowly. "I suppose . . . you're right." Although she thought she might disagree about Nidaba.

"Of course I'm right."

"So what do you think he'll decide should be done with me?"

"I imagine you'd best wait and see."

"If I dinna like it, I will refuse. I . . . I will leave the clan if I must. I willna be forced into anything, Nicodimus. Not even by my own laird."

"Wild horses couldn't force you into anything, Arianna."

She looked at him, and he smiled. "You may take it as a compliment, if you wish."

She smiled back at him, just a little. She liked the way he made her feel. But she hated his secrets. Still, she supposed it would take him some time to come to trust her, to see her as a friend, the way he did Nidaba. But it would happen. She would see to that.

There was a sound outside the door, and then Nidaba stepped back inside. "I've come to tell you we eat in an hour, and to ask you, Arianna, if you would like to borrow a clean dress to wear."

Glancing down at her attire, Arianna sighed in relief. "I . . . would like that very much. Though your gowns will likely drag 'round the rushes on me. I thank you, Nidaba."

Nidaba nodded, her face expressionless, then sent Nicodimus a look that told him his welcome here was over. As soon as they were alone, she opened an ornately carved chest and pulled out gown upon richly hued gown, none conventional or even fashionable. They were all simply cut, many daringly so, with no sleeves to cover the arms, and only one strap to attach atop one shoulder. Nidaba chose just such a gown, in a shimmering amber-colored material. "This one is shorter. I made it so, for ease in riding."

"It's . . . very beautiful."

Nidaba handed it to her, folded her arms across her chest and

watched with an unblinking gaze as Arianna undressed, and donned the
gown. Arianna felt like a wanton when she put it on, but Nidaba only
nodded her approval and reached for a silver comb.

"Sit," she commanded.

Arianna sat upon a stool, staring into a polished silver mirror that
must be worth a fortune. And to her surprise, Nidaba began to run the
comb through her hair. Arianna stared at her reflection, and that of the
dark woman behind her, and she sighed. "My mam used to comb my
hair this way."

"Why has she stopped?"

Arianna shrugged. "Nothing is the same since my sister died."

"And why should it be the same?" Nidaba asked. "There is grief now,
where there once was joy. You miss her. Your mother misses her. Why do
you not comfort one another?"

Arianna lowered her head, not saying what she felt. That it was her
fault, and she felt too guilty to look her mother in the eye, much less try
to comfort her, or allow herself to be comforted.

"No one knows the hour of their death, Arianna. You could not have
known your sister would drown that day. You nearly drowned yourself."

"You know about Raven?" Arianna asked, meeting Nidaba's eyes in
the mirror.

She nodded. "Nicodimus . . . has spoken of it."

Arianna swallowed hard. "Do . . . do you love him, Nidaba?"

Nidaba held her gaze in the mirror. "I have loved him for all of his
life," she said. "And protected him, as well. I sense you are dangerous to
him, young one."

Blinking, Arianna shook her head. "I would *never* hurt Nicodimus!"

Nidaba's gaze met and held Arianna's, and they narrowed very
slightly. "Then you have nothing to fear from me. But if you do hurt
him . . . I warn you, child, my wrath will know no bounds."

A cold chill rushed down Arianna's spine at those words.

Nidaba ran a slender hand over Arianna's hair, then gently pulled the
strands back from her face and secured the tresses with a jewelled comb.
She nodded. "There now. I believe you are ready for the meal."

Arianna stepped into the great hall feeling as if she were caught in a
dream. Or perhaps a nightmare. The gown she wore felt foreign and
strange, made of what Nidaba called "silk," spun by special worms in the
Orient. Fit for a goddess, it was, dyed an amber hue that reminded Ari-

anna of Nicodimus's golden hair. The gown hung from one shoulder, where it was caught with a brooch of glittering gemstones, leaving the other shoulder and both arms sinfully bare. One wrist bore the white bandages, but other than that, her arms were fully exposed, and it felt scandalous, but good. While the gown did drag through the rushes on the floor a bit, it was not nearly as long as she had feared it would be. She looked beautiful. And she knew it.

The moment she stepped into the hall, a hush gradually fell across the room as conversation ceased. Soon all eyes were turned to where she stood near the doorway. She seemed to have captured the attention of all those who had gathered in the hall for the evening meal. Even the laird himself stopped his talk to stare at Arianna. Was she so different then? Nidaba had arranged her hair in a most becoming fashion, with soft tendrils curling all around her face. And her eyes had been touched with some mystical powder to enhance their shade.

The laird stood near the hearth speaking with his two sons, Kenyon, who was just her age, and Lud, two years her senior. But it was not their eyes she sought, as she scanned the huge room. There . . . Nicodimus sat in an oversized wooden chair with a heavy brass goblet in his hand, but he'd paused with the drink halfway to his mouth and sat motionless, staring at her.

She licked her lips and boldly returned his stare, secretly wondering what to do next. Then the laird cleared his throat and Nicodimus blinked and quickly got to his feet. "Arianna. You look . . ."

"You look fit to take a man's breath away," Lud cut in, rushing to her side to offer an arm. He was a big lad of twenty years, with a belly that already bulged from too much ale. His face was ruddy, his hair, thick and uncombed.

"Nay, she looks better than that," Kenyon exclaimed. "She looks like an angel." And he came to her other side, also offering an arm. Kenyon was Lud's opposite, small and slight, fair of coloring, and always well groomed.

She glanced back at Nidaba, who only watched, her face expressionless. Not knowing what else to do, Arianna let the lads escort her to the laird's table, which sat on a raised dais at one end of the hall, where pitchers of mead surrounded platters piled high with steaming food. It looked to Arianna as though the laird's cook had been expecting a great many more mouths to feed tonight. There were several other tables on the floor nearby, just as laden with fare.

"Lovely as a sunrise," Laird Lachlan boomed, and headed for the high table. Nicodimus's approach was slower, his gaze enigmatic, as it slid from Lud to Kenyon, and back to Arianna again. Lingering on her. Nidaba watched him with her black almond eyes and expressionless face.

Nidaba and Arianna sat down, and then the men took their places. The others in the room quickly followed suit. Right away, beefy arms began reaching for the joints of meat and pastries. But Arianna's appetite fled at the thought of what Laird Lachlan might decree for her. Would he send her away? Would she have the spine in her to defy him if he tried?

Nicodimus glanced her way. "Are you not hungry, Arianna? Is it your arm? Is it paining you?"

She shook her head, and took a piece of mutton from the trencher set before her. "I'm nervous, I suppose. Laird, will you tell me what you've decided?"

"Food first, lass," he muttered around a mouthful of pork. "Talk later."

"I'm afraid I'll never be able to eat until I know what it is you're about to . . . *suggest* I do."

The feeding stopped momentarily. Lud glanced at Kenyon, and then the two grinned. "Never known our father to be one for makin' *suggestions*," Lud said.

"Aye," replied his brother. "Mostly he just gives orders."

"Enough," Nidaba said sharply . . . or, sharply, for her. But the lads fell silent. And Nidaba addressed their father. "Surely you can see the girl is frightened of what will befall her next, Joseph," she said softly.

"Nay, not frightened!" Arianna argued. "I dinna fear anything!" Her voice carried to the other tables. They all looked at her for a moment, perhaps surprised at such a declaration from such a small female. She focused her eyes on her food, waiting until they all went back to eating and the conversation grew loud again. Then, more softly, she went on.

"I canna wait endlessly for my fate to be sealed, Laird. I must know what you intend to do with me."

Drawing a deep breath, Joseph wiped the back of one hand across his mouth, then leaned back in his chair. "Very well, then," he said slowly. "The answer is obvious. Lass, what you need is protection. And a bit of taming, I might add. A man's name is like armor to a woman—his guidance, most needed. Especially in a lass as wild as you. You've got to get yourself a man. A husband."

Arianna felt her eyes widen, and she stiffened with tension. "You'll forgive me, Laird, but a husband is what the fool who cut me meant to be. I canna see that—"

"Now, lass, I said, you need a man. Angus MacClennan's a mere lad with half a brain an' less in the way of ambition. Bein' his wife would be no good for you. A woman with a nose for trouble such as you have needs a man stronger than she, not weaker."

It was too late now for discretion, for every man in the room was looking on in great interest. Blinking, looking around, desperate for any option to the laird's decision, she glanced wildly around the table. Her gaze met first Lud Lachlan's, then his brother's, and the expressions in their eyes as they stared at her made panic flutter in her chest. "Who . . . who . . . ?" She sounded like an owl. But she couldn't seem to speak. Not the laird's sons. Please, not his sons. She'd never liked them in that manner. Lud was a slightly pompous bully who pushed his younger brother around with his weight and size, while Kenyon fought back with his keen intellect. Lud was too big and brutish, Kenyon too small and effeminate to stir in her the kind of reaction, the hot longing that Nicodimus did. And besides, throughout their childhood, neither of them had often let her forget that they considered themselves her betters. Although they'd changed their attitude toward her since she'd reached adulthood . . . since she'd grown breasts, at least.

They had even saved her life that day in the loch. But they had failed to save her sister . . . though they'd tried. They had failed, and she supposed she shouldn't hold that against them, but she couldn't help it. Each time she'd seen them since the day Raven had drown, had only served as a painful reminder of that horrible day.

She turned toward Nicodimus, but he was sitting very still, watching Joseph, waiting for his next words. He looked as if he were holding his breath. Joseph returned his gaze before turning his attention back to Arianna.

"You need the protection of a husband, lass. And I need to see to the well-being of the clan. I can't have this sort of talk dividing us," Joseph said slowly. "An' while I'm unsure it's wise to do so, my sons have insisted I consider choosing one of them as your husband."

"Aye," said Lud. "You'd be safe wed to the firstborn and heir of the laird." His eyes, friendly before, looked hungry now. And having seen the way Lud devoured the meat on the table, she nearly feared he'd do the same to her.

"Laird . . . surely there must be some other way to ensure my safety than—"

"Or the second born, who is far closer to the right age for her!" Kenyon shouted.

"Oh, but I—"

"Or the chieftain himself," said Nidaba, very softly. And when Arianna sent her a surprised look, she thought Nidaba looked smugly satisfied. So she thought Arianna would be out of Nicodimus's reach for good now, did she? "Joseph's wife has been dead this past decade. It is time he remarry," Nidaba went on, ignoring the desperate look in Arianna's eyes. "So, Joseph, which will it be?"

Arianna shoved herself away from the table, springing to her feet. As she did, so did two of the laird's men, one with a shank of meat still in his hand. "Nay!" Arianna cried. "I dinna mean to be rude, Laird, an' I am grateful to you—and fond of your sons, but I could never—"

The laird held up a hand to silence her. With a commanding look, he ordered his men to take their seats again. "Alas, Arianna, there's no other way. I'll leave the choice up to you. One of my sons, one of my men . . . But one way or another, lass, there's goin' to be a wedding. An' soon."

She shook her head rapidly, her eyes welling with hot tears. And she could feel the eyes of every man in the place focused on her, speculative and cold. Then she glanced down at Nicodimus, who remained just as still as a statue, and whose face had gone stony. He met her eyes, had to have seen the plea in them, the fear.

"I'll leave here," she said at last. "I'll leave the village an'—"

"An' what lass? Make your way through the highlands alone?" the laird asked. "How would you eat? Or live? Nay, you'll marry. I promise whoever you choose, I shall see to it you're safe and protected, well cared for an' happy. An', lassie, you must know 'tis a great gift I offer you! My own sons, 'tis a match beyond your dreams."

"My dreams are far bigger than you could possibly know, Laird." Her voice grew quieter, until she had to swallow the lump in her throat in order to go on speaking. "An' I'm well aware of the gift you offer. I'm but a crazy wench with no prospects beyond marryin' a cobbler's son. Yet you offer your own sons. I dinna expect you to ken why I must refuse but—"

"Lass, you've no choice in the matter. I am laird of this clan. You will choose. Tonight. I'll speak to your father, an' I've no doubt he'll agree."

Blinking, turning her wide gaze from one of the men to the next, she felt as trapped as a hunted animal. And suddenly she felt as if she couldn't breathe. She drew in all the air she could, but it wasn't enough. Her chest constricted, and she pressed a palm flat to it, inhaling again and again. A pulse beat in her throat so hard it felt as if she were choking on her own heart.

Nicodimus got to his feet and went to her, searching her face worriedly. "Easy, Arianna," he whispered. "Breathe in slowly. Slower than that." He gathered her up, and took her back to her chair, then lowered her gently into it. "There's no need for all this upset. Joseph is only looking after you."

"I . . . w-want to go home."

His blue eyes softened. "Arianna, if you return home you'll not be safe. Your father is no fighting man. And with the talk in the clan being what it is . . ."

"I canna . . . I willna marry . . . not unless . . ."

"Unless . . . ?"

She got her breathing under control, sat up straighter, and turned to face Joseph Lachlan, while Nicodimus remained standing beside her chair. "If I must choose, then I'll choose right now," she said, her voice no longer shaking, but firm and strong. She turned to Nicodimus. "I choose you. If I must marry, I choose you, Nicodimus."

His face went as hard as granite, and his eyes turned cold. "I," he stated in a voice that made her tremble, "was not one of your choices."

She lifted her chin, turned her head quickly away so he wouldn't see the sudden, hot tears that sprang to her eyes at his quick, firm rejection. There was a satisfied look in Nidaba's eyes. "Then I'll nay marry at all," Arianna declared.

She got to her feet, walked directly toward the doors.

"Lassie!" the laird cried, getting up as well. "You mustn't go back into the village, 'twould nay be safe."

"If you wish to stop me, Laird Lachlan, you shall have to kill me." She jerked a heavy door open, stepped out, pulled it closed behind her . . . and then she ran.

Chapter 5

I could only stand there and watch when Arianna rose as proudly and regally as a princess, and left us all behind her without a backward glance.

There had been no mistaking the pain in those brown eyes. Deeply felt, but quickly hidden. I had hurt her. I hadn't meant to. My reaction had been gut deep, the instinctive lashing out at that which caused me pain. I had done wrong, I knew that now. She had felt trapped, and she had reached out to me for help. I should have seen her desperation, should have realized she was only reaching for me the way a drowning man would reach for a sliver of driftwood. I had callously slapped her small hand away. And why? Because of my own need to preserve my solitary existence. Because of my own weakness where Arianna was concerned. I was afraid, I suppose, of a girl as small and slight as a butterfly. Determined that I would feel no more for her than I did already, and causing her pain in my attempts to ensure that. I was afraid, yes, but not of her. I feared being hurt again. The agony of the last time was still with me.

Anya, fiery-haired, soft-spoken Anya, lying on a bed of furs, too hoarse and exhausted to scream anymore, while the clan elderwomen worked around her, grim expressions on their weathered faces. I'd been with Anya fully half my life, by then. For fourteen years, we had been as one. And no matter how often her brothers, Marten and Kohl, mounted raids on our village seeking vengeance, trying to steal her back, she'd remained safely at my side.

Jaymes had only just seen his twelfth year, and he huddled outside our hut, his face tearstained, his entire body shaking. Will paced, trying hard to be a man. To help, to be strong for his mother, his brother, and me. I couldn't even offer my sons any comfort. I was afraid right to my soul as my wife struggled to give birth to our baby girl, but to no avail.

Anya grasped my hand as I leaned over her. She stared up at me with her eyes of pale blue, and very softly, she whispered, "I never thanked you for taking me away from them, Nicodimus. You saved me, you know."

"I'd save you going through this now, if I could." Tears choked me, burned my eyes and my throat. *Saved her?* How could she say it? I had brought this on her. It was *my* child she carried, struggled to deliver. I was nearly out of my mind with the frustration of being utterly unable to help her. There was nothing I could do. Nothing, and it ate at my soul.

"Hush," she said. "It is nearly over."

My head came up fast in alarm when she said those words.

"I have had a good life with you. I have grown to love you, husband. And if I had to do it all over, I would change nothing. I promise you that."

"Anya . . . you mustn't speak that way. . . ."

"I will speak as I must. Time is short. You know it as well as I."

"No . . ."

She lifted a trembling finger, touched it to my lips. So brave. She even managed a smile for me. "Take care of the boys, my love. Jaymes is so gentle of spirit. He is not meant to be a warrior like you. And Will. Will is a bit too much of one. He needs to learn to master his emotions, to temper his anger."

"I know. I know, Anya. But you'll be here to see to that."

She shook her head side to side, just once. "Keep them away from my brothers, Nicodimus," she whispered. "Marten and Kohl must never come near my sons. They are cruel, arrogant men without a hint of conscience or decency. They made my life hell . . . until you came and took me away."

"They'll never come near our sons," I promised her.

She nodded and was silent for a long moment. Her pain, I knew, was constant now. There was no rest in between. No time to prepare for the next bout. She stiffened as if it were growing still worse. Clenching her teeth, her voice broken and hoarse, she whispered, "I love you, Nicodimus. I love you."

Then Anya closed her eyes. Her entire body relaxed for the first time since it had gone taut with the initial birthing pangs. I cried her name again and again, but to no avail. My sweet Anya was gone. I was moved aside by the elderwomen, who'd done all they could to help her, as they frantically tried to save the babe. But I knew in my bones it was too late for the little one as well.

Weak, nearly lifeless, I went outside to face my sons. I didn't need to tell them. They saw the emotion in my eyes, and they knew. Young Jaymes rushed into my arms and clung to me, sobbing so hard I feared he'd tear himself in two. Will turned away and walked into the forest alone. I stood still as stone and silently vowed never to love another the way I had loved sweet Anya.

"Nicodimus? Nic?"

Nidaba's voice penetrated my mind, her hand on my shoulder, shaking me. I blinked away the haunting memories that still had the power to tear at my soul, even after seven centuries, and faced the woman who had saved my life more than once.

"You cannot mean to go after Arianna," she said, her voice a harsh whisper. "She's trouble to you, to both of us, you know that." Already, Joseph was speaking with his men, his meal disrupted, along with his appetite, I imagined. He would send them after Arianna, though it would pain him to do so.

"How much trouble can she be, Nidaba? She's only a girl."

"She's an immortal High Witch, same as you and I," Nidaba all but hissed. "One without discipline or a hint of discretion. Reckless and bold—"

I came very close to smiling at that description. "I have to go after her all the same," I told Nidaba. "Joseph, leave your men to finish their meal. I'll fetch the girl back."

Joseph stopped speaking, studying me curiously and finally nodding. "Aye, the lassie would likely react better to you than to a dispatch of soldiers."

Nidaba sighed, shaking her head as if in disgust or exasperation with me. In silence I turned to do what I must to save another girl. Even though there was a part of me that didn't want to try . . . for fear I might fail. Again.

Nidaba didn't try to stop me, but I could feel her disapproval following me all the way across the rutted courtyard to the gates.

Arianna had a head start on me. I could not follow her, so I went to the place I thought she would most likely go: her father's cottage. The village was dark this night. Silent. No light emerged from the saddle maker's cottage, but I saw a shadow moving through its plank door. Arianna. I went still as she stepped out again with a small pack slung over her shoulder.

Gods, she intended to leave then.

Pausing outside the doorway, she turned back, and in the glow of the waning moon, I thought I saw a shimmer of tears on her face. "I dinna know where you are this eve," she whispered. "But where e're you be, I hope you ken my love. I'm sorry, Mam. I wish things could've been different."

There was no reply. I'd assumed those inside to be asleep, oblivious to what was happening without. But from Arianna's choked words, I discerned no one to be within the cottage. She hadn't even been allowed the luxury of saying a proper goodbye to her family. I cursed myself for being so cruel to Arianna and took a single step toward her, but she was already running again, fleeing into the night, heading toward the cemetery.

I sighed and stood still for a moment. Of course, she'd want to say goodbye to her sister as well. She would never leave Stonehaven without doing that. At least I knew where to find her.

I walked slowly, needing to collect my thoughts before I faced Arianna. I didn't know exactly what I was going to say to her when I found her. The wise thing, the *sane* thing for her to do, would be to obey Joseph and take a husband. Not me. Certainly not me, but one of Joseph's boys. They were both decent young men, and it was obvious either of them would be glad to have her as wife. It would solve all Arianna's problems. She could stay here, close to her family. The talk about her might go on, but not to such a dangerous degree. And certainly no one would dare to act on it.

And yet, some part of me rebelled at the thought of talking her into any of that. I couldn't imagine myself trying to convince her to marry either of the Lachlan lads.

So what options remained for her? Leave here, alone? Perhaps Nidaba would . . .

My musings as well as my steps came to a halt as the sounds of distant shouts reached my ears. Frowning, I glanced in the direction from whence the noise seemed to come, and saw an eerie red-orange glow lighting the night. My throat went dry. "Good Gods, is that The Crones' cottage?" It had to be. It was.

I broke into a run, rounding a corner so that the cemetery came into view. Arianna was not there. "No," I whispered. "No, she mustn't. . . ." Cupping my hands to my mouth I called, "Arianna! Arianna, come back!"

There was no reply. She must have seen the flames and headed out there. But she might not have heard the shouts, as I did. My senses were honed, sharpened, beyond mortal limits. Hers were not. Nor would they be, until after she'd tasted death for the first time, and revived into something new. She wouldn't understand what she might be walking into.

I whispered a spell of protection, and then I ran.

A prickling sensation ran up the back of Arianna's neck as she stood over her sister's grave, whispering her goodbyes. She'd realized, almost as soon as she'd left Lachlan keep, that the laird had been right. She *wasn't* safe in Stonehaven. It wasn't the gossip and the speculation about her that worried her. It was her father, and Laird Lachlan, and Angus—all of them trying so hard to marry her off as fast as lightning. Well, she wouldn't have it. And if it took running away to ensure her freedom, then that was what she'd have to do.

She could have borne wedlock, she supposed, had it been with Nicodimus. He understood her. No one else ever had, nor, she suspected, ever would. But he'd made it all too clear how he felt about the notion of being burdened with her as his wife. So she had little choice remaining. She didn't know how she would make her way, or even where she would go. She only knew she would survive. She never had any doubt of that.

She had glanced up at the sky as she'd contemplated which direction to take, and had glimpsed the fiery glow in the distance. The Crones! Their cottage must be ablaze!

Fear for the three women clutched at her heart, and she dropped her sack to the ground and raced through the village—the oddly *silent* village. It occurred to her that it wasn't all that late. Darkness had fallen, but there ought still be people about or some signs of activity. It was strange. Her own family's cottage had been empty, and it looked as if all the others were, as well. But perhaps the villagers, too, had seen the flames, and had rushed off to help douse the fire.

Imagine that—the fearful and narrow-minded villagers rushing off to help the outcasts. Never! Nay, it must be something else that had drawn everyone away this night.

Arianna's bare feet fell hard on the packed mud path through the village. She clutched a woven shawl around her shoulders to protect against the night's chill as she ran steadily. She could run like the wind. She'd always been proud of the fact, though she'd been told often enough 'twas unladylike to race with the boys . . . and unwise to beat them. The long gown Nidaba had loaned her slowed her only until she gathered its skirts up to her knees and held them bunched there with one hand. The night breeze rushed over her face and whipped her hair behind her. Her lungs worked hard, her heart harder, but she pushed on. Perhaps the balefire had got away from The Crones, she thought. Perhaps it was only some brush burning and not the cottage. Perhaps they weren't even home, but out gathering herbs, or . . .

She rounded a bend, and came to an abrupt halt as The Crones' cottage came into view. It was ablaze, every inch of it, with hungry flames shooting to the heavens. She could feel the heat from where she stood. And . . . and people. Arianna's own clan, all of them standing around, just watching it burn, some carrying torches. What in the name of . . .

She moved forward slowly, a frown creasing her brows, her eyes scanning the crowd for some sign of the old women.

She found them, not amid the crowd, but dangling high above it. Her stomach lurched so forcefully she doubled over and fell to her knees, gagging.

Celia, Leandra, and Mary each hung suspended by ropes from the sturdy limb of the giant oak that had shaded their home by summer and protected it through the cold winter months. Their bodies were completely blackened, charred, smoldering still as they turned slowly in the light of the nearby fire.

Overcome by horror and nausea, Arianna could barely understand the people muttering. Something about a lamb being born with two heads, and how it was a sign. Something about Angus MacClennan, and Arianna's refusal to wed him. Arianna knelt, heaving violently, shaking so hard she could barely remain on her knees.

Someone heard her retching and turned. "'Tis Arianna Sinclair herself," a voice yelled. The voice was vaguely familiar, though she was certain she'd never heard it raised in such an ugly tone. "She's been seen with the Witches! Out alone, at all hours, day an' night. An' she dinna drown when her own sister did!"

"A Witch just like 'em, no doubt," shouted another. "Did you see what she did to young Angus's face?"

"Aye, and he said when he cut her she bled only loch water!"

Arianna weakly lifted her head. The crowd turned toward where she knelt, and slowly began to move forward. She knew she was in more danger than she had ever been, and her stomach clenched with icy fear.

"God in heaven, nay!"

It was her mother's voice. Arianna managed to lift her head a bit higher, saw her mother and her father battling their way through the crowd to reach her. Her mother leaned over her, smoothed a hand over her forehead, and threw her arms around Arianna while her father stood at her side.

"My daughter is innocent!" her father cried, dropping to one knee, gripping her shoulder.

"Arianna," her mother whispered. "We tried to stop this. We did, I swear it to you, but they wouldna listen."

"Innocents dinna walk about alone at night, Sinclair," a voice accused. "Perhaps Arianna should join the other Witches in hell!"

Arianna managed to lift her head again, and saw the crowd moving still closer, while her mother hugged her hard, sobbing in terror. "I'll nay let them harm you, my girl! They'll have to hang us all!"

Stunned by the shock of seeing her friends so brutally murdered, and by the fear, her surprise took a moment to register. But then it did. This was her mother, the woman always so concerned with being proper and what the clan thought of her. On her knees, hugging her accused daughter, and defending her aloud! Tears stung her eyes. To have her mother defend her so fiercely and to show her love so openly! If only it didn't seem as if this would be the last moments they would share together.

Arianna looked up to see her father picking up a large limb from the ground. Lifting it high, he turned to face the threatening villagers. As if he'd fight them for her. But they'd kill him . . .

"Da, nay, you mustn't—"

And then a large shadow fell between Arianna and her neighbors. A tall, strong man, silhouetted by firelight. But she knew him just as she had always known him. She would know him even if she were blind.

"Nicodimus," she whispered, closing her eyes. "Thank the Fates."

"You can all stop where you are," he commanded. "Arianna Sinclair is under my direct protection, and the protection of your laird, Joseph Lachlan, as well."

His voice was harsh, powerful, and so icy it sent a tremor of reaction through Arianna, even though she knew she had nothing to fear from him.

"Any man who lays a hand on her . . . or any woman who speaks an ill word against her, will answer to me. And believe me, it will not go easy with them."

There was an angry murmur that grew louder. Nicodimus turned to her, ignoring the crowd. Gripping her shoulders, he helped her to stand. As her mother stood looking confused and afraid, and her father looked on in worry, Nicodimus searched Arianna's face. He pushed her hair away from her eyes, and brushed the twigs away from her borrowed dress. "Did any one of these pigs touch you, Arianna? Hurt you?"

She opened her mouth, but only a sob escaped. "Th-they *killed* them. They killed them. They—" She turned and pointed, and his gaze followed hers to where her beloved teachers dangled from charred ropes. As she stared, one of the ropes seared through, and gave way, sending one blackened corpse smashing to the ground.

"Celia!" Arianna shrieked.

Nicodimus pulled her close, tucking her head against his chest so she could no longer see. "They'll answer for what was done here tonight," he said, and he said it loudly enough so the crofters could hear. "Joseph will see to that. He won't tolerate murder being done in Stonehaven."

"An' just how is it you're speaking for Laird Lachlan," someone demanded.

"Aye," challenged another. "An' how is it Arianna Sinclair is under *your* protection?"

Nicodimus turned to face the crowd. "She's under my protection," he said fiercely, "because she is my betrothed. And I will kill any man who dares harm her."

Arianna stiffened in shock, dizzy now from the onslaught of so many emotions, all bombarding her at once. She was dimly aware of her mother's gasp, her father's perplexed frown, the shocked exclamations of the crowd. But all her mind could grasp at the moment were two things. That three innocent women had been murdered tonight because they were different. Women she had loved with everything in her. Women who had risked—and ultimately *lost*—their lives for her sake. And that Nicodimus had claimed her as his betrothed only to prevent her from being the fourth to die here tonight.

Oh, but his arms were around her now—strong, warm, and fiercely protective. Right now she never wanted to leave the haven they provided. Her heart pounded as if it would burst, and new tears welled to replace the old. He wouldn't go back on his word. He'd said he would marry her, whatever the reasons. And he would. She would be his wife. This man brimming with secrets . . . who yet made her feel she knew him as well as she knew her own heart. His wife. She was uncertain she could survive the pain she felt tonight. But if she had any hope at all of facing everything that had happened this night, that hope lay right here in his arms.

Hoofbeats sounded, and she lifted her head from Nicodimus's sturdy chest to see Laird Lachlan, his sons, and some forty of his men, come thundering into the clearing. The crowd broke apart. Cowards who didn't wish to be identified quickly melted into the trees. As far as Arianna was concerned they were all guilty. Every one of them had been a part of this evil.

"Joseph will see to this," Nicodimus whispered. "Come, you need to be away from here. This is no place for you."

Shaking her head, she drew slightly away from him. Yet his embrace remained as she stared up into his dark eyes. "Nay. I canna leave them like that." And as she spoke her gaze strayed to where two of her friends hung charred and blackened. And one lay bent and broken on the ground.

Nicodimus's palm cupped her cheek, turned her head gently, so she could only see him. "They'll not be left, Arianna. I promise you that. But remember all they taught you. Those bodies are but empty shells now. The Crones have moved on, and are beyond the touch of pain. They would not want you lingering here." One hand moved to stroke a slow path down her outer arm. "Gods, lass, you're shaking all over."

"He's right."

Arianna turned at the sound of her father's voice. "Come home, lass. I vow I'll let no harm come to you there."

Her lips pulled tight and her tears spilled anew. "Oh, Da . . ." Sniffling, she nodded. But when she looked down, she saw that her father still clutched the limb he'd snatched up in her defense. His hand held to it so fiercely that his knuckles had gone white. "You truly would have fought them all," she whispered in wonder.

Her father's brows rose in surprise. "You're my own child, Arianna. I'd fight the devil himself did he try to do you harm." His gaze lowered, but then he reached out and closed a hand around hers. "I love you, lass. I dinna always understand you. But I love you."

He hadn't spoken those words to her since her sister had drowned, and hearing them now brought a surge of emotion that left her weak-kneed. "And I love you, Da."

"Come, then. An' you too." He nodded to Nicodimus. "We have much to discuss, you and I."

"Aye, sir. That we do," Nicodimus replied. And without warning, he scooped Arianna up into his arms.

"I can walk," she said, her protest mild, for she truly wasn't sure she could make it under her own power. She still felt weak and ill. She was afraid she might vomit again before they ever made it back to the cottage.

"You tremble still," Nicodimus informed her. "Besides, let them all look on and know that I meant what I said. I want there to be no doubt among the clan of my intent."

She battled dizziness. "You . . . had little choice, but to say what you did, Nicodimus. I'll nay hold you to such a promise . . ."

He was striding now toward the village, a step behind her father and her mother. She thought his arms tightened just slightly around her. But he didn't look down. "I meant what I said." He said no more as he carried her among the crofts and back to her home.

The Crones, her heart moaned again and again. Gone. Executed like murderers when all they had ever done was try to live in harmony with nature by the old ways. The ways of their ancestors. Gods! It was so unfair! They'd taught her, initiated her into the ways of magick. Aye, they'd wondered at the strength of her power, but perhaps their true fear had not been of her, but for their own safety. Perhaps they'd sensed the disaster building. Perhaps they'd felt it coming. And though she hadn't wanted to believe it, the blame for all of this rested squarely on her own shoulders.

She'd been careless—rebellious. Almost dared the clan to discover her activities—to learn where she went at night, what she learned, and at whose tutelage. They'd suspected for some time. And if Arianna's thoughtless ways hadn't generated so much talk of Witchery in the clan then perhaps The Crones could have continued living here peacefully. Perhaps . . .

But not now. They were dead. Murdered.

"And their killers must die. . . ." Arianna whispered, blinking her eyes open, looking through floods of tears back toward the clearing they were leaving behind. "They must die!"

Twisting in Nicodimus's arms, she pushed against his chest so suddenly she broke his hold on her. She stumbled to her feet and snatched the dagger from her side—the dagger The Crones had given her, and had told her never to be without. She'd worn it hidden beneath her clothes. And now the time had come to stain its blade with the cursed blood of killers!

As soon as she had the dagger in her hand, Arianna ran. A feral cry rose from her, and baring her teeth, she lifted the blade high and charged forward, determined to slash to ribbons every man she came upon. "Murderers!" she screamed. "Murderers all, and if it's hell you believe in, then I'll gladly send you there!" She glimpsed movement in the trees, aimed her deadly attack that way . . .

. . . and was snatched up from behind. Nicodimus's strong arm clamped tight 'round her waist, while his free hand closed gently, but firmly, about her wrist. "Let go the blade," he said hoarsely into her ear.

"Nay! I'll kill them all!" She struggled.

He held her, and let her fight him until all her fight was gone. Finally, her hand went limp, the blade fell to the ground, and her body began to tremble anew. Violent, back-bowing spasms that racked her to her soul. She couldn't breathe, and felt as if her throat had closed off. "They killed them. They *burned* them, Nicodimus. They . . ."

"*Shh-shh.*" He turned her weakened body into his arms, held her close. She heard her mother's concerned questions, heard Nicodimus mutter, "It's the shock, Mara. I've seen it before. Come. She needs a warm bed, a cool cloth, and her mother's comfort. She'll be all right."

He carried her cradled in his arms. But not safe. She didn't think she would ever feel safe again. Not now that the enormity of it had finally hit her. The Crones were Witches, and because of that, they'd been brutally tortured and murdered. More than likely, their killers would be pardoned, for killing a Witch was not only legal, but morally acceptable.

And she . . . she was a Witch, too.

For the first time, she realized that that fact alone was enough to put her life in constant peril. She'd been in grave danger for some time now, only she'd been too blind to see it. Her mother had tried to warn her, her father. Nicodimus . . .

What about Nicodimus? Was he one, too? A Witch like her? He'd neither admitted nor denied it when she had asked. But sweet Goddess, if he were, then he had put his own life in jeopardy just now. By associating himself even more closely with her, his plan might go completely awry. Rather than restoring her good name, he might simply sully his own!

An image came to her mind. A vision too horrible to bear. Nicodimus, his body blackened and charred, dangling from a tree like The Crones. She released a horrified cry, and buried her face against his chest once more.

Chapter 6

She could hear their voices, deep and hushed. Nicodimus and her father seemed intent on their conversation. A candle's gentle glow painted her mother's face as Arianna lay huddled, trembling still, beneath a mound of covers. How long she had been there, she did not know. She only knew dawn must be close. She must have slept at some point, though she only remembered the startled way she kept coming awake, the horrors of the night glaring in her mind's eye. And Nicodimus, coming to her each time, soothing her.

Nicodimus had carried her here last night, and had laid her gently down. Before he'd turned away, his gaze had touched her face, searched it, and she'd glimpsed genuine worry in the deep blue depths of his eyes. Or . . . she thought she had. His fingertips had danced over her forehead, brushing a stray wisp of hair aside. "Rest now," he had whispered, and then he'd straightened away.

She could see him now, for their home was small, and only a half wall and a curtain separated this room, and her sleeping pallet, from the rest of the cottage. Still here. He'd stayed all the night through. But why? He sat in a crude wooden chair, dwarfing it and the table and the room itself, not so much by his size, which was substantial but not unusual. Nay, Nicodimus's force of presence was what made everything around him seem smaller by comparison. He need only walk into a room to have every eye turned upon him. Men looked upon him with respect and not a little fear. The women, with something far different in their eyes.

My Nicodimus, she thought suddenly, and a fierce surge of pride welled up in her throat. *Mine, though he knows it not.*

There was a fire burning in the hearth, and his hair gleamed with the flame's red-gold shimmer. He listened respectfully to all her father said in careful undertones. Nodding his head in reply, he himself spoke softly and glanced her way, catching her eyes and holding them for a long moment. There was something there, some tension she could not identify. Then her father spoke, drawing his gaze away again.

"Have they been talkin' the night through?" she whispered to her mother.

"Aye, lass. They've much to settle between them."

"Nay, they have nothing to settle. I can settle my own life, Mam."

Aging hands soothed Arianna's brow and placed a cool cloth upon it. "This sudden betrothal o' yours gave your da and me a shock," her mother whispered. "An' there remains much to be decided. Dinna worry your head about it, lass. You've had enough worry to last a lifetime."

Closing her eyes, Arianna lay back and sighed. She knew what they were discussing out there. Her. Her future, her life. When would they realize that she could make her own choices?

"There's something you must understand, Mam," she said slowly, and her mother looked down at her with a certain expectation in her eyes. As if she knew and dreaded what was coming next. But it didn't stop Arianna from going on. "Nicodimus only said what he did to keep them from killin' me," she whispered. And the memory of her dear friends, her teachers, hanging charred and lifeless from the mighty oak, whispered coldly through her mind. She shivered and closed her eyes, but forced herself to go on, refusing to be distracted. "He canna truly mean to wed me, Mam."

Her mother's hand patted hers. "Aye, perhaps he did speak in order to save your life. But he's a man of his word, is Nicodimus Lachlan, an' if he says he'll make you his bride, you can be certain, he means to do it. You've naught to worry about on that matter, lass."

Arianna sat up a little, but her mother's hands urged her back again. "'Tis unfair to expect him to marry me, Mam. He saved my life. I canna hold him to the lie he spoke to do it. I'm certain he thought he had no choice but to say what he did."

"Perhaps *you* canna hold him to his word, Arianna, but your father can. . . . Not that it's necess—"

"He wouldna!" She sat up in bed so fast the cool wet cloth fell from her forehead. "I'll nay have a husband who needs forcin' to the altar!"

Her voice had risen. The two men in the other room fell silent and turned to stare.

"You'll have the husband your da chooses for you, lassie," her father said.

"I'll have a husband who wants me as wife, or none at all." Flinging the covers aside, she got to her feet. Bare, they touched the dirt floor, and her toes instinctively curled against the dampness and chill.

Her mother's hands came to her shoulders, trying to pull her down again, but she stood strong. "Darlin', how do you know he doesna want you as wife?" she whispered. "You dinna ken, methinks."

"Nay, Mam. 'Tis you who dinna ken. I proposed marriage to him myself only yestereve. An' he made his feelin's quite clear." She stared at Nicodimus as she spoke.

His lips pulled at one side, as if he battled a smile. So he was amused by her objections, was he? Was that what her pain was to him? Amusing? Did he not know how deeply his rejection had cut her?

"Can a man not change his mind?" Nicodimus stood up from the table, his tone soft, but firm, his eyes holding hers captive whether she wanted to be held or not. "Arianna . . . I was taken off guard by your . . . offer. I admit, my reaction was cruel, and thoughtless. But I swear to you, I regretted my words the moment I spoke them."

Her eyes narrowed as she watched him. He was lying to her, she was certain of that. "I would speak with you alone, Nicodimus."

He didn't agree or disagree. He looked to her father, and her admiration of him grew another notch. For he was her father's better in every way, and yet determinedly gave him his due. "With your permission, sir?"

Her father nodded but once and came to take her mother's arm in one hand. He drew her to the door, and took the empty water pail from its wooden peg on the wall beside it. "We'll walk to the well and back," he said. His way of letting them know he wouldn't be far, and would return soon. He sent Arianna a stern look, while her mother's parting glance was only worried. She'd have offered them both a smile of reassurance, if she felt capable of smiling at all. But her stomach was churning, and a large empty pit seemed to have opened up in the center of her chest. What *was* this feeling? She'd never been nervous around anyone in her life, no man, no laird, no warrior. Yet the moment she was alone with Nicodimus, her hands began to tremble and the odd sensations in her belly intensified.

At the sound of the door closing behind her parents, Arianna's forced mettle deserted her. She let her legs give as they seemed determined to do anyway, and she sat down on her pallet gracelessly. Nicodimus could see through her false calm as if peering through clear water. It was no use pretending, not with him.

"You dinna want to marry me and we both know it, Nicodimus. So let's waste no more time with this foolish pretense."

He walked slowly into the room, stood so tall above her that she wished she'd remained standing. But if she rose now, she'd be far too close to him, so she remained as she was and tilted her head up at him.

"I don't intend to lie to you, Arianna. I'm going to tell you the simple truth. You are a spoiled, selfish wild thing and it is high time you gave some thought to the well-being of someone else besides Arianna Sinclair."

She sucked in a shocked breath, her chin coming up fast. "How dare you!"

"Like you, hellion, I dare anything. And I think you know it. Now go on, spew your defenses. Tell me how unselfish you are, and then tell me why you'll refuse me."

"I'll refuse you for one reason and one reason alone, Nicodimus! I'll nay have a man who needs be forced to wed me."

"I've never been *forced* to do anything."

His tone was soft, but impatient. He knelt in front of her, gripping her shoulders and turning her body until she stared right into his blazing eyes. "And this is no longer about what you want."

"And what do you ken of what I want?"

"Oh, I know. I can see it in those cat's eyes of yours, Arianna, just as plain as the sun on the Summer Solstice. What you want are declarations of undying love, and a man on his knees begging for your hand—"

"Nay, not any man. You, Nicodimus. Only you."

That seemed to quiet him for a moment. His face paled and his lips tightened, but he never dropped his gaze. He drew a deep breath that expanded his chest, and blew it out, very slowly, before he spoke again. "You'll never have that from me. I've no love to give, and I have never begged for anything in my life. But I'll wed you, Arianna. And because of our marriage, your father, the man who just proved himself willing to lay down his life for you, will be respected and his wealth will grow. And your mother, who nearly fainted in terror at that clearing last night, will be spared the grief of losing another daughter."

"She wouldna have lost me. I'd have run away, nay let the villagers kill me."

"If you had run away, you'd be just as lost to her. And your family name would be ruined, your father destroyed and known only as the sire of a fugitive Witch. Is that what you want for them?"

She lowered her head. "It mayn't have happened just that way."

"That's the only way it could happen. And *will* happen if you continue with this stubborn game you play. At the keep, Arianna, when Joseph bade you choose, you obeyed. You chose me. And if you regret that choice now, well, I'm afraid there's naught to be done. Your recklessness brought you to this. And now you've naught left but to deal with it."

Lifting her head slowly, she stared into his eyes, searching them, seeing a spark there, but so deep, so distant, she didn't see how she could ever reach it. Her voice quiet now, barely above a whisper, she asked him, "And what of us, Nicodimus? What sort of husband will you be to me?"

He rose then, turning slightly away, on the pretense of watching for her father's return. "You'll have my protection. I'll provide for you. And you'll bear my name."

"But nay your children," she whispered.

His head swung around. "Never that."

She lowered her head quickly when she felt the sting of tears burn her eyes. Gods but she did not cry. She *never* cried. And she blinked the dampness away. "Then . . . ours will be a marriage . . . in name only?"

Nicodimus came toward her, stepping close to the pallet. She got to her feet and turned her back to him, surreptitiously dabbing her eyes with one hand, reaching for a wooden comb with the other. He said nothing as she began drawing it through her hair.

"Is it because you dinna want me, Nicodimus?" she asked, very softly. "Am I nay beautiful enough to stir the desire of a man such as you? Have you nay once thought of tasting my lips, of holding me close with nothing between us save the heat of our own bodies?"

She felt his gaze on her, burning into her back. And boldly she turned to face him. "Tell me."

"My reasons . . . are my own. And an unmarried girl of your tender years—a maiden—shouldn't be asking such questions. You know nothing of these things . . . nothing of . . . wanting."

She lowered her head until her chin touched her chest. "If I know nothing of wanting, then what is this feeling burning inside me,

Nicodimus? Why do I so crave your touch, if desire is something I'm too young to feel? Why do I yearn to be in your arms? I want you, Nicodimus. And though you may deny it until the day you die, I think you want me, too."

She saw it clearly, the reaction that lit his eyes for but a moment, quickly concealed, a fire instantly doused. "I will set the terms of our marriage, Arianna. And as my wife, you'll honor them."

She stepped forward, closer to him, but didn't touch him. "Do you think you can live with me as my husband and never touch me? Never know me?" She laid her hand lightly on the front of his shirt, and slid it slowly up his chest.

His hand closed over hers, stopping its progress and moving it away. "We will not be residing together for long."

He could have slapped her and shocked her less. "I . . . but I . . ."

"You will reside in the keep, of course. And I will, as well, until I am certain of your safety. The talk in the clan will die down soon enough."

Her lower lip trembled, and she caught it between her teeth. "And then?"

"And then I go my way. I have . . . obligations. I come here only to rest in between them, Arianna. You know that."

"I only thought . . ."

"That I would change my life for you? No, Arianna. My destiny is set. Yours . . . has become entwined with it. Irreversibly so, I'm afraid, but not endlessly. There is no need for me to remain here once your safety is assured."

"I . . . I'll go with you!"

His surprise showed in his eyes. "Your family . . ."

"As my husband, Nicodimus, you will be my family."

He reached out to stroke her hair, gently, softly. "I cannot take you where I go, Arianna. There is only danger for you there. More, even, than there is here in Stonehaven."

"But where is this horrible place you must go? Why do you return there if 'tis so dangerous?"

"Because I must," was all he said. He took his hand away, and a darkness seemed to settle over him. A finality. There would be no arguing him around to her way of thinking.

"Then . . . you'll go. You'll leave me. Bound to a man I can never have, free to know no other. Am I to die a maiden, then, Nicodimus?"

"There is," he said slowly, "a long, long time before that possibility will arise."

She shook her head. "You are meant for me. This I have known since the day I first set eyes on you. And you *do* want me, Nicodimus. And you *will* know me. I vow it on all that I am."

He looked hurt by her words. Just a brief flash of some old pain flitted across his face. And then she saw anger. His jaw went tight, and he opened his mouth. She had the most peculiar feeling he was about to reverse his offer. She only held his gaze, praying he would not.

He did not speak, seeming to change his mind. She nearly sighed with relief, all the while gathering her courage. She *wanted* to wed him. But she wanted him to want it, too. Either way, it would not matter. She would be bound to him, aye, but he would be bound to her as well, she reminded herself. No other woman would know him. She would kill any woman who tried. It was her he would grow to love—Arianna Lachlan, his wife.

Finally, looking as if he were drawing on his last reserves of patience, he whispered, "So what of it, Arianna? Will you wed me or not?"

"Aye, Nicodimus," she said, before she could lose her hard-won courage. "Aye, I'll be your wife. If you'll give me your word that you'll be true to me. That you'll have no other woman. Including Nidaba."

He frowned at her. "That is an easy enough promise to make."

"I mean to see that you keep it," she declared.

"And to accept my terms?" he asked her.

"Terms? That you will never love me? Never touch me?"

He had to look away to answer. "Yes."

She moved to watch his face. And as she did, she knew that he was lying as much to himself as to her. He loved her already. Somewhere deep inside him, he knew it. She was meant for him, hadn't she sensed that from the very first? If The Crones had taught her anything at all, it was to trust her senses, the ideas that popped into her head like stray thoughts, the kind most people ignored. The wisdom of those old women had come from sources so ancient, even they had no longer been able to identify them. Yet they had lived by what they knew to be true.

The door creaked open and her parents stepped hesitantly inside, looking from one of them to the other, questions in their eyes.

All too aware that she had not agreed to Nicodimus's terms, knowing he was aware of it, too, she spoke aloud. "There is to be a wedding, then," she said, lifting her chin, holding his gaze and refusing to look away. "I have agreed to marry Nicodimus."

Nicodimus stared steadily into her eyes, and gave a nearly imperceptible nod of what she took to be approval, though there was more than a bit of wariness or perhaps, suspicion, in his eyes as he did.

"Thank goodness you've come to your right mind!" Her father's face split in a smile, and he clasped Nicodimus's hand in one of his own and shook it hard, slapping his shoulder with the other. "Welcome to my family, Nicodimus Lachlan."

"And glad I am to call myself a son of yours, Edwyn Sinclair," Nicodimus replied, to which her father beamed.

Mara hugged Arianna, and as she did, leaned near, and whispered, "What changed your mind, daughter? I've never known you to give in until you get what you want."

"I'm gettin' exactly what I want, Mam," Arianna said softly, watching Nicodimus and her father as they talked and gestured and planned. "A man who loves me. He doesna ken it yet, of course, but he will. In time."

"Bless me, but I believe you, child. Heaven help Nicodimus Lachlan. He canna ken all he's in for."

The celebration in Arianna's home that dawn was subdued and dulled by the grief so recently brought upon this clan. Dulled, too, I thought, by my own ominous thoughts. Arianna was a willful girl. She had given me fair warning that she would not abide easily by my dictates. The sooner I could get the vows said, and be safely away from her, the better.

It may sound foolish now. Arianna was beautiful, young, and just awakening to her body's yearnings. But she was dangerous to me, too. I knew my own heart too well. She was a girl I could come to care far too much for, far too easily—if I let myself. But I was certain of my fortitude. My lessons had been too hard won for my will to crumble at a look of yearning from a pair of beautiful eyes.

My Gods, I should have known I could never resist her for long. Should have known it that very day, as she looked me squarely in the eye and admitted her own desires: her desire to make love to me, to be my wife in every sense of the word. But foolish pride was my downfall. I told myself that a man who had lived seven centuries could easily win a battle of wills fought against a girl of seven and ten.

I could not have been more wrong.

Mara Sinclair took a bowl and pitcher of water into the small sleeping area with Arianna, and drew the curtain tight. Edwyn and I continued our discussion of the wedding and other arrangements. For his daughter's honor, as wife of the cousin of the laird, I would have a new cottage built for Arianna's parents. It was only fitting that my bride's family live in a dwelling grander than the one they now inhabited. And I would gift the family with food, sheep, and grain. All these things we discussed, as well as the date, a week hence, for the vows to be spoken. I was for having it done sooner, but Edwyn argued that there would be need of time to stitch a proper gown, and that it would only arouse more talk in the clan to have the wedding in such an unseemly haste. So I agreed.

I had a deep respect for Edwyn Sinclair. Always, I had liked the man, but since bursting into that clearing and seeing him there, standing alone, facing a murderous mob, defending his daughter with his life and a rotting limb, my respect had trebled.

Even as we discussed all these things, though, my senses were sharply attuned to what went on in the next room. I heard clearly the sounds of fabric against soft skin as Arianna removed her clothes. The trickling of the water as she bathed, and her own gentle sighs taunting me now and again. I grew agitated and restless, but tamped those feelings down and warned my foolish mind against them.

When at last she reappeared, freshly scrubbed, hair gleaming, in simple but clean garments, I saw a slight sparkle in her eyes. As if she had been aware of my attention the whole time.

But it dulled slowly, as she became aware of what was happening outside. Noise filtered into the cottage, voices, and Arianna hastened to my side as I opened the door to look without. Joseph sat mounted near the burial ground, three hastily constructed coffins in a wagon, beside him. The Crones. And a crowd had gathered at the cemetery gates. Voices rose in agitation, and Joseph shouted above them all. "They were murdered and shall be buried proper!"

Then the village priest, who stood directly in front of the death wagon, nearly nose to nose with the horse that pulled it, held his Bible high above him. "Not with good Christians, Laird. 'Tis blasphemy and will surely bring the wrath of the Almighty down upon us all!"

Before I could stop her, my timid bride rushed past me, bare feet flying as she raced toward the burial ground. She gripped the halter of the funeral horse, even as I ran forward. Her parents followed on my heels.

"You and your high and mighty notion of good and evil!" Arianna shrieked at the priest. "Where are the gallows, I ask you! Where are the executioners to make your faithful Christians pay for the sin of murder! Where?"

I caught her arm, tugged her back a step, but she jerked it free. "Nay, these fine women willna rest here among the hypocrites, for they were far too good to lie among refuse! 'Tis bad enough my own dear sister rests in such company!"

"Arianna, hold your tongue!" Edwyn shouted.

"I willna hold my tongue, Da. I canna."

Again I gripped her arm, and this time she relaxed at my touch, rather than fighting it. Turning slightly, she faced Joseph upon his horse. "Laird, I beg of you, dinna insist these women be buried here. They were taken from this life against their will an' before their time, tortured an' murdered because their beliefs differ from those accepted by the rest of the clan. Let their rest be as they would have had it."

When she turned, I could see her face. The tearstains on her cheeks. I'd never seen her cry the way she did for those three old women. And my heart seemed to soften.

"Did I know how they would have had it, lass, I'd gladly grant your request." Joseph shook his head sadly. "Alas, I ken nothing of their ways."

Arianna's lips curved into the saddest smile I had ever seen. "'Tis well, then, that I do."

A gasp went up from the crowd. They murmured against Arianna until I put my arm around her shoulders and sent a meaningful look over them all, meeting each pair of eyes, one by one. "You'd do well to heed my bride's words. She bears wisdom far beyond her years."

She glanced up at me in surprise, and I knew why. She'd been expecting me to quiet her. To order her to stop this nonsense, and tug her back inside, off the streets. Not to stand at her side and support her this way. But how could I not? I admired her so much that day. Gods, but I'd never seen the sort of courage this girl displayed. Even now that it had been made clear to her what happened to people outspoken in their differences, she stood among her enemies, and spoke loud and bravely against them. Even then she bore the heart of a warrior.

"The Crones would wish for a great funeral pyre to be built at the site of their destroyed home," she went on. "They would ask that these coffins be set atop it, an' that those who cared for them carry torches to ignite the flames." Slowly, Arianna turned, and stared off in the direction of the clearing where thin spirals of smoke still danced slowly skyward. The wind lifted her golden hair and sent it snapping, and blew her skirt about her naked ankles. A faraway look came into her eyes. "They would wish us to remember them, the good they did for us in life. I tell you true, I never could have survived the loss of my beloved sister were it not for the tender guidance of Celia, Leandra, an' Mary. They comforted me when no one else could." And then she faced the crowd again. "You, Maddy Hargrove, might think upon the time you nearly died giving birth to young Billy, an' how they came to you to ease your pangs an' save your life as well as that of your babe. An' you, Nathan MacGregor," she said, pointing an accusing finger toward the man and looking like an avenging angel. "You might recall the time they brought liniment for the cut on your leg which had already begun to fester. You might thank them that you still have a leg on which to stand."

Her gaze turned skyward, then. "By dark of night, we shall ignite the pyre. So the flames can dance an' spread their light far, even unto the eyes of the very Gods themselves."

"Blasphemy," someone whispered.

Arianna's gaze pinned the one who'd spoken. "Aye, an' was it blasphemy when Leandra stopped you as you walked, an' bade you hurry home an' tend the fire in your hearth? You obeyed then, an' found coals scattered on the floor, beginnin' to burn already, an' your wee children asleep in their beds, unaware."

Mara came forward then, a hand coming to rest upon Arianna's shoulder. "My daughter's views are not always my own," she said, her voice, unused to speaking above a meek and obedient whisper, wavered slightly. "But in this, I believe she is right. Or . . . if she's wrong, then perhaps we should call for the execution of everyone who used The Crones' ways to aid themselves. For if what they did was sin, then we all are as guilty as they."

"Well said, Mara Sinclair," Joseph declared with a firm nod. "Well said. It shall be as my cousin wishes it then." And by addressing Arianna as such, he was reminding them all of her new status in the clan and village. She might be different, but she was above them now. "'Twill be done. This night." He turned to where his sons stood behind him. "Lads, choose several strong men and take them to the clearing. Supervise them as they build this pyre." He glanced at Arianna. "Are there any special instructions you would give them, lady?"

She blinked in surprise, but quickly moved beyond it, falling easily into her new role. And no wonder. Hadn't she always sensed she was different from the rest? "Aye," she said. "The wood for the fire should be of oak, ash, and thorn. An' none of the men are to speak an ill word of The Crones as they stack the wood. This pyre is to be built in their honor, to see them out of this lifetime. 'Twould nay do to have their names besmirched during its building."

Kenyon and Lud glanced at their father, and he nodded once, firmly.

"So be it then. The bodies will remain in my care, under guard, until nightfall."

He swung his horse around as if to go, but Arianna called after him. "Laird?"

He turned in the saddle. "Aye, lass?"

"I . . . Thank you. You are indeed a fine man, and an honorable one. I am more sorry than I can say for my behavior at the keep yestereve."

"Say no more," Joseph said with a gentle smile. "'Tis forgotten." Then he frowned. "You should ken, lass, the men who led the others in this murderous spree last eve are restin' now in my dungeon, and will remain there until they face their punishment."

She nodded. "An' what will that punishment be?" she asked, her throat sounding dry, her voice raspy.

"Much as it pains me, lass, those old women were murdered. As soon as the gallows is built, they shall hang." There was a murmur among the others, but it silenced when Joseph looked to see who would dare question his authority.

A slow, soft sigh escaped Arianna, and she lowered her head. "'Tis as it should be."

"Thank you, Joseph," I said, and in spite of myself, I found I was holding my young bride's hand tight in my own.

Joseph nodded once, kicked his horse's sides, and headed away to the keep, while his sons hastened to obey his orders.

Chapter 7

❧

Only a handful came to see The Crones on their journey. Joseph, Kenyon, and Lud. Nidaba, Arianna and her parents, and Nicodimus. They all stood a few yards, from the pyre, heads lowered respectfully, each thinking their own thoughts, saying their own prayers or whatever it was they believed in saying at times of parting. All of them let Arianna have enough room to grieve in privacy.

She stood apart from everyone, closer to the flames. It seemed to Arianna that she could hear the old women's voices as she stood very close to the funeral pyre and watched the flames dance for the sky. Leandra whispering that true love came but once, and that a person would always know it when it happened. Celia saying that was poppycock, that a woman must choose the man she would love, and set about winning his love in return. And Mary whispering that only the Fates themselves knew the answers.

Arianna thought perhaps they'd each had a part of it right. One could recognize love in themselves, but never know for certain if it would be returned. Doubts crept into her heart as she stood beside the fire. For how could she be so sure Nicodimus would ever love her, when even life itself was such a fragile and uncertain thing? Here a moment, and then gone. Fleeting as a stray breeze, and just as difficult to cling to. Life, love, joy. All so tentative, so slippery. She'd learned nothing if not that. Too much had been ripped away from her desperate grasp to doubt it.

Nicodimus could be torn from her as well. And it could happen all too easily.

Heat razed the front of her while the night's chill breath fanned her back. Firelight danced on her face, and her cheeks burned a bit, but she didn't step away. She only stared up at the burning coffins and heard the sharp snaps and cracks of the fire's teeth as it devoured them. The hiss of the green wood, the deep throated growl of the flames. Cinders rose like new stars flying heavenward to take their places among the rest in the inky night sky.

"Aye," she whispered. "Go, my sisters. May your souls rest and reflect and find the serenity you sought here among strangers. May you share all you learned with the exalted, and the ancient, and the enlightened. And may you return still closer to the state of perfection toward which we all strive. Live, love, die, and live again, my sisters. Merry meet, and merry part. I will miss you, until merry we meet again."

Hot tears slid down her cheeks, and Arianna opened the cloth in which she kept the flower petals she'd brought with her. These she scattered amid the flames.

A soft brush of warmth at her side made Arianna look down from the fire's brilliant yellow and orange glow. Nidaba stood beside her, her dark skin alight, her lined eyes shining the flames' reflection. She wore a white tunic, and silver crescents dangled from her ears, while a larger one hung from a chain 'round her neck. The ruby stone she wore in her nose gleamed red in the firelight. In silence, her eyes on the spot where the fire kissed the sky, Nidaba began to mutter in her own tongue. And the words had a music and a beauty to them that was . . . holy.

Her hand closed around Arianna's, sending the now familiar jolt through her. Slowly Nidaba lifted both her hands high, one of them still clutching Arianna's. "Farewell, innocent ones. Follow the moonlight into Inanna's embrace," she intoned in her jewel-rich voice.

Nicodimus came to Arianna's other side, clutched her other hand, and lifted his in similar fashion. "Go in peace," he said softly. His voice sent a tremor up Arianna's nape as it always did. Nicodimus's voice was like a physical touch.

Slowly, six hands lowered. Nidaba faced Arianna, bending her head slightly.

"Thank you for that," Arianna whispered.

"The loss of one is a loss to all of us, young one. Mortals seem to have much difficulty grasping the truth of that."

"Mortals? This is the second time you've used that word."

Looking up, meeting Nicodimus's eyes over Arianna's head, Nidaba licked her lips. "It is a lesson best learned on the other side, I think. That is all I meant."

"I see." She didn't. Not really.

"I am sorry for your pain, Arianna. Truly."

Arianna lowered her head. "I thought . . . you probably hated me."

"I do not hate. Except when my mind slips." She shrugged. "But how long can one live, really, without feeling the icy touch of madness every now and again?"

Arianna frowned and searched her face. "Madness? Nidaba . . . ?"

"What's this talk of madness?" Nicodimus asked, and he looked worried. "You're the most sane woman I know, Nidaba."

Nidaba lowered her head, and laughed very softly. "Speak to me when you've existed as long as I have, love."

When Nidaba's eyes met Nicodimus's once more, Arianna wondered anew at the depth of the link she sensed between the two of them. She experienced an unwelcome and unbidden stab of jealousy.

Nicodimus's strong hands closed on Arianna's shoulders from behind her. "Your garments are beginning to singe, little cat. Come away from the fire."

Turning to face him, Arianna caught her breath anew at the sheer beauty of the man. The way the firelight played on the angles of his face . . . the way it gleamed in his eyes. She tilted her head to one side. "What did you call me?"

"Little cat. It is what you remind me of, Arianna. With your curious eyes and volatile nature. Claws that can lash out in the blink of an eye to do a man to death. Your independent nature. In many, many ways, you remind me of the creatures."

Eyes narrowing, she studied him. "Then 'twas not an insult?"

"No, Arianna. 'Twas a compliment."

Her smile was slow, genuine, if tinged by sadness. "Then I thank you."

"You are very welcome." His palm flat at the spot directly between her shoulder blades, he urged her away slightly. A fallen log seemed to have become the gathering place for the others in attendance. This was where Nicodimus led Arianna. Easing her down to sit upon it, then standing beside her like a servant attending his queen as she rested on the throne.

Joseph approached her first, took her hands in his, and kissed them gently. "'Tis sorry I am that this happened, lass. I should have seen it coming. Should have done more to prevent it."

"Nay, Laird, you—"

"Ah-ah. None o' that. You're my cousin now, same as Nic. You'll address me as Joseph, an' nay by my title. As shall your family."

Lowering her lids to hide her surprise, she simply nodded. "You mustn't blame yourself for this . . . Joseph. Even I dinna see this coming, an' more than anyone else, I should have done."

He held her hands firmly for a long moment. "I suppose we all wish we'd have known, but the truth is no one could have. I only wish 'twere under more joyful circumstances I could welcome you into my family, lass. But welcome you I do."

"Thank you, Joseph." Leaning up, she kissed his cheek. And the laird's smile was broad for a moment.

Less so, his sons, as one by one, they too came to her, kissed her hand, and welcomed her to the fold. Both seemed sad to see her pain, but their pride was far more wounded, she suspected, that she had refused to have either of them for her husband. Their eyes were shadowed, their mouths drawn and petulant, though she could see them trying to school their expressions.

Nidaba only met her eyes, and turned to leave with Joseph and the lads. The whole time Nicodimus stood his post by her side. He'd watched the boys carefully, closely, and had gone just slightly stiffer when they had approached her. Now he relaxed that minute amount she shouldn't have noticed in the first place. But she had noticed. She noticed every detail about him, even a hitch in his breathing.

Her mother and father had moved closer to the fire. Mam to toss flowers of her own upon the flames, simply because it was what Arianna had told her to do when she'd asked how to show her respect. Da simply stood with his head bowed, hands folded low. A moment of prayer and farewell.

She was silent, watching them. Nicodimus seemed more intent, though, on watching her.

When they returned, her mother said, "Come, child. We must get you in out of the night air, afore you take a chill."

Arianna bowed her head. "You spoke up for me, this morning, Mam. Despite what the clan might have thought of you, and despite that your own beliefs more closely mirror theirs than my own."

Her mother's hand stroked a slow path over Arianna's cheek. "I havena been the best mother to you, lass, since . . . since Raven . . ." Her voice broke.

Arianna knew how difficult it was for her mother to speak her sister's name, and she rose in one fluid movement to wrap her mother in a fierce embrace. "Nay, Mam, you've been the best mother in the world. 'Twas I who closed myself away."

"I was too crippled by my own grief, child," Mara went on. "But I do love you, lass. I never stopped. An' I'd lay down my life for you to this day, without a moment's hesitation. I love you, Arianna. My firstborn daughter. You're my soul, dinna you know that, lass? My very soul!"

Tears choking her, Arianna clutched her mother tight, and nodded hard. "Aye. Aye, I know. An' I for you, Mam. Even when I seemed distant, that remained true. I love you."

They embraced for a long moment, the emotions so powerful, Arianna couldn't tell which body was trembling, her own or her mother's. Perhaps both. But when they stepped apart, she looked at her father and saw his eyes were unashamedly red and moist. He met her gaze and nodded once, and she understood. I, also, he was telling her. She went to hug him as well.

Then she straightened. "I canna leave just yet," she told them. "I need to stay, to hold vigil by the fire until the flames burn out. 'Tis a tradition older than any of us, an' I wish to carry it through to the end."

"But lass, 'tis dark! An' the night air—" her mother began, but her father touched Mara's shoulder, and she bit her lip.

"She's a grown woman now," he said. "She can decide for herself how best to show respect to her friends who've passed on, so long as 'tis safe." At this he glanced at Nicodimus, who'd been standing apart, silent, until now.

Arianna met his eyes, saw the fireglow dancing in them. "She'll be perfectly safe," he said. "I'll stay for as long as it takes."

Alone with her, in the darkness, beside a blazing funeral pyre. It was not the wisest decision on my part. But I was learning more about Arianna every moment, and I knew full well she'd have stayed with me or without me. I still had concerns for her safety. While the crofters may have softened slightly toward her, their tongues would still wag were she seen out alone at night. Especially here.

She stood watching in silence as her parents walked back along the path toward the village. Within a few moments, the night swallowed them up, and yet she remained there, back to the fire, eyes fixed on the distant darkness.

"Are you all right, Arianna?" I asked.

Blinking away her thoughts, she nodded, and met my eyes. "My mam and my da . . . They love me again."

I almost smiled. Would have, except I thought it might hurt her to realize how her innocence amused me. She pretended such fierceness, such toughness. When in truth she was as tender as a babe. "They never stopped," I told her.

"I was certain they had."

Tilting my head to one side, curious, I took her arm and led her back to her stately throne—the fallen limb—and sat beside her. "Why?"

Shrugging, she shook her head.

"Because of your sister's death?" I prodded. I found myself wanting to know. Then realized it wasn't just this matter I was curious about. I wanted to know everything about Arianna Sinclair. Her deepest feelings, her darkest secrets. Everything.

"'Twas my fault. She drowned trying to save me. But I've told you this."

"Yes, and I've told you it was no more than an accident. Your family could never have blamed you, Arianna. Likely they were beside themselves with relief that one of you had survived, when for all they knew, the loch could easily have taken you both."

She nodded slowly, deep in thought. "But . . ." Then biting her lip, she stopped herself.

"Go on," I said.

She shook her head. "Nay, Nicodimus. I dinna speak of this. 'Tis my own demon that haunts me, an' I'll nay share its curse with you."

As she said these words, she turned her gaze away from me, staring instead at the fire. And I felt a shield go up, as if she were protecting herself from me, from the pain of the past, from intrusion.

Cupping her chin, I turned her to face me again. A more beautiful creature I had never seen. Arianna in firelight was something to behold.

"There is no demon you cannot share with me, Arianna," I told her. "I'll not judge you, nor laugh at anything you say. Perhaps . . . perhaps I can help you to exorcize the beast that haunts your eyes."

The eyes of which I spoke narrowed. "And why would you want to do that?"

Her questions, as usual, cut to the bone. "I . . . It is what a husband does."

"Nay, Nicodimus. 'Tis what a lover does. Not a husband who is but a name. But a tender, caring man, out of concern for the woman he loves."

I licked my lips, tried to swallow as my throat went dry. "Arianna, you've mistaken my intent completely."

"Have I?"

The wind played in her golden hair as she searched me with her wise eyes. It was more and more difficult to believe the girl had yet to see twenty years of life. "You have," I said. "I cannot be your husband in the way you would have me be, little cat. But I'll be more than a name to you. I'll be your friend."

She frowned a little, a tiny pucker appearing between her delicate brows as she considered this. "My friend?"

I nodded.

"Because you care about me?" she asked, looking again into the flames, but peering at me from the corner of her eye as she awaited my answer.

"I always have," I admitted.

Her lips curved into a smile. "'Tis a start."

The words startled me, as did the smile. "It is the whole of it, Arianna. Do not read more into my friendship than what is there."

She nodded hard, as if in firm agreement, but I knew better. I knew her too well, in fact.

"Will you tell me then? Your feelings about your sister?"

She nodded again. "Aye, I'll tell you. When you love me, Nicodimus. When you love me."

She rose slowly, and pulled her shawl from around her shoulders, to spread it upon the ground. Sitting down upon it she tucked her legs under her, and used her arms upon the log as her pillow. "I will rest now," she whispered.

I only nodded, and watched her for a time. She hadn't slept much the night before. Her grief had been too raw to allow it. I was glad to see her eyes this heavy, her head this relaxed. When her breathing became deep and steady, I knew she truly slept, and knew how badly she needed it. So when she shivered, I sat down close beside her. I did not wish for the cold to interrupt her rest.

I had not expected her to curl against me, drawn instinctively to the warmth of my body. I had not expected her head to rest upon my lap, nor her arms to curl tight about my waist. And when they did, I had no idea what to do about it.

I sat there a moment, looking down at the vision twined around me, debating inwardly. Finally realizing that this woman was to be my wife. I do not think it had hit me fully until that moment, when she rested against me, a warm weight of softness and beauty. I was to be not only her protector, but her husband. It would take every ounce of will I possessed not to make her my wife in every sense of the word. Every ounce of will.

Yet I was the strong one. I was older, wiser, and far more powerful. She needed my help, not my desire. I could handle my own body and its incessant demands. To prove this to myself, I relaxed there on the ground, and put my arms around her, held her gently against me. Kept her warm.

And died a thousand deaths before I finally fell asleep.

When Arianna stirred awake, she felt his arms pull her closer to him. As Nicodimus came slowly awake, his body went hard and tight, and his eyes when they opened, blazed with something she had never seen in them before.

For just an instant, its intensity frightened her, and she pulled away with a soft gasp.

Nicodimus closed his eyes, and when he opened them that look was gone. He said nothing. She wasn't certain of what to say either. Suddenly arousing this man's passion took on a frightening new prospect. She hadn't realized what a powerful force she might be bringing to life. Could she deal with his passion? Could she ever satisfy a man such as he?

He wanted to know her innermost feelings about her sister. But she could not yet confide in him her certainty that the Gods had made a mistake that black day. That they must have meant to take her, Arianna, the eldest. The troublemaker. The rebel. Never could they have intended to take the most gentle, tender soul ever to draw breath. She knew inside that it should have been her to surrender to the murky depths of the loch. Not Raven. And that perhaps, had she not fought so hard to survive, the greedy loch would not have taken her precious sister in her stead.

That was the secret she kept, and it was hers alone.

But even now Nicodimus's dark gaze searched her face, probing and seeing far too much. And there was more there. There was a heat blazing behind his gaze. One so intense it was frightening. And yet exciting to her.

"The—the fire has burned out."

"Yes," he said, watching her through narrowed eyes as she rose to brush the dust and twigs from her skirts. Nervous hands fluttered about her hair, smoothing it. She darted quick glances all around. Busying herself by picking up and shaking her shawl, and then arranging it with exaggerated care around her shoulders.

"Arianna," Nicodimus said, very softly.

She went still and looked down at him. He sat, still resting with his back to the log.

"You needn't ever be afraid of me."

She tried a smile, but it was forced. "I'm nay afraid of anything, Nicodimus. Why on earth would I be afraid of you?"

"You know why. I promise, you're safe with me . . . and safe *from* me. All right?"

Looking at the ground, she whispered, "An' that's supposed to make everything all right, is it? But what if I dinna want to be safe from you, Nicodimus?"

When he didn't answer, she brought her head up, met his eyes. "I dinna, you know. Not at all."

"Nonetheless, you shall be." He got to his feet, and it was his turn to busy himself. He checked the smoldering ash which was all that remained of the fire, making sure no spark had spread. It occurred to her that Nicodimus might be as nervous as she had been. As shocked and shaken by the flare of awareness between them, as well.

But no. Nicodimus would not be shocked nor shaken by anything.

"Walk with me," she asked softly, deciding to go easier on him, just in case. Perhaps he only needed time to adjust to the idea that he loved her and desired her and would until the end of time. "Tell me of our wedding day. What will it be like?"

He finished what he'd been doing and came to stand beside her, looking relieved. "It will be everything you wish for, Arianna. You need only tell me what you want. The chapel will be decked in wreaths and buds, and the—"

"Chapel? But Nicodimus, I canna marry you in a chapel."

"But—"

"I'm not a Christian. I'm a Witch, and proud to be one."

He took her hand. "You mustn't speak it aloud that way, Arianna. It is unwise, you know that now."

"There is no one to hear me but you, an' I trust you with my life. Nay, I wish to speak our vows beneath the blazing fiery sun, our bare feet caressing Mother Earth's soft greenery and the air kissin' our faces, and the sea as our altar."

Nicodimus lowered his head. "The marriage needs to be recognized by the clan, and by the Church, Arianna. Such a one as that would not be."

"Then . . . canna we have both? One for the benefit of the Church and the clan, and another just for the two of us?"

He stared down at her. "We only need the one. The legal one, Arianna. For that's all there will be, that and friendship. No binding of two souls together as one, as you no doubt have in mind."

Closing her eyes to the disappointment, she sighed deeply. "Then 'twill nay feel like a marriage at all."

"Nor is it meant to. Only to look like one."

Her hand fluttered to her chest, very briefly. She fisted it and lowered it to her side again, an act of will. "Perhaps we should speak of something else."

"Perhaps," he said.

Nodding, she lifted her chin, staring straight ahead as they moved, side by side, along the path. "Tell me about Nidaba."

Nicodimus seemed surprised by the question, for it took him a moment to answer. "What do you wish to know?"

"How long have you known her?" She looked at him.

"I . . . it seems like forever. Surely for most of my life."

A vague answer. She wondered why. "Where did you meet?"

Searching her face, he tilted his head. "You're a curious little cat, aren't you?"

"Do I not have a right to be curious about the other woman in my husband's life?"

He shrugged, perhaps conceding the point. "'Tis a tale you may well enjoy, little one. The first time I met Nidaba . . . no. I will tell you about the second time. It was—"

"Why?"

He broke off, glancing down at her. "Like you, Arianna, I have some things in my past that are . . . too painful to talk about. Do you understand?"

She searched his eyes, saw the old wounds there, and nodded. "Aye. I ken it all too well. Go on, then, an' tell me the tale."

"I was traveling alone through the arid lands far to the east, when I was set upon by a group of desert bandits. Twenty of them, mounted on camels, surrounded me, swords drawn, demanding my horse, my gold, and my food and water. It was a three day journey to help, and that on horseback. On foot I'd have had no chance."

Arianna had stopped walking and stood staring at him, her eyes wide as she listened. "What did you do?"

"Drew my sword and prepared to fight. Actually, they began coming at me, long curving blades of their swords flashing with such skill I could barely follow them with my eyes, much less dodge the blows. And then there was this . . . this sound."

"Sound?"

"Yes. A cry, high-pitched and keening, rather like the shriek of an eagle before it swoops down upon its prey. The attackers whirled, and I turned to look as well. Pounding down upon us was a figure swathed in white robes to the point where only the eyes were visible. Each hand wielded a deadly blade, and they swung like windmills overhead as the white stallion thundered with guidance from neither hand nor rein. The bandits scattered. She didn't even have to kill any of them. They vanished like a distant mirage, and she sheathed her swords by crossing them in front of her and driving the left into the right sheath, and the right into the left. She was amazing to behold."

"She?" Arianna whispered. "Nidaba?"

"Yes. I didn't know it right away, of course. I blurted my thanks, but she only nodded and motioned for me to follow her. Only when we were safely inside her desert home, a veritable fortress, really, did she remove the headdress and reveal herself to me."

Arianna blinked. "She's . . . she's a very beautiful woman, I think."

"I have always thought so, too."

"Did you . . . did you and she . . . ?"

He touched Arianna's hair. "Nidaba and I are friends, Arianna. Only friends."

Her heart soared . . . but then began to sink a bit. Because she thought that if Nicodimus had been able to resist the allure of an exotic beauty such as Nidaba, she was in for more of a challenge than she realized. That Nidaba hadn't wanted him never occurred to her. No woman could fail to desire Nicodimus. Not ever. He was perfect in every way.

"You're very deep in thought about something," he observed. She started, unaware he'd been scrutinizing her face for several moments.

"Aye, I suppose I am." She shrugged. "It's occurred to me how very little I know about you, Nicodimus. You know every detail of my life, no doubt. But of your past, of your history, I know nothing."

His eyes became shuttered, and when her gaze searched them, he looked away. "You will," he said. "In time, I'll tell you all about myself."

"Would you care to begin now?"

He sent her a quick glance, then looked away. "Here, your mother is already awaiting us. Worried for your well-being, no doubt." He waved toward the distant figure, and Arianna saw her mother standing outside the cottage, waving back.

"She knows I'm perfectly safe with you," Arianna said with a sigh. "As your secrets seem to be, as well."

"You needn't be worrying about my secrets, little cat. 'Tis our wedding you ought be thinking of, planning for."

"Oh, I am," she said softly. "Believe me, Nicodimus, I am planning all the while."

His smile was warm, genuine, but there was a hint of something unreadable in his eyes. "Good."

Oh, but he wouldn't think it so good when she finished. Or perhaps he would, but not right away. She would fashion the most beautiful gown any woman had ever worn. She'd bathe herself in flower petals and smell like heaven to him. Her hair would gleam like gold. When Nicodimus bent to her lips, as he must—aye, he *must*—she would kiss him as he'd never been kissed before.

How she would manage that, she wasn't certain. She had never *been* kissed by a man before. But perhaps . . . someone could tell her how to best go about it.

If only The Crones . . .

Lowering her head, she sighed her regrets. Her teachers were gone. She would have to fumble through this as best she could. But come her wedding night, she intended to lie with her husband. In his bed, in his arms, whether he liked it or not. And she would, or her name was not Arianna Sinclair.

Chapter 8

I watched Arianna change during the next few days, and the change at once relieved and troubled me. The pain that had for so long shadowed her eyes began to fade. The ghosts that haunted her, seemed to have been chased into a dark corner—for the moment, at least. She no longer spent hours each day sitting alone in the cemetery, and even the agony of The Crones' final fate seemed to be easing.

I actually heard her laugh one day, as she and her mother walked arm in arm along the heather-covered moor beyond the keep. Such a rare sound, and so beautiful, that it startled me into stillness. I found myself edging nearer, straining to hear it again, curious as to what had caused it.

"They have repaired the rift between them, have they not?"

I turned abruptly, unaware of Nidaba's silent approach. She moved like a cat and stood beside me now, observing the mother and daughter as I did.

"I believe," I replied, "that they are even closer than before the death of Arianna's sister."

"Good. The girl will not cling quite so tightly to you then."

I frowned, drawing my gaze away from Arianna to focus on Nidaba. Her gaze held no contempt as she watched Arianna and her mother talking and laughing below. No dislike. It was only narrow and watchful.

"Why do you dislike her so much?" I asked.

Nidaba looked at me sharply. "Does it seem to you that I dislike her? I do not. The girl has spirit."

"Then . . . ?"

"It is the two of you together I do not like, Nic. You're not going to be good for her. Nor she for you. You'll destroy each other before you finish this ruse."

I shook my head at her. "I only want to protect her—"

"By keeping the truth from her? The truth of what you are, Nicodimus? Of what *she* is?" Nidaba's eyes again narrowed, falling on my young bride once more. "She ought to know, to have time to prepare."

"There is a long time before she will need to prepare for such as that," I told her.

"Only the Gods could know for sure. And you are not a God, my friend."

Her words troubled me. For I had seldom known Nidaba to be wrong about anything.

"Look at her," she went on. "You know full well that her laughter is not entirely due to her newfound closeness with her family, Nic. That kind of joy comes from only one place in a woman's heart. The girl is in love with you, and dreaming of things you have told her will never be. You cannot both come out of this unscathed."

My lips tightened. "I do not wish to hurt her."

Perhaps, I thought, I should tell Arianna again how it was to be with us. But two things kept me from doing that. First, the knowledge that Arianna Sinclair would believe exactly what she wanted to believe no matter what I might say to the contrary. And second, the simple fact that she was so incredibly beautiful when she was happy. Her smile, the sparkle in her eyes, the spring in her step, the confident tilt of her head. I loved seeing her this way. I did not want to be the one to put the shadows back into my lady's eyes.

She and Mara came 'round the bend in the steep path and saw us standing near the outermost wall. Arianna's smile died slowly as she met my eyes, searching them.

"Nicodimus, whatever is wrong? You look troubled."

I was troubled. For just an instant the thought had occurred to me that perhaps I *could* learn to love the girl. Could be her husband in the way she dreamed I would be.

And yet, I could not. I was a hunted man. More Dark Ones sought my heart than that of any other immortal, so far as I knew. Nidaba was older and more powerful, yes, but she'd lived so discreetly that few knew of her existence. My heart was the prize many Dark Witches sought. Two in particular, who had made it the mission of their endless lives to put an end to mine. Arianna would be in constant danger at my side.

Beyond that, I knew I was incapable of loving her. My heart was far too wounded to produce the tender emotion in any real quantity. Ironic, I thought, that a heart so damaged could be so prized by so many.

Frowning slightly, Arianna came closer, her small hands touching my cheeks. "My love, you are pale. Are you taking ill?"

My stomach clenched tight as the endearment fell from her lips. I glanced sideways, but Nidaba only stood in silence. "Arianna, you mustn't call me that," I said at last.

"And just why not? 'Tis what you are, and our weddin' day is on the morrow. Aye, sure and you might as well get used to it."

I closed my eyes. Such a stubborn girl. A smile tugged at my lips. "Aye, sure and I might as well," I said softly, imitating her beautiful speech.

"Is it teasin' me you like then?" she asked, stepping back a bit, hands going to her hips, eyes flashing with mischief.

There was, I realized, very little about Arianna that I *dis*liked. "I wasn't teasing, little cat. How goes the sewing, hmm?" I fell into step beside her, with her mother on the other side of her, and Nidaba walking along at my other side. We moved beside the blackberry briars that lined this side of the keep's outer wall. They blossomed just now, and their scents were heady and sweet.

Arianna shot Nidaba a sidelong glance, and smiled. "Nidaba has gifted me with the most wondrous material, and the gown is perfect, as you will soon enough see."

Any gown would be perfect if she were wearing it, I thought. We circled the keep, moving past the cobbled well, toward the gates. I paused, as a tiny shiver of warning skittered over my nape. What . . . ?

"I'll wear flowers in my hair," Arianna was saying. "And there will be such revelry afterward! Joseph has been more than generous, an' he has the cooks hard at work already. . . ."

As she went on, I glanced up, caught Nidaba's eye. She nodded just once, almost imperceptibly.

She felt it, too, then. The truly ancient among us could sense when another was nearby. And I sensed it now. Lifting my head, I scanned the horizon. But saw no one. Nothing.

"There will be barrels an' barrels of heather ale," Arianna was saying. "An' roast boar, venison, beef, an' mutton. Pastries to savor. Wine will flow, and fruits spill over. 'Twill be so . . . so . . ." She was looking more and more curiously from me, to Nidaba, and back again. "What *is* wrong with you two? You look as if you've seen a ghost!"

Snapping out of my state, I gripped Arianna's elbow in my hand. "Come, let's get you inside," I said, leading her and her mother through the gates, and across the courtyard toward the keep. I looked about as we moved among the men there, checking each face, but seeing only clansmen.

"But I dinna understand," Arianna protested. "What is it?"

"Do you not feel the rain coming, Arianna?" Nidaba asked, her tone unconvincing. "The air grows damp."

"You'd not wish to take a chill on the day before your wedding, now would you, little cat?" I asked her.

"You both be addled! 'Tis lovely outside!"

"Now, daughter, dinna argue with your bridegroom," her mother chided, but she, too, looked unconvinced.

I simply kept moving until Arianna and her mother were safely inside the keep. It was happening; the one thing I feared above all else. One of the Dark Ones had finally found me here—traced me to my only haven. Gods forgive me if I had brought disaster upon this peaceful village. Upon my friends. Upon my woman.

My woman.

Gods, why had I allowed myself to think of her that way?

When we entered the keep, Arianna turned to face me, her eyes no longer filled with mischief or joy, but that deep wisdom she was too young to possess. "A word, Nicodimus, in private."

Eager to be away, I nodded all the same, and sent a glance to Nidaba. She quickly excused herself, and Mara muttered something and vanished toward the kitchens.

"All right then," Arianna said softly. She came close to me, gripped my hand in both of hers. "I ken something is wrong. An' I can plainly see you're hidin' it. Now, tell me what it is."

Not for anything would I have spoiled the day to come for her with worries such as those plaguing me now. Gently, I stroked her hair with my free hand, as if I could soothe her the way I could soothe Black when he grew agitated or afraid. "Nothing is wrong," I told her. "Truly."

Tilting her head to one side, she searched my face with her velvety eyes. "Why are you lyin' to me, Nicodimus?"

Drawing a deep breath, sighing, I lowered my head. "All right. It's . . . sometimes, Arianna, I get . . . feelings. This, I know you understand."

Her eyes widening with interest, she nodded. "Aye, I do. The Crones taught me to trust those feelings, never to doubt them."

"And good advice it was," I told her. "Out on the path just now, I had the feeling that . . . that we were being watched."

Arianna frowned, nodding sagely. "Aye, I've had the same feelin' once or twice today, myself." She looked up into my eyes, worry clouding hers. "Who do you suppose it could be?"

She was too young to have such a sense of other immortals, I thought. But then again, she always knew when I was near, didn't she? Amazing.

"I do not know," I said, and it was only partially a lie. True, I didn't know *who*, but I damned well knew *what* sort of creature was watching us. "But I intend to find out."

Her eyes were narrow upon me. "You think this person . . . could be a danger to us?"

She saw too much. Read me far too well for me to lie to her easily. "I don't know. Perhaps. I cannot tell you because I'm not even fully certain myself. I am going to ask you trust me in this matter."

Nodding, she lifted her head again. "I do trust you, Nicodimus."

"Then please, Arianna, stay here tonight. Your family as well."

Blinking in surprise, she nodded. "Aye, Nicodimus. All you had to do was tell me the truth. If you fear there is danger, then I believe you. I will never doubt your word . . . so long as you speak the truth."

I very nearly smiled at that. Would have, had I not been nearly sick with worry. "Will you always know, Arianna, when I am not speaking the truth?"

"Only when you are as obvious as you were this time," she said. She smiled at me, and I knew I was forgiven.

"I shall go and fetch my father," she said softly, closing one hand around mine and squeezing. "We'll pack up our things for the wedding tomorrow, and—"

"No, Arianna. Let me go for him. It will be for the best." I started to tug free of her grip.

She held me fast. "You truly do sense danger, dinna you, love?" She searched my face. "Is there danger to you waiting outside these walls as well then?"

I looked her squarely in the eyes. "No, Arianna. I will be perfectly safe." Gently I tugged my hand free, and headed for the door, even as her eyes narrowed on me. And I think she knew, once again, that I had not been honest with her.

Gnawing at her lip and pacing the great hall did nothing to alleviate Arianna's worry, which seemed to intensify the moment the doors closed on Nicodimus's strong back. She recalled again the wisdom of The Crones. *Never mistrust your feelings, lassie. They be the core of your womanhood. The voice of your heart.*

Nicodimus was in danger.

Arianna stood a bit straighter, feeling a jolt of protectiveness surge through her so powerfully she felt as if she grew inches taller. Her chin thrust outward, she headed for the doors, pausing only once on the way, just long enough to glance behind her. But Nidaba was nowhere in sight, nor was her mother, nor any of the others, save a handful of servants spreading fresh rushes over the floor. She was more grateful than anyone would ever know for the privacy.

She ran a hand over her hip, and felt the reassuring lump there, where her dagger was strapped. Then she drew her shawl closer, and slipped away. Nicodimus was her man. She would be damned if she would stand by and let any harm come to him.

She crept, following on foot, ducking behind trees and bushes and any cover to be had, for she knew too well that Nicodimus would be furious if he saw her.

He did exactly as he had said he would. Rode to her home, fetched her father, and settling both Edwyn and the satchel he'd rapidly packed atop Black, Nicodimus led the stallion back to the keep gates. All this she witnessed from a spot high on the hilltop between the keep itself and the village proper, just at the edge of the woods, hidden amidst the trees.

But her husband-to-be did not go into the keep with his future father-in-law. Instead, he saw Edwyn through the gates, then remounted his noble Black and turned. He came toward Arianna, riding slowly, eyes narrow and scanning the horizon, peering into every clump of shrubbery in search of the watcher.

Arianna cringed backward farther, unable to believe she could hide from so piercing a gaze. But even as he rode slowly nearer, she forgot to fear discovery. For another shape rose up behind him. Another man, mounted upon a horse as pale as death.

Her eyes widening, she stepped out of her hiding place, and shouted a warning. But instead of heeding her, Nicodimus continued toward her, obviously surprised and displeased to see her there, and unaware of the danger coming upon him from behind. The white horse began to run, its rider a fearsome brute of a man, all swathed in a black cloak that covered his colors, did he wear them. His face was hidden behind a beaked black helm that completely covered his head. The reddish-brown tail of some unfortunate animal flew from the spiked top of the helm, like a banner. He thundered on, swinging a spiked mace in deadly circles. Arianna lunged forward, drawing her blade, even knowing she could never reach the man before he reached Nicodimus.

The mace flew directly at Nicodimus's head. But nothing happened. Eyes widening in shock, biting her knuckles to silence the cry that leapt to her lips, Arianna shook her head in confusion. Nicodimus had dropped low, over the side of his mount, just as the weapon came at him. Gods, he must have known all along.

Leaning low, he continued riding toward her, and when he swooped down upon her, he snatched her right off her feet, and settled her safely in front of him. One arm held her tightly to his chest, and he whirled his mount around, even as the other man thundered closer. Nicodimus continued to cradle her protectively with one arm as with his other hand he jerked a leather covered shield from the saddle, holding it before her.

The black-helmed stranger drew his pale horse to a stop, but the animal danced and pawed impatiently. Black tossed his head, shook his mane, and blew his angry retort.

"Who are you?" Nicodimus demanded. "What do you want of me?"

"You know what I want," was the answer, spoken so softly and yet so chillingly it sent shivers up Arianna's spine.

"I've no quarrel with you."

"The Dark and the Light live in constant conflict, Nicodimus. It is the way of things, with our kind."

Arianna turned to stare up at Nicodimus's face, but she saw no fear there.

"Then you know my name. You have me at a disadvantage."

There was a nod. Then the mask's beakish point seemed to aim her way. "Is this the latest leman, then? Or is she to be a replacement for the wife you stole away from her family and murdered?"

Arianna's breath caught in her throat. "W-wife?"

"Do not dare to speak of my wife," Nicodimus said, and he sounded even more dangerous than the other. "Or I'll kill you here and now."

"If you think you can."

"Oh, I know I can." He reached to his hip, hand closing on a weapon there, a dagger or blade. "And do not be so certain that the helm you wear hides your face from me. When your words tell me who you must be." He started to lift his weapon, but then he went still, looking down into Arianna's eyes, and she knew her tears showed. "I'll not do this. Not here. Not now. This woman and her clan are no part of our conflict."

"Perhaps you're right. About the village," he said. "As to the woman . . . Well, once I've cut out your heart, Nicodimus, she'll be mine to do with as I please. To the victor go the spoils, or so I was once told."

Nicodimus narrowed his eyes. "Show me your face, coward, that I might know which of my two oldest enemies I am going to have to kill."

"Not just yet I think. We'll meet again, Nicodimus. We'll meet again." He nodded toward Arianna. "As will you and I, pretty one."

She cringed closer to Nicodimus's chest, even as the man whirled his mount and thundered away. Pale hooves sent tufts of sod in their wake and left deep scars in the ground. Then Arianna turned into Nicodimus's arms as the full brunt of shock and fear finally hit her.

He clutched her shoulders, shook her gently as he stared into her eyes. "Why must you disobey? You could have been killed, Arianna! For the love of —"

"I'm sorry," she said, voice firm, even if her eyes were damp. "I should never have come out here armed only with my dagger. My Goddess, what help could I have been to you with only that for a weapon? I ought to have found swords, a mace like the masked man carried, a lance. . . ."

Nicodimus stared at her, opened his mouth, then clamped it shut again and shook his head. "I believe, Arianna, you're missing the meaning."

But she wasn't. "What did he mean, Nicodimus? About a wife you stole, an' murdered? What was he talkin' about?"

He dropped his gaze and looked away. "Come, let's get you back to the castle where you'll be safe."

"I'll go nowhere until you tell me. I know you have secrets you will not share, Nicodimus. But surely even a man as secretive as you would see a previous marriage as something he should discuss with his bride."

He held on tight to her waist, and nudged the horse into a trot. "It was a long time ago, Arianna."

"And you stole her from her family?"

"I rescued her from a den of brutes who beat her and treated her as their slave."

"He said you murdered her."

He looked down at her sharply. "No doubt he sees it that way." Then his throat moved convulsively as he wrenched his eyes away. "Sometimes, I do as well. It is true enough. Anya died trying to give birth to my daughter. So I suppose it could be said she died at my hand, yes."

"Nicodimus, nay!" Arianna pressed her hands to his face, forcing him to look into her eyes. "Nay, my love, you must never say such a thing. Never." Frowning at the pain that he tried so hard to keep hidden behind his eyes, Arianna forced away her own. "My Goddess, you loved her, dinna you?"

The skin drawn taut over his cheekbones, he gave a curt nod. "Yes. I loved her."

"And that is why, then. That is why you canna love me. Your heart belongs to another. Gone she may be, but alive within your soul." Lowering her head, she relaxed against him, eyes falling closed. "I understand now. I'm sorry for you, Nicodimus. So sorry. For I know your pain all too well."

"Arianna . . ."

She lifted a hand, pressed a forefinger to his lips. "Say nothing, love. There is nothing to say. You canna deny what you felt for her, no more than I would ask you to. I understand, now. I do, I vow it."

One large hand stroked down along her outer arm. "I know you do, little cat. I know you do." He touched her face, then drew his hand away quickly. "Tears, Arianna? I never saw you cry in your life until these last few days."

"'Tis only the shock, Nicodimus. The fellow frightened me well and clear to my bones. Next time he'll nay catch me so unprepared. Let him threaten you again, and he'll find himself skewered on my blade."

She dared peer up at him. Saw his lips curve a little. "You must promise never to disobey me this way again, Arianna. That man is a trained warrior."

"Aye. You know who he is."

He nodded. "One of Anya's two brothers, Marten or Kohl. I cannot be sure which of them. But either is as deadly as the other, and each is a danger to you, Arianna."

"I can learn to fight."

"He would kill you without a second thought." He looked deeply into her eyes. "He would kill you, Arianna. And I would not be able to live with that. So promise me you'll stay out of my battles. Let me fight them on my own. I'm very capable, you know."

She looked at him steadily. "That man will come back. He wants to kill you."

"I'm not going to let him do that, Arianna. But it's my battle. His and mine, and you are no part of it."

"He made me a part of it when he said what he did."

"Listen to me." He held her closer, harder, and a certain fierceness came into his eyes. "I will never let him touch you. I swear it to you, Arianna. You are safe with me."

Smiling slightly, she stroked a hand over his cheek. "Aye," she whispered. "You do care just a little."

Averting his eyes, he dropped a very chaste kiss upon her forehead. "More than is wise," he muttered, and kicked the horse into a gallop.

Her wedding day dawned clear and bright, like a new promise, and Arianna welcomed it. Her mother frowned at her when she refused to break her fast but didn't argue. For once, it seemed, she understood. Arianna seemed no more capable of eating than of coherent thought. She paced the spacious chamber assigned to her, until her mother went down to break her own fast and Nidaba came in her place.

"You sent for me?" Nidaba asked, closing the chamber door, turning to face Arianna.

"Aye." Arianna stopped pacing and gathered her courage. "I need to ask something of you, Nidaba. An' I fear you'll turn me down, for I know you disapprove of my wedding Nicodimus."

Nidaba averted her eyes. "It is not my place to approve or disapprove of your marriage, child."

Arianna lowered her head. "But you do, all the same. I hope you will change your mind one day, Nidaba, for I have come to admire you above any female I have known." Arianna looked up again to see the normally unreadable eyes wide with surprise, the lips slightly parted. "Does that surprise you? You're a strong woman, Nidaba. Independent. Getting along in this world somehow all on your own. And Nicodimus has told me of your skills in battle."

Nidaba schooled her features. "What is it you want of me, child?"

Arianna titled her head. "What do you know of this dark enemy Nicodimus encountered yesterday?"

Nidaba's eyes shifted away, toward the window. "Likely less than you do. Why?"

Arianna shrugged. "I dinna suppose it matters. Only that my husband could have been killed. An' if it had come to that, I'd have been of no help to him."

Meeting Arianna's eyes this time, Nidaba smiled. "You think Nicodimus needs your help, little one?"

"I only know that if he ever *should* need it, I want to be able to give it." Arianna squared her shoulders, lifted her chin. "I want you to teach me to fight, Nidaba. An' I dinna want you tellin' Nicodimus about it, for I know he would likely object."

Blinking several times and tilting her head to the side, Nidaba studied her for a long moment. And then, without an argument or a question, she simply said, "Yes."

Arianna gasped. "Yes?" She couldn't believe the woman had agreed so easily.

"Yes. It is a skill you'll need to master sooner or later anyway. So, yes. I'll teach you. In secret."

Smiling broadly, Arianna clasped Nidaba's hand. "Thank you, Nidaba."

Nidaba only nodded, and turned toward the door. She paused with her back to Arianna. "I . . . could stay, if you like. Assist you in preparing yourself for the wedding."

Arianna felt as if she might finally have gained a measure of acceptance from the strange, powerful woman. "I would like that very much. You could shadow my eyes again, aye?"

Turning, Nidaba nodded, and offered Arianna a tentative, and very slight smile, for the first time.

She came to me on the steps of the keep's small chapel, and I caught my breath. For the first time I saw the full extent of the danger represented by this one small woman. For the first time, I realized, I would never be able to withstand a full-scale assault on my senses such as the one she seemed determined to launch. Oh, I had thought I could. I had told myself so. But now I knew what a fool I had been to believe it, even for a moment.

Arianna wore silk as white as snow, which had been cleverly shaped to cup and lift her breasts, and hug tight 'round her small waist. Snugly covering—but not really covering—her arms were sleeves of delicate lace, which allowed incredibly seductive glimpses of creamy skin. Her hair had been rinsed in henna, so it gleamed like sunshine, and spilled about her shoulders, threaded through with tiny flowers—heather, forget-me-nots, and baby's breath. Her eyes—lined by the unmistakable hand of Nidaba—seemed somehow older, wiser, and a hundred times more sensual than before. And they shone with nervous excitement. Her lips were full and rosy and shining.

She came to me, and I could not take my eyes from her. Not to look toward the village priest as he spoke his words over us, nor even to spare him a glance when I repeated my vows. I could not stop staring at Arianna. The little cat who had somehow been transformed into a regal bride. Maiden bride. *My bride.*

Before my eyes she promised to love me, to obey me, to remain loyal only to me. In her small face was such solemn sincerity that I knew they were not just words. Not to her. She meant every vow she spoke. She would honor them. Her promises were real, and she would expect mine to be as well.

Honoring my vows to her . . . would not be difficult, I realized slowly. Keeping them would be no chore at all.

A tear slipped from her doe-brown eyes and glistened upon her satin cheek when I put my ring upon her finger. I leaned forward, brushed my lips across her face, and kissed the tear away. "It will be all right," I promised softly. Surprise and what looked very much like hope lit her eyes as she stared at me. Then at the priest's word, she let them fall closed and swayed very gently toward me. I caught her up in my arms, and pressed my lips to hers. It was to have been tender, our wedding kiss. It was to have been sweet, and reassuring.

It became something far different. Because her soft lips trembled ever so slightly when mine pressed against them. And her hands, featherlight and hesitant, fluttered and then pressed against my back. Then her body seemed to melt into mine. My hands had rested gently at her waist, until that soft sigh and tiny tremor that went through her. Shyly, she dared use her tongue to trace the shape of my lips. Then I forgot exactly why I had been determined to kiss her so gently. I forgot everything: who I was, who she was . . . and what we both were. My arms locked 'round her, and pulled her roughly to me. My mouth opened over hers, and my tongue pushed between her lips, stroking deep. I pressed her hips to mine, shamelessly rubbing against her as I drank my fill from her mouth. And even as I plundered her, I felt her response. Shock, yes, but arousal, too. She arched against me, arms twining 'round my neck, fingers digging their way into my hair. She tilted her head to grant my mouth greater access, and parted her lips willingly to my invasion. Her breasts squeezed so tightly to my chest that I could feel the pebbling of her nipples even through our clothes, and I imagined the feel of them between my fingertips . . . my lips.

The priest cleared his throat . . . loudly.

Slowly, I raised my head, parting my lips from those of my responsive little bride. But I didn't take my arms from 'round her. It took only a glance into her stunned and confused eyes to know that I could not. She would likely collapse if I let her go now. Her hands were trembling, her knees quivered. Her eyes were glazed and shining and wide. Her lips swollen and wet and hungry. She was breathing in quick, shallow little puffs. And she pressed one hand to her belly as if to calm the riot going on within. Desire was what she felt, I knew that. Though I was unsure she could correctly identify it. I knew no one else in the chapel would have any trouble. Particularly if they noticed the bulge beneath my kilt.

What had I done?

She held my gaze, and the stunned expression in her trusting brown eyes gradually gave way to a tentative smile. She slipped her small hand into my large one and we turned to receive our blessings from the clan crowding the chapel, filling all the pews and spilling out the door. Everyone in Stonehaven had come to see us joined.

Almost everyone.

The intruder was not here. For that I was grateful.

Chapter 9

I could not frown upon the revelry Joseph had planned for the bridal feast. The doors to the keep had been thrown wide, and huge platters mounded with roasted meats, fish, and savory pastries were set upon all the tables lining the great hall. The entire clan was here to partake of the festivities. Jugs of heather ale, mead, and even precious wine were passed around freely, and mugs overflowed as all imbibed generously. Torches were lit in the courtyard as the celebration grew and spilled out beyond the confines of the hall. There was even a minstrel who moved hither and yon, strumming his lute and singing of love everlasting.

It was sad to hear of such things as those of which the mistrel sang, when I knew full well nothing was truly forever. I'd seen too much come and pass to believe otherwise.

But the wine and ale flowed like the twin rivers of Nidaba's homeland, and the food never seemed to run low. Feasting, dancing, singing, all of it ran together. Arianna was tugged away from me early on, pulled into the embrace of her family, and false-faced villagers (who, I reminded myself grimly, had been all too ready to see her hanged and burned only days ago) with well wishes.

I found myself torn. One side of me wanting to go, to enjoy the festivities and let Arianna find her own way back to me. The other side, unable to do so. Unable to stop craning my neck to find her through the crowd. To make certain she was well, and safe, and not afraid nor tormented in any way.

Spotting her, I shook my head. Since when did Arianna Sinclair—Arianna *Lachlan*—allow anyone to torment her? It was a silly thought. And yet, she'd seemed so vulnerable today. So utterly open and vulnerable . . . to me. Only to me.

I gave up trying not to, and made my way through the crowd to her. I found her in deep conversation with the whelp who had cut her to see if she would bleed. My ire rose, my hand clenched into a fist, and my teeth, in all likelihood, bared.

"But that's when I realized what a fool I had been," the whelp was saying. "An' I'll never be able to apologize enough for hurtin' you. Never in all my days."

"Not if you live to be a hundred and ten," I put in, stepping close to Arianna, and in spite of myself, slipping a possessive arm around her shoulders.

"Oh nonsense, Nicodimus," Arianna said with a soft laugh. One that was off in some way, one that spoke of mischief. She was up to something. I looked down and saw that gleam in her eyes, and knew I should quiet her, and fast. I eyed the near-empty mug in her hand and wondered how many times it had been filled with wine. Her cheeks were pink, her eyes more sparkling than usual, and we had yet to sit down to the feast.

"I can forgive you, Angus. If you can forgive yourself. After all, you must feel a terrible fool for what you did. Far worse than the pain you inflicted on me, was the uselessness of the entire endeavor."

"*Arianna* . . ." I warned.

"Uselessness?" Angus echoed.

"Aye, that foolish old superstition that says a true Witch willna bleed if you cut her."

"S-superstition?"

"Aye, indeed. You saw for yourself the murder of The Crones. You . . . were there, were you not?"

Angus lowered his head. "Aye, I was there. An' ashamed I am to admit I did nothin' to prevent it. I know you were fond of them."

"Yes, well, many of us were," I said, tugging at her arm.

"If you were there," Arianna rushed on, "then you must have seen their blood flow."

His head coming up fast, Angus looked at her, wide-eyed. "What's this now?"

"Aye, the ladies didna go to the noose without a struggle. They fought, and were cut, and when they were, Angus, they bled." She lifted her brows high. "Just. Like. Me."

"*Damnation,* Arianna . . ."

Angus interrupted me. "Then . . . then they were nay Witches at all?" he asked, eyes bulging.

"Oh, but they were. They were true Witches, through and through." Arianna tossed her hair behind her shoulder, and finally allowed me to pull her away, leaving Angus gaping and pale faced behind us.

I tugged her behind a tapestry, my hand firm on her arm, and made her face me. "What the hell do you think you're playing at?"

Her smile didn't so much as waver. "Putting the fear of the Goddess into him. Dinna fear, Nicodimus, I admitted to nothing."

"No, just planted the seed in his fertile mind. He'll be convinced you're a Witch before nightfall."

"And what's wrong with that? I *am* a Witch."

"What's wrong with that? You saw what befell your mentors, Arianna, and yet you ask me what's wrong with that?"

She glanced down at my hand on her arm. "You are hurting me."

I eased my grip instantly, but didn't let go. "I ought to be shaking you! Arianna, you're so reckless! So impulsive, so—"

"So perfectly safe," she interrupted. "As your wife, I'm safe. They wouldna dare harm me now, an' well you know it. So why do you care if I exact a bit of revenge for the wrongs done me an' mine? Hmm? What harm is there in letting young Angus spend the next several nights in a cold sweat, fearing my Witchly retribution? 'Twill do him no harm!"

I sighed, exasperated with her to no end. "'Twill do you harm, woman. Especially if he talks to others about the thoughts you've put into his head. This whole episode could turn itself back upon you, Arianna."

"Nay, it canna. For I have never felt safer than I do with you, my husband. An' I plan to spend the next several nights wrapped up tight in your arms." She snuggled close, twining her arms 'round my waist and resting her head on my chest. "Surely no harm can befall me there."

I stared down at her. My throat went utterly dry. Her eyes, heavy-lidded and gleaming from beneath thickly curling lashes, were filled with promise . . . and desire. Clearing my throat, I managed to force words through my lips, though they emerged rather hoarse. "You know that is not the way it will be. I have told you this."

"Aye, you have. But that was before our wedding kiss. An' I thought perhaps you'd changed your mind."

"I gave you no reason to think that," I said firmly, clasping her shoulders to move her slightly away from me.

"Nay? I rather thought near mating with me in front of the priest an' the entire clan was reason to think so, Nicodimus. Forgive me, though, if I misread you." Anger flashed in her eyes now.

I closed my eyes as painful memories reared up. I couldn't live it again. Didn't want to know her in that way, to come to cherish her any more than I already did, only to lose her. It would hurt too much. I would not love again, not ever. I had vowed it and I would keep that vow, for sanity's sake.

"I'm sorry. What you're thinking of can never be."

Her gaze fell, but not before I'd seen disappointment and pain cloud her expression. "Then let Angus rouse the suspicions of this clan. Let them come for me. If I canna be with you, I'd just as soon be dangling from a limb."

She whirled 'round as she said it, and stomped off toward the high table.

She was angry. Well, let her be angry then. It would be for the best.

I strode after her and joined my bride at the high table. As I sat down, she tore a leg from a roasted capon, and bit into it with a fierceness that was completely unladylike.

Arianna donned a nightshift so bold she could not believe she had the nerve to look at it, much less wear it. A wedding gift, presented to her by Nidaba during one of the more quiet moments of the celebration.

Sheer, made of a fabric she'd never seen before. Black, it hung to her ankles, but hid nothing. Every part of her was visible through the soft fabric. Arianna peered at a polished silver mirror, biting her lip. Even looking at herself dressed this way brought color to her cheeks. What would seeing Nicodimus looking at her do?

She snatched a blanket from the bed, and hastily tossed it around her shoulders. For now. Surely the courage to let it fall to the floor would come when she needed it. When Nicodimus . . . her husband . . . came through the chamber doors.

Her husband. Gods, to think of that man as her own. It was nearly too much for her mind to comprehend, and yet it was true. Or nearly true. She had yet to be his wife in the most important way. She had yet to lie in his arms, with less even than this scrap of cloth between them. She had yet to feel him inside her, filling her. Closing her eyes, she released a shuddering breath. It would be magick. True magick.

He would come to her. He would come to her soon.

Putting down the mirror, Arianna examined the room in which she and her husband were to spend their wedding night. Joseph had wisely assigned them to a chamber far from those used by the others. They would have complete privacy. Stone walls rose on all sides, with but a single window looking out and down to the outer walls, and the loch and woods beyond. She could not see the village from here. On one wall, a hearth stretched broadly, and a fire laid ready for the touch of a spark. Much like the fire inside her laid ready for the touch of her true love's hand.

His lips.

His body.

She closed her eyes against the roiling in the pit of her stomach . . . and lower. She was dizzy. Too much wine, surely.

When would he come? He should surely be here by now . . . if he intended to come to her at all tonight.

She whirled and stepped toward the door, even opened it a crack and peered out into the flickering, torchlit halls. But no sign of Nicodimus did she see.

He *would* come to her . . . wouldn't he? He'd said he would not. He'd said her dreams of being with him could never be. But she'd been certain he would at least come in long enough to wish her good night . . . on their wedding night. And when he did . . . and when she let the blanket fall away and he saw her in this scandalous shift, he would be unable to leave her to her lonely bed. He would take her, making her his woman in every way.

But no footsteps echoed in the halls. No sound at all came to her.

"Oh, Nicodimus, please," she whispered. "You wouldna leave me alone tonight. Not tonight, of all nights . . ." A tear burned in Arianna's eye as slowly she realized that was exactly what he intended to do.

The sound of hoofbeats accompanied a chill night breeze, through the window, and she hurried there. Hands braced on the stone sill, she leaned out, staring down into the darkness, to see the rider galloping away. Horse and rider both . . . unmistakable to her longing eyes. Nicodimus. Leaving his wife behind.

Her tears burned away under the blazing heat of her anger. Arianna let her blanket fall away, and snatched a dark, hooded cloak from her chest. Throwing it around her, she yanked the door open and strode out into the cool corridor. He would *not* leave his bride behind on their wedding night. She would not allow him to.

I felt like a brute for the first time in my life, that night. Arianna . . . She was more than I could hope to resist, and I dared not face her. I knew too well what would happen between us if I went to her in the chamber where she waited. If I looked into those brown eyes and saw the raw yearning there as I had seen it earlier today when I had spoken my vows to her. If I touched her and felt the innocent trembling reaction of her body to mine. I knew she wanted . . . craved . . . what I could never give her. Not just coupling. I could provide that easily enough, and likely would have, had there been any way to keep her heart uninvolved. But it would not be possible with Arianna. It would mean more to her than the satisfaction of a physical hunger. It would mean I owned her, heart and soul. And that was a responsibility I did not want.

If I were to be utterly honest, I might admit that I feared for my heart and soul's well-being as well. Perhaps even more so than for hers. She intrigued me, enticed me, tempted me, in a way no woman ever had. No, not even my precious Anya. Arianna was so unlike my first love as to be a different breed altogether. Anya had been tame and timid. Arianna was wild and untamable. Anya had endured my touch, enjoyed it even, out of her desire to please me and her love for me. But Arianna was a bundle of passion awaiting release.

No. I could not go to her. I feared her, it was true. I felt as if she could easily destroy me, and lay to waste the solid stone wall I'd spent centuries building around my heart.

I knew now what I had done. I almost smiled when I realized that I had had a hand in destroying my own defenses by having put myself into this predicament. Her husband. By the Gods, I was the girl's husband now.

I rode Black hard, far away from the keep walls, into the forest beyond, and still farther, picking up the timeworn, but still familiar trail that led to my place. The sacred place of my people, and of those who came before them.

The Stone Circle.

When the towering pillars rose before me, I felt the first hint of peace beckoning me nearer. Tying Black's reins to a tree limb, I unlaced and removed my boots, out of reverence for the sacred site. My head bowed low, I stepped between the stones and entered the sanctuary.

Power pulsed here—from the stones, perhaps, or maybe from the ground itself. No one knew if the construction of the circle gave it the power, or if the power had been what had made the Ancient Ones choose this site. Perhaps neither was true, and it had been the constant use of this place for worship and ritual that had imbued it with magickal energies. I only knew the power here was real. A force I could feel thrumming like heady wine through my veins the moment my bared feet touched the soil within.

Moving to the center of the circle, I sat cross-legged and willed myself calm. Consciously, I slowed my breathing, deepened it, and one by one, relaxed every tense muscle in my body. I lowered my chin, closed my eyes, and opened my senses.

Gradually, the peace of the place worked into me. The sounds of the forest—for it was alive around me—made their way to me. The gentle breeze whispering amid the trees, and the stones themselves. The songs of nightbirds and crickets chirping. I could think clearly here. I would see the way I must proceed with Arianna. I had no wish to hurt her, and I knew I had that power. I had no wish to be hurt by her . . . and yet I suspected that power could belong to her all too easily. In silence, I sat. Until the silence was broken by a voice, deep and loud, calling my name from without.

"Nicodimus!"

My head came up fast, eyes wide, but sharp in the darkness. He stood outside the sacred place, a dagger already gleaming by the pale light of a crescent moon in his hand.

"The time has come."

Slowly, I got to my feet, my hand inching toward my own dagger, the one I never dared to be without. For this was my life. I never knew when a challenge would come.

He took a step forward. I held up a hand. "Not within the circle," I said, my voice low. "This is sacred ground."

He shrugged, his face invisible behind the beaked helm. "I've no care where I kill you, Nicodimus, so long as it gets done."

"Are you so certain you're ready to die, Marten?" I asked him, moving forward, coming out from amid the stones ten paces before him. "Or is it Kohl, behind the mask?"

"I am not certain at all that I wish to die," he said, his voice tinny and hollow. "But then I have no intent of dying, so what does it matter?"

He sprang then, and though I'd no wish to take a life here in this place, nor on the night of my wedding, I had no choice but to try my best to kill the man. For unless I did, he would surely kill me.

He plowed into me like a maddened bull before I could react. The pointed cone of his helm rammed my midsection and sent me stumbling backward, doubled over. Instinctively, I drew my knee sharply upward to pummel his face. An ill-planned move, since it only resulted in the beak-ish helm piercing my knee clean to the bone, by the feel of it.

I went down to the ground, and still he kept coming, roaring like an animal as he brought his blade down hard and fast. I rolled away, and his blade found dirt instead of flesh. Scrambling to my feet, even as he yanked his dagger free of the earth and began to straighten, I plunged my own blade deep into his back. My head clear now, I sought the spot where the bottom of his helm met the top of the breastplate he wore. My aim was true. The blade sank deep into the place between neck and back, and the force with which I drove it sent it clean through my enemy's spine.

He cried out but once, a cry that seemed cut off almost before it be-gan. Then he went still. Motionless. Not a breath whispered from him. Not a sound. And yet he lived. Paralyzed and unable to breathe, but alive still. I sensed it.

I drew my blade from him and straightened, rolled him over with my foot, and crouching low, removed the helm. Blood poured from the thing, dampening the ground beneath him. And for a moment, it held my attention, and the familiar surge of regret swamped me. Spilling blood, taking lives, it had never set well with me. I did not like to be the instrument of death. Not even to one as evil as he.

But then my gaze went to his face. The bulging, unblinking eyes. The mouth, agape as he suffocated. And I stilled, as recognition flooded me. Kohl. One of Anya's two brutish brothers, as I had suspected. One less to torment me all my days.

Gripping his shoulders, I searched his immobile face, frozen in its dy-ing grimace. "You were no immortal when I first knew you," I said to him. "And well I know how you gained your immortality, Kohl. By mur-der. What I wish to know is, how did you learn of this? Who taught you the way to steal unending life? Who?" But my voice trailed off, as I real-ized he could not answer me. And besides, what answer did I need?

It was obvious what had occurred, and it had been for a very long time now. Somehow Kohl and his brother had learned the secrets of the immortal High Witches. Somehow they had learned that to become one, they need only take the heart of another. And they had done so, long ago. A short time after Anya's death, as near as I could guess it. They had made themselves into a deadly pair of Dark High Witches, and likely I had been their reason for doing so. They had yearned to avenge their father's death, and then their sister's. On me. What did it matter who had taught them?

I lowered my head, closed my eyes, and thought of Anya. Lifting my head again, I saw the life slowly fading from Kohl's face. "I'll not take your heart until you die, Kohl," I said slowly. Knowing full well that had our positions been reversed, he'd delight in carving my own immortal heart from my chest while I still lived. "I'll do it before you have time to revive. You'll feel no pain. Make your peace, Kohl. You'll not be waking from death this time. Your life is over."

He blinked once and I sensed he would have spoken had he been able. To curse me? To thank me? How could I know? But taking his heart was the only way to ensure he stay dead. For immortals, be they Dark or Light, would revive from any death, so long as their hearts remained within them. And the hearts themselves would beat long into the future, even when removed. Imprisoned in small boxes, they were the stolen sources of the Dark Ones' power. My own immortality was earned in another way, for I was of the Light. My power came from the Source of all power, not from doing murder. I had no need of Kohl's heart nor the power it held. But I must take it all the same. And burn it, for that was the only way to release his soul.

The light in Kohl's eyes finally died. And still I waited, just to be sure. When his body began to grow cool, I removed his breastplate, and carved into his chest.

Arianna borrowed a horse from the stables Joseph kept within the keep walls. She headed out in the direction she had seen Nicodimus take, and then followed the deeply embedded tracks of his horse's pounding hooves. Once she had picked up the trail by the light of the moon, it was easy enough to guess where he was headed. To the Stone Circle. The Crones had shown her the place once. They had spoken of it with great reverence, but seemed afraid of the power they said the place held.

It was not difficult to find the place again. And when she neared it, she knew Nicodimus was nearby. She need only come within a short distance of him to feel his presence. And she felt him now. That tingling awareness that seemed to brush over her flesh. The dark sense of him fill-

ing her. Gods, how she loved him. Wanted him. Craved him the way
some men craved their whiskey. Strong, he was, but so tender. His touch
would be gentle and powerful all at once. He would teach her what this
yearning in her belly meant. And how to quench it. He was the only man
who could.

"Gods, how I love you, Nicodimus," she whispered. "Never has any
man touched my soul as you have done." And now, oh, now, if only he
would touch her body in the same way. Her fantasies of him had carried
her this far, but they were no longer enough. She *needed* him . . . not in
her mind, but in her arms, in her bed, inside her.

She closed her eyes, and the now familiar feeling of moisture gathered between her legs. It had been happening frequently of late, this new
sensation, the dampness. The empty feeling, yearning to be filled.
Maiden she may be, but learned as well. The Crones had spoken of such
things, taught her what her mother would not. According to them, the
pleasure to be had in mating was intense and wonderful and not at all sinful. A woman, they said, would experience as much pleasure as a man,
and it was natural that it be so. Not shameful, not immoral, but good
and right, and as our Creator intended. For did not the entire Universe
come about by the mating of Goddess and God? Was not our Source
truly the union of the two? As above, so below. All is but a reflection of
itself.

She wanted to feel that magick with Nicodimus. She wanted to be
one with him. It was meant to happen. She knew it was. He was the missing part of herself. She was his. He would realize it one day. He had to.

Shaking herself out of the deep contemplation into which she had
fallen, she dismounted from the dun mare she'd taken, and moved forward, bare feet brushing the ferns and woodland grasses and mossy
stones. And slowly, bit by bit, she emerged into the clearing.

Then she went still, and caught her breath. At first she saw only the
Stone Circle, the sight of which filled her with as much awe and reverence now as it had the only other time she'd glimpsed it. It seemed to
have been created by a race of giants, for she could think of no other
creature capable of standing such massive structures upright, much less
securing them deep enough within the earth to remain that way.

But then the scene taking place within the circle caught her attention,
and her blood congealed at the horror of it.

Two men, within the sacred circle. One lying still atop a pile of brush,
like a miniature funeral pyre about to be lit. He was obviously dead. His
chest had been laid open, and his clothing was soaked in blood. The

other man stood above him, his hands held high, and in those hands rested a bloody mass that nearly made Arianna retch to see it.

She whirled away, clinging to a tree with one hand, moving behind it as if to shield herself from the gruesome sight. Head bowed low, eyes closed tightly, she fought to catch her breath as her stomach churned. But something compelled her to look again. Something forced her to see . . . to know . . .

Slowly, she forced her eyes open, and lifted her head. Peering around the tree, she made herself look. Really look and see what was happening. And when she did, a soft sound rose in her throat entirely against her will.

The man standing was Nicodimus. And the thing in his hands . . . was a human heart.

A heart that was still quivering . . . beating. . . .

The sound she made was half gasp, half cry. And when she uttered it, she clasped a hand to her lips. But too late. Nicodimus's head turned sharply, his keen eyes scanning the woods, and landing unerringly upon her. His lips parted, as if he would speak, and he reached toward her with a hand stained scarlet.

Arianna backed away, shaking her head, unable to speak or even to cry. Good Gods, what was this? What sort of Witch was he? And what kind of evil drove him to . . .

She did not want to know. Suddenly she feared the man she had always loved. His secrets were far too many and too deep . . . and darker than she had ever imagined.

Even as he took a step toward her, Arianna whirled and raced away, frantically untying the reins before leaping onto the mare's back and wheeling her about. Kicking the mare's sides, she galloped into the forest.

She must run, she told herself. She must! For the hands that held a ghastly still-beating heart skyward in some sick offering to whatever Gods lived in Nicodimus's soul, must never touch her. Never!

Chapter 10

Hastily, I built a pyre within the circle. Hastily, for I'd no wish to have Kohl revive before I did what must be done. His wounds would heal, and I would be bound to kill or be killed all over again. Already I felt my own torn flesh begin to tingle, mending itself as it always would—no matter the injury—unless my own heart were taken from me.

Slinging his lifeless body over my shoulder, I laid Kohl upon the pyre, and there I took his heart. Flint ready in my pocket, kindling laid, I held the heart high above my head, and whispered the words I had long used for such grim occasions as this.

"By the powers of the Ancient Ones, by the force of my Creator, and by my will, I commend this body to the fire, and this heart to the flame, and this soul to its Source. Go forth, Kohl, and ponder the lessons of this lifetime. And return, one day, to live again, enlightened by all you have learned. Go in peace, my brother. As I will it, and with harm to none, so mote it be."

For a long moment, I held the heart high, pushing my will into it, feeling it begin to slow, to release its life force bit by bit. But even before I could place it upon the pyre, a soft sound startled me out of my state of intense concentration. A sound so pained, so hurting, that it cut right to my soul. I snapped my head 'round in search of the source of that cry, knowing even before I saw her there, that Arianna had found me, had seen this wretched deed I did. And the knowledge brought with it a fierce surge of regret.

I spotted her there, clinging to a large oak, staring at me from beyond it. Her eyes were wide with surprise and shock and something I had hoped never to see in them. Fear. Fear of me. I tried to speak, not knowing what to say, even lifted a hand toward her, but she turned and fled as if she'd seen some monster instead of her husband.

And indeed, she likely believed she had.

With a heavy heart, I returned to my grim task. For to leave it unfinished would make me the exact monster my wife seemed to believe I was. It must be done. I would deal with Arianna later, though I had no idea how or what I could say. I should, perhaps, have told her what I was long before now. But I had not. Now I had no choice.

Calming my frantic heart, I placed Kohl's atop the pyre, near his feet. Then kneeling, I struck the flint until it produced a spark and ignited the kindling. There I waited until the flames danced high, and the body was too far consumed for there to be any hope of someone coming along and snatching it out in time. The heart, too, sizzled and oozed as the flames roasted it, burned it, then reduced it to smoldering ash.

Only when all was complete, did I dare leave and go off in search of my runaway bride, to try to explain what she had witnessed. And I must hurry, before her emotions made her do something foolish. For her to learn the truth was inevitable. For her to learn it like this, unforgivable.

Even now, I was uncertain just how much I should tell her. She was so young, and so incredibly vulnerable to me. To tell her what I was, how I must live, was going to be shocking enough to rock her right to her soul. But to tell her that she was the same . . . I was not sure I could bring myself to do that. Not yet. I resolved to wait, to see her reactions to the first of my frightening revelations before deciding if she were ready for the rest. The truth. The frightening, shocking truth, of what she was. An immortal High Witch, who would one day be forced to commit the same violence she'd just seen me do. Or have it performed upon her by one of the Dark Ones.

The knowledge could easily destroy my fragile little cat. And for the first time I realized that if it did, it might well destroy me, too.

I returned to the keep only to be told that Arianna had left with a small pouch of her belongings. Joseph's sons had already set out to search for her along the roads leading away from the village. But I didn't think she would leave Stonehaven. Not yet. I knew Arianna, or thought I did, better than anyone. So I went to the places where I knew she would go for solace. Her parents' home in the village, the cemetery where her beloved sister lay buried, the shores of the loch.

And finally, to the site of The Crones' cottage. That was where I found her. Alone, sitting on a small boulder with her knees drawn to her chest and her arms wrapped tight around them. Her face lowered, her dress absorbing her tears. Trembling and frightened, I found her. More kitten than cat just then. Vulnerable and afraid. I knew I would have to treat her gently, or see her bolt.

It twisted my heart into a knot to see her hurting, to know that her pain belonged to me.

The night wind whispered her name as I stepped slowly closer, and then I repeated its loving refrain.

"Arianna."

Her head came up fast, brown eyes wide, unblinking. Cheeks red with tear tracks, full lips trembling. "Leave me alone, Nicodimus." Her voice shook with emotion, with fear. Of me.

"I can't do that. I . . . I need to explain. What you saw, it wasn't . . ."

Her eyes narrowed on me, seeming to pierce right through my skin. "Wasn't what? Murder?"

Sighing deeply, I turned and sat beside her on the boulder. My elbows resting on my knees, bent forward at the waist, not looking at her, I said, "It was not murder. Kohl was trying his best to kill me, and I had no choice but to defend myself."

"By cuttin' out his heart?" Her voice broke on those words, and when I turned my head to look at her, I saw the grimace on her face, the horror of the memory in her eyes.

"It was . . . necessary."

"What sorts of Gods do you serve, Nicodimus, that would require such a gruesome sacrifice?"

I closed my eyes slowly. "I'll tell you, Arianna. If you'll listen, I'll tell you my secrets. Things you likely won't believe. But true, all of them, utterly true."

She said nothing, so I lifted my gaze to hers again, searched her face. And she said, "Goddess help me, for I am a hopeless fool. I want you to explain it all away, Nicodimus. I want to believe in you again. So I'm listenin'."

I nodded, drew a breath, nodded again. "All right. All right, then. But first . . . first, Arianna, know this. I would never hurt you. Never. Do you believe that?"

Again her eyes met mine, probed, searched. A little less fear, and more of her natural curiosity lighting them. "'Tis difficult to believe in the tenderness of a man I just saw holdin' a bloodied heart in his hands . . . a heart that . . ." She closed her eyes, gave her head a quick shake. "But that's impossible."

"Nothing is impossible," I said softly. "Nothing." It was going to be difficult to explain all of this to her. "What did you see, Arianna, that you believe impossible?"

She tilted her head to one side, remembering, and a little shiver worked through her. "It appeared that the heart was . . . was still beatin', Nicodimus. But 'twas only my shocked mind playin' tricks on me."

"You've no idea how I wish that were the case."

She blinked. "What are you sayin'?"

Drawing a breath, I said, "Let me begin at the beginning, Arianna. I only ask that you not run from me . . . at least, not until I've finished. The things I'm going to tell you will shock and upset you. But they are things you need to know and understand. Things I . . . likely should have told you a long time ago."

She thought a moment, then nodded once. "All right. I suppose 'tis little enough to ask. You've saved my life on more than one occasion. I owe you as much."

"You owe me nothing."

"I differ with you on that point. But let's nay argue. Just tell me these secrets of which you speak, an' make me understand why you butchered that man so brutally. For I trusted you, Nicodimus, an' what I saw frightened that trust away. I only want to understand, an' find it again."

"You want me to restore your faith in me," I said slowly, clarifying it in my own mind. Wondering if she'd be better off if I stopped here and now. But no. She had to know. We shared a fate, she and I.

"I was born into a tiny clan that once made its home here, at the site of this very village. And the year was seven hundred and fifty."

She smiled then. Smiled broadly, and punched me lightly on my arm. "Be serious, now, Nicodimus. An' stop jesting with me. 'Twould make you o'er seven hundred years old."

"Seven hundred and fifty, Arianna."

She stared at me. Her smile faltered and died.

I said no more, and gave her a moment to digest that bit of information. She clearly didn't believe me. It was evident in everything from the

sudden worry clouding her magnificent brown eyes to the slight stiffening of her muscles. No doubt the question of my sanity was even now
occurring to my lovely bride. And I disliked seeing it there.

"You mean," she began, slowly, cautiously, "you *feel* that old. But of
course, you are not."

"Do you remember, Arianna, the way I looked when you first set eyes
on me?"

She nodded at once. "Every detail," she whispered, then quickly
turned her head away and I saw her cheeks color prettily, despite the
darkness.

"And have I changed in all that time?" I asked her. "Aged at all?"

She frowned, pondering. "I . . . have often wondered how you hide
your age so well."

"I hide my age so well because I do not age. My body hasn't aged
since I was twenty and eight, Arianna, and it never will." I paused, turned
to face her and took both of her hands in mine. Warm, they were. Soft as
satin, with nimble, slender fingers that were quick and clever. I loved the
way her hands looked—small and strong, yet willing to nestle into the
grip of my larger ones. I liked closing mine around them, holding her.
And I didn't give it any more thought than that. Though I recall very
clearly the word that whispered insistently and in an unfamiliar tone, a
possessive commanding tone, through my mind. The word was *Mine.*

"Arianna," I said. "I am . . . I am immortal."

Her head dipped slightly, eyes seeming to plumb mine even as they
narrowed to mere slits. "Immortal?" she whispered. And now her hands
turned, her beautiful fingers lacing with mine, and she squeezed.
"Nicodimus . . . love, you know that canna be." Then one hand broke
free, and her fingers gently probed and rubbed over my head, through
my hair, searching every inch. "You may have been injured in the battle,"
she said quickly. "With that man . . . Kohl, you called him. Oh,
Nicodimus, I know you didna do murder back there. I was only shocked
to see such violence, an' afraid, an' still very upset with you for leaving
me alone on the night of our wedding, an' so my emotions got away
from me, I suppose, an' I—"

"Cease."

She did. Biting her lip, she stopped the stream of nervous words that
had been spilling out of her without censure. I think she knew even then
that there was some truth to what I said. How much, she could not know.
But she needed to speak, and fast, to keep me from saying any more.

"I am not injured. I was, but 'tis healed now."

The worry in her brown eyes deepened. "No one heals so quickly," she said softly. "Where were you hurt, Nicodimus? Show me, and let me tend the wounds."

I nodded. "Yes. Yes, I must show you. 'Tis the only way to get past your disbelief. There is much you need to know, my little cat, but we cannot proceed until we rid you of your skepticism."

"Aye," she said slowly, humoring me. "Aye, just show me. I am your wife, and tendin' your wounds is my duty. Let me help you, love."

I nodded, and turned away from her, so my back blocked her view. Then, moving very quickly, I drew my dagger with its jeweled hilt, and pushing back my sleeve, I drew its blade across my forearm.

"Nicodimus, nay!" Arianna leapt to her feet, seeing what I had done, but not in time to prevent it. Weeping aloud, she reached for the deep gash in my flesh, as if she would grip it tight and try to stop the bleeding. But I drew my arm out of her reach, held up a hand.

"Just wait, Arianna. Just wait." With one hand I smoothed her hair, my eyes on the gash, watching it. But when I heard her sobs I looked up, saw the distress, the twin rivulets of tears. She was shaking all over. And I was suddenly full of regret. I reached for her. "Arianna . . ."

But her eyes were widening, and focused unblinkingly on the cut. And when I looked down again, I realized the blood flow was slowing visibly. Arianna took a stuttering breath as it stopped entirely, then stepped backward with a soft gasp as the skin 'round the edges of the wound began slowly, bit by bit, regenerating.

"Please," I asked her, when she took another halting step backward. "Please, do not be afraid. It is what I am, Arianna. This is what I am."

She searched my face, stared deeply into my eyes, her own growing less fearful by slight degrees. Her feet moved, but this time to bring her closer, and she reached out a tentative hand, to touch, drew away, and touched again. "Oh . . . oh, my . . ." she whispered, and sank to her knees at my feet, drawing my arm with her, clutching it in hers. She lifted the hem of her robe, and before I knew what she was about to do, wiped the blood away from my arm. Then she watched, trembling on her knees as the cut slowly healed. Her fingers trailed over the new skin, soft, erotic, sending a bolt of awareness straight to my soul, like lightning searing hot and shattering.

"Good Gods, 'tis true. . . ." She lifted her huge, innocent eyes to mine. "But how? How can this be?"

"For a very long while, I did not know. I still do not know all of it. The why of it, or how it all works. I only know that long ago, in my village, I believed myself to be an ordinary man. I hunted, I fought. I was a warrior, skilled and proud, and would have been chieftain of my clan one day. I had a wife and two strong sons."

At this point, Arianna's head snapped up. "Not just a wife then. But a family," she whispered. Slowly rising until standing, she faced me. "Tell me of them, Nicodimus. Tell me of your family. And of the woman who captured your love."

Nodding, I lowered my head. "Her name was . . . was Anya."

Arianna's small hand came to my face, cupping it, fingers tracing my cheeks. "You loved her," she whispered. "Nay, dinna look as if you regret it, husband. You've told me of your love for Anya before, an 'tis a relief to know you loved once. I'd begun to fear you were incapable of it."

I shook my head, considered telling her she had the right of it. That I was incapable of loving . . . now. But then decided I had hurt her enough, and my revelations would soon do so even more. Enough of causing her pain.

"How long were you together?" she asked, taking my hand now, leading me back to sit on the boulder as if she were the experienced sage, and I the innocent. She urged me downward, then curled her legs beneath her and sat on the ground at my feet, close to me. Her body leaning against my thighs.

"I was but four and ten when I found her. She was the daughter of an enemy chieftain. Our men took her father's life in battle, and I found her in her village, being beaten by her two brothers, Marten and Kohl. She'd been mistreated all her life. So I took her."

"As prisoner?" she asked. No judgment in her tone, just curiosity.

"The choice was hers. I took her, yes, but I may have left her behind, had she asked it of me." I shrugged. "Or perhaps not. At any rate, she did not object, so I took her. And back in my village, I made her my wife, and gave her my promise that no man would ever raise a hand to harm her again. 'Twas a promise I kept."

Arianna's hand touched my thigh, and she dipped her head, as if she were studying her fingers with great interest. "Was she . . . very beautiful?"

"She was comely. Small and frail. With the temperament of a mouse, Arianna. Wary and afraid, but eventually she came to trust me, and to love me. We had a good life together. She cared for my needs and I for hers. She gave me my sons, the most precious things in the world to me."

Arianna blinked and lifted her eyes to mine. "She sounds like my opposite. She couldna have been more unlike me."

"'Tis true enough," I told her.

And she quickly looked away, hiding her eyes from my scrutiny. "Tell me of the children."

"Jaymes was the younger. Timid and tall for his age. Sickly. But bright, beyond measure. He was constantly working figures, numbers and such. He could draw any likeness, and play the pipes like Pan Himself. Will was the elder. Strong, a warrior, a strapping lad with a temper to match. It was all I could do to keep that one in line. Had he lived much longer, he'd have been fully capable of besting his sire in a fair fight."

Darkening with understanding and sympathy, her eyes turned up toward mine again. "Oh, Nicodimus. You lost them."

I closed my eyes. "I lost them all. Anya died struggling to give birth to our third child, a wee girl who never lived to draw her first breath. After four and ten years with her, I didn't think I could live without her, but somehow I did. My lads needed me, then. I had no choice."

"You are very strong," Arianna whispered. "I've always known that about you." Her arms had somehow twisted 'round my waist, and her head rested on my thigh. "An' a fine father you must have been to those lads."

"I tried. By the Gods, Arianna, I tried. But Jaymes died when the Black Death swept through our village later that same year. And a year later, Will and I were cut down side by side, in battle with the same clan from whence I'd taken his mother."

"Oh, Nicodimus . . ." she whispered, head rising, hands stroking along my back. "Oh, my love, I am so very sorry. I know this grief that lives in you. I know it well."

"I know you do," I told her, studying her eyes seeing the tears pooling there. "You've felt it, too."

"So you and Will were wounded . . . in this battle?" she asked.

"No," I said. "No, Arianna, we were . . . we were killed."

She sat up straighter. "No, my love . . ."

"Yes. I'd a blade thrust straight through my heart, Arianna. There was no question. I died beside my son on the field of battle. But moments later, I lived again. Consciousness returned, and with it a blinding flash of pain and light. My body arched until I thought my spine would snap, and I dragged in a desperate gasp that failed to satisfy my starving lungs. I opened my eyes and stared, first at the blade which skewered me still, and then at my beloved son, lying lifeless at my side. And a rage filled me such as none I had ever known. I gripped the hilt of the sword, and pulled it from my chest. I howled in rage that Will should be dead, and I alive, with no one left, no one at all. Even before my grief abated, I felt a tingling sensation, saw the bleeding stop, and watched in awe as the mortal wound in my chest healed itself.

"Someone saw me then, and shouted that I'd been dead, my body already cooling, only moments before. I was confused and maddened with grief, and so I ran. I ran away."

Soft, cooling palms skimmed my face, and big brown eyes, brimming with tears, traced my features with healing tenderness. "Aye, Nicodimus. An' you've been runnin' ever since. From love. From carin' of any kind. Because it hurts to love and lose, you've decided nay to love at all."

I nodded, amazed, and not for the first time, by her insights. "You are very wise for one so young."

"'Tis nay my age which makes me know your heart, Nicodimus. 'Tis my own grief. I, too, wished never to suffer loss again. I believe 'tis why I drew away from those closest to me. Even my own dear mother." As she spoke, she lay her head down once again.

I looked down at her, blond hair spread over my legs as her head rested gently there. "Then perhaps you do understand."

"To have lost my sister nearly destroyed me," she went on, lifting her head now, and stroking my cheek with one hand. "I canna imagine the pain of losing a child . . . much less two of them, an' your newborn . . . an' your wife."

I closed my hand over hers on my face, and gently moved it away, for her touch was eliciting more emotion from within me than I had realized was hidden inside. "'Tis the way of things, for me . . . for my kind."

Her hand stilled in midair, eyes widening. "You mean you're nay the only one? There . . . there are others?"

I felt my lips pull into a smile at her innocence and wonder. "Hundreds," I told her. "And all of us cursed to outlive all of those we love."

Blinking rapidly, she finally averted her face. "I could never exist that way," she whispered, her voice choked with emotion. "Never!"

And my throat went dry, because I knew she must. But I couldn't tell her that. Not yet.

Eventually, she looked back at me. "I ken now why you canna love me, Nicodimus. I'll never ask it of you again."

I looked into her eyes, as dark and fathomless as the night itself, and I felt an odd tug in the center of my chest. It felt like . . . regret. But that made no sense, whatsoever.

But she gave me no time to examine the feeling.

"Where did you go?"

I only looked at her blankly, still pondering my own heart. "Where did I—"

"When you ran away," she clarified, staring up at me, wide-eyed and rapt with attention.

"Of course." I focused my mind back on my tale. "I wandered for a time, stopping at crofts and working for a meal and a place to lay my head before moving on again. Eventually, I decided to make my way back to my village, my people. I'd been searching for answers, but I'd found none. I'd been traveling aimlessly over the whole of Scotland for well over two years. And I was still no closer to understanding why I lived. But I had noticed things, changes in me. Though these things only served to puzzle me more."

"What sorts of changes?" she asked, nearly breathless now with anticipation.

"They were gradual," I explained. "There was a certain sharpening of my senses. My eyesight grew keener, and I began to see in darkness as well as I did in bright light. My hearing became . . . acute. My sense of smell became as honed as that of the wolf, and I seemed able to taste things more thoroughly, even things on the air. Physical feeling intensified, and with it, physical strength and stamina beyond that of any ordinary man. And then there was the healing . . . any wound I had would heal within a short while, just as I have shown you here this night. And while I suspected I could not easily die, I had no idea that I was immortal."

"How could you?" she asked. "Who would ever imagine such a thing?" She shook her head slowly, her gaze turning inward. "Even though you've shown me this miraculous healing power, I still canna quite grasp the fact that you canna die."

"I can die, Arianna. Just not easily, nor in the usual way."

She perused my features, her brown eyes narrow. "Go on, tell me what happened, how you found the answers you sought."

I rose from the stone to pace away from her. Apparently in thought, but truly because her embrace affected me far more than it should. Far more than I could bear.

"When I returned, it was to find my village destroyed. The crofts of my people burned, the crops lying exposed to the burning sun, withered and ruined, the livestock butchered, their carcasses stinking and bloated. And their owners, for the most part, alongside them in the same or worse condition."

"Oh, Nicodimus," she breathed. "Gods, I'd have collapsed in devastation."

I turned. She'd risen, but stayed near the rock, looking as if she'd like to run to me, to offer comfort, but perhaps, knowing better. "That is very close to what I did. Later, when I managed to move again, I erected a huge pyre, placing upon it the bodies of my clan—my friends and neighbors, my elderly father and my cousins." I lowered my head, shuddering at the memory. "I think I knew even then that the men responsible were Anya's brothers, Marten and Kohl. They'd vowed vengeance on me since the day I took their sister, and only the births of our sons had prevented them leading their clan against us sooner. Evil, they may have been, but even they had enough decency to refrain from embarking on a battle that might wound their own kin."

She nodded slowly. "But once your precious Will was gone, their restraint went with it."

I nodded, my lips tight, my stomach roiling with the memory. "After the fires burned low, I went to the ancient Stone Circle, where the holy men of my clan would go to commune with the spiritual realm, and find peace and wisdom. Common men such as I rarely ventured into the sacred space, but I still had no answers to the questions burning in my soul. And somehow, I thought I would find them nowhere else."

Eyes widening, Arianna tipped her head to one side. "The same Stone Circle where I saw you tonight?"

"Yes, little cat. I vowed I would remain there until the Gods themselves spoke to me, or I would die slowly within its embrace. And there I sat upon the ground, day and night, with neither food nor water. I sat there through rain and storm, through the chill of night and the heat of midday, until my mind became dulled with hunger, and my body parched with thirst. Until I became too weak to sit up, and so lay down instead, my knees curled to my chest, my body trembling. And still I waited, demanding the Gods either speak to me or take my life."

Arianna did come to me then. She stood very close, one hand sliding up my arm. "Obviously, they did not take your life."

"No. They gave me the answers I sought, in the form of a group of men whose roots went back in time, to unknown beginnings. The Druids. Holy men. As it happened, my vigil fell near their springtime rites, the one the Pagans call Beltane. And so they came from their secluded havens, to summon forth the spirits of the trees, and to dance in celebration of the spring."

"And they found you there?"

My hands had found their way to her waist, tiny in the span of my palms. I think I put them there to keep her at a safe distance, but it almost transformed into an embrace. It felt incredibly intimate, standing this way, holding her waist, her hands on my outer arms, her little face turned up to mine.

"One of the hooded, aged men carried me to the edge of the circle, and poured water down me, fed me, wrapped me in a blanket. Then left me there to witness their peculiar rites." I closed my eyes, remembering. "The fiddler played, and they danced and chanted. It was something of rare beauty and power."

I could see her face twist in confusion. No doubt she wondered why I would later sully such a sacred, mystical site with the blood of my enemy. But I would come to that.

"When they left again at dawn, they carried me with them. And at their temples, hidden deep within the forests, they patiently taught me what I was."

"What, Nicodimus? What are you?"

So much eagerness in her eyes. The fear was less now, than it had been before.

"I'm a Witch. An immortal High Witch, Arianna. Far different from village Witches such as The Crones were. Most don't even know of the existence of the High Ones, the immortals."

She took my hand, and led me beside her along a path deeper into the woods. "How did you become this way?"

Her small hand was not cold, nor trembling, but strong, and firm. As if she could somehow comfort me. And amazingly, she was doing just that. "There are two ways," I told her. "It is said that when one dies while attempting to save the life of a Witch, that person will return to his next lifetime with the gift of immortality. He is born, and grows older as any mortal would do, until he experiences physical death for the first time. When that happens, he doesn't remain dead . . . but instead revives to life once more. And from that moment on, he will not age. His senses will sharpen, and his strength will grow. The older he becomes, the stronger he will be."

She nodded, listening intently. "You said there is one way you could experience true death, Nicodimus."

"Yes. Only should someone remove my heart from my chest, will my death be permanent. And even then, it isn't true death, for the body, though lifeless, will never rot away, and the heart, though bodiless, will beat on . . . perhaps forever."

She stopped walking, and with a soft gasp lifted her hand to her breast. "'Tis a nightmare!" Then she blinked . . . and slowly looked up at me. "Then . . . that man in the circle, whose heart you cut out . . ."

"Yes," I told her. "He was immortal. But not like me, Arianna. He was one of the Dark Ones, made immortal by far different means. For as I told you, there are two ways to obtain this endless life, and the second is far less pretty than the first."

She released my hand, and wandered toward the banks of a swift running stream, there to sit down on the soft moss, spreading her skirts beneath her. "Come," she said, patting a spot beside her. "Tell me."

I stood where I was, staring at her, so small and delicate to my eyes. "Perhaps I've shocked you enough for one night, Arianna."

"I'll nay rest until I know all of it," she promised. And again, patted the moss.

Sighing, I went to her, settled down beside her. "All right. Since I know your stubbornness to be legendary, I will go on. But if it becomes more than you can bear—"

"I am far stronger than you know, Nicodimus. Far stronger."

Looking into her eyes, I sighed and relented. "Where there is good there is also evil. You know this."

"Aye," she said. "There can be no light without darkness. 'Tis the way of things. Of nature itself."

I nodded my agreement. "Thus with Witches. There are evil ones among us, those without conscience, without love in their souls. When they find out the secrets of High Witches, they cannot resist seeking out immortality for themselves."

"And how can they gain it, Nicodimus?"

"By killing one of us. By taking the heart from our chest, and holding it captive in a small box. So long as they possess the heart, they possess the immortality, and the power of its rightful owner. In time, the heart will weaken, and the Dark Witch with it. So they are compelled to take another, and another. It is the only way they can live on."

"I see." She said it slowly, thoughtfully. Then, drawing a deep breath, met my gaze straight on. "You say you are one of the Light Ones, Nicodimus. And yet I just saw you take a living heart."

I stiffened. That she could, even for a moment, believe me to be one of the Dark Ones. . . . I nearly spoke without thinking, nearly told her of the birthmarks we all bear, the Light upon the right flank, the Dark upon the left, in order to prove to her my innocence. But I bit the words back in the barest instant before I would have spoken them. For if she knew of the birthmark's significance she would have to know that she was as I am. Immortal, just like me. And I was convinced my tender cat was not ready for that information. Not yet. Hadn't she already told me she'd rather die than to outlive all those she loved?

"I took his heart because it was the only way to ensure he stay dead. And I did not keep it, Arianna. I burned it on a pyre, the heart as well as the body. For that was the one way to free Kohl's immortal soul."

She inhaled deeply, lowering her pretty chin, but then her head came up again, eyes wide. "Kohl? Nicodimus, this man was the one who attacked you before . . . he was . . ."

"My brother-in-law," I said, nodding slowly. "I have no idea how he learned the secret, but he and his brother did so. They both managed to take living hearts and capture immortality for themselves. And it makes sense to me that they did so. If they had learned I was immortal, they would have gone to any lengths to become the same. Their only wish was to live long enough to kill me, the man who killed their father, humiliated them before their own clan, stole away their sister. They blamed me for Anya's death as well. And they always vowed they would have vengeance on me one day."

"What of the other one, Nicodimus?"

I shook my head. "If they had been together they would no doubt have attacked me as one. Unfair, but they have never been men of ethics or honor. And Marten is a far more accomplished Witch than Kohl. He's even mastered the art of setting fires with but his will over the centuries. I'd have had much more trouble defeating Marten. No, Arianna, if Kohl attacked me alone, then his brother must be far away."

Her hand came up to stroke my face. "I'm sorry for you, Nicodimus. It must be truly horrible to know you have been hated so much for so long." Then she shook her head slowly. "And to live being hunted by the Dark Ones. For that is how you must live, is it not?"

"Yes. It is. Coming here, to this place, has always been my escape from that life. But one of them found me, even here."

"Aye," she said. "But that one is no more."

"I never meant to bring the darkness to this place. . . . To you . . ."

Her smile was gentle, and small. "I dinna doubt that, Nicodimus."

"But where one can find me, others may well follow."

She sat a little straighter. "They will have me to contend with, do they wish to harm my husband," she declared.

And that made me smile. But then she hugged me quite fiercely, her arms tight around my waist, her head pressing to my chest. "Dinna laugh at me, Nicodimus. I mean what I say."

My arms went 'round her, seemingly of their own volition. Such a strong, stubborn woman. She touched something deep within me. The scent of her hair seemed to tangle itself 'round my senses, and tug me gently closer.

"Take me to the Stone Circle, next full moon," she said softly. "The Crones were afraid to perform magickal rites there. But I wish to feel the power you spoke of, to know it for myself."

It was not in my power to deny her. I thought then, that anything she asked of me, I would gladly do.

Anything . . . except love her. I must never do that.

Never . . .

Chapter 11

Arianna understood. Now so much more than before. Perhaps Nicodimus would love her . . . if only he could. But he could not. Oh, she did not believe for a moment that his heart had died with his family. No, his heart was strong in him, and filled with tender emotions. She had seen the pain in his eyes as he'd spoken of his lost family. One could not hurt if one were incapable of loving. Indeed, she had begun to think her husband had more love inside him than anyone she had ever known. But not for her. Nay, not for her. He could not risk loving her, nor would she ask it of him. For he knew—and now she did as well—the consequences loving her would bring. He would be forced to watch her grow old, while he remained young and strong. He would have to watch her die, leaving him behind. Immortal and utterly alone.

She thought on these things as she rode before him on his fiery black stallion, her back pressed to his chest, his hand at her waist. She thought on these things and more. And she realized that she had to give up her dreams of making him love her. For his sake. She loved him too much to ask him to suffer such unspeakable anguish because of her. She would not ask it of him again.

He glanced down at her, concern etched on his face. "The things I've told you tonight . . . they've shocked you."

She thought on that for a moment. "Shocked, aye. But enlightened, as well. I ken your heart more now than ever I have, Nicodimus. An' 'tis glad I am you finally shared your secrets with me."

His steady gaze made her wish for more than could ever be as he replied, "I always intended to tell you all of this. I only . . . thought to wait until I judged you ready to hear it. I thought . . ."

"You thought a girl so young and flighty too immature to deal with these truths. You thought I would run in fear of you, or give myself nightmares."

He frowned, a hint of guilt appearing on his face. "I only thought to protect your tender heart and mind from such dark truths as these."

At that, Arianna smiled. "My heart is far from tender, Nicodimus. I am strong. Far stronger than you know."

"And far more vulnerable than *you* know, little cat."

"Nay. 'Tis not so. In time, you'll see."

He returned her smile, but his was doubtful, tentative. And slowly a more serious expression replaced it. "I've trusted you with these secrets, Arianna. And secrets, they must remain. Understand that."

"Aye," she replied. "Nicodimus, I ken full well the need for secrecy in this. An' I would die of torture before revealin' a word of what you've told me this eve. I swear it to you on the name of my sister."

He blinked as if in surprise at the vehemence in her voice. But she meant what she said, and used the only words she could think of to convince him of that. He believed her, she thought. For he nodded firmly, and turned his attention back to the path ahead.

The keep rose dark and towering before them, and only as they drew near did she think of something she had not asked. "What of Nidaba? Is she . . . is she a High Witch as well?"

He glanced her way. "Nidaba's secrets are not mine to share. But if you ask her, Arianna, I believe she will be as honest with you as I have been. She does not show it, but I sense that deep down she is fond of you, for some reason."

She lifted a hand to her breast as if wounded. "Am I so onerous that this surprises you?"

He met her eyes, a reluctant smile tugging at his lips. "Naught you might do could surprise me," he said. "And you know full well you're the farthest thing from onerous. It is simply that Nidaba tends to . . . shy away from intimacies, bonds of any kind where caring is involved."

"Aye," she said, smiling back at him now. "Except with you." He conceded the point with a nod, and Arianna told herself she'd no right to feel jealous.

Side by side they rode through the gates, and dismounted. Nicodimus took the reins, and led his horse into the stables. And he didn't object when Arianna walked with him into the dark, hay-scented outbuilding. He removed the saddle, the bridle, reached for a rag and began rubbing his stallion briskly.

She felt a bit guilty for not having taken proper care of the mare she'd borrowed earlier. And while Nicodimus worked on Black, she went to where the dun mare stood, and brushed her coat. When Nicodimus gave Black some grain, she gave some to the mare as well, and thought she saw approval in her husband's eyes.

Arianna tilted her head when he faced her once more. "I suppose your aversion to closeness must not extend to animals. For I believe you think more highly of your horse than your wife."

She was teasing. But Nicodimus didn't jest with her in return. Instead he took both her hands in his, and stared into her eyes. "You must never think that, Arianna. I do care for you. More than is probably wise."

Her hands warmed where he held them, and her heart seemed to quicken its beat. But she closed her eyes and reminded herself she must be strong. Must not give in to the yearning of her body . . . nor to that of her heart. "You needn't spew lies to comfort me, Nicodimus. I've told you, I am the strongest person I know. An' now that you've explained your past to me, I'll be content to be your wife in name only. I ken why 'tis necessary, an' I willna go back on my word." He parted his lips to say more, but she shook her head firmly. "Nay, no more. Save your carin' for your horse, husband. I've no need of it. Truly. You saved my life by wed-din' me, an' 'tis enough. More than enough."

He frowned at her, studying her there in the darkness as if unable to comprehend her words.

"Dinna you ken, Nicodimus? I'm only agreein' to the terms you laid down afore our marriage. I'll nay try to make you love me, only to watch me age an' die while you remain alone. Is this nay the very thing you wanted of me?"

As they walked together out of the stable and began crossing the courtyard, which was, for once, void of any clansmen, his frown deep-ened and he nodded. "Yes, I . . . I suppose it is."

"Then you have it." She lowered her head, bit her lower lip. "How-ever, I would ask one concession of you."

"One concession?" He crooked a single dark brow. "Now you have me curious. Go on, what is it?"

Lifting her chin, she cleared her throat and met his eyes. "I believe the laird and Nidaba would exercise discretion, but as for Kenyon an' Lud, I have doubts. Besides, servants are known for gossip, an' there are servants aplenty in this household. An' the rest of the clan, coming an' going all the while."

"Indeed," he said. "There are. And they do gossip."

She nodded firmly. "Aye. Were it known my husband preferred sleepin' in the hall or the stables to sharin' my bed, I'd be shamed, Nicodimus. Ridiculed an' a cause for amusement to the entire clan."

Nicodimus kept his gaze trained on the ground rather than on her, no doubt displeased with the direction her thoughts had taken. But she forced herself to go on.

"I would ask, Nicodimus, that you at least make a pretense of feelin' . . . affection for me . . . of our marriage bein' a real one, rather than a lie designed to protect me from my own rebellious ways. Allow me to salvage my pride, an' walk without shame among my clan." Still he said nothing. Her voice softer, she rushed on. "After all, 'twill only be for a short while. Only until you leave me again, as you said you would."

He brought his head up sharply, his eyes intense now.

"I'm sorry," she said. "I've angered you. If you find the idea so distasteful, Nicodimus, then please, put it from your mind. I'll deal with the ridicule. The Gods know I have before." She turned away, striding toward the keep, a short distance away.

Nicodimus's hand on her shoulder brought her to a stop. "No, Arianna. 'Tis I who am sorry. My anger was with myself for not thinking of this sooner. Already, I've given the clan reason to talk, by riding off alone on our wedding night the way I did. I'll not give them any more."

She didn't turn around, for if she did, he would see the tears that burned inexplicably in her eyes. "Thank you, husband."

"I will say I went riding to give you time to prepare for me," he said, softly. "And as for your own jaunt tonight, the tale will be . . ." He thought for a moment, and when he spoke again, his voice was different. Quieter than before, and slightly coarse. "The tale will be that my passion for my chaste young bride was such that it frightened her. That she ran away, and that I fetched her back home only to ravage her still more."

As he spoke, his hand on her shoulder moved in what might have been an unintended caress. Soft, his touch. Calloused, his palm on her tender skin, she felt it even through the robe that covered her. The words he spoke brought a foreign longing alive in the pit of her stomach, and made her feel breathless and warm.

"'Tis . . . a good tale," she whispered. "I . . . I am feelin' a mite ill, Nicodimus. My stomach is behavin' quite badly just now. Flutterin' an' . . . odd."

When he said nothing, she chanced a look over her shoulder at him. He offered a strained smile, and swept her hair away from her forehead with a featherlight touch. "You'll be fine," he told her gently. "The feeling . . . will pass."

He didn't sound certain of that. Nonetheless, he turned her 'round, and gripping her elbow, walked her to the doors. But when they strode through the great hall, they were greeted by worried questions from a half dozen people. Joseph, Nidaba, and Kenyon and Lud, all while a handful of Joseph's men looked on with speculative expressions.

Nicodimus met her eyes once, and she saw the silent message in them. His pretense would begin now. Ignoring them all, he scooped Arianna up into his arms, and strode with her to the far end of the room and the stone stairway there. And as he did he spoke, his tone intimate, but loud enough so they could hear. "I'll be gentler this time, my love. I promise." And before mounting the first step, he bent and pressed his mouth to hers.

Arianna's heart nearly beat a hole through her chest. And yet that great emptiness remained. Oh, if only this were real. If only it could someday be . . . real.

I only wanted to protect her. No, that wasn't entirely true. I wanted her. I knew that. My body craved hers the way any healthy man's body would crave that of a beautiful woman . . . especially knowing that woman wanted him, too. Before, I had been half convinced Arianna would seduce me into her arms . . . into her bed . . . before we'd been married a week. I had told myself I would resist her, but I had already known I could never withstand her charms for very long.

But tonight . . . tonight everything had changed. *She* had changed. Suddenly so willing to agree to my terms. Vowing to leave me alone, and to have me play the part of the passionate husband only in front of the others. And I had realized then that not having her, not taking her, was again a possibility. Attainable, perhaps with ease.

That knowledge made me want her more than ever, however foolish such a thing may seem. So that when I spoke the tale I would spread among the clan, I saw the images of it in my mind. Fetching my runaway bride home, and carrying her up to our chamber to savor every inch of her, to exercise all of my husbandly rights. I had grown aroused beyond endurance at the thought, and more so when I realized she had as well. Stomach ailment, indeed. My innocent bride did not even recognize raw desire for what it was.

When I scooped her up, held her against me, promised to be gentle, and then tasted her succulent mouth, my desire for her burned still hotter, and for just an instant on that darkened stairway, I allowed myself to savor the fantasy . . . then became lost in it.

Hands tangling in her hair, I pressed her mouth open wide, and licked inside with my tongue. My hands began to caress the parts of her I held, one in perfect reach of a firm, rounded breast, and the other stroking her outer thigh. I felt her nipple harden against my palm, and nearly groaned with the force of the need that rocked through me. And all the while my feet carried her faster to the top of the stairway, then down the corridors. I kicked the chamber door open when I reached it, and strode through to lay her down upon the waiting bed.

It was her hands on my chest that finally made me realize what I was doing to her. My little cat lay breathless, her face flushed, eyes wide and staring up at me. I straightened slowly, pushing a hand through my hair as I turned away. Averting my gaze in shame, I walked to the door, pushed it closed. "I . . . I apologize, Arianna."

On a breathless sigh, she whispered, "I . . . I'd no idea you could be so . . . convincing. For a moment I thought you meant to . . . to . . ."

I looked back at her, but she clamped her lips tight and said no more. How was I to do this? Spend the night at her side and not touch her? It would surely take a saint to accomplish such a feat. I was no saint.

She tried a smile, though it was confused and tremulous. "Surely every person in the place was convinced as well," she suggested. Then slowly, she got to her feet. "'Tis so very warm here, dinna you think? I vow, 'twas not so when I left earlier."

She pulled at the ties that held her robe in place, and tossed it aside without a care.

What I saw then . . .

I could only stare for a long moment. "Arianna," I whispered. I sank to my knees to keep myself from moving any nearer. But I was unable to take my eyes from her body, for it was utterly revealed to me, every part of it, by the sheer fabric she wore. "By the Gods, woman, what do you think I'm made of?"

Blinking, she glanced down at herself, and then went so red the blush was like fire. "Damnation!" she cried, and she spun around, and snatched the coverlet from the bed to hold over her.

But it was too late, for the image of her was burned into my mind. And I knew it would haunt me. Breasts, high and proud, with full, sweet curves, and nipples elongated and dusky rose in color. The pendant she wore resting in between. A belly, flat and tight, and the silken triangle of hair between her slender thighs. Her perfectly rounded buttocks, and the tempting darkness in between. When she'd turned away, she'd aroused me even more.

"Where," I whispered, my voice barely more than a tormented croak, "did you get that . . . that shift?"

Holding the coverlet tight to her, refusing to face me, she answered, and her voice trembled. "Nidaba. I . . . I thought 'twould make you want me as I do . . . did you. I . . .'twas before I knew, Nicodimus. 'Twas before I agreed to . . . I dinna mean to . . . I simply forgot what I was wearin', you see." She lowered her head. "Sweet heaven, but I've never been more ashamed."

Somehow, though shaking with desire, I managed to get to my feet. Still, I kept my distance. "You've nothing to be ashamed of, Arianna."

"'Twas an underhanded trick I'd planned to play on you. Indeed, you must think I've no shame at all. I dinna intend—"

"I know. It is all right." But the knowledge was there . . . what she'd been planning. To seduce me in her innocent way. By the Gods, had I come to this chamber tonight instead of racing away on my horse like a fool . . . I closed my eyes against the desire that raged in me like fire in my blood. And still it came. Against my will, I heard myself say the words I all but bit my tongue to prevent.

"Let go the coverlet, Arianna."

She stiffened, her back to me. "What?"

"Let go the coverlet."

"But . . . but Nicodimus, you said you dinna want . . ."

"I am your husband, am I not?" I whispered. And I knew better, Gods, I knew better than to go on with this. "You wanted me to see you in this gown, and I find . . . I want to see you."

"I . . . I dinna ken you."

"I saved your life. Twice now. Do this for me. Release it, Arianna. Show yourself to me."

Her head tipping up slightly, she unfolded the coverlet in front and opened her arms, paused for just a heartbeat, and let it fall to the floor. I heard her breath catch in her throat when I whispered, "Good. Now turn 'round."

Slowly, she turned. Her chin high, and her eyes alight with too many emotions to name. Pride was there. Desire, too, and perhaps anger at my tone of command. And yet she had obeyed. I knew her too well to think she would have if she had not wanted to.

She stood still as I perused her, more thoroughly this time, slowly, feasting with my eyes on every part of her until her face was red and her breaths shallow and quick. Quicker now, as I moved foward. I was driven by sheer, base desire. My honor, along with any sense of self-preservation, and perhaps any hint of sanity, had fled me now. I only felt need. Hunger. Heat.

"How is your stomach now?" I asked her, when I stood so close I could feel every breath as she exhaled.

"It feels as if a flock of sparrows were set loose inside," she whispered.

Lifting my hands, I ran the backs of my fingers over her breasts, over her nipples. She sucked in a breath. So I turned my hands, and used my fingers, caught the distended peaks between them, and squeezed lightly.

"Nicodimus!"

I increased the pressure until I could feel the thrum of the blood pulsing where I pinched her. Until her every breath was a whimper of longing. And then I eased it, pressed once again, eased, pinched hard, and released her.

She was breathing in short, quick little gasps. "I-I-I dinna understand . . ."

"Shh-shh. You will." I slid my hands down her body, over the whisper-soft nightshift, caressing her belly, her hips, her outer thighs, then slid around to the insides of her legs, and ran my palms slowly upward again. "Part your legs for me, Arianna."

With a gasp that was half sob, she did as I said. I trailed my fingertips upward, and then over the soft mound of hair between her legs. A light touch that made her tremble. Then I parted her folds, and dragged my fingertips over the moist center of her. She released a sigh that stuttered out of her, and a soft "Oooh . . ." I repeated the stroking, a little harder each time, and then I found the tiny nub, the key to her pleasure, and rubbed it hard beneath my fingertips.

Arianna shuddered, her juices wet my hand. I moved my fingers inside her, dipping and stroking, rolling and pinching that pulsing nub harder and harder between my fingers. And she threw her head back, and clutched my shoulders with her hands, and cried my name aloud. I closed my arm tight 'round her waist and held her to me when her knees would have buckled. Working her with my fingers while she shuddered in sweet release. I held her longer still, close in my arms while her body trembled, and relaxed, and her breathing eased.

"What did you do to me, husband?" she asked in a whisper.

"Lie down on the bed," I croaked, my hands on her shoulders, pushing her gently backward as I spoke, for I could not wait. I could not wait to have her. No longer.

She didn't move. Her feet planted, she lifted her head, narrowed her eyes on me. "Nay, I canna."

"You . . . ?"

"I'll nay lie down on the bed for you, Nicodimus. For though you tell me 'tis what you want, I ken you far better than before. An' you dinna want this."

Looking down at her fiery eyes, her moist, succulent lips, I shook my head. "I want it," I told her. "And so do you."

"Nay, you're mistaken there, husband. What you did to me . . . felt like heaven. But if you think mating without any love is what I want, you're sadly mistaken indeed." And firmly she closed her hands over mine, where they rested 'round her tiny waist, and took them away. She turned from me, snatching up the dark robe she'd discarded before, and pulling it around her like armor. Hiding herself from me.

"I cannot love you, Arianna," I told her, lowering my head. "I know you deserve more—"

"Aye, on that you are correct. I do deserve more. But the fact remains, Nicodimus, that though you vow you canna love me, I could quite easily love you. Even more madly than I already do. An' this," she said, waving a hand toward the bed. "This will only make me more likely to do just that. An' perhaps already has." She dropped her gaze as she spoke the last words on a hoarse whisper.

Pushing my hands through my hair, I turned and paced away. I couldn't look at her, look at the bed, without feeling aroused beyond what was sane. I was awash in shame for losing myself to passion and forgetting to protect my fragile little cat's tender heart. "You've the right of it."

"Aye, I do. Just as you wish to protect your heart from being broken again, Nicodimus, I must look out for my own. I'll nay surrender it to you knowin' already that you'll crush it beneath your boot heel. A fool I would be, did I do such a thing."

"And I would be a cruel bastard to ask it of you," I told her softly. "I . . . Arianna, I didn't mean to be . . ."

"You dinna mean to be cruel, Nicodimus, but 'tis cruel you were. First you told me you dinna want me, though it cut me to the quick to hear you say it. An' now, when at last you've convinced me 'tis true, an' best for us both to accept it, you change entirely. Just when I promise to be your wife in name only, just when I steel myself against feelin' anything for you, you go an' . . . an' . . ."

She turned quickly away, but not before I'd seen her squeeze her eyes tight to prevent the tears spilling over. I touched her shoulders, turned her back 'round to face me again. "I lost myself. You . . . you are a most beautiful woman, Arianna. And if you thought I didn't desire you, if that was what my words made you believe, you were wrong. It was more that I didn't *want* to desire you. But . . . but one look at you . . . in that . . . that scrap, and I simply lost all reason . . . and control. I apologize."

Her eyes widened, and color crept into her cheeks. She dashed at the drying tears, and smiled tremulously. "Then . . . you're saying you couldna help yourself."

"A moment of madness," I told her. "I have few weaknesses, Arianna. Did you ask me what they were, I'd be hard-pressed to name them. But I'm finding I do have one. And that weakness is you. I'm sorry if my desire confused or frightened you, little cat."

"Dinna be sorry for that, Nicodimus. That you find me . . . desirable . . . makes my heart swell. An' my head, as well, I fear."

"You've every reason to be proud. You're a remarkable woman, in so many ways."

"Aye." She lifted her head, met my gaze head on. "That I am."

Her ready agreement made me smile. I must have been insane. Any other man would have been worshipping at her feet by now, promising her the moon if she'd only love him forever. I, on the other hand, was wishing I could erect barriers to keep her away from my heart, for she seemed to sling arrows at it with every glance, every smile, every word. I knew I had good reason to put up defenses. She was young, far too young to know her own mind, her own heart. Far too young to commit to me in any real way, or be expected to honor that commitment . . . for eternity. Far too young and too beautiful and full of fire to be satisfied by a tired old man such as myself for very long. She'd destroy me if I let myself love her. I would lose her. There was no doubt in my mind of that. It frightened me, right to my bones. Never had I been afraid of any foe. Of any beast or any danger. Never had I doubted my ability to survive.

But I would never survive a war of hearts with Arianna Sinclair. Arianna . . . Lachlan. My bride.

She cleared her throat, and drew my gaze. Innocence personified, with spun gold hair, velvet brown eyes, and satin skin kissed by the sun. She did not look like my potential executioner. A man unafraid to face down a rampaging lion, I thought. Ironic that he trembles in fear of a mere kitten.

"Perhaps 'twould be best if we dinna share the same chamber after all," she whispered.

Her words startled me out of my thoughts. "No, little cat. You're constantly proving yourself the wiser of the two of us, and you were right about the gossips and the damage they could do. I'll stay here, and I promise, lady, I'll not ravish you while you slumber."

"I never thought you would," she said softly, but kept her eyes carefully averted.

She should have, I thought. Because it wasn't beyond the realm of possibility. Sighing deeply, I snatched a tapestry from the wall. Then, drawing my blade, I sliced two lengths of thong from my boot laces, and bound one to each corner. Soon, the tapestry hung suspended in the midst of the room, dividing the portion where she would lie in the bed from the place where I would rest, alone and miserable, upon the floor.

Chapter 12

I treated Arianna like a princess after that, more careful than I had ever been with anyone, so eager was I to protect her tender heart. I regretted letting my passion grow almost beyond my control, and was determined to offer amends. I was only making matters more difficult for myself, of that I was keenly aware. And yet I could not seem to stop my feet from treading eagerly upon the path to my own destruction.

She . . . mesmerized me. I took such pleasure in her company. Her wit, her laughter, seemed to fill the keep with a spirit which had never lived there before. Or, perhaps, not in a long while. Since the death of Joseph's own wife. But there was more than just this. Before my eyes, Arianna grew from the frightened, wild and rebellious child still mourning her sister, to a young woman filled with life and confidence. Part of what influenced her was, I believe, the companionship Nidaba and I offered. Two who shared her beliefs and practiced her faith. No longer did she question the legitimacy or even the sanity of it.

And more than that, too. Arianna was now a lady, my wife, and everyone in the household treated her as such. There was some resistance at first, but as I had already learned, no one could remain indifferent to Arianna for long.

It wasn't just me, I knew, who was slowly being drawn into the enchantment she spun. Within a fortnight she'd endeared herself to every servant, and many in the clan had gone from whispering suspicions about her to singing her praises, while others had at least grudgingly accepted her. Even the laird's men soon looked upon Arianna with fondness and affection.

Mara was so proud of her daughter. This was another part of Arianna that seemed to be flourishing here—the loving daughter, devoted and attentive to her parents. She had dresses made for her mother, and personally oversaw the early stages of construction for the home Joseph and I were having built for her family. Each day, without fail, she rode into the village to visit her parents. Often she would bring them back with her to dine at the keep, and sometimes she would take me along with her to eat at the humble cottage with them. She even attended morning mass at the village church with them on occasion. I knew how she detested it, so it moved me even more that she should do this just to please them.

The love in that tiny family grew steadily, day by day. And I was somehow included in that love. Arianna's father and I spent a great deal of time together in the stables discussing Joseph's horses as Edwyn repaired saddles, and even hunting together now and again. The man seemed to look upon me as a son, and an old scarred place in my heart seemed to soften and become tender all over again.

But it was not the strengthening bond between Arianna and her family, nor between her family and me, that unnerved me. No, more than anything else, it was my own unwilling fascination with her. I grew more and more reluctant to be away from her, and found myself seeking out her company at every opportunity. When she visited her family, I went along more often than not. Even to mass at the village church. I knew she was spending time with Nidaba every day in secret lessons of combat. I often hid myself to watch. The way she moved, the way she learned so quickly, her grace, her strength . . . all of it entranced me. When I exercised Black, I took her along, and our rides became more for sheer enjoyment than for the good of our mounts. Seeing her beside me upon a galloping mare, her hair flying in the wind, sent such sensations through me that I barely knew how to contain them. Or to understand them. And while these feelings frightened me, even while the warnings whispered through my mind, my heart rejoiced in them.

I told myself it was only friendship I felt for my young bride, a fondness like that of a brother for a sister. And yet I knew, deep down, these were lies. For I wanted her. More with every breath I drew, I wanted her. And each night as I lay in my nest of cushions upon the floor my discomfort and frustration grew. My young, beautiful bride only an arm's length from me, asleep in the bed we were meant to share, seemed to beckon me even from within the realms of her dreams. And often, I would part the makeshift curtain between us, just to look on her as she slept. When she rolled toward me, a soft sigh escaping her slightly parted lips, her hair spread over her pillows, I ached inside. When moonbeams streamed through our window to bathe her in silvery light, I held my breath as I watched her sleeping.

The moon waxed toward full, and with each night, I grew more and more uneasy. For I had promised her we would observe the full moon together, at the Stone Circle, and I felt a certain anxiety growing stronger and stronger within me. What I feared, I did not know. But there was a sense I had always possessed that warned me when danger was near. And I felt it now, looming larger with each night.

Until finally, the moon was full, and I knew the time was at hand.

Arianna was . . . remarkable that Esbat night. She wore a white tunic gown of the style I'd seen worn in Greece on my travels there, no doubt given to her by Nidaba. Silver clasps held the gathered fabric at her shoulders, a silver belt hugged 'round her slender waist. Her long, graceful arms were bare, save the bracelets she wore. And her pendant was fastened, as always, about her slender neck. For the first time I examined the pendant more closely, and the detail of it, the Moon Goddess reclining in the curve of a cradle moon, made me catch my breath. For it was the sort only worn by High Witches . . . but she did not know she was one.

She looked up at me as I entered our chamber, eyes wide, smile uncertain. Then she rose slowly as my eyes remained riveted. Her hair caught up with a silver clasp, then spilling free 'round it. A black cloak I'd given her for tonight was draped over her arm.

"Am I dressed suitably?" she asked me, her voice soft, hesitant.

"You . . . chose very well, Arianna." I'd seen an artist's conception of the Moon Goddess Diana once, and it had looked very much the way Arianna looked now. Silver adorning her, dressed all in white. As for myself, I wore my finest kilt, beneath a dark hooded cloak, and this night, I had donned my own pendant, so similar to Arianna's.

My gaze returned once again to the pendant she wore, I wondered what she knew of its significance. "Arianna . . . that necklace. It is . . . very unusual."

She fingered the piece, her touch reverent, fingers dancing over the circle, and the star in its center, and the cradle moon and reclining goddess that adorned its outer curve. "'Twas one of three gifts The Crones gave to me when I'd studied with them for a year and a day," she said. "'Twas at our last ritual together. I will cherish it always."

I nodded, not telling her I was wearing one very much like it, tucked beneath my cloak. Nor did I tell her that most of the High Witches I had known did as well. I did not usually wear mine when I was here at Stonehaven. I had no wish to advertise what I was to those few who might, somehow, know what the pendant symbolized. It was becoming painfully obvious that more knowledge existed out there than I had ever suspected. The Crones . . . could they have known of our existence? They had given her a High Witch's dagger as well that night as I'd watched in silence.

But how? And if they suspected what Arianna truly was, why had they not told her?

Then again, I thought, why hadn't I?

Perhaps they, too, had believed her too young, and not yet ready to know the truth.

"Come," I said softly, banishing the other thoughts. "It nears midnight." Taking the dark cloak she held, I draped it about her shoulders. It was silken, large, and loose, and had a hood. I had one like it.

"What is the meaning of the cloak, Nicodimus?" she asked as we moved into the corridors and through them, and finally out into the night.

Reaching behind her, I tugged the hood up to cover her golden hair. "It is practical. We blend with the night and are less likely to be seen. The Druids wore white ones much like these during ritual, and I followed their custom. However, with the advent of Christianity and Witch-hunters, I thought it wise to change it to black, at least for the journey to and from the sacred site."

She glanced up at me as we moved side by side over the meadows and into the woods beyond. "Ah. But what of your own people?" she asked as we picked our way along the old path. "Did they wear cloaks for their rites?"

"No. My clan were of the barbaric sort. We spoke to our Gods in solitude, and wore nothing at all, save the colors with which we painted sacred symbols over our bodies."

She blinked as if surprised, then smiled to herself. "I can see why you thought the Druid method might be preferable tonight, then."

I glanced down at the hint of laughter in her voice. But as I did, an image crept into my mind. One of my beautiful Arianna, naked and proud, unashamed, raising her arms and turning her face up to drink in the moonlight. And the image grew. Until I saw myself kneeling before her, dipping my fingers into pots of color, and drawing the ancient sacred symbols upon her pale, soft skin.

I shivered, and she looked up quickly. But when I said nothing, she faced forward again.

Soon the stones of the circle towered before us, and without being told, Arianna stopped and bent to remove her slippers before stepping inside. I nodded my approval and removed my own boots. Then I entered, and tugging the pack from my shoulder, I emptied it, setting its contents upon a large flat stone table in the northernmost quadrant. Wine, and two cups, four candles, and a staff.

"What magick will we work this night, Nicodimus?" Arianna asked me, her voice childlike with excitement.

I smiled down at her in the moonlight. "What do you wish for?"

She lowered her head at once. And I knew I had spoken too quickly. I knew what she wished for. And she knew it was impossible. Yet she spoke it all the same.

"I wish for your love, Nicodimus, but I ken that can never be. I wish for your touch . . . but nay for the consequences of knowing it. For those would only be pain for us both. An' I'd nay use magick to gain either of those things, for were they not given freely, they'd be worse than useless to me."

I did not speak. I could not, for I knew not what to say.

She lifted her head again, eyes meeting mine. "So instead I'll wish for something far simpler an' more mundane. A cooling North wind, to ease the dreary autumn heat."

Relief that she could smile in spite of the pain I'd caused her—was still causing her—made me breathe again. "Then a cooling wind it shall be. A wise choice, for the heat is wearing on the clan, making their tempers short. You've called forth the winds before?"

"Aye," she said. "With The Crones to guide me. Thrice we did so, an' each time the gentle breezes came within a fortnight of our casting." She tilted her head. "An' you, Nicodimus?"

I nodded once. "Usually the winds come within a day of my conjuring." I bent to make the preparations, building a small fire in the center of the circle, and lighting it. Then I placed a candle in each of the four directions, just at the edges of the circle. Returning to the center, I sat for a time, gazing into the flames. Arianna did likewise, and I knew she was letting her mind go quiet, gathering the energies around her. It seemed we both felt ready to proceed at the same moment, for we looked up simultaneously. And in silence, I took a flaming limb from the fire. I walked to the North candle, focused on the energies of Earth, and lit the candle's wick. Arianna met me in the center, taking the limb from my hand. She moved to the East candle, closed her eyes for a moment, and lit it. I could almost feel the Air move as she summoned its elemental energies to join us here. I repeated this process in the South, for the element of Fire, and she in the West, for Water.

Meeting at the stone table again, we locked gazes, and I saw something in her eyes . . . the swirling reflections of moonlight and fire. A shiver worked up the back of my neck. I took a breath, poured the wine, handed Arianna her cup. She held it up, as if to capture the light of the moon in the glistening scarlet liquid, as she chanted.

> *I am one with the light from above.*
> *An' one with the force from below.*
> *One with the beasts of the wild*
> *One with the green things that grow.*
> *One with the moon, one with the sun*
> *One with the Earth and the Sky*
> *One with All since afore I was born,*
> *An' will be long after I die.*

Then closing her eyes, lowering the goblet, she drank its contents. I downed mine as well, and walked her back to the fire. Dipping a hand into the deep pocket of the hooded cloak I wore, I drew out a palmful of herbs, and tossed them into the flames. They hissed and heated, burned fragrantly.

Smiling, Arianna reached her small hand into my pocket, and repeated what I had done. Then I faced North, palms up in front of me, and chanted in a long forgotten tongue the words to call the North wind.

Her eyes as she watched me were huge and luminous. And before I knew what she intended, she faced me, and pressed her palms flat to mine. The tingling contact rocked through me, right to my core, and the warmth remained long after that initial shock faded.

I felt it then. A power like I'd never known surging from below and above at the same time. And the place where it gathered until it nearly burned, was the very place where Arianna's palms pressed flat to mine. For just a moment, I swore an amber glow emanated from our joined hands.

There was a deep humming sound, as the wind picked up force, blowing through the trees, whistling over twigs, and groaning past limbs. Then it grew to a roar. The mighty oaks 'round us seemed to bow beneath its force. Arianna's hair blew and danced and her white gown seemed alive. Leaves and twigs swirled 'round us like miniature cyclones, and the air cooled so rapidly my skin shivered. My gaze swung 'round, seeking shelter. But before I could think on that further, the air filled with snow. Snow! In the midst of a highland autumn!

It coated my garments and melted there, wetting me to the skin in a matter of seconds. Amazed, I faced Arianna.

But my little cat stood with her face turned up to the snow, and her arms outspread as it fell on her. Turning in a slow circle, she faced me again, a look of wonder in her eyes as her hair grew damp, and crystalline flakes sparkled on her cheeks like tears. Smiling, then laughing aloud, she flung her arms 'round my neck.

"Do you see what we've done!" she cried. "Nicodimus, this is powerful, this magick we work together!"

Her body close to mine, my arms tight 'round her waist, I nodded against her snow-damp hair. "I've never seen the like."

She drew back just a little. Enough so she could look up at me, her face only inches from mine. "The Crones said 'twould be so. They said the power of magick is strongest when there is balance . . . between feminine and masculine energies, such as those of a man an' a woman."

"Yes." I nodded my agreement. "I've been taught much the same . . . and yet it has never been quite this . . . startling."

"Ah, Nicodimus, do you nay ken, even now? 'Tis nay just any combination of man an' woman who could bring about such a force as this. But of you an' me, husband. Two who . . . belong to each other."

"Arianna . . . I—"

She held up a hand. "I know, dinna speak it. I know you canna love me," she whispered. "An' I've no wish to hurt you. But I know you want me as I do you, Nicodimus. An' I'm tired of protectin' myself from future hurt by refusin' to live life. I'm tired of fightin' against feelin's over which I've no control. 'Tis like fightin' against nature."

I stared down at her. She stepped back another pace, and drew the cloak from her shoulders, tossing it to the ground. "I know you canna love me, husband. But I can love you." Her hands went to the shoulders of the tunic, freeing the clasps there, and the dress fell down to her feet as if washed away by the snow. "Let me love you," she whispered. "Just this once . . ."

I stood staring at her. Perfect, her skin glistening with the snowflakes that drifted down on her. Breasts round and soft, nipples growing stiffer with each icy flake that touched them. She stepped over the discarded dress, closer to me.

And what was I to do? How could I . . . or any man, resist such an offering? Before I could even consider my answer, my hands were on her, palms skimming over the wet skin of her belly, cupping her breasts, caressing her. I drew her tight to me, and bent my head to capture her mouth. I tasted the snow on her lips, and the warmth beyond them when I pushed my tongue inside. I fed at her mouth as her yearning body pressed against mine, and I dreamed of drinking every melting droplet from her skin. I slid my lips to her cheek and down slowly over her neck. She tipped her head back and moaned softly as I nipped and suckled the tender skin there.

Lower. I licked the beaded moisture from her shoulder. And all the way down her arm to the inner bend of her elbow, and she cried out when my tongue darted over that sensitive flesh. I moved to her hand, sucking the moisture from each finger, and then kissed a hot path across her belly and began again at her other arm.

She was trembling, clinging to me in order to stay upright when I moved at last to one tender breast. I took my time, circling the peak slowly with my tongue before finally closing my lips on the crest. I drew on her there, and she shivered. I suckled harder, and her fingers curled in my hair. I bit lightly, and she pressed herself closer.

"Nicodimus," she whispered. "Oh, but you give me such pleasure. An' I . . . I dinna ken how . . ."

I bit again, and this time she tugged against my teeth, whimpering in rapture at the sweet touch of pain. My hand slipped between her legs, and I touched her inner lips, tracing them, feeling the moisture there for me. I drew a forefinger higher, circling the tiny nub that was the key to her pleasure, and then touching it, rubbing it, pinching it so that her knees began to buckle, all the while still feeding at her breast.

My other arm 'round her waist anchored her to me, else she'd have surely fallen to her knees.

"Nay," she whispered, and it was a plea. I pinched her harder, and her voice grew hoarse. "You must tell me what to do, Nicodimus. Tell me how to please you."

I closed my eyes in sweet anguish. "You please me, Arianna, with every breathless whisper, and every sigh and every touch." I slipped my fingers inside her, gently, carefully. "And to see you in the height of pleasure will please me even more."

"Make love to me, Nicodimus," she whispered.

I lifted her then, and carried her to the stone table. My cloak I flung down beneath her, then I lay her upon it. Quickly I took off my clothes until I stood naked in the falling snow. And gently I parted her legs and watched as the snowflakes kissed her secret places. Then I bent to kiss and lick every droplet away until she squirmed and cried out and opened wider to my questing tongue.

I moved upward until I lay atop her, and carefully, I entered her slick, tight passage. The wind swirled icy cold 'round us, and the wet snowflakes fell upon my back. I moved deeper into her, and still deeper. I felt her pain, brief and sweet as I tore through the barrier of her maidenhood, and I held her still beneath me, waiting, giving her time.

Timidly, hesitantly, she moved her hips against mine, taking me deeper. And again, drawing away and moving once more. Fire licked at my loins, and I took her then. Deep and hard and fast, I took her, and she lifted her hips to meet my every thrust. I kissed her fiercely, swallowing each breathless whisper, each sigh, each moan. And finally, her entire body tensed around me, squeezing and drawing on me, convulsing around me until I felt myself shatter inside her. I pumped my seed into her, and with it, it seemed, my very soul. And then I eased my body down beside hers, and held her, and wondered how I could ever let her go again.

Oh, Gods, she'd done it. She'd made her way into my heart. I knew, with everything in me, she would break it before she was done.

Chapter 13

"'Twas wonderful, Nicodimus. I . . . thank you."

He sat up slightly, blinking at her in surprise. But then his face changed even as Arianna lay in his arms, feeling more alive than she ever had. He frowned, tilting his head to one side. "What . . . what is that sound?"

Arianna listened, but heard nothing. "I canna hear—"

"Shh-shh." He held up a hand, sat a bit straighter. "Horses. Oh, Gods, battle!" He surged to his feet as Arianna's heart leapt into her throat.

"But Nicodimus, I hear nothing!" Even as she said it, she rushed to retrieve her garments.

"It is yet another part of being immortal, Arianna. The sharpening of the senses . . ." He struggled into his own clothing and drew his dagger, then came to stand over her, his eyes alert and scanning the trees around them as she finished dressing. As if he'd protect her should any threat appear.

And that gave her to know he truly believed there was trouble afoot. "Nicodimus . . . what is happening?"

He closed his hands around hers and stared intently into her eyes. "I want you to stay here. Right here, Arianna, wrapped in the cloak and concealed amongst the shadows of these stones. The clouds have covered the moon. If you are still, no one will see you, even should they look, and you will be safe—"

"Nay! I'll nay stay safe while you rush into danger!"

He shook his head firmly. "I must go, little cat, and there's no time to argue with you. The village . . . I believe the village is under attack. Joseph and the boys . . . Nidaba—"

"Mam!" she cried. Suddenly it seemed her stomach turned in on itself. For now the sounds were reaching her ears as well, and in the distance, an eerie glow began to reach into the dark sky, despite the falling snow. She screamed aloud, hands pressed to either side of her head as panic took hold of her heart.

"I'll see to your family, I vow it, Arianna. Please, please, remain here, safe."

Trembling from head to toe, she nodded, knowing even as she did so that she lied to her husband. She lied blatantly. For no force on earth could have kept her from her family.

He studied her face for one lingering moment, then drew her dark cloak tight about her, and led her to a shadowy niche between two of the standing stones, where one had toppled slightly and leaned against another. "In here. You'll be all but invisible, in here."

She nodded, eyeing the cavelike space. Then Nicodimus gripped her shoulders and pulled her against him. He kissed her long and hard. "Stay safe," he said, and his tone was one of command. "I'll come back for you."

"Aye, Nicodimus. Go, now. Go do what you must."

With a quick nod, he turned to leave her. But she rushed after him, a sudden knot of cold fear hitting her fiercely in the chest. Flinging her arms around him, she fought to control her sobs. "Oh, my love, please take care. Stay alive, for though I've fought against it I—"

"I know," he said softly, stroking her hair. "I know. Go now, hide and await my return."

She nodded hard, pressed her lips once to his warm neck, then fled to the spot where he had told her to hide. He watched until she had crawled into the darkness between the stones, and only then did he hurry away.

But the instant Nicodimus was out of her sight, Arianna crept out of her hiding place, and picked her way quickly and silently through the woods, taking the shortest route to the village. And as she went the sounds of battle grew louder. Shouts, screams, thundering hoofbeats. The snap and hiss of fire. The snow fell and fell, and as she finally drew nearer the village, she realized the shouts and cries were coming less and less frequently with each step she ran. Until, only the hoofbeats, and the crackling of flames remained.

What she found when she emerged from the trees made her heart turn to stone.

Cottages burning, flames licking at their thatched roofs, and hissing against the snow; fueled by something that burned despite the wetness from above, but burned more slowly because of it. And as she raced closer, she saw torches born by men on horseback who thundered through the village. Swords and clubs smote the few crofters who ran like frightened animals through the muddy pathways. And when the clouds skittered away from the face of the moon, she saw the bodies, battered and bloodied. *Everywhere.*

"Mam? Da?" she whispered. Her own family's cottage stood in the distance. Arianna paused to bend down and scoop up a discarded blade as she moved urgently toward it. Her dagger was at her hip, aye, but she wanted something bigger. The sword hung heavy in her hand, too long for her, its tip dragging through the mud when she stumbled. She expected to be struck down before she reached her parents, and quickened her pace at the thought. But the darkness and her cloak must have been her aids, for none of the rampaging beasts seemed to notice her. Most were far too busy, looting the homes, murdering the few who remained alive, and putting the torch to every building in sight.

She heard a cry from within her parents' house. Her mother's cry . . . a cry that was cut off before it ended. With a growl of absolute fury, she lifted the sword high, raced forward, and burst through the door.

Her mother lay upon the floor, limp, her head bloodied, while a soldier bent over her, tearing at her dress. Without hesitation, Arianna brought the blade flashing down with all her might, aiming for the man's neck.

He cried out only once as his blood shot from his veins, and then he crumbled at her feet, his head tipped at an impossible angle. Arianna stepped over him, giving him not a second look. She rushed to her mother, knelt over her, gripped her shoulders.

"Mam! Mam, 'tis all right. I'm here now an' . . . an' . . . Mam?" She shook her mother, but saw now what she'd failed to see before. Or refused to. The once bright eyes were already filmed over by the glaze of death. Staring sightlessly, their light forever extinguished. "Nay!" Arianna cried. "Nay, this canna be!"

Rising to her feet, she backed away, turning her gaze from the sight of her mother there on the floor, only to see her father lying still in a corner, a dagger in his belly, a pool of blood around him.

Arianna's head began to spin. She did not want to believe any of this, for it could not be real. She had barely survived losing her sister, but to lose her parents, too, and just when they'd begun to mend the rift between them? Nay, 'twas too much to bear.

She lifted her head to gaze into the dark, snow-damp night, and saw the herd of swine who had brought this destruction upon her people, her family, her clan. Looking down once again at the sword in her hand, she muttered, "I will kill them. Aye, I'll kill them all!"

In a fury she raced into the wet snow, bare feet slapping through the mud, as she attacked one man after another. Her rage drove her, gave her strength. She killed more than she could count. Until at last, when she lifted the blade high above her head about to bring it down on another of them, she felt her body pierced from behind, and went still, her mouth agape, eyes bulging. Looking down, she saw the point of a blade protruding from her belly, blood flowing to soak the white tunic dress she'd worn to please Nicodimus.

Nicodimus. Gods, where was he? Where on earth was he?

She dropped to her knees, and knew death would come soon to claim her. So be it, then. 'Twas preferable to going on, dealing with such a crippling loss. No one left to her but a husband who could never love her. A husband who would leave her in the end just as Raven, her sister had done. Just as her beloved teachers and her parents had each done in turn. She would lose him. She had lost them all.

Better than living, was dying just now. Better than living . . .

Arianna fell, facedown in the mud—never having glimpsed the face of the man who had killed her.

I never should have left her alone. It was a mistake that led to my destruction, and for it I take full blame. Things may well have ended differently had I kept my promise to protect her family. But those promises were words I never should have spoken, wrenched from me without forethought, and my judgment was poor. I wanted only to comfort her, to take away the pain I saw in her soft brown eyes. To take away the fear. To be her hero, I suppose. Foolish. Foolish to make promises I could not keep simply because I loved the girl.

Yes, it was true. I loved her. In spite of my best efforts not to. Ari-

anna had conquered me. I hated the feeling, the vulnerability it created in
me. And yet it was that feeling that drove me to protect her and all those
she cared about. A feeling that made me willing to face battle—to face
anything at all—for her.

So I spied the flames, heard the thundering beats of hooves, and
knew the village and clan were under attack by a large number of soldiers, whose motives I could not imagine. But I simply knew that this
was no ordinary raid. I raced to the keep for weapons, and to stir Joseph
and his sons in case they remained asleep and unaware. Every man in the
household would be needed to defend the village. Every last one.

I broke from the woods, and raced across the moor, up the hill to the
front gates, my lungs burning, my body alive with immortal power.

It was only when I found the gates flung open that I slowed, and took
more careful stock of things.

The huge wooden door leading into the great hall was not open, but
lying flat—a battering ram made of half a tree trunk dropped upon it.
And from the gaping, dark windows, thin spirals of smoke whispered
forth.

"Nidaba," I whispered. "Joseph . . ."

Forcing myself to pause, to take care, I slipped inside, keeping to the
shadows. The intruders were long gone, now. But everywhere I looked
were signs of their carnage: broken bodies were strewn on the rushes,
slaughtered like sheep. I found Joseph at the base of the stone stairs, still
in his nightclothes. His neck broken. His sons had never even made it
out of their chambers. Both of them lay dead within. And of Nidaba . . .
of Nidaba there was no sign.

My heart clenched and my blood boiled. Damn these bastards, whoever they were! Attacking a peace-loving clan, murdering Joseph, a man
who had shown nothing but kindness and understanding to all who'd
known him. My friend. He had been my friend, and one of the few I still
possessed.

But I had no time to mourn, nor even to bury him. Kicking open the
bolted door of the weapons room, wondering why the invaders had not
bothered to loot it to the bare walls, I snatched a sword and scabbard and
belted them in place. Ignoring the rest, for I'd no need of maces nor
shields nor crossbows, I strode quickly outside again, needing the air to
cleanse the stench of spilled blood from my lungs.

Glancing toward the stables, I saw the tongues of flame beginning to
lick up the sides. No doubt the straw and hay inside had been smoldering
even before I had arrived. The doors stood closed up tight, as if the bas-

tards had not even bothered to steal the horses, but simply wanted to destroy them. Destroy everything associated with this clan.

Gods, who could have cause to hate the clan so much?

I ran, yanking the stable doors open, and in only seconds, managed to send several horses galloping to safety with no more than a slap of my hand. The last few were panicked by the flames, and I had no time to lead them free one by one. Not when Mara and Edwyn were in their cottage at the mercy of the attackers. I gripped Black and leapt upon him without benefit of saddle or rein. He obeyed as easily as he always had, and leapt free of the burning building with barely a flick of his eye. He'd seen fire before, Black had. The stallion knew no fear.

Leaning low, I kicked him into motion, and we sailed through the night, pounding ever nearer the village, but my heart sank as I saw the yellow glow battling the snow-drenched darkness, and I whispered the names of my wife's parents as I raced closer. I drew my sword, rounded a bend in the road, and then tugged Black to a halt as I saw the destruction. The death all 'round me. The ruin. There was nothing left. Nothing.

And the soldiers were gone. They had rained terror and destruction down upon an unsuspecting, peaceful clan, and then left just as quickly as possible. Tears burned in my eyes as I moved closer to the saddle maker's cottage. Because there was no hint of life from within. No one moved or breathed. I heard no tears, no cries for help, though the thatched roof was already alight with flame. No moans of pain. I knew death, and this was it. I felt it in the very night, heightening my awareness with every wet snowy droplet that struck my skin. I was the only man alive here.

Black halted in front of Arianna's former home, and I dismounted slowly. My boots sticking in the blood-soaked mud, I stepped inside. And then I felt the pain rip through me as I saw them. Mara, her head caved in. Edwyn with a mortal blade wound to the gut. And in the corner . . . who was that?

A soldier, one of the attackers, his head nearly severed. Someone had fought back then. Tried to help. But too late, too late.

My eyes burned with unshed tears as I thought of telling Arianna that her beloved parents had been brutally killed. I had been unable to tell her the truth about her own nature, to spare her the pain of knowing she would one day outlive all those she loved. But now that day had come all the same, and there was no way I could spare her this. No way.

And I'd promised her. I had *promised her* that I would protect them.

"I'm sorry, Arianna," I whispered. "Damnation, if I had only come here sooner. If I had only . . ." But I shook my head, for my words and my regrets could not change what had befallen her family tonight.

Edwyn . . . he had been as kind to me as if I were his own son. And Mara . . . I recalled her smiling face, the reborn joy in her eyes as she and her firstborn had found each other again.

Gone, now, both of them. Their precious lives snuffed out without a care, without a cause.

My every instinct told me to go after the vermin who had wreaked such tragedy on Stonehaven. They had headed north, and their trail—the hoofmarks of so many horses—would be easily followed. But I needed to return to the Stone Circle, to Arianna. Thank the Fates, I thought, that I had left her there. The soldiers had headed in the opposite direction. She was safe. They would pass nowhere near her.

Stepping outside, I reached for Black's mane to pull myself up, but as I did, I glanced down, and a gleam caught my eye. Not a blade, but something silver, stomped into the mud. Instinct caused my stomach to quake, and I dreaded what I would find. I bent, and picked it up.

A silver pendant with a cradle moon adorning one curve. Exactly like the one Arianna had been wearing. And it had been lying here, right outside this house of death—her parents' home.

"No," I whispered. "No, it cannot be hers. She wouldn't have come here, she couldn't have. . . ." Terrified, I scanned the bodies crumpled hither and yon, but I did not see the ethereal white tunic she had worn, nor the gleam of her spun gold hair. Not at all. Still, my gut was telling me what my mind already knew. It was hers. She had been here . . . and something terrible had befallen her.

I draped her pendant 'round my neck to join my own there. Then, leaping upon Black, I whirled him around, kicked his flanks hard with my heels, and headed at breakneck speed back toward the Stone Circle. But the emptiness in the pit of my stomach told me even before I reached the sacred place, that I would not find my bride there, either.

A jolt bent Arianna's body backward so suddenly and so acutely she felt as if her spine would snap and her lungs burst from the force of her gasp.

Then slowly, her body eased again, and she opened her eyes. But even as she did, memory came flooding back, and she squeezed them tight against the onslaught. The attack. The bodies. Her parents lying dead . . .

"Nay, it canna be," she muttered, and turned instinctively into the shoulder upon which her head rested. The arms around her tightened, and a deep voice whispered, "There, lass, it will be all right now, I promise you that."

And that voice, she realized, head coming up fast, eyes widening, was *not* Nicodimus's.

He held her to him, seated behind her on a horse; a large man, and strong from the feel of him. She found herself staring into pale blue eyes that reminded her of a wolf in winter, and ashen hair that gleamed nearly white in the moonlight. Not with age, but with the fairness of its hue. His face was soft, with a gently rounded chin and cheekbones, and a bulbous nose. No harsh angles, no cragginess like her Nicodimus. But softness. He seemed a gentle soul, this man who held her in his arms.

And yet she stiffened, pressing her hands to his shoulders to hold herself away.

"Aye, lass, 'tis natural you'd be confused now. But you've naught to fear from me, I promise you." He studied her face. "'Twas your first death, was it not?"

Her brows bunched together, she whispered, "First . . . death?" And then she recalled the sensation of being run through, the horror of looking down to see a blade thrusting out of her own belly, and of falling dead into the mud.

Dead.

"Nay," she whispered very softly. "Nay, 'tis nay possible. I . . . I *died*. I . . ." Lowering her chin she saw the bloodstains all over the front of her tunic, and even the slit in the cloth where the blade had torn through. Hooking her fingers in that tear, she ripped it wider, and then searched her skin, her belly, for some mark or cut or flaw. But only found the stains of drying blood. She pressed her fingers to the spot where it seemed she could still feel the phantom pain of the wound . . . but there was nothing there. No injury. Not so much as a nick nor a scratch.

Wide-eyed, she lifted her head once more.

"You canna mean to tell me you dinna know, lassie! You're immortal. A High Witch, just like me. Nicodimus must have told you. . . . Damnation, he dinna tell you at all, did he, child?"

She blinked rapidly, searching her mind, hearing the warnings it whispered. "Immortal? Nay . . . nay, it canna be. . . ."

"You're the living proof that it is, lass. It is. You're alive, and unmarred by the blade. I found you lifeless in the mud, but knew you for what you were, and vowed to take you away from all the carnage. And from the reach of Nicodimus."

Nay. She would never be beyond the reach of Nicodimus. He would find her. He would come for her. But this man . . . this man knew his name. "You . . . you know my husband?" she asked.

"Aye. He's been my arch enemy for centuries, lass. One of the Darkest of the Dark, he is—"

"Nay!" Arianna felt her anger rise to drown out her confusion and grief. "My Nicodimus is good and pure, and I'll kill any man who says otherwise!"

He studied her for a long moment, drinking in, it seemed, the anger flashing from her eyes. "I can see you believe it to be true. I vow, lady, at least now I understand why a woman like you would bind herself to a man such as he. You simply dinna ken the truth."

She narrowed her eyes on him. "I'll never believe a word spoken against my husband," she all but hissed at him. "Who are you that I should take heed of a word you utter?" Then she tilted her head. "You're one of *them*, aren't you? One of those who attacked my village!"

He nodded slowly. "Aye, lass, though it pains me to have to tell you. I am their chieftain."

"Bastard!" Arianna clenched her hands into fists and pounded his chest. But he easily caught her wrists and held her still, though she struggled. His horse came to a halt.

"I dinna fault you, lass. Indeed, I canna. But if you'll only hear me out. I tried to get to the village in time to halt the bloodshed. I tried, I vow it on the name of my own father. But I was too late. And my men had already done that poor defenseless village to death."

Grief made her weak, and she stopped her fighting. "Aye, and they'd done my mam to death, as well, and my da along with her. An' I vow I'll see every one of them die before I rest."

His eyes, soft with sorrow, moved gently over her face, and releasing her wrists, he stroked her hair. "Gods, but I'm sorry. More sorry than you can know. The men . . . they were crazed. Their chieftain—my older brother, Kohl—was murdered . . . by your husband, lass. By our lifelong enemy, Nicodimus, that Dark Witch of old."

"'Twas nay murder! Nicodimus had to kill him in order to stay alive!"

He shook his head. "An' I suppose he gave you some reason why he had to take my brother's heart as well, did he not? But pretty one, only the Dark take the hearts of their victims. Only they and no others."

She shook her head, confused. Nicodimus had told her that . . . but then he'd said he'd had to take Kohl's heart to set his spirit free.

"The men adored Kohl," this fellow went on. "And they . . . took vengeance on the village. One lad knew what was about to occur, and raced off to find me. But I dinna arrive in time, and the men, without a leader . . . acted in anger and unleashed a mighty fury upon Stonehaven." Again, he shook his head slowly. "It pains me more than I can say that your family perished in the attack, lass."

She studied his face. "You're naught but a liar," she whispered, but his words made her wonder. Not about Nicodimus—nay, never that, he was good and true, and she loved him—but about the rest. Perhaps this man *had* tried to stop what had happened.

Then more things clicked into place in her mind. "Your name is Marten. Nicodimus told me about you . . . the brother of Kohl, and of Nicodimus's wife of so long ago. Anya."

"Aye, I imagine he told you much. I only hope you'll nay believe the worst of me too easily. Nicodimus . . . he hates me. It has always been so."

"An' you hate him in return," she whispered. "Nonetheless, he dinna tell me that he was one of the Dark Ones, nor that you were one of the Light."

"Nay, lass. Nor did he tell you that you yourself were an immortal High Witch just as we are."

She blinked. "He . . . he knew?"

"Of course he knew."

Shaking her head slowly, she knew it couldn't be true. "Nay, he'd have told me if he knew. He . . . he trusted me with all the other secrets. Why would he keep this one from me? Nay, he'd have told me. He would!"

"Perhaps," Marten said slowly. "I suppose 'tis possible he dinna know of your nature. Tell me, did he ever see the mark of the crescent moon upon your flank, child? The one that marks all immortals as who and what they are?"

She felt the arrows of his words piercing her soul. The crescent birthmark. Nicodimus bore one. So did Nidaba, and so did she. He knew that. So if it was the mark of immortality . . .

"And has he ever touched you, lass?"

Frowning harder, she said, "I dinna ken your meanin'. What are you—?"

"Take your hands from my shoulders, pretty one. Just for a moment, an' you'll understand."

Still confused, she did, sitting away from him slightly, taking her hands from his shoulders.

"Now, put them back again."

With a nod, she lay her palms lightly upon his shoulders once more. Immediately, a jolt of something passed through her. The same sort of jolt she felt when she touched Nicodimus, or Nidaba.

"The initial contact you make with any other immortal will give you just such a sensation, child," Marten explained slowly, patiently. "So even if Nic had never seen your birthmark, he'd have felt what you were the first time he touched you. Do you ken?"

She nodded, very slowly. So it was true. Nicodimus had known what she was. He had to have known. And yet, she defended him. "If he did keep the truth from me, then he likely had reasons for doin' so."

"Aye. No doubt he and that she-wolf of his planned to take your young heart, once it grew powerful enough to sustain one or the other of them."

"Dinna be foolish!" she shouted. "Nicodimus is my husband, and Nidaba my friend!"

"Aye. And the two of them sharing a bed for nigh on eight centuries now, lass. Can you not see what is before your face?"

She felt as if he'd punched her in the belly with a fist made of cold iron. Blinking with reaction, battling tears, she whispered, "Nicodimus . . . and Nidaba?"

"Lovers, child. Lovers all along, even right under the nose of my sweet-natured sister, who died more of heartache than childbirth all those years ago. For she knew."

She shook her head slowly. "Nicodimus . . . he loved Anya."

"Loved her? Nay, child, he took her. Destroyed her village and her family and took her as his captive. By force, he took her."

She lifted her gaze. "Just the way your men destroyed my village, Marten? An' just the way you've now taken me?"

"Aye, lady. I'm afraid so. I'm sorry your life is being turned 'round because of it, but justice is justice, and for Nicodimus, 'tis long overdue."

Dropping her chin, releasing a sigh, she whispered, "You're so wrong about him."

"An' if I'm wrong about him, then where is he? Hmm? He was nay among the dead, I can tell you as much. Neither he, nor the dark woman who owns his heart and soul. Nay, lady, he dinna come looking for you, nor so much as try to protect your family. He vanished, he and his Nidaba. Vanished, without givin' you a second thought. He lied to you, little one. He lied to you about what he truly is, and kept the truth of your own nature a secret from you. And then he abandoned you. He's not worthy of a woman so fine as you are. Oh, sweet lady, I dinna even know your name."

Blinking, eyes burning, she whispered, "My name is Arianna. Arianna Sinclair . . . Lachlan."

"Arianna," he said slowly. "Dinna cry, Arianna. He's nay worthy of a single tear from such as you."

But the tears fell all the same.

Her captor pulled her gently closer, his touch exquisitely gentle, his body warm and soft. "I'll make it all up to you, lady. I vow I will. You'll know nothing but joy whilst you reside in my keep. Nothing but joy."

Chapter 14

I stood in the center of the Stone Circle, hands clenched, arms taut and quivering as I howled my rage. My cry echoed through the forest and the surrounding moors, bounding from the silent monoliths that surrounded me. And yet no one heard. There was no reply.

Arianna was gone. Gone.

"I'll find you," I promised hoarsely when the echoes of my fury finally died away. "I swear to you, Arianna, I'll find you, no matter where they've taken you. And when I do I'll kill the bastards. I vow, if they've harmed a hair on your head, I'll . . ." My voice dropped to an anguished whisper. "Gods, don't let them harm her."

I lowered my head, staring through pools of tears at the pendant I clutched in my hands. Tears. How long had it been since I'd shed them? A century, perhaps? Longer?

Dammit to hell, why was I still pretending? "I love you, lass," I finally admitted in a whisper, wishing for all the world that I could just hear her voice, that joyful lilt, one last time. "I love you. I should have told you. But I will, I vow it, I will. And I'll make it right again, make all of this up to you—somehow."

My hand fisted 'round the pendant, and then I brought it to my lips, and kissed it to seal my vow. Silently, I fastened it 'round my own neck.

Then I mounted Black, drew the horse about, and kicked his sides. Black lunged into a gallop, and I headed north, as I knew the attackers had done. Their trail was well laid and easily followed. I would catch the blackguards before this night was through.

"Stop looking for him, Arianna," her captor said, his voice soft, his eyes gentle. "Nicodimus will nay come for you. The sooner you accept that harsh truth, the better 'twill be."

She shook her head slowly. "He will. He'll come for me, you'll see." But would he? Maybe the more important question was, *could* he? Oh, but she was no fool. She knew well enough what was happening here. This Marten and she were alone, no one within sight nor earshot around them. Yet there had been dozens upon dozens of warhorses and soldiers in the village. So many men. Obviously, they had all ridden off in another direction, perhaps to plunder some other village, perhaps to battle some other clan. But wherever they had gone, it was obvious Marten's goal lay elsewhere. His horse's hooves, she noted, were wrapped in thick layers of cloth. And he guided the beast over the hardest terrain, where leaving a sign of their passing would be all but impossible. Marten pushed onward at a terrible pace. The miles seemed to fall away between Arianna and her home, along with all she had known there. All she had ever held dear, all she had loved. Perhaps Nicodimus would be unable to find her, even if he tried.

If he tried.

And what if he didn't? What if all the things Marten had told her . . .

But, nay. That could not be. She knew Nicodimus. Knew him . . . and loved him. She believed in him. Aye, he had kept things from her—vital things she should have been told. She was immortal.

By the Gods, she was immortal. And unsure now, what that meant to her. How it would change her life. She only knew that even the girl she had been only hours before was now lost to her. As lost as her mother and father. As lost as her dear sister. She no longer knew who Arianna Sinclair Lachlan might be, who she would become.

Gods, why had Nicodimus not told her?

She sighed, closing her eyes. If Nicodimus had kept so vital a truth from her, then he must have had some reason. He must have!

He would come for her. And when he did, she realized slowly, through the haze of grief and shock that clouded her mind . . . when he did, she could be with him . . . forever.

Aye, forever. He would not have to watch her grow old and die, as she had believed, for she was immortal, just as he was. And could be with him!

If . . . if he wanted her.

Doubts assailed Arianna then, new ones that had not occurred to her before. For Nicodimus had known these things all along, hadn't he? So maybe he did not want her after all.

I followed the horde of men for three nights before I finally caught up to them. I had not expected them to be moving so quickly. They had left no survivors behind, and had no reason to assume they were being pursued. Why, then? The question dogged me. Why such haste?

If they knew, somehow, that I was following, if they were ready and waiting when I finally arrived at their camp . . .

But, no, it didn't matter. Whether they expected my attack or not, my course would not change. I had to rescue Arianna. I had to find her. Hold her in my arms again, and know that she was all right.

It was full night, the fourth one of my journey, when at last I heard the sounds in the distance that told me they were near. Keeping to the thickest patches of forest, I moved Black slowly, quietly nearer, until I could see by the pale glow of distant fires that they had set up camp for the night. Good. Good.

Tying Black in a grove of pines, I crept closer, walking softly, using the skills I had learned as a warrior long ago, and wondering as I neared what I would find awaiting me in Arianna's eyes. I had promised to protect her family, but I had failed. And more than just that ate at my soul. For those butchers had killed every clansman they saw. No one was spared, no prisoners taken. The lifeless corpses of beautiful young women had littered the muddy village road alongside those of their families. So why, then, had they taken Arianna alive?

And what if they had not? What if she, too, had been cut down, only to revive again? What if they had only taken her captive when they'd realized that they *could not* kill her?

What if she knew now, what she was? What I, in my arrogance, had kept from her?

I paused to lean against a tree, swamped with a sudden weakness brought on by regret. "I should have told her," I murmured hoarsely. "By the Gods, I should have explained it all to her, whilst I still had the chance . . ."

But it was too late for regrets now, and when I lifted my head again, I could see the camp of my enemies. No less than fifty men in this troop, I judged. Four separate fires burned, and men surrounded each. Some eating, some drinking. Some still as stone, contemplating the flames. Some already lying down. And at the center of them all, a ragged tent had been erected, with men standing guard at each of its four corners.

"Arianna," I whispered, and my heart tugged as if trying to leap from my chest. She must be alive! That well-guarded tent had to be where they were keeping her. Every inch of my body seemed to stretch forward. My feet itched to run to her. And only by a supreme act of will did I manage to hold myself back. To draw a breath, and crouch down beside the large tree, and wait.

The hours crept by. Too slowly, too damned slowly. It seemed ages before the men in the camp truly slept. All except for those standing guard outside the tent. I could not hope to outfight fifty armed soldiers. Four, on the other hand, should pose no problem. But I would have to move quickly, carefully, and in utter silence. They must not be given the chance to sound the alarm.

I crept closer, then moved silently among the sleeping men, picking my way with great care. Still concealed in shadows, so the men guarding the tent could not see me. Not yet. But I could see them, for my vision in the night was excellent, honed by the kiss of immortality.

I took another step, then went still as I saw one of the men turn toward the tent flap, as if in response to some sound from inside. I strained to hear, and finally did, even from this distance. The voice was a whisper, barely more than a breath.

"Please. Only for a short while. I am so cold and afraid, and alone . . ."

No, I thought in silence. By the Gods, what did she think she was doing?

Even as I willed him not to, the man to whom she spoke gave a nod, and ducked inside. While the other three exchanged lewd grins, and muttered their speculation. Fury built in my blood, a hot, pulsing thing. The bastard was alone in that tent with my wife. My woman. My Arianna. He would not live to see another sunrise.

In a moment, he poked his head back out, and I could see that his chest was bare now. My jaw clenched, teeth grated, hands fisted.

"Why dinna the three of you go an' fetch a bite to eat?" the man asked softly of his companions. "A mite o' privacy is called for at the moment."

One of the men frowned. "We were told nay to leave our posts," he argued, keeping his voice low.

"Aye, so you were. But if you do this for me I'll return the favor . . . in just a while when your own turn comes 'round."

The other man's brows rose high. "The lady's willin' to take each of us?"

And the man inside the tent gave a shrug. "The lady's a prisoner. Who cares if she's willin'?" He grinned broadly, his meaning plain.

The other three exchanged glances. "I dinna think it wise," said one. "The chieftain, and Master Dearborne as well, warned us against that one. They say she's evil, same as the outlaw Nicodimus."

Another man nodded. "Aye, and the lad Nedmond himself witnessed the demon, cuttin' the heart from the very chest of Master Kohl."

"Ah, she's but a woman. You can well imagine Laird Marten is takin' what pleasure he wishes from his own captive wench! An' I intend to do the same."

Nicodimus stiffened. Marten . . . Gods, he should have known Marten would come to avenge his brother.

But there was no time to think, for the other men sighed, and nodded their agreement. "Dinna be too long," said one who hadn't spoken before now. "An' dinna untie the wench, either."

The bare chested one grinned again. "Nay, my friend, I willna. I prefer them bound, I do." Then he ducked back inside the tent, likely to ravage my wife.

I drew my dagger as the three men wandered away from the tent, heading toward me. I saw the fire they'd chosen, one with a barrel of ale standing nearby, and a pot half full of stew near enough the flames so it would still be warm.

I got closer, crouched down, and waited, though it nearly killed me to do so.

Two of them dipped out a cup of the stew, and sat down, while the third went straight for the ale, a short distance away. Even as he drew the foaming brew from the spigot, I crept up behind the other two. A silent slice, and the first one's throat was cut along with his windpipe. The second never knew a thing was wrong until his mate's legs began thrashing and the stew he'd held tipped to the ground. He glanced sideways, his eyes widened, and my hand covered his mouth even as my blade drove into the base of his neck, cleanly severing his spine. He did not move or breathe again.

His cup full of ale, froth spilling over his hand, the third man turned with a smile and started toward them, frowning when he glimpsed his comrades lying still on their backs. As he paused, squinting at them through the darkness, and then moving closer, I crept 'round until I could come up behind him. I knew the instant he saw the blood, the second he realized death had visited his camp this night. For his body went taut and his head turned as if to shout to the others. But the sound never emerged, for my arm clamped tight 'round his neck from behind, and my hands gripped his head and twisted hard. He went limp when his neck snapped. I lowered him to the ground, and he looked for all the world as if he were sleeping.

Then I turned toward that tent again, and the blood thundered in my temples as I moved quickly, quietly forward. If the bastard had touched Arianna, if his hands were upon my woman, his death would be slow.

Wrenching the tent flap open, I leapt inside, dagger drawn.

The woman before me was standing, naked except for the shift she was pulling on, over her head. The guard lay at her feet, his face frozen in a surprised grimace. He wore nothing except the dagger that protruded from his chest, and the blood that slicked his skin.

"Arianna," I whispered, reaching for her.

Her head and arms poked through, and she straightened the shift around her legs, turning to face me. Not Arianna. Not her at all.

"Nidaba? But . . . but I thought—"

"Exactly what the bastards intended you think, no doubt," she whispered. She gripped my hand. "Come, we must go before we're found out."

"But Arianna . . ." I began.

"She is not here, Nicodimus. Come. *Now.* I'll explain as we go." And she drew me from the tent.

In silence we made our way from the camp. Nidaba led me to where the soldiers' horses were picketed, helping herself to one as I quieted the others. I loosed the remaining mounts, and led them into the forest, before slapping their rumps and letting them run free. We raced quickly to where Black was tied, and were far away before we heard the shouts of alarm. Far enough away so I knew they would have no chance of catching us.

"Where is she?" I asked Nidaba.

She lowered her head. "Their leader took her, Nicodimus. His home is to the south, from what I was able to overhear. A keep called Kenwick. Do you know it?"

I did not. But it would not stop me. "Their leader," I said with distaste. "Marten. The bastard has hounded me for the last time. I do not know this Kenwick, but I will find it," I vowed. "And when I do, Marten will die."

"He knew you would follow the others," Nidaba said slowly. "So he sent them in the opposite direction, with me as their prize."

I glanced at her quickly, for once forgetting my own anguish. "Nidaba . . . did they harm you?"

She averted her gaze. "They were ordered not to touch me until I was safely in the dungeons of this . . . Kenwick Keep. I was to be delivered unharmed to a man called Dearborne, for what, I do not know."

"They were *ordered* not to touch you," I repeated, watching her face closely. "Was it an order they obeyed, Nidaba?"

For a moment, she was silent. Then she only whispered, "Most of them did." She met my gaze and said no more. And I knew she would not. "This is far from the matter at hand, Nicodimus. There is something you must know. Arianna . . ."

I closed my eyes as she paused, drawing a breath, sensing what was to come.

"She was run through," Nidaba told me. "She experienced death for the first time, my friend. And likely revived to realize the truth."

I closed my eyes against the pain that flooded my soul. "I feared as much. I should have told her."

"There is naught to be done about it now. She knows. And likely knows you did as well, and kept it from her. You should be aware of it before you face her again."

"Why did he take her, Nidaba? Why, when I'm the one he wants?"

"I do not know, I only know he took her and rode south. If it were Arianna's heart he wanted, surely he'd have simply taken it and been done with her."

"A heart so young would be of little use to a Dark Witch as old as Marten," I protested.

She nodded. "I have thought of that. And realized, Nicodimus, even before I knew who he was, that perhaps it is your heart he is after. Now I am even more certain. Arianna is simply serving as his bait. If you go after her at Kenwick, you will be walking directly into Marten's trap. Just the way he wants you to do."

I looked up sharply. "I've thought of that, as well. But if he wanted me to follow him to Kenwick, then why the ruse to lead me away?"

Nidaba shrugged. "To give him time to prepare? To set this trap of his in such a way that there will be no chance for you to escape?"

I knew she was trying to warn me, to prepare me. To dissuade me from rushing headlong into disaster, perhaps even death. But it did not matter. Nothing would keep me from Arianna. Nothing.

"I have no choice in this. She is my wife, you know this, Nidaba. I must go after her."

"Even if it costs your life?" she asked, softly, for she already knew the answer. "Even . . . if it costs you your immortal heart?"

"I love her," I whispered, the confession draining me. Saying it aloud to Nidaba solidified the feelings in my heart. With the confirmation came the fear, more intense, more vividly real than before. Certain disaster awaited me, I knew it in my gut. Yet I was powerless to divert it. "Gods help me, Nidaba, but I love her."

Closing her eyes, she nodded. "I feared as much. I . . . can only hope she's worthy of that love," she whispered.

"I only hope," I said, my voice hoarse, "I didn't wait too long to realize it. For though she loved me once, Nidaba, she could very well hate me by now."

His keep would have held Lachlan Keep twice within its solid walls. Huge blocks of chiseled rock towered high above the tall sturdy outer wall. Kenwick was a dark, dreary place. Large, but made of dark stone, with few ornaments and only a small number of torches for light. The gate itself seemed to have been built of entire tree trunks. Surely not even an army of men could gain access to such a fortress.

But could Nicodimus? Would he even attempt such an impossible feat?

Upon her arrival she was given into the hands of serving girls, not one, but two of them. A few men lingered about the great hall. One who wore a dark robe with its cowl pulled over his head stood silent and watchful. He made her shiver, that hooded man.

"You are a lady, Arianna of Stonehaven, and as a lady you shall be treated," Marten said, as he waved the serving girls closer.

"I am a prisoner," she replied.

Marten lowered his head, and his eyes seemed saddened. "'Tis my hope that will one day change. That you will grow to be happy here, Arianna. And that you will wish to stay. But until that day comes, aye, lassie, you are my prisoner."

She shook her head firmly, tears burning in her eyes. "I will never wish to stay with you. My only wish is to be back with my husband again."

One of the serving girls, the younger one, by the looks, caught her breath. Marten glanced up at her, a sharp reproach appearing, then vanishing in his eyes. He cleared his throat. "These are your servants, Arianna. They will attend to your every need. Lydia and Kathleen." He indicated each of them with a wave of his hand. Lydia was younger, with dark hair and eyes, and she reminded Arianna of the sister she had lost. Her beloved Raven. The thought gave her heart a painful twist. The other one was of her own dear mother's age, she guessed.

Looking again at the hooded man, she asked, "And who is this?"

Marten said nothing, but the man moved closer, lowering his cowl to reveal a thin, aged face. "I am Nathanial Dearborne. I am Marten's . . . spiritual counselor."

Marten cleared his throat, and the old man moved away.

"Your lady is in need of a bath," Marten addressed the servants. "And garments suitable to her station. I leave her in your care."

Lydia came forward and curtsied before me. "Come, my lady. You look weary and worn. Let us tend you."

Arianna glanced up quickly, and saw her first chance for escape. Surely the two women could not hold her by force. Not against her will.

Marten looked into her eyes, and seemed to read them. Without looking away, he lifted a hand behind him, crooked a finger. At once a burly man came forward, standing at the ready, weapons at his sides.

"You will attend the lady as well, Gorden. And dinna allow her out of sight even for an instant, for she has yet to realize that this is her new home. Until she does, I fear she will bolt at the first opportunity. And does she escape, Gorden, I'll have your head. Do you ken?"

Gorden nodded, his eyes flicking over Arianna briefly. She shivered at his cold glance. As if she were a possession to be guarded, or an animal in need of tending.

"I regret this is necessary, Arianna," Marten told her softly, and he lifted her hand and brushed his lips across the back of it. She shuddered in revulsion. "Perhaps the day will come when it no longer is."

She knew her disappointment showed in her eyes. Her hopes for escape crushed, at least for now. But she would not stop trying, nor stop seeking an opportunity. If she were patient, and cunning, one would surely come.

"It willna matter how many guards you place upon me, Marten. Nicodimus will come for me. Nothin' will stop him."

Marten spared her a pitying glance and stroked her hair, but she shied away from his touch. "Poor Arianna, clingin' to false hope. But you'll see soon enough that your husband will nay come for you. Because he doesna care. But I do, lass. I do."

Turning away, she hurried off, unsure where she was going, only needing to be away from this man who spoke so horribly of her beloved Nicodimus. Lydia caught up, gripping her elbow gently and steering her in the right direction. "Come, my lady. This way." And then leaning close, she whispered very softly, for Arianna's ears alone. "Take heart. My dear mother used to say that true love always prevails. Dinna give up hope, no matter what Laird Marten says."

Arianna glanced sideways at the girl, and sensed she might have found an ally here, in this strange, impenetrable prison. And perhaps, in time, a friend. Having one might make the short time she would be forced to spend here a bit more bearable. But there would not be *much* time, either way. For Nicodimus would come. She clung to that hope.

But when a full week had passed, with no sign of her husband, hope began to fade.

Each day she was dressed in fine, costly gowns, her hair styled in ringlets, and glittering jewels and gold adorned her fingers, her wrists, and even her earlobes. Gifts, all of them, from her captor. They felt to her like chains more than jewels, but Marten insisted she wear them. She dined in the style of royalty, seated at the high table, Marten's table. Unlike Joseph Lachlan, this laird seemed to hold no fondness for eating among his clansmen, and his table stood far apart from theirs, all the way on the opposite side of the gray and somber great hall.

Marten's table was near a hearth, where a fire always burned. No one else dined at the high table except for Dearborne. The man seemed to be considered of great importance to Marten. She was not certain why. The others sat away from that warmth, and if the evening were cold, and the men uncomfortable, it seemed not to disturb Laird Marten at all.

The chambers she had been given were large, but just as gloomy and dark as the rest of the hideous place. And always, wherever she went, her guard, Gorden, stood to one side of her, watching. Always watching.

His dark eyes watched her as she dressed, or undressed, or bathed. Lingering where they would, for as long as he wished. It seemed he had his master's consent to ogle her.

Each evening, Marten came to her, and spoke for long hours of Nicodimus's past deeds, all of them evil. And of Nicodimus's longtime lover Nidaba, and the way he would touch her, and likely was spending every night in her arms. He would talk on and on, while she was forced to sit and listen to the details of the things her husband was likely doing with his lover, even now.

A dark cloud settled over Arianna as the days passed by, slowly, so slowly. Her hopes faded with each night that Nicodimus did not burst through the gates, sword in hand, to rescue her. She cried often. It seemed each time she did, Marten appeared there. As if someone were reporting her every whisper to the man. He would speak soft words, words of comfort, and make promises that he would one day end her terrible pain, mend her poor, broken heart.

At last . . . at long last, she realized the truth. Nicodimus was not coming for her, for if he were, he would have been here by now. But she could not stir a tender feeling for Marten, nor did she wish to do so. She could never love another as she did her Nicodimus, nor would she even want to. And she would not live her life as Marten's possession, no matter how richly she would be kept.

Without hope, her mind seemed to sharpen. And at last, she was able to think clearly once more. Without Nicodimus to depend upon, a bit of the rebellious girl she had been stirred back to life in her soul. Stirred from beyond the depths of grief and shock that had, for a time, silenced her. And Arianna came to understand that she had no one to depend upon but herself.

Silently, she vowed never to forget that lesson again, nay, not for as long as she lived.

Secretly, Arianna began to plan.

She need only pretend. She need only convince Marten that her feelings had changed, and that she was willing to stay with him, to be his woman. And once he believed the lie, his defenses would relax. Gorden's constant watchful eye would turn away from her. And that would be the time when she would make good her escape.

But she would need to be convincing. Marten was no fool, and would not believe easily. So she began slowly, offering him a slight smile when he spoke to her at mealtime. Forcing herself not to draw away when he took her hand, or touched her face. Even seeking him out once or twice in the castle, and claiming she had been lonely and wished his company. She asked him to tell her about her new nature as an immortal, and to explain to her the tingling jolt that rocked through her each time he touched her.

And finally, one day when they were alone in the great hall, Marten kissed her without warning. Arianna knew she would never have a better opportunity. She swallowed her revulsion, and linked her arms 'round his neck, letting her body go soft, and parting her lips in invitation. She felt his reaction. His body hardened, and his heart hammered in his chest as he held her tighter, plundering her mouth in a way that made her want to retch. But she held her ground, refusing to let him see the truth. She pressed herself against him, closed her eyes, and told herself it was necessary. Necessary. She would do anything to get free of him.

Anything.

When at last, he lifted his head away, she breathed heavily and deeply, and stared deep into his eyes. "I have missed being held in a man's arms," she whispered.

His eyes filled with fire, he slid a hand up the front of her to cup her breast. And when she gasped in surprise and disgust, he took it to be a gasp of sheer pleasure. "Give yourself to me, Arianna. And I promise, you'll nay miss a man's touch ever again. For I will touch you often, and thorough, and well."

She released all her breath. "Aye, Marten. Aye. Touch me. Touch me everywhere."

His smile was one of victory, one of possession and ownership and pride. But also, one of doubt. "I am nay so certain I believe you, lass."

Her confidence wavered, but she stiffened her resolve. "How shall I prove myself to you?"

He looked at her, his hot gaze roaming from head to toe. Then slowly, he reached out, and began unlacing the front of her gown. Panic made her heart race, but she only stood still, eyes closed. Whatever was necessary, she reminded herself. For her freedom.

His hands worked steadily, but slowly, so she had ample time to object. When the laces were loosed, he spread the bodice open still wider, and then clenching the fabric in his fists and giving a brutal tug, he tore the dress wider still. Her breasts spilled free, bared to his hungry stare.

He touched them, his hands cupping and squeezing them, his fingers closing on her nipples, and tugging at them. "I want you very badly, Arianna," he said, his voice thoughtful as his hands worked, pinching her, kneading her. "Do you want me, too?"

"Aye," she whispered.

"Then tell me. Make me believe you, Arianna. Convince me of this desire you claim."

With everything in her, she resisted, and yet forced herself to speak the lies to him. "I want you, Marten. More than I've ever wanted any man."

He smiled again, and bent his head and nursed at her breasts, first one and then the other. Arianna placed her hands at his head fast, instinctively, her intent to push him away. But she fought her heart and won. Instead she held him to her, tipped her head back, closed her eyes, and sighed loudly. Marten's hand caught her skirts and pulled them up high on her thigh, and higher, baring her down below, and plunging his hand between her legs. He worked her there with his hand, rubbed her hard and fast with roughened, cold fingers, as his mouth tugged and his teeth nipped at her breast. And she whispered, "Please, Marten . . . please . . ."

A sound, a broken gasp, gave her to know someone else had entered the great hall. Mortified, she looked up quickly. And then her soul seemed to shatter, for Nicodimus stood in the open doorway, sword in hand, eyes . . . so tortured she couldn't bear it. He only stood there, staring in anguish as Marten laved her breasts and drove his hand ever deeper.

"Nicodimus, nay!" she cried. "It isna—"

Marten bit down hard, and she uttered a sound that was a cry of pain, but she knew it would not seem so to Nicodimus. To her husband. And even as she pulled against Marten's hands and his mouth, she saw another form—a dark, hooded form—enter behind Nicodimus. Nathanial Dearborne! She cried a warning, but too late. The Dark One moved fast, lifting a blade, and plunging it into Nicodimus's back.

He sank to his knees. With a sudden desperate push, Arianna finally jerked free of Marten's embrace, and ran to Nicodimus, falling down beside him. His eyes were already beginning to glaze over. . . .

"Nicodimus, 'twas an act, all you saw! I vow, 'twas only a trick!"

"And a fine trick it was, Arianna," Marten called, his voice tinged with glee. "Our plan to lure him here worked perfectly, wouldn't you say? You did it so perfectly. You shall be well rewarded."

Nicodimus shook his head very slightly, his fading eyes holding hers. "How . . . why, Arianna . . . ?" he whispered. And then the light in his eyes died out.

"Nicodimus, nay! Nay! I love you, I vow to the Gods, I do. No one else. Only you!"

But he didn't hear her. He was beyond her words now. Marten was laughing as he came forward. He said, "Your plan worked perfectly, old man. And I thank you. Now, at last, I shall have the most powerful heart in existence. And I will have vengeance on my dear brother-in-law as well."

He yanked Arianna by her hair up from where she knelt on the floor. "And for you, my little liar . . . Gods, you know you almost had me believing you." His fist smashed into her face, and she crumbled to the floor atop Nicodimus. Consciousness fled in a sudden rush of blackness. Gods, if only she would never have to wake again.

Chapter 15

I could not believe my eyes when I saw her in the arms of another. Not after she'd sworn to me that she would never give herself to any man but me. Not after she had spoken of her love for me so many times. And when I glanced to the side and saw that the man who held her was none other than Marten, I drew my blade. *He must die!* My mind screamed the command. He had stolen the hearts of innocents and fed on their power for seven long centuries. He and his brother, both determined to kill me, to have their vengeance, had murdered Joseph Lachlan, his entire family and clan. There was nothing they would not do to destroy me.

And nothing they could have done to torment me more than what Marten was doing now. Ravishing Arianna—my wife—right in front of me. My mind exploded in a blinding rage, so white hot I ignored the senses I should have been heeding. And the attack came from behind.

As I lay dying, Marten congratulated my wife on her plan having worked perfectly. I looked up into her eyes, which were wide and afraid. Her entire body trembled as she held together the gaping front of her dress and shook her head slowly from side to side.

It did not fit. The way she looked, simply did not fit with what she had done. But there was no time to ponder that, indeed, no time for anything at all. My time was over. I died as the blood drained from my body, and knew as the light faded that this would be my final death. For the bastard would have my heart this time.

Marten would have my heart . . . or as much of it as Arianna had left for him. For truly, she had the bulk of it. I could feel it bleeding in her small, slender hands.

When Arianna regained consciousness, it was to see Marten lying dead upon the floor. And farther away, near the door, Dearborne, that frightening old man, was just straightening away from Nicodimus, a bloody, still-beating heart cradled in his palms.

She screamed her husband's name and raced forward. But the old man only backed away as she hurled herself down upon Nicodimus's bloody form. The gaping wound in his chest, the scarlet wetness staining his clothes, the utter lifelessness of his body, all of it too terrible to look upon. And there was his dagger, still clutched in his fisted hand.

"Do not be so upset, child. You're young. You'll find another," Nathanial Dearborne rasped.

Rage welled up in her. Rage and violence, and a burning lust for the killer's heart. "You tricked him," she whispered. "You and Marten. This entire scheme was created just so you could kill Nicodimus."

"How very astute of you, Arianna. Yes, indeed, I've been planning this for a very long time. I was there, you see, when the brothers learned of their sister's death, and heard the tales of their brother-in-law, whom they detested, having apparently risen from the dead on a field of battle. It was I who told them the way to gain immortality for themselves. I who showed them how they might live long enough to have their vengeance. Of course, Marten believed Nicodimus's heart would be his." He glanced at the dead man. "He had no idea I was only allowing him to do my work for me, nor that I would collect the prize for myself. And his own heart will be my bonus in just a moment. I win," he said. "I always win."

Arianna's fingers inched forward, and she eased the blade from Nicodimus's dead hand. Then she turned her head slowly. Dearborne had placed her husband's heart in a small box, and this he dropped into a drawstring sac that hung at his waist. Then he pulled out his blade, already stained with Nicodimus's blood, and started toward the dead Marten.

"You're mistaken," Arianna whispered, straightening to her feet. "You dinna always win. You willna win today."

Dearborne stopped where he was, facing her, his silver-gray brows lifted high. Then he smiled. "Child, you cannot mean to challenge me. You're barely a newborn."

"You'll nay leave this castle alive, Nathanial Dearborne," she whispered. And then she charged him.

Nathanial's eyes narrowed, but he drew his dagger to defend himself. However, he had obviously not expected so furious an attack. Arianna was driven by rage, a fury more powerful than his need for a living heart had ever been. He fought, yes. To preserve his life. She fought for the loss of her love, and there was no power stronger. Her anger seemed to surge from her in waves that sent him staggering. She had no care for her own life, and was so numb that she did not feel the blows he returned. There was nothing, nothing but rage, all of it directed at the old man.

"He died thinkin' I betrayed him," she said, panting, slashing with her blade. Tearing through the old man's robes, and his flesh more than once. "I'll ne'er have the chance to tell him the truth. An' all because of you!" She slashed again, slicing his chest clear to the bone.

Gasping, staggering backward, the old man shook his head. For the first time, Arianna saw fear in his eyes. He continued backing away until he reached a heavy chair, then he spun, snatched it up, and threw it at her.

The piece was far heavier than a man of his age should have been able to so much as lift, much less use as a weapon. She hadn't been expecting it, but should have recalled what Nicodimus had told her about the increased strength and honed senses of immortals. The chair hit her hard, and drove her backward, smashing her into the wall. She shook herself, shoving it away and surging to her feet again, only to find Dearborne gone. He'd fled from her, leaving the door wide open on the carnage he'd left behind.

Gone. And Nicodimus's heart gone with him. So final. It was so final. Her husband was dead, and the enormity of that was more than she could bear.

A sob was wrenched from her breast as Arianna once again went to her husband. Her fault, she realized. Her fault, all of this. If only she had obeyed him, if only she had stayed safe in the Stone Circle as he'd bade her do. Oh, if only . . .

But he was gone now. He had explained enough to her so that she knew this. He would not revive. His heart had been taken from him and he was lost to her now. Just as Raven, her sister was lost to her. And just as her dear parents were, as well. Arianna was alone. More alone than she had ever been.

A low moan made her turn fast. Marten! His heart had not been taken, and he moved slightly now. Slowly, he opened his mouth as if to draw a breath—and she recalled that stunning, painful first gasp she herself had drawn, upon waking from the dead.

She lunged toward him, flipping the dagger in her hand so she held the blade end, and brought the jeweled hilt crashing down on his head.

He did not move again.

He would, though. Unless . . .

Biting her lower lip, she bent over Marten, and with her dead husband's blade, she sliced through the fabric he wore, baring his chest. She positioned the blade, point down, above his heart, closing both fists 'round the hilt. Grating her teeth, she closed her eyes tight, and drove the blade deep into his chest.

The body went rigid, and when her eyes flew open wide she saw the blood bubbling forth from around the embedded blade. She saw his eyes bulging, pain burning in them.

Shaking her head slowly, grimacing and trembling, she jerked the blade free of him, and rose, backing away. "I canna," she whispered. "Gods forgive me, but I canna cut a livin' heart from a man's chest!"

Marten slumped back into temporary death, as Arianna fought not to choke or faint. She couldn't do either of those things. She was immortal. A High Witch, alone in the world. She would need to be strong to survive. She would need to eliminate her weak stomach as well as her soft heart. She would make herself hard and powerful, and no foe would ever take her. No man would ever use her.

But first . . .

She looked at her husband once more. His face still and relaxed as if he were only sleeping. First she would see he had a proper burial. And it would be in the place he loved best.

The servants had fled. She would have to work on her own. She fetched a silken coverlet, tucked it beneath her arm and went outside to seek a horse and wagon.

She'd traveled only an hour, Nicodimus's lifeless body in the back of the wagon she drove. When she came to a stream, she stopped, and carefully, lovingly, she stripped away his torn, bloodied clothes. Then she bathed him, as much she thought, with her tears as with the cold water. As she did, her gaze fell upon the twin pendants he wore.

With trembling fingers, she lifted one of them, fingering it with sobs all but choking her. He must have found it. He'd had one like it, all along. It must be . . . it must be something worn by High Witches. And he'd donned hers . . . almost as if he'd cared for her after all . . .

Aye, and he must have, or he wouldn't have come for her. Died trying to save her from Marten. But she'd made him hate her in the end.

Swallowing her tears, she lifted one of the two pendants from his neck—the one that seemed older, more dulled with age, for it was his—and lowered its chain over her own head. She pressed a kiss to it, and then to her own pendant, which she left upon the body of her beloved.

"Remember me, Nicodimus, wherever you are. And perhaps . . . someday . . . forgive what I did here this day. For I love you. I love you still."

Tears rolling fresh down her face, she continued bathing her husband's violated body.

When he lay clean and glistening with droplets, she wrapped his body in the silken coverlet she'd taken. It was a deep blue. A fitting shade, she thought vaguely. A sad color.

When all was finished, she reached for the wagon to pull herself once again into the seat.

"Arianna!"

She turned fast, finally realizing she was not alone, and saw Nidaba thundering toward her on a horse.

"I've just come from Kenwick!" she shouted as the mount slid to a hasty stop and Nidaba leapt to the ground. "There was blood everywhere, and no more than a quivering servant to be found. Gods, what happened there?"

Arianna opened her mouth to speak, but found the words would not come. Nidaba gripped her shoulders, shook her. "We were coming for you, Nic and I. He kept ordering me to stay behind, but I refused. Then he slipped away last night while I slept. Damn him for being so protective! He knows full well that I—" She stopped there as her gaze fell upon the silk-wrapped body in the back of the wagon. She fell silent, searching Arianna's face. "Oh, Gods no. Tell me it is not him," she begged.

When Arianna still said nothing, Nidaba rushed to the wagon, and pulled the silk away from Nicodimus's face. "Oh, no," Nidaba whispered, her voice gone soft and coarse. "Oh, please, no . . ."

"I am sorry, Nidaba. 'Twas my fault, truly. Marten . . . and this other immortal, Dearborne, they set a trap for Nicodimus. An' it worked, just the way they both intended it would. I . . . I . . ."

"You cost him his life! Damn you, Arianna!"

Arianna lowered her head, unable to deny the charge. "If I could exchange my life for his, I would gladly do it," she whispered.

Nidaba stepped away from the wagon, and stood facing Arianna. "I ought to kill you myself," she whispered. Her entire body quivered with rage, her face was snow white and her dark eyes gleamed.

"If you wish," Arianna said softly. "I'll nay fight for my life. I ask only that you finish what I've begun. Bury him, Nidaba, at the Stone Circle he so loved. An' if you've a hint of mercy in you for me, you'll lay me to rest beside him there. For I loved him. I love him still."

"You loved him so much you let him die for you," she seethed. "The one servant I found blubbered that Nic had burst through the doors to find you in Marten's arms. Marten, the man who hated Nicodimus above all others! What were you doing with him if you loved your husband so, Arianna?"

Her shoulders slumped, Arianna whispered, "I was bargaining for my freedom. Like any common whore." Hands trembling, she took the blade she now carried at her side, and held it out to Nidaba. "Use Nicodimus's dagger," she said softly. "'Twill be fittin', dinna you think?"

Snatching the blade away, Nidaba growled fiercely, and finally lifted it high above her head, and drove it downward, toward Arianna's chest. Arianna stood motionless, awaiting the blow. But it never came. The blade sank instead, into the wooden side of the wagon just behind her. "Stay clear of me, Arianna Sinclair," she whispered. "Stay clear of me, for if I see you again, I *will* kill you!"

Spinning away from her, Nidaba took a step toward her horse, only to fall to her knees. For a long time she remained there, sobbing so hard she scarcely breathed except to mutter "Nicodimus" over and over again, brokenly. She shook all over, and her cries grew louder all the while. Until finally, they abated, and she went utterly silent. It was as if there were nothing left inside her.

"The man who killed my Nic," she said at last, "You said his name was Dearborne?"

"Aye, Nathanial Dearborne."

Nidaba nodded. "The same who wanted me brought here as his captive for some sick reason. Well he shall have me then. He shall have me and rue the day he harmed my beloved Nicodimus!"

She lunged to her feet, mounted her horse and rode away at a murderous gallop.

Arianna felt no relief that Nidaba had left her still alive. It would have been easier had the woman simply ended it. Her limbs heavy, like lead weights, she tugged Nicodimus's dagger from the wood. Then dragged herself into the seat to continue the journey.

She buried Nicodimus in the center of the ancient Stone Circle near the place that had once been her home. She covered his beloved, silk-wrapped body with earth. Then she sat upon his grave, drew his dagger, and grasping a handful of her long, golden hair, began sawing. Lock upon lock fell to the ground around her. And tears upon tears fell with them.

Eventually, she left that place. Left Scotland. Left all she'd known, and began her new life as an immortal High Witch. For the first time, she understood the pain Nicodimus had known so long ago, when he, too, had lost all those he'd loved, only to find that he must live on. No wonder he had been unable to love her. Unwilling to risk his heart that way. She understood now. She knew that she would never love again, either. But for far different reasons.

Oh, she feared the pain, the loss, just as Nicodimus had. She feared it. But it wouldn't matter if she feared it or not. She was incapable of loving another as she had loved her Nicodimus . . . as she still loved him.

One day, she vowed, she would find Nathanial Dearborne again, and make him pay for what he had done. And one day, perhaps, if her long ago spell had worked, she would find her beloved sister again, as well. That dim hope was the one thing that gave her the strength to keep going.

Until then, she had nothing to do, except prepare. She would learn. To fight, to kill . . . to survive.

PART TWO

Chapter 16

Arianna spent almost two hundred years alone. More utterly alone, she thought, than the last star to fade in the morning. And in that time, she nursed a hatred for Nathanial Dearborne and for Marten, that rivaled the sun for its blazing fury. She didn't see Nidaba in all that time, and didn't search for her. The woman hated her with good reason. Besides, seeing her would only be a painful reminder of Nicodimus and the brief, sweet time Arianna had spent with him. In his arms. Loving him, even though he couldn't return her feelings.

But that was history. She was no longer a seventeen-year-old girl in love. She was different now. She didn't look the same; she'd kept her hair short and liked it that way. Though perhaps if she looked very deeply, she would find somewhere inside, buried in the deepest part of her being, the notion that she left her hair short in memory of Nicodimus. In some kind of meaningless penance for the long ago mistakes that had cost him his heart.

She didn't *sound* the same. The lilt of the highlands had long since faded from her voice. She was hard, solitary, and she spent every moment she could honing her skills with a blade. She fought. She killed. She survived, with one thought foremost in her mind. Someday she would cross paths with Dearborne and Marten again. And when that day came, she would kill them for what they had done.

But almost two centuries after Nicodimus's brutal murder, something happened that softened Arianna's rocklike soul, and restored a sense of joy to her existence; in the summer of 1691, she found her sister. Raven at long last, lived again. Arianna's long ago spell *had* been true. Raven looked the same, bore the same name, and Arianna recognized her at once. And even though Raven didn't know who Arianna was at first, there had been an immediate connection, and a slow rebuilding of the bond they'd once shared. For over three centuries, they remained together almost continuously.

And then, a year ago, in 1998, another figure from the distant past had reappeared in Arianna's life. Nathanial Dearborne. He'd been determined to kill Raven, to take her heart for his own. He'd hated her for capturing the love of the man he'd thought of as his son. He blamed Raven for turning Duncan against him, and sought vengeance. But he hadn't counted on Arianna's presence, nor her intervention. Dearborne's attempt on Raven thwarted, he had run back to his rooms to gather his belongings and flee Arianna's wrath. . . . At last, her chance to avenge Nicodimus had come. . . .

Arianna walked into the room while Nathanial Dearborne gathered up the tiny wooden boxes, all of them filled with stolen, still beating hearts. The sources of his strength, his very life. For a moment she only stood in the doorway, watching him as he packed the hearts in a case, and began reaching for the volumes of journals that lined the shelves. It amazed her that her hatred for him could still be so strong, after four hundred eighty-seven years . . . for that was precisely how long it had been since she'd seen the bastard plunge his blade into Nicodimus's back.

Arianna drew a breath, and stilling her emotions, began to speak. "You took the man I loved," she all but growled. "And I'll kill you for it."

Dearborne froze, then turned slowly to face her. And Arianna knew he feared her. She'd nearly bested him when she'd been but a fledgling immortal, after all. He had to know she could kill him easily now. He'd always known. It was why he'd been so carefully avoiding her for so very long. She could see it in his eyes.

"Don't be so certain, Arianna," he said to her slowly. "I was unprepared for you before. But never again will I underestimate the power of hatred."

"It wasn't the power of hatred, Nathanial. It was the power of love." He took a step forward, but she moved to block the door fully. She stood there with her legs shoulder width apart, knuckles on her hips, chin high. "Hatred has no power. The power that nearly killed you then was the power of love. My love for one of the many you murdered. And it's that same power that will destroy you now."

He took a step backward, setting his packed case on the floor to free his hands. She watched his every move, ready to react. "Which one was he, this victim of mine? It's been so long . . . I can scarcely remember them all. Was he the barbaric Celtic warlord? The Mayan Shaman?" He shrugged. "Not that it matters. They all died on their knees, begging for mercy."

"I can hardly wait to see how you do," she said, and drew her dagger, held it lightly, tossed it from one hand to the other. "But to remind you, his name was Nicodimus, and he died with the blade of a coward in his back. And you remember him perfectly well. I know you do."

His Adam's apple moved as he swallowed his fear—or tried to. "Will you kill me unarmed, Arianna, or give me a chance to draw my blade?" His hand inched toward the leather pocket at his side.

She narrowed her eyes. "I'll kill you in a fair fight or not at all," she told him. "Go on."

He drew the weapon from its sheath. Not his dagger, but she didn't see in time. Dearborne pulled out a handgun, and even as Arianna gasped and tried to dart out of its line of fire, he leveled the barrel and pulled the trigger.

The bullet hit Arianna in the chest like a freight train, driving her backward through the open doorway, and into the hall. The pain exploded even as the floor fell away, and she realized she was tumbling head over heels down the stairs. Her body crashed and pounded, twisted and turned, and when she came to a stop at last, her limbs were bent beneath her, broken, and she knew the healing wouldn't have time to take place, because Dearborne wouldn't let it.

It was over. She had failed . . . failed Nicodimus. Again.

She opened her eyes and saw the evil bastard standing over her. "It's a shame you prefer a fair fight," he said. He crouched low, tore open her blouse and she could do nothing to prevent it. "I prefer a sure win, myself." And then she felt the fiery tip of his blade slicing her flesh.

"Raven . . . will kill you for this . . . ." The thought of her sister's grief was nearly as painful as the rest.

"Oh, I'm sure she will try." Dearborne tilted his head thoughtfully.

"Do you ever wonder about the bodies of slain immortals, Arianna? They die, but don't really. They remain ever new, ever young. Do you suppose their minds are still alive, as well? Do you suppose they *know* they've been buried alive?"

She did wonder, had wondered endlessly, ever since Nicodimus had been taken from her. But she had no more time to wonder, because Dearborne chose that moment to drive his blade into her chest to the hilt. Arianna's mind exploded in a screaming blast of agony . . . and then she descended into blackness.

But it was a blackness that faded.

The next thing Arianna felt was the jolt that seemed so much like electrocution. Her back arched sharply as she sucked new breath into her lungs. And as she relaxed and blinked her eyes open, it was to see her beloved sister staring down into her eyes. Fear and shock raged inside, and Arianna clutched at her chest, which throbbed and tingled. "How . . . how did you . . . what . . . ?"

Raven stroked her hair. "It's over, Arianna. You're all right." She smiled through her tears. "You're really all right."

Raven hugged her close, but Arianna couldn't stop her own violent trembling. "B-but . . . he took my heart."

"I know, I know, darling. But now I've taken his. And yours . . . yours beats still, back inside you where it belongs."

"But—"

She was interrupted then, by Duncan, her sister's lover, the man who'd once thought of Dearborne as a father. "It was Nathanial," he said. "He seemed to want to clear his conscience before he died. So he told me how to bring you back."

"But how could he know that?" Arianna asked, amazed. "I didn't even know that such a thing was possible, and . . ." She blinked then, as the magnitude of what this meant hit her fully. "He has other hearts here."

"Well, yes," Raven said. "Weak ones, nearly lifeless, some of them, but—"

"Don't you see?" Arianna sat up slightly, grasping her sister's shoulders. "My Goddess, Raven, don't you see what this means?"

Raven hadn't seen. Not fully. Not then. But Arianna had. She'd taken all those captive hearts, knowing that one of them, one precious heart, belonged to Nicodimus. And if there was a chance in creation that she could return it to him, restore him as she had been restored . . . she had to try.

She'd taken Dearborne's journals as well, pored over them. And what she found in them horrified her. The man had considered himself some kind of scientist. He'd taken other immortals captive, kept them and experimented on them to find their strengths, their weaknesses, all with the intent of becoming the strongest of them all. He had killed and revived his victims time and again, observing the effects, making notes. He had taken hearts, and returned them, just to see what the results would be. His notes made mention of one "subject" in particular. One he called only "the dark woman," whom he'd tormented longer than any other, before she had finally escaped him. Dearborne had written that this woman had been the oldest High Witch he'd ever known, and that even her strong mind had begun to flirt with madness, in time. He had intended to kill her once and for all when he'd finished with her, but she'd managed to break free before he'd done so. As she read those words, Arianna thought of Nidaba. The last time Arianna had seen the woman, she had been going after Dearborne.

Gods, could this victim have been Nidaba? That strong, proud immortal Arianna had admired—and envied—so greatly?

Arianna, Duncan and Raven, had burned Dearborne's body. But before incinerating his heart, she'd performed an incantation over it, willing all its stolen power to return to the captive hearts where it belonged.

Once that was done, Arianna left her sister behind to begin the longest journey of her life. Armed with the six captive hearts, all beating strongly now in their little boxes, and the reams of information recorded in the journals of a madman, she set out to locate the bodies of Dearborne's victims, and to try to restore them to life.

But the first one . . . the very first heart she returned to its rightful home . . . would be that of Nicodimus. The man she had loved and lost. The man who believed she had betrayed him. The man . . . who had been her husband.

Chapter 17

Arianna stood upon the hill overlooking Stonehaven. It was rebuilt, isolated—backward by modern standards, space-aged in comparison to the way she remembered it. The ship had seemed to take forever to cross the Atlantic, and though she'd been impatient, there had been no other way. She certainly couldn't have boarded an airliner with six human hearts beating in her carry-on bag.

In her hands she held the small wooden box that contained the heart of Nicodimus Lachlan. Its beat had been weak, barely there, until she'd cast the spell to return all Dearborne's stolen power to its rightful owners. Now it beat strong and steady. And now she would try what her one-time husband had told her no Witch could do.

She would try to raise the dead.

The wind blew, riffling her short hair, brushing her cheeks with the scent of heather and the sea. Midnight now. The Witching Hour children spoke of in whispers on All Hallows' Eves. She walked slowly into the woods, leaving her vehicle, a small Jeep, parked nearby. A heavy backpack hung from her shoulders, and the jugs of rainwater suspended from either side of it bounced against her hips, and made it even heavier. But she had grown strong in four centuries of immortality. The weight was no burden to a High Witch as old as she. Deeper and deeper into the woods she trekked, until she located the site where the sacred Stone Circle had once towered.

Those monoliths were tumbled down now. A few remained upright, leaning drunkenly inward. Some lay flat and broken, large chunks missing, ruined by time or overzealous tourists who stumbled upon the circle and thought to take some of its magic home with them. Sacred souvenirs. The place was overgrown by vines and brambles. Few even knew it existed.

Arianna paused at the very center of the circle, where she had buried Nicodimus. Closing her eyes, she remembered him as he had been, and in turn, herself as she had been. She was not the same anymore. There was, she mused, a large difference between a girl of seventeen and a woman who had existed for centuries. But one thing remained the same. Her guilt. She blamed herself for Nicodimus's death just as surely as *he* had blamed her for it while the life drained away from him. And what she did now, she did to right the wrong she had done him. And for no other reason.

"You likely won't even know me now, Nicodimus," she murmured. According to Dearborne's hideous journals, others had been revived. Some right away, some more slowly, but all to varying degrees of confusion. And they had been relatively recent kills of his. The madman had noted that the longer he allowed an immortal to remain in death, the more disoriented they were upon their resurrections. Arianna herself had been dead only moments when she'd been revivified.

But Nicodimus . . .

Nicodimus had been lying in this dark mockery of death for centuries.

Even without that, he might not recognize her. Her once long golden hair was cropped short now. Her voice no longer carried the lilt of Scotland, and every shred of innocence had been burned from her eyes.

She no longer vomited at the thought of taking a heart. Indeed, she'd taken many. Quickly, coldly, and without remorse. For it was the way of things. She had come to learn that very early on in her new life.

Above all else in Arianna's mind, was the knowledge that if Nicodimus *did* somehow know her, and remember her, he would likely hate her for what she had done. His last glimpse of her had been in the arms of his darkest enemy. The man who'd hunted him all his life, and from whom he had come to rescue her. And he had died because of it.

"It doesn't matter," she told herself again. She had been telling herself the same things over and over all night as she'd made her preparations. "It doesn't matter. I'm righting a wrong. It isn't as if I still love him. It's been centuries. And that love belonged to an innocent girl—a girl who died along with her family back in that tiny cottage on that darkest of days. A girl . . . who no longer exists."

With a sigh of resignation, refusing to acknowledge the slight trill of anticipation singing through her veins and making her hands tremble, she set the box with its precious contents down, and shrugged off the large backpack. She set the water jugs aside, quickly loosing the knots that held them. Then, unzipping the pack, she took out the foldable shovel, the flashlight, the four white candles, and the soft, down-filled sleeping bag.

The moon sailed high, and the night breeze made the trees 'round her seem to whisper. Trees sacred to long ago Druids. Oaks, tall and mighty, so old they'd seen entire races come and go. These very trees had been in attendance at Nicodimus's burial. It was fitting they look on now, at this, his restoration.

Her hands still shaking, Arianna began to dig.

She hadn't buried him deeply. Her preternatural strength had only begun to manifest then, and besides, she'd been emotionally and physically drained. So firmly entrenched in her misery, she'd barely been able to hold her head up, much less dig a proper grave. But she had made it deep enough so that Nicodimus would be safe. No animals would have reached his perfectly preserved body.

She pushed the blade in with a foot, scooped out mounds of soil and flung it behind her. Over and over she did this, never tiring in the least. As the hole deepened and widened, she dug more carefully, inserting the shovel with great care, feeling for his body lying helpless, lifeless beneath the black earth. Her heart pounded harder with every bit of dirt she removed—but not from the exertion.

Finally she glimpsed a rotted scrap of deep blue satin. Her breath caught in her throat, and she fell to her knees, picking it up carefully, shaking the dirt away and then running her fingers over the fabric. "Nicodimus," she whispered.

Using her hands, now, she clawed more soil away, and finally saw one large hand, icy cold and so . . . so very still. Coated in dirt, damp with it. A sob escaped her as she brushed the dirt away. She dug faster, frantically now, scraping the dirt away from his forearm, then upper arm, and shoulder . . . until at last, she uncovered his face.

Earth was caked upon his skin, but she whisked it away. Soil had crumbled into the creases around his closed eyes . . . Gods, how she wanted to see them open again! She continued working, refusing to give in to the foolish urge to just sit and stare at him. She could not be discovered here. How would she ever explain herself? No, she must work quickly, and put her emotions aside. Close them off. Refuse to feel. It was easier than it might have been once. She had been practicing this very thing for a long time, after all.

When his body was free of its earthen tomb, she paused briefly, brushing the soil from her hands and staring down at him. He lay motionless, in some kind of suspended state. Neither alive, nor fully dead. Bathed in moonlight at the bottom of an uncovered grave, caked in earth. Naked, except for the few scraps of satin that remained. And the pendant—her pendant.

Her breath caught in her throat at the sight of it lying there, and it was as if the centuries, the very ages, melted away. The pain of losing him was as fresh and new in her heart as it had been on that day.

And yet, it had been so long. It had been so long since she'd looked at this man. Since she'd touched him.

Stop it!

Closing her eyes briefly, Arianna put a mental stronghold on her heart, and listened only to her mind. The practical voice telling her, step by step, what must be done. She had planned this all carefully. She knew what to do, how to proceed.

She went to the sleeping bag, unzipping it and laying it open, just to the left of the grave. Then she moved around to stand near Nicodimus's head, her feet in the grave on either side of it. Bending low, she gripped him underneath the arms, and tugged him out of the hole, onto the damp, mossy ground. The wound in his chest lay open, gaping, and filled with soil and stones, but no insects, thankfully. Evidently the insects had sensed this was no ordinary body to be feasted upon, and had stayed away. As she scooped the dirt and stones away, she wondered what Nicodimus felt, if anything, what he thought—if thoughts were still something of which he was capable. What he remembered . . . or would remember when he revived.

If he revived.

Over four hundred years. Gods, even Dearborne had never attempted to raise an immortal this long dead.

"It will work," she whispered, squaring her shoulders. "It *has* to work."

Arianna set the white candles around him, and lit them, one by one. Then she dug into the very bottom of the backpack for the large bowl and the clean cloths she'd brought along. Kneeling beside Nicodimus, she poured water from one of the jugs into the bowl, dipped a cloth, and held it, dripping, above his face. She squeezed gently, and the water trickled over him. Soil streamed away in dirty rivulets. Bending closer, she began to wash him.

Like history repeating itself, she thought, and the memories came vividly. Memories of the last time she'd washed his lifeless body this way . . . at a stream as she'd carried him back here to be buried.

Just like last time, tears mingled with the water. When the first one dropped from her face to his, it startled her. She stopped what she was doing, sat up straight, and touched her own cheek, only to find it damp. "You're a fool, Arianna. A hopeless fool," she told herself.

She bathed Nicodimus's face, and his neck. She washed his hands, gently working the soil away from each strong finger and from the creases in between. His arms and his chest, she cleansed. No movement came from him. No life. She spent a great deal of time on the wound in his chest, the place where his heart would rest once again, when she had finished. One entire jug of the fresh rainwater she had brought went to this purpose. She rinsed the gaping place again and again, and shone the flashlight upon the open wound, to be sure it was perfectly clean.

Then she moved lower, washing his strong thighs, and the place in between. His calves, and his feet. She rolled him over, and cleansed the ages of soil from his back and buttocks. And with the remaining water, she rinsed his hair, running her fingers through it to scrub the dirt away.

Finally, all was ready. All that remained was to replace his mighty heart. Arianna paused to brush a lock of gold and russet hair from his forehead. "Come back to me, Nicodimus. Fight your way back, if you must . . . but come back."

Closing her eyes, drawing a deep, steadying breath, she reached for the box with trembling hands. It was small, intricately etched with symbols and designs. Engraved upon the lid of each of Dearborne's tiny prisons was a single letter. She could only guess, only hope, that the N on this one stood for the initial of its rightful owner. Nicodimus.

Carefully, she lifted the lid, and gathered the heart in her hands. Lifting it high, tipping her face up to the moonlight, she held it, and it seemed to Arianna that its beat grew stronger as she spoke. "By the powers of the Ancient Ones, by every force of the Universe, I restore this heart. I revive this body. I resurrect this man. Nicodimus, I call you forth. Return to life. Live, Nicodimus. Live. *Live!*"

Slowly, she lowered the heart into his body, positioned it carefully, and took her hands away. "As I will it, so mote it be," she whispered.

She sat back on her heels and waited, watching. She stared until her eyes watered, willing his chest to heal, his body to accept and embrace its heart. But nothing happened.

Tears once again stood in her eyes, but she angrily blinked them away. "It might take time," she reminded herself. "That's all. Just time." Nodding hard in affirmation of that belief, she gently eased Nicodimus's body onto the waiting sleeping bag, and folding it over him, zipped it up. One by one she snuffed the candles, and packed them away. She attached the empty jugs to the sides of the backpack. She scraped the earth back into the empty grave, and the bits of rotted silk along with it. Then she folded the shovel and put that in the pack, as well. She packed the basin, the soiled cloths, the flashlight. All that remained was a length of rope. This she tied to the sleeping bag at either side of Nicodimus's head, then looped the rope around her waist, and set off.

The journey back to her Jeep seemed endless. His weight behind her seemed to increase with every step, and even with her tremendous immortal strength, she grew tired. Not physically so much as mentally. She wanted the journey over. She wanted him safe inside, out of sight. At last her vehicle came into view, just as the first blush of purplish predawn light painted the horizon.

Nicodimus was heavy, even for one with her power and strength. But not too heavy. She wrested his body into the car, closed the rear door, and leaned against it for a moment, sighing in relief. It was done. Or all but done.

But would it work? Would he awaken?

And if he did . . . what then?

With a sigh of resolution, she vowed to deal with that when the time came. Climbing behind the wheel, she started the engine, and drove over the rutted track and down into the village of Stonehaven; to the cottage that sat on the site of her onetime home. The place where she'd been born. Where she'd lived. Where she'd found her parents brutally murdered.

She had returned here several times over the centuries. Drawn back like a moth to the candle's flame. She had come back to the memories; the pain, the hurt, the loss. As if testing her resolve to feel none of it anymore. She had purchased the lot on one of those many visits, and had a modest home built there. She rarely visited it anymore—simply paid a local resident to see that the place was cared for, kept up. But somehow, she couldn't seem to let it go. It was as if that place were her one remaining connection to the mortal, headstrong girl she had been, and the happiness she had once known. It was as if selling it would be cutting herself off at the very root.

The house was a simple, two-story structure, with clapboard siding painted white, and black shutters at the windows. Closed now, those shutters. All of them. It wouldn't do to have anyone peering in just now. The house had two bedrooms and a bath upstairs, and one below, in the back. That would be Nicodimus's home . . . for now.

She peered again at the paling horizon as she shut off the engine. She'd best hurry and get him inside before the villagers began to wake. Quickly, she moved to the rear of the Jeep, opened it, and tugged him out. She paused only long enough to shut the doors, then dragged him quickly over the flagstone walk to the house. His body bumped up the three front steps to the door, and she opened it and pulled him through. With a surge of relief, she closed the front door, and turned the lock.

"Almost done," she whispered. "Perhaps it's good you're taking your time about waking, Nicodimus. I doubt you'd like being dragged around by a female."

She peered down at his pale face, but saw no change. Trying hard to keep disappointment from consuming her, she dragged his body across the living room floor, and through the door at the back, into the bedroom there.

She let him lay on the floor alongside the bed, while she hurried back to close and lock the bedroom door, just in case. And finally, she tugged back the covers, opened the sleeping bag, and with no small effort, maneuvered his limp form into the bed. Only then did she look again at the wound in his chest, eager to make sure his mighty heart hadn't been jostled out of place. It hadn't. It remained precisely as she had placed it. Was there more color to the pale, steadily beating heart than before? Was the tissue around it pinker? Or was it only wishful thinking?

No way to tell. Patience, she must have patience.

Drawing the covers over him, tucking them gently around him, Arianna finally slumped into the chair beside his bed, where she would wait . . . for as long as it took. Much like a funereal vigil, she thought. Only . . . in reverse. In times of old the bereaved would sit up the night through with the recently deceased corpse, the idea being to remain until the soul had surely left the body.

Arianna's strange vigil . . . was the wait for Nicodimus's soul to return. If indeed, it had ever been gone.

The silence of the room seemed to expand as she sat there. Until she could hear the beating of her own heart, and his, and no other sound.

Arianna drew Nicodimus's hand into her own and held it. The hours passed slowly, endlessly, and after more of them than she cared to count, she lost her battle with exhaustion and closed her eyes as sleep crept in to pull her under.

I emerged from a state of *nothing*, to a state of *everything*. Every part of my body burned. Every bit of my skin sizzled. My head felt as if a spike had been driven through my skull, and my chest, as if it were about to burst. The gasp I dragged in was noisy and painful. And then, just as suddenly, I went limp. Weak. Terrifyingly weak.

I opened my eyes.

A woman rose to her feet from where she'd been sitting in a chair beside the odd bed in which I lay. A beautiful woman. Her hair was cut oddly short, but golden in hue, and her eyes were as wide as all the world, and brown as a doe's. She clutched my hand in hers. And I felt it. I . . . I *felt* it!

"Nicodimus," she whispered. And one trembling, very warm hand touched my face. I thought I glimpsed teardrops dampening her eyes, but she blinked those away quickly enough, and leaned closer. "Nicodimus," she said again. "Can you hear me?"

"Yes." My lips formed the word, but the only sound that emerged was a rasp of air. I closed my eyes in frustration. The name she called me by—*Nicodimus*—yes, it was familiar to me. But my mind seemed lost in a fog I could not explain, and that my own name would seem so strange startled me. Who was I?

A coolness touched my lips, whilst a soft, strong hand lifted my head. A drinking vessel, made of glass and filled with water. I sipped from it, then drank deeply, closing my eyes once more. The liquid felt good on my parched throat. So good.

When the water was gone, the woman lowered my head again to the softness that pillowed me, and set the vessel aside. "How do you feel?" she asked me.

I had to think on that for a moment, for so many feelings were coursing through my body that it was an effort to identify any one in particular. "Weak," I finally answered. "Heavy. My head . . ." I tried to lift a hand to press to my temple, where a dull throbbing sensation lived, but found my hand barely moved. It rose slightly only to fall again, limp and useless at my side. I believe my eyes widened in alarm.

"It's all right, Nicodimus." She took my hand again in hers, and lifted my arm, bending it at the elbow, then lowering it again, bending, then lowering. Over and over. Then she began moving my fingers one by one. Her touch as gentle as a caress. And slowly, more sensation returned to the arm, the hand, though the rush of it was tingling and intense to such an extreme that it made me grimace. She then moved to the other side, manipulating that arm, that hand. By the time she finished, I found I could indeed move. Slowly, weakly, but my limbs were at least functioning now.

She moved lower, to my legs, tugging the covers aside, and as I lifted my head with great effort to glance down at her as she worked them, I saw that I was naked.

"Lady," I whispered, in a voice so choked and raw it was unfamiliar to me. "You might at least leave me covered."

She met my gaze and smiled very slightly. "I've never known you to be shy before, Nicodimus." But she tugged the covers over me from the lower part of my waist to the upper part of my thighs.

She knew me, this woman. That smile had triggered a reaction in my mind, but it was a reaction so fleeting I could not identify it.

"Who are you?" I whispered. "What has happened to me that I am so weak?"

She'd been massaging my feet, wriggling my toes, drawing the feeling back into me as if by magick. But she paused at my question, looking up slowly this time, her smile gone. "You don't remember me then? Or anything that has happened to you?"

Staring into the huge velvety wells of her eyes, I searched my mind, but found nothing. I shook my head slowly.

"Try, Nicodimus. Try to remember."

I closed my eyes, strained to find the information in my brain, but to no avail. "I am sorry. I cannot."

She nodded slowly, returning to her station at my side. "Would you like to try sitting up?" she asked.

I nodded, and her warm hands slid underneath me. She eased me upward, into a sitting position, but dizziness spun my brain in circles, and this time I did press my hands to my head.

"It will pass," she whispered, still holding me. "Easy. Take it easy."

I clung to her voice as if to a lifeline. And knew I would have tilted right off the bed had her hands not been my support. But in a few moments, the rush of dizziness passed. I lowered my hands, lifted my head tentatively, and opened my eyes. Yes. It was gone now.

But her hands remained at my shoulders.

"I . . . It is better now. Gods, what ails me?"

She drew a breath, and I sought her face. Small, with an elfin, turned up nose, and wide full lips. Eyes wide set and almond shaped, cheekbones high and sculpted. And yet she did not answer me. And it occurred to me then that she was very oddly dressed.

"It would be better," she said softly, "if you could remember on your own."

I frowned at her. "Then you'll tell me nothing?"

"I'll help you to remember, Nicodimus."

"Then do so, woman! I did not even recall my own name until you spoke it to me!"

"Calm down." Her hands on my shoulders moved higher, to the tops of them, and began a smooth, rhythmic motion of pressing and easing and moving in circles. It sent the breath rushing out of me, made me to bend my head forward. Her touch . . . it felt good. Soothing.

"Look at your right flank," she told me, still rubbing. Her hands slid behind me now, her thumbs pressing against the base of my neck, then lower as she rubbed the unbearable aching from my back.

I looked where she told me and saw the birthmark I bore. The berry-colored mark of the crescent moon. Something sparked like a near-dead ember in my mind.

"We all bear a similar mark, Nicodimus. I bear one just like yours. Now, look at the pentacle you wear around your neck."

Lowering my chin, I did. A pendant, with a quarter moon on one curve of the circle that surrounded it, and a woman—a Goddess—reclining there.

I lifted my head, and eyed the strange woman's neck. She wore a pendant just like mine.

"What are you, Nicodimus?" she asked me very gently, those eyes probing mine.

"I . . . I am a Witch." The words rolled off my tongue without forethought. "I am an immortal High Witch."

She nodded. "Yes. As am I. You see? It's coming back to you." Her voice was so soft, so encouraging to me. "Now, tell me, if you're immortal, how can you die?"

I frowned, searching the murky, blackwater depths of my mind. "I . . . my heart. I can only die if a Dark One takes my . . ." Alarm flashed in my mind then, and I found myself instinctively reaching to my side, for what, I did not know. A weapon. Yes, a dagger.

"It's all right. I am not a Dark Witch, but a Light One. Do you know how to tell the difference?"

Eyeing her warily, I nodded. "The crescent appears on the right flank in the Light, the left in the Dark."

Nodding slowly, she reached down to the odd fastening of the breeches she wore. Blue, they were, and of sturdy make. Yet they hugged her body obscenely close. The fastener slid lower, an ingenious device with teeth of metal, and she pushed the breeches down, revealing a scrap of shiny, flimsy material underneath. A minuscule pantlet that covered her perfectly rounded backside, and concealed her woman's charms from me, though not by any great degree. Turning, she showed me the mark on her right flank. Then turning again, she revealed the left, as smooth and flawless as satin.

"You see?"

I blinked, but could not take my gaze from her body. "Yes. I see."

She pulled the breeches up again, fastening them. No modesty, I thought. Not in this female.

"Someone took your precious heart, Nicodimus," she told me slowly. "A Dark Witch. I found him. He's dead now. And in his home were countless journals filled with secrets of our kind, which he spent centuries compiling. From him, I learned that it is possible to restore the life to one who has been killed in this way. By retrieving the heart, restoring its power, and replacing it in the body of its owner."

As she spoke, she pressed her palm to my chest.

"I . . . I was dead?"

"As good as dead, yes," she whispered. "But now you are alive."

I was not certain I believed this far-fetched tale she told. And yet, were it true, I owed her a great debt. Far greater than I would ever be able to repay. "I . . . Thank you." I shook my head. "You are a stranger to me. I do not even know your name, and yet you did this for me?"

Her smile wavered. "I'm not a stranger to you, Nicodimus. We knew each other once. But you'll remember, in time. My name is Arianna."

"Arianna," I whispered. "Arianna." There was something about the name, but my mind refused to tell me what. I gave my head a shake, frustration eating at my gut. "Tell me, Arianna. Have you performed this feat before, on others? This raising of slain immortals from their graves?"

She held my gaze, shook her head. "You are the first. But that other one, he had done it many times."

"And were those he restored this confused, this weak and dizzy, when they awakened?"

She averted her gaze from mine as she spoke. "All awoke confused and weakened. Some to greater degrees than others. But it passed, Nicodimus, in each of them. And I'm confident it will in you as well."

"Yes, but when?"

Her hand, trembling slightly, stroked my hair. "I cannot say when. Be patient, Nicodimus." She offered me a smile that was meant to comfort and reassure. "Come, try to stand. See if you can walk at all."

I was hesitant, but I turned obediently when she pulled me to the side, and my legs dangled over the edge of the bed. Then she came to stand in front of me, wedging her thighs between mine to get closer to me. Her arms slid beneath mine, and around to my back. "Now slide toward me," she instructed.

I did so, wondering at her lack of shyness in pressing her body against that of a near-naked man. I felt a stirring of awareness in my loins, but my body did not respond in any physical way. No hardening took place. And what I felt was, I sensed, but a faint shadow of true desire. Not because she was less than desirable. She was very desirable. My mind knew that. My body simply seemed slow in acknowledging or reacting to the information.

My feet touched the cool floor beside hers, and my body straightened slowly upright. She held my chest tight against her, waiting, as I tried to get my balance and test my legs to see if they would support my weight.

I was shocked at how much effort this cost me. How weak-kneed I felt. Yet I managed to stand. She moved to stand beside me, rather than in front of me, all without letting go, but the change in her position caused the cover she'd placed over my body to fall away.

She ignored that. And I decided if she were not offended, I would not worry over something so insignificant as modesty. It was, I knew, the least of my troubles just now.

She slipped an arm around my waist, holding me hard against her, and then she began to move, very slowly. "Just once around the room, for now," she said. "Then you can rest until your strength returns."

My feet did not move from the floor, but rather slid along it with each step she took. The floor covering was odd. Thicker than any tapestry or floor covering I'd ever seen, and soft, but not like any fur I'd known. It was no more than ten paces to the doorway at the end of the room, and yet by the time we reached it, I was drained and struggling to remain upright. To my shame, I was leaning upon the slight woman far more heavily than she should be able to bear.

But immortals grow stronger, their senses more acute, with each passing year.

The voice of my mind whispered this information to me. I realized it was true, and that the knowledge I had once possessed was still within me, awaiting recovery. It reassured me a great deal.

Arianna paused at the closed door, turned me carefully, and then waited, giving me time to rest before starting back to the bed.

It gave me a moment to examine the room. I saw the bed. A large affair finer than any I had ever seen. The wood seemed like oak, but it gleamed with a luster unknown to me. A shine so bright it reflected the light of the oil lamp on the table beside it. The table, too, shone like glass, though it again was wood. There was a window at one end, but its curtains were drawn tight, affording not one glimpse of the world without.

We walked back to the bed, and Arianna used one hand to pull the covers back out of the way. Soft quilts, but different from those I'd known. And crisp white linens underneath, spotlessly clean. She eased me onto the bed, and I lay back gratefully. But was shocked anew at the plushness of the plump pillows, and the way the mattress seemed to cradle me like a cloud. Surely these were not stuffed with straw. No, they definitely smelled different. Their scent was one that seemed new and clean, and yet foreign to me all the same. She must be, I mused, a very wealthy woman, to afford such luxury. And yet, this place did not appear to be a castle. The room was small, its ceilings low. Still, it was far finer than any cottage I had seen. Far finer.

Arianna tugged the covers over me. "I'll bring food," she said. "You need to eat and drink a great deal in these first hours. It will help get rid of the lingering weakness."

I nodded, wondering if I could stay awake long enough to sample her fare. Surely I ought to have had enough of sleep, if I'd been dead, even for the short while it must have taken for her to find the secret in my murderer's journals and restore my heart to my body.

"I am hungry," I said.

"Of course you are. Now, I'll only be a short while. Please, Nicodimus, promise me you won't try to get up while I'm away. Just lie here and rest, all right?"

I stared at her, fussing over me like a mother over a sickly child. I dared not admit to her that I was afraid of falling asleep. Afraid I would not awaken again.

"I give you my word, Arianna," I said.

She squeezed my hand and turned to go, but I found myself gripping her hand stubbornly. Tilting her head, she gazed down at me.

"Do not be long," I said softly, hating that she might realize how confused and afraid I was.

At first I glimpsed pity in her eyes. But then she chased it away with a smile. "You really are hungry, aren't you? I promise, I'll be so fast you'll barely have time to miss me."

I returned her smile. I liked the woman. Odd, she was—as were many of her words and phrases, her clothing, her hair, and many, many other things about her—but direct, too. And seemingly very concerned with my well-being.

She glanced down at my hand on hers, and bit her lower lip. "You'll be all right," she told me. "I promise." Then she tugged her hand gently from mine, and hurried from the room.

Arianna pulled the door closed behind her, leaned back against it, and quickly blinked her eyes dry.

He was alive! Nicodimus was alive! Gods, the magnitude of it stunned her to the soul. Every emotion she'd ever felt for him had flooded back into her being as soon as she'd looked into his deep blue eyes again. For a moment, she'd forgotten that so many years had passed.

And that he'd died hating her.

She knew she mustn't let herself forget those things again. Eventually, he would remember. And there could be no doubt in her mind that he would hate her all over again.

Or would he?

Worry gnawed at her as she hurried through the small house and into the kitchen, yanking a platter and glass from the cupboard, and utensils from the drawer. He was in far worse shape than any of those written about in Dearborne's journals had been. Oh, they too had been weak at first, but according to the notes, their memories had returned within moments, and their strength to a far greater degree as well. Nicodimus had lain in the grip of death for far longer than any of them had, though. Surely it was only a matter of time before he recovered fully.

She closed her eyes, and willed it to be so—even as she feared the opposite would prove true. Dammit, maybe she should have kept the journals rather than boxing them all up and shipping them back to Raven in the States, for safekeeping.

But no. She'd read them so thoroughly, and so often, that she had practically memorized their contents. They'd be no help to her now.

Arianna filled the platter with food. She had guessed Nicodimus would awaken ravenous, and she'd planned for it. She piled slices of ham and roast beef on the platter, added soft rolls, potatoes, and vegetables, then slathered the lot of it in gravy. She popped the feast into the microwave, and pressed a button.

Watching the modern wonder heat the food in record time, she mentally reviewed the precautions she had taken. She hadn't wanted Nicodimus to be shocked upon awakening. He had no idea how much time had truly passed, and Arianna thought it best he not learn the truth until he'd had time to adjust to simply being alive again. So she'd covered the bedroom's light fixture with a pretty scarf, and draped another over the wall switch. She'd placed furniture in front of every outlet, to prevent him seeing them and growing curious. She'd closed the shutters and drawn the drapes on the room's single window. It was a rear room, not near the road that passed by in front of the house. And it was solid. With the door closed he shouldn't detect the traffic passing by—what little of it there was here.

Not at first, anyway. Gradually, though, his immortal senses would regain their former acuity. He would hear the passing cars then. She closed her eyes and drew a breath. The timer *ping*ed. She would just deal with that when the time came. One problem at a time was more than enough to handle.

She filled the glass with milk, took the platter from the microwave, and headed back into the bedroom.

Nicodimus blinked at her in surprise, his gaze going from the heaping, steaming platter to her eyes again. "Surely you did not have time to prepare such a meal as that?"

"I had it ready and waiting, Nicodimus. I knew you'd need sustenance." She moved closer as he slowly, painstakingly, sat up in the bed. The covers fell away from his chest, and her heart tripped over itself in response to the sight of him. Glorious, as he'd always been. A flare of desire sparked to life deep in her belly. Gods, how pathetic was she? That she could want him still, just as she always had. And yet, why had she thought that would be different now? Why had she been foolish enough to believe the years would have changed that?

She hadn't prepared herself for this. She wasn't even certain she could have.

She set the platter on his lap. He frowned at it for a moment, then gripped the stainless steel fork in his fisted hand and turned it slowly. "What sort of tool is this?"

She could have kicked herself. Her first mistake. Gods knew there would be more. "It's a fork," she said. "It's to eat with."

He eyed the fork, turning it this way and that. "I have seen one before . . . in . . . Greece, I believe. But they were not the custom in my country. I never saw the need." Shrugging, he speared a hunk of meat with the fork, and drew it whole, to his lips. He bit off a chunk, while gravy dripped from the rest back onto the plate.

Arianna settled into a chair beside the bed, grateful that he seemed more interested in the food than in the fork. He ate with gusto, cleaning the plate, and using the remains of a roll to swipe the last droplets of gravy away. Then he chugged the milk and set the glass aside, wiping his mouth with the back of his hand and sighing in content.

"My praise to your cook," he said, nodding at her.

"I don't have any cook," she replied automatically.

He seemed surprised by that. "Then you are truly a woman of many talents."

Not as many as he thought, she mused, but she couldn't very well tell him the food had been purchased already made, and needed only heating up. "Would you like some more?" she asked.

He pressed a hand to his belly. "No, I am sated. Thank you. It seems I am growing more deeply indebted to you all the while."

She shook her head quickly. "No, you mustn't think of it that way. You were . . . You are my friend, Nicodimus. I would do as much for any friend."

"Then you are an exceptionally generous soul," he told her, but as he spoke his eyes seemed heavy.

"Lie back now," she whispered, leaning over him to take the dishes away, pulling the covers over him once again. "Rest."

"But there is so much I still do not know." His protest was mild, and spoken even as he settled himself into the nest of pillows.

"You have time, now. I promise you. So much time. It's safe to go to sleep Nicodimus. You'll wake again feeling stronger and more like yourself than you do now."

"That would be more reassuring," he muttered, "if I knew who 'myself' might be."

She smiled as his eyes drifted closed. "Oh, I can tell you that much, at least. Who you are, Nicodimus, is the finest man I've ever known."

His eyes opened, and he stared deeply into hers. "I fear I shall never equal such high praise."

"You already do," she told him. "You're strong and brave, honorable and honest. Intelligent and loyal."

"You . . . sound as if you know me very well."

"I did . . . once." Closing her eyes, she shook the lingering sadness away. Sadness for what she'd lost so long ago, when she had lost him. "Go to sleep now. I'll stay with you. I'll be right here when you wake."

His breath escaped on a drawn out sigh, and his eyes fell closed once more.

Chapter 18

Memories came to me slowly as I slept. Dreams came to me. Dreams of a woman . . . a beautiful, fragile woman called Anya—my wife—and of two sons, Jaymes and Will. The images fluttered in my mind like a breeze through the branches of a leafy tree. None solid, just brief glimpses. A small village, the hut where we lived, Will and Jaymes hunting at my side. The happiness we'd shared.

I sought for some memory of Arianna—something to tell me who she was, and what she had been to me. For I sensed that there had been something . . . more than friendship between us. But what came was a feeling of foreboding. A certainty that the woman was not to be trusted—the feeling of pain . . . deep, intense pain, that I sensed she had caused. It was vivid, this feeling. So real that I woke to the grim certainty that she was no friend of mine, but perhaps an enemy of the most dangerous sort. That all of this caring was but a ruse, a trick of some kind.

Yet, as I opened my eyes, it was to see her there, asleep in a softly stuffed chair. She did not look like a dangerous enemy. Nor had she acted like one, thus far.

I was confused. More now than I had been before. The images creeping into my mind were disjointed and made no sense. All but one . . . a single piece of knowledge that lay there, bright as the glaring sun at mid-day, and just as undeniable.

Arianna stirred and opened her eyes, her gaze meeting mine, and the words tumbled from my lips without forethought. "I remember you now," I said. "You're the woman who killed me."

Her brown eyes widened as she rose from the chair. But behind the shock in her expression, I saw the guilt. Obvious guilt. It was true then.

"Nicodimus, no. I know it seemed that way to you at the time, but—"

"Where is my wife?" I demanded of her. "Where are my sons? Tell me where they are."

Closing her eyes slowly, standing motionless, she shook her head. "You . . . you remember them then."

"I love them," I whispered. "It should be my Anya, my heart, tending me now, not my betrayer."

She lowered her head as if in great pain. "She would be here if she could. But it's not possible just now, Nicodimus. I'm afraid you're stuck with me."

"The hell I am," I muttered. I flung back the covers, swung my legs to the side, and made as if to stand, but my knees buckled quickly, and I collapsed in an ungainly heap upon the floor.

She was beside me in an instant, gripping my arms, but I shoved her hands away. As she stood back, looking down on me helplessly, I gripped the edge of the bed and managed to drag myself back into it. Weak as a kitten! And completely at her mercy. It infuriated me.

"You mustn't try to get up," she told me, standing by the bed, hands clutched in front of her. Her knuckles were white, her arms trembling.

"I'll not lie here at your mercy, woman," I replied harshly. "I'll not become dependent for my very life upon my enemy."

Her expression grew hard and cold. "Right now, Nicodimus, you have no choice in the matter. You're too weak to leave here. And until your strength returns, here is where you'll stay."

I clenched my jaw until my teeth ached. Frustration burned in my belly. This weakness . . . I was a warrior, damn it. A fierce fighter, a skilled hunter. I was not this weakling who required a mere woman to tend to my every need.

"Don't look so devastated, Nicodimus. You're healing fast. Your body will be well again, soon, and I hope your mind along with it. The answers you demand will come. And when they do, and your strength has returned, you'll be free to leave here."

"I've no wish to wait that long," I muttered.

"No doubt tolerating my presence will be a great burden to you until then, but as I said, you have no choice." She dropped her gaze, turning away. "I'll get you some breakfast."

"Where is Anya!" I demanded in desperation as she started for the door.

She froze, her back to me. "I cannot tell you that. When you're ready to remember, you will."

She left, giving me no time to issue the threats hovering on my lips. I wanted to leap from my sickbed and close my hands around her tender throat, to choke the answers from her if need be. She knew the answers to the questions burning in my mind. I could see plainly that she did. I wanted to make her tell me of my wife and my sons. But I was unable. Weaker than a woman, when I had once been the strongest man in my clan. I could have howled in frustration.

The tale she'd told, of having brought me back to life by replacing the heart in my chest . . . it was untrue. It was no more than a well-spun web of lies. She was responsible for my downfall, she'd all but admitted as much. Why would my enemy wish to help me now?

No, she had reasons for what she did now. Reasons for keeping me here, keeping me from my family, and from knowing the truth. Some plot, some scheme I couldn't begin to fathom. Else why would I feel this certainty of her past treachery burning so strongly in my gut?

I would find the truth behind the lies she told. I would!

Arianna sank down at the kitchen table, burying her head in her hands. Her back ached from the night spent in a chair, and her heart ached from Nicodimus's rejection of her. His mistrust. When she ought to have been prepared for it. She had told herself that she was, that she would be able to handle it when his memories of her began to return.

"He has every right to hate me," she muttered. "I knew that before he ever awoke."

And yet she'd hoped . . . foolishly, perhaps, that it would be different now. Stupid. She was stupid and her heart was behaving like the heart of the young girl he'd known. It would only get worse when he remembered all of it. The true extent of her betrayal, as he had perceived it. He would hate her even more when he remembered seeing her in the arms of his worst enemy. And Marten's words as Nicodimus lay dying. She ought to prepare herself for that. Until this very moment, she'd thought she knew what to expect and how to cope with it. But now . . . Gods, she hadn't expected it to hurt this much!

At least she knew now the true reason he'd never been able to love her. It went beyond his past pain. The truth was, he'd never stopped loving his wife. His Anya. He loved her still. Remembered her, even when he'd forgotten everything else.

It was going to devastate him all over again when he remembered Anya's death, and his sons' as well. And he would refuse to let her offer any comfort at all.

A knock came at the front door, and Arianna lifted her head slowly. Brushing the tears from her eyes, giving a quick glance toward the back of the house to be sure Nicodimus hadn't dragged himself into sight, she rose and went to answer it.

Her beautiful sister stood there, brows instantly furrowing as she searched Arianna's face. And then Raven was hugging her close. "What's happened? You look terrible, Arianna, what's happened?"

Arianna hugged her sister in return, looking over Raven's shoulder to Duncan, who stood just behind her. Sighing, she stepped back. "Come in. How on earth did you find me?"

"Not easily," Duncan said, ushering Raven through the door. "We've been trying to catch up to you since you left Sanctuary, but you've been difficult to catch up to, Arianna."

"I might not have been, if I'd known you were looking," she said, raising a brow in question.

"We finally gave up and went back home," Raven explained. "Then the package arrived, containing Dearborne's journals . . . with this address on the return label."

Arianna sighed resignedly. She should have known her sister would follow her here. "The journals, yes. Did you . . . did you read them?"

Raven closed her eyes and nodded, no doubt recalling the horrific tales those journals held. Then she faced Arianna again. "Did you find him?" Raven asked. "Did you find this man you were so determined to resurrect?"

Arianna nodded tiredly, and led them into the kitchen, and to the table. Raven and Duncan sat down, and she put a pot of coffee on to brew, and a kettle for tea, which Duncan still preferred. "I found him."

"And?" Raven leaned forward in her chair.

"He's weak, confused. His memory is sketchy. But on one thing, he's very clear. Nicodimus hates me, blames me for his death, just as he did then. But . . . I'd expected as much."

"Oh, Arianna." Raven got up quickly and came to take the kettle from her hands. "Sit, darling. Rest. Let me do this."

She ushered Arianna into a chair and took over.

"Why don't you just tell him the truth?" Duncan asked softly.

Arianna lifted her head and looked at him. "You don't even know what the truth is, Duncan. How can you be so sure it would do any good?"

He offered her a gentle smile. "I know you well enough to know you didn't betray him the way he seems to think you did. You couldn't. Not a man you love."

"Loved," she corrected quickly.

Duncan sent Raven a swift glance, a silent message. "Okay. If you say so."

Arianna leaned back in her chair, shoulders slumping. "He doesn't even remember that his first wife and his sons are dead, Duncan. He keeps asking for them, and I just can't . . ."

As her voice trailed off, Duncan covered her hand with one of his. "Don't you think you ought to tell him, Arianna? Wouldn't it be for the best? I know it might seem a cruel thing to do, but it seems to me it's more cruel to let him go on not knowing."

Arianna shook her head. "His memories are coming back slowly. He'll realize soon enough." She shrugged. "Besides, I doubt he'd believe a word I said at this point."

"But Arianna, you saved his life!" Raven protested, turning from the small range and coming back to the table.

"I don't think he believes that, either. He'd be out of here if he had the strength to leave."

"Well then, thank goodness he doesn't! Arianna, he remembers the world as it was centuries ago. He has no clue how to get by in it today."

Arianna nodded slowly. "I had planned to help him, to teach him . . . but . . ."

"No matter. What do you say I pay the fellow a visit, hmm?" Duncan asked. "Perhaps he'd feel a bit better talking to another man."

"You're welcome to try," Arianna whispered.

With a nod, Duncan got to his feet, but Arianna gripped his hand. "Be very careful what you say, Duncan. Nicodimus has no idea how much time has passed, and I'd prefer he not know just yet. He has so much to deal with already."

"I won't give anything away, I promise, though I disagree with you on the wisdom of that." He squeezed her hand.

"Tell him I'll bring his breakfast soon."

Duncan nodded and left the room, following the directions Arianna gave for finding her houseguest. Arianna rose to begin preparing a meal for the lot of them, and Raven got up as well. "Don't cook. Let's walk to that lovely little bakery in town and get bread and pastries for breakfast, instead."

Arianna smiled at her sister. The sunshine on her face would feel good today. But then she sent a worried frown toward the back of the house.

"It'll only take us a few minutes," Raven insisted. "I'm sure Duncan can hold his own against a man who can barely stand upright for that long." She looked deeply into Arianna's eyes, her onyx ones filled with reassurances. "You're not on your own anymore, big sister. Duncan and I are here to help, and we'll stay for as long as you need us."

Blinking away the unexpected rise of tears, Arianna finally nodded. "All right. Let me just put on some fresh clothes."

When the door opened, I looked up, expecting to see the wounded eyes of my captor again—and they *had been* wounded. As if my suspicion of her caused her inexplicable pain. If she truly were my enemy, then why would she react that way to my accusations? It made no sense. And yet the certainty that I had indeed hurt her remained.

But it was not Arianna who entered my prison. Instead, it was a man I did not know. Tall he was, dark of hair, with a well-muscled frame that bespoke strength. As I had possessed once. His clothing was as strange as Arianna's was to me. I stiffened, instantly suspicious of him.

"Easy, big guy. I'm a friend."

I did not relax, though his eyes were indeed friendly as he perused me. "If you are a friend, you will take me out of this place," I suggested.

He smiled. "As soon as you're strong enough, I'll do just that—if you still want to go. You have my word on it."

I narrowed my eyes on him. "Who are you? If I know you, I have no memory of it."

He came closer, extending a hand. "Duncan Wallace," he said. I took the hand he offered. His grip was cool and firm, and the jolt that passed between us gave me to know he was an immortal, like me. "And this is the first time we've met."

"Then you are a friend of Arianna's?" I asked him.

He hesitated. "She has been a friend to me, yes."

"Trust her at your peril, Duncan Wallace," I told him grimly.

He sighed deeply, drew up a chair and took it with ease. "I do trust her," he said. "But she seems to think you don't."

"I do not. And with good reason."

"Wronged you once, did she?"

I nodded. "No doubt you disbelieve it."

"No," he said. "I believe it. Arianna is impulsive and wild and often reckless. But her heart is good. And if she did wrong you, Nicodimus, then I believe she regrets it with everything in her. And she's trying very hard to make it up to you now."

Those words gave me pause. I lifted my brows, searching his face for a sign he was lying to me, but saw only openness and honesty in his eyes. "Has she told you the details of how she betrayed me?"

Duncan shook his head. "No. Do you remember them?"

"No," I said. "Only small bits of certainty that she did, and that it cost me dearly."

Duncan drew a deep breath and sighed. "Perhaps it would be best to reserve final judgment until you remember what truly happened. Maybe . . . maybe there's some explanation for what she did."

"It is so infuriating to not remember!" I closed my eyes tightly.

"I know. I've been in a very similar situation myself, you know. And not so long ago."

This caught my attention and I eyed him again. "Truly?" I asked.

He nodded hard. "That's why I thought I might be of some help to you now. I know how maddening it is to have bits of memory that tease at the edges of your mind, only to vanish again before you can grasp them. I know how difficult it is to put those bits together in some way that makes sense. But it will come together, in time. I promise you."

I believed him. And for the first time since I had "awakened," I felt some semblance of hope come to life in my chest. I was unwilling to believe fully in a man who was a friend of my enemy, and yet I felt instinctively that he could be trusted. That he wished to aid me in this, just as he said he did.

"How long?" I asked him.

His lips thinned. "I wish I could tell you. In my case, it was only a matter of a couple of weeks. It might very well be less with you."

"Or it might be a good deal more," I said softly.

"It's only time, my friend. You're immortal. Time is something you have in abundance."

I nodded. "Patience, however, is not," I said.

He grinned at me. "We must be related then. Distant cousins, perhaps?"

A reluctant smile tugged at my lips. I could easily come to like this strange man. "What land are we in, Duncan, that the natives dress so strangely?" I nodded at his clothes. The sturdy blue that covered his legs, much like those Arianna had worn. And the garment on top that buttoned up the front and tucked into them.

He seemed taken aback by my question, and relief filled his eyes when the door opened again and Arianna entered, carrying heaping platters of fragrant baked goods. Another woman, taller, and very dark of hair and eyes, entered behind her, carrying a tray laden with drinking vessels and containers of brew that steamed.

"Breakfast has arrived," the dark one announced cheerfully. The two women lowered the feast to a nearby table, as I eyed the newcomer. A woman of rare beauty, she was. And her coloring reminded me of someone else. Another woman, very dark and tall. Slender as a reed, I thought, as a brief, flickering image of her crept into my mind. She'd loved me very dearly . . . and I her, but . . .

The image vanished as quickly as it had come, and I blinked away my frustration.

"Who are you?" I asked the woman.

Arianna parted her lips, but before she could utter a word, the woman said, "My name is Raven," she said. "I'm Arianna's sister."

My brows lowered, and my mind whirled. "But . . . but Arianna's sister is dead . . ."

Three pairs of eyes widened, and Raven clapped a hand to her mouth. But already, more memories were returning.

Marten had watched Arianna and her female companion as they walked the short distance to the bakery, and again as they returned to the small house, their arms loaded down with food. He'd always hoped to come across the beautiful Arianna again, someday. The few times he'd had word that she'd been seen in any given place, however, he'd arrived only to find her gone. Or, if he did glimpse her, she would be in the company of this other woman. He supposed he could have found her, if he'd put his mind to it. And yet he hadn't. He didn't like to think too deeply about why that was. But he knew, and the knowledge was a bitter pill indeed. She'd been very convincing that day so long ago. And in the time he'd held her captive . . . he'd come to care for her in a way that was completely foreign to him. When she had come to him, when she had returned his ardent kisses . . . there had been a few brief moments when he'd allowed himself to believe she cared for him as well.

The truth of her motives had cut him deeply. Her rejection . . . it had shamed him. So much that he still felt pain when he recalled it.

Part of him feared that when he saw her again, he would see pure hatred in her eyes as he had seen that day. It was an experience he had no desire to relive. So while he had fantasized about seeing her again, he'd done nothing to make it come about.

Now, however, events had taken a strange turn. Perhaps he would take this chance to have her, at last. He'd always wanted her. She, he reminded himself, had rejected him, tricked him, used him. Now that she was here, and he was so close to her, he found he had an urge to extract his revenge. Perhaps he would at that, when he finished with his other business.

Every year on the anniversary of Nicodimus's death, Marten visited his burial site to dance on his grave and gloat over his victory. It had been easy enough to find the burial site of his oldest enemy. For a beautiful young woman driving a wagon alone, with a satin-wrapped body bouncing in the back had been a remarkable sight in those days. So the few people who'd seen Arianna pass by had remembered her.

It ate at him that he'd never had the chance to take Nicodimus's heart himself, to drain it of its very life. Dearborne had stolen that from him.

He'd heard old Dearborne had finally met his match. He was nearly as glad to see that old immortal dead as he had been Nicodimus. He'd hidden from that old man for centuries, in fear Dearborne would find him and kill him for no more reason than the sport of it.

At any rate, this year, Marten's annual visit to the grave of Nicodimus had been different. This time he'd found the grave empty, barren, though refilled with freshly turned earth. And thoughts began to pound at his brain.

Dearborne, the treacherous cur who'd used him and would have likely killed him had the opportunity not been wrested from his grip, had hinted that the second death was not necessarily the final one for immortals. That there was a way even *it* could be reversed. And if anyone would know, it would have been that old man. For he'd captured and toyed with countless immortals in the time Marten had known him. He'd made use of Marten's own dungeons for his gruesome experiments on Light High Witches, before killing them in the end. He reminded Marten of a cruel cat, the way it will torture and tease a mouse until there is so little life left in the creature that the sport is gone. Then the cat will devour it.

Yes, Dearborne had hinted, but he'd refused to tell Marten what he knew. And he'd kept his precious journals under lock and key. But now . . . now the thought Dearborne had planted in Marten's mind returned. Was resurrection from the second death possible? Could an immortal whose heart had been taken, be revived? The possibility tormented him, especially when he saw that open grave, and learned that Arianna was right here in this town. Had Arianna somehow learned of Dearborne's secrets, and used them to revive his blood enemy? Was that bastard Nicodimus once again alive and breathing?

If he was, Marten vowed, he would not be for long. And there was only one way to find out. Watch Arianna. If Nicodimus were alive somewhere, he would come to her, sooner or later. The beautiful Arianna would serve as bait for Marten's trap.

Just as she had done before.

Arianna could have choked her sister for the slip. But it was an honest mistake. Raven had known Nicodimus as a child, in another lifetime, one that had ended centuries ago. Naturally she would have no memory of that. And Arianna had only given her sister the sketchiest of details about her own brief time with Nicodimus. No, this was her own fault, not her sister's.

"I'm so sorry," Raven whispered, backing away, eyes wide.

"No. Don't be." Arianna moved closer to the bed where Nicodimus sat, as still as stone. "You know, Nicodimus is going to need clothes. Why don't you two go into the village and see what you can find? My purse is in the kitchen."

Raven nodded, understanding. Duncan gave Arianna's shoulder a squeeze before they both turned and left. Alone with Nicodimus, Arianna wondered how much to tell him, how much he already might know.

"I . . . assumed I had only been in the grave a short while," Nicodimus said softly, slowly. His gaze seemed turned inward as he searched his mind. "But if she is your dead sister . . . grown now . . ." He lifted his gaze. "Did you revive her in the same way? I . . . I thought you said I was the first?"

Arianna sighed, pushing a hand through her hair. "No. No, Nicodimus. My sister drowned when she was but a child. That memory will likely return to you soon. She wasn't immortal then. She didn't die because some Dark One had taken her heart as you did. She died . . . trying to save my life."

Nicodimus closed his eyes, nodding slowly. "And so returned to her next lifetime as an immortal."

Arianna nodded. "Yes. And I had to wait until she was reborn into that new lifetime to find her again."

His brows rose, but other than that, there was no reaction. "Your sister is grown," he murmured. "Born again, and a woman grown." It was as if he were clarifying this in his own mind. "Immortal, this time."

She nodded. "Yes. She's one of us now."

"And her age?"

He wanted to know how much time had passed. He wanted her to tell him. Gods, it would be so hard for him. She didn't answer him. She couldn't.

"I remember my Anya," he said slowly. "Young and fair. Hair like fire. My sons, just lads . . . but they must be grown now. And Anya . . . older . . . 'Tis more than my mind can grasp. She . . . she was pregnant with our third child when last I recall seeing her. A girl." Then his brows bunched in concentration. "But how could I know the child was a girl unless . . ."

"Nicodimus, don't push yourself," Arianna pled, but it was too late. His head came up suddenly, eyes wide and anguished as the memory hit him. She saw it come, saw the utter pain that made his face into a mask of torment.

"Oh, Gods, she died! Anya died and our babe with her!" He pressed his hands to either side of his head as his eyes moved rapidly from side to side, seeing nothing but the memory, she knew. His breaths came fast and short. "She died, she died in childbirth. Oh, Anya, sweet Anya . . ." Tears brimmed in his eyes, and he lowered his head, covering his face with his hands.

Unable to bear seeing him in so much agony, Arianna went to the bed, sank onto its edge, and put her arms around him. She hugged him close, stroked his hair. "I'm sorry, Nicodimus. I'm so sorry, more than I can tell you. I wish . . . I wish I could take this pain away."

He straightened slowly, staring hard into her eyes. "What of the boys, Arianna? What of my sons?"

She blinked, and shook her head. "I . . . in time you'll remember. . . ."

His hands clutched her shoulders hard, more strength in his grip than she had realized he possessed, and his eyes stabbed into hers like daggers. "Tell me!"

Closing her eyes, Arianna took a deep breath. "There was a

plague . . . it claimed the youngest. And your firstborn died at your side during a battle."

He released her all at once, tipped his head back, his hands like claws clutching at his face. His cry was one of such intense despair she felt tears streaming down her own cheeks. And she could only sit there, crying, watching him fight the pain, for a long time.

When at last his body stopped trembling, and his breaths came more evenly, he faced her again, eyes red-rimmed and dull with grief. "Why did you do this to me?" he asked her. "Why did you bring me back to this grief? This heartache?"

"I . . . I thought—"

"My family is gone. I belong with them, but instead I live on, alone and too weak to do more than lie in this cursed bed! Damn you for this!"

"You were not with them, Nicodimus!" Arianna got to her feet, determined to make him understand. "And you'd lived for a long time without them when my foolishness got you killed. But even then, you were not with them. You were lying in a shallow grave in some state of limbo. Not dead, but not alive. Trapped there, in some in-between place . . . forever. I . . . I only wanted to free you from that."

"There was another way!" he shouted, glaring at her in undisguised fury. "You could have freed me by burning my heart and my body. You could have returned me to my family!"

She lowered her head. "Yes, I could have. But I didn't. I foolishly believed you would prefer life to death, Nicodimus."

He shook his head slowly, his back bent, shoulders slumped. "At least . . . there was no pain there," he whispered.

"No, there wasn't. No pain. No joy. No pleasure. No life at all."

He sighed, a deep, wounded sound. "Why did you bring me back?"

She closed her eyes. "Because I owed you. I wronged you, and it was the only way I could see to make it right."

Grating his teeth, stiffening his spine as if making ready to receive a blow, he asked, "What is the year in which I now live, Arianna? Just how much time did I lie mostly dead in the grave?"

She felt her eyes widen. "I . . ."

"Tell me. And speak the truth. I must know sooner or later, you realize that. Simply tell me, for the love of the Gods!"

Nodding, she bit her lower lip.

"Tell me," he went on when she didn't speak right away. "I am not a fool, Arianna. I see that the window is blocked from without. I see what care you and the others take when speaking to me. It is obvious now that time has passed. The way you speak, the clothes you wear. . . . It is all very different. Has it been a decade?" He stared hard at her. "A century?"

He waited for her to give him the answer. Waited, and silently demanded she tell him what he needed to know. "It has been," she whispered at last, "nearly five centuries."

"Five?"

Lifting her gaze to meet his, she nodded slowly. "The year is nineteen hundred ninety-nine," she told him. "We are at the dawn of the third millennium."

He sat there, still and silent, searching inside himself for understanding.

"You'll be all right, I promise you, Nicodimus. I'll help you to adjust, and to learn, and you'll be fine. You're a strong man, an intelligent man, and—"

"A man who cannot walk across a room without help from a woman. A man held captive by his own betrayer."

"I am not your captor, Nicodimus," she whispered. "And I didn't betray you. Not the way you think—"

He shook his head slowly. "Take a dagger to my chest, woman. End it here. Undo what you've done. I've no wish to linger in this place."

She swallowed hard. "Now you're feeling sorry for yourself. I won't let you do that. It's not like you."

"And what do you know of me?"

She leaned close to him, touched his cheek with her palm and turned his face so she could stare into his eyes. "I know you well enough to know that this pain will ease. Never end altogether, but ease. I know your strength, Nicodimus. It's unlike that of any other man I have ever known. And I know, too, that even now, somewhere beneath this crippling grief, you're curious to see what the world is like, how it has changed after all this time."

He pulled from her touch, averting his eyes. "You know nothing."

She shrugged. "Maybe not. But I do know you won't get strong again unless you eat. And the food is here, waiting, untouched. I don't imagine your appetite is very good just now, after all these shocks. But force yourself, Nicodimus. If for no other reason than to hasten the time when you'll be able to walk out of my house, and never have to see me again."

He sent her a narrow-eyed glare. "That is all the reason I need," he muttered, and reached out to snatch a pastry from the tray. "Leave me in peace," he said. "Give me that much, at least."

She nodded, heaved a sigh, and headed out of the bedroom, closing the door behind her.

And as she stood there with her back to the living room, she knew she was no longer alone in the house. Someone else was here . . . and not Raven or Duncan. There hadn't been time for them to return from their errands in town.

She turned, a shiver of foreboding working up her spine. A woman stood facing her. A woman she hadn't seen in a very long time. Dark and exotic as ever, but no longer beautiful. Nidaba's hair hung in tangles, dirty, its sheen faded. Her eyes were sunken and hollow. Dark circles surrounded them, and she wore a dress that seemed to be rotting with age before Arianna's eyes. Even her jewelry—and she wore as much as she always had, right to the ruby stud in her nose—was dulled by the touch of time.

"*You,*" Nidaba whispered. "I told you once I would kill you if I saw you again."

"Nidaba. Gods, where have you been? What's happened to—"

"*Where is he?* What have you done with Nicodimus's body?" She shot forward on unsteady legs, her hands clutching Arianna's shoulders. "I went to visit his grave and he's gone! I should have known it was you! I should have known! Tell me, wench, where is he?"

Arianna pulled free, only to stagger to one side, banging into a small stand. A vase tumbled to the floor and shattered with a loud crash. And still Nidaba came at her.

"My Gods, Nidaba, what's happened to you?" The darkness of insanity seemed to glow from within Nidaba's once flawless eyes. "Calm down. Nicodimus is fine. He's fine, Nidaba."

"Fine? He's dead, and it's all because of you! You!" She made a growling sound in her throat, teeth drawing back from her lips in an ugly snarl, and she came at Arianna with her hands bent clawlike.

Arianna reacted instinctively. Years of fighting for survival had given her reflexes too strong to override. She reached to her side for the dagger that hung there, concealed by her blouse, but then her hand froze. She couldn't harm Nidaba. Not the woman who had been some kind of heroic figure to her once. Something horrible had happened to put Nidaba in this maddened state.

Suddenly the haunting words written in Dearborne's journal came floating back to her mind. "No," she whispered. "Gods, it *was* you, wasn't it?"

Nidaba brought her clawed hand flashing down as if to strip the skin from Arianna's face. Arianna lifted her hands to cover her eyes in self-defense.

But Nidaba stopped suddenly, one hand still gripping Arianna's shoulder, and she stared wide-eyed at something beyond Arianna. Slowly, Arianna realized Nicodimus stood behind her. She felt his presence, as she always had.

"Nicodimus?" Nidaba whispered. "How . . . ?"

"Release her, Nidaba."

Arianna turned, sighing in relief when Nidaba's hand fell away. Nicodimus stood near the open bedroom door. He wore a blanket tied around his middle, and one hand was braced on the door frame to hold him upright.

Arianna took a step toward him, but Nidaba shot past her, and Nicodimus enfolded the trembling woman in his arms and held her close. "There," he whispered. "It will be all right, Nidaba. It will be all right now."

Arianna stood watching them, and remembered all the poisonous things Marten had told her . . . that the two were lovers, that they had been for centuries, and that there was no room for anyone else in Nicodimus's heart. She hadn't believed it then . . . not completely. But now . . . now she wondered.

Nidaba sobbed in Nicodimus's arms, sobbed as if she would never stop. And gently, Nicodimus stroked her tangled hair and murmured words of comfort to her. His eyes met Arianna's over Nidaba's head. Some unspoken questions in them. *What has happened to her? Are you responsible for this, as well?*

Arianna only shook her head slowly. She didn't know. She didn't know what hell had befallen Nidaba. Not for certain. But she had suspicions. Dark, nightmarish suspicions that made her sick to her stomach.

Had Nidaba been one of Dearborne's captives? The dark woman he spoke of, who had escaped him after months, perhaps years, of torment?

The front door opened, and Duncan and Raven stepped inside with packages and bags in their arms. Arianna met their puzzled glances, and held a finger to her lips for silence, as Nicodimus slowly drew Nidaba back through the door and into his bedroom.

Chapter 19

Nidaba. The memory of her came rushing back to me all at once. I knew her. She had been closer to me than anyone in my life. My friend. My one and only friend at many times during my long, lonely life. My *best* friend, always.

She clung to me, crying softly for a time as I eased her into the bed I'd been occupying myself. And then she clung to me still as I sat down beside her. She didn't speak a coherent sentence in all the time I held her. Only sobbed, and kept repeating my name. Other words, phrases, made no sense to me. And I knew her mind was more than simply troubled. I feared for Nidaba, my heart ached with it.

She calmed, gradually, begged me not to leave her alone, and finally, she cried herself to sleep in my arms.

She had been the strongest woman I had ever known. To see her reduced to this quivering, childlike state of hysteria frightened me right to the core.

Arianna entered the room. I could have snapped at her for intruding, but I knew it had been some time since I'd drawn Nidaba in here. She had been patient, I supposed. Considering this was her home, and this strange woman had attacked her on sight. No doubt she'd have Nidaba thrown into the streets now. Or try to. I would not let that happen without a fight.

Arianna didn't speak, just stood quietly near the door, apparently ready to leave the room, should I order it. I looked up at her. Her gaze seemed very vulnerable, and slightly wounded as it lingered on Nidaba's sleeping form, her head all but in my lap, her arms locked 'round my waist.

"She was the one who found me with the Druids, where I'd gone to nurse my grief. It was she who convinced me to live again, when I only wished to die. I had lost my wife, my sons, my unborn daughter, and then my entire clan had been destroyed. I had revived to a life I did not understand," I said, very softly, for I did not wish to wake Nidaba. Still, she shuddered now and again with residual sobs.

"She was the one to take me from that temple, when my studies with the holy men had ended. She was the one who taught me the many things they could not."

Arianna walked farther into the room, and her eyes seemed to well with sadness, not the anger I had expected, as she gazed at Nidaba. "What things didn't they teach you?" she asked softly.

"To fight, to kill. To stay alive," I told her. "I laughed at first. I, a warrior, being taught to fight by a mere woman. I remember the narrow-eyed look she gave me when I said those words. The haughty indignation. But indulgent." Reaching down, I stroked Nidaba's hair, and gently moved her arms from around me, easing her into a more comfortable position upon the pillows. "She has always been indulgent with me. And so we fought our mock battles and I realized that fighting the most skilled mortal warrior was not even close to battling an immortal. But I learned fast."

"I imagine you did," Arianna said.

"We have parted many times, gone our separate ways, but always, we find each other again. I love her," I stated emphatically, as I slid from the bed, keeping my blanket anchored like a kilt around my hips. "I love her the way I imagine you must love your sister."

Arianna stared at me, then eyed the sleeping woman again. "She does not cling to you in a way that seems exactly sisterly to me, Nicodimus."

I blinked as her meaning came clear to me. "What you are thinking is incorrect, Arianna. Though why this concerns you I cannot know. My memories are broken, but of this, I am certain. Nidaba and I have never been lovers." I tilted my head, studying the color in Arianna's cheeks, and the glint of jealousy in her eyes. Unmistakable. "But I wonder now, what of you and I?"

Her gaze flew from Nidaba's sleeping form to my face, eyes going wider. "What do you mean?"

"What were you to me, Arianna?"

She shook her head vehemently. "Far less than Nidaba was," she whispered. "Or Anya or your sons. That much should be obvious."

"Why?" I asked, moving still closer to her. "Because I remembered them before you? Tell me, Arianna, did I know you before them, or after?"

She looked up slowly. "After. A long while after."

I shrugged. "Then it could very well be that my mind is pulling the past to me in order of chronology, rather than of import. Could it not?"

She bit her lip, looked away. "I think not. And besides, it's unimportant. What is important is Nidaba." She looked again at the sleeping woman. "Poor thing. She was so strong when last I saw her. So fierce. To see her like this . . ." She lowered her head, shaking it slowly.

I nodded, seeing the sincere worry in her eyes. Could this woman truly be evil if she cared deeply for Nidaba? Even after Nidaba had attacked her, in her own home?

"When was it . . . that you saw her last," I asked, as eager for answers as Arianna seemed to be.

She hesitated and looked up at me. "It was right after . . . after you had been killed by a Dark One named Nathanial Dearborne. I tried to kill him, but he fled, taking your . . ."—her eyes focused on my chest—"your heart with him."

I felt my own eyes widen with surprise. "You fought him?"

"I was out of my mind with rage." She shook her head. I wondered that a girl as small and delicate as she would try to avenge my death on an immortal strong enough to have defeated me in battle, but I said no more.

"I took your body back to the ancient Stone Circle to bury you. It was a place you loved very much," she said. "On the way, I stopped near a stream to bathe you and wrap you in a satin coverlet. That was when Nidaba came along. And I . . . I had to tell her you'd been taken from us."

I nodded slowly. "She would have been devastated by the news."

"She was. She screamed to the heavens, blamed me, told me she'd kill me if we crossed paths again, very nearly decided to do it right then and there."

"You didn't fight her?" I asked suddenly, certain I had known no immortal who could outfight Nidaba.

"No."

She did not elaborate, leaving me to wonder what, exactly, had transpired between the two.

"When she left," Arianna went on, "she demanded the name of the man who had killed you. I was certain she would go after him herself. And if she found him, Nicodimus, she didn't kill him. I know that, because I saw him again only recently. Duncan was the one who finally ended his cursed existence."

I nodded thoughtfully.

"You must find out if Nidaba spent any time with this Dearborne," Arianna said softly. "When she wakes, if you feel she is ready, ask her, Nicodimus. But ask her very gently. And if she reacts strongly, then let the matter rest. Don't press her."

I narrowed my gaze on her. "Why? What do you know of this man?"

She focused on Nidaba again. "He kept journals. He was obsessed with becoming the strongest immortal alive, and to do that, he felt he must learn of our every weakness. It was through his studies and notes that I learned how to replace a heart, to bring a victim back, as I did with you."

I nodded. "But there is more."

"Yes, there is more. He . . . kept captives at times. Immortals he would weaken through many methods. Pain, torture, starvation. He would kill them by mortal means, and make detailed notes on how long it took them to revive, and whether multiple deaths and resurrections seemed to weaken their hearts. Sometimes, he took hearts, only to wait a time and replace them." She closed her eyes and shuddered. "He used them to experiment on, Nicodimus. The notes of these experiments read like the transcriptions of nightmares. And I fear . . . I fear Nidaba might have been in his hands, for a time."

I felt my blood boil in my veins. "Where are these notes?"

"They're at my sister's home. I can have them sent here, if you wish. You're free to read them, Nicodimus, but I can tell you already you will not find what you're looking for. Dearborne didn't name the captives he kept. Nidaba's name was never mentioned. There is no way we can know for certain . . . unless she tells us."

I closed my eyes in pain. Gods, the thought of Nidaba going through such torment! "If the man lived still, I would kill him myself."

"He deserves a thousand deaths for what he did, Nicodimus, but he had only one. I burned his heart to release his spirit. Had I known then, what crimes he'd committed, I might not have had the generosity to do so."

I paced toward the bed, vaguely surprised that my legs seemed to be functioning more readily than they had until now. "What will become of Nidaba now?" I asked softly.

"What do you mean?" Arianna asked. "She'll stay here, with us, of course. We can care for her. Perhaps in time . . . her mind will heal."

I turned toward Arianna, searching her face for the villainess I had believed her to be. But found no sign of it in her deep brown eyes. "She attacked you," I said. "She threatened to kill you. Might have done so, had I not come out in time."

"She loves you," Arianna returned, her voice gentle. "And she needs our help."

I nodded slowly, watching her face. "You . . . did not fight back, when she attacked you."

"*You* love *her*, as well, Nicodimus. I couldn't take away another person you love. I could never do that."

She confused me, this woman, who admitted betraying me, admitted costing me my life, and yet seemed to be nothing but goodness to her core. And beauty. Pure beauty such as I could scarcely bear to look upon.

"She should sleep for a while," she said quietly. "You're getting stronger. Perhaps you'd like to bathe, and put on something besides that blanket while she rests."

I glanced down at myself and nodded. "If she wakes . . ."

"I can lock the door in case she bolts. And station Duncan outside in case she needs anything. But truly, I think she'll sleep for a long time. Look at her. She's exhausted."

I nodded my agreement. "I think . . . perhaps the door should be left ajar. If she's been held captive in the past . . ."

Arianna nodded. "You're right. We'll leave it unlocked and open a bit."

"Good. Then . . . I shall bathe."

She smiled gently, and took my hand. And at her touch, the familiar jolt rocked through me, but something else accompanied it. Another jolt. A physical awareness so very powerful it left my knees weaker than they had been before. Her skin . . . her scent . . . her touch . . . all were familiar, and tickling to life some distant memories from deep beneath the surface of my mind. A flash, and no more. A sudden recollection of my own feeling of intense arousal, of longing. Her mouth beneath mine as I tasted and probed its recesses. Her breath near my ear, promising things, whispering secrets my mind still struggled to keep from me. *You will love me one day, Nicodimus. You will love me just as I love you. You'll see.*

* * *

She watched his expressions as she led him through the house to the stairs. She wanted him to use the upstairs bathroom. There was a bath below, of course, but they'd be less likely to disturb Nidaba with the noise if they used this one.

His gaze danced around each room they passed through, fixing on light fixtures, the refrigerator, the switches and plugs in the walls, the stereo system, and other things he couldn't possibly identify. The television set was, thankfully turned off just then.

"What's up?" Raven asked as they started up the stairs.

Nicodimus leaned heavily on the bannister, so Arianna paused to let him rest a moment. "Nicodimus is ready to be out of bed. So we're going to try a bath and a shave."

"Here, you'll need these." Duncan quickly snatched up a pair of shopping bags. "Meanwhile, what about our . . . other guest?"

Arianna felt a rush of pain. "Nidaba is a friend . . . or was once. When I last saw her, she was going after Dearborne. And from the state of her now . . ."

"Oh no," Raven whispered. "Gods, no, tell me you're not thinking . . . what we read in those journals . . ."

Arianna nodded at her sister. "It's possible. I can't be sure, but my senses are telling me it's true. I thought of Nidaba when I first read Dearborne's account of the prisoner he called 'the dark woman.'" Sighing, Arianna pushed the gruesome memory from her mind. "She's resting now. But the bedroom door is unlocked. Just keep an eye on her, will you?"

Raven nodded.

Nicodimus turned to Duncan. "Nidaba is dangerous in this state," he warned. "Take care."

"I'll be careful. Don't worry," Duncan said. "Go on, enjoy your pampering. We'll yell if we need you."

Nodding, Nicodimus began moving up the stairs again, slowly. At the top, Arianna led him into the small bathroom and eased him onto a chair at the vanity.

"It is," he murmured, "as if I've entered an entirely new world. I see everything, yet recognize . . . almost nothing."

"It must be very upsetting to you. It will get easier, I promise."

He nodded, but looked doubtful.

"I guess we'd better start at the beginning. We use a power called electricity for just about everything now. It's the same kind of energy that creates lightning. Mankind has learned to generate the power, and it is connected by wires to most homes. With this power, we no longer have to use candles or oil lamps for light." She moved the light switch on the wall, and the lights came on in the dim bathroom. "See?"

Nicodimus stared up at the lights overhead, and the rounded bulbs lining the top of the mirror. "No," he said. "I do not see at all."

"I'll show you the wires later, and try to explain in more detail how it works. The same electricity powers the pumps, so we can have water pumped in as we want it. It also heats the water, if we like." She leaned over the tub, closed the plunger, and turned on the water, adjusting the temperature and letting the tub fill.

Nicodimus watched it with awe. "It is amazing. Truly amazing."

He turned to the sink, seeing the spigots there similar to the ones in the tub, and reached up to turn a knob. Then he jumped backward when water shot out.

"It's all right," Arianna soothed. "Go ahead, play around with it a bit. Get a feel for how to work it."

"I have seen such things before. The bathhouses in Rome. But the water there was heated by the earth. . . . Hot springs fed the baths." Nodding, he turned the knob further, increasing the flow, then cranked it in the opposite direction to turn it off again. He tried the other knob, getting hot water this time, and nodded in understanding as he shut it off. Then he pointed toward the toilet. "And what is this?"

"Um . . . that's a toilet. You um . . ." She opened the lid. "You sit on it, to uh . . . answer nature's call."

He tilted his head, then his brows rose as he understood. *"In the house?"*

Smiling, she nodded. "Look." She flushed the thing, and he watched the water swirl and vanish, only to refill again.

"Where does it go?" he asked her.

"A tank buried underground outside." She pointed to the roll of paper. "You use this to . . . uh . . . clean up afterward. It goes down, too."

He shook his head in wonder. Arianna liked not seeing open hostility and suspicion in his eyes for a change. She went on, showing him the razors and shaving cream, the hair dryer, the soap and shampoo. The toothbrushes and how to use them. When finally the tub was filled, she turned to the door.

"You are leaving me?" he asked. He didn't sound worried, just surprised.

"I . . . thought you'd want some privacy."

He studied her face. "You have bathed me before, Arianna. Twice now, I believe. Surely you are not embarrassed by this now?"

As he spoke, he dropped his blanket, and stepped into the steaming water. He lowered his glorious body slowly into the tub, and leaned back with a sigh. Arianna tried, but she couldn't take her eyes off him.

"You uh . . . you were dead then, Nicodimus. Both times."

"And those were the only times you ever saw me in a state of . . . undress?" There was speculation in his eyes as he studied her face.

"No," she admitted.

"Then we—"

"We aren't going to talk about that, Nicodimus."

"Why not, Arianna?"

She looked down at his body beneath the rippling water. "For many reasons. The main one being that you'll remember everything on your own, and I think it's better for you if you do."

"And the other reasons?"

She swallowed hard. "It was a painful time for me, Nicodimus."

"Because you wanted me, and I did not return the feeling?"

She met his gaze suddenly. "Because I loved you, and you did not return the feeling. Wanting me was never a question." She turned again, gripped the doorknob.

"I think, Arianna, it still is not a question," he said softly to her back.

Arianna felt her eyes widen. Swallowing hard, she stepped out of the room and into the hall, and closed the door firmly behind her.

So that was why she had resurrected me from the very bowels of death. She had loved me. *Had* loved me. *Once.* A very, very long time ago. How she felt about me now, I did not know. How *could* I know? Certainly all she had done for me thus far, from bringing me back to life, to taking me into her home and caring for me, seemed to indicate that she still cared for me. But caring and loving were quite different matters.

I was getting stronger at a rapid pace now. By the hour, it seemed, I felt the life force moving more powerfully through my body. And she had told me that once I was able to do so, I would be free to leave here.

To leave her.

Never to have to look upon her face again, as she had so eloquently put it.

But I had a new interest in staying. I did not want to leave until I had unlocked all the secrets of Arianna. Of our past together, of what she had been to me, how and why she had betrayed me and cost me my life, and what . . . if anything . . . she felt toward me now.

And Nidaba. What horrors had befallen my beloved companion, Nidaba?

I bathed thoroughly, washed my hair in the water, using the sweet smelling stuff she had called "shampoo." I likely used more than was needed, for the suds the stuff created nearly suffocated me, and I had to turn the water flow on once again and thrust my head beneath it to rinse it all away. Huge white mounds of froth floated upon the water in which I soaked, rendering it useless for rinsing. But quite fragrant for all that.

Finished, I dried myself with the thick, soft "towels" she had left for me, and performed the shaving ritual with some difficulty. The little razor seemed too small for my large hand, and I longed for the honed edge of my dagger instead.

Briefly I wondered what had become of my dagger. Stolen, no doubt, by the bastard who'd killed me. I would have to acquire another, for as my memory came clearer, battles of the past emerged in rapid succession in my mind. And I knew that for an immortal to go about unarmed was foolish beyond words.

Next, my chin bleeding from several small wounds, I approached the clothing Arianna had left for me. One by one, I examined the items in the neatly folded stack beside the water basin. A shirt of soft fabric, with little round discs sewn at the sleeves and along the edges up the front, much like the one Duncan wore. It was fairly obvious how to don that, so I did. There were no laces for closure, and after studying the garment more closely I realized that there were tiny openings in the cloth that the little discs could be pushed through to hold the edges of the garment together. Next was a small white scrap of cloth with three openings. Two of which seemed to be for the legs, and one which was hidden by a flap. It must be . . .

I nearly laughed aloud as I realized its intended use, and tossed the small garment to the floor. The day had not dawned when I would need to maneuver my rod through a minuscule portal when I required use of it! Ludicrous!

The final item was of the sort Arianna wore. "Jeans," she had called them. Sturdy and well made, with a metal fastener at the front, and a little round metal disc atop it. I stepped into these easily and tugged them up to my waist, drawing them closed and feeling how tightly they hugged me. I was unused to clothing of such close fit, but I assumed this was the mode of the day, and I must adjust. I toyed with the odd fastener, but found no way to make it work. Finally my fingers stumbled over the tiny handle at its base, and I deduced that I needed to pull this upward. I did so.

Tiny metal teeth bit into the flesh of my manhood and I howled! Hopping in agony, I tried to grasp the minuscule handle again, to tug it downward this time, but I could not seem to find it.

The door burst open, and Arianna stood staring wide-eyed at me. Then she lowered her gaze, and her hands flew to her lips—to hide her amusement, I was certain.

"Get this thing off me, woman, before it cuts clean through my—"

"All right, all right, just stand still." She dropped to her knees at once, and the moment I stilled, her nimble fingers gripped the evil little implement of torture and gave a tug.

Sharp pain screamed through me, but the device let go its teeth. My hands went instantly to cup my groin, my face contorted in residual pain.

Arianna looked up at me. "How bad is it?"

"It damned well feels as if I've been cleaved half through," I muttered, sucking air through my teeth and stomping one foot twice as if that could somehow ease my pain.

She looked at the floor, eyeing the white undergarment I had tossed there. "No wonder. That's what underwear is for, Nicodimus. Well, one of the things it's for, at least."

"I might suggest you tell me things of such import a bit sooner, in the future, lady."

Again her full lips pulled into a smile she quickly hid. Still kneeling, she touched my hands. "Move them aside and let me see."

I went still, my jaw dropping.

"Oh, come on. Now don't try to tell me you're shy, Nicodimus. I know better. Let me see if you've been completely emasculated." I grunted in derision, but moved my hands aside. She examined me for a moment. She touched me, and I caught my breath at the surge of energy that sizzled from her hands when she did. But it was brief, all too brief. Then she stood and nodded. "It's just a tiny scratch. You'll be fine." Was she slightly breathless?

"Of course I will. The healing will take place in moments." I disliked that she had seen me howling in pain over such a seemingly minor injury. However, it truly *had* hurt incredibly. Already, though, the pain was easing, and my flesh tingled as the skin began to regenerate itself. Or was that simply the tingling sensation remaining from her touch?

"Take them off," she told me, "put on the underwear, and be careful when you use the zipper. Okay?"

"Zipper. So that's what that vicious contraption is called."

She nodded. "You need any help?"

"I believe I can manage to dress myself, Arianna."

"You could have fooled me," she said, eyeing the shirt. I looked down, and realized it hung crookedly. I had misaligned the little discs. I sighed, and shook my head, feeling doubts as to whether I would be able to adjust to this new world. I hadn't even left her house yet, and already I was floundering.

Her hand came to my cheek, soft, warm. "You're going to be fine," she told me as if she had sensed my misgivings. "You're smart, and you're strong, Nicodimus. More so than any of the other men I've met in this century. You'll put them all to shame, I promise."

That soft-spoken faith in me did wonders for my spirits. I had already recalled the years I had spent grieving my wife and sons. And while it made me sad, it gave me some peace, too. It took the edge of newness from my sorrow, and helped the shock to ease away as well. I had been without them for centuries. I had learned to go on. And I would have to do so again, now.

A knock sounded at the door. Then Duncan's voice followed. "Is Nic okay in there?"

"Fine," Arianna called. "Cut himself shaving."

"Shoot, I do that everyday," Duncan returned. "I say we go on strike, grow long beards and never shave again."

I felt myself smile. Arianna had chosen not to embarrass me by revealing the truth; and Duncan, it seemed, thought nothing of the explanation she had given him. So commonplace, this shaving accident, that he had made a jest of it.

"I believe I shall join you in that movement," I called to him.

Arianna's palm skimmed over my cheek, and meeting my eyes, she shook her head side to side. "That would be a shame, Nicodimus. Covering up this face . . . it would be a crime."

Instinctively, I caught her palm in my hand, and drew it around to my lips. I kissed her there. Her eyes grew dark and smoky before she lowered them and quickly drew her hand away. "I'll leave you to change," she told me, and stepped out of the room again.

I sighed after she'd gone. Truly, there were feelings surfacing within me that I did not understand. If this woman had been my enemy, if she had betrayed me, if she had caused my death—none of which she denied—then why would my body react to hers the way it did? Why would I now feel myself wanting her ever more strongly each time I looked into her eyes? Why would these tender, aching feelings keep welling up inside? It made no sense.

I shook my head. The memories would come. Soon, they would come. Perhaps I would understand my emotions better then. One thing was certain. I would not leave this place until I did.

Marten grew more and more frustrated as he watched the small house at the edge of Stonehaven, awaiting his opportunity.

Nicodimus was alive! There inside that small house. Marten had followed Arianna, and he'd been watching ever since. He had even crept close enough to peer through the cracks between the shuttered windows—and he'd glimpsed his enemy inside.

Alive. Fully, completely, alive.

It seemed impossible, but he could not deny what he'd seen with his own eyes. So he watched, and he waited.

So many people around! Yes, he'd like to wreak his vengeance on Arianna for trying her best to make a fool of him. But she wasn't his main quarry. Nicodimus was. The thief who'd stolen his sister so long ago, and left his father mortally wounded and dying, and he and his brother without a woman to tend to their needs. It had been Anya's place, her duty to care for them.

Nicodimus was old and his heart was powerful—or had been once. As he peered through the windows, Marten thought it was again, and growing more so all the time. Marten wanted that power, craved it for his own. But the two strangers, immortals both of them he sensed, stacked the odds strongly against his success. And then the Dark One had shown up—insane or nearly so. Nidaba. He'd heard tell of her before. Dearborne had once claimed she was the eldest immortal he'd known of. He'd wanted her for his experiments. Whether he'd ever had her, Marten did not know. But he had no wish to lock daggers with her now.

Too many. Too many for him to take on alone. He would likely be killed himself before he managed to get to Nicodimus, if he stormed the house the way his instincts told him to do. No, he needed a plan. A way to get them outside, to scatter them, leaving his quarry alone and vulnerable.

Nicodimus was still weak. Though healing, his body was still weak. And Marten wanted to spring on the ancient immortal before he grew strong again.

At first, Marten had thought to wait, that the others would leave eventually. But when days had passed and they still hadn't done so, he knew the time had come to make his move.

Every Witch had some innate skill that stood out in him, and that skill grew stronger when the Witch in question was an immortal High Witch.

Marten had such a skill. One he had honed down through the ages, until he'd achieved near perfection. It was that skill, he realized at last, that would bring this standoff to a head. He could drive them from the house most easily.

His skill was the art of telepathic combustion.

Marten could make things burn.

Chapter 20

Nicodimus held the remote control in his hands, and thumbed buttons as his eyes remained riveted to the television screen. "Amazing," he kept muttering. "No matter how often you explain this, I still do not understand."

He looked, Arianna thought, like a man out of time. Big, and finely developed, but from work rather than workouts. A balanced, muscular power that emanated from him even when you couldn't see what lay beneath his clothes. But Arianna had seen. And she wished she could again.

Lying beneath him as he moved on top of her, around her, inside her, had been like riding the untamed fury of the elements. He was the physical perfection and strength of earth. He was the life and breath of air. The sizzling heat of fire, and the depth and silken caress of water. Gods, no wonder she'd loved him from the moment she'd laid eyes on him.

He stood now, wearing jeans and a black T-shirt, which had become his uniform, though he admitted to missing his kilt. She'd promised to get him one. Frankly, she couldn't wait to see Nicodimus in a kilt again.

Nidaba rested in a large beanbag chair in the rearmost corner of the room. She had refused to don modern clothes. Arianna had tried to convince Nidaba to bathe and wash her hair, but the woman had only finally given in when Nicodimus had begun telling her about the wonders to be found in the bathroom.

If she were familiar with indoor plumbing, she didn't say so. In fact, she refused to say anything at all about where she had been, how she'd managed to get by for all the centuries since Arianna had last seen her. When asked, she retreated behind a wall of silence, and her eyes went blank.

Sensing it might be too much for her to bear talking about, Arianna stopped asking.

Arianna had found a black dress of similar cut to the one Nidaba had been wearing, and she'd replaced the tattered one with it while Nidaba had been in the bath. Nidaba wore that now. Her own had been so old it had fallen to bits when Arianna had tried to wash it. Nidaba gave no indication whether she had noticed the change or not.

She brooded, Nidaba did. Her gaze was always hostile. Her reactions were nervous and startled all the time. She simply sat, watching. Silent and watching.

Arianna went to her with a plate of food now, holding on tight to the sides of the dish in case Nidaba tried to knock it to the floor with a swipe of her hand, as she had done no less than three times in the past week. "Are you hungry, Nidaba? Would you like to eat?"

Nidaba gave the plate a thorough looking over. Fried chicken tonight, with french fries. Nicodimus had fallen in love with greasy modern cooking.

"I detest it," she said, "all of it!" but she took the plate out of Arianna's hands and ripped into a chicken leg like a lion ripping into a rabbit. "Why do you not roast your meat as is proper?" she mumbled around the food. "Why must you try to kill us with this horrible fare? It is unfit to eat!" Within seconds she'd stripped the meat to the bone, and was yanking up the second piece. She paused, and glared up at Arianna. "Do not think I am fooled by your make-believe kindness, wench. You may have taken Nicodimus in with your wiles, but not me! I'll not let you destroy him again. Not again!" Then she went stiff and her eyes widened.

"What is it, Nidaba?"

At Arianna's question, Nicodimus turned from the television set to look at Nidaba's frightened face.

"The window! Someone is watching from the window!" she shrieked. The food flew from her lap as she leapt to her feet. The plate shattered, French fries and chicken bones scattering over the floor, and Nidaba ran into the bedroom. The door slammed hard behind her.

Arianna sighed. Duncan and Raven had hurried in from the kitchen at the noise. "She throw another tantrum?" Raven asked softly.

Nodding at the mess on the floor, Arianna bent to begin picking it up.

"Let me," Duncan said. "You'll cut yourself." He moved her aside and tended to the mess himself.

Nicodimus met Arianna's gaze as she sighed and sank into a chair. "I just wish I knew how to get through to her," she whispered.

"I mentioned Dearborne's name to her," Nicodimus said softly, glancing at the door as if afraid Nidaba might overhear. "Just as you suggested I should. But she became like stone. As if she could neither hear nor see me. Just went still, barely breathing, it seemed." As he spoke, he moved to the window to stare through the glass, looking around in wonder at the town outside. "I see no one."

"I doubt anyone was there," Arianna replied, but she too, looked when Nicodimus moved away. "She's so frightened. I feel sorry for her."

"Oh, Arianna, for goodness sake, how can you?"

Raven's exclamation drew all three sets of eyes. But she only rushed on. "She's mean, and she hates you, and she threatens you at least ten times a day. It's obvious she wants Nicodimus all to herself and sees you as her only obstacle. My Goddess, Arianna, I can barely sleep nights for fear that creature is going to sneak into your room and murder you to get you out of her way."

"That is not going to happen," Nicodimus said quietly.

Arianna tore her gaze from her sister's to stare at him. But he said no more. So she turned back to Raven again. "It's not like you to be so cruel. The woman is ill, Raven."

"The woman is insane, Arianna. And if I had my way, she'd be out of this house before she starts acting on these delusions she has that you are to blame for what happened to Nic almost five hundred years ago. She wants you dead. I can see it in her eyes."

Arianna lowered her head. "Maybe she does. But they are not delusions, Raven. As much as you love me, you cannot admit that I am less than perfect. But I am, and my mistakes did cost Nicodimus his life."

"And you haven't punished yourself enough for that all these years? Is that it? Do you feel you have to let her punish you now, too, just so you can feel you've suffered thoroughly enough?"

Arianna sighed heavily, but said nothing.

Nicodimus moved closer to her, and took her arm gently in his big hand. "Is that true, Arianna? Is that why you allow Nidaba to stay? Due to some sense that you must pay for whatever you did to me in the past?"

She looked up slowly and met his gaze. "No, Nicodimus. It's nothing to do with that, I just—"

Nicodimus held up a hand for silence, and without taking his eyes from Arianna, he said, "Duncan, Raven, if you would not mind . . ."

"We'll give you some privacy," Duncan said quickly, and taking Raven's arm, he led her up the stairs to the bedroom they shared.

"Come," Nicodimus said when they had gone. "Sit with me for a time."

With a sigh, Arianna did as he asked. She sat down on the small sofa. Nicodimus took a seat beside her, his body turned toward her, and gathered her hands in both of his. "It is long past time we had this talk, do you not agree?"

Not meeting his eyes, she nodded. "I suppose so."

"I have not told you this, Arianna, but I have had . . . memories. Of you. Of us."

She looked up quickly, drew in a short breath.

"I remember only small glimpses into the past. Riding together, this one is clear. You had long, golden hair. It flew behind you in the wind and captured the sunlight. I could barely keep my attention focused on guiding my mount because it was so beautiful."

She blinked in surprise, a lump coming into her throat so suddenly she nearly choked.

"And there are other things, too. I remember how I loved listening to you talk. I remember your voice, and the song of the highlands in your speech. And your quick temper, and your impulsive nature and how often I feared it would get you into trouble."

She smiled a bit, nodding at him. "It often *did* get me into trouble. But you were usually nearby to get me out again."

"I remember holding you as you cried at your sister's grave. I remember when some lad cut you to see if you would bleed, and the fear and horror I felt as I tended the wound." He shook the remembered fear away. "You were furious at him."

"*You* punched him in the nose," she said softly.

He smiled. "I should have done more." He met her eyes, and his smile died slowly. "I remember making love to you, in a sacred place surrounded by stones, Arianna. In the midst of the falling snow. And I remember what I felt for you then—"

"Don't." She got to her feet quickly, putting her back to him. "Stop now, Nicodimus. Your thoughts are confused. You didn't feel anything for me then."

"But I did." He got up, and came behind her, his hands sliding over her shoulders as he turned her gently. "I still do."

She closed her eyes as tears threatened. "You will change your mind when you remember the rest."

"It will come soon enough," he said. "But it will not change my mind. I was suspicious of you at first—"

"With good reason! You came to hate me before you died, Nicodimus."

"But you've shown nothing but kindness to me, and to Nidaba as well. No, Arianna, I could never have hated you. If anyone has cause to hate, it is you who have cause to hate me. For you loved me, freely and generously, you loved me. This I remember very well. Yet I, in my stubbornness, continued to deny feeling anything for you in return, even when I—"

"Please don't," she whispered. "If you say it now only to take it back later . . . Nicodimus, I don't think I'll ever get past it."

"Perhaps I don't want you to 'get past it'. But I will not say the words if they frighten you so. I will hope instead that my heart can speak for itself."

He drew her closer then, and bent to press his lips to hers. For the life of her, Arianna could not pull away. He kissed her so tenderly, so gently. And when she parted her lips on a shuddering sigh, and wound her arms around his neck, he kissed her harder. Deeper. He pulled her hips tight to his own, and drove his tongue into her mouth, tasting all within his reach, plundering her until her head was spinning and her heart, pounding.

And then he lifted his head away, and his eyes sparkled down into hers. "I would like very much to hold you in my arms tonight, Arianna. I want to take you to my bed. Will you let me?"

She couldn't speak. So she only nodded, then panicked and the words spilled out before she could stop them. "I will never love you again, Nicodimus. I won't let you break me that way. Not again."

He stared at her, and finally sighed and shook his head, "I hurt you very badly, then, didn't I?"

She nodded in jerky motions. "I gave you all of me, all I had to give. But it was never enough for you. And you only threw it back in my face."

"Then I was a fool. And whatever you did to me in the end, was likely well deserved, Arianna."

Lowering her head, she shook it slowly. "No. You warned me after all. You told me you could never feel anything for me. I just couldn't accept it."

"Nor should I have asked you to." He searched her eyes, saw the way she trembled, she was certain of it. "I want you very badly, Arianna."

"I . . . I . . ." She stared up at him, incapable of refusing him. She was his, tonight and every night, if he wanted her. She hated feeling powerless, craving him this much when she ought to know better than to fall into the same old trap. Loving a man who could not love her back. It was self-destructive. And painful. And she deserved better, dammit.

"No, Arianna," he said softly, his eyes roaming her face. "Not tonight. Not now, with this unsettled between us. You'd give still more of yourself if I asked you now, wouldn't you? No, don't answer. I will not ask any more of you. Not now, not like this."

"Nicodimus?"

He shook his head. "Go on, little cat. Go up to your bed. And do not worry about Nidaba. I will hear her if she moves from her rooms. I will keep you safe, I vow it."

Little cat. He did remember. Arianna drew a deep breath, hating the weakness only he could bring to life in her. Damn him. She was strong. She didn't need him to love her, didn't even need him to forgive her. Much less to protect her.

She didn't!

And she didn't love him, either.

Only a fool would love a man who'd rejected her as many times as Nicodimus had rejected Arianna.

Only a totally hopeless fool. And Arianna was nobody's fool.

Marten focused his intent on the small house. His eyes bored into it as he drew the heat up from the core of him, holding it and letting it build. Hotter. Stronger. Sweat broke out on his face and arms. His breaths came short and fast, and his body shuddered with the effort of containing the energy. And yet he held it inside him as it grew. His body heated, and he knew his skin was turning bloodred. A white-hot haze filled his vision, brighter, blinding, but still he did not blink, did not close his eyes.

Finally, with a shout, he released the energy. It shot forth, a ball of spectral flame that penetrated the house at its base, near the back. As it flooded out of him, Marten went weak. Nothing remained inside him, no strength, no energy, and his body sank limply to the ground. He lay there, still, waiting. His strength would return in a few moments. It always did.

While he waited, he watched the house as his vision slowly cleared and returned to normal. He saw the soft glow from within. Saw it build. Watched it spread.

Marten smiled.

Arianna lay awake in her bed, restless and troubled. So Nicodimus wanted her again. It was no surprise, or at least, it shouldn't be. He'd wanted her before. He just hadn't loved her. And although he might think that had changed, she knew better. She had spent too much time convincing herself he could never love her to believe so easily now. Once he remembered, it would all change.

And why would he bother with her anyway, when it was obvious his feelings for Nidaba ran far deeper, and were far older than anything he could ever feel for Arianna? He spent countless hours with Nidaba. Whenever she ventured out of the room she'd claimed as her own, he would be at her side, talking to her about the amazing things he'd seen or learned about in this new world. Or reminiscing about the past, recounting various adventures they'd shared together. Asking gently if she remembered.

She always did.

He spent time with Nidaba in her room as well. Less now that she was venturing out more often, but still, a lot of time passed with the two of them holed up back there. Arianna didn't like to think about what they were doing. She'd barely restrained the urge to walk in on them and find out. At least Nicodimus didn't sleep in there with Nidaba. He'd taken to spending his nights on the sofa. Insisted on it, in fact, though Arianna had offered her own room to him. Maybe because it was closer to Nidaba. Maybe because he could get up and slip into the bedroom with Nidaba in the night, and no one would know. Maybe . . .

Maybe it was none of her business. She had no claims on Nicodimus.

Well, one claim, but it hardly deserved consideration. Still, technically at least, she was his wife.

He didn't know that yet. Hadn't remembered that far. But he would, in time. And she wondered what he would make of it when he finally did remember.

The scream from below ripped through Arianna's psyche so deeply that she was on her feet before she was aware of moving at all. She yanked the bedroom door open, smelled the smoke, and felt her heart leap within her chest. Racing into the hall, she peered down over the railing into the living room, and saw Nidaba tugging with all her might on Nicodimus's arm.

"Fire! There's fire! Come with me!" Nidaba shrieked.

Nicodimus only pried her hands away, and pointed to the front door. "Go, get outside, now! I have to get Arianna!"

"Damn Arianna! She'll only get you killed again, Nicodimus! Come with me now!" She gripped him again, clung to him.

Again he freed himself, shoving Nidaba forcefully toward the door, and turning he started up the stairs.

"I won't leave you," Nidaba was screaming.

Nicodimus ignored her, stopping halfway up when he glanced up and into Arianna's eyes. "Go," Arianna told him. "Get Nidaba outside. I'll get Duncan and Raven and join you."

He shook his head firmly, just once, and a cloud of smoke wafted up between them. Nicodimus took the stairs rapidly, even as Arianna turned to race through the hall and pound on her sister's bedroom door.

Nicodimus came up behind her as she pounded and screamed, but there was no answer, and it was hot here. Hotter by the minute. From below she could hear the roar and crackle of flames now, accompanying Nidaba's panicked shrieks, and a glow hovered beyond the smoke like some evil eye.

Nicodimus moved her aside and swiftly kicked the bedroom door in. Smoke billowed out of the room, and he held one arm before his face as he charged inside.

Numbly, Arianna realized the fire must have started in Nidaba's room, just below this one. The crazy woman must have set her house on fire! But Raven . . . Duncan . . .

They were not in the bed, and only when Nicodimus bent to the floor did she see them lying there. They had apparently been overcome by the smoke as they made their way toward the door.

"Raven!" Arianna rushed forward, even as Nicodimus hauled Duncan up, and flung the unconscious man over his shoulder.

Arianna gripped her sister under the arms and lifted her. Thank the Gods for preternatural strength. Though slender, Raven was both taller and bigger than Arianna. Were she mortal, she'd never have been able to manage it. Even now, Arianna struggled, but she held her sister close to her, and dragged her feet over the floor, through the door into the hallway, following Nicodimus's lead.

"Stay close," he called, and she could hear the rawness of his voice. Her own eyes burned and watered, and her lungs seemed starved for air. Nicodimus reached the top of the stairs, but looking down, Arianna saw only a pool of fire.

"My Gods, Nidaba!" she cried, wondering if the woman had gone outside, or if she still cringed by the door allowing the fire to devour her.

"This way," Nicodimus said, turning around. He headed back to Arianna's bedroom, and straight through it to the window. Without hesitation, he opened the window and thrust Duncan's upper body through. "Were you not immortal, my friend, I would not attempt this. And I fear it shall be painful, all the same." Then with a shove, he launched Duncan into the night.

Arianna heard sirens wailing. The village's volunteer fire department, no doubt. Another spectacle of modern life for Nicodimus to wonder at.

Her bare feet began to blister, and as she looked beneath her she saw tongues of fire licking up through the floorboards. Her sister's weight was taken from her arms, as Nicodimus pulled Raven into his own. Carefully, he maneuvered Raven's body through the open window, dropping her just as he had dropped Duncan.

"Come," he rasped, gripping Arianna's arm. "Hurry."

The flames licked higher, and she heard the floorboards cracking beneath her blistering feet.

"Now!" he commanded, jerking her forward. She hooked one leg over the sill, gazing back at him. She held his arm. The floor wouldn't hold long. She didn't want to leave him. He wouldn't make it in time.

"Nicodimus—"

He gave Arianna a mighty shove, and she sailed through the night, hitting the ground with a bone-shattering impact that rattled her teeth and sent pain searing through her body. But even as she managed to draw a pain-racked breath and stared back up, she realized he hadn't followed. The window was a dark hole, now, and Nicodimus no longer stood there. Beyond the darkness, she could see only the dancing flames.

"Nicodimus!" Nidaba screamed.

Arianna whirled to see the woman standing nearby, staring up with anguished eyes at the spot where Nicodimus had been. Near her feet, Duncan was slowly stirring awake, as Raven shook him and spoke to him. The both of them were all right. And Nidaba, too. But Nicodimus . . .

"You've done it again, haven't you, Arianna? You've killled my son all over again!"

Arianna blinked, stunned by the words, confused, but unable to devote even a moment's thought to the crazy ramblings of a madwoman. "The floor must have given way," she muttered, calculating in her mind, where he would have landed if it had. The kitchen, he would be near the kitchen. She raced round to that side of the house while Nidaba shouted in some unknown language after her. Curses, no doubt. Hurled in the tongue of the desert lands from whence she came. Arianna gave one brief thought to hoping the woman was too crazy to cast a decent spell, then put Nidaba from her mind and kept on running.

The town's only fire engine came to a squeaky stop, and men piled out. But she had no time for them. Arianna found the hatch door in the ground and jerked it open, racing down into the pitch darkness of the basement, and then up its inside stairs to the door that opened into the kitchen. Smoke here, but not as much. Heat, too, but maybe . . .

She pressed her palms flat to the door. Hot, yes, but not blistering. Bracing herself for a blast, she opened the door. A wall of fire danced before her eyes. It coated the kitchen walls like living paint, and licked out across the floor in pools. She eyed the gas powered range, thought of the propane tanks just outside, and dropped to her knees to avoid the smoke. "Nicodimus!" she cried. "Nicodimus, where are you?"

She couldn't see. Perfect night vision was worthless when smoke burned her eyes like acid. So confusing was being in the heart of this fiery beast, that she no longer knew which way she was moving, just kept crawling along on all fours, choking out his name before drawing in more smoke-laden air.

Then she felt him. Warm, soft, his arm, yes it was his arm! She gripped it, and slid her knees backward over the floor, dragging his weight. Carefully, she moved, trying to retrace her path exactly. She moved a few feet, then she tugged, dragging his body over the floor, then moved a few more feet and tugged again, mightily, pouring all her strength into moving him. She shouldn't be this weak. It shouldn't be this difficult. But she knew it was the smoke, the heat. She was dizzy. She knew damn well she could die from smoke inhalation just as she could die by any other mortal cause. She'd revive again . . . unless the fire consumed her body—and her heart with it. If that happened, she'd be truly dead. Permanently dead.

And Nicodimus with her.

Blackness threatened, but she battled it. Dragging him still farther, she called on her Witchly senses to guide her to the basement door. She moved back farther, and pulled him along, and finally she ran out of floor.

It seemed to vanish from beneath her knees, and she fell, her body banging hard all the way to the bottom, her hand wrenched free of Nicodimus's arm.

No!

She pulled herself upright when the tumbling ended, realizing she'd fallen down the very stairway she'd sought. But without Nicodimus. She gasped, inhaling in a huge amount of the relatively clean air there, and lunged back up the stairs again. Gripping both of Nicodimus's arms, she pulled him back down the stairs with her. There she collapsed, finally unable to fight the darkness any longer. It closed in and she knew nothing for a time.

"What did you mean by that?" Duncan asked Nidaba after she'd stopped screaming.

"Never mind her, Duncan, we have to find Arianna!" Raven cried, her head pressed between her palms as she searched in vain for her sister. "My Goddess, I think she's gone back inside after Nic!"

The firefighters manned hoses now, aiming them at the flames and soaking the poor little house in an effort to save it. But Raven thought it was going to be a total loss. She didn't care, she just wanted her sister.

"That way," Raven screamed. "She went that way!" She started forward, only to be pulled firmly back by Duncan's strong hands.

"Look, there," he said, pointing to the open hatchway door. "I'll go. Stay here. I mean it, Raven."

She met his eyes, nodded hard, and watched in terror as he raced away. "Be careful!" she cried.

Duncan ducked into the basement, out of sight. Trembling, Raven glanced behind her, only to see Nidaba curled into a small trembling mass on the ground. She had come to hate the woman. It was unlike her to hate anyone, but Nidaba had been heartlessly cruel to Arianna ever since she'd arrived here. And Raven didn't take kindly to *anyone* who mistreated her beloved sister.

But now, seeing Nidaba in this much pain, Raven was touched in spite of herself. She moved forward, bending close.

"My son, my Nic," Nidaba was muttering, and Raven felt her own eyes widen as understanding dawned, almost blinding in its brightness.

"By the Gods," she whispered. Was this just more insane rambling from a lunatic driven beyond reason? Or could it possibly be true?

"They'll be all right," Raven whispered. "Duncan will get them out . . ."

"Don't touch me!" Nidaba jerked violently away from Raven's hand on her shoulder. "I hate you, I hate you all!"

Raven knelt beside her, and Nidaba lifted her head, her wet, red-rimmed eyes fixing on Raven's, the ruby in her nose glinting the fire's reflection.

"No, you don't," Raven said. "You just love Nicodimus. But we all do, too, don't you see that?" Raven fought a sob. "The man I love is in there, too, and my sister . . ."

Then, without warning, Nidaba collapsed against Raven's chest, shuddering with sobs that seemed too powerful to contain. Unsure how to react, Raven put her arms around the woman's shoulders and just held her while she cried. "I cannot lose him again," Nidaba sobbed. "I lost him twice . . . and I cannot lose him again."

"You won't, I promise, you won't."

Nidaba shivered, lifting her head, looking at Raven, and for the first time since she'd met the woman, Raven saw some fleeting kind of lucidity in her eyes.

"He died for the first time when he was but nine years old," she whispered. "I didn't even know what I was then. . . . He . . . was all I had."

Raven frowned, puzzled, and gently brushed the hair away from Nidaba's eyes. "When was this?" she asked softly.

"So long ago . . . so very long . . . millennia passed before he was reborn as an immortal High Witch. But I knew he would be. . . . I knew, for he died stepping between a soldier's sword and his mother's heart. He died to save my life. So did I, but I revived, and my son . . . my precious Nic, did not."

"My God," Raven whispered. "My God, you really are . . . You're his mother?"

"Nicodimus!" Nidaba cried, rising to her feet and staring through rivulets of tears at the inferno. "Don't leave me, Nicodimus, not again!"

Raven turned to gaze back at the blazing house. And then Duncan emerged, Arianna hanging limply over his shoulder. And as he came up the last steps, Raven saw that he was dragging Nic behind him.

Nidaba collapsed on the ground then, retreating, perhaps, to insanity. And for once, Raven thought she understood why. Millenia, she'd said. Gods, could anyone live that long and remain sane? She left the woman alone with her ghosts, and ran forward to help Duncan carry Nic and Arianna to safety.

"They'll be all right," Duncan assured her as she eased her sister's body from his arms into hers. He bent to scoop Nicodimus up. But Duncan had taken in a lot of smoke. It coated his mouth and nose in black soot, and he moved slowly, awkwardly, choking often, pausing to catch his breath. Eventually, the two managed to carry Nicodimus and Arianna back to where Nidaba had been waiting.

Raven lowered Arianna to the ground, and Duncan dropped Nicodimus beside her. "The fire didn't get to them," Duncan said. "They'll revive."

"Thank the Gods," Raven muttered. She bent over her sister, stroking her soot-streaked face. "You see Nidaba? I told you they'd be okay."

As she spoke, Raven looked up. Nidaba was no longer where she had been before. Turning her head, Raven scanned the area, but still, there was no sign of the strange woman.

Instead, she spied a jeweled dagger, thrust into the earth, and a small scrap of paper pinned there by its blade. She frowned at Duncan, who quickly went to pull the dagger up. Duncan scanned the note, then met Raven's eyes. "Nidaba has been taken by someone named Marten, who says he'll release her only to Nicodimus. 'Come alone,' it says. 'You know where to find me.'"

Duncan frowned, his face tight with concern. "Do you have any clue what this is about, Raven?"

Raven shook her head slowly, but her eyes burned with tears of worry for the woman she sensed she had never really met until tonight.

Chapter 21

"Nic, come on, wake up."

I heard Duncan's voice just before my body went rigid, and the life force flooded back into me. Then I went limp, lying still on the damp ground, opening my eyes slowly.

Before me were a massive machine with flashing lights, and men wielding lengths of soft tubing that spouted water at the house. The house . . . Arianna's home was a sodden, charred mass now. A ruin. Tongues of flame shot forth still, but the fire was nearly extinguished. The sight of it stirred some memory. A brief glimpse of a similar scene from the distant past. A flicker, then gone, leaving me with a sickening feeling in my stomach. I turned my head, not wishing to look on that sight any longer, only to see Arianna lying beside me on the ground. Still.

"Arianna?" I sat up immediately, moving closer, bending over her. Her face was dusted with soot, her hair dulled with it. I touched her face, lifting my gaze to her sister's. "I do not understand. I pushed her from the window."

"But you were still inside," Raven said softly. "She went back in after you. We couldn't stop her."

Something twisted in my heart. "She could have burned," I whispered. I gathered her limp body gently into my arms, pulling her upright, so she rested against my chest. One hand at the small of her back, one cupping her head and holding it to my shoulder, I rocked her back and forth. "You're such a fool, little cat. Risking death for a man you say you do not love. I think you lie."

As I held her, she went stiff, sucking in a great gasp, then relaxing in my arms once more as she came awake. "Nicodimus?" she whispered, her voice hoarse.

"Right here. It is all right. Everyone is safe." As I said it, I realized I had not seen Nidaba, and sent a questioning glance over Raven's shoulder to Duncan.

The man nodded. "Yes, everyone got out of the house."

Good. Nidaba was likely frightened by the noise and lights and people. She was probably hiding somewhere nearby.

One of the men who'd been fighting the fire came toward us with a stack of blankets. "The house is lost," he said, and his voice was thickly laced with a Scottish lilt. "But there be rooms for you at the inn. No charge. An' by the time you get there, you'll find a change o' clothes a'waitin'. Some o' the local ladies keep such things on hand for emergencies such as this."

"That's very kind. Thank you," Raven said.

In my arms, Arianna was still shaking. Still, I thought, trying to sort through the confusion in her mind. I'd been here with this woman for several days now. And with each one that had passed, my feelings for her had grown. All the suspicions, all the instinctive sense that I must not trust her, and even the knowledge that she had indeed been somehow involved with my death, did nothing to dampen the feelings growing wild within me. There was something about her. Her keen mind and quick wit. Her boldness and intelligence. Her kindness and generosity. Her temper—even that drew me to her. She was small and quick and, I sensed, passionate. I had made love to this woman once, though the memory of it was vague and sketchy now. Knowing it only served to make me want her more, a desire that burned hot within my soul, and seemed to grow daily. But it was more than lust I felt for this woman. A great deal more . . . perhaps more than she wanted me to feel.

I felt it all the same, and sensed she did as well. And I would tell her so, if only she would let me.

It was, however, something she did not wish to hear. And I would respect her wishes. For now. Only for now. She loved me, though she might deny it. I knew that. She had risked her life to save mine tonight. She loved me. She simply needed time to accept the idea.

I took one of the blankets from the stack the man had left with us, and wrapped it around her shoulders, brushing ash from her hair.

"Nic, we um . . . we need to talk. Something has happened," Duncan said.

Arianna's head came up, her eyes alert now, and searching the area around us. "Where is Nidaba?" she asked.

Raven averted her eyes. "Nidaba . . . told me some things a few moments ago. Things you both need to know . . . especially you, Nic."

I frowned, wishing Nidaba would show herself and ease this sudden kernel of worry that seemed to be gnawing at my belly. "What did she tell you?" I asked.

Licking her lips, Raven lifted her gaze to meet mine. "She . . . she's always been very close to you, hasn't she? Very protective of you."

I nodded. "Yes. Sometimes to the extreme."

"But she's never told you why, has she?"

"No."

Raven bit her lip, nodded slowly. "I didn't think so. Do you know why you were born into this lifetime as an immortal High Witch, Nic?"

I nodded. "Of course. I must have died trying to save the life of another, in the lifetime before."

"Right. Well, Nidaba . . . she was the one whose life you saved."

I blinked in surprise, glancing quickly at Arianna. She said, "It doesn't surprise me. I always knew there was an incredible bond between you two."

"More than you could even guess," Duncan said.

I glanced his way. Raven cleared her throat. "Nic . . . When you died to save her life, Nidaba was . . ."

"Was . . . ?" I prompted, when she stopped mid-sentence.

"She was your mother."

I heard Arianna's soft gasp, even as Raven's words made their way to my ears. It felt as if my heart jumped into my throat. I parted my lips, but could not speak, could not even breathe for a moment.

"Sweet Goddess," Arianna whispered. "Your mother . . . Oh, it all makes so much sense now."

The large vehicles began to rumble away. My gaze seemed to search the darkness around us as if I were seeking some sense, some explanation that could be found there. There was none, of course. There was the house, reduced to smoking, sodden ash and charred beams that dripped and hissed away the last of their heat. There was Arianna's driving machine sitting out of harm's way, and apparently untouched by the flames. There were three people watching me as everything I had believed in my life simply melted away beneath a revelation too shocking to comprehend.

And there was Arianna, still in my arms. I suddenly held her more tightly. "My mother," I whispered, staring at Raven in disbelief. "She said this?"

"Yes. She was your mother, an immortal High Witch, but she didn't even know that at the time. You were nine years old, she said, when she was attacked by some soldier. . . . She didn't say why. Just that you leapt in front of her, and were killed by a blow from his sword. And that it was a very long time before you were finally reborn in Scotland."

My head low, I shook it slowly. Arianna sat up slightly, and ran one palm gently over my cheek. "Why?" I asked of no one in particular. "Why would she not have told me these things . . . ?" Arianna only shook her head, her big brown eyes wide with concern for me.

"I don't know why, Nic," Raven said. "But I think it's true. I . . . I know Nidaba is not in the best of mental health right now, but I saw her eyes when she was speaking, and . . ." She drew a breath, then nodded hard. "She was speaking from the heart, I know that much."

"No wonder she hated me so much," Arianna said. I looked into Arianna's eyes, saw the pain there, the reflection of my pain, and perhaps Nidaba's as well. So caring, this woman. The most caring I'd ever known. "I understand everything now," she said.

"I do not," I told her. Reluctantly I released Arianna's small, warm body, and got to my feet. "I must speak to Nidaba. Where is she now?"

Raven and Duncan exchanged a worried glance. Then Duncan extracted a small scrap of paper from somewhere beneath the blanket wrapped around him, and handed it to me. I frowned down at the words . . . English, I thought but unfamiliar to me. I could not read what was written there.

"We only left her alone for a minute . . . just long enough to pull you two out of that basement," Duncan said. "I guess that's when he got to her."

My head came up fast, and just as quickly, Arianna jumped to her feet beside me, and snatched the note from my hands.

"Marten," she whispered.

"Marten?" The name brought his image clearly back to my mind. My nemesis. My onetime brother-in-law, and lifelong enemy. "That bastard is still alive? Damn him. Are you saying . . . Gods, are you saying he has taken Nidaba?"

"It looks that way," Duncan said. "Read him the note, Arianna. Maybe he can make some sense of it."

Arianna met my gaze, and I saw her reluctance. But she nodded, and read aloud. "'Nicodimus, I have taken your precious Nidaba. I will kill her if I must, but I fear taking the heart of a lunatic might well infect me with her madness. Still, I will risk that, if you force me. I am willing, however, to make a trade. Nidaba, unharmed, for you, Nicodimus. Come alone, old friend. You know where to find me. Marten.'"

I stopped my pacing and lifted my head. "But . . . I *do not* know where to find him. What . . ." Then I let my question die on my lips and gazed at Arianna. She looked quickly away, shielding her eyes from my probing stare.

"Arianna, if you know what this means, tell me."

She only shook her head, still not meeting my eyes. "I don't know."

"You must know!" I went to her, gripped her shoulders, and stared into her eyes. "Arianna, please."

"I don't know, Nicodimus. It must be something from the past, something you still haven't remembered. But if it is, it's something I didn't know about."

I saw something in her eyes. A shadow that seemed to hide her soul from me. I did not know if she were telling me the truth, or why she would want to lie. I did not feel as if I knew anything just then. Everything I'd ever believed seemed to have been shaken to the core by Raven's revelations. "I must find her," I whispered.

"We'll find her," Duncan said, his voice firm and strong. "He can't have taken her far. Arianna, maybe you can at least give us a physical description of this Marten character to go on."

Arianna nodded, but I saw the way her jaw was set, and the determination in her eyes. I also saw the suspicion with which Raven was eyeing her. She, too, thought Arianna knew more than she was saying.

But why? Gods, could she be jealous of my affection for Nidaba still? Even knowing the woman had been my mother?

My mother. Gods, I could not get over it. Nidaba, my own mother.

"So what is it, exactly, that you're keeping from Nic?" Raven asked.

Arianna looked up fast. Nicodimus and Duncan had gone off into the woods beyond the town in a hopeless attempt to track Marten and Nidaba. "I don't know what you mean. . . ."

"You damned well do, and I won't let you deceive me, Arianna. Not me, of all people. I know you better than anyone. I love you better than anyone, and I'm not going to let you get away with this any more than you would if our situations were reversed. Now what is it?"

Arianna dropped her gaze, unable to withstand the impact of her sister's accusing eyes. She was shaken, right to the core. All this time she'd been half convinced that Nidaba wanted Nicodimus for herself . . . when she'd been his mother all along. Protecting him just as any mother would do for her son.

"You know where Marten took her, don't you?"

Arianna shrugged. "I have an idea."

"And you don't plan to let that poor woman die in Nic's place. I know you better than to think that. You're going to go after her yourself, aren't you? Aren't you, Arianna!"

Arianna sighed deeply, knowing better than to try to fool her sister on this point. "What choice do I have? She's his mother, Raven. He loves her, and he needs her, especially now."

"He loves *you*, Arianna."

"No. He thinks he does, but that will change once he remembers. . . ."

"Oh, for the love of heaven, you're so blind! The man adores you! That's not going to change because of something that happened centuries ago."

Arianna shook her head. "If he goes after her himself, Marten will kill him. It's that simple. Hell, that snake would probably kill them both."

"And if you go after her, he'll kill you instead."

"No. I can beat him. Nidaba is unbalanced, and Nicodimus is still weak. But *I* can beat him, Raven. And I will—for Nicodimus. Just as you would do for Duncan. You know you would. Don't even try to deny it."

Raven lowered her gaze, unable to argue with that simple truth. "Yes. I would. Because I love him. And you love Nic the same way, don't you?"

A stabbing pain pierced Arianna's chest as she nodded. "Yes. I love him. But I can't have him, I can't make him love me, and I'm not going to try. I've made that mistake before, but I learned from it. Yes, I love him. . . . I love him enough to let him go, Raven."

"And enough to die for him?"

Arianna didn't answer that. Instead, she just looked away.

"Fine, go after Marten in Nic's place if you must. But not alone. I'll go with you. And Duncan will, too. With three we'd have Marten outnumbered."

Keeping her gaze carefully averted, Arianna nodded. "You must promise not to tell Nicodimus. We'll have to slip away, without his knowledge. He's still not strong enough to do battle."

Raven eyed her warily. "All right. Agreed."

"Good then."

"Why do I get the feeling that was far too easy?"

Arianna shook her head and plastered a false smile on her face, hoping against hope her sister would believe her lies. "We'll go tomorrow. We both need rest after this night's mayhem."

"Yes. All right." Raven paced away, then back again.

"Let's get to the inn then. The fireman said they would have rooms for us."

"One room," Raven said. "One large room. I don't plan to let you out of my sight tonight, Arianna."

Meeting her sister's gaze, Arianna murmured, "You're going to have to, love. I plan to spend this night in the arms of my husband. Just in case my plan goes wrong. It might be the last chance I ever have."

"Your . . . ?" Raven's eyes widened as she searched her sister's face.

Arianna simply nodded. "Nicodimus and I were married once, a long time ago. He doesn't remember it yet, but I do. I'll never forget." She lowered her head, to hide the color she felt staining her cheeks. "So give me this night with him. And tomorrow, we'll do what needs doing."

"Oh, Arianna." Raven enfolded her sister in her arms, and held her tight. "Why is it you feel you have to try so hard not to love him?"

"Because he can never love me back. I thought . . . I thought if there were no love, there could be no pain. No hurting and longing for what I could never have. But it was never a choice, really. I've always loved him."

Raven stroked her hair. "Things will work out. Have faith, sweetheart."

Arianna lowered her head to Raven's shoulder. But she was out of faith, and determined, at last, to right a very old wrong. She couldn't have Nicodimus's love, she knew that, had accepted it. But she could save his life, and she could give him back his mother. She could make up for the mistakes she'd made in the past. And she would. Even knowing full well that it might be the last thing she ever did.

Marten had left no sign. Duncan and I searched for hours, to no avail. We found no track, no path, no clue. I thought of Nidaba, of the horrors she must have suffered in the past, likely at Dearborne's hand,

and of how she must be feeling right now . . . a captive once more. Anxiety for her, and a deep fury against Marten, boiled in my belly.

"We might as well go back," Duncan said, a hand on my shoulder. "Maybe Arianna has remembered something more about all this by now."

"Arianna will not tell us any more than she wants us to know," I said wearily. "She's always been the most stubborn girl I . . ." I stopped speaking for a moment, and Duncan looked at me, waiting. "I remember her stubbornness. The way she would sneak away from her mother's home by night to study the ways of magick with The Crones. Even knowing the danger such actions brought with them."

Tilting his head, Duncan studied my face. "The Crones?"

I nodded, Arianna's face clear in my mind now. The way she had looked then. I had followed her, spied on her to be sure she was safe. I'd seen her with the old women, her cheeks bathed in the glow of their balefire. "She looked the same . . . but different somehow. Physically, she hasn't changed, except that she has cut off her hair. But there was an innocence in her eyes then. She seems . . . hard now."

"Not so hard as you might think," Duncan offered. "With her sister, she's as soft as a breeze."

I nodded in agreement. "Her hardness is selective then. She dons it to protect her heart from the likes of me."

Duncan couldn't seem to think of a response to that. Instead he said, "Tell me about these old women who taught her their ways."

I nodded, searching for the memories, finding them where before there had been but shadows. "They were Witches, mortal ones. Even before she knew of her own nature, Arianna sensed her power. She was determined to learn about it, about what it meant, and why she possessed it when others did not. She sought out the knowledge in the only place she could find it. The Crones were outcasts, feared by the clan, but left alone for the most part."

"Still," Duncan mused, "it must have been risky for Arianna to spend time with them. Especially in those days."

A darkness settled in my brain, and a chill shivered up my spine. "It nearly got her killed," I said. Then I blinked and searched my mind some more.

"This is a new memory, isn't it, Nic?"

I nodded. "It was the fire, I think, that brought all of this back to me. I recall . . . I was searching for Arianna, and could not find her. And . . . there was smoke, and noise coming from the edge of the woods where

The Crones lived. I went there and . . ." I pressed my fingers to my fore-head, as if to force the memory clear, and then I lifted my head, felt my eyes widen. "The clan murdered them. Hanged The Crones and burned their bodies. It was like a nightmare. Charred remains dangling from the limb of a mighty oak. The house in ruins. The entire clan, milling about, some bearing torches . . ."

Duncan grimaced. "You're right. Seeing Arianna's little house burn tonight likely jarred some of this loose for you."

I didn't care what had caused the memory to return. I only needed to follow it, for I sensed its import. "Arianna was there. Gods, she was dev-astated, and furious. The crowd turned its attention on her as she shouted accusations at them. Someone cried out that she had been seen with The Crones, that she was likely a Witch as well, and should suffer the same fate." I lowered my head as the breath rushed out of me, and felt again the sick-to-my-stomach fear that had assailed me then. "I re-member her father, standing in front of her, ready to defend her against that murderous mob with no more than a fallen limb as a weapon. He'd have had no chance against them all. But I stepped in to protect her as well."

"How?" Duncan asked. His gaze riveted to mine, he seemed fasci-nated by the tale. "Two men against an entire clan? How did you defend her against that?"

I closed my eyes as the past rushed over me. "I was known as close kin to their chieftain. They wouldn't have dared defy me. But I knew Ari-anna would be in grave danger again the moment I was gone. I had to link her to me in a way so permanent and so real that she would be safe, even without me at her side."

Opening my eyes, I stared up at the stars, and saw the past unfolding in my mind. The dress she'd worn, the flowers in her hair. The excited uncertainty in her eyes. "I married her," I whispered. "By the Gods, I married her. Arianna . . . Arianna is *my wife*."

I felt as if my legs would buckle beneath me, and suddenly Duncan was there, gripping my shoulders, and easing me downward until I sat on a partially rotted stump. The fragrance of the moist, decomposing wood and moss rose up to wrap around my senses, but my mind refused to stop whirling.

"Your wife? For the love of heaven. She never told us any of this." He shook his head in wonder. Then he eyed me again. "It's all just a bit too much to deal with in one night, isn't it, Nic? Discovering a mother and a wife, all at once? Are you okay?"

"I . . . Gods, why didn't she tell me?"

Duncan hunkered on the ground beside the stump. "I could hazard a guess. If you want me to?"

I looked at him and nodded hard.

"Arianna is . . . a proud woman. No, that's an understatement. It's more than pride. At any rate, if you only married her to keep the clan from murdering her, then she must have known it. Right? I mean, frankly, knowing her as I do, I'm surprised she even agreed to it."

I frowned fiercely, searching my mind. "She did not agree . . . not at first. But in the end she realized she had no choice. Her mother and father urged her to accept, and I pushed her as well. Her only other option would have been to run away. To leave all she knew and loved behind, and to try to exist on her own. In the world as it was then, she would have been in just as much danger that way as she had been that night at The Crones' execution."

Duncan nodded. "So she agreed . . . knowing you didn't love her."

I blinked and met Duncan's eyes. "I was a fool. So determined to protect my heart from the touch of hers and the pain I believed that touch would bring. Gods, I set terms. Can you believe that? *I* laid out terms, expecting *Arianna* to agree to them."

"Might as well set terms for the wind as to how it should blow," Duncan remarked, shaking his head and smiling slightly at the very idea. "Arianna sets her own terms."

I nodded wryly. "Yes. She did then. She agreed to wed me, but informed me she would never be content with the rules I laid out: that she would be my wife in name only, that I would never be capable of loving her, or being her husband in the truest sense of the word. She said . . . she said she would make me love her. That my defenses would crumble beneath her slightest touch. That it was I who would surrender to *her* terms, and that I should be aware of it from the start."

Duncan smiled fully now. "You should have run for the hills, Nic. You never stood a chance, did you?"

"If I ever thought I did, I was fooling no one but myself," I admitted. "My pride . . . it wasn't pride really. It was fear. My old wounds ran deep. I had lost my wife, my sons, my family. I had no wish to let her reopen those wounds, and I knew that she could. That she would if I let her. But I could never admit that I was afraid of a young girl like Arianna."

"Don't feel too bad, Nic. I was scared to death of her sister." Duncan got to his feet again. "But I have a feeling you should be telling Arianna all of this, instead of spilling your guts to me. Don't you?"

"I suppose I should." I rose slowly, brushed the dust from my jeans. But there were more images making their way back to me as we walked toward the village. No clear memories, but a sense. A sense that Arianna had indeed conquered my heart, and that once she had held it in her small hands, she'd crushed it mercilessly. The old fear of her crept over me once more. The feeling that I must protect myself from her this time, or suffer complete destruction at her hand.

And yet, I had no desire to obey my mind's warnings. No desire at all. Let her trample my heart if she would. I would not resist her. Not this time.

I was shivering when we arrived back at the site of her burned house. A chill of foreboding ran all the way to my soul.

Arianna and Raven were waiting there, but looking far better than they had when we'd left them. They were clean and dressed in fresh clothing.

"Any luck?" Raven asked.

"No, none at all." Duncan touched the blouse she wore. "Very pretty."

"Some of the locals donated some fresh clothes to us. And Arianna and I have rooms waiting at a local inn for the night. There are clean clothes waiting for you both there, as well."

"And a hot shower, I hope," Duncan said.

Arianna had a hold on my eyes that wouldn't let go. I could not look away, and found I did not want to. She took my hand, and saying nothing, led me along the streets and through the town to the inn.

Chapter 22

The inn was a large building, likely once a farmhouse, with brown slabwood siding, and a railed stairway leading up to solid doors, painted red. When we went inside, Raven led Duncan directly up the stairs, leaving Arianna and I alone below.

Arianna seemed nervous. Naturally, she would be, I reminded myself. She'd just lost her house to fire, and likely the sight of the flames had elicited the same memories in her mind as they had in mine.

Licking her lips, she led me to the foot of the stairs, then paused and looked up at me. The nervousness fled however, and her full lips quirked upward into a teasing smile. "You're still covered in soot," she said. "And your hair is practically gray with ash."

I returned the smile, though still sick with worry for Nidaba, and reeling with shock from the night's revelations. "You can see then what I would look like as an old man."

"You already are an old man."

I lifted my brows. "True enough. But you are an old woman, as well. I suppose I can no longer argue that you are too young for me, can I?"

Her smile faded, and she broke her gaze. "You remember that?"

"I have remembered a great deal tonight, Arianna." I reached out to stroke her hair, then paused, noting the dark smears of soot that coated my hand. "I will bathe first, and then . . . we will talk."

"All right." She seemed to lift her chin a bit as she started up the stairs, and not meeting my eyes, she said, "Our room is this way."

Our room? My mind leapt on those words. Did she mean . . . could she want . . . but . . .

She was moving quickly away from me, and I hurried to catch up. Turning at the top of the stairs, she moved along a corridor, paused at a door, and inserted a key. Then she opened the door and stepped inside.

The room was a simple one. There was a large bed, a pair of over-stuffed chairs, and a television like the wondrous one that had been in Arianna's house. She was already moving through, opening an adjoining door, calling over her shoulder, "The bathroom is right here." But I was focused again on the bed: one bed. Only one.

Shaking myself, I went to join her in the bathroom.

"No tub," she said. "Just a shower stall, but I showed you how to work that at home."

I nodded mutely.

"Your clothes are here." She patted the top of a folded stack of garments. "Towel is on the rack." With that she quickly backed out of the small bathroom, leaving me with a head full of questions, and not a single answer.

Sighing, I reached into the stall to turn on the water and adjust its temperature. I hurried through the process of bathing, though I did a thorough job of it. I was eager to speak with Arianna . . . with my wife. To find out just what she intended to do about tonight's sleeping arrangements. Perhaps there had been only the one room available, I thought as I scrubbed the soot from my body, and watched the dark water swirl down the drain. But surely if that were the case, she'd have spent the night with her sister, and sent Duncan to share this room with me. Unless Raven objected to that. Then again, I did not think Raven the kind of woman who would deny her sister anything she asked.

I shampooed my hair, ridding it of the ashy residue, and was rinsing the lather away when there came a tap on the bathroom door.

"Are you almost done?" Arianna called.

"Yes."

"Can I come in?"

I went still, standing motionless beneath the spray. Soap bubbles trickled down my face, into my eyes, and still I could not move. "Yes," I finally managed.

The curtain of the shower was pulled closed, but I heard the bathroom door open, heard her small, soft footsteps as she came inside. And then closer. "I . . . got some more soot on me when we were back at the house," she said, her voice very soft now. Almost timid, which was so unlike her it made a shiver dance over my spine.

Bracing myself for her rejection—for it would certainly come—I spoke softly. My voice seemed incapable of anything louder just then. "I would like nothing better than to wash it away for you, Arianna."

She did not answer. Reaching up to the curtain, I curled my hand around it, and drew it slowly open.

She stood there before me, not a stitch of clothing covering her beauty. Her cheeks were pink, her eyes wide and shining. My eyes devoured her, from her blush-stained face to her slender neck, and lower. Her breasts, round and peaked, and perfect. Her waist, narrow and tempting. The shadowy hollow of her navel, and the silken curls between her legs. Beautiful legs, slender and strong, and small bare feet, toes curling and relaxing over and over.

"I see no soot," I whispered.

She licked her lips. "I lied. There isn't any."

I clasped her waist in my hands and pulled her into the shower with me, turning her so that she stood directly beneath the spray. The water coursed over her, drenching her hair and running down her face. Her arms curled around my neck, and every part of my body seemed to tingle with new life, as she stood on tiptoe, and pressed her lips to mine. Her mouth tasted sweet, her tongue, warm and moist as I stroked it with mine. Wet flesh pressed to the front of me, her breasts warm, nipples taut against my chest.

I slid my mouth from hers to drink the moisture from her jaw, and her neck. "My beautiful Arianna," I muttered. "My beautiful wife."

I heard her soft gasp, felt her body stiffen. "Then you remember that, as well."

"I remember that. How I ever forgot it, I will never know." I bent over her, capturing a breast in my mouth, tasting it, teasing its hard crest with my tongue while I held her tight to me. Her taste . . . yes, I remembered this as well. And more. I fell to my knees before her, and as the water rained down upon us, I kissed the droplets away from her skin. Licked it away from her belly, her hips, her thighs. Then I pressed my mouth to her center, darting my tongue inside to sample the salty moisture there.

Moaning softly, she clenched her hands in my hair, and parted her thighs, opening to my gentle invasion. Inviting me to take more of her. I swelled and ached for her, wanted to devour every bit of her, and I drove my tongue deeper. The taste of her was maddening to me as I stroked her, sucked at her, used my lips and even my teeth to make her tremble and shake. She whispered my name, then cried it out loud when her plea-sure reached its peak, and when she would have backed away I caught her buttocks in my hands and held her still, pressing my face tight to her and licking deep. Refusing to let her go, flushing her with my tongue until she was shaking so hard her knees buckled beneath her, and she would have collapsed had I not been holding her so tightly.

Gathering my shuddering lady into my arms, I carried her from the shower, reaching back to shut off the water. I took her to the bed, and lowered her to the mattress. Then I eased myself atop her, parting her thighs with my hands, pressing them wide for me. I slid inside her. She was warm, and wet, yes, but tight. Very tight, and still convulsing with the echoes of her climax. Slowly, I began to move deeper, and when I had filled her, I pulled back again. Very slowly. In a moment, she was moving, too, her hips arching up as I thrust into her, pulling away as I drew back. Her legs wrapped themselves around me. Her arms impris-oned me. I bent to feed again at her mouth as I moved faster, drove harder. She reached the pinnacle again even as I felt my seed spilling into her, drawn from the depths of my soul, it seemed. Draining me dry.

I lay there inside her for several long moments, during which neither of us spoke. The very blood in my veins seemed to sing with joy, and my soul itself sighed in sweet release. Sweet union.

I moved to lie down beside her, and she curled into my arms, her head nestled upon my shoulder.

"Arianna," I whispered. "Sweet little cat, does this mean that you—"

Her fingertips came then to press softly to my lips. "No talk now, Nicodimus. Not now. I want to fall asleep in your arms. Let's save the talking for tomorrow."

I frowned, but agreed. There was nothing, *nothing*, I would not do for her. So if she wished to sleep in my arms, that was what she would do. And in the morning, I would convince her somehow that my love for her was true, and abiding, and too strong for any ghosts of the past to threaten.

Arianna slipped away before dawn. Doing so was far easier than she had expected it to be. She stood for a long moment beside the bed, in the darkness, just looking at him. Nicodimus lying there with his eyes gently closed, his magnificent chest rising and falling in the rhythm of slumber. That was the way she left him, and the image she would carry with her of him, in her mind. She found she didn't want to face Nicodimus when he woke, didn't want to see what might be in his eyes when he opened them. Not the misguided notion he had that he had ever cared for her . . . loved her. And not the memory that might very well have returned by then, and the hatred that would come with it. To see either of those things would hurt too much to bear. Both would tear at her heart and leave it bleeding. So when she slipped away it was with a sense of relief.

And longing. Bittersweet longing for something that could never be. Something that *had* never *been*. She'd been foolish enough to hope for it once. But she was harder now, and wiser, and she knew the difference between fantasy and reality. And yes, it hurt, but the pain would be far worse if she let herself fall into that bottomless pit of hoping again. Her feet were firmly on the ground. She knew exactly where she stood with Nicodimus.

She also knew where to find Marten and Nidaba. The keep where Marten had taken her all those years ago—the place it had taken days to reach on horseback. Now it was only a couple of hours away by car. She could locate Kenwick again, she was certain of that, although she had never tried to do so in the years since.

She exited the inn by a rear door, and stepped out into the dead silent, still streets of the sleeping village. A soft purple hue colored the sky, and the only sounds were the occasional cry of a nightbird, and the fluttering wings of insects swooping by. Morning was still a couple of hours off. It would give her all the time she needed.

She walked briskly back to the remains of her house, and thanked her stars that she never worried about such things as taking the keys from her car in this peaceful little place. Within a short while, she was heading south, along a road that hadn't even existed the last time she'd traveled this way. But the direction was right. Easy enough to keep the coast in view. Easy enough to recall the odd shape of the hills that surrounded that place.

And easy enough to wile away the time the journey took, reliving every moment of the night she had spent in Nicodimus's arms. It had been so good. So beautiful. She had no regrets, not one. It had been right to make love to him. Right, and perfect, and wonderful.

By the time she reached her destination, the sun was up, brilliant and orange and fiery in the sky. It spilled like liquid fire over the rugged hilltops, and painted the lush grasses in shades of crimson and gold.

Arianna stopped the Jeep along the roadside and got out. Shielding her eyes, she stared at the spot amid those craggy hills where centuries before, the dark, hulking form of Kenwick had risen like a brooding giant pointing at the sky. Now there was nothing.

"Gods, what if I was wrong?" she whispered, squinting, straining to see. "What if this isn't what Marten meant at all? It doesn't look as if the keep is even standing after all this time."

Doubts crept in. If she had been wrong, it could cost Nidaba's life, and as much as the woman seemed to hate her, Arianna couldn't return the feelings. She remembered too well the woman Nidaba had been. The strength of her tempered by wisdom—strength a young rebel had admired to no end. Nidaba . . . she'd been unaware of it, but Arianna had idolized her for a time. She'd tried to emulate her, wanted to be like her.

Nidaba was a broken woman now. Wounded so deeply she'd curled up inside herself and seemed unable to find her way out again. But she would. In time, and with Nicodimus's help, she would. Arianna would at least make sure she had the chance to do just that.

She couldn't turn back now. Not until she made sure nothing remained of Kenwick.

Stiffening her spine, she struck out on foot across the land, plotting her course mentally as she went and aiming for the spot dead center of the surrounding hills, where that keep had once stood.

The terrain was rough and rocky as she climbed higher and the grass thinned. The chill morning breeze battled with the fiery sun, so she was alternately hot and cold as she pushed on. It took no real effort for Arianna though. In fact, she took it with ease, enjoying the stretch and flex of her muscles, and the increased flow of her blood. She had been cooped up too long in that cottage in Stonehaven. She had been inactive, playing nursemaid and housemother to her guests, and reining in her natural tendency to run wild.

She guessed she had been reining in a bit more than that, too. Her emotions had been imprisoned inside her since Nicodimus's return from the grave. Even now, they beat at their prison bars in protest, straining to break free. But she knew better than to let them out. Not now. She needed all her focus now, all her attention for the battle ahead.

If she let her feelings reach the surface, she feared she would be useless in a fight. She would be kneeling on the stony ground, aching for a man she could never have. Moon-eyed with a love she had sentenced to death long ago. She'd been so blind. Her feelings for Nicodimus were just as alive as he was. They had been all along. Merely dormant, waiting.

She had resurrected her own weakness, her only vulnerability, when she'd resurrected Nicodimus.

Arianna topped a rise, and peered downward into the basinlike clearing. Crumbling stone walls staggered below, some towering to a height of fifty feet, while others barely held themselves upright at three. Stone masonry littered the ground. What remained of the place seemed almost ready to crumble. Yet she spied the arching entryway, its wooden doors long gone. Dust by now. Beyond that opening, a yawning darkness seemed to beckon.

She crept closer, glancing at the ground, seeing a rusted iron hinge lying there. Then drawing herself up, she stepped through, and ventured into the cavelike depths of the keep's ruin.

Her eyes adjusted quickly, as always. She stepped over broken stones and a broad beam that lay across her path. Her very breaths seemed to echo here. The sound of every step she took seemed magnified a thousand times. Deeper she trod, and deeper, following the only path possible, a twisting, writhing, ever-narrowing path that seemed to have been cleared deliberately. For no structure could crumble in just this way. And as she moved forward, she realized she was also moving *downward*. The angle sharpened, leading her into the bowels of the very earth.

"The dungeons," she whispered, startled at the loudness of even that slight sound here. This silence must be like death itself. But she soon saw that her prediction was an accurate one. The tunnel opened out wider, and the dirt floor leveled off.

She paused at the edge of this wider place, sensing danger. A man stepped out of the shadows to stand in front of her.

Marten.

"Well, now," he said. "This is pleasant, but not what I expected. Where is Nicodimus?"

Arianna drew her dagger. "He is not coming. You'll have to face me, Marten."

"Will I?" He stepped away, vanishing, it seemed. But she knew he'd only ducked into the shadowy recesses of the crumbling dungeon.

Arianna followed slowly, stepping with care, scanning the darkness, then blinking in the sudden light as she rounded a corner. Torches flickered from where they'd been thrust into chinks in the stone walls. Before her, Arianna saw a nightmare.

Nidaba lay still, strapped down to an ancient table. The pendulum high above her was drawn back and seemingly suspended in the blackness. But its blade hung low. And though it was rusted and pocked with corrosion, its edge gleamed in the dancing torchlight, as if recently honed. Yes, honed by the hand of Nidaba's heartless captor, no doubt.

Nidaba's eyes met Arianna's and held them. "Kill him," she said, and her voice was level, and for once, seemed perfectly sane.

"That would be a very bad idea."

Arianna's gaze shifted to where Marten stood beside the table, his hand wrapped around a tall lever.

"One tug," he said, unnecessarily, for it was already obvious. "One tug, and the blade will swing. I've adjusted it carefully, Arianna. It will slice her tender belly on the first pass. On the second, it will sever the organs, and by the third pass it will neatly cut her in half." He shrugged, a slight smile toying with his thin lips. "Well, maybe not so neatly I suppose. In any case, it would be difficult even for an immortal to revive after being cleaved in two." He lifted an eyebrow. "Then again, it might be rather amusing if she did. I might enjoy seeing that before I finally take her heart."

Arianna's grip tightened on the dagger she held. "Are you so afraid to face a woman that you'd resort to this? Release her, Marten, and fight me, if you dare."

He simply shook his head. "It is not you I want," he said. "It is my dear brother-in-law. Nicodimus. I've waited centuries to kill him."

"You'll have to wait longer, because he's not coming. I told you—"

"Oh, he'll come. He'll come when he realizes I now have both his women in my . . . tender care. Put the dagger down, Arianna. Now."

Nidaba shook her head. "Don't listen to him! Kill him, Arianna, or he will kill Nicodimus! Do it!"

"I'll pull the lever. Take one step toward me, and Nidaba suffers unbearable pain while you watch. Drop the weapon, Arianna." His hand twitched on the lever.

"Marten, listen to me," Arianna said, trying to keep her voice calm, but shivering at the way it echoed in this place. It was as if a dozen ghosts mocked her, repeating her every word in deathly whispers. "Nicodimus won't come. He can't. He doesn't remember this place. He doesn't even know I've come here. The centuries of death did something to his mind, and his memory is not—"

"You are an accomplished liar, Arianna. Do you really think I would believe you again? No, you fooled me once. Pretending to want me. Throwing yourself into my arms the way you did, all just so that you could win my trust and try to escape. I had truly begun to care for you, did you realize that?"

"You don't know how to care for anyone but yourself, Marten. You murdered my family! How could you think I would have ever forgiven that?"

He shrugged, averting his eyes. "No matter. Put the weapon down, Arianna."

She swallowed hard, darted a glance at Nidaba.

"Let him do as he will with me," Nidaba whispered. "I beg of you, do not trade my son's life for mine!"

Marten glared at Nidaba. "Shut up, woman!"

"I will not shut up! My son died to save my life once, and I cannot bear to let it happen again! Kill him, Arianna! Forget about me, and kill this cur! Now!"

Arianna clutched her dagger and lunged toward Marten. He jerked the lever instantly, and the blade lurched forward with a terrible groan, only to come to a creaking, shuddering stop again, mere inches from Nidaba's belly. Nidaba's eyes were shut tight, her jaw clenched in readiness.

Arianna froze where she was.

"It's up to you," Marten said. "But I feel I must warn you, Arianna, I am running low on patience. Dangerously low. Put it down."

Nidaba's eyes opened, damp with unshed tears. She turned her head toward Arianna. "No," she whispered. "You mustn't. No, no, no . . ."

"I'm sorry. I have to. Forgive me, Nidaba. I can't watch you suffer such an agonizing death." Arianna faced Marten again. "All right. You win." She dropped her dagger to the dirt floor. Its tip sank into the rancid, packed earth.

Marten smiled, but his hand remained on the lever. "Very good. Now, come here. We have plans to make, you and I." She remained rooted to the spot, and he held up a hand. "Come here, Arianna. Or I'll kill her all the same."

Chin lifting slightly, Arianna went to him. The dank place was filled then with the soft sound of Nidaba's sobs, echoing endlessly.

I woke with a feeling of dread. Something horrible had happened in my dream, but though I tried, I could not remember what. It had to do with Arianna . . . and with death.

My death.

I strained to recall the details, but they eluded me like thieves in the night. Sighing in frustration, I opened my eyes, reaching for her, needing to hold her close to me and feel her there and know that it wasn't real. That it was only one more taunting memory of a past that was long dead.

But Arianna was not there.

"Arianna?"

No answer.

I got up slowly, looking around the room, eyeing the door of the adjoining bathroom, which stood open. I saw no movement inside. A slow fear spread through my veins and I moved faster, hurrying to the bathroom to look for her. "Arianna?" I called again.

The bathroom was empty. Her clothes, I realized as I turned to scan the bedroom in search of them . . . gone. I snatched up the clothing I'd never donned the night before, threw them on haphazardly, and ran back into the bedroom. I yanked open the door, stepping into the hall just as Duncan and Raven came 'round a corner from their own room, smiling, hands joined.

"Where is Arianna?" I all but shouted.

Their smiles died. Duncan looked puzzled. Raven, terrified. "I assumed she was still with you," Duncan said, his frown deepening as he looked past me into the empty room my wife and I had shared the night before. "You mean she's not—"

"Gods, I was afraid she'd do something like this," Raven said, interrupting him. "I knew it! I never should have believed her!"

I rushed forward, gripping Raven's hands gently in my own and striving for patience. "Tell me."

Bowing her head, Raven closed her eyes. "She knew where Marten had taken Nidaba . . . or . . . she thought she knew. But she wouldn't tell me. Nicodimus, she felt you were still not strong enough to fight Marten and win."

"So she went to fight him in my place?" I asked, my stomach clenching. *"And you let her?"*

Raven's head came up fast. "Of course I didn't *let* her! She promised we'd go together, this morning. She said we'd stand a greater chance that way."

"And you believed her? Believed she'd allow you to risk your life in a battle with an immortal as old as I am! She's your sister, Raven, and you didn't see through so obvious a lie as that?"

"Come on, Nic, this isn't Raven's fault," Duncan said, his hand on my arm. "When Arianna sets her mind to something, she's as stubborn as they come. If you know her at all, you ought to know that."

I sighed and closed my eyes. "I know that. I am sorry, Raven. But

Gods, she can't fight Marten alone. He's older than she, more experienced in battle. The last time he took her, he held her for . . ." Then I blinked, and looked up slowly. "The last time he took her . . . yes. Yes, I remember now! His men attacked our village . . . murdered her parents, and everyone else in their path. And he took Arianna. He took my wife the same way I had taken his sister so many years before. It was vengeance, in his twisted, perverse mind."

I paced the hall, pressing one hand to my forehead as I sought the memory.

"Where, Nic?" Duncan asked urgently.

"I'm trying. . . . I remember following the trail of his soldiers. But it was a trick. The soldiers headed north, leaving an obvious path for me to follow. But Marten struck out alone with Arianna. He went south. . . . Yes, two days' ride—south. There was a keep . . . on the coast. . . ."

Duncan gripped my arm. "Can you find it again?"

I looked up and met his eyes. "I *must* find it again. And I will."

We had no choice but to travel by car . . . that amazing vehicle I had only observed from the windows of Arianna's house until now. Duncan quickly procured one from a local man, explaining that it was an emergency.

Raven and Duncan eased me into the rear seat of the machine, and I held on and battled nausea as Duncan manned the controls, setting the beast into motion. Such speeds! It was dizzying, sickening, and yet I paid little heed to the protests of my head and stomach as we bounded over the rutted dirt roads of the new Scottish countryside. I was glad of the contraption that could, by some miracle, reduce a two day journey to one of mere hours. It would get me to Arianna sooner.

It would carry me to my wife . . . sooner.

As we traveled, I directed Duncan as best I could, my memory still hazy. But more and more came back to me. I recalled this same feeling of rage and dread and helplessness filling me in the past. The thought of that vermin having Arianna. The love I felt for her, burning inside me. It had been there before. I knew that now. I may have told Arianna I could not love her, but love her I had, and still did.

I'd done too thorough a job convincing her of my lie, then, hadn't I? For even now, she believed it. Even now, she thought my love an illusion. But it beat in me strong and sure, and old. Very old. She had changed me. I'd been a bitter, lonely man, living to fight, fighting to live, existing in a world that held no joy for me. She had given me joy again.

Such joy. Gods, just looking at her face, seeing her smile had filled me with it. Touching her, holding her delicate form in my arms . . . I had been born again, it seemed. Brought back to life long before she resurrected my body in this strange, new century. For I had been dead then, before I'd known her.

As I would be now, did I have to live on without her.

"I am coming for you, Arianna," I whispered. "Hold on, my love. I will be with you soon."

Raven turned in her seat, and clasped my hand in hers. "She'll be all right," she said, teary eyes at odds with the confidence in her voice.

"She has to be."

"Do you understand what you are to do?" Marten asked softly, eyeing Arianna, suspicion in his gaze.

"I keep telling you, it won't matter. Nicodimus is not coming here."

"And I keep telling you, he will. It is fate, I believe. Things must come full circle. It's the way of the Universe. This will end just as it began. He *will* come for you, Arianna. And when he does, he will find you in the arms of your lover. He will be beaten, utterly, long before I take his heart. I want him to suffer the ultimate defeat at my hands, and you will perform your part *exactly* as I have told you. You will recite the lines precisely, and *convincingly*, Arianna, or Nidaba will pay the price. Now again, do you understand?"

Arianna stared at him, hatred blazing from her soul. Nidaba remained strapped to the table, gagged now so that she could not cry out. No longer in sight, though. Marten had brought Arianna back to that place where she'd first spotted him. The place where the tunnel widened, lit now, with a torch of its own, leaving Nidaba helpless and silent, in the dim, flickering light of a single, dying torch. The frayed length of rope tied to Marten's wrist led back around the corner to that deadly lever. He need only pull to cause Nidaba excruciating pain before ultimately ending her life. And he would, unless Arianna did exactly as he said.

But it wouldn't matter. Arianna wouldn't be forced to play out this gruesome act, for there would be no audience. Nicodimus did not remember.

He must not remember!

Marten pushed her to the floor, then took a seat beside her. "Now we wait," he told her, "for your hero to arrive. And when he does, Arianna . . ." Marten smiled grimly in the dancing light, and she could see the evil emanating from his small, piglike eyes. "He will die. And this time, he won't be coming back."

Chapter 23

We stopped the vehicle each time I thought I saw a familiar place and got out to explore. But I was so disoriented. Things had changed. Not just by the appearance of villages where none had been, and the utter absence of some that had existed long ago, but by the building of roads, the disappearance of forests, the leveling of hills. Meadows thrived where barren moors had rolled before. Pastures that had once been dotted with grazing flocks, now grew up to woodlands. I could only follow the coast, wondering if even its shape had changed. If the constant barrage of the sea had eroded it away to the point where I would not recognize even its familiar form.

But at last, I spied the odd-shaped hills poking into the sky like a circlet of spikes, and I knew this was familiar. Within them, a keep nestled, protected from attack by its natural fortress.

And then, Raven pointed and sat up straight in her seat. "Look! Arianna's Jeep!"

I saw it. But no sign of Arianna anywhere near it, nor from within. I got out at once, racing to the machine to check for her presence all the same. Knowing I would not find her there. My heart fell, and my hands clenched into trembling fists at my sides. Without a word, I turned and began walking toward where I thought the keep had been. In silence, Duncan and Raven followed. I knew that they, too, were wondering what we would find here. Arianna's lifeless corpse, sentenced to death without her heart?

Her heart. Gods the thought of Marten draining the life force of the most vital woman I had ever known. But I could not allow myself to think that way, for the pain of it was nearly crippling. I *would* get her back. I would find her again and restore her to life just as she had done for me. I would, no matter what.

"Nic, hold up," Duncan said, his voice a harsh whisper, his hand on my shoulder. I stopped walking, and he pointed past me. "Look."

I saw it then, the ruins of the keep. It struck me anew how very long it had been that I'd been away . . . from life. From Arianna. To my mind it had been only days ago that I had come here, stood in this very spot, quivering with rage just as I was now.

"That looks like the way in," Duncan said.

I took only a single step before he gripped my arm. "Wait, Nic. It could be a trap. God knows the bastard will be expecting us. It's why he took Nidaba in the first place. He'll be in there, waiting for you."

"Then I will not disappoint him," I said, starting off again.

"Nic, will you use your head?" Raven cried.

Again I stopped, turning this time to face the two who had become more than just my allies in the past several days. They had become my friends. I knew their concern for me was genuine and heartfelt. And likely wise. But wisdom did not concern me. Getting to Arianna was my only thought.

"Look, we'll go 'round this thing, see if there's another way inside," Duncan suggested. "That way we can approach from two directions at once, maybe catch this Marten character off guard."

I nodded. It was a good plan. One that made perfect sense. "Go then. I'll wait here. Signal me when you are ready to go inside."

Duncan eyed me, and finally nodded once. "Be careful," he warned me. "I intend to."

With that, Duncan and Raven raced off around the crumbling remains of broken stone. The moment they were out of sight, I started inside. I could not wait. Not while visions of what Marten might be doing to Arianna played havoc with my mind. I would kill him.

Kill him!

The tunnel I entered was long and winding, littered with debris. Silence was impossible, and I knew that if Marten were listening—as he surely must be—he would hear my approach. Dagger in hand, I moved on all the same. I peered around each corner, fully expecting ambush.

At last, I emerged into a spot where the tunnel widened, and there I saw the last thing I had expected.

Arianna, in Marten's arms. Not fighting him. Not kicking or pulling away. Her arms were twined 'round his neck, and he was kissing her. And *she* was kissing *him*. A red haze of fury colored my vision when at last he lifted his head. And he stared at her, never looking my way, though he had to know full well I was there.

But then, so must she.

"I am so glad you came away with me at last, Arianna," Marten said.

Arianna said nothing. She turned her head toward me, and I saw in her eyes a message, words she could not speak, feelings spilling with the tears. "It has always been you," she said softly, her voice breaking. "I've never loved any one else the way I love you."

The words, apparently spoken to Marten, yet her eyes were on me. That was when the final memory returned to me. I saw it all unfold in my mind in the mere space of an instant. I had crashed through the doors of Kenwick, surprised to find them unbarred, and I found my wife in Marten's arms. I had seen the same message in her eyes then—just before I was leapt upon and killed.

As I had lain dying, Marten had gloated, "Our plan worked perfectly, Arianna." And for one brief instant, I had believed it. I had *believed it.*

Just as I was no doubt meant to believe it now.

I let my body sag, let my head lower, and my hand and my weapon with it, fell to my side. "So this is the way of it," I muttered.

"Nicodimus, no—" Arianna began. I saw Marten grip her arm painfully and nod toward his hand. Glancing downward, I noticed what I hadn't before: a length of hemp tied 'round his wrist.

"Tell him, Arianna," Marten said.

She closed her eyes to prevent the tears spilling over. "I . . . I never loved you," she whispered, her words hoarse and broken.

I had to wait until Martin let her go, before doing anything at all. He was hurting her, I could see that. And the implications of that rope on his arm . . .

I dropped my dagger to the floor. "Then I have no reason to fight, Arianna. No reason . . . at all."

"That will make this much easier," Marten all but crowed, his face alight with the anticipation of his triumph.

"Come then," I said. "Take me if you will." I opened my arms out to my sides and waited. He would have to release Arianna to come to where I stood. And that rope, whatever it was, as well.

He paused, glancing down at the rope with a hint of alarm in his eyes. "No, Nicodimus. *You* come to *me*. You must at least wish to say goodbye to . . . to your faithless wife."

But I wouldn't. For it was what he wished me to do. Instead I sank to my knees, hoping my act would be a convincing one. I lowered my head and made my shoulders shake as if with the force of sobs too violent to contain.

"So be it then," Marten said. "I never intended to let the Dark Woman live anyway."

Even as I lifted my head to see what he meant, Marten removed the rope from his wrist with a flick of his hand, clenched it in his fist, and gave it a brutal tug.

Arianna screamed in utter horror, and another scream came from the depths of this place. A faint one that was terror-filled, and very brief. Arianna leapt on Marten, even as he charged at me. He carried her on his back as she pummeled and clawed at his face and eyes. My hand closed 'round the dagger I had dropped. Marten flung Arianna from his back, lifted his dagger high, and brought it down at me. I drove mine upward. It pierced him just beneath the rib cage, at a sharp upward angle, and I buried it to the hilt, and gave it a twist for good measure.

He froze where he stood, eyes bulging, blood surging over my hand. Then he staggered backward two steps. I yanked the blade free as he did. He fell to the dirt floor. Beyond him, Arianna knelt with her head bowed. Getting to my feet, I went to Marten, bent over him, and quickly cut the heart from his chest. I flung it into the dirt at my feet, and left it there, to be disposed of later.

Arianna needed me now.

I wiped my hands as best I could, and went to her where she knelt, sobbing. Gripping her shoulders I pulled her up and into my arms. "Arianna, it's over. He's dead, my love. You're safe now."

But she was limp in my arms, and trembling violently, uncontrollably.

I eased her away from me just enough to stare down into her haunted eyes. "He made me say those things, Nicodimus . . . I never meant . . ."

"I know that."

She frowned hard at me. "You . . . you know?"

"Just as I knew the last time, Arianna. Even as my life slipped away from me, I knew you could not have betrayed me with him. I believed in you. With my very last breath, I believed in you, Arianna . . ."

She shook her head, eyes wide. "You knew? Even then, you knew . . . ?"

"I knew."

But then her face crumpled, and she sank against my chest. "Oh, Nicodimus. Nidaba! Gods, what Marten has done to poor Nidaba!"

She continued sobbing, crying, but I could no longer understand her words. Something about the rope, something about a pendulum. All but carrying her, I followed the trail of that hemp, 'round the corner. And as we moved onward, she pulled away from me, turned her back, covered her eyes. "I can't look! I can't see her that way! Oh, Gods, Nidaba, I'm so sorry! I tried, truly, I tried. . . ." Again her words degenerated into unintelligible gasps and sobs. She bent nearly double, arms folded 'round her middle as if she were in pain. Choking on her tears, she seemed lost to me.

I could not comfort her, so I turned instead, to see the fate of Nidaba. The mother I must have known as such once, but could only remember as my friend. My dearest friend. My most cherished companion.

A table, straps dangling from its sides, stood empty before me. A blade, suspended from far above, swung in ever decreasing arcs, back and forth above it.

And beside it, on the floor, I saw Duncan, getting to his feet, brushing himself off, and reaching down to help Raven to her feet as well. And then the two of them bent down, and I saw a slender hand reach up, and then another, to clasp theirs. They pulled, and Nidaba rose to her feet with the regal grace of a desert queen.

"I tried, Nidaba. Oh, Gods, I'm so sorry!" Arianna was still whispering brokenly.

"You not only tried, child, you succeeded," Nidaba said softly.

Arianna went still and stiffened. Nidaba came closer, moving with the grace and dignity I remembered so well, and hadn't seen in so long. She settled a hand on Arianna's shoulder. "I'm all right. Alive . . . at least. And I owe you my thanks, Arianna," she said.

"Nidaba?" Slowly, Arianna turned around, and then she flung herself into Nidaba's arms, and held her so hard I thought both women might well break.

After a time, they stood apart again. Arianna, stroking Nidaba's hair away from her face, searched the older woman's eyes again and again as if to be sure she was truly real and not some vision. "How did you escape that horrible blade?"

"Duncan and Raven came in through some other way. They freed me just in time."

"Well, not quite in time," Duncan said, glancing down at his arm.

I saw that it was cut and bleeding. He'd risked his very life to save Nidaba. To save . . . my mother. "I am in your debt, Duncan," I told him.

He only nodded. Nidaba took Arianna's hand in hers and stared into her eyes. "My . . . my mind . . . is not as strong as it once was, Arianna. It was becoming less so even before my time as Nathanial Dearborne's captive, and I fear the things I experienced then have broken it beyond repair. But there are some . . . lucid moments. More so, since I found my Nicodimus again." Here she paused to look at me with tear-filled eyes and a trembling smile.

"You'll heal, Nidaba . . . Mother," I said gently. "I'll see to it. You'll be well again."

Her gaze lowered. "Perhaps," she whispered. "But I fear the life span of a High Witch's mind does not equal that of her body. How long can one live on and remain truly sane, do you suppose?"

I swallowed the lump in my throat. "How long have you lived?"

She sighed wearily, bowing her head. "Four thousand years, my son."

I could only stare at her, dumbfounded. By the Gods, she must be the oldest of us all. Was she? Or were there others, even more ancient than she?

Nidaba faced Arianna again while I stood there, trying to digest the magnitude of a life span so long.

"There is something I should have told you long ago, Arianna, when I met you on the road to Stonehaven, taking my son's body to the Stone Circle. But I was too distraught to think clearly, and I . . . I blamed you for his death."

Arianna lowered her head. "As you should have. I blamed myself."

"But it was not your fault. And the one thing you didn't know, Arianna, the one thing you deserved to know, was that he loved you then."

Arianna lifted her gaze to mine, then quickly looked at Nidaba again, her eyes wide.

"He told me so many times as we searched for you. He told me that he loved you, and that he had never admitted it to you. It was driving him mad that he had never told you the truth of his feelings, and his greatest fear was that he would never have the chance."

Arianna shook her head in wonder. But Nidaba simply pulled her closer to me and placed her hand in mine. "Tell her, my son. You love her still, do you not?"

I nodded once, my eyes on Arianna's. "I do. I always have." Arianna parted her lips, but I hurried on before she could speak. "No, let me finish. I remember it all now, Arianna. Everything. Everything about you. I was like a dead man already before I returned to Stonehaven that last time. But you wouldn't allow me to remain that way. You made me feel again, for the first time since I lost my wife and my sons. You brought joy back into my life. You made me whole, Arianna. And I realized it on the night I lost you. You are my heart, little cat. You are my love, and I will spend the rest of my days making up for the pain I caused you in the past. I swear I will . . . if you will let me."

Her tears spilled over, and Arianna spoke through a watery smile. "I swore I would never love you again, Nicodimus. But the problem is, I never stopped. Not ever. I couldn't. I never will."

I smiled down at her, and then I swept her into my arms. My woman, my wife, my very soul. My Arianna. I kissed her, and I knew that at long last, I truly was alive.